THE ODOR OF ETHER DRIFTED IN
THROUGH THE NIGHT

Ether is more or less an accustomed odor in a hospital. But ether coming in out of the night is a different thing. And nobody in the west wing had been operated on that day. That was the odd thing about it.

My starched skirt swished across the room after the sergeant. Light came on as he touched a switch and he pulled down a sheet which covered the humped-up figure of the man on the bed. The smell of ether was strong, almost overpowering, so the room seemed to waver dizzily around me.

But the figure on the bed would never move again. He wouldn't smile or flash his teeth. He was no longer handsome. It was Lieutenant Parly and his throat had been cut.

Also by
MIGNON G. EBERHART

Another Man's Murder
Family Affair
Hunt with the Hounds
Murder in Waiting
Next of Kin
The Patient in Cabin C
Postmark Murder
Run Scared
Unidentified Woman
The Unknown Quantity
Witness at Large
Wolf in Man's Clothing

Published by
WARNER BOOKS

MIGNON G. EBERHART

MAN MISSING

WARNER BOOKS

A Warner Communications Company

DEDICATION

To a great newspaper woman and a great lady,
Mary King Patterson

All persons and events in this book are entirely imaginary.
Nothing in it derives from anything that ever happened.

AUTHOR'S NOTE

The background of this book may be traced in some degree to my experience on a naval base, where I spent some time while my husband was stationed there as an officer. But that experience did not include murder. Nothing like this ever happened on the Base and I think it extremely unlikely that it ever would!

In fact, all my memories of the Base, the Navy personnel and their families living there, and the many experiences we shared as one family, are very happy ones. A reward for writing this book has been the renewal of those memories and of warm and lasting friendships. None of the people on the Base, I'm sorry to say, appear in this story for the primary, writer's reason that real people simply do not fit a fictional plot. But I'd like to salute all of them, wherever they are. And I hope that I have not taken too many liberties with fact or fancy in trying to describe what *might* have happened—one hot summer's night, with sand blowing from the desert, the Base secured against intrusion, and tons and tons of ammunition lying out in the silent darkness of the hills.

M.G.E.

1

Something was wrong and I didn't know what it was. But something, somewhere, was wrong.

I looked down the corridor ahead of me as I sat at the chart desk. All was quiet; there were no red gleams of signal lights anywhere. At the west end of the corridor an open door let in a night breeze which was gradually cooler, and refreshing after the heat and wind of the day. I couldn't see or hear anything to account for my feeling that something had not been done. So I examined the charts, taking them from the file one by one, making sure that no temperature, no pulse, no medication had been forgotten. While I was new to the ways of a naval hospital, still all hospitals are much alike, so I checked carefully, found nothing undone and looked at my watch, which said 2 o'clock.

My name is Sarah Keate; I am a nurse, but it would require an Act of Congress to permit me to become a regular Navy nurse. A nurse cannot enlist in the Navy if she's past forty and I am that and then some. However, an emergency had arisen (the emergency being the fact that the lieutenant usually on night watch in that wing had broken her leg when getting out of a jeep after a dance at the officers' club the previous week), someone was needed at once to take her place, I happened to be visiting the naval base and was obliged to volunteer my services. So I was taken on, with the status of temporary civilian employee, until another nurse could be transferred to the base and take the lieutenant's place. Naturally I knew nothing of the special rules and requirements of a naval hospital, but the basic requirements of all hospitals are very much the same and, so far, nothing had gone wrong.

But for the last hour or so I hadn't been easy in my mind. And I didn't know why, unless something I couldn't remember or analyze had touched the sixth sense of warning which an experienced nurse acquires. Of course, the watch had begun rather badly with the lights going out unexpectedly while an electrician was repairing an electric grill in the diet kitchen, and just as, in the little drug room next to it, I was measuring a sedative. The result was I dropped a sufficient quantity of sedative into the glass to quiet permanently even Marine Sergeant Brown, for whom I was preparing it, and Sergeant Brown was a remarkably sturdy character. I had to empty the glass and find flashlights so the corpsman and I could patter ghostily upon our chores until the lights came on again. But that was for only a few moments and since then, except for the heat and the corpsman's headache, everything seemed to be in order. However, I went methodically through the charts again.

At the moment there were not many patients in the west wing, although there were some fifty-odd beds in the entire hospital—which as a matter of fact was called a dispensary but to me was and remained a hospital. The wards were in another section of the low, rambling building; the rooms in the wing I was temporarily in charge of were either single or double rooms. I was not alone. Navy nurses are of officer status and their duties are mainly administrative; corpsmen perform the usual nursing chores. Since there were so few patients in that wing I had to assist me during night watch only one corpsman, Jenson, who had a headache due to watching a heated baseball game between the sailors and marines under an even hotter sun. Consequently, after concluding his routine tasks he had retired to a small coat room beyond the drug room and diet kitchen, with some aspirin tablets. He was, however, within immediate call. Inasmuch as I had been Superintendent of Nurses in a large city hospital for more years than I care to admit, I daresay I felt that I was not likely to come upon an emergency I couldn't cope with—a mistaken idea on my part.

I put away the charts; clearly there was nothing wrong.

It was still too early for the 3 o'clock coffee I permit myself not only to keep me awake during the long hours of night watch, but also to relieve the tedium—which seems now an extraordinary word to describe the night then under way. I rose and walked the length of the corridor, passing the black spaces that were doors to the sick rooms, most of them open, to catch the night breeze. I reached the door at the west end of the corridor and looked out.

It was Saturday night, always hilarious, I had discovered, on the base. There were lights in the officers' club and a dance still in progress, for I could hear the music. There were scattered lights among the married officers' quarters—small brick houses set among grass and shrubbery and trees which provided a man-made oasis, quite literally, in the desert. I could see lights in Captain Somers' house, which was considerably larger than the others, since he was Commanding Officer of the base; I knew, for Kitty Somers, his wife, was my hostess, that there was a poker game in progress. For a moment I regretted my present task; during the weeks of my visit on the base I had taken rather a fancy to poker.

Nearer, lights outlined the long, low building which was quarters for bachelor officers, called B.O.Q. Doubtless those who were not at the dance were listening to the radio, writing letters, or more probably engaging in a pastime which was referred to as shooting the breeze.

The silence in the sleeping hospital made it seem rather far away from the lights and the faint sounds of dance music. I was suddenly, strongly aware of the miles of desert that lay around us toward the north and east, and the lofty mountain ranges which hemmed us in at the south and west. And hemmed us in, as a matter of fact, with an immense powder magazine. The naval base was a Naval Ammunition Depot—N.A.D. Wanaha, to be precise—and I had not yet grown accustomed to the unnerving proximity of quantities of explosives, all stored away in what were called igloos (bunkered and spaced at strategic intervals to prevent chain detonations), and loading plants, out in the surrounding desert. This section was of course the most important section of the base, its reason for being; it was called simply "the Area," off limits for many of us, and guarded night and day by marines with remarkably agile trigger fingers, and (at night) Doberman pinschers, trained for attack.

But everyone else on the base was quite accustomed to life on top of a powder magazine. They assured me nonchalantly that they had never had a blow, which seemed a casual way to speak of such a contingency. And I knew that the most elaborate and careful precautions were taken to prevent its occurrence.

"Black powder," the Safety Officer had told me once

cheerfully, over a poker hand, "has ten times the volatile power of TNT." He looked at his cards. "It's sensitive. I'll take two cards."

Sensitive, I thought; wasn't that just fine! I swallowed rather hard and failed to see a potential flush, an oversight which cost me 36 cents. The stakes were small in our little games, but they were fought for violently.

I turned abruptly as if someone had nudged me and looked along the corridor again, and again there was nothing but an empty, white-walled corridor and black spaces that were doors. Nothing wrong.

So while I have no nerves, little imagination and far too many years' experience as a nurse, I put my uneasiness down to nerves. The three preceding days had been extremely hot, with a wind off the desert which blew sand everywhere and never stopped. Sand in our teeth, sand in our hair, little drifts of fine sand along doorways and window sills. So tempers were a little frayed and nerves were pulled fine—mine, I decided, too.

Besides, what could happen?—barring an attack of temperament on the part of the black powder, an eventuality which I devoutly hoped would not occur. Obviously nothing. In my mind I ran over the sick patients; not one of them was then on what could possibly be regarded as the danger list. The nearest thing to it was Lieutenant Parly, alone in one of the rooms along the north side of the corridor; he was a young one-and-a-half-striper who had got a concussion and some broken ribs when his car, going at high speed from Wanaha City back to the base, had turned over in the sand. He was off the danger list, and had been improving steadily, almost too rapidly and fretfully, indeed, for the night before he'd worn out Jenson's feet and my patience. Of course, adhesive straps and body casts do have a tendency to itch, especially in hot weather, but I'd have felt more sympathy for Lieutenant Parly's demands if he'd been wounded in battle, or injured in the normal course of duty. An accident incurred while racing back to the base from Wanaha City with his pockets full of gambling money (and himself rather too full of alcohol), was different.

He was an extremely handsome young man, too handsome, in a dark, romantic way, with wavy hair, overfull and rather shallow blue eyes, a black toothbrush moustache, and a smile that revealed flashing white teeth. But the flashing teeth didn't make up for his nagging complaints; Lieutenant Parly had not endeared himself to me.

Wanaha City, I should explain, is not a city at all but a one-

10

time mining town, which had experienced numerous ups and downs. Once a prosperous and booming gathering place for miners, fantastic in its robust life, it had lapsed into a deserted and forgotten street of dilapidated frame buildings with the closing of the once busy and prosperous silver mines in the mountains and valleys beyond it. At the time of the selection of the site for a naval base and its subsequent building, Wanaha City had again taken on life; during the years of World War Two, when the base had a full and indeed crowded complement of staff, sailors, marines, Waves and civilian employees (of whom there were many), Wanaha City had burst into frenetic activity itself. This died away again, gradually, at the end of World War Two, only to resume, although on a less crowded and vigorous scale, during the war in Korea. Wanaha City was the only town within easy driving distance of the base; its restaurants and stores provided objects unprocurable at Ships Stores and Post Exchange, dinners out for officers' wives who were tired of cooking, and officers and personnel who were tired of mess-hall dining.

The fact that gambling was legal in Wanaha City did not detract from its popularity. Every restaurant had its roulette wheels and crap games, as well as a mysterious game which is played by the use of what look like bird cages. I had, of course, experimented in a minor but I must say very interested way with all of them, and once at the green-felted crap table had acquired a handful of silver dollars owing to sneezing as I was placing my small bet and getting it on a different space from that which I had intended. The next time I tried it, however, I regret to say a little rake came out and pulled every one of those shining big dollars away from me, which rather discouraged further experiment.

But the main reason for Wanaha City's attraction to all of us was a simple one: there was no other place to go. A leave to San Francisco or Los Angeles had to be, because of the distance, at least a two-day leave. Any evening we could drive the ten miles to Wanaha City, have a gay dinner, dance, chat and gamble in a mild way, and return to the base.

The officers and, of course, their families were free to come and go as they wished; the enlisted men visited Wanaha City when they had liberty and referred to it as going ashore, which seemed peculiar. They also called it Wanaha Beach, although there was never anything less like a beach.

But then, many Navy ways were and remained abstruse to me. Even time. Twelve o'clock midnight is midnight to me, not 24:00.

For the most part, naturally, social life was limited to the

11

base. There were constant small cocktail parties and dinner parties, poker and bridge. Naturally, too, in so small and restricted a community as the officers and their families made, they saw much of each other—too much sometimes. But small feuds which arose died rapidly away; you can't refuse to speak to your next-door neighbor, or somebody who is certain to be your bridge partner any evening. In the main there was a kind of family loyalty among them; there might be private little quarrels, but they all stood together, nevertheless, and had and solved the same problems.

Because I was Kitty's guest, I had seen much of the officers and their families, but this was a small circle. The entire personnel of the base included a battalion of marines, several battalions of Navy enlisted men, Waves, a handful of nurses, and a very large group of civilian employees, who worked mainly at the loading plants.

A section of grass and trees surrounded the officers' quarters, the Waves barracks, the administration buildings, church, school and hospital. This entire section was called "the Row," although, in fact, it was roughly oval. The red brick houses, many of them alike, were set with nice regularity within the oval and connected by paved streets winding over the grassy, parklike space. The whole of it was surrounded by a business-like wall. The Row was set off from the rest of the great sprawling base. There was a wide gate and sentries; even I, a visitor, had been given a pass which alone permitted my entrance to the base itself and to the Row.

The music from the officers' club came to a loud and gay climax and stopped. The abrupt silence aroused me. The lights in the Captain's house had gone out without my perceiving it, so the poker game there was breaking up, too. I shivered a little in my thin white uniform, for the night was turning cooler, and debated closing the door. Indeed I moved to put my hand on it, intending to do so, when a door somewhere behind me closed. It closed very softly, so softly that there was an effect of surreptitiousness. I whirled around.

No one was there. The corridor was rather shadowy, for the only light was the green-shaded lamp at the chart desk at the very end of the long hallway. But certainly no one moved along it, anywhere.

It was odd, for none of the patients was likely to be moving about at that hour, opening and shutting the sick-room doors.

It was not that there had been a rash of broken legs; indeed, most of my patients were ambulatory. But the fact was that every single one of them (except my little pet Lieuten-

12

ant Parly) slept long and heartily. Once they got past the initial discomfort of removed appendices, sunburns or strapped-up ankles or casts, everybody in the west wing seemed to have a positive gift for zestful, heavy slumber. It was only with considerable effort on the part of Jenson, who was ruthless in that respect, that we managed to get them awake in time for morning temperatures and breakfast trays. I didn't then think of Jenson and the possibility that he might be moving about the corridor; I was still unaccustomed to the constant presence of a corpsman.

However, since the patient, whoever it was, could scarcely have failed to see me (for I am, to say the least, no shadow, especially in my white uniform, which does nothing to minimize a somewhat substantial figure) and since, if he wanted anything, there was always a signal light attached to his bed which could be snapped on in the fraction of a second, I thought no more about it. I closed the door—bolting it merely because I was trained long ago to bolt any door which had a bolt.

Then I strolled back along the corridor and decided to indulge myself and have my coffee ahead of time. There was no sound at all from the rooms on either side of the corridor except an occasional peaceful snore.

The small diet kitchen for the west wing is not far from the chart desk, running south, parallel to the rooms on that side and to the drug room. There is also a coat and storage room and then I remembered Jenson in the storage room, and glanced into it. He was there, stretched out in two chairs, his head at a neckbreaking angle, sound asleep. He was a tubby little man with pink cheeks and a bald and just then sunburned head despite his youth. He was almost as new to the Navy as I was in the point of experience; indeed, he had been a corpsman for only a matter of weeks; but he was conscientious, good-natured and as a rule, untiring.

I went on into the diet kitchen, a narrow room, white and shining with its enameled cupboards. I put a saucepan of water on the grill and reached for powdered coffee. The window reflected me, with my abundant red hair—streaked with white, to be honest—my white cap, the shining walls of the tiny room. Everything done and checked off, nothing forgotten—

Wait a minute! I *had* forgotten something, and that was a visitor.

She was one of the Waves, Ensign Sally Wilson. She had come in just before 10 and the day nurse had mentioned her when she turned over the wing and the orders for the night to me. Visiting hours were over, she had said apologetically, but Sally would be leaving in a minute or two; she'd gone on then with the orders. I hadn't seen Sally or any visitor leave but obviously she had gone long ago.

So that was the forgotten detail that had been bothering me and it was really nothing at all! Perhaps, I thought morosely, the Navy was right in refusing to accept nurses over forty. Certainly I was showing signs of decay. I straightened my cap irritably, stuck my finger with a pin, and discovered that the electric grill still wasn't working and no amount of turning switches would make it work. There was going to be no coffee that night—and no hot milk, beef tea, or other solace with which to placate pretty Lieutenant Parly. I put the coffee away again and started back to the chart desk, and as I entered the corridor someone went out the door at the end of it.

I saw the moving reflection of the green-shaded desk lamp, as if it were very far away, flashing once as the glass-paned door closed. I had a glimpse of a khaki-colored sleeve and the clear flash of gold braid on a shoulder board.

That was all. The door closed and the small green dot that was the lamp reflection steadied itself.

Clearly one of the boys had got bored with the hospital and taken himself quietly out of it for a few hours, intending to return before he was missed. Since this wouldn't do at all, I went down the corridor in hot pursuit. By the time I reached the door and pulled it open, however, he was gone. There is a small entrance there, a kind of porch, only a step up from the path and banked with shrubbery. I went out onto it and peered in every direction for a fleeing figure and there was none. By now the base was quiet. The houses were dark; the only lights were the small street lights at intervals along the winding roads, and a dim area of light from around the corner of the wing, coming, I knew, from the lights above the gate and sentry. My gallivanting patient wouldn't go that way, for the sentry would stop him and demand his pass.

But he had vanished, very swiftly, into the night and there was no use trying to find him. I'd have to make a check of the patients, and then watch for his return. I closed and bolted the door, which the A.W.O.L. patient had, of course, been obliged to leave unbolted, and then I saw the small red gleam of a signal light over one of the doors.

It was Jenson's duty to answer it, but I've done too much nursing to stand on ceremony. I went to attend it. As I approached the door I saw that it was the room occupied by Buffalo Bill.

I need not say that this was not his real name; he was Sergeant Bill Brown, top sergeant in the marines. From one or two allusions I had at first believed that he was called Buffalo Bill in recognition of a certain talent with firearms, but it later developed that the name referred to some incident, long in the past, in connection with a thing like a tractor which, however, goes over water and is called a buffalo. What the incident was I never knew; but Buffalo Bill was an apt nickname for Sergeant Brown either as a human tractor or as a fighter. He was all of twenty-two, big, tough, and never left you in doubt for one instant as to what he thought of anything.

I opened the door quietly as one does in a hospital. Then I gulped, slid into the room and closed the door behind me. The light was on, Buffalo Bill was sitting on the bed, looking vast in pajamas, his legs dangling. And a .45 revolver lay beside him.

"*What are you doing with that?*"

He eyed me. His broad face was flushed, sleepy and angry. Even his light hair, which would curl in spite of the shortest marine hair cut on record, I'm sure, looked porcupinish and angry.

"What are *you* doing running up and down the corridor?" he said, instantly turning defense to attack. "You woke me up."

"Put that gun away."

"Why did you come into my room?"

"Your signal light is on, of course. What do you want?"

"No, I mean before that. Before I turned on the light—"

"I wasn't—I didn't—"

"A few minutes ago. You woke me up—"

"I did no such thing. Give me that revolver—"

He put a hand like a ham down on the gun. "*Somebody was here.*"

"Nonsense. You had a nightmare."

"Listen, sister—" he lifted the gun and waved it, in an absent but impressive way. "I hear anything close to me at night. I've got ears like a cat's. I woke up. Somebody was here in my room."

"Well, I wasn't," I snapped. "You imagined it—unless the corpsman—but he's asleep."

He blinked at me, and accepted my denial. "Okay, then who was it? I don't like people creeping around at night."

I saw his point. Neither did I. I said, "There's nobody here now. Either put that gun away or give it to me, or—besides you've got no business having a gun here—"

15

He put the gun down and patted it. "Where I go, this gun goes," he said simply. "Naturally, I like my rifle better. But this is okay."

I eyed the gun; he eyed me. Then he said unexpectedly, "There's something wrong here tonight."

It rather took my breath. "W-what! I mean—where? What do you mean?"

He rubbed the other hand over his hair. "I don't know. Something—"

The troublesome fact was, of course, that men who have seen heavy combat duty do develop an even more acute sixth sense of danger than that of a nurse. This boy had returned from Korea only a few months ago. I took a hard grip on common sense. "There's nothing wrong," I said crisply.

"There was a hell of a row in the next room," he said slowly. "I heard it through the window. But that was before—" He rubbed his curls in a perplexed way, eyed me and said, "There's a funny smell coming in that window. Anybody been operated on around here today?"

"Funny—" I went to the open window at the head of his bed and sniffed. And there was a slight but pungent, sweetish odor of ether drifting in through the night.

Ether, of course, is more or less an accustomed odor in a hospital, along with soup and antiseptics. But ether coming in out of the night is a different thing. The surgery was in a remote wing. Nobody in the west wing had been operated on that day. That, of course, was the odd thing about it. I sniffed and it was ether, no mistake about it; faint, but definite. Then I knew that Buffalo had got out of bed as he wasn't supposed to do and was limping across the room. I whirled around to stop him and he was bending over near the door. He picked up something from the floor, looked at it, his vast shoulders quite still and rigid, then turned to me. He had a knife in one hand, and his revolver in the other. The knife was an enormous and wicked looking clasp knife. The blade was open. He dangled it by a chain fastened to a ring on the handle. He said, "Guess I'd better take a look—" and opened the door and limped out into the corridor.

My starched skirt swished across the room after him; by the time I reached the door he had disappeared into the next room. Light came on as he touched a switch and I ran into the room in time to see him pull down a sheet which covered the humped-up figure of the man on the bed. Then I was at his side. The smell of ether was strong, almost overpowering, so the room seemed to waver dizzily around me.

But the figure on the bed would never move again. He wouldn't smile or flash his teeth. He was no longer handsome. It was Lieutenant Parly and his throat had been cut.

"Sure got clomped, didn't he!" observed Sergeant Brown.

At that instant a soaring, wailing sound shattered the night silence, rocked the hospital and the base, wailed and soared deafeningly all around us. It was the disaster whistle.

2

Once or twice before that I had heard the disaster whistle, so I knew that when it blew things happened, very rapidly and according to plan. A man on duty in the administration building signaled the O.D. (which means Officer of the Day and, so far as I could see, of the night, too) and the fire department, manned by sailors. The O.D. then reported to the C.O. (Commanding Officer, this time, who was Harry Somers), the nature of the disaster—accident, fire, or—heaven forbid—a blow. And meanwhile, everybody waited, their faces very still, listening. If there was no sound of detonations—and if the earth didn't rock and windows come crashing in upon them, the chances were that the whistle meant an accident or a fire alarm, also likely to be disastrous in their way, but not on so catastrophic a scale as a blow might be.

So even then, Buffalo and I listened rigidly while the disaster whistle stunned our ears. But the walls didn't really shake; the windows didn't crash. And the knife, dangling from Buffalo's vast hand, glittered in the light. There was a red stain, still wet-looking, along the blade and around the handle.

I thought, but that's murder. He's been murdered.

Buffalo, listening, said, "Must be only a fire."

And abruptly the disaster whistle stopped. There was for an instant almost a painful silence. Then the sergeant pulled the sheet up again, shielding the tragic and horrible thing on the bed. He put his arm around me and, limping, propelled me into the corridor. "Take it easy. Only a fire or something. Some Wave left her electric iron turned on. Here—"

Jensen bounced out of the storeroom, rubbing his eyes. Without knowing it, wafted along by Buffalo's great arm, I had reached the chart desk. I was sitting back in my chair feeling very odd. The telephone was there, Buffalo had it pressed against his ear and was saying something into it that I couldn't hear, and the ambulatory patients were popping curious heads out of doors. Several red signal lights went on. In fact, for a moment or two there was a certain amount of confusion, and I'll not pretend that I so much as tried to control it. It was all I could do to control myself.

Buffalo said, "Okay—okay—" And put down the telephone. "Okay, fellows," he snapped in his best drill-sergeant voice, which was almost as loud as the whistle. "False alarm. No fire, no blow, nothing. G'wan back to your bunks. Loot—" He fastened on a young two-striper, very sleepy and disheveled. "Get those fellows back to bed. Snap into it." His eyes flicked Jenson. "What are you goggling about! Get busy." Jenson opened his mouth, shut it and flapped at the patients like a nervous hen.

The young lieutenant gasped, overlooked rank, and his pajamas twinkled along the corridor to Jenson's assistance. The other patients hesitated, however, alert and instantly aware of something unusual going on, resisting both Jenson and the lieutenant, watching Buffalo, watching me. I think it only chance that Buffalo gave his revolver a twirl. "You deaf? Get back to your bunks." He chose to explain. "Somebody touched off the whistle by mistake. Accident. No fire, nothing. Now then—back to bed."

It was a tribute to Buffalo Bill rather than to Jenson or the young lieutenant that they obeyed, although in a leisurely and grumbling way. But they did drift slowly back to their rooms. Buffalo Bill nudged me—with the revolver, as a matter of fact, but I don't think intentionally. "Better keep quiet for a minute, sister."

He went to speak to the young lieutenant, who apparently as ranking officer in the wing was the voice of authority, and then brought him back to the chart desk. "Okay now, sister," Buffalo said to me. "You'll want to report to the O.D." He took up the telephone again. Apparently the girl at the switchboard demurred. "Sure, I know—but you ring the O.D., sweetheart, or I'll cut your th—" He stopped, nearly strangling himself with the effort, and said, "Get him!" The parade-ground snap was like a whip in his voice and in a second or two he handed the telephone to me.

"*What*—" began the young lieutenant. The sergeant's eyes had a slaty gleam. "Quiet," he said. "Go ahead, sister. Tell him—"

I did.

The O.D. didn't believe me. "Murder! That's impossible! Are you sure?"

18

I was sure. I must have convinced him. "I'll report to Captain Somers. Keep things under control—"

My hand was shaking so I had difficulty replacing the telephone until Buffalo took it out of my hand and clicked it into place.

The young lieutenant turned a glazed regard to Buffalo. *"She said murder—"*

Buffalo, a man of few words, replied. "Lieutenant Parly. Throat cut."

"Th—throat—"

I didn't know that Jenson had floated back to the chart desk until he gave forth his first utterance which was, "Ye-owww," right in my ear and not helpful.

"Did it with this." Buffalo dangled the bloodstained knife before the lieutenant (his name was Graves) and the young lieutenant grasped the edge of the desk and stared at the red, shining wetness of the knife blade. Jenson, his sunburn standing out now in scarlet patches, said, "Ye-owww" again.

"Brace yourself, Loot," Buffalo said. "The girl at the switchboard listened in. There's going to be hell to pay—"

Young Graves braced himself with an obvious effort, looked at me, looked up and down the corridor, and said, "Who did it?"

Neither of us replied, for obvious reasons, and the sergeant's prophecy was almost certainly the fastest one on record to be fulfilled, for Lieutenant Edith Pillsbury, her cap over one ear, came running from the passage that led from the west wing to the main corridor and office. "The girl at the switchboard says—" she began, and saw the knife.

I think it was Jenson who caught her and lowered her, since there was nowhere else and I couldn't move out of my chair, to the floor, where she gave a low moan. There's no keeping a secret in a hospital where every word re-echoes and multiplies itself against bare walls. Heads were popping out doors again. Jenson sketched a frantic gesture with his hands and ran to shoo them back, a futile procedure, for they popped right out again and Buffalo and the young lieutenant exchanged a few words and the young lieutenant went down the corridor, extracted a couple of men from the avid observers and took them into the room where Lieutenant Parly lay. Murdered.

Edith Pillsbury scrambled to her feet. "Something—happened to me," she said in a queer voice. She took a gulp of air. "We've got to do something."

"Okay, sister," Buffalo said over his shoulder. He was standing with his back to us watching the corridor, the gun still in his hand at what I understand is called the ready. "Okay, sister. Everything's under control." He was this time addressing Edith Pillsbury, who moistened her lips and turned to me. I said, "I've reported it. I've reported it—"

Jenson ran to open the west door and Harry himself arrived and not the O.D., for which I was grateful, although I restrained myself from running to meet him. He flung back the west door (he was fully dressed, probably owing to the disaster whistle), and ran, followed at ten feet or so by the Exec, Jim Warring. Their appearance silenced the entire wing. Heads popping out of doors became rigid and still. The Captain paid no attention to them but hurried toward me. I tried to rise and my knees wouldn't hold me.

Harry Somers is a small, slim man, with a thin, weathered face, very bright, observant eyes and an air of command, and I was never so glad to see anybody in my life. The sergeant moved his gun toward his forehead in an odd kind of salute; Edith Pillsbury stiffened to attention; Jenson stopped flapping and I think wrung his hands. The Exec caught up with the Captain and checked himself, and Edith said, "Sir, we have to report—"

There'll be hell to pay, the sergeant had said, and he was right.

The Captain's presence, however, had a salutary effect upon all of us, which says much for Harry Somers. He snapped a few questions at me and at Buffalo—Who? Where? When had we discovered the murder? He took the knife from Buffalo's great fingers, examined it in one swift glance and wrapped it cautiously in a handkerchief. "No idea who did it?"

We hadn't. The Captain turned around to face the corridor with its staring faces. "All right, men. Keep to the rooms assigned to you till further notice. Jenson, enforce that. Lieutenant Pillsbury, don't let the rest of the patients hear of this tonight. Lie to them, do anything, but keep 'em quiet. Sarah, stay right here. Sergeant, show me the room. Jim"—he looked at the Exec, young Commander Warring—"you'd better come along."

A gleam of respect came into the sergeant's slaty eyes. "Yes, sir." He started off down the corridor.

Jim Warring snapped to attention, too, but gave me an anxious look. "See here, you look—there must be some whisky around."

"I'll get it, sir," Edith Pillsbury said instantly, and contrived, even then, to smile at him, Jim being rather an objec-

20

tive in a quiet but resolute way among the nurses and Waves. She adjusted her cap to a fetching angle. "I'll see to Miss Keate."

"Right. Thanks." Jim Warring followed the Captain. Buffalo and all of them disappeared into the room where Lieutenant Parly lay dead.

Jenson said, "My golly, every damn signal light!" and bounced to answer them.

Edith found the whisky; it was in the diet kitchen. She poured a generous drink, looked rather wistfully at it as she gave it to me, cast a more wistful glance at the door where Jim Warring had disappeared, said, "Never a dull moment. I'd better get on the job," and flashed away.

I sipped at the whisky, choked and sipped again. I have been a rampant teetotaller all my life, but it seemed to be the thing to do at the time. For the fact was that not only was I suffering, perhaps not unreasonably, from a sense of shock, but I knew something of what lay ahead of us. It was not the first time I had made the acquaintance of murder.

I do not mean that I move in murder circles. Nor do I seek out crime. I do my best to avoid it. But a trained nurse, so to speak, gets around. In the course of her profession she dips into wide and varied waters, and sometimes for me this has included very muddy pools indeed. Consequently, while murder was certainly not an old friend, it was, in a way, a rather familiar acquaintance. However, if I have ever been of any slight assistance in solving the puzzle of a crime, I fear this is due as much to curiosity (and a more or less observant eye) as to the strict sense of justice which has most charitably been attributed to me.

It has also been said, again very kindly, that I have a certain small deductive ability; this is not true. I wouldn't know what to do with a mysterious poison except throw it down the drain very promptly and I would turn over a suspicious fingerprint at once to the nearest policeman. I have only nursed for many years; I have seen people at close and sometimes critical range. I'll not say that I cannot add two and two with a fair degree of accuracy, but I make my mistakes, too.

So the only thing I saw just then was a rather appalling view of the investigation—the grim apprehension, the inevitable tragedy, the latent dangers ahead of us—and it was no pleasant view.

Someone said quite clearly into the abrupt silence, "Down the hatch with it, old girl." I didn't know who said it; faces were still in the doorways with—at the moment—a certain longing expression in all of them. But I thought it excellent advice and sipped again, with such immediate results that I retrieved my cap from the back of my head and rose, deeming this an emergency if there ever was an emergency, and intending to go to Jenson's assistance. However, as I did so, Jim Warring came out of the closed room and came to the desk.

"Feeling better?" he said to me, and picked up the telephone. I listened while he called Commander Roslin, the head doctor; Commander Nagel, the Security Officer, and several others whose particular duties I didn't know, and also telephoned to somebody else and directed him to call a staff meeting at 6 that morning. Then he telephoned to the administration building, where I knew there was a twenty-four hour duty. "How's Smith?" he said. "—Okay. Captain says bring him to the hospital. Right. The doctor will be here." He cut off the connection, thought for a second and then lifted the telephone again. This time instead of calling a number he asked for Lieutenant Pillsbury. "Edith, you've got a new patient coming in. Ensign Smith. —No, he's got a bump on the head. I don't think it's serious—Rosy's on his way here. In this wing? Okay, I'll tell Miss Keate."

He put down the telephone. "Edith says to put Smith in one of the vacant rooms. He'll be here in a few minutes." He thought for a moment, frowning at the glass surface of the desk.

Commander Jim Warring was an attractive young fellow, in his thirties perhaps, but young for his job as Executive Officer of the base, and young to have experienced combat in two wars. He was unmarried and lived in the B.O.Q. and was so frequently in and out of the Somers house that he seemed like one of their family. I liked him. He was sensible, kind, said very little and was a good bridge partner. He looked now, though, very worried—as indeed he had every right to be.

But I didn't expect him to say what he then abruptly said. "Look here, Miss Keate. They're bringing Ensign Smith here —you heard me. He was on duty at the office tonight and got a—well, a bump on the head. It knocked him out. The Captain and I were there with the O.D. when they got us on the telephone and you told the O.D. about—" he jerked his head back toward Lieutenant Parly's room. "The fact is—well, whoever got into the office and knocked out the ensign was the guy that touched off the disaster whistle." He stopped and looked at me and said, "And now Parly's murdered. Funny, isn't it?"

It wasn't the right word for it. Still, it was as good as any. "Do you mean that—that whoever murdered Lieutenant Parly—"

"I don't know. Nobody knows who knocked out Smith or what happened to him. It was easy enough to get into the office; all he had to do was walk in. Smith apparently was in a chair beside the switchboard, dozing maybe. Smith came to while the disaster whistle was blowing, stopped the whistle, got the O.D., sent back the fire trucks. They were waiting to find out what had happened and where to go. Captain ordered a relief for Smith but he—" he paused—"the Captain thinks it a good idea to put Smith somewhere where he can't talk. Think you can see to that? I mean while you're on duty. I'll warn the day nurse too. And Jenson."

I nodded. Jim looked rather doubtfully at me. "Sure you don't want a relief right now? We can get one of the nurses out—" But the shortage of nurses being what it was, the day staff needed rest. And would get, during the coming day all too little; no doubt about that.

I said no, I'd finish the night watch. Jenson trotted past with a thermometer and a frantic glance at us. And suddenly I realized that nobody was watching from the doorways; Jim's presence had sent them hurriedly to cover. Probably they couldn't hear. And I was afraid I had something which might be important to tell him. Or to tell the Captain. He moved and the light flashed on the three gold stripes on his shoulder boards and something tightened somewhere in whatever it is that we call instinct. After a moment I said cautiously, "Jim, do they know who killed him?"

He shook his head and stared at my now empty whisky glass. All the men on the base were deeply tanned by the blazing, unremitting sun, but he was rather gray below the tan and certainly tense. "No way of knowing so far. Captain will want to talk to you, get all the details. He'll have to set up a Board of Inquiry, question everybody." He sighed. "It's my job, too. I—" He was sitting on the edge of the desk; he got up, frowned, and suddenly said in a low voice, "Look here, Miss Keate. Have you—that is—well, you haven't seen Sally Wilson here tonight, have you?"

"Sally!"

He nodded.

"Sally—" I tried to collect extremely scattered wits. "No. But—that is, I think she was here. The day nurse said so when she went off duty. But Sally must have left—oh, almost as soon as I came on duty."

"That would be at 22:00?"

"If you mean 10 o'clock, yes. Jim, I'm sure she left right away—"

"Didn't you see her?"

"I was busy. I didn't notice. Why—" I began, and stopped, for I knew why Jim was interested in Sally's whereabouts. I had seen them together riding in Jim's little car, Sally's light hair blowing, or sitting rather close to each other at the movies, or dancing at the Saturday-night parties in the club.

Jim said, "So the day nurse knew she was here. I suppose she'll tell it; they'll have to question her about Parly."

"Sally didn't have anything to do with Parly. She didn't even know him, did she? Besides—*murder*—"

Anger flashed into his eyes. "I didn't mean Sally—"

"I know," I said hurriedly. "I didn't either. That's the point."

The flare of anger died away, but he looked very sober. After a second he appeared to have come to a decision. "Look, Miss Keate—I'm about to ask you to do something that—that isn't—but I'm going to ask it anyway. If the day nurse doesn't remember Sally coming here—forget it yourself, will you?"

"But—but Sally—"

"Will you?" Jim Warring asked.

So I had to settle an inner debate. It has always seemed to me that the least an innocent bystander can do when he finds himself in any sense a witness is to tell the truth, and the whole truth. Concealment or evasion is not only unfair and contrary to civic duty, but it is also very likely to boomerang. I didn't for a second question Sally Wilson's innocence; it was preposterous even to speculate as to whether or not she could have been, in any possible way, a part of murder. But at the same time, it is my nature to cling to principles. Besides, the truth couldn't hurt her. I looked into Jim's young —and very dark and troubled—eyes and finally said, "Why?"

"Because I don't want them to question her," he said promptly. "She had nothing to do with this and I'm not going to have her dragged into it."

Prompt. Too prompt? I said uneasily, "Did she know Parly?"

Somehow I didn't think Jim Warring would find it easy to lie, so I couldn't be sure whether or not there was a kind of flicker in the very intent eyes holding mine. In any event, he said with a shrug which looked easier than it may have been, "Everybody knows everybody here on the base. But you know as well as I do that Sally Wilson wouldn't—" He stopped and for an instant a picture of murder seemed to rise between us. The room, too near us; murder, too recent. Lieutenant Parly.

I didn't want to look at it; neither, I think, did Jim.

He leaned over the desk toward me. "There's a reason, Sarah."

Of course. Otherwise he wouldn't ask it and ask me at the same time to trust him and trust Sally. So I promised, conscience scarcely giving a dying flutter as I remembered the way Sally looked, dancing with him—her face all alight and glowing and very, very young.

And at that point there was a sound down the corridor, the west door opened and two sailors trudged in carrying a litter with Ensign Smith sitting bolt upright in the middle of it, clutching his cap to his chest and looking extremely indignant.

There occurred, in fact, as apparently he found himself in the hospital willy-nilly, a slight ruckus, with Ensign Smith trying to get out of the litter and the sailors forcibly and, indeed, rather enthusiastically restraining him. One of them gave a slight howl as if a shoe had encountered some portion of his anatomy. Jim Warring went to quell the commotion, and the heads that had popped out of the doorways at the sound jerked back again when they observed that Jim was still on deck. (An apt phrase in this instance; I daresay there is a contagion about Navy vocabulary.) There was a vacant room in the corner, near the door. Jenson bounced to meet the little cavalcade and he and Jim and I got Ensign Smith settled, on the bed if not in it.

Commander Roslin, who must have run all the way from his house to the hospital, came in the corridor door, panting, and promptly took over. He looked at Smith's head, which had indeed quite obviously suffered a heavy blow, examined it and told Ensign Smith he was lucky he had a hard skull. "Unusually hard skull," said the doctor with professional interest, upon which the sailors grinned at Ensign Smith, who glared back at them, and trudged away. Jim said to the doctor, "The Captain's waiting for you, but better get Smith fixed up first—" and the doctor sent Jenson for a razor and dressing tray.

I went to close the corridor door after the sailors, who were exchanging quiet but pungent remarks as to the thickness of Ensign Smith's skull which it appeared they had always suspected. The two slim young figures in white, their

25

gob caps slanted jauntily at the same angle, disappeared around the corner of the hospital and I lingered for a moment in the doorway.

From there the oval looked like a Christmas tree; there were lights everywhere and cars speeding along the roads. Certainly the news of the murder had gone like wildfire over the entire Row, if not yet the entire base. I remembered Kitty saying once, rather wryly, that if she turned off the lights at midnight, locked the door, pulled down the curtain and sneezed, the next morning everybody on the base would ask her how her cold was. Even the Waves barracks were lighted from stem to stern and a little group of officers, one of them tastefully attired in what looked at that distance like a towel, was standing out in front of B.O.Q. talking excitedly.

I thought of young Sally Wilson, over in the Waves barracks (and the flicker in Jim's eyes when he had evaded my question as to whether or not she knew Lieutenant Parly). And I thought of the arm in khaki uniform with the gleam of gold braid on the shoulder board which I had seen, closing that door.

That was, just then, my problem. In that hurried instant I had quite naturally believed him to be a wandering patient, but on second thought I knew he wasn't. He had had, I was sure of it, three stripes on his shoulder board, and none of my patients was of the rank of commander.

Indeed the only man of the rank of commander who was at all likely to visit the hospital at night was the doctor, Commander Roslin, and I had reason to believe it was not the doctor.

3

My heart was thumping very uncomfortably. I must be sensible, I told myself. I would have to tell the Captain, of course. But first I must check the patients, make sure that they were all present and accounted for.

The door to Lieutenant Parly's room was still closed. I glanced in the room beside me where, now, Jenson was shaving a spot on Ensign Smith's scalp and Ensign Smith was telling him to take it easy with the razor or he'd break his neck. Jim and the doctor were in one corner having a low-voiced and a very serious conversation, if the doctor's shocked face was any indication of its nature. Faces were watching again from almost every doorway and as I passed a little murmur of question went with me to the chart desk where again I sat down.

I must get my thoughts in order; I must have all pertinent facts ready for Harry Somers. So exactly what were the pertinent facts?

Or more accurately, were they pertinent?

I had felt uneasy and troubled, but I discounted that. First because I had put it down to nerves, second because if it was due to my subconscious, endeavoring to remind me of Sally Wilson whose presence I had forgotten, then I had promised Jim Warring I'd continue to forget it.

There was the soft opening and closing of a door. That could have some possible connection with the murder, I didn't know what—certainly the murderer would try to escape from Parly's room as stealthily as it was possible to do. Still it might conceivably be a clue of sorts. I'd tell Harry Somers that.

And what else? The odor of ether—odd. Drifting in through Buffalo's window. From Parly's window? It was stronger in Parly's room. Had it been used to silence him before the murder? Prevent his outcry? If so, that was odder still. In fact I didn't then want to explore its implications. I went on.

There was the knife, of course. The Captain already had that and knew what Buffalo could tell him about it, which was little enough.

But the important fact was the man who had walked out the door at the end of the corridor. And that could be all too significant. My knees began to shake and I had to wipe my forehead with the back of a suddenly cold and unsteady hand. It is not, I may say, a pleasant experience to be within hailing distance of a remarkably brutal and stealthy murderer—especially at the moment when he is escaping the scene of the murder, probably, indeed almost certainly and literally, red-handed. And I knew every man of the rank of commander on the base—knew him and liked him.

Well, those were the facts and the only ones. Otherwise there was simply nothing that anybody could call a clue.

So I sat there staring down the corridor, and eventually the faces in the doorways grew bored with looking at me and listening for the door to Lieutenant Parly's room to open, and withdrew. Commander Nagel and several other officers arrived, all of them looking rather white and excited, and

I directed them to Parly's room. The doctor finished with Ensign Smith's dressing and Jenson came trotting out with the debris, which undoubtedly included some of young Smith's red locks, and went to the washroom. Jim Warring and the doctor lingered in Smith's room for a moment, in order, I suppose, to have a stern word with him as to the advisability of keeping his mouth shut until the Captain questioned him. Then they came out and went to Lieutenant Parly's room, where again the door closed. Jenson came back into the corridor and I sent him to check the patients in the wing and make sure they were all present and accounted for. "The Captain wants to know," I told him, somewhat anticipating the truth, but it would be Harry's first inquiry.

Jenson gave a resigned sigh and disappeared into the nearest room. Young Lieutenant Graves and the two men he had taken into Parly's room appeared, all rather pale and meek-looking and went into their respective rooms. Buffalo Bill limped out of Parly's room, gave me a look, jerked his thumb upward in an encouraging way and went to his room. I was interested to note that he had no gun; probably the Captain or Jim had relieved him of it. I had an impression too that he and the others had been told not to talk. And then as Jenson returned Harry came out of Parly's room and came to me.

"All present, sir," Jenson said snappily. The Captain gave him a blank look and took up the telephone. "Tell Lieutenant Pillsbury to take over here," Harry said to the girl at the switchboard. He turned to me. "I want to talk to you, Sarah. Jenson—"

"Yes, sir."

"Lieutenant Pillsbury will take over here for the rest of the night. She'll be here in a minute or two. All right, Sarah—"

So I went with him, past the closed, blank door of Lieutenant Parly's room and out the west door at the end of the corridor. Lights were everywhere. The cool night air struck our faces. Harry gave a tired sigh. "This is going to be the very devil," he said. "We'll go home. Kitty's up, waiting. I've ordered a staff meeting at 6. I want to be able to report all of the facts I can get. Now then—"

We started along the paved street toward the lights in the Somers quarters. As we passed B.O.Q. there was a sudden silence among the group of officers. One of them, Commander Gary, an ordnance officer who headed the department of manufacturing and packing of ammunition, came to meet him. "Yes, Commander?" Harry said.

28

"We were wondering—that is, if it's true, sir—"

"Lieutenant Parly was murdered. There's a staff meeting at 6."

"Yes, sir."

We walked on, taking the branching lane toward the Somers house. When we were out of earshot of the group in front of B.O.Q., Harry said, "All right, Sarah, begin at the beginning—"

I told him quickly everything there was to tell. Our footsteps were quiet on the paved lane. Dawn was not far away; distant mountain peaks were barely touched with light.

The sound of a door opening and then closing very softly. Buffalo's signal light; his insistence that someone had been in his room, waking him. The scent of ether—here Harry gave a brief nod—then the knife, on the floor in Buffalo's room, and our really horrible discovery. "But, someone," I said, "left the west wing; he went out the west door. That was before I went to Buffalo Bill's room—"

Harry stopped short. "*What?—Who was it?*"

"I don't know. I thought it was a patient. I went after him, but he'd already disappeared. It was just after that that I saw Bill's signal light."

"But it wasn't a patient? That's why you had Jenson check—"

I took a long breath. "He was wearing an officer's uniform. I saw gold braid, just a glimpse of it on his shoulder board."

Harry's face was a sharp, pale outline. "*What rank?*"

"It was only an instant—I saw the door move, the glass reflected the green light on the chart desk. I saw his sleeve, khaki-colored, and—and there were three stripes on his shoulder board."

"Three—"

I nodded, miserably.

"*But that—*"

"Yes, I know."

He stared at me for a moment, his face drawn and stern in the dim, cold light before the dawn. "Are you sure?"

"Yes—"

"Rosy! Commander Roslin—"

"No. He was too tall. His shoulder was too high against the wall. The doctor is short and tubby—"

"Then—who was it? Could you recognize anything—"

"He must have been about six feet tall. But I didn't see anything else."

"But—a commander—" He stopped. We walked on, both silent.

It would limit the suspects in a frightening way. An officer, a commander, one of the small group, all known so well and familiarly among themselves. Harry said suddenly, "I can't think of one of them I don't trust. I can't think of one of them who would—" He didn't finish.

I said unhappily, "He might have been in the hospital on some—some errand. He may have known nothing of the murder. He—"

Harry said, "I'll have to question them. I—but I can't believe—" He stopped again as we turned into the path that went through shrubbery borders toward the big brick house, with its gabled windows and vines, that loomed up against the sky ahead of us. There were lights in the windows and Kitty was waiting on the porch. She came to the steps as she heard our footsteps crunch on the gravel. "Harry—oh, you've brought Sarah! It's true, then?"

Harry nodded. "How about some coffee, Kitty? I've got a staff meeting at 6."

Kitty, her dark short curls disheveled, her pretty face white, put her hand on his arm. "And it was Parly!"

Light fell from the door directly upon them. I saw the look they exchanged, an anxious look certainly, troubled and incredulous, but also significant somehow, as if a mutual knowledge flashed between them. Kitty took a sharp breath. "Parly!"

Harry put his hand upon hers. "All right, Kitty," he said gently. "We don't know who did it, yet. We'll find out. Now then—"

"Of course," Kitty said and put her head up. "Come in, Sarah. The servants are up. I'll tell Suli." She hurried down the hall toward the kitchen and Harry led the way to his study.

Kitty Somers was a true Navy wife and the study gave mute evidence of it, for she had early developed the gift for making any quarters where they found themselves homelike and comfortable. There were bright Indian rugs on the floor and gay slip covers on the deep lounge chairs. There were photographs everywhere. There always are photographs in a Navy home; they are tangible links with others of the great Navy family. Harry sat down at his desk and put his hands over his face so the light shone on his dark hair and touched the gray.

Harry Somers had had long and fine years of service in the Navy; indeed, he had a Navy Cross. I had known him since he and Kitty were married, the year after he graduated from Annapolis. I had known Kitty since she was scarcely a gleam in her father's eye and despite the difference in age between us, and the many years during which Kitty had followed Harry over the world and Kitty and I had kept in touch only with letters, still we had kept in touch.

So when she invited me to come to her at Wanaha Base for a long visit I had come at once. And found both of them very little changed—Harry a little older, a little graver with the years of increasing responsibility. Kitty a little plumper, a little more sober when she thought of their son (now graduated from Annapolis in his turn and serving a tour of sea duty), but the same Kitty, pretty, gay, adept and by now well trained in her position of Commanding Officer's wife. She had a quick temper which she had learned to control; occasionally a sharp and impulsive tongue. But I think she was popular and well liked wherever they were sent and I knew that she was liked and respected on the base.

I heard her little heels clicking along the hall and Harry took his hands away from his face and sat up straighter as she came into the room. She had a tray in her hands, which she put down on the desk. "I told Suli to bring breakfast for us here," she said, and poured coffee for us. She took her own cup and sat down on the sofa. Her dark eyes were fixed on Harry, waiting. He lifted the coffee cup to his lips. None of us spoke until Kitty could wait no longer. She said unevenly, "It would be Parly—"

"Kitty—" Harry began.

"—of all the people on the base!" She had a red silk dressing gown pulled around her; the white lace on her nightgown showed at the front. She pulled the dressing gown closer around her with a kind of shiver and put out an unsteady hand for a cigarette. "At least," she cried, "he deserved it!" There were tears in her voice and in her eyes, but there was anger, too. Harry saw it and got up. "Now, Kitty—"

"All right. I'll stop. But he was a rat and you know it."

"He was one of my officers, Kitty. And he was murdered—"

"He was—" Kitty burst out, met Harry's eyes and checked herself. "What happened?"

"Sarah will tell you all there is to tell."

"*Sarah*—" With one of her quick and disarming changes of mood Kitty cried anxiously, "Oh, Sarah, I'm so sorry. It must have been horrible for you."

Harry said to me, "Tell me again, Sarah—everything. Don't ask her questions, Kitty, until she's finished."

So, sipping hot coffee and grateful for it—and for the house and the comfortable, pleasant study, grateful for the presence of Kitty and Harry—I told them again. It still seemed, as the O.D. had said, impossible; it couldn't have happened. But it had happened.

"*Ether*—" Kitty cried and turned to Harry. He said, "There was an empty can which had held ether on the floor under the bed. A towel in the washroom adjoining the room had been soaked in it. Probably knocked Parly out. Gave whoever murdered him a chance to do so—well, quietly. No struggle. No call for help."

Again there was something about that I didn't want to pursue.

Kitty's face was suddenly stiff and white. She reached with a queer, blind motion for her coffee cup, lifted it, put it down. "Go on."

She didn't say anything when I got to the knife, but Harry interrupted then. "Clasp knife. Regular issue. No identifying marks so far, unless there are fingerprints. Anybody could have had one—almost everybody does have one."

But when I told of the man who had left the wing, the man in khaki-colored uniform with three gold stripes on his shoulder board, Kitty gave a kind of moan. "Oh, Harry— There's only—well, Commander Gary, Rosy, Commander Nagel—"

"He was fairly tall. About six feet, Sarah thinks. That lets out Nagel and Roslin."

Kitty blinked. "There's Baker. He's about six feet. And Cranshaw. Or—"

Harry turned to me. "How about lieutenant commanders? Could it have been two and a half stripes?"

"N-no." I thought back to that instant's flash of braid. "No. Three."

They eyed me, however, rather dubiously, so I began to question it myself. Three stripes or two wide stripes and one narrow stripe? "I think—I'm sure it was three."

Harry said slowly, "And Jim, of course. He's six feet. But —is that all, Sarah? Everything—?"

It was all, except the fact that at some time the previous evening little Sally Wilson had visited someone in the wing — Who, I thought suddenly? Who?—and I hadn't seen her leave.

I ought to tell them, of course. Not only was Harry the Commanding Officer; he and Kitty were my friends and I owed them loyalty in all things. Why had I let Jim Warring extract a promise from me? Yet Sally Wilson could have had nothing to do with murder; it wasn't really important. All that went through my mind as Kitty turned to Harry. "What are you going to do?"

"It's the very devil," Harry said again. "We'll investigate. Try to settle it. Find out who murdered him and—" He paused, looking very bleak. It diverted me from Sally Wilson.

"What happens?" I asked them. "Is it a matter for civil authorities, the police, or—or what?"

"It's up to me," Harry said shortly. "It's like a ship. I'm Commanding Officer."

"But the—the investigation?"

"First I appoint a Board of Inquiry. They investigate and try to find the cause of death. Like an inquest in civilian life. I report to the District Office. It goes to Naval Intelligence and the F.B.I. If we can't settle the thing ourselves, fix the blame, they send officers here. . . . Usually it doesn't come to that. Trouble, I mean. But murder—" he rubbed his forehead. "I can't say I've ever had murder in my command. However, usually evidence comes out pretty quickly. Someone will know something."

"This isn't like a—a brawl," Kitty said sharply.

Harry rubbed his forehead again. "No," he said, bleakly. "In fact in my experience it's unprecedented—" The telephone at Harry's elbow rang. He answered it. "Captain Somers.—Oh, Jim—" He listened, his brown face showing tired, fine wrinkles. "I see. Well, that's bad.—All right."

He put down the telephone. Kitty, leaning forward with her pretty white arms clasped around her knees hard as if to prevent their shaking, said, "What—"

"Edith Pillsbury says the ether was probably taken from the drug supply in the west wing. Checked it just now."

My own cup clattered on the table as I put it down. "Who—"

Harry shook his head. Kitty cried, "Ether! But why would they have a can of ether in the west wing? The operating rooms are in the east end—"

"Removes adhesive," I told her. "Harry, nobody went into the drug room. I'd have seen—"

"Edith says it's gone. Jim talked to the day nurse; she says it was there yesterday. Says she used it for something about 9 last night."

One hour before I went on duty. Not much leeway. I said slowly, "I suppose someone could have gone into the drug room while I was busy—just at first when I came on duty. Or even later—I stood at the door for a while, looking out. That was when I heard a door open and close."

"The drug-room door?" Kitty asked.

"I don't know. No, it seemed nearer."

Harry said, "We'll have to question the men in the west wing—Jenson—"

"He was asleep," I told him. "In the storeroom. He had a headache." There was still something in my mind which I wouldn't permit statement, either in spoken or unspoken words. Evading it, I said, "Someone might have entered the wing from the main corridor, tiptoed across past the chart desk to the drug room and out again. But it doesn't seem likely. I think I'd have heard or seen—"

Harry said, "No. There's a girl on the switchboard, just beside the main door, all night. As you know. She says nobody came in after she went on duty at 10. Nobody went into the west wing from the main corridor. She's sure of that. Jim talked to her too."

So that settled that. I said, "Maybe Jenson saw somebody—" But I doubted it; he'd have said so. Besides he was sleeping savagely during the time preceding the murder, or at least preceding the time when a man had quietly walked out the west door of the corridor and I had seen him leave.

"Jim's questioned Jenson," Harry said, tapping his fingers absently on the desk. "Jenson didn't know a thing."

"I could have told him that!" Kitty snapped, reviving for an instant. "Jenson's never known anything!"

I was rather pleased at her natural tone, but at the same time I was inclined to think that Jenson knew almost everything that went on anywhere. Harry said, "Look here, Sarah, this goes against the grain, but we've got to question everybody. What about the sergeant? The one they call Buffalo?"

"What about him?"

"I mean—" Harry's mouth was a tight white line. He thought for a moment and then said bluntly, "He had a gun with him. Had no business having it."

"I know. I was trying to make him give it to me."

"Yes. We had a little difficulty persuading him to give it up. Not much; he knows orders are orders. But still—Sarah, would you have any reason to think he might have quarreled with Parly?"

I stared at him. "No!"

"You see, there are only two likely motives, a quarrel, or," Harry said rather sadly, "a case of battle fatigue. Something the doctors haven't so far noted."

"Buffalo?"

"Sometimes it doesn't show up at once, you know. But once in a while a genuine psychiatric case gets on the loose, runs amuck. Unexpectedly. Breaks out like this or other ways."

Kitty took a quick breath that was like a muted scream. "Harry! Not here—"

"It's possible anywhere. Does happen. Not often, but sometimes."

"Not Buffalo!" I said.

Kitty's dark eyes shot to me. Harry said, "What's wrong with Buffalo?"

"He's got a bad knee. Kneecap shattered in Korea. Operated and fixed up with plastic. He's been having trouble with it."

"No signs of nerves?"

"None. Oh, he's impatient. Sedatives are ordered for him when the pain gets bad. That's all."

Harry looked at me. Kitty said, "But—but most of the men in that wing have been in combat, haven't they? It could—" she swallowed hard—"it could be anybody!"

Harry rose. "We'll have to question them all." He glanced at his watch. "I've got to be going."

"Harry!" Kitty cried. "Breakfast—"

"It'll wait, honey." He was at the door and Kitty sprang up and ran after him, her arm sliding around his waist. I heard them murmuring together as they went to the door. Then Kitty came back.

She stood for a moment in the doorway, a really lovely figure in her red dressing gown, very young-looking with her black curls and pretty face. Suli, one of the two Filipino houseboys, came pattering down the hall in the soft slippers he always wore and she stood aside to let him carry a tray into the study and put it on the table. He was very small, clad in spotless white duck; he had a smooth, young brown face. "Breakfast, missy," he said to Kitty, gave me an alert, curious look and pattered away again.

Kitty came into the room, stopped at the tray, looked down at it as if she didn't see it and then with a sweep of red silk closed the door to the study.

"Suli hears everything," she said. "Sarah, you don't know —we didn't tell you. It didn't seem important. Just one of those things. But now—" She came close to me, tears welling into her eyes. "Sarah, Parly *was* a rat. He had a bad record. Everybody'd had trouble with him. But this—" She swallowed and a tear ran down her pretty cheek. "He's been a

35

devil. You see, with a record like his, he's been passed over for promotion. Harry couldn't recommend him for another half stripe. A full lieutenant. He told him why; his fitness report was barely satisfactory. In fact Parly's whole attitude was so bad, let alone his performance of duty, that Harry had to tell him finally he'd either have to straighten himself out or get out of the Navy. That is, it's automatic, the next time he's passed over. And—and Parly—he's been saying that Harry didn't deserve his decoration. His Navy Cross. Parly said that he knew somebody on Harry's ship during the war, I mean World War Two, and that it was another man that ought to have got the Cross. Nobody believed him, of course. Except—well, you know, things do get whispered around. Jim Warring got wind of it, talked to Harry and had Parly on the carpet. And he—oh, Sarah, he was a worm. He said, yes, sir, and no, sir, and that whoever told Jim was lying. He denied it all. Harry told Jim not to make too much fuss about it, but to stop it; tell Parly it was his last chance. So Jim did. But Parly—the rumor didn't die down. Harry was going to have to take steps. And Parly—"

The tear dripped dismally down on her red dressing gown. "He's got a relative, an uncle, in the Navy Department; he's top brass. And Harry's in line for rear admiral."

"Oh—"

"Yes. Parly was always—well, bragging about his uncle and of course that didn't go down very well with any of us here, but at the same time, just because of his uncle, there was a kind of spurious authority about it. I mean nobody believed him and yet—"

The telephone rang again. Kitty wiped her eyes with the back of her plump white hand and went to answer it. Her voice, to my admiring surprise, became at once polite and cool. She talked and listened and talked and I didn't hear a word of it, for I was thinking of Lieutenant Parly.

There'll be hell to pay, the marine sergeant had said. And Kitty had said, "It *would* have to be Parly. Of all the people on the base."

She put down the telephone. I said, "Kitty, how many people know about this lying rumor?"

"Everybody, I should think. At least, they'll know about it now. You can't keep anything like that quiet. Murder—"

4

I sprang up and took her shoulders in my hands. "Kitty! Nobody could say Harry did it! The Commanding Officer! Harry—with a record like his!"

She looked at me; I could feel her try to steady herself. "No. Except—oh, Sarah, people will say anything! If there's even talk—question, suspicion, don't you see what it might do to Harry? He said somebody must have quarreled with Parly. Well—if that isn't a quarrel—"

"Kitty, you mustn't think—you mustn't talk like that—"

"I know." She wiped her eyes again. "That's right. I've got to control myself." She took a long breath. "That was one of the Waves on the phone. She wants to see me. She wouldn't say why, except it was urgent. I had to let her come. Will you talk to her while I go and wash my face? I mustn't let anybody see me like this. . . . Now then, eat some breakfast, Sarah."

I patted her arm. "Good girl." She gave me a wavering smile and whisked away.

I didn't like it. I didn't like it at all. It seemed to me that it would certainly be quite simple to prove young Parly's malicious whispering to be a lie. The Navy does not present a high decoration for nothing and certainly whatever deed of courage and valor for which it is presented is a fact, substantiated and established. Why had young Parly so maliciously but so obviously lied? That answer, from even my slight acquaintance with Parly, was easy; he was, as Kitty had said, a rat. And he hated Harry Somers, simply because he demanded performance of duty as an officer.

While there are many—heartbreakingly many—heroes in uniform, a uniform does not automatically make a hero. That requires something else. And something which, in my opinion, Parly was notably lacking.

I wished angrily that I could see Parly's top-brass relative myself; I'd soon put him straight if he had any delusions about young Parly. Blood may be thicker than water, but if the relative were the man he ought to be, he'd be ashamed of his nephew. And automatically on Harry's side.

It was, as a matter of fact, a sensible conclusion. Perhaps I've always been in love with the Navy, but certainly I had

37

every reason to respect the service and the men who make it what it is. So if young Parly's relative was top brass, then he was also a man of proved honor. That went without saying and it comforted me.

Besides, I thought, in all probability he and any other relatives of young Parly had had their private troubles with him; even a very young man doesn't turn into a shirker and a liar overnight. He doesn't develop into a whiner and a troublemaker in a minute. It takes some time.

I had had myself with Parly only petty and rude complaints and general whining. But Harry Somers was an experienced commander—experienced, reasonable, one who demanded that duties be well and promptly performed, but a man who was willing to take time, trouble and patience with any of his men—in this instance, Parly.

And certainly the revengeful lies of a young j.g. who already had a doubtful record were not likely to weigh much against a man of Harry Somers' integrity and record. It was a lie which automatically showed itself as a lie. I would say all that to Kitty.

Suli knocked, opened the door, said something, and Sally Wilson came into the room.

It brought me back with a jolt to my own problem of conscience. "Sally!"

"Oh—Miss Keate! I came to see Mrs. Somers."

She had run all the way apparently, was breathing hard and there were two bright spots of color in her cheeks. She was an exceptionally attractive girl, not far from being beautiful, with smooth light hair, a nice mouth and chin and very direct, dark blue eyes. Her summer uniform, seersucker so finely striped that it looked a clear cool gray, was crisp and neat. Her hat with its seersucker cover, her black oxfords and black handbag were spotless and trim. She was so pretty and slim that the crisp uniform set off her sweetness, like a frame for a picture. I couldn't blame Jim Warring for trying to keep her out of a murder investigation. On the other hand— well, on the other hand, I was afraid I was going to have to drag her into it. I didn't want to.

"There's a reason," Jim had said, and for the first time it struck me that it might be a reason which would not reflect favorably upon Sally. I didn't like that either. I said hurriedly, with a kind of compunction, "Mrs. Somers is upstairs. She'll be right down. Have you had breakfast?"

She glanced at the tray and gave a little shiver. "No. . . . No, thank you. Miss Keate. I'll—I'll wait—"

Kitty opened the door. Again I felt a wave of pride and

admiration, for she had changed swiftly into a yellow linen dress; she had brushed her hair and put on powder and lipstick and a string of small pearls; she looked composed, friendly—and capable of consulting with anyone with kindliness and wisdom. She smiled and said, "Good morning, Sally."

Reveille sounded just then, clear and sweet through the morning air. It was light outside. Sunshine streaked in bright shafts into the room where the curtains did not quite meet, and paled the lamp on the desk. Sally, in that mingled light, looked extraordinarily pallid. I went to the curtains and pulled them apart so the clear, bright morning sunlight filled the room. I turned out the desk lamp and Sally said, "Mrs. Somers, I've got to tell the Captain something. And I—I thought—if you don't mind, it would be easier to tell you first."

Her young hands were clenched together behind her. Her chin was high. Kitty said, "Why of course, Sally. Sit down."

But Sally wouldn't. "It's about Lieutenant Parly."

"Oh," Kitty said. "Oh."

"You see," Sally's mouth was unsteady but her words were clear and rapid. "You see, I—I knew him."

"But everyone—" Kitty began, and then said sharply, "What are you trying to tell me?"

"I was at the hospital last night," Sally said with that forced rapidity, like a child confessing. "I talked to him."

There was a sharp little silence. Then Kitty took a breath. "Sit down, Sally, and tell me—"

"Yes, I want to. It—" Sally sat down as Kitty did and linked her hands hard together in her lap. She moistened her lips. "You see, Mrs. Somers, he told me—he said that he—he said that he had something to tell me about my husband."

I sat up abruptly. Kitty said, "Husband! I didn't know you had a husband. I didn't know you were married—"

"I—" Sally's eyes wavered for a second; she looked down at her hands, bare, I saw then, with no wedding ring. "Yes. He was—there was an accident. He was in Naval Aviation. He was a pilot. It was a small plane and he—it burned."

"Sally! I'm sorry. I didn't know."

"Nobody knew," Sally said. "I mean it's on my record, of course. But—I haven't been here long, you know. I was transferred from Washington. And nobody here seemed to think of it or to—to know about it, so I didn't say anything. Except —I told Jim—I mean Commander Warring. I told him. But—" she looked up at Kitty. "Somehow the girls, the Waves and everybody got the idea I was Miss Wilson, not

Mrs., and they—I didn't want to talk about it. It seemed, I don't know how to explain it, but it seemed to—make it unreal. Far away. It was easier to forget." She paused and added simply, "Johnny's accident, I mean."

She looked down at the bright Indian rug. Yet it seemed to me that there had been a flash of something like shock, remembered or brought to life again, in her dark blue eyes.

Kitty said slowly, "My dear—I'm sorry."

Sally looked at the rug. "I didn't think it mattered. I didn't think I was doing anything I ought not to do. I was so grateful, you see. It was different in Washington. All the girls there, everybody I worked with knew about it and—I don't know how to explain. They were so kind, and so careful not to say anything that would hurt me or remind me that sometimes it did remind me. I couldn't forget and—and so when I got here and nobody seemed to think about it I—I let it go. I didn't say anything. And then after a few weeks I—well, I didn't do anything. I'd thought at first that somebody would notice it, in my record you know and—but nobody did. So I just—" she swallowed—"I just didn't speak of it."

But she had told Jim Warring, I thought; the reason for that was clear.

"Well," Kitty said, "I shouldn't think that's a crime. You must have joined the Waves later. After your husband's death—"

"Yes. But here at the base—I didn't mean to—to go under false colors. It just happened," Sally said again, stiffly.

"You didn't intend to," Kitty said pleasantly. "So long as your records are clear, I don't see how it could matter." But she was waiting for more; she bit her lip as if she wanted to say, "What about Parly?"

Sally said, "And then—well, it was this way. Lieutenant Parly—I knew him a little, of course. And he—he had known Johnny. That was at San Diego."

"Yes?" Kitty's plump hands were tight on the arms of her chair.

"And—" Somehow I felt then that Sally was arranging her words with care, as if she'd thought them out, rehearsed them and was now afraid she'd forget the lines she had rehearsed. She said, "Lieutenant Parly sent word to me that he'd like to see me about Johnny. He said there was something he thought I would like to know."

She stopped. And again I thought there was a curious stillness in her face. Like the incredulous stillness of shock.

Kitty said, "So you went to the hospital to see him?"

"Yes. Yes, last night."

This, I thought, was the crux of it, the reason for Sally's story. Sally looked straight at Kitty. "I—I don't— When I got there he was tired and a little—not very agreeable. He—" She stopped. Kitty said, "Go on, Sally."

Sally said slowly, carefully somehow, "He said he'd seen Johnny just before he left. That was at San Diego. Johnny's plane was found in the mountains—burned. Lieutenant Parly said he'd talked to Johnny and that—" her voice lowered— "that he thought I ought to know Johnny's last words. He—but then he didn't tell me. He was—in a sort of mood. It was as if he meant to—to tease me."

There was another pause. Then Kitty said, "That was very cruel."

"He—" Sally looked at her hands. "But he talked about Johnny and the morning Johnny left. He said that Johnny might have picked up somebody to go with him on the flight. A hitchhiker. I—I hadn't known that. When they told me, I mean when I got the official notification, they said nothing of anybody else in the plane. It was only Johnny I knew about." Her voice dropped to a whisper. "They sent me his things then, later."

There was another silence. I knew Kitty was thinking hard, questioning, arranging in her mind, the few and sadly simple facts. "When did this happen, Sally?"

Sally's voice was low but clear. "Three years ago. We hadn't been married long, you know. Only a few months. I'd known Johnny since I was a little girl. We lived in Virginia, not far from Washington. We were married and then in just a few days, really, Johnny was sent to San Diego. We hadn't even had time to find an apartment or anything like that. I lived at home and Johnny lived there, too, when he could. But I was going to San Diego to join him. I didn't go with him. My father is alone and he wasn't well. I was to wait for a few weeks before I went to San Diego. But then—it—they told me what had happened. So I—I didn't know—it was so terribly sudden and final and—but anyway, then when Father was better, I got into the Waves. I was stationed in Washington. I kept thinking about Johnny and—I wanted to come west, I don't know why. Perhaps because that was what we had planned, Johnny and I. And besides there in Washington everyone knew about it. I couldn't—I don't mean I wanted to forget it or to forget Johnny. I couldn't forget Johnny. They lived near us, Johnny's people, I mean. Johnny and I—ever since we were children we'd known each other. I couldn't ever forget Johnny." She paused. Her young mouth set itself almost as if she were taking some inner but

41

resolute vow. "I can never forget Johnny—" she said, half-whispering.

"Of course not," Kitty said.

Sally's eyes lifted to Kitty's. "I wanted to get away, somewhere where everybody didn't know about it and—so I asked for a transfer west, in this country if possible, and they sent me here."

Kitty said slowly, "You want me to tell the Captain this?"

"Oh, would you? I ought to have told everyone, right away. But—and then Lieutenant Parly last night—I did go to the hospital."

I said, "When did you leave, Sally? I didn't see you."

She gave me a rather bewildered look. "I—I don't know. Not exactly. I was—I didn't want anyone to see me. Lieutenant Parly had—I was upset. I think I left a little after 10. I'm not sure." She paused as if trying to remember the time more exactly. Then she gave her head a little shake and pushed back a wisp of fine light hair with a disarmingly childish gesture. "But just as I went into the corridor the lights went out."

"Lights!" Kitty looked at me and I nodded. "The electric grill in the diet kitchen was being repaired. The lights were out—oh, several minutes." So that was why I hadn't seen Sally.

Sally said, "I went out the west door. I—hurried. I went to my room. I was—crying, I guess. I didn't go back to the dance. Then this morning I heard about it."

I said slowly, "Did Parly say anything about—say, a quarrel with somebody? Was anybody else in the room? Did anyone come in while you were talking to him?"

"No."

I made another try. "Was there anything at all, Sally, that might suggest—you see, they don't know who murdered him and they've got to find out. Anything, no matter how small, that seemed unusual to you or—"

Sally got up with the swift, frightened movement of a bird. "There wasn't anything!"

She had told Jim Warring that she'd been married and that her young husband was dead; naturally she would have done so the moment Jim began to show any special liking for her company. And Jim had said, there's a reason. I had believed him. I said, cautiously, "Did you tell Jim Warring that Lieutenant Parly had sent for you and why?"

"Yes. He said of course I must see him." A faint flush crept up into her cheeks, but then as suddenly it drained away, so her face with that resolute, lifted chin was startlingly white.

And that too was what Jim ought to have said. If he was falling in love with Sally and knew it, then he'd do exactly that, for Sally's sake and for his own. And for, if it came to that, the clear understanding and happiness of another marriage. He'd have to make sure that Johnny was in the past for Sally, and that everything was done that ought to be done.

Then I saw that Kitty was watching her intently, still waiting. She said, "Is there anything more, Sally?"

Sally turned to her. Again her words seemed to fall into a rehearsed and not too well-remembered pattern. "When I heard of the murder, I knew I had to tell the Captain that I had seen Lieutenant Parly. In the hospital, I mean. And—and why."

"I'll tell him," Kitty said.

"Thank you." Sally gave a quick little sigh, like a child who has confessed all. (Or had she confessed all?) She said swiftly, as if eager, now, to escape, "I'm on duty. I've got to go. . . . I expect the Captain will—will talk to me about it?"

"I think he'll have to talk to everyone who saw Lieutenant Parly yesterday," Kitty said evenly. Sally turned to the door and Kitty rose to go with her. "If you remember anything—ahything at all that might give the Captain information of any kind—"

Their voices died away in the hall. In a moment I heard Kitty's high heels tapping back to the study. She came in, gave me a long look and said, "That girl's not telling everything."

The trouble was, it was in my mind too. Yet I had an obscure desire to defend Sally. "She was frightened."

"Yes."

"She felt as if she'd been passing herself off as an unmarried girl. In effect lying."

"Well," Kitty said, "she was."

"But you can see how it happened. In Washington, near her home, she must have been constantly reminded of Johnny. People can suffer through kindness as well as anything else. Every time any of her friends started to speak of—oh, a dozen things, they must have remembered Sally and tried to turn the conversation to something else. All that. And here there was nothing like that. It was a new life to her. As if the past and Johnny had been put away and she could go on and make another life for herself."

Kitty went to the window and looked out. Her neat yellow dress outlined her pretty figure. The sun made a nimbus of light around her dark hair.

I said after a moment, uneasily, "What will Harry do when you tell him?"

"He'll talk to her. Question her. He'll have to."

"Of course. But—"

"I suppose," Kitty said, "we'll have to check on her story."

"It's in her record. I mean that she was married and—"

"I mean about Parly. Whether or not he really knew Johnny."

"Oh. . . . She couldn't have made it up, Kitty. Why should she?"

"She was there," Kitty said over her shoulder. "She was in his room last night. Nobody saw her leave. The lights—that doesn't really fix the time and she knows it. She could have left much later."

"She didn't murder him."

"She'd have to give some account for being there. She must have come while the day nurse was still on duty. The day nurse would remember and tell it. Even if you didn't see her."

Compunction twitched at me again; I hadn't seen her, but I'd known she was there. However, now that Sally herself had told her story, it didn't matter. I said again, "She wouldn't have murdered him. You didn't see him, Kitty. A woman couldn't have—" Something stopped me.

"Anybody could have killed him," Kitty said. Her face being turned away from me, her voice sounded hard. "Harry said they thought someone had used ether to make him unconscious and then murdered him. A woman could have done that."

And that, of course, was what I had refused to put into words. My heart sank. Kitty was too smart for me.

I tried to rally. "But—but, Kitty, there'd have been no reason for Sally to murder—"

Kitty turned around so swiftly that there was a force, something resolute and almost threatening, about her plump body. "There could have been any number of reasons. Suppose she isn't telling the truth. Suppose she *had* to get rid of Parly!"

I stared at Kitty. "Why?"

"Reasons—I don't know! She's been seeing Jim Warring." Her dark eyes were bright and cold. "Suppose Parly—"

"Suppose what?"

She shrugged. "I don't know."

"You can't mean that she might have been somehow involved with Parly!"

"How do I know she wasn't! Or—well, maybe he could

44

have stopped her marriage to Jim—it's easy to see she likes Jim."

"Johnny—"

"Johnny's been dead for three years. She knew him since she was a child. Perhaps she was fond of him, certainly she was—but it could have been a boy and girl affair. She's older now, more matured. Suppose she's fallen in love with Jim and it's really love for the first time. And Parly—" She eyed me again with that implacable cold look. "Suppose she had to get rid of him!" She said again.

"Kitty!"

"Don't look at me like that. The girl wasn't telling all the truth. You can't deny that. There are too many loopholes. She says Parly sent for her, said he wanted to tell her something about her husband and then didn't. Does that sound likely?"

"Well—" I said slowly. "Parly was a liar and a trouble-maker. He was petty and mean; I know that myself. Sadistic perhaps in a petty way. Yes—I think it could have happened like that."

"So Sally Wilson went home and cried all night!" Kitty said scornfully.

"Yes, I think that could have happened. If for no other reason because she may be in love with Jim and talking to Parly brought Johnny back and reminded her so she felt disloyal to Johnny and—"

Kitty interrupted. "You're making a case for her. You've always got a soft spot in your heart for somebody you like. And you're a sucker for young love."

Kitty, normally, was a sentimentalist and matchmaker, bar none. I said tartly, "What about yourself?"

"If you think I'd let anything or anybody hurt Harry, I won't!"

"But *Sally*—"

"She was there. She was with Parly. He was murdered. And she's scared! You can see that."

I could. Murder is shocking, yes; even the murder of someone known as slightly as, by her account, Sally knew Parly. It had been painful and difficult for Sally to talk of Johnny, stirring up again the memories and grief that Parly had recalled to her the previous night. Yet did any of it quite add up to the odd effect about Sally—of some deep and secret shock, some inner, desperate resolve?

Kitty took a sharp breath, "Between Sally Wilson and Harry—I don't care about Sally Wilson." And Harry—Harry's everything to me; her lifted head, her eyes, the firm line of her pretty mouth said it so emphatically it was like a shout. She went to the tray and began to gather up the breakfast things. "You didn't eat anything, Sarah."

"I wasn't hungry."

"No—what a night you had! You must sleep now. I'll keep the house quiet. It's Sunday so the marine band doesn't practice today."

5

As I drew the curtains in Kitty's pleasant, orderly guest room to shut out the dazzling sunshine, the nervous tension which had kept me going suddenly let me down. I was so numb with weariness I could scarcely get out of my white uniform. Even the marine band, which had an unnerving habit of practicing furiously on the green outside B.O.Q., couldn't have kept me awake.

But then, trying to sleep and thinking instead, a curious and indeed very terrible thing occurred to me. The cold fact was that the only people who, so far, might conceivably have had a motive for killing Lieutenant Parly, were Harry Somers, Sally Wilson—and Kitty herself. Kitty with her utter devotion to Harry, her quick anger, her sometimes wildly reckless nature! Parly had lied about Harry; could Kitty have believed that he could have succeeded in spotting Harry's fine and unblemished record? Could Kitty, wild with anger . . . No! I rejected it, shocked by the process of my own mind. It was an outrageous question.

And I couldn't believe that young Sally Wilson could have taken a knife . . . No. That wasn't possible, either.

Outside I could hear the usual morning sounds of the base, late because it was Sunday. A light thud on the porch below my windows told me that the day's newspapers had arrived, tossed neatly onto the porch by a nonchalant sailor making his rounds. I might say that I could never accustom myself to sailors delivering the newspapers. I wondered what was going on in the hospital.

By then they must have removed Lieutenant Parly, notified the powerful relative. At that moment in staff meeting they were deciding the course of investigation.

How many of the officers present, listening to Harry, offering suggestions, knew of the lying, whispered rumor

Parly had started? All of them probably by now. But they knew Harry too; none of them would suspect that Harry Somers, Commanding Officer of the base, would have stooped to connive at murder.

Of course, any commander, especially one like Harry, inevitably makes enemies—not many, and only among the few, the very few, whom his duties require him to admonish, reprove and keep in line.

I hadn't told Kitty the comforting and certainly logical conclusion I had reached as to the unlikelihood that Parly's spiteful little story would be credited by his august relative, whoever he was, or indeed by anybody in Navy circles. That morning she was shocked, her quick nerves on edge. Once her emotions were under control, she'd see it clearly. Probably Harry had pointed out the fact to her many times.

And I wanted to talk to Jim Warring about Sally. Or was I, I thought morosely, a meddling busybody? And then I remembered Lieutenant Parly as I had seen him last, and tried not to—and faces and words, the long, night-lighted corridor, the sound of the disaster whistle, Ensign Smith's red hair and the sailors, and Jenson paddling up and down the corridor, and Harry's face with the fine lines around his mouth and Kitty's tears all blended together in circles. I didn't wake until mid-afternoon.

Consequently I missed a day of swift and decisive activity on the base—as well as a day during which excitement ran high. Rumors, of course, had sprung up like the gusty desert wind, and ranged from suicide to an attempted enemy attack.

The staff meeting, however, resulted in prompt measures which stopped the more dramatic rumors. Although all during those hot and uneasy days and nights, a multitude of other rumors sprang into life, were whispered over the base and then, most of them, died away again. The most stubborn of these was a recurrent story of a homicidal maniac at large— which resulted in, I must say, a certain amount of justifiable apprehension. It is not really very pleasant to feel that any unexpected step on a porch might be that of a stealthy and random murderer. Or that any face, even a face which is familiar and known, may shield the disordered intent of murder.

However, that morning steps were taken. A bulletin was issued, saying briefly what had occurred. A Board of Inquiry was appointed—the Security Officer (Commander Nagel), the Legal Officer, Colonel Sinclair of the marines, Jim himself and one or two others. Security measures throughout were tightened. Investigation was begun. All the men in the wing were questioned; Lieutenant Parly's known acquaintances were questioned. He was quartered in B.O.Q.; the officers living in B.O.Q. were questioned. His belongings were searched. A longer task was the sifting of records of base personnel for some clue, some faint evidence that might conceivably bear upon Lieutenant Parly, or the murder. This included, of course, Lieutenant Parly's record, both at the base and at former assignments. It also included, I later learned, Sally Wilson's record, Jenson's and, of course, Buffalo Bill's.

Sentries of the previous night were questioned. Ensign Smith was questioned as to his unknown assailant—who, however, so far as Ensign Smith told them, remained unknown. In brief, the questioning was so wide that it included in the end almost every one of the officers and their families, Waves, nurses, and all those quartered in what was called the Row. It was probably an impossibility (certainly it was not possible within the space of one day) to question every person in the restricted area of the Row; it was not possible to question individually all the enlisted men, the marines and the many civilian employees. But that day there was a general order to the effect that anybody who might have seen or heard anything during the night which could conceivably bear upon the murder, or even which was out of the ordinary, unusual in any way, should report it at once. Sentries everywhere were doubled.

The fact that there were sentries on guard at every minute of the day and night simplified the problem in a rather unpleasant way. The base itself was not only well guarded; there was only one road into it. This road wound for miles through mountains and then between desert and mountains; it entered the base directly, went straight between the cluster of houses (administration buildings, hospital, church, school and Waves barracks, which was set off from the rest and called the Row), on one side and the barracks for enlisted men and marines (and Ships Stores, moving-picture theater, commissary, recreation hall) on the other side, to Wanaha City. This road was always under heavy guard. No one could have entered the base at night without being stopped by a sentry. No one could have left it.

And within this guard, the Row itself was set off by another guard at the gates.

Thus there were only two alternatives. Whoever had murdered Parly was passed by the gate sentry, or he already lived within the Row. And consequently was one of that relatively small and extremely close little community—all known well and familiar to one another. Every officer, including all commanders, lived in the Row. I wondered how Harry would approach that short roll call of commanders. I wondered when he would question them, what they would say. And when—or if—Harry would tell me the results of that inquiry.

This was just then the most urgent and ugly point of inquiry, but there was much more than that to be undertaken, and all of it entailed an enormous amount of questioning, checking, sifting which would take days to accomplish.

The shorter route of investigation, at least what they obviously hoped would prove to be a shorter route, lay in investigating the circumstances of the murder and Lieutenant Parly's acquaintances, seeking a motive.

Unluckily, it developed all too soon that most of those with whom Lieutenant Parly had come in contact at one time or another had had what could be called a quarrel—which was not so much a reflection upon our tempers on the base as it was evidence of Parly's far from charming character and activities. It was no easy task that had been placed upon Harry and the other officers.

The house was quiet when I awoke and instantly remembered, too well and fully, the previous night. Suli, as was his custom while I had been working at the hospital, had placed a lunch tray outside my door. From the silence in the house I took it that Kitty was out, but when I emerged from the shower I heard the murmur of voices on the porch below my window and, after I had lunched and dressed, I went downstairs.

It was by then getting toward late afternoon with the sun still pouring goldenly upon the base but the shadowy eastern slopes of the mountains were already blue and purple. I heard Harry's voice at the telephone in the study but Kitty was on the porch, in the long porch swing. Jim Warring sat beside her. Colonel Sinclair, the Commanding Officer of the marine battalion, was sitting morosely near the cocktail table.

Jim was talking. ". . . windows are out. All the screens in the wing were closed and locked on the inside. Nobody went past the main entrance, and the desk and switchboard there. No—if it was somebody outside the hospital he had to come and go by way of the west door of the corridor." He saw me and sprang up. "Hello, Miss Keate."

Colonel Sinclair gave me a disgruntled and troubled nod. Kitty said, "There you are, Sarah. Have a drink."

Jim poured me a Coca-Cola and at my questioning look

49

Kitty shook her head. "Nothing! Nobody saw anything! Nobody knows anything! Except that Parly was murdered." She looked and undoubtedly was tired and, as always with Kitty when she was anxious, quick and sharp in speech. I took the glass Jim handed me. Colonel Sinclair, nursing a highball and eyeing the blue slopes of the mountains, said, "I tell you there's nothing—nothing at all in Buffalo Bill's record to suggest a brain storm. He's a steady guy. Fine sergeant. Magnificent record. I think Harry can believe every word he says. No question of it." He sipped his drink, nodded his massive gray head and said, "Buffalo didn't do it."

"Well," said Jim, "I don't think so myself." He turned to me. "It's been a busy day," he said, and outlined the various measures they had taken, but did not mention any special inquiry among those officers of the rank of commander.

Kitty swung her little foot and stared at the tip of her slipper, and Colonel Sinclair drank and eyed the mountains. The sky was a clear, enormous blue; from where we sat we could see the base flag, red, white and blue, floating high and beautiful against the sky. "The upshot of it is," Jim said finally, "we're just about where we started. Parly could have been murdered by one of the men in the west wing; some of them have alibis after a fashion—Buffalo and Parly were the only patients who had private rooms. The other rooms, as you know, were occupied by two or four men—but, of course, we don't know exactly when Parly was killed. The doctor thought from a half-hour to—say, two hours before he saw him. He couldn't pin it down—Parly was etherized, by the way, as we thought. They did a post-mortem. But while several of the men report being awake, talking, seeing each other at various intervals during the night, still it's perfectly possible that the murderer could have been one of those men, who could have been up and about while his roommate was asleep. So far, though, we've found no motive among them. Jenson saw nothing out of the way. The girls at the switchboard and main desk, there at the main entrance, are sure no one went into the corridor leading to the west wing. So—" he sighed. "So there we are."

"What about the sentries?" I asked.

"Drew a blank there, too. There were the usual little parties returning from a drive or Wanaha City. None of them after about 1. Nobody without a pass. Everybody accounted for. Most of the people in the Row were at the club dance."

He stopped abruptly and there was a curious, sharp silence which for a moment I didn't understand and then I understood too well. Everybody in the Row was suspect. So, already, they were trying to establish alibis. It gave me an odd sensation of unsteadiness, as if the earth had given itself a sudden shake under my feet. Or as if I had inadvertently stepped on quicksand.

And also, in the same moment, I was appalled by a sense of the quantity of detail the investigation into murder must involve. There were too many people to be sifted down, questioned, their stories to be compared. Yet in another and even more appalling sense, there were too few. If they limited the suspects to the people living in the Row, that meant—well, it meant Kitty and Harry and Jim and the Colonel—and the men in B.O.Q. and all the officers and their wives living in the small clusters of red brick houses, with the neat little porches hung with green vines. It meant the Waves in the long barracks across the green, visible through gaps in the trees, with lights beginning to twinkle from behind the windows. Sally Wilson was there.

My thought seemed to have wings which touched Kitty. She leaned forward, her hand clasped around her pretty ankle, an odd look, part defiance, part something angry and cold in her dark eyes. She said to Jim, "Sally Wilson left the dance to go to the hospital, to see Parly—"

It was news to the Colonel, who jerked his massive head and sharp gray eyes toward Kitty. It wasn't news to Jim. He took a moment to put his glass very carefully upon the table. Then he rose. "I've got to go," he said politely to Kitty. "Thank you for the drink. Tell Harry I'll be at B.O.Q."

His eyes were angry too, and likewise defiant, so they seemed to meet Kitty's gaze with a spark. Before she could speak he turned to me. "How about walking over with me, Miss Keate?"

I rose hurriedly. "I need exercise. Yes, yes, of course—"

Kitty, with a baffled and still angry look, watched us go. As we walked down the graveled path I could hear the Colonel's voice in what seemed to be a question. We got out onto the paved, winding road. The sun was sinking lower, swiftly as it always did toward the high, sharp rim of mountains. Across the valley we could see its light still upon a distant rim of hills, touching them to rose and purple and blue. The sky was blue too, edged with a clear lemon color. All around us the Row was taking on its twilight quiet. Father Andrew came out of the church, last to leave after evening service—which, I learned later, was remarkably well attended that day. The sunlight, striking across in horizontal beams, made a halo of the fluff of hair around his bald head, a chance illusion which modest and gentle (but firm) Father Andrew would himself have been shocked to observe. He wedged the door open, saw us, waved his hands in a friendly and apologetic way, as if he'd like to talk to us but hadn't time then, tucked up his black cassock and set off at a jog trot toward the gates and another service in the motion-picture theater.

Instead of crossing toward the B.O.Q. Jim directed our steps toward the church. Its old bricks were a gentle, faded crimson in that remarkably clear yet soft light. Its steeple pointed to the sky where all at once an evening star shone out. Jim said abruptly, "I phoned to Sally. She . . . Of course it's a horrible sort of thing. She's upset. She didn't seem to want to talk. But she said she had gone to see Kitty."

"Yes. I was there."

"Well," Jim said, "I'd have stopped her, I suppose. Not very smart of me. I was wrong to ask you to keep it quiet. It would have come out anyway. Besides, I couldn't have stopped Sally. What did she tell you?"

We sat down on the steps of the church and something of the evening serenity and the beneficence of the church touched us. I told him Sally's story, briefly, while he stared at the path, his tanned profile without expression. "I see," he said. "Did Kitty believe her?"

I hesitated; that was wrong too. When you have something to say, it's better to say it. "Kitty didn't think she was telling all the truth."

6

There was a little pause. Then Jim said obliquely, "You've heard about Parly and the Captain?"

"Kitty told me. It's all nonsense, Jim. Nobody's going to take the word of a boy like Parly. Besides, don't they get all the facts nailed down before they give a decoration?"

Jim laughed. "Oh, Lord, yes! There's no question of Harry's decoration not being earned." He sobered. "The problem is a different one."

"You can't mean this relative of Parly's would make trouble! A man like that!"

Jim eyed me, half smiling again, probably both at my ignorance and my earnestness. "It's his uncle. No, he's all right.

52

Nobody in the Navy more respected. He's on the board for promotions. Harry talked to him this morning."

"What did he say?"

"Well," Jim said slowly, eyeing the lofty peaks of the mountains which were by then outlined as sharply as if they'd been cut from paper against the last of the sunlight. "It wasn't easy for Harry. He had to tell him what happened. Then he had to tell him—uncle asked—what kind of record Parly had made."

"Bad."

"Yes. The boy was a problem. Harry told him the truth—had to; it shows anyway. Uncle didn't seem surprised. Told Harry Parly's mother was his sister. Said as a matter of fact that they'd always had a spot of trouble with the boy. Said, quote, his fool of a sister, unquote, didn't bring him up right. Indulged him too much—all that. Said he'd tried to do everything he could with the boy. Said he was sure Harry had. Oh, he was decent as all get out."

"Did Harry tell him about Parly and the decoration?"

"No. I urged him not to. Harry agreed—at least he didn't say anything, but probably he'd already decided not to."

"But he'll hear it and—"

"I don't know. Seems to me that there are some things it's better to let die of their own lack of substance. I had Parly on the carpet, you know, as soon as I got wind of his dirty little tricks. I told him we wouldn't have it. Reprimanded him. He denied it. Harry said not to make an issue of it. Beneath Harry's dignity as a matter of fact. Not that Harry stands on dignity; he's got too much sense. However, there wasn't much I could do beyond giving Parly a good stiff talking to and warning. You can't go too far with something like that; you've got to stop it, of course, but it's bad psychology to give it too much importance. I'd have had to bring somebody in who'd face Parly with the story, who'd heard it from Parly —all that. First thing you know the whole base would ring with it. I put the fear of God into Parly—or hoped I had. Harry said to leave it at that."

It made sense, of course. But I said indignantly, "The old days of the Navy had something to recommend them."

Jim smiled briefly. "Discipline, you mean? Bread and water and the hold. I must say it would have been easier. But you've got to give a man a chance. I told him he'd have to straighten himself out or get out of the Navy. We can't let that kind of thing go on. We don't want bad Navy material and won't have it," Jim said simply and with finality.

"But uncle . . . Did he think uncle's rank would protect him?"

"Oh, Parly, the little—well, he's dead now. Anyway, he made a reference to uncle. I told him he'd be the first to kick him out. I told him that uncle wouldn't have made any allowance for relationship, in fact he'd have to bend over backward to show impartiality. He couldn't have permitted himself the patience Harry had shown. That was all. Parly went away—sullen and furious. That night was the night he had the car accident. Harry said to let the thing ride, give Parly a chance."

I thought for a moment. "What did his uncle say about the murder?"

"Seemed to think Parly had quarreled with somebody. Oh, he was shocked, of course, but decent—very. Didn't want to interfere—said it was in Harry's command. Didn't know of any special fact about Parly—I mean nothing that would suggest a motive. Said he heard from Parly only through his sister. Said he'd talk to her, tell her."

My fool of a sister, he had said. But I was sorry for her just the same. The clear sweet notes of the bugler sounded over the base and I turned as I always did to watch colors, red, white and blue against the lofty sky, float slowly downward. Peaceful, serene, so the moment was like a blessing and a prayer. The bugle stopped and it was as if something had said the week's work was over; tomorrow's work will begin; be at peace.

There was a kind of lump in my throat. I thought of all the men on the base devoting their lives to keeping that flag afloat. As Harry had done and only wanted to continue to do all the days of his life. Harry—and the Colonel of marines, and all the tough, fighting leathernecks. The sailors. The officers in those lighted small houses, all of them experienced, all of them fired into a hard and resolute pattern by combat and years of service.

It wasn't fair for one bad apple in a barrel of fine ones to threaten the fine ones. Yet someone had murdered young Parly.

The sun dropped down behind the mountains, swiftly and finally. At once the blue slopes of the mountains seemed to move upon the base, so the soft twilight spread over the trees, the lights in the houses were brighter, the shadows were deep and blue. I could see lights twinkling too from the long, rambling hospital—from the west wing.

"I'll have to get back to Kitty's. You said the problem was different."

Jim roused from deep thought. "Oh, that. Yes. You see—it's not easy to explain. I'll try to make it clear, but it's one of those things—well, in short, you know that Harry's in line for a rear admiralship."

I nodded. He went on. "Parly's lying little nonsense wouldn't touch that. Nobody would believe it. Anyway it's proved a lie before he uttered it. Uncle—if or when he hears of it—will feel like the devil, horribly ashamed, all that. But, at the same time, we've had trouble. Administrative trouble with an officer, one of our men. And murder. The board that decides important promotions has got a job on their hands. They've got to be right in their estimate of men. They've got to weigh and consider every scrap of knowledge of those men that they can sift out and analyze. They've got to stick to the men who can command other men and have proved it. Harry's got a magnificent record. But this—well, it's true that it's one of those things that couldn't have been prevented. Happened in spite of us. Nothing Harry or I could have stopped. But it happened. There was trouble," Jim said with a kind of sigh. "Why? What was it? Circumstances all reported in detail, yes. But there was trouble. And very serious trouble. Maybe," Jim said as if he were quoting, "maybe we'd better pass over Somers. At least this time." He turned to me. "Two times and he's retired."

"You mean if he's passed for promotion two times?"

He nodded. "It's automatic. Used to be three times; now it's two. It would kill Harry."

It seemed chilly suddenly, darker. I said after a moment, "No, it wouldn't kill him. He's tough. It would only break his heart."

"Same thing," Jim said shortly. "And the fact is the board would only be doing their duty. So it's got to be cleared up. And fast."

"Jim, how many people know about this story of Parly's attacking Harry?"

"Too many."

My heart was thudding. "But they can't—they *couldn't*—" I didn't want to say it.

Jim gave me a quick, hard glance. "Accuse Harry of murder? Certainly not. What could he gain?"

Nothing, of course. But Jim's denial was so swift and hard that it sounded defiant.

I rose. I could see flickering lights springing up in the dining room of the Captain's quarters. Suli was lighting the candles.

Jim rose too and faced me. "Did *you* think Sally wasn't telling all the truth?"

"I—well, no, Jim," I said miserably. "You see—as Kitty said, there was a sort of—of gap in the story. Sally said that Parly had sent for her; he told her he wanted to tell her something about her husband. And then he wouldn't say anything, yet she went to her room and cried all night and—she looked more deeply shocked and troubled than she ought to have looked, even at murder. . . ." If it was the murder of a man who meant nothing to her. I didn't tell Jim that.

He said, "That's what she told me. I knew she was going to see Parly—she told you that. I had taken her to the club dance; she left just before 10 to go to see Parly. It seemed to me right that she should. I want her to be—" He took a breath and seemed to square his shoulders. "I want her to be sure."

Sure that Johnny Wilson might stay in her memory but not usurp her heart, not any more, not for the rest of her life? Sure that the past was the past? A heart divided: he didn't want and wouldn't take that from Sally. Yet how was Sally, how was anyone to learn that reconcilement? I can't forget Johnny, Sally had said, half-whispering, as if making a promise, a decision, within herself.

But I didn't, quite obviously, know enough about love. Jim said, "I think she'll love me if she lets herself. I think she loves me now. So that's all that matters." I put my hand on his arm. He said, "She was so young when she married Johnny. They'd known each other all their lives. I think perhaps it was that. I think that in fact Sally, as a woman, still has to learn about love. And as for me," he said, suddenly boyish, "she's my girl. I've had it. She's my girl for the rest of my life."

We walked slowly along the path in the twilight; my hand was still on Jim's arm and he seemed to like it there. As we came to the curve that led to Kitty's, he put his hand over mine. "Thanks. I'll get Sally to talk to me. I promise you. But whatever she tells me—or doesn't tell me—well, I'm for Sally. You do understand that?"

I understood, all too well. I walked back to the Captain's quarters slowly and deeply troubled. Kitty had said I was a sucker for young love; perhaps I am. But I liked Sally with her square little chin, her loyalty, her direct blue eyes. And if I'd ever had a son I'd have wanted him to be like Jim Warring.

I knew that he was not only for Sally; the Navy was his love and his life too. What would he do if he had to decide between them?

I pulled myself up, at that, with a jerk. For Sally hadn't

killed Parly; she couldn't murder—murder I thought incredulously—anybody!

Jim had not mentioned the three gold stripes I had seen. So either Harry had told him in confidence or he had not told him at all. That, too, stirred something apprehensive deep down in my consciousness. I knew that Harry trusted Jim with many of his administrative problems; had he decided not to trust him with this? Why?

I avoided any mental speculation as to an answer.

Colonel Sinclair, his wife Marie, and Commander Gary and his wife Ruth were on the porch with Harry and Kitty; Suli was bringing out cocktails. I remembered only then that Kitty had said something about asking them to Sunday supper. Clearly she'd decided to go on with it, not put them off; carry on as if nothing had happened. Or, more exactly, as if what had happened could not concern Harry in any personal way.

I knew, of course, both the Sinclairs and the Garys fairly well. Colonel Sinclair was older than many of the officers on the base; solid, hard-driving, passionately devoted to his men. Marie was a large woman, with a long rangy face, short, reddish-gray hair and pale green eyes that saw everything. She was, however, kind and sensible with a forthright if rather sharp tongue.

The Garys were younger; if we'd had a siren on the base, it would have been pretty Ruth Gary with her smooth dark hair, sleeked back to a knot on her white neck, and long-lashed dark eyes. Ruth said darling and dear indiscriminately and had a way of patting uniformed arms softly and giving languorous glances from her dark eyes which exasperated some of the other wives, but made the Gary quarters extremely popular among the junior officers. There was no harm in Ruth; she merely had a flair for charm in capital letters as she had a flair for style, so she always looked as if she'd spent far more on clothes than a commander's pay could be expected to provide. She wore that night a sleek black linen dress, with bangles at her wrists and ears, which made Marie's inevitable flowered-print silk look dowdy and overfancy.

Commander Gary, tall, dark and rather taciturn, was obviously proud of Ruth's charm and indeed almost painfully devoted to her. That night, however, his devotion appeared to wear a little thin, for once or twice he frowned and all but snapped at her.

It wasn't a pleasant meal. We couldn't ignore the murder, yet the men were so tight-lipped and silent that we couldn't

57

talk about it either. The candles wavered in the night breeze and I tried not to think of the dull gold stripes on Commander Gary's shoulders. Suli slippered around the table with the vast tray of condiments. We had Rijsttafel that night, a real challenge to anybody's digestive talents, and I was helping myself recklessly to coconut, chutney, shredded almonds and a few other of the eighteen—I counted them—equally daring trimmings, when Ruth said she intended to lock all the doors that night.

"Darling, if it's somebody gone berserk—"

Commander Gary interrupted. "Stop that, Ruth."

"But it's possible, sweetie-pie," she said, with a kind of shiver. "It does happen—"

Harry said to me, "Oh, by the way, Sarah, the new nurse arrives tomorrow. She'll go on duty at once."

"So you've got only one more night at the hospital." Ruth eyed me blankly. "Well, that's too much. I wouldn't go near the place."

"Ruth," her husband said warningly.

Kitty said Sarah had been the greatest possible help. Harry said something too. We went out on the porch for coffee, with the deep black desert night all around us now. And all too soon it was time for me to get into uniform and go to the hospital. The Garys were leaving at the same time and we went together, trudging along the winding road. They left me at the west door and Ruth looked at the door and at me and Commander Gary took her arm as if to check anything she might say and said shortly that all of them appreciated my help, and good night.

So I went into the corridor of the west wing to take night watch for the last time, and I was thankful—but I was sorry, too, which was odd, and not only because nursing is my job, not only because I'd felt an odd sort of satisfaction in being permitted to do it. The fact was, I had an urgent sense of something unfinished. A chore not completed.

And something that had to be completed, because Harry had to be cleared. And there was Sally Wilson. And Jim.

The corridor was already quiet; the day nurse waited for me at the desk to give me orders for the night. She did so quickly and left; she didn't mention the previous night. But before she left she took up the telephone and gave the number for B.O.Q. "Lieutenant James said he'd take me home," she told me rather apologetically. And whisked away.

So it was going to be like that. Afraid to cross the lighted, grassy space to the Waves barracks. I'm going to lock the doors tonight, Ruth had said. The night before someone had crept stealthily into the wing, furtively along the bare, quiet corridor.

I wouldn't think of that. I busied myself with orders; Jenson bounced past and stopped to talk and I cut him off shortly. In another hour or so the entire wing had sunk into its usual heavy sleep, at least I sincerely hoped so.

All was quiet, yet in spite of myself I kept feeling that I was being watched and once or twice felt sure that there was some movement, somewhere near. When I looked, however, there was never anyone but Jenson and after awhile he disappeared and the night hours settled into their long quiet course.

I couldn't settle down myself, however, and after I was so sure that I'd heard a kind of rustle somewhere in the corridor that I let my coffee (early that night, indulging my own nerves), boil over while I poked my head out of the diet kitchen to look and listen—and saw nothing and heard nothing—I drank what was left of the coffee and went to Buffalo Bill's room. I had an extraordinary reason. I am not forgetful; indeed, it has been hinted that my eyes and ears are too sharp ("Old eagle eyes," was, in fact, one comment—made, however, by a little student nurse when she thought mistakenly that I was out of earshot). And, to quote the same generic source, I have a memory like glue. But Buffalo Bill had said something to me, there in his room the night before, which I could remember without, so to speak, remembering. Something noted at the time, forgotten, blotted out by the fact of murder. But something—wasn't it?—that might be important.

It was an elusive, but a tantalizing half-memory. So I finally went down the corridor to Buffalo's door. Jenson, his immediate duties accomplished, had long ago disappeared in the diet kitchen, there I suspected to smoke a cigarette with the door closed.

I knocked softly on the door to Buffalo's room, avoiding the sight of the closed and undoubtedly secured and locked door to Parly's now empty room. If Buffalo were asleep, I'd tiptoe away again. I opened the door a crack and listened.

There was no gentle snoring, no relaxed sound of breathing. I pushed the door a little wider. The room was dark but a faint streak of light from the corridor fell directly across Buffalo's bed, which was empty.

I went into the room. No one spoke, no one moved. But as my eyes grew more accustomed to the darkness I saw Buffalo kneeling at the window, his great shoulders almost blocking it off. His rigid attitude struck me with a queer stab of something like terror. I crossed the room and put my hand on his shoulder.

Without a word, without a sound, with a lightning movement so it was all in one he shot upward. And bells rang; birds sang; whistles blew. I saw as brilliant a collection of stars as was ever seen by mortal eyes as I swooped away into utter blackness. In a word, I was knocked out.

7

Out of a kind of ringing blackness there came first, perhaps not unreasonably, a certain surprise. Then I began to be conscious of other things. Lights pressing against my eyelids. A voice saying something I couldn't understand. Cold water splashed wildly on my face so my collar was drenched and cold. I opened my eyes. Buffalo Bill, huge and clumsy in his pajamas, was bending over me. He had a glass of water in his hand and was about to splash that over me, too. I said somewhat hurriedly, "Don't," and sat up against the bed.

"I didn't mean to! Oh, I *didn't* mean—I'm sorry! I don't know what—I didn't mean to, Miss Keate."

He waved the glass of water and thereby drenched my ankles. He looked as if he was going to cry. I took the glass with some energy and put it down on the floor and both his great hands shot to his head where he pulled and tugged at his hair. "I don't know why—I didn't realize it was you. I just—Oh, *gosh*—" He cried and pulled his hair and groaned.

I struggled upright, reached for my cap on the floor and then stood, leaning, however, against the bed and feeling rather peculiar and dizzy. Buffalo remained in a tragic huddle, crouched on the floor, beating his head now quite literally. "It was your hand on my shoulder. I didn't hear you come in. I didn't know anybody was here. I just—I just slugged. I didn't know I was going to."

"Well, I'm all right," I snapped, although rather feebly. "Get up and stop that nonsense." I tested my nose and cheekbone; nothing was broken, although it felt like it. He gave me one shrinking, all but tearful glance, and thumped his head and groaned again.

"Get up!" I said. "You didn't kill me. But why on earth—"

He got to his feet slowly and indeed very awkwardly compared with the lightning-swift speed with which he had swung at me. As he rose, the door opened and Jenson stuck his face in. His eyes were bright and curious. "Anything wrong?"

The marine sergeant muttered something I really can't bring myself to repeat. I said, "No, it's all right. I had a little accident."

I just ran into a truck, I thought bitterly. I just tangled with a concrete mixer.

"I thought I heard somebody groan," Jenson said. His eyes quickened and he stepped into the room to peer at me with a fascination which I do not usually attract. "Golly, Miss Keate, what's the matter with your eye?"

I could feel it puffing. I snapped, "I ran into a door."

He peered closer. "You're sure going to have one hell of a shiner," he said in an interested way.

A growl came from Buffalo Bill and Jenson looked startled. I said, "Get me some—"

"Whisky?" Jenson said brightly.

"Certainly not!" I snapped. "I'm in charge of the wing. I'm responsible for it." But I wanted to get rid of Jenson; there was no sense in the story going all over the base. I said, "Spirits of ammonia. Put it on the chart desk."

Buffalo rumbled again in an indescribably menacing manner and Jenson backed away. "All right. All right. I only wanted to—"

"Get out," Buffalo said succinctly.

Jenson did so hurriedly. And then Buffalo collapsed on the bed and looked at his great hands angrily. "How could I! I didn't mean to—I didn't—" He took a long breath that threatened to burst his pajama jacket and then said simply, like a rather sad child, "I've got to learn to stop fighting."

Well, of course, it was what he had been trained to do. You can't train boys for fighting, you can't teach them to protect themselves, instantly and swiftly in combat, and then expect those hard young bodies and lightning-swift nerves to forget all their lessons.

I tested my nose again, it being rather prominent and what might be called an exposed target. Buffalo sat in dejected silence and stared unbelievingly at his hands. "I felt your hand on my shoulder and I—I just swung. I wouldn't have hit you for anything—"

"Oh, shut up!" I said crossly, and then as his blue, bewildered eyes met mine I said, "Sheer reflex. I shouldn't have approached you like that." And I wouldn't do it again, I resolved grimly. Never monkey with a buzz saw. Don't pull the pin of a hand grenade.

He gave me such a miserable look that I couldn't bear it. "It was my fault," I told him. "See here, son, if you hadn't been trained to do just that you'd probably not be alive today. It was sheer muscular reflex, the kind you ought to have." He just looked at me with miserable, young blue eyes and I sat down somewhat weakly. Upon which Buffalo jumped up, all swift co-ordination now. "Spirits of ammonia," he cried, and limped out the door so quickly that I didn't stop him.

He was back in a moment with a glass in his hand and holding it for me to drink, his hamlike hands now as gentle as a kitten's paws. Jenson, or Buffalo himself, hadn't stinted me on the spirits of ammonia. I gulped as the pungent draft struck my throat. Buffalo Bill fussed over me like a mother hen. I wiped my eyes cautiously, got the glass tactfully from his hand and told him I felt better and to get off his leg.

He sat down again on the bed, a huge hulk of sorrow; I said, "What were you looking at? At the window, I mean."

"What?" he said, and seemed to travel back a long way. "Oh, that."

It was not enlightening. Neither was the suddenly rather guarded look in his eyes. "You were kneeling there at the window. So intent that—what were you watching out there?"

Buffalo's hands were suddenly very steady and hard on the bed. "Nothing."

"But—" His sudden wariness was like invisible barbed wire projected between us. "Was somebody out there?"

"No," he said quickly. "Not a soul. Nothing."

I looked at him. But there couldn't be anybody—well, prowling around the hospital. Could there be? Not with sentries doubled. Not with everybody on the alert, watchful. Not after last night.

Besides, if he'd seen anybody, or heard anything, he'd tell it. Wouldn't he?

He said with unexpected adroitness, "I was—I don't know —thinking about last night. Wondering why I hadn't heard it. The windows are so close—I mean mine and the one in Parly's room. Seems funny I didn't hear anything."

"But you did," I reminded him.

"No. No, I didn't."

"You said that something was going on. You said—" And then the fugitive and tantalizing memory chose to leap out of obscurity. I leaned forward. "*That* was why I came to talk to you! I couldn't remember, but now I do. You said there'd

62

been a row next door. In Parly's room! What was it? What did you mean?"

His eyes were candid, but he didn't want to look at me. He got up, limped to the window and stared at the black screen. "I don't remember saying that. I don't remember hearing anything."

But he had said it. I was now sure of that. I waited a moment. Then I said cautiously, "He had visitors yesterday, didn't he?"

"Oh—yes, I guess so. Seems to me I remember voices." He turned back, picked up a package of cigarettes and folded it neatly and carefully.

"Whose?"

"Well, of course, Jenson; he's got kind of a squeaky voice. And the day nurse—"

"Did you know Sally Wilson was there?"

He didn't look up from the cigarette package. "Sally? Was she there?" He paused, slightly embarrassed, and said, "I should say Ensign Wilson. I guess I always think of her as Sally. Yes, she was there, and there was an electrician fixing Parly's fan. Parly gave him hell about it. That was in the afternoon. I don't remember Sally. I mean Ensign Wilson."

I don't know why I thought he remembered perfectly, but I did. "Sally wasn't here in the afternoon. She came at night, that is, before 10. But she left right away. If you heard her leave, it would be a good idea to tell the Captain. Merely as a formality; you see, nobody happened to see her leave and—"

His eyes were wide now with an angry light in them. "Do you mean they think *Sally*—"

"No. It's only because they are questioning everybody and —and trying to get alibis for the people who were known to have seen Parly yesterday or people he knew and—and all that." It was rather lame.

But Buffalo's broad face flushed. "Oh, sure I heard her leave," he said promptly. "Must have been just after you came on duty. Yes, I'm sure of it. I heard your voice in the corridor. You were telling Jenson to do something or other. Yes. Sally left and—and I'm sure somebody came into his room after that. I didn't notice much. A man's voice. Maybe one of the fellows in the hospital. But that was early. I went to sleep and—what time was he killed? Can the doctor tell?"

"Within a couple of hours, I believe."

"Then Parly was killed between about midnight and about 2:30, when we found him?"

"That's what they think."

"Sally was gone long before that," he said flatly, and sat down on the bed again, with all the yielding and communicative grace of a stone wall. It occurred to me that he might be able to substantiate Sally's explanation of the reason for her visit to Parly. "Did you hear anything of their conversation—I mean Sally's and Parly's? It would help Sally. She's told them about it and—"

"No," Buffalo said.

"Look here, son—" unconsciously I quoted Jim—"I'm for Sally."

He studied me for a moment, his eyes bleak and watchful. He said then, slowly, "She's a nice kid." Doubtless it was unintentional, but his fist doubled up.

I gave it, I daresay, a rather nervous look. But I had to go on. "Buffalo, I don't want Sally involved in this thing, not in any way. She's explained her reason for coming to see Parly. If you heard anything, any scrap of talk that would substantiate—"

"Oh, I see!" But he stared at the bare and polished floor for a moment before he said, reluctantly and indeed rather carefully, "I could hear a few words."

"What?"

"Well, once I think she said she—she didn't believe something. And there was something or other about a letter. Nothing much but—" His blue eyes, wary now and cold, lifted to mine again. "What's Sally's explanation?"

"That squares with it," I told him quickly. "It seems Parly knew her husband, Johnny Wilson. He was killed in an accident. Parly wanted to talk to her about him."

"I see," he said again, eyed me and then nodded briskly. "Okay. You can tell the Captain that I heard that. And I heard Sally leave."

And that's all I'm going to get out of you, I thought tersely. And at that instant, Edith Pillsbury knocked lightly and opened the door. "Jenson told me you'd had an acci— Goodness! What an eye!"

"I ran into a door. In the dark." I rose. "You'd better have a sedative, Sergeant. I'll send Jenson with it."

Edith looked slightly baffled but also fascinated. Like Jenson. "It's swelling like everything."

I went into the corridor. She followed me to the chart desk. "Don't you want to put something on it?"

"No," I said, perhaps forcibly, for she said, all right, it was my eye, and glanced along the corridor.

"Is everything going all right tonight?"

"Oh, dear me yes! Splendid. Couldn't be better."

She ignored my feeble irony. "That's good. I was thinking of last night. Captain says not to talk about it. But how can we stop it! Well, I'll get back to duty. All my wing is as bright and lively as a Saturday-night dance. But I suppose the men here didn't get any sleep last night." She yawned. "You're lucky," she said, and swished away, her uniform rattling crisply, along the narrow corridor which led from the west wing to the main entrance and desk.

Lucky. The men, I regret to say, called her the Pill, which was inevitable, but I felt just then that there was also a certain appropriateness.

Jenson came out of the kitchen and asked me if I wanted coffee and I said no, I'd had some. "Can you see out of it?" he asked with interest.

"I can see you'd better get busy," I said tartly. "It's time for Graves's medication."

I followed him into the drug room and, after he'd gone, measured a sedative for Buffalo, resisting a mean impulse to retaliate by doubling the dose and thus give him in effect what I understand is called in certain circles a Mickey Finn. I sent it to him by Jenson and sat down at the desk and studied the charts as minutely as I could with one eye.

But Edith had put a curse on us. Just as I was trying to sort out in my mind the little, the very little Buffalo had told me of Sally's talk with Parly, the whole wing seemed to wake and turn restless. Red signal lights popped on with a frequency and persistence that kept Jenson and me busy for the rest of the night. Along toward dawn Ensign Smith developed an unexpected temperature. Indeed, I thought dismally, the entire situation was rapidly deteriorating and I was very likely to deteriorate right along with it, only faster. My cheekbone ached all the way to my back hair.

There wasn't any reason that I could see for Ensign Smith's temperature. He thrashed around nervously, his cheeks were red and hot and he wouldn't sleep; yet it wasn't enough rise in temperature to justify calling the doctor. However, when I went to his room again, about dawn, he had gone to sleep and roused fretfully when I advanced the thermometer. "If you'd just let me alone," he mumbled, half asleep and blinking at me. "I don't know anything about it. I didn't kill him for a—" His eyes focused on me. "Where'd you get that eye!" He sat up, staring at it, and his mouth being open I shoved the thermometer in it and pushed him flat again.

The temperature had dropped back to normal. So that was all right. And then with Jenson beginning to rouse the patients who had eventually drifted off to sleep again, and enduring their customary and freely expressed disapproval, and me getting the charts in order for the day nurse, it was all at once morning.

And the end of my last watch in the hospital. I would have felt a keener regret if the day nurse hadn't arrived, fresh and revoltingly cheerful. "Good morning," she caroled, "good morning—" and stopped. "Gosh! Whose fist did you run into!"

"Here," I said tersely, "are the charts. Smith's had a temperature—"

I departed promptly, without even a backward look at the familiar hospital corridor. I let myself out the west door. The sun was streaking across the grass and reveille sounded as I opened the door to Kitty's house—quietly so as not to wake anybody.

They were downstairs, however, early as it was, in the dining room, with coffee already on the table. Kitty heard me. "Come in, Sarah. Coffee's ready for you—*good gracious!*"

She stared, her eyes wide and horrified. Harry got up from the table dropping his napkin. "*What happened?*"

"If you've got a good battle going on anywhere," I said crossly, "just send in the marines."

"Well," Harry said judiciously, "that's what we do sometimes."

"What do you mean?" Kitty cried sharply.

"Oh, I brought it on myself. But he'd heard Sally—some of it anyway . . ." I poured coffee for myself and told them while I drank it. It seemed to me that it went a little but a valuable way toward substantiating Sally's story.

What I didn't anticipate—and ought to have done—was the long queer look Kitty gave Harry when I'd finished. And the way Harry's face tightened and his eyes grew worried.

Kitty leaned over the table toward him. "Harry, if that's battle fatigue, if that boy's as nervous as that—"

Harry got up. "I'll talk to him," he said quietly. "I think he's all right. Seems sound enough to me. As Sarah says, sheer reflex. Don't worry, Kitty." He started for the door, neat and erect in his uniform, turned back to say, "Steak," clearly not as a dietary suggestion, and went away.

Kitty was biting her lips, kneading a bit of toast, her eyes wide and speculative. Suddenly she cried, "But—but if he's like that—why, *he* could have killed Parly. The knife was in his room. He was next door to—"

The telephone rang and terror, nothing else, licked across Kitty's face. But Suli, in the kitchen, answered it and came to say it was for me. I took it in the study, my hand on Harry's desk, which was fortunate because it was the day nurse and she wanted to know why I had unlocked the window and the screen in Parly's room during the night.

"I didn't. I didn't go into the room! It was locked—I mean," I corrected myself, "secured."

"Well," she said after a moment. "Somebody unlocked it and got into the room, too. Last night. You ought to see the room. It looks like a hurricane had struck it. Rosy's fit to be tied—" she cut herself off. Somehow I felt that Dr. Roslin was standing at her elbow. My impression was confirmed when she spoke again, more formally. "Commander Roslin wants to know if anybody went into the room last night."

"No. That is, I didn't see anybody. Not anybody at all. I don't see how—"

She cut me off. "Thank you." The telephone clicked briskly in my ear. I put my own down slowly and hung onto Harry's desk. If anybody had got into Parly's room—by way of locked door, locked window, locked screen—then he was invisible. And so silent that in that quiet, night-lighted wing, I had not heard him.

But the door had been locked. The window and screen had been latched on the inside. He'd have had to have the key.

And Buffalo Bill had seen him! That was why he had been at the window! Kitty was standing in the doorway, clutching her red dressing gown around her, watching me and waiting.

8

When I told her she said, "Buffalo Bill!"

Buffalo Bill who had been kneeling at the window, looking at nothing, he had said. Listening to nothing. Yet so rigidly concentrated on watching and listening to nothing that he had not heard my approach.

"It was Buffalo Bill," Kitty said again. "He was nearest Parly's room. He could have unlocked the door. Or got out of the window and into the next room and— Did you ask him why he was at the window?"

"Oh, yes. He said there wasn't anything." But he had closed up like a clam, too.

Kitty, eyeing me, said, "You like Buffalo! How can you

defend him after he gave you that eye! It shows he's not stable, not—"

"I don't think he got into that room last night. I don't think he killed Parly."

Her eyes flashed. "But you think he knows something. Don't you? You think he's in on it—"

"In on what, Kitty? A conspiracy to do away with Parly?"

"N-no. I didn't mean exactly that. Oh, I don't know what I mean. Except Buffalo had the opportunity. He's proved what a nervous state he's in. He—" She stopped, thought and said sharply, "*Why* would anybody get into that room last night? What did he want?"

That, of course, was the point. She went on swiftly, "There must have been something Buffalo—or somebody—" she interpolated hastily as I opened my mouth to say it wasn't Buffalo—"or somebody wanted. What was it? Harry and all of them examined the room. They went through it and all of Parly's belongings. Everything he had in the hospital. Everything he had in his room at B.O.Q. What would anybody want out of that room?"

There was no answer to that. And I thought again, how could anybody have got into that room during the quiet night just past? So I didn't hear it, didn't see it, knew nothing of that visit. I had imagined, at times, certain stealthy movements in the corridor, but it had been sheer imagination. Hadn't it? There was never anything or anybody there when I looked.

But Buffalo Bill had seen something. I'd have to tell Harry that I was all but sure of it; Harry would question him. However, I very much doubted whether Harry would get any more out of Buffalo than I had. I didn't even explore the problem of why Buffalo had refused to talk of it. I said wearily, "Well, there's nothing we can do. I'm going to get some sleep."

At once Kitty was all concern. She made me swallow some breakfast; she got me off to my room; she pulled the shades and went away.

That was Monday, another hot, windy day with the sky like a brass bowl above us and fine drifts of sand everywhere. I couldn't compose myself to sleep at once; indeed I was only catching the very skirt of sleep when the marine band started on the green outside B.O.Q., tootling away with "The Halls of Montezuma," with which they always began and ended. It is a noble hymn; indeed it increases the pulse and brings a kind of lump in your throat and you think of Guadalcanal and Tarawa and Iwo Jima—and Belleau Wood, if you are as old as I am. It is not, however, conducive to slumber. They followed it magnanimously although not so spiritedly with "Anchors Aweigh." Somewhere in the middle of "The Wide Blue Yonder" I did go to sleep.

The base hummed around me on its usual busy routine. Ammunition was detonated out in the desert and I didn't hear it, which was unusual. It was the nerve-shattering custom on the base to detonate damaged ammunition. During the first week of my visit the thunderous boom and crash had sent me under the bed, waiting for the house to fall in on me, but when I discovered that there was a specific rhythm, a count (for the purpose of allaying any such alarm as mine), I learned to count but I held my breath while counting too. But that morning I was only dimly aware of the windows rattling and fell into exhausted sleep again.

That day, of course, as during the previous day, speculation and excitement ran high, with little groups of women gathering on the porches of the red brick houses, to be driven inside by the sand and heat and to talk endlessly of the murder while the men were not present to put a brake on such chatter. Certainly there was a kind of unspoken order which had gone out, suggesting such a brake, but human nature is human nature; it couldn't have been stopped short of individual gags for every person on the base.

And again that day Harry, Jim and the Board of Inquiry carried on that meticulous, patient job of investigation.

The sun was lowering when I awoke and the wind had gone down, which was a mercy. Sand lay in fine drifts everywhere, on the window sills, on the pillow and even my nose and teeth felt gritty and I was sure that I brushed it out of my hair. When I looked at myself in the mirror I had a shock; it had never occurred to me before exactly why a black eye is called a shiner. I had some sunburn lotion with a powdery white base and did my best with it, achieving a ghastly effect which, however, was a shade less ghastly than the truth. When I went downstairs to the porch, Suli was sweeping carefully with a dampened broom. Kitty was on the porch; there was the usual sunset cocktail tray and Harry had got back from the office and was sitting beside Kitty— his face gray from sand as much as fatigue. Kitty gave a gasp when she saw me and Harry said, "How is your eye?"

"Better," I said, lying.

"What *did* you put on it?" Kitty asked.

"Calomine lotion. Is there any news?"

There was.

The new nurse had arrived, Harry told me, and was to go on duty at 10. And there had been developments.

"About your little Wave," Kitty said and poured me some ginger ale. She glanced at Suli. "That's all, Suli," she said, and the alert little Filipino gave me a bright glance and gathered up his broom and slippered into the house. Kitty was looking both sulky and eager. She said, "It's a queer story—"

"Wait, Kitty. First—" Harry fished a neatly typed memorandum from his pocket. "We've been trying to make a sort of timetable, trying to fix the time of the murder as exactly as we can. Will you listen, Sarah, and see if this checks with what you remember?"

I was seething with impatience to hear about Sally, but when there's a certain steely look in Harry's eyes somehow one remembers that he is the Commanding Officer. I nodded and he read, "Eleven hundred: about then you felt that something wasn't quite right, you didn't know what, but you felt uneasy and checked all the charts to be sure that nothing had been omitted. Right?"

"Y-yes. If you mean about 2 o'clock. That is, I'd been feeling uneasy for some time. No real reason for it."

He made no comment as to that, but went on. "Then you went down the corridor and stood for awhile at the west door. The officer's club dance was still going on."

"That's right."

"While you were standing there the dance stopped. And about then you thought that you heard a door somewhere along the corridor open and close."

"Yes. I had just made a motion to turn, and was about to close the door."

"So someone in the corridor behind you might have seen your movement and ducked out of sight to avoid being seen by you?"

"Yes. Yes, I suppose into Buffalo's room—"

He interrupted, "The club dance ended a few minutes after 2—they meant to stop at 2 but went on for a few minutes. But lights were out within ten minutes. So it was about, say, twenty minutes or so after 2 when you went back to the diet kitchen. How long were you there?"

I thought back. "Five minutes, perhaps. I can't say exactly. When I came out I saw the man in uniform leaving—"

"We'll put that at about 2:25. You followed him to the door, then Buffalo's light went on. You went to his room and talked to him—how long?"

70

"Three minutes at the most. Harry, if it was the murderer in Buffalo's room—"

"I'm coming to that." I'd forgotten that one did not interrupt or question the Commanding Officer. Harry's crisp yet absent tone reminded me; clearly he spoke in just that tone merely from habit, but I had a wicked impulse to salute and say, "Aye, Aye sir!" I thought it healthy to restrain it. Harry said, "The disaster whistle blew at exactly 2:33. So that works out. You discovered Parly seconds before the disaster whistle. Consequently the murderer had time to escape the hospital, make his way to the administration building, and knock out Smith and touch the whistle."

I risked a question. "And after that?"

Harry sighed and put away the slip of paper and became an old friend, not the Commanding Officer. "That nobody knows. It's likely Parly was killed some time before you found him; the doctor says certainly a half-hour but possibly as long as two hours. They talked to Buffalo Bill today. They questioned the patients in the west wing. The person who admits to having talked last to Parly—aside from the murderer—is Jenson. But you'd expect that. He went into his room about 11. Usual night care; says nobody but Parly was in the room. So he thinks the lights went out for those few minutes about 10:30. Does that check with your own memory of it, Sarah?"

I thought back and after a moment said it did. "It was only a little while after I came on duty. I didn't look at the time, but I was measuring a sedative that Jenson was to give Buffalo Bill. It was his night medication. So it must have been about that time."

"How long were the lights out?"

"Not long," I said slowly. "It seemed longer, I expect, than it really was because we had to hunt out flashlights and all that. At the most, though, I'd say five minutes."

"Then that checks with Sally's story," he said. "She says she left while the lights were out. So that was about 10:30 and Jenson went to Parly's room at about 11, after the lights had come on again; he says only Parly was in the room."

So he had questioned Sally; I wanted to hear more of that, but Kitty said, "There's the bathroom. There's that little closet. Somebody could have hidden there—"

"Parly would have told Jenson if it was somebody he didn't want to see—say, the murderer. And Jenson went into the bathroom once or twice. Jenson was sure that nobody was in Parly's room then."

It still didn't narrow the time during which the murder

71

had been done. Harry said, "None of the boys in the wing admits to having visited Parly or spoken to him from the corridor during that evening. Somehow I think they're telling the truth. I don't know. We tried to work out alibis for as many as we could but it wasn't very satisfactory. Most of them were asleep. Wouldn't have known it if a roommate got up and killed Parly. Of course, some of them obviously couldn't have done it; we limited the inquiry to the ambulatory patients. But we got nowhere really, nothing conclusive; the only evidence was a negative sort of thing—that is, nothing developed in the way of any close association of any kind with Parly—no quarrel or anything like that. No motive." He sighed. "It's not conclusive; still, those things do leak out, and I'm inclined to think that we can eliminate the patients. Not only because of a lack of evidence suggesting one of them but because Sarah—well, you've nursed so long, Sarah. You've got a kind of sixth sense about your patients. I think that you'd have known it if one of them had done anything at all that was unusual. I think that trained sense of yours would have roused the instant one of them so much as sneezed." He was smiling a little, watching me.

I said tartly that they snored plenty, but in a way he was right. It's something that comes with nursing. You may not hear a fire engine on the street, in the night; you may not know there's been a thunderstorm. But if a patient starts to twist and turn in his bed, or murmur in his sleep—or even if all at once he gets a temperature, somehow you know it.

At the same time, I had let a murderer walk into that wing—somehow, some time—and then walk out again. I said, "You can't count on that, Harry. Somebody murdered Parly and he was one of my patients—"

Harry said, "And you knew it. Oh, I don't mean that you knew he was murdered, or that there was somebody in that wing who ought not to have been there; not with your mind. Not anything precise or factual. But your instinct told you something was wrong. And somebody was watching you, trying not to let you see him. You knew it without knowing it. So you tried to find out exactly what it was. I'm a believer in instinct," he said simply. "I've seen it operate in battle."

It was, of course, an explanation for the nagging uneasiness which I had tried to rationalize away, blaming Sally's unseen departure, blaming the weather, anything. Perhaps Harry was right. But if so, I had signally failed to heed its warning. I said tartly, "Instinct didn't operate very successfully for me! I never thought of murder!"

Harry didn't reply to that. He went on: "Buffalo's theory

is that whoever murdered Parly had come out of Parly's room—cautiously, first looking along the corridor—intending to leave by way of the west door. He saw you standing in the doorway and dodged into Buffalo's room. He waited there—probably for some time before Buffalo in fact roused —until he thought the coast was clear, when you came back and went into the diet kitchen. The murderer left the knife in Buffalo's room, first wiping off his fingerprints and with the intention not only of getting rid of the knife, but involving whoever was in the room in the murder. False evidence, so to speak. He waited and you didn't come out of the diet kitchen so he took the chance and hurried along the corridor and almost made it. If you hadn't come out of the kitchen just when you did, he'd have got away without being seen."

"Oh, yes, I think that's likely. I heard the door open and close. Buffalo Bill was certain that someone had been in his room. But I suppose he didn't thoroughly wake up until he heard the door close and whoever was there had gone—"

"In a commander's uniform," Kitty said from the dusk.

"Yes," Harry said after a moment, "yes. There's no news on that yet, either."

I moved uneasily and my chair creaked. "Did you tell the others—I mean the Board of Inquiry—about that?"

"Certainly."

"What did—" I swallowed rather hard. "What did they say?"

He shrugged. "Checked it, of course. No results."

"I did see him."

"I know. By the way, I've given them your account, but they may want to get it direct from you."

Like an inquest, he had said, in civilian life. I sighed. "All right. What about the disaster whistle?"

His shoulders moved in a kind of weary shrug. "Cover, again. The murderer had to get away. Confusion would help, bring out the fire department, curious people, everything. Give him a chance to mingle with them and get away. He went from the hospital, I think, to the administration building; door was open, all he had to do was walk in. Obviously he knew the layout; knew exactly where Smith was and that he was in the room alone. Waited his chance to get up behind Smith, hit him over the head—we don't know with what— but anyway hit him, touch the whistle, and then get away."

Kitty stirred impatiently in the shadow. "Tell her about Sally."

Harry sighed. "We've been looking into the records all day, checking—" He got out his handkerchief and wiped sand from around his nose. "Checking everything we can. It's a long job. But as to Sally Wilson, she was married to this young Johnny Wilson. He was a Navy flyer. He was killed in an accident. Young Parly was at San Diego and may have known him slightly, probably did know him. That much checks all right, but—"

Kitty said, "Tell her about the money."

"Money!" I said, startled.

"Well," Harry said, "yes, I'm going to, although there's nothing there, Kitty—"

"Tell her," Kitty said, lifting the glass and fixing a long and enigmatic look on the purpling eastern slope of the mountains.

"Well, Johnny was carrying a large sum of money for the paymaster. Ninety-three thousand dollars to be precise. It—when the plane was burned the money was burned too, of course—"

Kitty interrupted again. "They couldn't find it."

"They couldn't find anything that looked like the burned remains of it," Harry said. "It was a bad job, the accident I mean. They only identified Johnny Wilson because it was his plane, his assignment. They couldn't even find his dog tag; maybe he wasn't wearing it. By the time they'd located the plane it had been burned and everything in it beyond a recognizable stage. Oh, of course, there are always ways of identifying a plane, metal parts may be twisted and smashed but they are identifiable. Nothing else was."

There was a long silence. Poor Johnny Wilson, and poor little Sally. Nothing identifiable; nothing left at all of that youthful brief marriage. Harry said presently, "Sally's got a good record. Works in Commander Gary's office; he says she's excellent. Parly was at San Diego. It's not only possible, it's very likely that he knew Johnny and talked with him just before Johnny took off—"

"Wait a minute," I said slowly. "She said something about a hitchhiker. She said that Parly said that somebody may have got a ride with Johnny."

Kitty hadn't overlooked that and neither had Harry. "Yes. So Kitty told me. So Sally told me." There was a kind of defiance in his glance at Kitty. "She impressed me as a straightforward girl. I think she told the truth."

"Not all of it," Kitty muttered, watching the hills.

Harry went on. "She was upset, naturally. Sat there like a little girl and looked scared. That was natural too. But honestly, I don't think she cut Parly's throat. It wasn't a—a woman's crime." A kind of bleak shadow settled over his face.

74

"Sally couldn't have killed him," I said. It had become a formula: Kitty paid no attention to it. She crossed one pretty ankle over the other and swung her little foot.

"Ether," she said in a kind of murmur, eyes on the hills. "He was unconscious. The doctor said he was full of ether. So anybody could have done it. Sally—"

Harry put his hand gently on her knee. "Kitty, why? There's no reason. He told her he'd seen Johnny. That was all. Why should she kill him?"

"Jim," Kitty said flatly. "She's in love with Jim and if Parly could have stopped it, if he—"

"Nonsense, Kitty." His voice was gentle as always with Kitty but there was again a note of something steely below it. Kitty closed her lips tightly and swung her foot faster. I said, "*Was* there a hitchhiker?"

Harry shook his head. "If so, he wasn't deposited anywhere; Johnny Wilson hadn't made a stop; he was flying direct from San Diego here as a matter of fact, bringing the money. Paymaster here has to have a lot of cash. Then Johnny was to go on to Elwell Naval Base."

"There wasn't—" I began, fumbling for something, I didn't know just what; it lay too far below my outward consciousness—"there wasn't—well, another body in the burned plane. Besides Johnny?"

Kitty's foot stilled. Harry said, "No. Only Johnny."

So then there could have been in fact no hitchhiker. But it bothered me, oddly, just the same. I said, "And that was all Sally said."

Harry nodded. "She said that Parly had said something of seeing a hitchhiker, somebody wanting to hop a ride with Johnny. That was all she knew—"

"All she admitted . . ." Kitty murmured, and stopped as Harry's hand pressed her knee. But then she took a quick breath and flashed around.

"Don't try to stop me, Harry! I've been thinking of it and thinking and—suppose Parly was the hitchhiker and he got away with the money and—"

"Kitty! He couldn't—"

"And then—and then—" Kitty took a quick breath; her eyes leaped to me and to Harry; she cried, "Suppose Sally knew it! And she—"

"Stop that, Kitty," Harry said sternly.

I said, "Kitty, it was Parly who was murdered! Even if there was a hitchhiker and even if it was Parly and he got away with the money, Sally wouldn't have had a reason to kill Parly. If anything like that could have happened, it's

75

Parly who would have had a motive for killing Sally. But Sally—" Then I saw what had flashed into her mind. And what she didn't really accept for an instant.

Harry saw it, too. Savingly, he laughed. "Kitty, Kitty! Would you make Sally and Parly in a conspiracy! Sally sharing money with Parly; Sally covering up Parly's theft, Sally murdering Parly to—I suppose to keep it quiet. I can't think of anything else. Would you accept all that to protect me!" He laughed. But he took her little hand just the same. "Kitty, look at me. First, I don't need such a drastic theory for protection. Believe me. Second, that's as far-fetched a notion as any beautiful and altogether lovely wife ever thought up in her loyal little heart, because third, it isn't true—"

Kitty wouldn't be won over. She looked angrily at Harry. "You let yourself go overboard about Sally. Because a pretty girl looks at you with big blue eyes and says she doesn't know anything at all about the murder of a man she's just visited and that she—"

"And I'll tell you why it isn't true," Harry said, as if Kitty had not spoken. "Parly was not on the plane with Johnny. I asked. They checked back. Date, duties, everything. Parly was not in Johnny's plane."

"Oh," Kitty said finally, staring at him. "Oh."

I took a long breath. The trouble was that while I wouldn't have put it past young Parly to have got himself involved in something unpleasant in the extreme, yet he couldn't have had a hold of any sort over Sally. And Sally couldn't have killed him. I always came back to that. I said to Harry, "You said there wasn't any news about any commander at the hospital."

Harry released Kitty's hand. "They checked with every commander on the base. It was the only thing to do. Not one of them admits having visited the hospital for any reason at all that night. And," he said slowly, "I have to believe them. Yet you did see that uniform, Sarah. We'll have to go on with lieutenant commanders, even lieutenants, in the event you didn't see the stripes clearly. And it may have been a perfectly innocent errand. But we've got to get to the bottom of it."

There was another silence. Then I said, "What about last night? Who got into Parly's room?"

"There's a dead end there, too. Jenson knew nothing about it. I questioned Buffalo Bill about that, too. Told him I thought he might have seen whoever it was who got into Parly's empty room. He was at the window, you said. But he said he hadn't heard anything out of the way, hadn't seen anything, and stuck to it." He lifted his glass, eyed me and said, "Was that your impression?"

"Not—exactly," I had to tell him. "He seemed to close up when I asked him about it."

"Well—" Harry sipped his drink thoughtfully and then said, directly, "Is there anybody he'd want to protect?"

There was. It leaped into my mind and almost to my lips. Sally. Sally, again. She's a nice kid, he'd said, and there was something about it that seemed to me now like a declaration. And a defense. Sally.

I wasn't going to tell Harry that. Besides, I told myself quickly, it was only an impression. I shook my head. Kitty said, "What would anybody want in that room, Harry? You went all over it, didn't you? You and Jim and everybody? Why would anybody get into it and search it? The nurse said it looked as if a hurricane had struck it. Whoever got into the room must have wanted either to find something or to destroy something. What?"

Kitty, I thought crossly again, was too smart.

Harry replied wearily, "Oh, the room was searched. But nothing was taken. Nothing was any different, nothing missing that was there before. And nobody," he said with a sigh, "seems to know anything at all about it."

I decided, without any clear reason, to steer away from that subject. "How about Ensign Smith and the disaster whistle? Does he know who hit him?"

"No." Harry frowned a little as if in indecision. Then he said abruptly, "A rather odd thing has come up. That is, it was no secret, but it didn't come to my attention until today. Smith was with Parly when he was injured."

"Smith!" Kitty cried.

"They were coming home from Wanaha City. Smith says Parly picked him up on the main street, gave him a lift home. Car turned over. Smith hailed another car and reported it. Smith wasn't hurt."

There was another long and thoughtful pause. I said finally, "Was that all he told you?"

Harry shrugged. "That was all. Said Parly was driving too fast. He'd been drinking. Said he didn't know anything about what Parly had been doing that night. Smith saw him as he came out of El Rico's. Said he was talking to some girl, Smith didn't know who, he didn't pay much attention, on the sidewalk. Parly came toward his car, saw Smith and offered the lift back to the base. That was all."

Some girl. "A girl in uniform? I mean one of the girls on the base?"

Harry shook his head. "Smith didn't think she was in uniform. Says he didn't really notice. But he'd have recognized—" his eyes twinkled slightly as he glanced at Kitty—"he'd have recognized Sally," he said gently.

Kitty looked sulky and wouldn't smile. I said slowly, "Was that all Ensign Smith told you?"

Harry's eyes sharpened. "Yes. Why?"

"I was only thinking. He had a temperature that night. No reason for it unless he was—well, excited. Worried. And once when I took his temperature he said something about—he was half-awake, I'm sure, though—he said he didn't murder Parly, he wouldn't have murdered him for a—"

"For a what? What was he talking about?"

"He woke up then. He didn't say any more."

"I see," Harry said. "I see. Well, we'll question him again."

"He could have knocked himself out," I said slowly, digging back into such criminal lore as had come my way. "It has been done. So nobody would suspect him, I mean."

Kitty and Harry both gave me rather shocked and horrified looks, as if I had plumbed the depths of human perfidy. But after a moment Harry said bleakly that he supposed it was possible and they'd talk to Smith again.

Suli came out of the house.

The little figure in white, his slippers flapping softly on the floor, came toward us. I don't know why there was an effect of slow motion, so we were transfixed, watching him as if Nemesis in white duck and slippers was approaching us, but there was.

And we were right. Suli stopped in front of Harry. "Captain, sir—a man. The dry-cleaner. He wants to see Captain, sir, pliz."

Harry said shortly, "All right, bring him out."

The man was in the hall, just inside the door, waiting, and came at once. He was tall and thin and worried-looking; his shirt had damp patches over his shoulders. But we didn't really look at him, for he carried a uniform coat, a khaki-colored jacket, over his arm. He spread it out on the porch swing beside Harry. "I'm sorry, sir. But I think you ought to see this."

Kitty gave a queer kind of scream. Harry took up the sleeve of the coat and across the wrist there was a dark, rusty stain, stiff and dry.

I know a bloodstain when I see it. So did Harry. So, I suppose, did all of us. Suli sucked in his breath. Harry said, in a hard, somehow painful voice, "Whose blouse is this?"

The thin, worried man made a motion to turn it over, but

78

Harry forestalled him and moved the jacket so we could all see the three gold stripes on the shoulder board. The dry-cleaner said with a kind of apologetic gulp, "It belongs to Commander Warring, sir."

9

Kitty whispered, "That's blood—"

Harry said sternly, "How did you get hold of this? Tell me everything you know about it."

I never knew his name, this worried man; he ran the dry-cleaning establishment, outside the busy little Row and across the highway, a small shack wedged in between the PX and the motion-picture theater. He was a civilian employee, I knew that; he was not in uniform; but when there were deliveries to make sailors made them. Usually all of us took articles, dresses, coats, uniforms to his place, and called for them hurriedly ourselves. He carried on a brisk business in uniform cleaning. He cleared his throat now, anxiously. "It was your order, sir. You said if anybody knew or heard of anything unusual, and *that*—" his faded blue eyes shifted to the uniform and he didn't need to say that blood on a coat sleeve was unusual indeed.

"Go on," Harry said.

But it was a short and inconclusive tale. The coat had been simply left on the doorstep, certainly an undesirable ward, some time Saturday night or Sunday night; the shop was closed after 9 on Saturday until 7 o'clock Monday morning. The coat had been gathered up and he had not seen it himself until late Monday afternoon when he had been sorting out cleaning for the next morning. "It was blood, you see. So I— I didn't know what to do. Commander Warring's name is on the blouse here . . ." He put out bony hands but Harry had found the name on a tape neatly stitched inside. "It was Commander Warring, so I was in two minds as to what to do. But then—well, it was blood."

"Yes, yes, I see." Harry said. Kitty was very white, her eyes fixed on the dry, stiff rim of rusty brown. Suli, waiting curiously near the door, sucked in his breath in a whistle. Harry said, "Yes, that was right. I'll take care of the blouse. I am sure that Commander Warring will know exactly how it got there, some accident and— Yes, that was right to bring it to me." His look said, you can go now.

The dry-cleaner backed away. "I don't want to get Commander Warring into any trouble, sir, but—"

Harry rose. "No, no. I'll see to it. I don't want to hear about this from anybody else. Understand me? You've told me and that was right. Now keep quiet. I mean that."

"Oh yes, yes, sir." He backed toward the door and Suli opened it. Harry said to Suli, "That goes for you too, Suli. Understand?"

"Oh, yes, Captain, sir. . . . This way."

The dry-cleaning man and Suli's white-clad figure disappeared into the house, toward the kitchen. Harry folded up the coat and Kitty watched him. He rose. "I'll just talk to Jim," he said, and went into the house, carrying what he called a blouse, but was a coat to me.

"*Jim*—" Kitty said then, in a frozen way. "*Jim*—" Her eyes gave me one flicking glance. She picked up her highball glass. And both of us waited until we heard Harry in the hall again.

He came out on the porch. "Jim's coming over here."

"What did you do with the blouse?"

"Locked it in my filing cabinet."

"Harry—" Kitty began and stopped.

"There'll be some explanation," Harry said evenly. "Sarah—" he stopped too, and I knew why. He didn't want to say, could it have been Jim you saw? Suddenly I saw myself in court—or in court-martial, whatever it would be—star witness against Jim.

I had to wait a second or two while Harry's eyes waited too, watching me. Then I said, "I don't know, Harry. I couldn't swear to anything—except a man in uniform."

"And the height," Kitty said with a catch in her voice. "Jim is close to six feet. And the shoulder boards. Oh, Sarah—"

Loyal Kitty. She'd throw anybody to the wolves to protect Harry, but not Jim. Not somebody who was so close a part not only of Harry's official family, but in another and deeper way a part of their own family life. She cried, "Sarah, you *can't* give evidence against Jim. Isn't there something—I mean you *can't* be sure of the height! You *can't* be sure it was really three full stripes! Two and a half—"

"Now, Kitty," Harry said, "let's wait till we talk to Jim. Don't jump to conclusions. Besides," he sighed, "we've only begun the inquiry. All sorts of things can come to light. At any minute, any second—"

Kitty's back stiffened. "Of course. Yes, of course. Yes, of course—"

But then we waited while the bugler sounded taps, clear

and sweet through the desert evening. We watched the flag flutter down the pole. We saw Jim, hurrying across the green from B.O.Q. and along the road. He turned, running into the path, disappeared behind shrubbery and then came at a leap upon the porch. He gave us one swift glance. "What's wrong, Harry?"

Harry rose. "We'd better go to my study," he said.

They went into the house.

It was rather a disappointment; I wanted to hear the conversation.

Kitty was disappointed, too. "Might as well talk to him here," she said angrily. "Jim didn't murder anybody. No need to be so formal and official about it."

"I expect he wants to show him the coat."

"Blouse!" Kitty snapped, and seethed with impatience while we waited. I seethed, too. Lights were beginning to show here and there over the base. The sun dropped down with its usual abrupt finality behind the mountains, and the curtain of twilight descended promptly as if to mark its exit. Kitty replenished her highball with a nervous and rather lavish hand and then didn't drink it, but suddenly rose, avoiding my eyes, and went into the house, closing the door rather quietly. It was a long while before she returned, looking irritated.

"Not a thing," she said in a frustrated way and sat down.

"Did you listen at the door?"

"Certainly. But I couldn't hear a word."

"Really, Kitty—"

"Nonsense!"

So we waited and it grew darker. Kitty's pink cotton dress and white sandals and white face became light blurs in the dusk. At last Harry and Jim came out again and somehow their relationship had changed.

There was nothing visible, nothing tangible, but a difference. A difference which Harry seemed to try to bridge, for he told Jim to pour himself a drink; he went to sit beside Kitty on the porch swing. Jim appeared to try to meet Harry's effort; he poured a drink for himself, and sat down in one of the wicker lounge chairs. All was as it usually was, friendly, informal—and yet it was not the same at all. Harry said, "Jim says it's his blouse all right, but he doesn't know how it got there. Last time he saw it, it was hanging in the closet of his room at B.O.Q. That was a couple of days ago."

"You didn't take it to the cleaner's at all?" Kitty burst out.

Jim shook his head. "No. It's a fairly new uniform. Palm Beach cloth. More expensive than I usually blow myself to.

Thought I'd save it for dress-up occasions when whites were not in order." Jim's face was rather stiff and, I suspected, white under his tan. His eyes were fixed on his glass.

Harry looked at him. "Jim, I had to ask you about it."

"Yes, sir."

The sir was proper, of course; but as a rule, when it was not a question of orders, they called each other Jim and Harry.

Harry said, "I needn't say that I believe you, Jim. So, therefore, somebody took that blouse out of B.O.Q."

Jim said nothing.

Harry said, "The question is who?"

"Anybody could have done it," Kitty cried. "Anybody in the world can walk into B.O.Q. and help himself—"

Jim turned his highball glass carefully. "Impersonating an officer is a serious misdemeanor."

"So is murder," I said shortly. "I don't think anybody who is going to murder somebody would stick at stealing a uniform."

Jim glanced at me briefly and I thought with a flash of gratitude. Kitty cried, "That's right. Why, a woman could have taken it and worn it! A woman—"

"Six feet tall?" Jim asked.

"Well, it would have made a disguise. And Sarah could have made a mistake about the height—" But her voice trailed away doubtfully, and there was a little silence. I wished miserably that I had never seen that door open and flashing of light on shoulder boards. But I didn't think I'd made a mistake and obviously nobody else thought so, for presently Harry said, "It's the very devil. Think hard, Jim; somebody at B.O.Q. must have seen you or known you were there—"

"Sorry," Jim said. "I'd like an alibi myself, but it's as I told you. I took Sally to the club about 9:30. She told me Parly wanted to see her; we talked it over and she went to the hospital. I stayed at the dance a while; she didn't come back. I strolled over past the hospital and then around past the Waves barracks. I didn't see Sally, so I went on to B.O.Q. Nobody in the lounge saw me; my room's the first door on the left, before you pass the door to the lounge. Then the disaster whistle blew. Cranshaw was O.D. I was curious, tried to get Cranshaw and Smith and couldn't. So I got up and dressed and met you outside B.O.Q."

Harry said after a moment, "Well, we'll work on it, Jim. Somebody got that blouse. Meantime—"

"Meantime you'll have to report it to the Board."

"I'm afraid so."

"Right." Jim put down his glass. "Is that all, sir?"

But Harry rose and walked with Jim down the steps and along the driveway. And when he came back Suli was in the doorway saying that dinner was served.

"It's late," Kitty said regretfully. "You were up so early, Harry. You've got to get a long night's sleep . . ."

Harry put his arm around Kitty and smiled. But as we went into the house he paused to speak to Suli in a curt, stern voice I had never heard him use. "Suli, remember, you're to keep quiet about that blouse. If a word about it gets out—"

"Oh, yes sir," Suli said, bowing.

After dinner we had coffee on the porch, and then Kitty made Harry go to bed. "You've got to get some rest. I'm going to turn off the telephone and tell the man at the office that he can't wake you unless the—the whole place goes up!"

"In that case," Harry said dryly, "it would be too late." He paused to kiss Kitty unexpectedly and she clung to him a little. His light, quick footsteps went along the hall to the stairs.

And with Harry out of the way I felt the opportunity had come for a little errand of my own. It was not a promising errand; I think I undertook it only because of the ugly business of Jim's coat—I should say blouse. I had to do something. I paved the way cautiously. "Kitty, I'd like to get a breath of fresh air. I've slept all day and—"

"I wouldn't take a walk," Kitty said curtly. She had gone back to the porch swing, out of the little path of light from the doorway, so I couldn't see anything but her light dress, but I didn't like the strained note in the voice that came to me from the shadow. Indeed, I wouldn't have cared to take a walk either, not through the deep blackness of the night, past shrubbery, along the winding roads.

"I thought of a drive—"

She sounded surprised. "A drive! Why, of course, Sarah! If you—that is, certainly." The prompt and kindly hostess in Kitty emerged. "I'll phone for the car. I'll go with you."

I didn't want that. "Oh, don't bother. I'll just ride out toward Wanaha City and back. Clear out the cobwebs—"

"All right, if you don't mind. I'd really like to stay here and see that nobody bothers Harry. I'll phone for the car. You'd better take a wrap. It'll be cooler driving. And don't forget your pass."

So in perhaps ten minutes I was on my way, in Harry's official car with a jaunty young sailor for a chauffeur, to Wa-

83

naha City and a most nebulous sort of undertaking, for I wanted to find the girl who had been with Parly when he picked up Ensign Smith.

All I knew was that there was a girl and that she wasn't one of the girls on the base. Not a Wave, not a nurse, not one of the few civilian employees in the offices. Smith would have recognized her at once. But there was a girl. And I suppose instinctively I had been waiting for a girl to turn up; Parly had struck me as a lad who would have girls. And since he was talkative and boastful, that girl might—just *might* know something. It was a tenuous lead, so exceedingly unlikely to produce results that I hadn't even wanted to tell Kitty my purpose; if I failed to find the girl, as in all probability I would, nothing was lost.

We passed B.O.Q., lights spreading out from its low windows and open door. It would have been so easy, I thought, so simple, for someone to enter that low, rambling building at a time when all the men living there were out, and take Jim's coat. Yet, as he had said, it would be a serious offense to impersonate an officer.

I wondered what Jim was doing. I thought of Kitty's quick remark to the effect that a man's uniform would have been a simple and effectual disguise for a woman; Kitty had a faculty for hitting the nail squarely on the head. A disguise, yes, which a woman could have adopted. However, it would have been an extremely dangerous disguise; one quickly apparent, instantly attracting suspicion, failing in its own purpose by drawing attention to itself. Only in a very dim light, only at a distance, only at the briefest possible glimpse could it have deceived anybody. Certainly I didn't know any woman on the base who was six feet tall or anywhere near it. Little Sally Wilson was at the most five feet three or so.

I wouldn't think about Sally just then and I wouldn't think about Jim and the blood on his coat—and the way he looked and tried, obviously, not to.

We passed the hospital. Lights were shining there too, through the thickly planted shrubbery and above the west door. Tonight the new nurse would take my place. I had an impulse to tell the sailor to stop, and to go into the west wing and question Ensign Smith myself. Was he sure he didn't know the girl? What did she look like? Was there any possible bit of description he could give me? And what exactly had those rambling, half-conscious expostulations meant? If anything. But that was Harry's province.

We stopped for the sentry who scrutinized my pass and peered into the car to satisfy himself as to my identity, which as a rule they did not do. Once beyond the gates, we turned to the right onto the winding highway toward a dim radiance, visible even at that distance through the remarkably clear air of the desert night which marked Wanaha City.

I had a plan, of course, but it was almost as nebulous as the task I had launched myself upon. Since the girl was not one of the girls on the base, she had to live in Wanaha City. Barring a wigwam in the desert, which seemed unlikely, there was simply no other place to live.

She had been in Parly's company, and again since there was simply no other place to go, it was likely that they had been together at dinner in one of the restaurant-cum-gambling places. Since Parly had been seen by Ensign Smith outside El Rico's, I would start there.

When we reached Wanaha City and the increasing radiance turned into a dozen brilliant neon signs along its short main street and I told the sailor to let me off at El Rico's, he gave a slight start. The car swerved toward an approaching car, he retrieved it in a split second, but said, "Yes'm," over his shoulder. He stopped the car outside the great neon sign which practically blotted out the sky, and sprang out to open the door for me. "Wait for me," I told him.

"Yes'm." He hesitated. "Are you sure you wouldn't like me to go in with you?"

"No. That is—no, thank you."

"Yes'm." His eyes were bright and curious. "I'll be right out here if you want me."

I was rather touched. He was absurdly young, with his gob cap jaunty over one ear.

A burst of sound fell upon me; the juke box was going loudly, the place was full, the gaming tables were all crowded. It being Monday night there were not so many uniforms as toward the end of the week; still there were numerous sailors and marines enjoying liberty, beer, steaks, roulette and dice. There were some booths along the restaurant side of the big room, shielded by partitions between them; I went to one of them, which commanded a wide view of the room, sat down, and when an ancient waiter, his brown face shriveled by sun wrinkles, came to my table, I ordered ginger ale. He nodded, swiped at the table with a napkin, and rocked away at a bowlegged gait which suggested a youth spent on horseback. Noise and voices, laughter and the click of the roulette wheel swam about me confusingly. When the waiter returned I had a five-dollar bill in my hand. His sun-faded eyes sharpened.

"I wonder if you could tell me—" I couldn't lower my

voice; the noise in the room was too loud; I had almost to shout it. "Do you remember seeing a young man, a lieutenant in the Navy—his name was Parly—"

The brown face shriveled until it was a mask. "Guy that was killed? Sure. Used to come in here."

"Yes. Well, I wanted to speak to his—his girl friend."

The shriveled face and the faded blue eyes were suddenly chilly. "Oh," he said.

"Yes. Can you tell me who she is?"

He didn't say anything for a moment. The music stopped and a sailor nearby got up and went to put another nickel in the juke box. Music burst upon us again and I released the bill and shoved it toward the waiter. He swiped it up with another nonchalant dash of his napkin. "She's not far away," he said enigmatically. "But you'd better talk to the manager. You pay your check at the cashier's desk." He rolled swiftly toward another table.

Not far away. I looked all around. There was a girl in a booth opposite, with a young sailor patting her hand in what I can only call a persuasive manner. At another booth I saw one of the lieutenant commanders with his wife, both busy with steak and fried potatoes. Then the group around the roulette table shifted and I could see the dealer, who was a girl.

This was nothing unusual at Wanaha City; many of the restaurant and gambling places employed girl dealers. This one was fair, with her hair drawn back tightly to a kind of pony tail and tied with a black ribbon. Her pretty face was rather pale; she bent over the table, watched the bets and then spun the wheel again. The group closed up around her.

And then I saw Sally Wilson, sitting alone at a small table.

10

Sally was in her uniform, very sleek and trim. She had a glass before her to which she was not paying much attention, for she was watching the room. Scrutinizing it indeed and everybody in it, her pretty face as rigid with concentration as that of the girl at the roulette table. A party of sailors burst in the door and she turned to look closely at each one. She was waiting for somebody, I thought. Who? Jim?

I glanced around the room again and I couldn't see Jim anywhere. Sally sipped at her drink and rose, carrying the drink in her hand, and wandered slowly out of sight behind the noisy groups around the gambling tables.

The waiter had said, you'd better ask the manager. Had he said it in the usual laconic but significant western way, which means so much more than it says? Who was the manager?

There was a cashier behind a counter and huge cash register; there was a sort of cage with grilled windows where chips were turned into cash. Behind this cage a door appeared to lead to an office of sorts; I could see a calendar on the wall and one corner of a large safe.

Sally had completely disappeared; I couldn't see so much as the top of her smooth blonde head. After a moment I, too, wandered across the room, threading through groups of sailors, marines and some scattered ranchers and cowboys in blue jeans and high-heeled boots. When the cashier in the cage was involved with some marines who wanted and, needless to say, got silver dollars, I walked around the end of the counter and into the office. A man with his feet on the desk and a battered Stetson hat on his head looked up and said, "Sorry lady, I can't give credit."

He was a young man, very lithe and brown, with extremely sharp blue eyes.

"Are you the manager?"

He nodded once. Without so much as a flicker his gaze took in my glass of ginger ale and, as it soon developed, my black eye. "Listen, lady. You'd better give it up and go home. There's nothing to it, you know. Gambling. You're sure to lose in the end."

"Young man, I assure you—"

"I'm telling you. How do you think I'd run a place like this if it wasn't for suckers! The house always wins in the end. Now you take my advice. A woman of your age—" He shook his head, his blue gaze fixed itself on my eye, and he said in a fatherly and reproving manner, "Besides, I don't like fights. Especially women—"

Something didn't exactly snap within me, but my hand twitched to come into smart contact with his ear. Instead, I thrust my glass under his nose. "That's ginger ale. I want to ask you about a girl. That is—Lieutenant Parly on the base must have brought her here and I—"

I didn't finish, for his eyes turned suddenly iceberg cold. He rose with one lithe motion and closed the door. "What do you want to know?"

"I want to talk to the girl."

He eyed me. Beyond the thin pine door we could hear the hum of voices, the surge of music from the juke box. Suddenly I was aware of what I understand is called a six-shooter, lying in a careless way on top of the desk. I said, "That's all I want. Will you tell me who the girl is? I know she's here somewhere and—"

"Who are you?"

"I'm a nurse. Sarah Keate. I was on duty when Parly was murdered. He was with a girl here the night he was in a car accident and I thought she might be able to tell me something about him."

He waited a moment. Then he said in a soft yet really deadly voice, "I can tell you all you want to know about him. He was a . . ." Well, a so-and-so, and a this-and-that. I listened, rather approving it, as a matter of fact, until all at once he stopped, and said, "I beg your pardon, lady," and removed his hat. "What I mean is Parly was no good. You can't talk to the girl. She's my sister."

"Your—"

"That's all." He opened the door.

"Why can't I talk to her? I only want to—to ask her about him. Nothing that—" He looked at me and I looked at him. The juke box paused for an instant and then began to roar out "The Caissons Are Rolling Along."

He closed the door again. "Sit down," he said politely, but still in that remarkably soft, gentle—and deadly voice.

I sat down. He leaned against the door, very lean and thin, but tough-looking in his blue jeans and white shirt. His hair was startlingly blonde above his tanned face and his eyelashes and eyebrows were very light too, as if bleached by the sun. But there was nothing sunny in his blue eyes. "Look here, lady. I'm going to tell you a thing or three. Parly was a—" He swallowed hard and said with obvious restraint, "A no good sun-of-a-gun. He got around my sister with his flashy looks and a lot of highfalutin' talk about himself and his family and all that. She wouldn't believe me when I told her he was no good. I run a nice place. Anybody will tell you Dave Winters is okay. So's my sister and anybody will tell you that, too. I didn't like the way Parly was acting. I've seen something of guys like that. So I don't mind telling you that I—" He checked himself and seemed to substitute other words. "I told him to leave her alone. She thought he was serious. She began to talk about marrying him and going east with him and—" He rested one lean hip on the desk. "She wouldn't listen to me. She liked him and when she heard he was killed—no, you can't talk to her, lady. She's got to forget about him. I'm not going to have her questioned. I'm not going to have a word said against her. That clear?"

It was clear. No question of that. I said, "But see here, Dave. I mean Mr. Winters—"

He said, with no flicker of a smile, "Dave will do."

"They don't know who killed him. They've got to find out—"

"Bonny doesn't know a thing about it."

"Bonny—"

He looked annoyed. He said tersely, "My sister. Name's Wanaha Bonanza Winters. Named for a silver mine my grandfather had; it petered out." He watched me as if expecting me to smile and ready to give me another black eye if I did. Needless to say I didn't. He added, "We call her Bonny. I didn't mean to let it slip out. And I'm not going to let you or any of those boys in blue at the base put her through the works."

We eyed each other again, while all I had ever heard of western tempers, swift and final acts of justice, even vigilantes and bloody feuds about claims flashed through my mind.

But there was only one thing I could see to do. "You see, Dave, it's my duty to tell the Captain that your sister knew Parly. Probably she doesn't know a thing about him that would give the Captain any information about his murder—"

"She doesn't," he said shortly, but his eyes had narrowed.

"But he'd have to question her. He and the—the Board of Inquiry. Wouldn't it be as well to let me talk to her, first? I'll tell him anything she tells me—"

"There's nothing she knows about his murder."

"All right. But she just might know something about—say somebody he had quarreled with. Something he—oh, something he was going to do. I don't know what. Except she'll have to be questioned, so why not let me talk to her—"

My voice petered out like the Wanaha Bonanza mine. If a rattlesnake had blue eyes and levis he would have undoubtedly looked exactly as Dave Winters looked at me just before he struck. "Getting tough, aren't you?"

"Even if it wasn't my duty to tell the Captain that Bonny knew Parly, he'd find out sooner or later. Somebody will tell him. I promise you, if I talk to her, to make it as easy for her as I can."

Dave waited a moment; then he hitched to the other hip and said absently, yet as if it bore upon the conversation, "I was in the Army myself."

I thought it over, allowing for the laconic significances of western turns of speech. Finally I saw. "Parly wasn't typical of the Navy. In fact he'd got into some trouble. He was told he had to behave or get out of the Navy."

He made no comment about that; if there was approval it was unspoken. But he said, "You've got me, nurse, and you know it. Okay. I'll think it over. I'll let you know."

There was, of course, no reason why I could not simply go to the girl myself and talk to her. Yet in another way I couldn't. I said, "All right. You can phone to me. I'm staying at Captain Somers' quarters."

"Okay." He slid off the desk, opened the door and I went out. So that was that. If I hadn't talked to the girl, I had found her, in a way, at the first shot, which was lucky. Wasn't it?

I didn't feel too sure of that. I looked around for Sally.

Someone had taken the booth I had left but the little table where Sally had sat was vacant, so I sat down there. Sally's fair head wasn't anywhere to be seen through the shifting groups of people. My eyes fixed idly upon the roulette table nearest me and the girl dealer—as they call the croupiers at the roulette tables. And as I watched an odd little incident occurred. A jovial young sailor cocked his hat over his ear, bent over the girl dealer, put his arm on her shoulder, and in the flicker of a second simply disappeared below the roulette table. A waiter stood nonchalantly dusting off his hands beside the girl dealer. She gave the barest glance downward, looked back at the table and said, "Number eighteen. Red."

So that was Bonny. I was sure of it. Brother might let little sister work in his business establishment, but nobody was going to take any liberties with her.

It was all swift and matter of fact. The waiter idly watched the game. A wave of laughter broke out around the table to which Bonny paid no attention at all. A hand or two went down to help the young sailor to his feet. Some shouted, laughing remarks followed him as he took his way rather sheepishly to the dice table. And the girl dealer was Bonny.

She was a very pretty girl in spite of the strained tightness of her light hair and the absurd pony tail; she wore a white shirt, like her brother, and blue jeans. Her small face was rigidly concentrated on the game; she had sun-bleached eyelashes and eyebrows, a drift of freckles over high cheekbones and a wide mouth which looked as if a smile suited it better and more habitually than its present tightness.

Someone moved between us shutting off my view; I looked

around the room. There were many vaguely familiar faces, once or twice someone recognized me and spoke to me—the young lieutenant commander and his wife, whose names I couldn't remember, a boy with one stripe on his shoulder. None of them showed any surprise to find me sitting alone, which was not the custom in Wanaha City; I suppose they thought I was with a party who were trying their luck at the tables. Shore Patrol, two sailors with S.P. arm bands and guns at their hips, stalked sternly around in a circuit of the place and out again. Sally followed them out.

I saw her, making steadily and somehow very quietly, sliding between groups, toward the door and away.

I followed her. There was no use trying to talk to Bonny that night; I'd wait for Dave to speak to her. It seemed very odd that Sally was alone.

As I say, it was not the custom for any of the women on the base to visit Wanaha City, let alone sit around tables, alone. Part of it was base custom, and part of it was a bow to an even stronger western etiquette; women did not visit gambling places alone. When I got out onto the street, brightly lighted from the competing neon signs of the other restaurants and gambling rooms, Sally's slender figure in its crisp gray uniform was entering El Capitan's—as big, as flourishing, as noisy, as El Rico's. So I went into El Capitan's and there she sat at a nearby table, watching the door.

She saw me. For the barest fraction of a second I thought she was going to jump to her feet and run away. But then she said quickly, with a kind of catch in her voice, "Why, Miss Keate! I didn't see you—" She glanced past me. "Are the—the Captain and Mrs. Somers with you?"

"No, I'm alone." There was no point in beating around the bush. "I saw you in El Rico's and followed you over here. Are you waiting for Jim?"

"N-no. I'm alone, too." She made, somewhat belatedly, a little gesture toward the chair opposite her. As I sat down, her blue eyes traveled to the door again. The Shore Patrol marched in and again sternly made their way around the room. Sally's eyes traveled around the room, too, but not after them. She was looking for somebody, no question of that.

Naturally I looked too. But while, as in El Rico's, there were faces which seemed familiar, still there was nobody I could name.

I said, "I'm about to go home. I have the Captain's car. Can I give you a lift?"

Her blue eyes came back to me with a little jerk. She hesitated. Then she gave an oddly weary sigh. "Yes, thanks, I may as well go."

"Who brought you?" I asked, suddenly curious.

She rose. Her face was tired-looking under the bright lights and drained of color. "I took the bus. There at the gate."

That struck me as rather odd too, in that it implied a definite purpose in coming to Wanaha City. I didn't think she had been suddenly overwhelmed with an urge to watch the gambling. If someone had happened to say to her, "We're going over to Wanaha, come along for the ride," it would have been a more usual proceeding. But to go out to the gates, wait for the bus which trundled back and forth between the base and Wanaha City at thirty-minute intervals all day and up to midnight, all that implied purpose.

Perhaps she saw the question in my face; at any rate she said rather quickly that she was ready to go if I was and we left.

My sailor chauffeur seemed relieved when he saw me approaching the car and pleased when he saw Sally. He saluted smartly and flung open the door with a flourish. Neither of us spoke all the way back to the base, with the rosy radiance above Wanaha City fading away behind us, and the black desert night all around, our headlights cutting a bright path through it. We met and passed a few cars, not many. Off at our right lay the Area, distant, black and mysterious—and packed with latent and powerful explosives. It occurred to me that the Area was scarcely less packed with explosive and dangerous power than were the unfathomable emotions of human beings. Who had murdered Parly? To what particular explosion was murder due?

I was tired and I had accomplished exactly nothing. My small wave of self-congratulation as to the identity of Bonny Winters had vanished completely. I kept seeing the blood-stained cuff of Jim's coat and wondering what the Board of Inquiry—to say nothing of the District Office, F.B.I. and Navy Intelligence, if it came to that—would make of it. And the girl beside me, as still as if every nerve within her counseled caution, hadn't told all the truth. She hadn't told all the truth of her interview with Parly before his murder. And she hadn't made any explanation at all to account for her visit to Wanaha City, wandering from one gambling place to another—quite as if there was somebody, somewhere, she was trying to find.

I told myself I could be wrong about that. I told myself

that I was having an attack of the vapors—not, however, a customary affliction with me. We reached the lights around the base, stopped at the gate to show our passes and in a moment we drew up with a sweeping curve before the Waves barracks. The sailor swerved the car around and the lights flashed brightly across the banked shrubbery around the door and a man moved swiftly back into the shadows of the shrubbery, out of the light.

11

The sailor brought the car to a halt with a jam of brakes. Sally scrambled out the door. I cried, "Wait, Sally. Somebody is there—back in the shrubbery—"

Sally was out of the car, "No, no! There isn't anybody—"

The sailor jumped out of the car, started toward the lighted doorway, paused to stare and came back. "I didn't see anybody, Miss Keate."

"But I saw him! I saw his legs—"

"Thanks for the lift," Sally said swiftly. "Nobody's there, Miss Keate. It's all right—"

I put out my hand to stop her, but she was running along the lighted path. She flashed between the thick clumps of shrubbery and through the doorway. I could see her in the lighted hall.

The sailor said, "Honestly, Miss Keate, there isn't anybody. The murder's got the women sort of nervous. It was the lights flashing across. You thought some shadow—"

I thought I had seen legs and a furtive shadow slide back into the masses of shrubbery, which not only surrounded the entrance but encircled the whole long building. Yet it could have been an illusion of swiftly moving lights and shadows. The sailor's hand was on the door. "Want me to take another look?"

"N-no. I must have been mistaken."

He got back behind the wheel; we circled and came out on the lighted, winding road. Nothing moved anywhere. Certainly there was no point in reporting something I hadn't really seen—rousing the base, stirring up the exact kind of hysteria which Harry Somers was trying to prevent. If every woman on the base let her imagination run riot we would live in a constant state of alarm.

93

Our lights caught no moving, furtive figure anywhere. We arrived at the Somers house. I said good night to the sailor and thanked him, and went quietly into the house, so as not to wake Harry or Kitty. Kitty, however, was in the study waiting for me. And there was no use trying to telephone to Sally because Waves barracks don't run to the luxury of room telephones. Besides, what did I want to say? I only wanted to be sure you were in your room? Nonsense. I had seen her safe within the hall. And I hadn't really seen anybody waiting there in the shrubbery.

Kitty unsnarled herself from the sofa. "Where *have* you been? I thought you'd be back long before this."

"I stopped in at El Rico's, watched the gambling awhile." If I so much as mentioned Bonny, Kitty wouldn't wait for Dave, she wouldn't wait for anything; she'd be very likely to set out for Wanaha City and Bonny that instant.

Kitty's eyes narrowed. "That's an odd thing for you to do."

"It's late. I'm going to bed." I gave what must have been an unconvincing yawn, for Kitty snapped. "If you won't tell me you won't! But I'd like to know what you've been up to." She turned out the desk light with an exasperated click and I started up the stairs where, of course, we both had to tiptoe and say nothing for fear of waking Harry.

I went quickly into my room and shut the door almost in Kitty's pretty but suspicious face.

But then hours passed and more hours and I still couldn't sleep.

Yet it was a quiet night on the base—almost too quiet. The wind had gone down, and once as the hours crept along I heard the eerie, jackal cry of coyotes away off somewhere in the desert.

I wondered how the new nurse was making out in the hospital. I thought about Jim. I thought about Sally—and wished she had told me why she had chosen to prowl through the gambling places at Wanaha City. I thought of the shadow I had seen, there in the shrubbery, and in the silence and darkness began to feel that I was right and Sally and the sailor wrong and a man really had slid swiftly out of sight.

But if so why was he there? What was he waiting for? Rather, who was it he waited for? Sally?

But she'd hurried into the barracks; she hadn't stopped an instant.

If I *had* seen a man there in the glancing light, then it was someone the sentry had passed. Someone who lived in the Row.

I didn't know whether that made me feel better or worse. Except I wished Sally hadn't put it aside quite so—well, so quickly. As if she didn't want me or the sailor or anyone to make a search through the shrubbery. On the other hand, if she thought I was nervous, mistaken, too quick to see something that wasn't there at all, wouldn't she do just that—tell me I was wrong and hurry into the barracks?

The sailor had been positive. His eyes were younger and sharper than mine. Oh, forget it, I told myself. There was nothing to be seen.

Probably Dave would let me talk to Bonny; there wasn't much else he could do. But suppose Bonny knew nothing at all that could possibly suggest a reason for Parly's death. And it was no business of mine to try to see her. I was a meddlesome busybody. No other word for it. The thing for me to do was pack up and leave before I managed to do something that couldn't be undone. Murder wasn't anything to meddle with. Certainly I had no right or authority to take to myself the role of investigator.

Suppose Dave Winters had decided to take things into his own hands and execute a rather summary justice. He had made no secret of his feelings about Parly; suppose he had decided to get rid of Parly before he broke Bonny's heart or wrecked her life as Dave Winters clearly felt he would do. But if—put it plainly, I told myself—if Dave Winters had murdered Parly he wouldn't have admitted his feelings so frankly. From prudence he'd have concealed them.

And then my thoughts leaped to Jim again and his bloodstained coat. He, at least, had no possible motive for killing Parly.

The coyotes wailed again off in the night and sounded like lost souls jeering revengefully at the night and the stars and everything in the world. I rose and put cotton in my ears.

Morning was brilliantly sunny and extremely hot. There was no wind, which was a mercy, but the sun beat down; there was not one cloud in the sky and everything below it seemed to bake in a dry and exhausting heat. That morning there were services in the little church for Lieutenant Parly, after which his body was to be taken away and loaded, as a matter of fact, on one of the long ammunition trains which wound in and out, every day, across the desert to the base and back again to ships waiting to receive more ammunition.

The little church was packed.

There was a certain protocol in the seating. Harry and Kitty had their usual front and prominent pew and I sat with them with a white veil of Kitty's draped over my white hat and, I hoped, somewhat concealing an eye which had turned a not at all tasteful plaid in green and yellow. Jim sat beyond Harry. Owing to the prominence of my position as well as to the occasion, I couldn't turn to look at others in the church, although I longed to do so.

Father Andrew conducted the services and in view not only of the circumstances, but of young Parly's by then rather widely known characteristics, was obliged to stick sadly to generalities. He was unwontedly solemn and troubled, consequently; his kind voice pleaded as sorrowfully as if he himself were responsible for the whole thing. It was a short service.

Opinion was that the padre had preached a good sermon. Everyone called him the padre—as unself-consciously as they said, "Glad to have you aboard," when guests entered a house, which was certainly a house and not a ship. Or topside when they meant upstairs. Or bulkhead when they meant a wall, or chow instead of food, or ladder instead of stairway, or deck instead of floor, or snafu or scuttlebutt—of which latter there was just then a considerable supply; particularly, I might say, snafu.

We trailed out of the cool dimness of the church into the blazing heat of the sun. The men went back to office and loading plant. Kitty and I walked slowly back to the Somers porch and took off our hats. Suli brought us iced tea. And Bonny Winters came to see me.

I didn't recognize her when she came up the path and emerged at the steps of the porch. She was wearing a thin blue cotton dress instead of shirt and levis; she had done up her preposterous pony tail of hair into a neat little bun; she was carrying gloves and a little blue hat in her hand and looked altogether decorous, serious and a little shy. Not at all what you would expect of a lady dealer in a gambling house.

She also looked very young and the freckles stood out across her pale face. Her eyes were smudged as if she'd been crying. It was when I saw that, and while she was hesitating shyly on the step, that I recognized her.

Kitty rose to the occasion. "I am Mrs. Somers. Are you looking for me?"

I said, "Miss Winters! I am Sarah Keate. This is Mrs. Somers—"

Kitty said how do you do, pleasant but puzzled, and asked her to sit down and have some iced tea. Bonny sat down as if she didn't know what else to do; locked brown, sturdy hands together and looked at me. "Dave told me about you. Last night. So I—I came to the funeral, you see, and I—I wanted to see you."

Kitty gave me a swift and penetrating glance. "Last night! Dave—"

"Dave Winters," I said shortly. "Bonny's brother."

Kitty's dark eyes shifted to Bonny. "Why, you're the girl at El Rico's! At the roulette table!"

"Yes," Bonny said. "Dave owns El Rico's."

"Do you want to talk to me alone?" I asked Bonny.

But Kitty forestalled that. "Never mind me," she said flatly and poured iced tea for Bonny, put it into the girl's hand, settled herself on the porch swing and folded her arms with obviously every intention of staying there.

Bonny said, "It's about Lieutenant Parly. Dave said—you were his nurse, I—I wanted—"

She stopped. Tears were filling her eyes and she was trying to hold them back. But if I had any idea that she was going to tell me anything the shoe was, so to speak, on quite the other foot. She said, "I wanted to ask you about him. I mean about—it. Nobody seems to know and I—I had to come to you."

There was nothing to do but answer the child as kindly as I could, with Kitty sitting there, watching and listening so hard that she didn't move so much as an eyelash and Bonny's tragic, bleak blue eyes fastened on me. It was a painful five minutes. I told her as little as I could. And then when she put up her hand and wiped her eyes with her little white cotton gloves, I said, "You see, it struck me that he might have told you something that would give the Captain some—some clue. I mean, suppose Lieutenant Parly had quarreled with somebody or—"

She was her brother's sister; she swallowed hard and said politely, "Thank you. I had to know. You see—I liked him and—"

Kitty leaned forward, "Were you engaged to him?"

"N-no. That is—" A flush crept up over her high cheekbones. "It was sort of—of understood. I mean, he hadn't exactly asked me but I knew he—he would. And he meant it. Dave says he didn't but he did. I know he did. He told me about—about his mother and his uncle—"

"Yes," Kitty said rather dryly, "his uncle."

"He's somebody big in the Navy. And he asked me how I'd like living in the East and—he was going to resign from the Navy and—"

"You don't resign from—" Kitty began sharply and caught herself. "What was he going to do?"

"Well, with all that money coming to him, he wouldn't really have to do anything. But I told him that was wrong. My grandpa used to say work was something everybody had to do. He said it was a sort of obligation." She dabbed at her cheek with a white cotton glove.

I said, "Drink your tea, Bonny."

"Yes'm," she said obediently, and touched the glass with her lips. The freckles were not standing out quite so sharply now and her lips, bare of lipstick, were taking on a little color.

Kitty said, "I expect you saw Lieutenant Parly frequently."

"Oh, yes." She nodded her head.

I didn't really want to question the child just then, but the words came out. "Did you say he was going to have some money?"

She nodded again. "Yes'm."

"You said—all that money."

"Oh, yes. He told me. Thirty thousand dollars now and—"

"Thirty—" Kitty began, and Bonny went on, "And more later. He said—" Tears welled up again, "He said his wife would never have to worry about money. He was so pleased and—and sort of excited about it. You see, his mother had never had enough money and so much of the time, in school and everywhere with boys who were rich, he always felt outside of things, you know, and—" She stopped.

Kitty said, "Navy families aren't often rich, you know. Where was he going to get this money?"

Bonny drank tea, rather slowly and deliberately. When she put down her glass she looked exactly like Dave. "I'm afraid that's all I know about it." She rose with finality. "Thank you very much, Miss Keate. Thank you, Mrs. Somers. I'll be going now—"

"Bonny—"

She was already on the step and she didn't intend to remain another second. That was perfectly clear. I said hurriedly, "Bonny, when did he tell you all this? I mean about the money?"

"When I saw him that afternoon. The—the last time."

"*Saturday?*"

"Oh, yes," she said simply. "They said he was better. I phoned and they said he could have visitors. So I went to see him." Tears rolled down her cheeks all at once. Dabbing at them she ran down the porch and away.

"Well—" Kitty said. "Saturday!"

"In the afternoon."

"Yes, but she was there!" Kitty eyed me. "So you weren't going to tell me."

"There wasn't anything to tell."

But she had it out of me, of course, although it was true, that there was little enough to tell. However, I didn't mention meeting Sally at El Rico's. Kitty needed no possible small fuel to add to the smoldering suspicion she had already built in her mind around Sally.

And after I had told her the little I knew of Bonny, she sat for a long time swinging her little foot in its neat white sandal and pushing one hand through her short dark curls. Finally she said, but tentatively, "Parly was giving Bonny a line, that's clear. She's an attractive girl. . . . I suppose Dave *could* have killed him."

"He'd have had to get past the sentries, get hold of Jim's coat, get into the hospital, take some ether—get away again."

"Somebody did all that."

"I can't see Dave doing it. He might have shot it out with Parly—on the street or in El Rico's or—or anywhere. But—"

She gave me a shrewd glance. "There you go again. You like him. You like Sally. You like Buffalo Bill. You like— Sarah, there's a murderer here, on the base, somewhere. Somebody killed Parly."

12

Somebody killed Parly. It brought back Parly's room at the hospital, like a grisly picture superimposed against the brilliant sunlight, the green turf below the porch, the languid, green shrubbery.

All about us the base went on with what seemed its normal routine. Baking under the hot sun. A power mower going somewhere. The red, white and blue of the flag drooping without any motion at all against the brassy sky. The red brick houses around the Row seemed very small, with the mountains as a background; the green vines over their screened porches looked dusty and dry. Away off in the desert there was a long kind of boom and scrunch, followed by another, another and then a long pause, while the glasses on the table stopped tinkling. I said at last, "It's queer about that money. *What* money?"

"We'll tell Harry," Kitty said. "But I don't think there was any money really. It sounds like more of Parly's line."

It could have been exactly that. Suli came to announce lunch and Kitty sighed as she rose. "There's the Red Cross meeting here this afternoon. Don't forget you're to give them a talk about bandages."

Harry lunched as usual at the officers' mess, so Kitty and I had a quiet, indeed an extremely quiet lunch together, both of us thinking and one of us, me, thinking in circles that only turned upon themselves.

The Red Cross meeting started at two and the officers' wives arrived promptly. They arrived indeed right on the dot and there was a stiffness and formality about them from the beginning which was not at all usual, our meetings being all too subject to breaking down into hilarity or gossip (I mean to say scuttlebutt) until Kitty or Marie brought them quickly back to order. I didn't myself notice the odd air of formality at first; it was Kitty, with her trained sense of social nuances, who began to get small scarlet spots in her cheeks and brought the meeting to order with considerable dignity and formality herself. She then turned the meeting over to me, with yards of dressings, and Marie Sinclair for a model on the dining-room table. But even my demonstrations, which wrapped various portions of Marie's anatomy (and brought out prickly heat which Marie protested vehemently) were all accomplished in polite, dead silence. And when at the end of it Suli brought out cookies and fruit punch, nobody loitered over it, as was their custom, but instead, and with various excuses, took a rather prompt departure. Nobody loitered, that is, except Marie who resumed her flowered-print dress in the dining room.

"Well!" Kitty turned from the step after the last little group had left, to face me with blazing eyes above those scarlet patches. "They've been talking!"

"Talking—"

"About Harry, of course. And Parly— Oh, Marie!"

Marie came out of the house and sat down. And if I'd known what she was going to say, I'd have put one of the bandages around her throat and tightened it, hard. "Somebody," Marie said, "has got to speak to that new Wave. The one with the light hair that Jim's been going around with. Sally Wilson. I wouldn't have believed it if I hadn't seen it with my own eyes."

There was a quick flicker in Kitty's face. "What's Sally been doing?"

Marie got out a powder compact and dabbed at the

prickly heat on her arm. "It was last night. The Colonel and I were playing bridge at the Gary house. We came home latish—about midnight. The Colonel was worrying about things, you know, they're all upset about it and doubling sentries and all that, so he thought he'd just take a swing around the Row before we went home. We drove past the Waves barracks and just as you turn there onto the road again, the lights shone against the east side, there where there are all those trees and shrubbery, and I saw Sally. With a man. And both of them jumped back out of the lights." She closed the powder compact with a snap. Her large, light green eyes went to Kitty and then to me.

Kitty said, "Who was the man?"

"We couldn't tell. But I saw Sally clear enough. She was facing me. You know as well as I do there's no excuse for that kind of thing. The girls have all kinds of liberty. And whenever there's a party they can check in at all hours. But Monday night! And ducking out of the lights like that! I thought I ought to report it to Lieutenant Hagshaw." She glanced at me. "That's the Waves commanding officer. But the Colonel told me not to. He took a very lenient view—well, you know how men are. A pretty face! He said let her see her boy friend if she wanted to. None of my business. But it wasn't Jim Warring. I'm sure of that. And I didn't like the way she jumped out of sight," Marie finished stubbornly.

The trouble was that there was a queer kind of uneasiness and sincerity in her face and in her voice. Gossip she might, and on occasion did. But there was something else.

Again like a hot little puff of wind where wind there was none, something seemed to come out of the still, sunny afternoon, out of the desert beyond, out of the mysterious reaches of the mountains and their now purple slopes and touch us, very lightly. Somewhere on the base there is a murderer.

Kitty's pretty face was as still as a candle and as pale. Marie took a sharp breath. "It's horrible, isn't it! It could be anybody."

She didn't need to say what could be anybody. Had I had, in fact, a shadowy glimpse of him, outside the Waves barracks the night before? Had Sally talked to him—later, when she thought I had gone?

I tried to assemble some kind of coherent thought. "You said it wasn't Jim," I said to Marie. "How do you know? If you didn't see him—"

"Oh, I saw him," she said. "That is, I knew it wasn't Jim. But I don't know who it was. And I wouldn't recognize him again. I just knew it wasn't Jim. That's all."

And, of course, it made more sense than it may sound like; you recognize people you know without knowing exactly how you recognize them, certainly without consciously adding up all those hundreds of details which make for instantaneous recognition. A detective once told me that and it's true.

Marie got up. She patted her reddish-gray hair nervously. A patch of prickly heat stood out on her face suddenly, rather as young Bonny's freckles had done. "The Colonel was right," she said abruptly. "I ought to have kept my mouth shut. It was one of the boys at B.O.Q., of course. Couldn't be anybody else. I'm sorry I said anything, Kitty. Forget it. Well, I've got to see about dinner."

"Marie!" Kitty said. "Tell me the truth. Is there—talk?"

Marie gave Kitty a bright glance and looked quickly away. "About Sally? Oh, no, I haven't told anyone but you—"

"You know what I mean. About Parly and—and Harry?"

Marie brushed an invisible grain of powder off her rather massive bosom. "Nothing," she said slowly, "that amounts to anything. It will die out. Nobody really thinks Harry—" she bit her lip and left lipstick on her teeth. "I mean—really, Kitty. It's only because they have to talk about it and Parly —everybody knows Harry had some trouble with him—"

"If anybody dares to say Harry killed him, I'll—I'll—" Kitty's hands were doubled into fists.

Marie said quickly, "Nobody would say that! I'd stop it. So would the Colonel. Believe me, Kitty, I've really got to go home and get dinner."

She went quickly away. Her print dress disappeared down the path. After a long pause Kitty said in a queer, tired voice, "I knew it! The minute they began to arrive for Red Cross. But there's never anything you can put your finger on. Never really anything you can stop!"

"Nonsense!" I put more robust cheer in my voice than I felt. "As Marie says, it will die down."

"Maybe," Kitty said after a moment. "Maybe. But Marie tells the truth. Sarah, who do you suppose that man was— the one with Sally?"

There was no answer to that so I made none. And after another long silence, Kitty said slowly, still in that queer, brooding voice, "Marie was scared."

"Yes. Yes. Everybody's on edge."

"She's a gossip. Sometimes she adds a little to make a story more interesting. But she—when all at once she was sorry and wished she hadn't said anything I—then I believed every word of it. If it was one of the men in B.O.Q., he wouldn't have ducked out of the light. Not just like that. I could—" Kitty swallowed. "I could see it! Couldn't you?"

I could. Marie's story was curiously graphic, more frightening than she had intended it to be. "What are you going to do? Tell Harry?"

"Yes," Kitty said slowly. "Sally didn't tell us all the truth about Parly and Harry can't make me think she did." She turned to me with a kind of burst. "Sarah, I don't want to see that girl accused of murder! I'm not after her scalp!"

I felt sorry for her. "I know, Kitty."

"It's—Harry," she said needlessly. "You saw. This afternoon. We've got to do *something!*"

After that we didn't talk much. The sun dropped lower toward the sharp edges of the mountains. But I didn't like the way Kitty sat, staring at nothing, swinging her foot nervously, her face implacable—a plump, pretty and seething volcano. Yet I couldn't say, Kitty, wait. Don't do anything. Wait.

Harry came home, tired and gray. Kitty took one look at him and didn't mention the chilly and silent Red Cross meeting, the murder, Bonny Winters, or even Sally. We had cocktails; taps sounded clear and serene over the base; the flag fluttered slowly down. Lights came out among the cluster of houses and we went into dinner. But after dinner, out on the porch again where now that the blazing sun had gone it was cooler, we had coffee and Harry talked about the murder.

"It's been a hellish day. We've got all we can do on the base any day and this Parly affair—"

"Is there any news?" I asked.

There was, he said quietly, and there wasn't. But so far they had come to a dead end. He drank some coffee. "I had the corpsman at the hospital—you know, Jenson—in my office again. Questioned him; nothing. Had another long talk with Buffalo Bill; nothing new there. Checked up all his medical reports; no indication of nervous condition. No reports yet on fingerprints—"

"Fingerprints!" I said sharply.

"Oh, yes. The Security Officer, Nagel, knows how to take them; he did that Sunday. We sent them airmail, dispatched them to the F.B.I. and BuPers. The F.B.I. checks for certain fingerprints. BuPers keeps the master jackets for Navy personnel."

"BuPers?" I said. "Jacket?"

103

"Bureau of Personnel. Individual records."

A jacket was a blouse, and a record was a jacket. Well, it was all right with me, but confusing.

"It'll take some time to try to weed out any fingerprints that ought not to be there," Harry said wearily.

"You'll find mine," I snapped.

"There you are," Harry said. "They can identify only the fingerprints there's a record of. Unless the F.B.I. has your fingerprints, Sarah—"

"As a matter of fact they have."

Kitty said, "Huh!" in a startled and inelegant way and Harry grinned.

I explained haughtily, "I was sightseeing one time. I visited the Bureau. I gave them my fingerprints. I thought it my civic duty. I think it's everybody's civic duty—"

"Okay," Harry said peaceably. "Okay."

I thought for a moment. "What about the can of ether?"

"The can of ether had been wiped off clean. There wasn't a print they could find on it. The knife—" Kitty stirred; I could hear the rustle of her dress. Harry said, "The knife had been wiped clean, too. Buffalo says he lifted it by the chain and didn't touch it. Jim took it and looked at it but he held it by the chain, too." He waited a moment; then he went on in a quiet and reasonable way. "It had to be done, of course. Nothing is easier than to check fingerprints among Navy personnel. But nothing at all conclusive may come from it."

"What about Jim's jacket?" I asked, meaning blouse.

"Nothing there either. We've questioned the men at B.O.Q.; nobody remembers seeing anybody go into Jim's room—but then they wouldn't have been likely to see anybody during the day, nobody's there except the men that clean the place and they were out by 4 o'clock on Saturday night."

"What did the other men feel about it? I mean the Board of Inquiry?"

There was a note of reservation in Harry's reply. "Much as I do, I think. Jim told them all he knew, which of course was nothing. But it—well, there it is. The only point is Jim had no motive."

It was, however, an important point. I told myself that and believed it. Yet as Harry had implied it was a tangible, visible piece of evidence.

Harry said, "I told Jim, you heard me, to try to remember somebody, something that would give him an alibi—only because it would clarify the situation. Jim still says he can't.

Says there were men in the lounge, he could hear them talking and playing the radio, but his room is the first one at the left, right beside the door. The door to the lounge is on the right farther down. So he didn't see anybody in the lounge and nobody saw him. I personally don't think there's much doubt that the murderer took Jim's blouse sometime during the day—or even the day before, Jim can't remember exactly when he last saw it—wore it when he went to Parly's room, and after he'd escaped he simply left it at the dry-cleaner's. To get rid of evidence or—like the knife—to involve somebody else."

But it was evidence. Oh, yes; concrete and damaging.

Harry lighted a cigarette. "They questioned Smith again and"—he glanced at me rather oddly, half-approving and half-puzzled—"you were right about him, Sarah. That is, he didn't say he knocked himself out. But he did borrow some money from Parly."

"Money!" Kitty said. I could feel her eyes flash to me.

"Seems he got in a game and was short and Parly loaned him a hundred."

"Oh," Kitty said flatly, after a moment.

"But, I don't think he cut Parly's throat to keep the hundred."

Kitty said suddenly, "Parly was—at least he said he was going to have money. Harry, listen." Her dress rustled from the shadows as she leaned forward. "Parly had a girl. Sarah found her. Her name is Bonny Winters and—tell him, Sarah."

So I did in full detail, except again I didn't mention picking up Sally. Or the man I was sure now that I had in fact seen, a furtive shadow among other shadows outside the Waves barracks. But when I stopped, Kitty said sharply, "And there's something else! Marie Sinclair told us. Tell him that, too, Sarah! It's really important."

So I told him that too, and I couldn't gloss over any word of it because Kitty was sitting there listening and would have nailed the slightest omission.

There was a long silence. Kitty shifted her position a little and her chair squeaked. Harry's face in the diffused light showed no expression at all. He said finally, "I'm sorry about that. We'll have to talk to the Winters girl and her brother. And Sally. In fact—I may as well tell you. Today Sally took a rather odd sort of telegram to the Western Union office here. The boy there sent it over to the O.D. He reported it to the Security Officer and to me."

Kitty's face came forward into the light, still and intent. *"What was it?"*

"I've got the copy. You can look at it. Come on, Sarah, you too."

We followed him into his study. He jerked on the desk lamp and put a paper on the desk in the light. Kitty and I leaned over to read it.

Kitty caught her breath. It was indeed an odd telegram. It was addressed to C. L. Sawyer, Hilldale, Virginia. It read, in Harry's neatly printed characters: REQUIRE CASH. LEHCPUNPACAM PETAIR EXPRESS. URGENT. SALLY WILSON.

Kitty's hands were spread outward on the desk; I saw them double up. "Code!"

I thought of all those vast stores of ammunition, of sabotage, of everything.

Then I went around the desk and began to rummage through a stack of newspapers and magazines.

13

Harry watched me. Kitty stared at the telegram. I found a late newspaper, a Los Angeles paper, and searched through it till I found the page I wanted. I spread it on the desk and took Sally's telegram. Harry came to my side. Kitty said, "What are you doing?"

And then Harry, following my forefinger down the columns, gave a dry little laugh and sat down. "I ought to have seen it myself. Thanks, Sarah—"

"You ought to have seen what?" Kitty cried, and ran to my side and I pointed them out.

"Am Pet?" she cried.

"It's the abbreviation. American Petroleum." I ran on down the stock-market list. "Leh Cp—that's Lehman Corporation. And here—yes, UnPac is Union Pacific. That's all. She wants somebody to sell stocks for her—"

"Oh," Kitty said. "Oh." She looked at the copy of the telegram, looked again at the abbreviated stock-market listings and said tartly, "You wouldn't expect a Navy family to know much about the stock market!"

Well, a trained nurse doesn't as a rule know much about investing money, either, and for the same reason: she doesn't have much to invest. But I've had some patients who not only pored over the market prices themselves, but made me read them, at length, and translated the abbreviations for me.

Harry chuckled. It was the first time in days I'd seen him laugh as if he meant it.

Kitty said crossly, "She must have a lot of money! Of course you can't tell in uniform. But—" She checked herself as if struck by a sudden surmise.

I knew exactly what it was and again Kitty was too smart and too quick for me. "What does she want that money for? She says urgent. She says require cash. What for? There's nothing to spend money on here at the base. There's nothing except—" She leaped swift as lightning. "Blackmail! If she murdered Parly—if somebody saw her—that man she was with last night and she didn't want to be seen with him and—blackmail!"

"It may not represent much money," Harry said slowly. "She doesn't say how many shares."

Kitty's mouth was stubborn. "Look! It's addressed to Sawyer. Not to her father. She doesn't want her father to know about it!"

"Probably Sawyer's a broker. Family banker. Lawyer."

"You'll have to find out what it means!"

"Yes." Harry's eyes were deeply thoughtful. Suddenly, with an air of decision, he turned to me. "You've seen something of murder cases, Sarah. I'll tell you frankly that we're getting nowhere. Partly perhaps because it's too—well, official. They think of records, red tape—and I suppose court-martial—and shut up like clams. And perhaps it's all too cut and dried. Maybe we stick to the book too closely. Sarah, I'd like you to help me. Will you see what you can get out of Sally about this?"

I said I would. I didn't have the faith in my ability to help that Harry seemed to have. And while it was my duty, I can't say that I always approach duty as such with alacrity. The fact was I wanted to talk to Sally myself.

So I said there was no time like the present and I started immediately for the Waves barracks before Harry could change his mind or Kitty offer to accompany me.

I might say here that I don't think Harry expected me to interpret his request for help with quite the latitude with which eventually I did see fit to interpret it. And I will not deny the fact that I set off along the winding, lighted road toward the Waves barracks with something of the zest of a battle-scarred old hound dog let off the leash. I didn't, naturally, give jubilant tongue to my feelings, and as I glanced across toward the lighted west wing of the hospital, it occurred to me that there were far too many trails. It was a sobering reflection.

For Buffalo Bill was still, so to speak, in a covert of evasions, if not outright lies. And I wasn't really satisfied in my mind about Jenson. But first I'd see Sally.

My white pumps made little thuds along the paved roads. B.O.Q. was lighted as usual with a radio going full blast. As I passed the Sinclairs' house I saw Marie and the Colonel sitting on the lighted porch, holding newspapers, but Marie was talking and the Colonel was listening, I felt sure, to an account of the uncomfortable Red Cross meeting. At the Gary house four people sat around a bridge table, but they were talking hard, too, not playing; Commander Gary and Ruth, and Edith Pillsbury, not yet due at the hospital, and Dr. Roslin.

The Wave barracks were set off at one end of the Row, a little isolated, so there was quite a long stretch of road, grassy spaces and trees between them and the other houses. There were lights at intervals along the road, but I stuck to the middle of it, avoiding the occasional clumps of black shrubbery. The Waves barracks were lighted and a radio was going there, too. The door was open and I walked back past a simple but formal sort of hall to a big and extremely informal lounge.

It was like walking into a nurses' dormitory. There were girls everywhere in all sorts of apparel; on the sofas, in the lounge chairs, on the floor; in uniform, pajamas, and very little at all; a buzz of conversation was going on, undeterred by the dance music. Somebody said loudly, ". . . if they don't get him soon I'm going to wire my congressman!"

There were some jeers and somebody else said, but seriously, "Oh, *do* shut up! I'm on night duty at the hospital—" It was the girl at the hospital switchboard, nights. She stopped as I paused in the doorway; in fact, everybody stopped and jerked around to look at me. I said, "Is Sally here?"

They eyed me curiously and rather expectantly as if I might be the bearer of news. Then the switchboard girl said, "Hello, Miss Keate. Sally—"she glanced around the room —"I guess Sally's in her room." She got up and went across to a girl who sat under a hair dryer and shouted at her above the hum of the dryer. "Sally Wilson. Somebody wants her."

The girl poked her head out of the dryer. "Oh, hello, Miss Keate. I think Sally's upstairs. I'll get her—" She emerged wholly, indeed almost literally so as she wore a towel draped over a brassiere and petticoat, her hair was done tightly in wet curls. "Want to come along?"

I followed her up some stairs and along a narrow hall. "I'm

her roommate," she said and opened a door. "Oh—I guess she's gone out."

The room was small, with two beds, two chairs, and two chests of drawers. I didn't exactly intend to take a look at Sally's possessions; at the same time, I heard myself say, "Is it all right if I wait for her? She may be back in a few minutes."

"Oh, of course." She slid a heap of clothing off one of the chairs. "Do you mind if I get back under the dryer? My hair's wet—"

I didn't mind at all. She trotted away and I waited till I thought she had reached the stairs. Then I closed the door.

I didn't have much time, and contrary to Kitty's and Harry's faith in me, I really hadn't much experience in what the police can accomplish in a matter of seconds. But I glanced at one chest of drawers which was laden on top with cosmetics, a heap of stockings, and a dangling pink brassiere and then at the other which was extremely neat, with silver-backed brushes and a tiny bottle of perfume and nothing else. Somehow that looked more like Sally, so I went to it. I was right, for there were two photographs, snapshots really, framed and hung above it. An elderly man in riding clothes, on horseback, with two setters and a glimpse of white fences and stables behind. Another showing the same man, this time beside a sundial with Sally a little in the shadow at his side. Between them there was a space which looked as if another and larger picture had hung there, for there was the small hole in the wall which had been made by a nail. I looked at the elderly man with interest; Sally's father probably, erect and smiling, with gray hair and a look of Sally around his chin and forehead.

Someone turned off the radio downstairs; I hadn't much time. So I opened the top drawer. I trust it is no reflection on my character to say that I did so without the slightest compunction and only that sense of the shortness of time—somebody, Sally herself, or one of the other girls might enter the room at any instant—restrained me from a methodical search of everything in the room. However, the top drawer held writing materials, and on top of a stack of envelopes there was a stock-market page, torn out and folded. I opened it and glanced along the rows; there were penciled checks against several stocks and some bonds. I scanned the list rapidly; there were not many checks, but every single one of them indicated what sundry patients had taught me to call gilt-edged stocks. So whoever had invested for Sally had invested wisely. And then I discovered that Sally herself had had a certain amount of training about money, for below the page from the newspapers there was a piece of paper with neat sums of addition. Lehman Corporation, so many; American Petroleum, so many; Union Pacific, so many—and the added sum of their quoted prices came to almost thirty thousand dollars.

So Sally wanted thirty thousand dollars. Urgent, she had said in her telegram; by air express.

Thirty thousand dollars. The exact sum Parly expected and boasted about to Bonny. Thirty thousand now—and more later.

There was no getting around the ominous signature of blackmail.

Why?

Someone was coming along the hall. I replaced the papers and closed the drawer and took another quick look at the photographs. And as the steps reached the door, a very singular thought came out of nowhere and all but rocked me back on my heels.

Sally's roommate came in. "Oh, Miss Keate, Sally went out. I don't know where she went but she told Lieutenant Hagshaw she wouldn't be back till 11. I thought I'd better tell you."

So I went to Wanaha City again that night.

I telephoned to Kitty from the little booth off the lounge and she sent the car and the same sailor driving it who had taken me to Wanaha City the night before. She also, thoughtfully, sent a coat and my handbag with my pass in it. "Mrs. Somers said you'd need it if you're going to Wanaha City," the sailor told me.

Inasmuch as I had not told Kitty my destination, this, although quite unreasonably, irritated me. So did the sailor, when we reached the red and green or orange lights of Wanaha's main street and he said brightly, "El Rico's, again?" as if I were a hardened gambler, a lost soul. I glanced back after I got out of the car and he was standing on the sidewalk, watching me and shaking his head gloomily.

In El Rico's the first person I saw was Sally, sitting again at one of the small tables near the door. But this time Jim Warring was with her.

The noise was a little louder, the tables a little more tightly packed than the previous night; there was a kind of rhythm about that, beginning with less din and fewer people on Monday nights and working up through the week to a tumultuous crescendo on Saturday nights. Neither Sally nor Jim saw me nor did they seem to be enjoying themselves or El Rico's, but the contrary. Sally was staring down into a Coca-Cola and

110

Jim pulling matches out of a little folder and breaking them with a steady application which the task really did not merit. He looked angry and Sally miserable; I wondered if they had quarreled and what about. I glanced past the cashier toward Dave Winters' little office but did not see him; Bonny was not at the roulette table.

I took a long breath and sailed toward their table. Sally looked up with a start; Jim said, "Sarah!" in a surprised way, and got to his feet and pulled out a chair for me. Sally smiled as if all at once she was very glad to see me and I sat down.

Jim said, "Are you out on the town, Sarah? What'll you have to drink?" He nodded at a waiter and ordered ginger ale, a drink of which my gambling-hall career was beginning to induce a certain satiety, and I had what I thought was a flash of inspiration. I dug into my handbag and got out a ten-dollar bill and put it on the table. "Gamble for me, Jim. I—" I glanced around the big room and chose a gaming table that was as far removed from where we sat as I could discover. "That one back there. With the bird cages."

Jim's eyebrows went up and then rather disconcertingly leveled off. "You mean you want to talk to Sally." He didn't look at Sally; I saw her hand close tightly around her glass. Jim said, "Okay. Delighted. And while you're talking to her you might ask her—"

"Jim—" Sally said softly.

"—what's wrong with me. She's just told me she's through with me. It's all right. That's the way she wants it. But she won't tell me why."

"Jim," Sally said in a whisper. "Don't."

He scooped up the ten dollars with a brown hand and I watched his tall figure in its khaki-colored summer uniform—with the three gold stripes on the shoulder boards—his lifted and angry black head disappear among the circle around the roulette table. Angry and hurt and consequently very youthful. It wasn't like Jim to speak in just that way.

And then I knew that the surmise which had leaped at me out of nowhere was probably fact.

Sally's face was white and she wouldn't look at me. I said, "Sally, where is Johnny?"

She looked at me then; her eyes flashed up wide with something very like terror.

"Where is he, Sally? Is he here, on the base?"

She moistened her lips. The waiter put down a glass of ginger ale and darted away. I couldn't witness that look in Sally's face; I concentrated on the bubbles rising in the ginger

111

ale and time went past and finally Sally said huskily, "What do you mean?"

I had to tell her, quickly and factually. "You've told Jim you were through with him. You wired home for money, a very large sum of money. Last night you were here and across the street, searching for somebody you thought might be in Wanaha City. Later on you met a man, outside the Waves barracks and you didn't want anybody to see you talking to him. And you had a photograph of Johnny in your room at the barracks and you took it down so nobody would see it and recognize Johnny. So I think he's alive and here, somewhere on the base." I looked at her then and felt as if I had struck her across the face. I said gently, "Tell me about it, Sally."

The pupils in her eyes were as black and terrified as a bird's held by a snake, a comparison which is not very flattering to me, but that's the way she looked. Finally she said, "Johnny—was in an accident. You know all about it."

I didn't think that lying was easy for her. On the other hand, of course, she might not be lying. I've made my mistakes. However, I had to go on.

"I expect you don't know that your telegram went to the Captain's desk. They thought it looked like a code—I mean, the list of stocks you wanted somebody to sell for you."

"My—" A wave of color came over her face. "That wasn't very bright of me, was it? I never thought of that. I thought that the abbreviations would—I mean it wouldn't sound like anything but—"

"It wouldn't sound like thirty thousand dollars."

"Thirty—how did you know that?"

I swallowed rather hard but told the truth. "I saw your notes. I looked in the top drawer there in your room. The Captain asked me to talk to you about the telegram. So I—that's when I saw that there was a photograph missing. It *was* Johnny's picture, wasn't it?"

She didn't reproach me even by a look. The child was quite literally stiff with terror. "That was Johnny. But I took it down because—well, I was seeing so much of Jim and—and—"

Not a good liar. I tried again, "Why do you want so much money?"

"Because I—" She took a quick breath. I saw her chin square itself. "I'd rather not talk about it."

"The Captain will ask you. The Board of Inquiry—"

"I'm sorry. I can't tell anyone."

112

"Why not, Sally?"

"Because," Sally said, her blue eyes like steel, "I won't. I can sell some of my own property if I want to. Nobody's going to stop me."

I waited, thinking hard and getting nowhere. Finally I said, "That's rather a lot of money."

"I—yes. It's almost all—I mean, my mother left me—" She floundered to a complete stop and bit her lip.

She'd been about to say it was almost all she had, which, of course, made it worse.

"You addressed it to somebody by the name of Sawyer. Why didn't you wire to your father?"

"Because I didn't want to. Carl Sawyer is a lawyer. He's got my power of attorney." She leaned toward me suddenly, catching her breath. "Did the Captain stop my wire? He couldn't have done that! It had to go. Did he stop it?"

"I don't know. He had a copy. I don't know—"

There was a still, white dismay in her face. "It's got to go! I'll send another! No, I'll phone—"

"Sally, why is it so urgent?"

She was eager now to be gone—to a telephone. She said quickly, "I don't want to talk about it, Miss Keate. Where is Jim? I must go—"

In other words, Miss Keate, mind your own business.

I said, "Sally, who brought you the message from Parly saying he wanted to see you?"

She replied to that quickly and rather absently, looking around the room for Jim, eager to get away to a telephone. I thought, now she's not hiding anything. "I don't know. There was just a note in the mailbox in the hall, there at the Waves barracks. It was there Saturday evening. I picked it up when I went to the dance. Jim was waiting for me and I didn't read it till we got to the club and—I don't know who brought it."

I considered that; a small problem but still it was troublesome. Her eyes met mine suddenly and with decision. "Miss Keate, Johnny was in the plane and he was— I told you—"

"Are you sure that it wasn't the hitchhiker who was found in the plane?"

"Hitchhiker—"

"Parly told you that he thought somebody might have gone on that flight with Johnny. Only one body was found. Was it Johnny—or was it the other man? If it was the other man whose body they found, where is Johnny? Why does he want so much money? Sally, I've got to ask you this. Did Johnny kill Parly?"

14

Jim said, "Who's talking about money?" and put down a clattering heap of silver dollars. "I did all right by you, Sarah." Without any change in tone or expression he said, "Did who kill Parly?"

Sally got up. "I'm going home."

Jim would know sooner or later. I said, "Sally, will you tell me the truth? Have you seen Johnny?"

Jim said, "*Johnny*—"

Sally's blue eyes flashed directly into mine. "No," she cried. "No! I'm going now."

"Johnny," Jim said again, in an odd flat voice as if he were talking to himself. Then he touched Sally's arm, "All right. All right, we'll go. Coming with us, Sarah?" His words were polite, and he was barely aware of my existence. I rose and went along with them and I don't think either of them knew that I was there. At the door I remembered all those silver dollars and went back barely in time to foil a waiter who gave me a reproachful look as I scooped up all but two of them into my handbag. By the time I reached the street Sally and Jim had disappeared and my sailor chauffeur came to meet me. He saw the way my handbag sagged from my arm, and as he opened the door he gave me a glance of respect. We went back to the base. I saw nothing of Jim's car, nothing of Jim and Sally and I felt as if I had tossed a highly explosive bomb right at them.

Yet maybe—just maybe—Jim would get the truth out of her. If Johnny had killed Parly (if it was Johnny, not Sally, who was being blackmailed), then Sally must be protected from the consequences of her own loyal but mistaken fidelity to Johnny.

Sensible conclusions are rarely satisfying and almost never comforting. My heart was as low as my heels. And I felt rather like one.

Also, I had failed Harry; the only thing I could do was put the whole question back into his lap. It was with no feeling of self-congratulation, but decidedly the reverse, that I crept into the Somers house. I emptied my handbag on the table near the door, intending to turn over my ill-gotten gains to the Red Cross, and although I tried to be quiet, Harry heard the tinkle of the silver dollars and came to the door of the study. "How did you come out?"

So I told him everything, then and there, making no effort to shield Sally as to the facts—although naturally when I'd finished I added a word to the effect that Sally's sympathies, obviously, had been worked on by Johnny. "He's her husband. There's no way of guessing what he's told her. She's loyal to him—"

Harry's fingers were tapping at the desk. His strong, hooked nose seemed to come down lower over his thin-lipped mouth. "She said she hadn't seen him."

"I think he's here," I said stubbornly. "I think he's the man she saw last night."

His brown fingers moved nervously up and down, the Annapolis ring catching the light. "There's nothing easier than to find out whether or not he's on the base. He can't be one of the officers, of course. Or one of the enlisted men. I suppose he could be a civilian employee at the loading plants but it's unlikely. A union card or records just could be forged—but as I say it's not likely. You say you think that she went to Wanaha City to look for him. The answer probably is that he's living there somewhere, if he's alive. But I *can't* really believe that, Sarah! His body was found—"

"Suppose it was the hitchhiker's body."

"We have no reason to believe there was another man. He was alone."

I felt as if I were dropping another bomb, but I said, "They didn't find the money. They didn't find any trace of it. Wasn't that unusual? Don't they find traces—"

He got up. "Are you trying to say Johnny stole that money, and murdered Parly because he knew it?"

"That's going further than I—" I thought for a moment. "It's a motive for murder."

"Yes." Harry paced up and down. "Yes, it's a motive. But if Johnny did that he'd have had to—crash the plane. See that this very problematical hitchhiker, the plane, everything was burned." He frowned at me absently and then shook his head. "That's not feasible. Think of the bare mechanics of it. If Johnny deliberately crashed the plane, he'd be very likely to kill himself, too. And exactly how would he make sure that the passenger—if there was one—would be killed and the plane burned, but that he could save himself and the money?"

I didn't know. "Was the body they found injured? I mean, as if the plane had really crashed?"

"You mean he might have landed and then killed the hitch-

115

hiker, and burned the plane?" He shook his head again. "I don't know about the body; I didn't ask. They said it wasn't recognizable. But the plane crashed all right. No question of that."

"Well," I said slowly. "Johnny had a parachute."

He looked at me as if I'd taken leave of my senses. "Parachute!"

"They always have a parachute, don't they? Suppose he—he knocked the hitchhiker over the head, dropped himself and the money by way of a parachute and—and just let the plane crash. He'd have expected it to burn and it did and—"

It seemed to me a simple and indeed the only practicable solution, but Harry very quietly sat down and put his head in his hands. "Sarah," he said in a strangled way. "You'd better go to bed. I'll think this over. I'll—do something about it. I promise you. But just now—"

"You're not going to get much out of Sally," I said, "but perhaps Jim can." I didn't add that Jim might choose to keep any confidence Sally gave him. And it was exactly then that I made a very serious blunder. It is hard even now to be philosophic about it. It's true that I couldn't have stopped events that were already, at that moment, in train. I could no more have checked an already lighted fuse. But it was a blunder.

Without further talk I started toward the door and Harry said, "Kitty's gone to sleep."

So I tiptoed up the steps and into my room, where my spirits really struck a new low. I'd been a great help, hadn't I!

All the same, Johnny was alive, somewhere. And he wanted money, so Sally tried to get it for him. She was in all probability telephoning for it at that moment. She'd see that Johnny got it, unless Jim took a hand in the business, and what could he do beyond extracting the truth from Sally, finding Johnny and—what?

It was about then, too, that I saw exactly what I had done in my little flurry of detectivism. I had provided Jim with a motive for killing Parly.

If Parly knew that Johnny was alive, if he knew or guessed that Johnny was guilty of murder and theft, then Jim had every reason for getting rid of Parly. Both to protect Sally and, they would say, to keep from Sally's ears the knowledge that Johnny Wilson was alive.

It wasn't a motive when you knew Jim Warring. It was nothing that he would have done. He'd have had it out in the open, come hell or high water. He wouldn't have crept stealthily into the hospital and killed a man. And even if he'd wanted to kill him, he wouldn't have killed him like that—not with ether. Not an unconscious, helpless man. Not with a knife. Not that way.

But I knew Jim or thought I did. All the officers on the Board of Inquiry knew him; they wouldn't—they couldn't accept such a theory as fact. But how about the District Office? How about the F.B.I. and Naval Intelligence?

Wouldn't such a motive weigh heavily against him with a jury, or whatever they call the men who act as a jury in a court-martial?

So everything was just too ducky for words and I'd been a great help to everybody concerned.

Had Jim been surprised when I asked Sally point-blank if she'd seen Johnny? But he hadn't murdered anybody. And I'd provide them with a motive for which (they might decide) he had murdered Parly.

I heard Harry come upstairs and go into his room, quietly so as not to wake Kitty. And I heard Kitty a little later coming very softly up the stairs.

At least I heard somebody, soft footsteps and the rustle of clothing, and opened the door just in time to catch Kitty at the top of the stairs. She had a coral pink sweater rolled up like a bundle in one hand and she almost screamed when the light from my room fell upon her. Then she flung her other hand to her mouth, made some kind of gesture toward me with the coral bundle and without saying a word went on quickly to her room and into it.

I followed her. "Where have you been?" I whispered.

"Sh—sh—Out for a walk. Good night, Sarah." It was her turn to close the door in my face and she did. But her mouth was trembling.

I went, fuming with curiosity, back to my room.

It was some minutes later that I knew I was frightened. Where had Kitty gone, and why? She wouldn't have gone out just for a walk, not at night; not after a man had crept into the hospital and murdered Parly, and the murderer was still at large and might be anywhere. Not Kitty. And she was frightened.

I believe that I argued myself out of that. She wasn't frightened; she'd only gone out to see somebody, Marie Sinclair perhaps, to talk to her about the mute and guarded suspicion on the base which still made itself audible somehow, concerning Harry. She hadn't wanted to tell Harry where she was going or why. If she looked frightened, it was only because she had steeled herself to walk along those roads at night, where every shadow might conceal a murderer.

Besides, it wasn't late; I looked at the clock and it was only a little after 10.

I didn't have any imagination but I was certainly, I told myself, letting something very much like it run away with me. Kitty would explain in the morning. And in fact no explanation was needed. It was none of my business, either. Except Kitty was impulsive. Except I had only that evening hoped that the seething volcano within her wasn't going to burst into hasty and possibly ill-considered action.

But I was already wound up too tightly to compose myself; the incident of Kitty released the key to a driving restlessness. I had to ask Buffalo Bill and Jenson at least one question. I could wait till morning, but in another way I couldn't.

At a quarter after 10 I decided to stroll over to the hospital. It was past visiting hours, but perhaps the new nurse would let me see Buffalo. He wouldn't be asleep yet. Jenson would tell her that I'd been the substitute nurse and I was a guest of the Somerses and I'd make up some excuse to see Buffalo. Perhaps I wouldn't even have to invent an excuse. Perhaps I'd see Jenson first and it wouldn't be necessary to see Buffalo. I was dressing by then, hurriedly, so my hands shook a little. At the last minute I, too, took a sweater and put it over my shoulders.

I turned off the light in my room, edged myself out the door and, clutching the railing, down the stairs and along the hall. I opened the door and the cool night air struck my face. I turned the night latch so I could return and tiptoed across the porch and down the steps, and hurried across the lawn so Harry, directly above, wouldn't hear my footsteps on the path. I must say I didn't care for the thickets of shrubbery and once when a branch touched my face softly I nearly screamed, as Kitty had done. But then I came out on the road and there were lights in B.O.Q. and lights in some of the houses, and of course the street lights along the road.

I took a course past B.O.Q. on the far side of the road. The radio wasn't going as usual and I missed its cheery assurance of people very near. Jim's car, a tan convertible with the top down, was parked in front of B.O.Q. His talk with Sally, then, had lasted an ominously short time.

Oddly the place seemed larger at night than during the daytime when the brilliant light brought even quite distant objects into a sharp focus. The houses seemed further apart. The areas of light beneath the street lamps seemed small and too infrequent amid the long empty spaces of velvet blackness. Even if I screamed, I thought suddenly, nobody would hear me. But nothing moved anywhere along those empty

118

roads. No shadow detached itself from heavy, deeper shadows.

I reached the road which curved toward the hospital and didn't see a soul anywhere. The west door was lighted but the rooms in the west wing were dark.

I went up the step to the entrance and discovered that I hadn't been breathing very easily and took a long gulp of air. The door was open. I could see the long corridor and the chart desk at the end of it with the green-shaded lamp above. A young woman in white was sitting at the chart desk. I took another uneasy gulp and opened the door. Her white cap jerked up at once.

She rose and came down the corridor to meet me. She was attractive, black hair and dark eyes, although on the plump side. We met and she said in a low voice, "Visiting hours are over."

"I know. I'm Sarah Keate—"

"Oh, yes. The substitute nurse. I'm Ensign Whitson." She eyed me curiously. "You were on duty when—"

"Yes. I—thought I'd like to see how Buffalo Bill is doing? I mean Marine Sergeant Brown."

"He's doing very well."

"I—that is—can I see him?"

"I'm sorry," she said implacably. "Visiting hours are over. You might come tomorrow."

The Navy is the Navy; no doubt of that. A brief impulse to walk coolly past her died at once; she'd have stopped me and made no bones about it. I said, "Well—I don't see Jenson."

Irritation flashed in her dark eyes. "You don't see him," she said crisply, "because he's not here yet. He's late. And if he thinks I won't report it because I'm new then he's quite mistaken . . . I'll tell Buffalo in the morning that you came to see him. Good night."

Somehow she had walked me back to the door which she now held open not only in a suggestive but a very commanding manner. She might have been an ensign, but she would undoubtedly add some stripes as rapidly as routine permitted.

I said, "Well, thank you," rather feebly and found myself out on the step again. And rightly. Oh, yes. But ruffled.

I daresay I had been Head Nurse in positions where my word was as good as law for far too long. The girl was right, but a spirit of rebellion was in my heart just the same. I went slowly back toward B.O.Q. As I approached it the radio inside the lounge burst into a loud and raucous squawk and was turned down but kept on going in a cheerful way, dance music from some night club, for as I trudged along it broke

119

off for an announcer's voice, "—comes to you from the some-thing-or-other room at the Fairmont—" and then swung into dance music again. A man came out of B.O.Q. with a little bag such as mechanics carry in his hand and swung himself into a car. Somebody in the lighted doorway said, "Thanks, boy. It ought to be all right now."

The man getting into the car shouted back, "All you need is some new tubes once in a while," and started his car with a rattle. I peered at the uniformed figure in the doorway think-ing he might be Jim. But the car backed around so the lights from it shone in my eyes and when it had rattled past me toward the gate, whoever was in the doorway had moved away.

Jim's room, I remembered, was the first on the left, the corner room. The windows showed no light, so I padded on. Indeed I had almost reached the path into the Somers house when a rebellious impulse struck me. If Jenson hadn't reached the hospital yet, I might intercept him on his way.

He was already late, of course. But quite obviously the new ensign had everything under perfect control. It wouldn't be a really heinous breach of discipline if I walked a few steps with him and asked one question.

Only one question, but it might be important. The Captain had asked me to help him, hadn't he?

I pushed away the disconcerting reflection that my efforts so far had had very unwelcome results. Yet it spurred me, too.

I could wait to see Jenson the next day; I had waited. But that was before I had known—or at least had had such strong reason to believe—that Johnny Wilson was still alive. It now seemed to me imperative to see Jenson.

But I didn't turn back. And in point of fact, it wouldn't have made any difference if I had. Perhaps my sense of hospital discipline was too strong for me; perhaps I didn't like the Row that night, with its long empty spaces, the deep black blotches around the clumps of shrubbery and under the trees. Instead, I trudged on to the Somers house and opened the door softly. And smelled a very odd sort of smell, odd and unpleasant. Like burning wool.

Harry had left a cigarette burning, had dropped it in a lounge chair. That was my first thought, so I tiptoed into the study to check an incipient conflagration. But even though I closed the door quietly and then turned on the light, I could find no burning cigarette anywhere. In fact the smell of burn-ing wool was less pungent. I went into the hall again. At the back of it a door led to the basement and it was an inch or two ajar. I went to it and opened it a little further and the smell of burning wool was sickening. I went softly down the stairs.

Halfway down I stopped. Kitty was down there standing at the open door of the furnace. Light from inside it touched her face to a yellow glow. She wore her crimson silk dressing gown, its sleeves rolled up beyond her elbows, and she was poking at something in the furnace with jabbing, desperate motions.

I went on down. "Kitty—"

She jerked around to look at me.

"What are you doing?"

I felt she wanted to push me away, but I looked in the furnace. She had a poker in her hand and she gave the smoldering, bubbling thing in the furnace another wild jab. It was her coral sweater.

Long streaks of charred material made canals through the material. A knitted wrist had burned off completely. Kitty said, with a queer kind of sob, "It's so hard to burn. It won't burn. It just creeps like that in streaks—"

"It also smells to high heaven," I said crossly, and took the poker from her and poked at it myself. Then I said, "Why?"

She wiped dark curls back from her face. "Turn it the other way. Then hold it up so the flames catch."

"*Why*, Kitty?"

"Never mind—"

"You'd better tell me." I lifted some of the seething, curiously ugly mass. A delicate strip of the soft wool dropped away as if it resented the flaming attack upon its loveliness.

Kitty went to rummage somewhere and came back with some fire tongs. "Let me. I've got to get it all burned. They're coming—the men from the District Office and from the F.B.I."

"To investigate? *When?* "

"Harry talked to somebody tonight, after you'd gone. They're coming here—I don't know when—" She shoved back her hair with her arm and cried incoherently, "I've got to burn it! They'll see—"

Something caught my throat as if it had hands. "*They'd see what?*"

"The blood on it," Kitty said. "It's Jenson—I found him."

"*Found—*"

She pushed the fire tongs against the sweater.

"He's out there! Near the hospital! He's dead! There was blood—I didn't know. I stumbled and then I looked and I got blood on my sweater. I can't tell Harry. I couldn't call anybody or tell them or— They'd say I did it or—because of Harry, you see. Oh, Sarah, help me. I've *got* to get it burned. Even if I washed it they'd find the bloodstains and—"

"What are you doing?" Harry said from the bottom of the steps.

15

He let us finish burning the sweater; there wasn't any way to drag it out of the flames then. He only gave it one strange look, after he made Kitty tell him what she was doing and why. Then he held Kitty for a moment, as if to assure himself of her safety. He touched her disheveled black curls and put his face down upon her tear-stained, plump cheek. He went up the stairs to the telephone in the study.

The buttons, of course, wouldn't burn. They could be raked out. "Why did you burn something in the furnace, Mrs. Somers? What was it?" I could hear the questions. I didn't tell Kitty.

When the thing was an unpleasantly liquid-looking heap, which is the way wool burns, as if the animal elements within it fought to the last for life, Kitty and I went upstairs. By that time Harry was gone.

We opened all the doors and windows to air out the smell, and then, without exchanging so much as a word or a look, closed and locked them again. It was as if we had not learned, yet, the recognition of danger, but it tugged at us, all the same, forcing us to acknowledge its presence.

Lights were springing up all over the Row by then and cars already were shooting along the roads toward the administration building and the hospital. I could see the headlights converging like floodlights upon a clump of shrubbery at the curve of the road from the gate, several hundred yards from the other road which went toward the Somers house and other houses.

Kitty wouldn't look. She lay on the sofa in the study, her face in the pillows. "Harry will tell them. He'll tell everybody I found him! It happened just exactly the way I told him, Sarah." She twisted so I could see her teary, flushed face. "I went to meet Jenson on his way to the hospital. I wanted to ask him if he had seen something, anything, that could be evidence. I thought he might be afraid to tell Harry or the Board, or anybody official. You remember what Harry

122

said about that. But I thought I could worm it out of him." She took an uneven breath. "I wanted to ask him about Buffalo Bill, too. Jenson saw more of him than you did or the doctor, or anybody. He'd have known it if Buffalo is dangerous, likely to blow up and—I had to do something!" she said, defiance in the one eye that was visible.

Well, I had wanted to ask Jenson one question too. But I thought then that my question was answered.

Kitty, fixing me with that one bright eye, said, "It was horrible, Sarah. I hated going out of the house and it was all so still and empty except the shadows around the shrubbery looked as if somebody might be hiding there. I tried to keep out of sight when I passed B.O.Q. and then I thought that Jenson would come by the road from the gate, of course; he lives in the barracks. I didn't see anybody all the way. I went to that curve, where the road from the gate turns into the hospital and I waited and all at once—" her voice wavered—"all at once I was sure that somebody was there. Close to me. It was a—a terrible feeling. I looked around and moved and then stepped on—on something and I looked down and it was a hand and it was Jenson. I knelt down and there was just enough light. I could see the blood on him. It looked black. I nearly fainted, Sarah. Really I did. Everything whirled around me and then all I could think of was—was the way the women acted this afternoon. So different and—so I came home! He was dead. There wasn't anything I could do for him. I didn't know how long he'd been there. I—" She buried her face in the pillow again and wailed, "And now Harry's going to tell them that I found him. They won't say that I murdered him or that Harry had anything to do with it. They'll just *look* at each other—"

"Kitty, stop!" The black curls went deeper into the pillow. "Listen, Kitty—I'm afraid that Johnny Wilson killed him."

The black head was very still. Then it jerked around and Kitty sat up. "Johnny Wilson! He's dead. He was killed—"

"I think he's alive and here on the base. I'd better tell you the whole story."

She sat there, huddled, scarcely breathing while I told her. "I was going to see Jenson, too," I finished. "I went over to the hospital and the new nurse wouldn't let me see Buffalo Bill, so I came back—I thought of going to meet Jenson, too! The nurse had said he hadn't got to the hospital yet. But I decided to wait till morning."

"What were you going to ask him?"

"Whether or not he had seen anybody at all around the hospital who could have been Johnny Wilson."

123

"Oh," Kitty said, staring blankly at me. "Oh."

"I think he had. Because if Johnny Wilson knew it, he had to get rid of Jenson."

"That answers your question," Kitty said after a moment. "You mean that Johnny must have seen Parly sometime here. Or that Parly saw Johnny. And so Parly sent for Sally to tell her. And that's what Sally refuses to explain."

"Something like that."

"But then—" Kitty said, thinking hard. "But then—" Her eyes snapped. "Did you say that the amount of stock she wants to sell comes to about thirty thousand dollars?"

"Yes. About the sum that Bonny said Parly was going to get."

Kitty took a long breath and rose and began to walk around the room pantherishly, her red silk skirt swishing like an angry tail. "Then Parly was blackmailing Sally. He knew Johnny was alive and—of course! He knew Johnny had in fact stolen that money!"

"But Sally still wants the thirty thousand and Parly is dead!"

"She could have murdered him to keep him quiet! She had a chance—"

"She left the hospital before Jenson saw Parly about 11."

"How do we know? Maybe—maybe Jenson saw her and she promised him some money to keep his mouth shut. And then she got scared and Jenson—she intended it for Jenson. But now she knows that Harry would inquire and would find out if she gave it to Jenson so she—" she caught her breath and whispered "—killed him."

I remembered the white despair in Sally's face. But then I took a grip on common sense. "She couldn't just walk up to him and stab him. He wouldn't let her."

"Somebody did," Kitty said, with the horror of her discovery in her voice.

I had to steady my own voice. "If Sally was going to hand over thirty thousand dollars to anybody, she'd give it to Parly as readily as to Jenson."

Kitty had an answer for that, too. "Unless at first she thought she could get rid of Parly, and then Jenson knew she did it and she got in a panic after you talked to her tonight and—"

"You've forgotten Johnny."

Kitty paused, her red silk skirt coming to a whispering stop around her. "Well. If she knows Johnny murdered Parly and now if *he's* murdered Jenson, she can't keep quiet about it. She'll have to tell. She'd be a—what do you call it?"

"Accessory after the fact."

"Yes. There are only two explanations, Sarah. You've got to admit that."

I didn't. "What are they?"

"It's obvious," Kitty snapped, having somewhat recovered her normal manner. "One is that Johnny Wilson murdered Parly. And Jenson knew something. That—or Sally murdered Parly, and now Jenson for the same reason. Women have done things like that. You can't say they haven't."

"I can't see Sally Wilson taking a knife in her hand and—"

"Parly couldn't have defended himself. He was under ether."

"Jenson wasn't. Do you think he'd stand still and let Sally put a knife in him? If that's the way he was killed."

"I don't know about that." Kitty looked sick and white again. "There was all that blood. He was lying on his face and it was all over his back. He had on a light shirt and—I thought it was a knife because anybody would have heard a shot and—"

"Kitty, are you sure there wasn't anybody else around anywhere?"

"Not anybody." She shook her black curls definitely. "There wasn't a car or anybody, anywhere. It was as still as if it were in the middle of the night. A sort of—" she gave a little shiver—"queer stillness as if everything was waiting for something."

I knew what she meant. I'd felt it too. We looked at each other for a moment and then Kitty, as if to break off the terror of that communication, went to the window. "They are still there—at the curve of the road. Sarah, did Harry tell you that he's sent for help?"

"No. That is, he said he'd try to find out whether or not Johnny could be alive. He didn't say the District Officers were coming." (Mrs. Somers, I thought irresistibly, why did you try to burn your sweater? So people wouldn't think you—or your husband—had anything to do with murder?)

Kitty said, "Harry and the Board thought at first that they could deal with it. They expected something to come up, some quarrel Parly had had, something like that. It usually does. That is, when there's any sort of trouble. Murder is different, of course. Murder—doesn't happen."

Except it had happened. Twice.

Kitty took an unsteady breath. "Just the same, they expected the thing to break. Right away. But Parly was murdered Saturday night and this is Tuesday night—getting on to Wednesday morning now," she added with a glance at the

125

clock on Harry's desk. "So this afternoon they talked it over and agreed to leave it to Harry and he phoned to the District Commandant tonight and they're sending some men from Naval Intelligence and from the F.B.I. And now—" She put her hand at her throat and stared at nothing. She was thinking, now it's Jenson.

But I thought, and they'll find Johnny Wilson.

I wondered how long loyal little Sally would try to protect him, how long her fighting, stubborn strength would hold out.

Kitty thought of Johnny, too. She cried, "What do you suppose young Wilson did with all that money? I mean, if he really did steal it. If he wants more money from Sally—that is, if she really does want it for him and it wasn't to buy off Jenson—why does he need so much money?"

There wasn't any answer to that.

"I want to see what they're doing," she said. So we went out to the porch where Kitty, avoiding my eyes and with a defiant jerk of her hand, unlocked the front door and then quickly went to fasten the hook on the screened door. From the porch we could watch the lights around the hospital and in the administration building and the whole Row, lighted everywhere now. We talked, of course, but not much. Toward dawn Suli came out with coffee and a large carving knife stuffed into his belt. Kitty looked at the carving knife. "What's that for?"

His eyes darted over us and then fixed themselves upon the tray. "Nothing, missy."

"Well, take it back where it belongs."

"Yes, missy." He might as well have said, no, I won't. He slid quickly back into the house. Just at that moment Suli was about the only person on the base (except Harry, of course, and Father Andrew, and Jim) whom I didn't suspect of being Johnny Wilson.

Yet that was patently absurd. Navy records were exact. But I wished I had had one glimpse of Johnny's photograph. I wondered if Sally still had the photograph or if she had destroyed it. But it didn't matter now, for she'd have to tell the whole truth. Harry and the Navy Intelligence officers— and perhaps Jim—would break through her wall of silence; she couldn't hold out against all of them. Besides, I told myself, they'd find Johnny.

It's curious how near Kitty and I came that night to the truth and yet how very far we were from it, too.

Harry came home just before reveille, shaved, snatched some breakfast and a fresh uniform, and left again. They

126

didn't really know anything, he told us. They had secured the whole base; nobody was to leave it even so far as Wanaha City until further notice. He had telephoned again, urgently, reporting Jenson's murder; Navy Intelligence officers and the men from the F.B.I. would arrive the following day, Thursday. Jenson had been killed, Dr. Roslin thought, exactly the way Parsons had been killed. He wasn't under ether, but he'd been stabbed through the back, again, probably with a government-issue clasp knife. The knife hadn't been found.

But he'd been killed, he told us, almost certainly only a short time before Kitty found him. He'd left the barracks, across the road from the Row, at about 9:30. The sentry had passed him; he'd walked on along the main road leading into the Row from the gate, and disappeared behind the administration building as he would have to do, approaching the road to the hospital. That was the last anyone had seen of him. The obvious conclusion was that someone had either met him, or had been waiting for him, just at the curve where the road branched into the hospital, where, later, Kitty had found him. Harry had also, he said, gulping coffee, told Jim to check with the base at San Diego and try to find out whether or not, by any possible chance, the body of the man found in the wrecked plane could have been that of somebody else, not Johnny Wilson. That would take time.

"I've got to go back to the office. The whole place is in an uproar. We've got to keep the lid on."

"Harry," Kitty said, "did you tell them that I—I found him?"

"Of course," Harry said. "Don't be silly, dear. Nobody's going to accuse you or me or— Now get that out of your pretty head!"

But he looked very gray and drawn, just the same. And didn't say a word, only drank scalding coffee quickly, as if he didn't even know it was practically boiling, while Kitty told him, in rapid, breathless little jerks, our own speculations about Sally; about Parly and Jenson and Johnny Wilson and the thirty thousand dollars.

I waited till she'd finished; then I said, "Can you get hold of a photograph of Johnny Wilson?"

Harry shot me a quick glance. "Of course. I've already asked for a complete record."

"When will it arrive?"

"As soon as possible, His permanent jacket is at BunPers in Washington. The District Office has only the records of men on active duty. Wilson's jacket should arrive Thursday or Friday at the latest."

"They must have trusted Johnny," I said, "to send him off with all that money!"

Harry gave me a surprised glance. "It's all in a day's routine. Why not? Of course, he ought not to have picked up anybody else, even somebody he knew—"

"He had to. If he intended to take the money, that was part of his plan—"

There was a gray shadow on Harry's face. "Y-yes. That's true enough. We'll know more when we get his photograph."

But meantime, I thought, meantime. I said slowly, "I asked Sally point-blank if Johnny was here and if she'd seen him. She said no. If he stole that money and she knows it, she'd have to decide whether to shield him—or not. It wouldn't be an easy decision. So far she has protected him. Perhaps he's told her some story to account for being alive and—"

"You are so certain of that!" Kitty cried. "How *can* you be so sure!"

I said to Harry, "If we know something of Johnny Wilson—something beyond his record! Something about *him*. What was he *like*? What—" I was fumbling for words. "What would he do? What did he think? *Would* he—well, take the money after the plane crashed and leave it and the man in it and—"

"If he's alive," Kitty said, "and murdered two men, then he'd do anything."

Harry put down his cup and rose. "He had an excellent record. The Commanding Officer at San Diego told me he was young at the time of his death, but he had the makings of a good officer. He was liked and recommended for promotion. That was about all he could tell me. It happened three years ago. Wilson's jacket went to Washington for the permanent file. It's a big base; big officer personnel—"

"Harry," Kitty said, "will they question me?"

"Of course. You, too, Sarah. Don't worry—just tell them the truth." He went away, a slight, wiry figure, but that morning looking rather stooped and old.

It was really a quite horrible day, hot again, with no wind and a blazing sun which seemed to suck up all of the usual, friendly life of the base. Nobody telephoned, not even Marie. Nobody came. We might have been living on an island in the desert, entirely to ourselves. We could see little knots of women gathering on porches; I saw Marie Sinclair cross the green and disappear into the Gary house. None of them came our way. As the blazing morning wore on Kitty began to get two scarlet spots in her cheeks again; her head was high and

128

defiant but there was a kind of angry—and frightened—glitter in her dark eyes, too.

In the early afternoon I went to the hospital and this time the day nurse let me visit Buffalo Bill. Merely because Ensign Smith's room lay at the right of the corridor immediately beside the west door, I glanced into the room as I passed it. It was newly made up, fresh and sunny and obviously unoccupied. I said to the nurse, "Where is Ensign Smith?"

"Oh, he was discharged this morning. Nothing much the matter with him, you know. Except," she said reflectively, "a sore head. In more ways than one. Hated being kept in the hospital," she added. She was looking rather pale and nervous. "Horrible, last night! Jenson—" Her eyes flickered nervously along the corridor and back to me. "Makes you feel as if they can't stop it."

She had, of course, been on duty the day before Parly was murdered. I had relieved her at 10 and taken the orders for the night from her. I said, "Well, there's one thing Jenson's murder seems to prove. The patients are in the clear. If none of them left the hospital last night, then none of them murdered Jenson. Or Parly."

She looked at me dubiously, "I suppose so. If it's the same—murderer."

I didn't think murder had broken out in a contagion like measles. "There can't be much doubt of that. Murder is a very unusual act."

"Good heavens, I hope so!" She eyed me, startled. And I said on a sudden tangent, "You remember Saturday—"

"I do," she said crisply.

"I was thinking of—oh, Saturday afternoon and early in the evening. Parly had visitors—"

"Just before I went off duty. Sally Wilson. I told you then."

"Yes. But—then there was another girl in the afternoon."

Her eyebrows went up. "Another girl! I didn't know that. Well, I'm not surprised. He was quite a lad." She thought for a moment. "But I don't remember another girl. I suppose I was busy and didn't see her. Visiting hours are okay, you know. I don't pay much attention—unless the doctor has given orders not to let a patient have visitors. Then we put the little sign 'No Visitors.' We'd taken it off Parly's door that morning." Her eyes sharpened. "He was quite a lad," she said again. "But I've seen plenty of his type. Who was the girl?"

"Nobody on the base. Her name is Winters. I expect you wouldn't know her." She shook her head. I added, "I thought perhaps her brother might have visited Parly too."

Her eyes were still curious but blank. I added, "Tall fellow, light hair and eyebrows. Tanned. He lives in Wanaha City—wouldn't be in uniform."

She shook her head. "I can't be sure about visiting hours. There's too many people in and out. But I don't remember anybody in civilian clothes. I'd have noticed that, I think. And from 7 o'clock on there wasn't any visitor but Sally." She sighed. "And I wish to heavens she hadn't been here. The Exec questioned me, you know. But I must say"—she cheered a little—"he was very nice about it. I explained that I wouldn't have let Sally see Parly after visiting hours if she hadn't been so—so—well, so sort of upset. As if she'd had some kind of—maybe it sounds funny, but as if she'd had a shock of some kind."

It was, of course, my own impression that morning when Sally came to talk to Kitty. The shock of learning that Johnny was alive—the childhood friend she had married, the young husband she had mourned. And the man who, alive, stood between her and a later, certainly deeper and more matured love.

It had been a double shock, in fact. For wherever Johnny was, Sally was determined to keep it secret; whatever he had done, she had determined to shield and help him.

Not an easy decision, I thought again; loyalty to Johnny had been, in the end, the argument she couldn't find it in her heart to fight.

The nurse said, "I expected a reprimand from Commander Roslin, and got it all right. Deserved it, I guess. But the Exec was nice about it. Said he understood how I'd felt. Of course," she added in a rather resigned way, "he's off his head about Sally. Everybody knows it. Too bad." She gave me a brief but twinkling grin. Jim, as an attractive and unattached bachelor (until Sally's arrival on the base), had been not unpopular among the nurses and Waves.

"Well," she said briskly, "if you want to see Buffalo, you know his room. But take it easy. He's in a fighting mood today."

She went cheerfully off down the corridor and I followed, toward Buffalo Bill's room. Dave Winters probably had not called on Parly. Certainly he wouldn't have made a friendly or sympathetic call. Yet, of course, if he *had* come to the hospital that night Jim's blouse would have provided at least a confusing item. A rather convincing kind of disguise. Suppose Dave had discovered the fact that Bonny, stubbornly, unheeding Dave's opposition, had come to see Parly as soon as he was able to see anybody. Suppose Dave had thought

130

that, maybe, just maybe, Parly was going to die and then when he'd learned that in fact Parly was going to get well, he'd decided to put a very final sort of stop to Bonny's affections. Or, more accurately, to Parly.

Suppose, even, he had somehow faked a pass—stolen somebody's pass, lifted it out of somebody's pocket, in El Rico's perhaps, among the crowded tables. It didn't seem likely. Yet Jim's blouse had some significance and whatever it was, it was important.

I paused at Buffalo's door, which was closed, and touched my eye rather gingerly. It was clearing up rapidly and I didn't want another one. I knocked loudly and as there was kind of a growl from the inside, I opened the door a somewhat cautious inch or two.

"Oh, it's you," Buffalo said. "Come in."

Lunch was over, but the trays hadn't been removed yet, for he sat in the armchair with a tray over his knees and a very glum expression on his face. He told me to sit down and asked me why they always sent around custard pudding at noon. "Slop," he said. "Baby food. Every damn noon. It's my knee that's bothering me, not my stomach. What's on your mind?"

"Is your knee any better?"

He moved it tentatively. "Oh, sure. Not well enough to take a stroll around the grounds and clobber Jenson."

"Nobody said you did." He gave me a bleak, blue look. "Somebody did," I said soberly.

He eyed the pudding, "Pink, too," he said in a tone of hatred, and very precisely and lingeringly turned it upside down on his empty plate, where it collapsed. "Jenson was a dumb little guy. But he was okay. He'd have made a good corpsman with a little more time." He looked at his knee thoughtfully. "I wouldn't be here now if it wasn't for a corpsman. Stuck with me, stuff whizzing around us. Fixed up my knee; got me back to the base hospital. . . . Jenson was a good little guy. But he shot off his mouth at the wrong time. And to the wrong person."

"Who—"

"That's the point." He glanced up at me. His jaw had a fighting line. "It's got to stop, sister. Somebody's going to get hurt."

I didn't point out that somebody—two people—had got hurt and it was nothing trivial. He said suddenly, "How's Sally?" He stopped, with an embarrassed cough. "I mean Ensign Wilson."

"Why do you want to know?" It was the wrong reply, but

I hadn't yet realized that everybody in the hospital—indeed everybody on the base that day—was in an explosive and somewhat dangerous mood.

His tray heaved and dishes clattered, but then he calmed down. "Shut the door, will you?"

I did. Buffalo Bill said, "I want you to bring Sally here. I want to talk to her."

"Well. All right. I don't suppose you want to tell me what you want to talk to her about?"

There was a short pause and to my stunned surprise I saw something very like a blush rise into Buffalo's hard-jawed face. It seemed out of order, unconventional in its way, for a marine sergeant to blush like that. "Why, Bill," I said. "Why, Bill—you like Sally!"

"Sure I do!" He shouted and then lowered his voice. "Sure I do. She's a good kid. But don't get any ideas. She's the Exec's girl. And anyway she—oh, well, she's not my—" He glared at me defiantly. "Maybe I'd like a girl like that. Maybe—but she's—" he swallowed. "She's too good for me."

"Don't be a baby!" I snapped. If I told him what I thought, which was that no girl in the world was too good for him, he would undoubtedly give me another sock with his hamlike fist. I said angrily, "Any girl would be proud—" And that was wrong too.

He growled at me. "Aw, shut up! I know what the score is. The point is she's the Exec's girl and she wouldn't look at another guy and—for gosh sake, stop looking like that! I'm not breaking my heart. What the hell! I just want to give her an even break."

"Bill," I sat down beside him. "Was it Sally in Parly's room the night after he was killed? Did you help her?"

He moved his bad knee restlessly and gave me a bright blue, very penetrating glance. "Sure."

There was a long pause. Trays rattled in the corridor. Finally I said, "Oh."

It was inadequate. Oddly though, it seemed to reassure him. "If I could get out of here, but—see here, sister. You've got to help. I don't know how you're going to do it. But I'll tell you what I want you to do and the way I want you to do it."

After a moment I said, "And you don't want me to tell the Captain or the Exec? Or anybody?" He didn't even reply to that, which in a curious way really bound me to silence.

"It's not very hard," he said, as if I hadn't spoken. "But you've got to take Sally over there to the Somers house and keep her there till this thing is—settled."

"*Bill!*"

His eyes were very bleak and direct. The steely, parade-ground tone was in his voice. "The guy that killed Parly—and Jenson—means business. Somebody's got to keep Sally out of his way."

My heart gave a kind of lurch. "I think you'd better tell me why."

"I guess I've got to. She came to see Parly the night he was killed. You know that. I heard a little of what they said. Couldn't help it—his window was open, I guess, and so was mine. Anyway she began to cry. Seems she was married to a fellow by the name of Johnny Wilson and he was supposed to have been killed in a plane he crashed, but he wasn't." His eyes fixed me for a second. "You already knew that."

"I thought so. I wasn't sure."

"Did Sally tell you?"

"No. She says she hasn't seen him. But she . . . Go on, Bill. What did Parly tell her?"

He waited for a second or two as if debating whether or not to question me further; then he said, "I couldn't hear everything they said. I just got a few words here and there. The gist of it was that Parly knew Johnny was alive, he'd had a letter about it. He read it to Sally but wouldn't give it to her. I guess it was from Johnny. It was then she began to cry. She must have liked this guy, Wilson, or she wouldn't have married him. It was tough for her; his crash and everything. But then," Buffalo said simply, "she'd kind of got over it and met the Exec. So what's she going to do? Johnny's alive and she's glad. But he's her husband and she's in love with the Exec."

In a nutshell, there it was.

"So what's she going to do?" He repeated. "Kind of a spot. But that's not all. There's some money in it somewhere." His blue eyes were icy cold. "Parly was going to get it. There was some talk I couldn't hear and then Sally said, loud so I heard it, all right she'd get the money. . . . I couldn't make out whether the money was for Johnny or not, but she said she'd bring it to Parly as soon as she could get it. And Parly was a guy I wouldn't trust with a—" He brooded. His angry yet troubled gaze fell on his knee and he said morosely, "With a beat-down plaster cast."

I agreed. "Go on, Bill."

"That's about all. She kept saying she had to see Johnny. So I guess Johnny's not far away."

"You mean you think Johnny murdered Parly—"

"Maybe," Bill said, his face like a rock. "My guess is from

133

what I could hear of it that Parly had something on Johnny." He waited a moment and then said, "What was it?"

If Bill could trust me, I could trust him. "There was some money in the plane that crashed. They never found traces of the money. They found a body; they thought, of course, that it was Johnny's but they couldn't identify it—"

"So Johnny got away with the swag. Parly knew it. And Jenson knew something—"

"What? Do you think he could have heard Sally and Parly?"

He shook his head, picked up a teaspoon and shoved the pink custard into a sagging little hill. "I don't think it was that. I think Jenson had some idea about the murderer. Something—evidence. Maybe he didn't even realize it was evidence. I told you: he was a chatty little guy and he was dumb."

I thought in all probability he was right. Indeed, it was the only motive for Jenson's murder which, so far, seemed likely.

"Captain Somers questioned Jenson several times. Apparently Jenson was perfectly straightforward in answering. He stuck to his story. He said he didn't know a thing about Parly's murder. Do you think he was lying? And intended—or in fact tried to, say, blackmail whoever murdered Parly?"

Buffalo frowned at the custard. "N-no. No, I think he was just dumb. The guy that murdered Parly is nervous and don't you forget it. Maybe he questioned Jenson and Jenson—oh, remembered something or—I don't know. But it looks like that to me."

There was another long pause. Then I said, "Why did Sally come here the night after Parly was killed? What did she want?"

He glanced at me in surprise. "Why, the letter. The one from—or about—Johnny. I heard her at the window of Parly's room. It was bolted on the inside. You can't work these window bolts from the outside. I heard somebody sort of working at it and I looked and it was Sally. I spoke to her. She was scared and upset and said she had to get something out of his room so I helped her. That's all."

It took me a little aback. "H—how? I didn't see you—"

"Sister, do you think I'd let you see me? Anybody who's been trained to duck shells can duck a woman."

"But—but the door was locked. I was in the corridor. The window was bolted—" But I had felt that I was being watched, too; I had imagined movements in the corridor. It wasn't, then, entirely imagination.

He grinned fleetingly, dove into the pocket of the white,

kimono-like garment he wore over his pajama trousers and showed me a very small piece of wire. "More training," he said enigmatically. "The locks on these doors wouldn't keep anybody out if he really wanted to get in. I got into Parly's room, didn't take more than a few seconds—"

"*Where was I?*"

"In that little room where you keep medicine."

"The drug room?"

"I guess so. It wasn't late. Jenson was trying to get them to turn off the radio, across the hall. I opened the screen for *Sally*. The window's low, I helped her over the sill. Then I helped her look for the letter."

"Did you find it?"

"Nope. It wasn't there." He eyed me truculently. "So I gave Sally a lift out the window again and latched the screen and locked the door and came back here."

"*You didn't!*"

"Oh, yes, I did, sister. You were putting away some charts then and the filing cabinet was between us. I don't know where Jenson was and I didn't want to see."

I had to believe him; it was obviously fact. Yet I felt rather as if I'd been stalked by the Whitestone Bridge and hadn't known it. He said, "Don't give it a thought, sister. We've had some training out in Korea. If you think somebody's going to take a pot shot at you, you move pretty easy."

I gulped. "And when I came into your room—"

"Sure. I was watching out the window. I just wanted to make sure Sally had gone back to the barracks okay. I told her it wasn't safe at night . . ." For the first time his blue gaze seemed to linger apologetically on my own eye, which was still slightly varicolored, but he didn't mention it.

"If there was a letter, it wasn't found. The Captain and Jim Warring and everybody searched the room after Parly was killed. If there was a letter—"

"There was," Buffalo said.

"Then they didn't find it. So whoever murdered Parly got the letter—"

"Because he knew what was in it," Buffalo said shortly.

"Then it was Johnny. It's got to be Johnny. But *who* is he? *Where* is he—"

"They'd better get busy finding out. And keep Sally out of his way till you do."

"Buffalo," I said, despairingly. "You think he's here somewhere on the base. So do I. Sally's trying to get some money. She's been meeting—at least once she met some man who didn't want to be seen. I mean, he jumped out of the way

135

when Colonel Sinclair and his wife happened to drive past and—never mind all that. The problem is, who *is* Johnny Wilson? He can't be one of the officers, here in the Row. Yet whoever killed Parly—and Jenson too—had to have a pass, had to be somebody they know—"

"Whoever he is, he's around. He's dangerous. Wait a minute. Has she got the money yet?"

Dangerous, I was thinking. Sally. "The boy at the Western Union office gave her telegram to the O.D." I explained it quickly, and absently, really, for I was still thinking: dangerous—Sally. "That was yesterday. I think she phoned to Virginia last night. Even by air express the money couldn't reach her till tomorrow."

It didn't satisfy him.

"Johnny wants that money. She believes and trusts Johnny. If she thought he clomped Parly, she'd tell the Captain, she'd have to. So—right now—she doesn't think so. She's sure Johnny's in the clear about that—whatever he may have done about the money. But suppose she's beginning to question it? Suppose she questions Johnny? If he sees even a question in her eyes, when that guy's got his hands on the money, he's—got to get rid of her. That's the way I see it."

16

There was a grim and inescapable logic about it. "Let me tell the Captain, Bill. Let me tell Jim Warring—"

"Sister, I'd have told them right away, but it would only make it worse for Sally. They'd question her. If she's got it into her head that she's got to protect Johnny, she'd do it. She'd refuse to tell them one single thing. But then she'd think about it. And the minute she thinks— Did he kill Parly? Did he kill Jenson?—that guy's going to know it."

Grim logic again. I was cold, that hot bright day. So cold my hands shook and yet my mouth was dry. I said, "But—they'd help. We've got to have that kind of help—"

"*No.* No, I've thought it all over. You're elected, sister. That's the drill."

"I don't—" I swallowed hard because there was a sort of tight band around my throat. "I don't know how."

He eyed the pink hill on his plate.

"Besides, suppose Sally won't let me. I've tried to talk to her. She won't talk. She—"

He looked up. "You've got to do it. I don't know how. But—" He started to get up and I took the tray and put it on a table. He heaved himself to his feet and wobbled his knee absently as if experimenting to see just how adequately it would carry him. He said, in a queer, rather hopeless voice, "Maybe if I could talk to her. No, it's better this way." His blue eyes met mine. He said in an odd, almost offhand way, "Thanks, sister."

So there it was. My responsibility. I went to the window and stared out across the stretch of bright, hot-looking lawn. Bill, behind me, waited. Finally I turned around. "All right. I'll do what I can. But you'll have to let me do it my own way. I'm going to tell Jim—"

"No. He's Exec. He'll have to report it—"

"I'm not so sure he'll report it," I said slowly.

"Oh." Bill eyed me for a long moment. "Oh."

Neither of us spoke, but communication was like a current between us. At last Bill said, "Okay. If you think he'll throw the book away and stick to Sally—"

Jim would stick to Sally. But I couldn't exactly see him, as Buffalo said, throw the book away. "I don't think anything!" I snapped miserably and with all too accurate truth.

But Buffalo's massive chest rose and fell in a long sigh. "I guess that's the best way to do it. Go ahead and give the word to the Exec."

"It's the only way. I'll go now, Bill."

He said again, in a very low voice. "Thanks, sister," as I went away.

The sun bore down upon me like a hot, dry blanket as I emerged from the west door and started along the road toward the Somers house. It was as a rule a time when all the men were in the office or loading plants, the children were in school, the women were seeking coolness behind drawn shades, so a kind of deserted and peaceful inertia seemed to fall upon the Row. That day it was different, although I couldn't have said exactly why except for a knot of men in uniform, talking absorbedly outside the long administration building, near the gates. The Waves barracks looked empty beneath the broiling sun and I wondered where Sally was just then. Probably at her job in Commander Gary's office in the administration building; she was safe for the moment.

But the terrible logic of Buffalo Bill's reasoning walked along with me as if it had a frightening presence of its own. I must see Jim at the very first possible moment.

There was a cluster of light dresses and excited voices on Ruth Gary's porch. Marie Sinclair came out quickly and ran across the green space to meet me.

"You'll get a heat stroke," I said crossly.

"I know. Let's get over there in the shade. Sarah," she said, "things aren't going right."

That was fairly clear; even what you might call strikingly true, but I didn't say so. We had moved below a towering clump of elms but it was hot there, too. She wiped her forehead. "I mean—nobody *says* anything, you understand. Not right out. But they—well, Kitty found him. Jenson, I mean They think it's odd—I mean for Kitty to go out like that alone. At night. None of the rest of us would have dared to—"

"They can't be such fools as to think Kitty murdered him!"

Her pale green eyes were bright and shallow in the reflected glare of the sun. "I told you. Nobody says anything right out. But all of them know about Parly and the Captain. And they're scared. So am I. It's—" she shivered, there in the heat. "But about Harry and Parly—that kind of thing can die down all right if there's no reason for it to flare up again. But sometimes—" She pressed her lips together for an instant and then said firmly, "Sometimes they can go on. It's been several days now since Parly was murdered. Everybody expected them to find out who did it and all about it right away."

"Some men are coming from the District Office to investigate. Harry sent for them."

"I know. But—Sarah, I've been in the service for a long time. It takes less than—" she made a curious kind of gesture, comprehensive as if murder and suspicion of murder had a presence, an invisible companionship, so it lay around us, as indeed in a very terrible sense it did. "It takes less than this," Marie said, "to break a man's service career."

I thought of the telephone that hadn't rung all that hot, long morning. I thought of the feverish spots of red in Kitty's cheeks, and her smoldering eyes. Marie said, with an odd, harsh intake of breath, "Besides there's the security angle. Sabotage. A blow. You're only a visitor. You don't realize that we're all sitting right on top of—"

"Oh, *don't* I!" I snapped rather bitterly. But it wasn't consistent to suspect Harry (even without putting it into words, only by the lifting of an eyebrow, a significant glance, a bare statement of fact which, yet, was horribly allusive), and at the same time to talk of spies and sabotage. However, terror is not necessarily consistent; it is something outside of human control. It may suggest anything. Marie said suddenly, "I'm going to see Kitty."

"Why don't you! Drop in for cocktails, you and the Colonel, the way you usually do. Show them you are backing them. Get the Garys and anybody else that feels as you do to come along."

Her eyes snapped. "All right." She sped away, back through the blazing sun to the Garys' porch and the group of women who had stopped talking to watch us.

I went on to the Somers house. Kitty was nowhere to be seen. Suli came pattering out from the kitchen, still with the preposterous carving knife in his belt, to tell me that missy was asleep.

I doubted that, but I didn't go to her room. Instead I telephoned to Jim's office, and was told he wasn't in, but that I could find him in the Captain's office, where naturally I didn't call him to enter upon what had to be a more or less confidential conversation. I thought for a moment, but the specter Buffalo's words had conjured up wouldn't go away. I telephoned to Commander Gary's office and asked for Sally. And she, too, was in the Captain's office. I put down the telephone.

Later, I learned of that interview—with the whir of the electric fan, Harry sitting at his desk, unconsciously rather stiff and formal, Sally erect in a straight chair, white and drained and frightened, Jim listening and powerless to help, for Sally stubbornly refused to answer Harry's questions. She wanted money, yes. Yes, it was a substantial sum. Yes, she had said she needed it urgently. But the reason was a personal one.

When Harry asked her if Johnny was alive, she said he'd been reported killed three years ago. When he insisted, asking if she had any reason to believe that in fact the report was a mistake and that Johnny was alive, she pressed her soft lips together and wouldn't answer. And when he asked her at last for a photograph of Johnny she said she had none.

"It doesn't matter," Harry told her. "I've sent for a photograph. It should be here tomorrow."

She hadn't replied to that at all. Jim, staring at the sentries at the gate just below the window, his hands clenched together until they ached, had turned then to look at Sally and she wouldn't meet his eyes. Harry finally let her go and she still wouldn't look at Jim, but walked out of the office, her square little chin high but her face very white.

I didn't know about that interview at the time, but I didn't really hope for much from it. I went up through the curtained, silent house to my own room. I took a shower, which was a mistake, for it only seemed to increase the sticky, baking heat, and then the sleepless, long hours of the past night fell upon me like a paralysis. Sally was safe for the time being. Jim would do something; I didn't know what, but something. I went to sleep, with the shades drawn against the sun and didn't wake until there were voices downstairs on the porch.

Marie had arrived, and not only Marie. I dressed hurriedly and went down and the murmur of voices grew as I neared them and when I got out to the porch it seemed to me that everybody on the Row was there.

I didn't know how Marie had accomplished it, unless she had acquired by a kind of osmosis certain talents of command from the Colonel. And of course public sentiment is a variable and extremely sensitive thing. The pendulum can and does swing furiously back and forth. Kitty and Harry as objects of suspicion and Kitty and Harry as objects of sympathy were two different things.

More exactly, perhaps, the growing undercurrent of question had been only that, and it was mainly projected by something very like a hard-held threat of hysteria. In their hearts they respected Harry and they respected Kitty. In their hearts perhaps none of them could in cold fact accept the premise that anyone, not only their Commanding Officer whom they knew and liked, but any one of them, living together so closely and familiarly, could have become a murderer.

At any rate, for the moment, public opinion was with Harry and Kitty. The whole Row was determined to show its friendship and loyalty—for the moment. So—for the moment—it was like a testimonial dinner, except of course, it had developed into something very like a cocktail party and Suli was running back and forth between pantry and porch, frantically trying to provide enough sandwiches and hors d'oeuvre. He had discarded the knife, I was relieved to note.

But Marie had succeeded too well. Kitty seemed quite as usual, friendly and composed, but Harry knew that the sudden and concerted arrival of practically everybody who lived in the Row had a reason and, of course, he knew what that reason was. He also knew that voices were a little higher, laughter a little shriller, and conversation very much faster and forced than it ought to have been. He was pouring a highball for somebody when I found my way through the eddies of uniforms and thin light dresses and brought up

140

beside him, and my first glance at his face told me that. He gave me a queer, grave—and rather sad look. "Is this your doing, Sarah?" he said quietly. "Or Marie's? Or Jim's?"

"Where is Jim?"

"He's not here. . . . Don't evade, Sarah. They've been talking, haven't they? And now they want to show that—"

"They're loyal to you, Harry."

"Yes," he said. His troubled eyes went across the porch, seeming to note each person there. "Yes. . . . I hope so."

The eddies of people had swirled a little aside from us. I said in a low voice, "You talked to Sally?"

"She won't talk. I gave her a chance to think it over. There's something wrong there, Sarah. You're right about that. She's stubborn but she's scared."

"Johnny—".

He debated and then shook his head. "I talked to the Commanding Officer at the San Diego base again. They are sure it was Johnny who was killed. Except—" he added, with a faraway look in his eyes—"except of course nobody could positively identify the body. . . . Oh, Colonel?"

Colonel Sinclair had moved up beside us. "I'll have another, Harry, just a spot. We've got the sentries doubled out in the Area. I've detailed M.P.'s for the Row tonight—"

I wandered back into the house and still didn't see Jim, so I telephoned to his office only to be told by the man at the switchboard that he'd left for the day. Then I telephoned to B.O.Q. and one of the junior officers who apparently hadn't known of the volunteer cocktail party (or had thought himself of an insufficient rank to join it without invitation) told me that Jim had come home but then gone out again, he didn't know where, but his car was parked out in front.

Perhaps, I thought, putting down the telephone, Jim was on his way to the Somerses'. It seemed an opportunity to intercept him. I went out through the kitchen where the cook and Suli both gave me rather frenzied, stay-out-of-our-kitchen-we-have-a-crisis look, and across the road toward B.O.Q., keeping the screen of the hedge along the driveway between me and the groups of people on the Somers' porch. Halfway along, I met Father Andrews, looking hurried and hot, his white collar wilted. He stopped to wipe his bald head and the halo of fringe around it. "I'm on my way to the Somerses'," he said. "I understand the entire Row has called on them this evening."

"It's proving to be a full-fledged cocktail party," I said. "I don't think anyone intended that." By anyone I meant myself and Marie.

But Father Andrews smiled gently. "I don't think that was the purpose. No, no. Quite a different motive, I should say. Very heart-warming. Yes, commendable."

He never saw harm until he had to, but then he would lash out with scorn and authority, his usually kind face unbelievably stern and wrathful. He wiped his head again, a troubled look suddenly in his eyes. "Miss Keate, I have a very serious responsibility. A very serious question in my mind. I feel that I'd like to talk to you about it. You know Captain Somers very well. You've known him, I understand, for a long time. And you know Jim Warring."

Every nerve in my body seemed to tighten. "Yes, Padre."

"I have been debating in my mind," he said slowly, "about my duty. You see I have every respect—yes, and admiration for Jim Warring. An able young fellow. A good commander. Yes. I cannot suspect him of complicity in these very terrible—" his eyes went to the mountains and he said slowly—"crimes. Blood guilt. No, I can't suspect him. Yet—Jenson, last night. We can't let these two terrible deeds go unpunished."

Little wires seemed to tighten around my throat. His troubled eyes came back to me. "I have told myself that I must have been mistaken. I have debated whether or not to approach Captain Somers. But the fact is—" he took a long breath. "The fact is I have reason to believe that Jim Warring knows something of Parly's murder."

17

I suppose I said, "What? Why?" or something like that. I wasn't aware of saying anything, but Father Andrew replied as if I had spoken.

The sun was lowering toward the sharp, blue rim of mountains. Its rosy light fell full upon Father Andrew's face which was both sad and stern. "I saw Jenson yesterday. Rather he came to see me. It was in no sense a confessional. He was one of my parishoners. He was troubled. He asked me to advise him. He—in brief, he said that he had had a talk with Parly shortly before Parly was murdered. It was, he said, about 11 o'clock that night when he went to Parly's room to give him the usual night care. Parly was in a talkative mood and, Jenson said, seemed pleased because—" His clear, troubled eyes met mine. "Because, he told Jenson, he was going to get even with Jim Warring. To quote Jenson, Parly said that he hated the Exec and that he knew something that would fix him. Parly was talkative and boastful. He said the whole base would be laughing if he told it, and that the Exec would do anything he could to keep him quiet. Jenson asked him what it was and Parly wouldn't say. Jenson said that he thought Parly was lying. He knew—" Father Andrew paused and then said simply, "I expect the whole base knew that Jim had been obliged to take disciplinary measures with Parly and why. Jenson said he told Parly to quiet down and go to sleep."

Parly had known of Johnny Wilson, alive and demanding money from Sally—whom the whole base knew was Jim's girl. It was in Parly's unpleasant little mind an ugly joke, with Jim on the receiving end of it.

Father Andrew said, "Jenson didn't want to tell anybody of Parly's statements. He hadn't really believed him; he felt that Parly was angry and spiteful. So Jenson didn't, as he said, want to get the Exec in bad. Yet it worried him to the point where he came to ask my counsel. I told him that he'd better speak to Jim about it. He is a fine officer; I was sure that he himself would tell the Captain. But—" he cleared his throat—"the fact is just then Jenson seemed to get a sort of— I don't know what. An idea of some kind. He stared at me as if he didn't see me and I waited and he said, 'I'd forgotten. *He* was there—I *saw* him!' Those very words."

"Saw *Jim?*"

Father Andrew nodded. "I'm afraid so, Miss Keate. He said—I think he said—'Maybe I'd better talk to him,' something like that. And then he left in a hurry. I never saw him alive again."

Jenson—tubby, worried, trying to do what he thought was fair. A good little guy, Buffalo had said; a little time and he'll be a good corpsman.

Father Andrew and I looked at each other for a long moment. I could hear the voices from the Somers house. The sun dropped lower. Finally Father Andrew said, "I don't want to accuse Jim Warring. At the same time, I believe Harry Somers to be a just man. He'll not act without facts. . . . Well, I can see that it is my duty to tell him. Thank you, Miss Keate."

I didn't know why he thanked me, unless for listening while he clarified to himself the anxious debate in his conscientious soul. He nodded at me and turned away, his shoulders sagging as if he carried upon them a very heavy load. He started on toward the Somers house.

What he had to tell Harry would be no news to Harry. Parly had been quite obviously, it seemed to me, gloating over the fact that Johnny Wilson was alive. Sally, Jim's girl, was still Johnny's wife.

The point was, what had Jenson remembered? Jenson had been asleep the hour or two during which Parly had been murdered. Hadn't he?

Or had he roused and stuck his head out of the storeroom door and seen—well, what? Whoever it was who crept out of Parly's room and then, as I made a motion to turn toward the corridor, into Buffalo Bill's room?

There was no way now to know that. But whatever it was Jenson knew, he had in some way admitted his knowledge. At the wrong time. To the wrong person.

I had by then strolled on past the B.O.Q., thinking so deeply that I hadn't noted the course of my steps. I had rounded the corner when I looked up and Jim sat on the little back steps of the B.O.Q. Sat there with his elbows on his knees, eyeing the Gary house.

He was looking so hard at the small brick house that he didn't hear me as I walked across the grass toward him, and sprang up only when I spoke.

"Oh. Sarah—"

It seemed a long time since he and Sally and I had sat at the little table in El Rico's and it was only the night before.

At that time—only the night before—Jenson had been going to the mess hall for dinner, listening to the news on the radio and the talk of the men around him, and all the time revolving in his mind whatever it was that his visit with the padre had brought (unexpectedly; to Jenson's own stunned surprise) to the surface. As if he'd gone fishing in obscured and confused waters and suddenly a fish had caught himself on Jenson's merely troubled and exploring line.

And then, after awhile, close to 10, for Jenson was not one to go on duty a moment before he had to, he had left the lights and company, had crossed the highway, been passed by the sentries at the gate who knew him well, and then as he turned into the hospital road—then what?

He had met somebody. Who?

Perhaps they had talked. What had been said? Why and how had he incurred the swift suspicion of a ruthless murderer? Had he, uncertain of the accuracy of his own memory, innocently in a way, questioned the person he encountered there in the shadowy curve of the road? Had he

144

said, *were* you in the west wing the night Parly was murdered?

Had he, by any chance, said: "I *know* you were in the west wing that night; what will you give me to keep quiet about it?"

Or, had nothing been said in words? Had the flicker of fear in his round face, the look of suspicion in his eyes betrayed the knowledge that had leaped into his mind? Somehow, that seemed the more likely hypothesis. And hypothesis it would in all probability remain. We might never know exactly how it happened, only—if the staff on the base, the men coming from the District Office to investigate were successful—why?

It wasn't, it couldn't be Jim he'd seen in the west wing. In Jim's presence I was sure of that.

I had sat down on the steps beside him. There wasn't anyone anywhere. The Row was like a deserted, forgotten town, still spruce with the lawns green and tended, curtains at the unlighted windows of the houses, chairs on the porches, all ready for reoccupation; yet, just then, completely empty as if a spell had been put on it. As if some invisible Pied Piper had induced every living soul in that wide and parklike area to follow in his train.

But if there was a Pied Piper, he had the face and name of murder.

Which was nonsense. The Row was deserted merely because so many of its occupants were at the Somers house. I said, "What did Sally tell you last night?"

He leaned his elbows on his knees so his brown face was in clear profile against the dying, rosy light in the sky. "Nothing. Exactly nothing."

"Did you ask her about Johnny Wilson?"

He nodded. "She wouldn't answer. I asked her if he was alive and that was the reason she didn't want to see me any more. She wouldn't answer. She said she wanted to get back to the barracks. I tried to explain to her why she had to tell Harry if there was anything she knew about Parly's murder. She just shrank back into the seat and—well, I took her home. There wasn't anything else to do. I told her that if Johnny was alive, we'd—we'd wait. Till she got her mind clear about what she wanted to do. About him, I mean, and me." Jim's jaw was a hard line. "I said whatever she decided was all right with me. I said—God knows what I said. None of it made any difference. She—then we got to the barracks and she got out of the car and went in."

I said after a moment, "It's you she loves, Jim. But she'd
145

feel loyal to Johnny, and the more determined to stick to Johnny, to help him, if that's what she thinks she's doing, just *because* she's in love with you."

He didn't reply to that; instead he told me of Sally's interview with Harry during the afternoon, with Jim himself a tense and anxious witness. "But the men from the District Office will make it tough for her. They'll have to. They'll make it," he said, "tough for everybody. It's their job to get at the facts. Besides there's the security angle. Half the base is sort of—listening."

"Listening?"

He said obliquely, "We don't have much secret stuff here. Once in a while we do a little testing, not much, nothing like—oh, Laressat, Caavisone. And, of course, Yucca Flat. All in this vicinity, but quite a distance from Wanaha."

This vicinity meant, of course, some thousands of miles. Suddenly the very immensity of the wide, spreading desert, the mountain ranges, the enormous distances of the West seemed to isolate the base and us in a curiously frightening way, as if we were alone and at the mercy of something we didn't understand. Which in its way was true.

Jim said, "But we could have a blow. The Safety Officers have done everything they can—tripled guards, set up new signals, everything. They've got so many marines out in the Area at night that they're practically falling over each other."

He eyed the Gary house, quiet and dark, off to the left.

I said slowly, "I had a talk with Buffalo Bill today. Parly told Sally that Johnny's alive. She promised to get money. Parly told her to give it to him. And Jim—Buffalo thinks Sally's—well, she's in danger."

He jerked around. "*Sally*—" He stopped and then said with a kind of steely quiet. "You'd better tell me everything."

So I did. I told him what I knew and what I only surmised. It was growing darker, the sun had plunged far down behind the mountains, but it seemed to me his face looked harder in that half light. Yet he watched the Gary house, not me, all the time. "There's only one reason why she won't explain the money or anything, Jim. Johnny got away from that plane and he took the money. They could never find traces of it. And now he's trailed Sally here and told her something—any sort of story to account for it. She's trying to get money for him. I don't know why, but he's given her some reason for it. Parly knew about Johnny. If Johnny murdered Parly to keep him quiet, if then he—he had to murder Jenson—" Was it Johnny Jenson saw at the hospital? It must have been

146

Johnny! And Jenson hadn't known it until while talking to Father Andrew something clicked in his mind, something added to something else. And it was too late now to know what it was. But what mask, what identity Johnny had assumed?

I said, "Buffalo is right! He'll not hurt Sally till she gets him the money. But after that—she's the only one who knows who he is or where he is and—once she questions his good faith, once she thinks: Did *Johnny* kill Parly, and Jenson—" I was all but quoting Buffalo.

Jim said, "What do you think I'm doing?"

"What—"

"The trouble is I've got to watch her without letting her know it."

There was a movement in the porch of the Gary house. Jim rose in one swift motion as if he'd been expecting just that. And Sally came out of the Gary house, closed the door very quietly behind her and started off, somehow very swiftly so it gave an effect of surreptitiousness, toward the Waves barracks.

"That's Sally!"

"She's been there for the last quarter of an hour. I phoned for her and she'd just left the barracks and I started out to meet her just in time to see her go to the Gary house—"

"But they are not there! They're at the Captain's—"

"Come on!" He hoisted me to my feet. We hurried after Sally. We passed the Gary house. There wasn't a sound inside. I knew that Ruth and Commander Gary were at the Somerses', yet I felt as we passed those blank, screened windows that somebody inside was watching us. Absurd, I told myself, hurrying to keep up with Jim's strides. But what was Sally doing in the Gary house?

Commander Gary was, of course, an Ordnance officer, head of the ammunition-manufacturing department. But he wouldn't have brought any records or notes that could be confidential to his house. Such records would have been kept at his office.

Sally worked in his office.

She was hurrying on ahead, a slender, swift figure in her neat seersucker uniform. We reached the road and Jim called, "Sally—"

She whirled around. She was perhaps thirty feet ahead of us and I could see her first look of shock and that she turned swiftly, as if trying to escape us. Jim ran toward her. "Sally—wait—"

She faced him. Her little chin went up and her whole
147

slender body seemed to stiffen. Jim put out his hand and she shrank back from it and looked at him with eyes so wide and blank that she was like a sleepwalker, aroused in a strange and terrifying forest. I came up with them and Jim said very gently, "Sally—oh, darling, don't look like that. I won't hurt you."

Her lips looked dry and stiff. She only looked at him. He waited a moment and then took her hand. This time she didn't resist and he drew her arm through his. "Look here, darling. I know Johnny's alive. He's somewhere here on the base—"

Still she wouldn't speak.

Jim said very quietly, "Let me help you, Sally. It might be helping Johnny, too. Give me a chance."

"*No! No—you can't!*" She pulled her arm away from him and gave a desperate glance toward the Waves barracks as if they were her only refuge.

"Sally, you've got to understand. You've got to realize that —God knows I don't want to accuse Johnny. But—Sally, it's murder—"

She had already questioned herself, and answered all those questions in her own way. "*Johnny wouldn't do that! Believe me! Not Johnny—*"

"All right," Jim said quietly, "all right. But listen to me, Sally. Whatever you are trying to do, you can't. I can't let you. You want money for Johnny. Why? Sally, let me give it to him. Let me—"

"I can't—I won't—" Her blue eyes flashed a look of sheer terror at Jim and she whirled around again as if to run from us.

Jim caught her by the arm. "You've got to listen. Can't you get it through your head that this is the Navy! This is murder! This is—for God's sake, Sally, the investigating officers will be here tomorrow. They'll question you. They'll question Buffalo Bill and—"

"Buffalo—" Sally said in a kind of whisper.

"He's told Sarah what he knows. He told her she could tell me. Parly knew that Johnny was alive somewhere. You promised Parly to get money—I suppose for Johnny. You're waiting for that money now. You're going to turn it over to Johnny. Where is he, Sally? Why are you doing it this way? Why won't you tell me—?"

She said in a queer chill voice, "Have you told the Captain about—about what Buffalo told you?"

"No," Jim said.

"Are you going to?"

"I—" The stern look left Jim's face. "I don't know."

I said suddenly, "What was it you wanted in Parly's room? A letter? From Johnny?"

And Jim said slowly, "Sally, I saw you go into the Gary house. I had phoned to you and—I understand of course that you must have had some errand for Gary, some memo he wanted or—or something," Jim said.

It was a question, but it also offered a very likely and reasonable answer. Except Sally didn't answer. She caught his arm with both hands. She cried, with a beseeching wildness which was like desperation, "Please, Jim. Give me a little time. Just a little more time and then it will be—" she swallowed convulsively and said as if she were trying to convince herself, "—all right. Everything will be, but—only a little time, Jim. If you love me, you said you loved me, you said—please, Jim. I've got to do what's—what's right. It *is* right. It's the only way. Jim—"

He was going to take her into his arms then and there. I didn't see how he could stop himself.

But somehow he did. "I do love you," he said. "I'll always love you. That's why I've got to make you understand. Do you think I want to have you watched, followed, guarded so we'll find out when you give that money to Johnny? Where he's hiding? What name he's using?"

Sally didn't move, yet it seemed to me the slightest flicker of something— Was it relief? Was it something else?—crossed her face. Jim went on as if forcing out the words. "You don't realize. You *can't* defy authority. You *can't* ignore orders. They are orders, Sally. You're an ensign. You've sworn to certain things—"

She cried, "I promise you that it's all right. I—it's nothing against anything I believe or I've sworn to or—there's nothing like that, Jim. It's—but I've got to do it this way. Only a little more time . . . Tomorrow . . ." She seemed to snatch wildly at something, hope, determination, I didn't know what. "Yes! Tomorrow. I promise you."

Jim said slowly, "I want you to go with Sarah to the Somers house. I want you to stay there. I'll fix it up with them and—"

"No!" Sally cried. "I can't. I've got to—I can't!" And with that she whirled around and ran toward the lighted barracks off ahead of us.

We didn't follow her. We watched her slim figure in gray going farther and farther from us, blending at last with the growing twilight until it disappeared within the lighted doorway of the Waves barracks. Then Jim turned and started

149

back along the road and I went with him, and he said, "I'd like to twist that guy's neck and I will if I get the chance."

There was at least one small but hopeful fact. "She doesn't think Johnny murdered Parly. She obviously is waiting for the money and he'll not do anything until he gets it from her and—she said tomorrow. You can't watch out for her yourself every minute. *Are* you going to have them—follow her? Trail her?" Such a course was sensible. In fact, it was the only thing to do. She'd lead them straight to Johnny. She'd try not to; she'd try to get to Johnny, somehow, so they wouldn't know it. But she wouldn't succeed. No, she'd lead them to Johnny; so the only sensible thing to do was watch her, follow her, keep her under the closest surveillance. And I hated it.

Jim said in a queer, tired voice, "I don't know. I don't know what to do. If she wants time . . . . But that's what she wants time for. To get the money and give it to him."

We reached the driveway leading to the Somers house. Voices and lights came out toward us. I said at last, "What are you going to do?"

Jim put up his black head. "I'm going to find Wilson."

18

Johnny Wilson. A boy Sally had known all her life, a boy who must have been like other boys. Young and happy and rather like Sally sometime, for otherwise surely she wouldn't have married him. And yet who somewhere along the road to maturity had taken a wrong turning.

People were leaving the Somers house. Marie Sinclair and the Colonel and Ruth Gary came along the path between the high shadowy hedges. Marie's voice floated toward us. ". . . Oh, nonsense! Come home with us and have a hot dinner . . ."

Commander Gary emerged from the gloom behind them. All of them stopped as they met us and I thought for a second that Jim was going to speak to Gary. Tell him that Sally Wilson had been in his house, for a good fifteen minutes during their absence.

He didn't. Marie said, "Oh, Sarah. I missed you."

Ruth put her hand on Jim's arm. "Darling, you weren't at

the party. It really turned out to be a party! Seems odd just now but—"

Commander Gary said, "Come on, Ruth." And another group came along the path and we went on up to the lighted porch.

The queer, high-pitched and false gaiety had broken down. Perhaps everyone knew it. At last only Father Andrew and Jim and I were left with Kitty and Harry on the broad porch. Its grass rugs were a little askew. The gay cushions on the chairs needed to be plumped up. There were glasses everywhere. Kitty, her face enigmatic, went around emptying ash trays. Harry said, "Stay to dinner, Padre. You too, Jim."

Father Andrew passed his hand over his bald spot. "I want to talk to you, Harry. I'd like Jim to hear it. The fact is I had a talk with Jenson—"

We sat there on the porch while he told them. Kitty sank down to a footstool, an ash tray in her hands and her pretty face very still and very white. I remember Harry, leaning forward with his hands linked together between his knees. And Jim who listened, his face in the shadow, who didn't ask any questions, who waited as we all waited while Father Andrew's gentle but inflexible voice went on. Parly had boasted of now being able to get even with Jim; and then Jenson had said, "*He* was there—"

Harry said, "Jenson didn't say Jim."

"No. But he'd been talking about you, Jim. . . . I'm sorry."

"It's all right, Padre. I wasn't there. Not until after they reported Parly's murder."

Father Andrew's gentle gaze was unexpectedly penetrating. Then he accepted Jim's denial. "I'm glad of that."

Harry said, "Thank you, Padre. Did Jenson say anything else?"

"No. I wish I had warned him. I—but I didn't think of—" He rose. "I thought I ought to tell you. I wanted Jim to hear it too. It seemed fair." He put out his hand and Harry rose and took it. The little clergyman looked up at him and the light fell strongly on his earnest, troubled face. "It's a bad business, Harry. Blood—guilt—"

He went away then and, as he did so, Suli's little white figure came to the door. He said that dinner was served and Kitty told him to put on a place for Commander Warring.

Jim went into the dining room as he had always done, so frequent and usual a guest that it was as if he were at home. Somehow, somewhere, the little constraint between him and Harry had either dwindled away, or in the shock and horror of repeated murder they had drawn instinctively together

151

again, to fight a common but an invisible and a terrible enemy.

I believe we talked some, not much. I do remember that there was still no fact that anybody had been able to dig up to explain Jim's blouse with its stained cuff, left at the drycleaners'. Harry said at last, "Anybody could have taken it out of your room! Nobody's around B.O.Q. during the day."

Kitty dropped her fork with a silvery clatter. "Sally! She could have taken it—" She met Jim's eyes and bit her lip.

I said hurriedly, "It wasn't Sally I saw in that coat, I mean blouse!"

Kitty's eyes dropped, but she was still defiant. "Suppose she gave it to Johnny. You're so sure he's here—"

Jim had a white line around his mouth. "If Johnny's alive, if she's trying to shield him because he got away with that money, she still wouldn't connive at murder. She—" He shot a glance at me, hesitated for a second and then turned to Harry. "I think he's alive, all right. And he's around here somewhere. And I—" He was trying to keep my faith with Buffalo; he was trying to keep his own faith with the girl he loved more than anything in his life—except his duty as an officer. It wasn't easy.

He faced Harry squarely. "Sir, there's something that has come to my knowledge. I'd like your permission to act on it myself."

Harry met Jim's eyes in a long, searching look.

Kitty caught her breath, stared at Jim and at Harry and cried, "Harry, he's in love with her! *Don't* let him do anything that—"

Harry's hand made a quiet motion. Kitty stopped. Harry said, "All right, Jim. If you see it that way."

"Thanks, Harry. I— Thanks."

"I'll have to know sooner or later. The men from the District Office get here tomorrow."

Tomorrow, Sally had said.

Jim said, "Yes, sir." And thought, I was sure, as I did, tomorrow! Not much time.

Kitty started to speak; her hard eyes were bright and sharp with demand. Then something in Harry's face seemed to check her.

But after awhile, when Suli had padded around the table filling water goblets and passing rolls, and gone back to the kitchen, she said, staring at the candle flames, that of course there was the marine band. Some one of them, during practice, could easily have slipped into B.O.Q., taken the blouse, hidden it.

"Where?" Jim said and Kitty said after a moment, "There are those cases they carry instruments in. A—a case for a French horn or a trombone—" Her voice died away indecisively.

It didn't seem likely. Yet it could have happened.

All of us heard the telephone ring, and Harry started to his feet. Suli came to the dining-room door. "Captain, please. Sentry at gate—"

Harry went to the telephone. In a moment he came back. "It's Dave Winters. The sentry stopped him. He wants to see me." He looked at Jim. "Let's hear what he's got to say."

They went out. Suli's alert, dark eyes went from Kitty to me and back again. He put down the salad and then, rather reluctantly, it seemed to me, pattered away. Both of us heard a car stop outside. We heard voices, but not distinctly. With a swish of her thin white dress, Kitty rose and went into the hall. I couldn't sit still. I followed her. So I heard, as she did, Dave Winters' voice, cold and very clear from the porch, "—so if you think Jenson was killed by the same man that murdered Parly, my sister has an alibi, and so do I. I had a fight with Parly. I suppose you knew about that."

"No," Harry said quietly. "I didn't. I knew that you—"

"I didn't want him hanging around my sister. He got sore once, so did I, and I knocked him down. I thought you'd heard about it."

"When was that?"

"A couple of weeks ago. He brought Bonny home one night and—" He shrugged. "That's all there was to it. But they said that you were trying to reach me. I thought that was why. Sure I had a fight with him. But I didn't kill him. It was a guy in the Navy that did that."

19

I wouldn't have said that I had moved or that Kitty had moved, yet somehow Kitty was pushing open the door and I was following her out onto the porch.

Someone had turned on the porch lamps, two of them on tables, which spread an amber glow against the deep blackness of the night beyond the screens. Dave Winters, easy and composed, yet hard and alert too, was leaning against a pillar of the porch. He was wearing a white shirt and levis again;

153

his sun-bleached hair, his tanned face loomed up sharply against the blackness behind him.

Harry said, "What do you mean?"

Dave didn't look at me or at Kitty, yet I knew that he had seen us both. "I'll tell you. I didn't want my sister dragged into this. I talked to her. I knew she'd tell me the truth, everything she knew about Parly. There wasn't anything that had anything to do with his murder. She went to the hospital Saturday afternoon, sure. He told her then that he was going to come into some money—"

Harry nodded and Dave saw that, too. "So you know about that?"

"Yes. She told Miss Keate."

Dave didn't look at me, but it seemed to me his eyes took on that extremely unpleasant rattlesnake expression. He said, "I decided I'd take Bonny somewhere—anywhere to get out of all this. We started out to go to San Francisco yesterday. We drove. You can't pin us down to an alibi for the time while we were driving. But we were at a filling station in Skagway Flat at exactly nine minutes after 10 last night. There was a clock at the filling station. You may not know that that's two hundred and sixty-odd miles from the base. If this Jenson was killed between 9 and 10 o'clock last night, no power on earth—especially my old coupe—could have got us two hundred and sixty miles in an hour's time."

Nobody spoke for a moment. Then Jim said, "Why did you come back?"

Dave's rattlesnake gaze went to Jim. "I heard it on the radio. At Humboldt City this morning at the motel where we stopped. You can check that. You can check with the filling-station fellow if you want to. We had to have an oil refill; I think he'd remember."

Jim said again, "Why did you come back?"

They were not at all alike, Jim and Dave Winters. Dave was light, so his bleached eyebrows and hair stood out like trimming upon his tanned face with its blunt short nose and wide mouth, like Bonny's. Jim was tanned too, but dark; taller and a little broader than Dave, and the few years' additional age and responsibility had given him something of Harry's ingrained habit of command. Yet just then there was a quality of something hard and young which communicated itself between them. Hard and alert and combative as if a spark or a word might set off a fight. Dave eyed Jim and replied almost lazily, "It stands to reason that the same guy that killed Parly killed Jenson. Murder's kind of an unusual thing. This—" he moved his head toward me but kept his

154

eyes on Jim—"this nurse was around inquiring about Bonny. So I thought I'd come back and just point out the fact that neither Bonny nor I had anything to do with Jenson's murder. But while I'm here—" he turned to Harry and drawled—"while I'm here I'll tell you this. Parly hated—" again the sun-bleached hair and tanned face jerked, this time toward Jim—"he hated Warring's guts and he was going to get even with him. He told Bonny that."

It was, of course, only what Jenson had told the padre. All of us, I think, missed the one point of significance. Harry said equably, "Yes, I think he did hate Commander Warring. He had been obliged to take disciplinary measures with Parly."

Dave's chilly blue eyes didn't move, yet I thought a flicker of approval touched them. He shifted from one lean hip to the other, got out a battered package of cigarettes, took one out, put it back and said, "Bonny didn't know how Parly was going to get the money. I asked her. But he talked to Bonny about money. He was going to get it somewhere. Talked as if he was about to get his hands on it. And he said that after he'd got the money, he'd fix Warring."

Harry didn't look at Jim. "Where was he going to get the money?"

From Sally, of course; from Sally. And Harry knew it. So he knew, now, from Dave, the essential facts of Buffalo's story. I felt better about that; I think Jim did, too, only more so.

Dave eyed Harry. "Bonny thinks it was from his family. Seems he had talked a lot about his family and all that. But I think he'd fixed some kind of deal."

Jim said sharply, *"Deal!"*

"Because," Dave said, "he told Bonny—he was a boastful son of a gun—he told Bonny that if he played his cards right he'd keep all the money. Just like that. His words. *All* the money."

Jim took a quick step forward. He and Dave faced each other like two duelists, prepared and ready to fight and yet, oddly, exchanging a kind of grudging respect. "Who was going to share that money?"

"Yeah, that's what I thought," Dave said laconically. "Looked to me like he was cooking up some kind of deal with somebody. And he was going to double-cross the other guy."

There was a long pause. The other guy. Johnny Wilson.

Dave said, "But the other guy got there first."

Jim said, "Look here, Winters, does your sister know who this other man was?"

Dave shook his head once.

155

"Well, then—can you make a guess? You must have seen Parly around—people he was with, all that."

"Oh, sure I saw him around my place. Saw too much of him. But I don't know who was in the deal with him. Might have been anybody. But the fellows he went around with were in uniform. Whoever killed Parly had to get into this place somehow. So that's why I say somebody in the Navy killed him. No use questioning me. Or Bonny. That's all I came to say." He turned around and suddenly western manners got the better of him. He gave me and Kitty a very polite bow. "Good night, ma'am," he said to Kitty. "Good night, ma'am," he said to me, and went down the steps.

His lean shoulders in their white shirt, his quick footsteps on the path, both dwindled away rapidly. We heard him jump into his car, down beyond the hedge; we heard it start with a wheeze and rattle off.

Kitty said slowly, "So Parly and—and whoever murdered him, both wanted money from Sally. The other guy got there first. And she still wants the money. So she's going to give it to Johnny. He's the—the other guy." She sat down on the porch swing and shook her head when Suli came to the door. "We'll skip dessert, Suli. Bring coffee out here."

"Whoever killed Parly," Jim said, "had to have a pass."

"Maybe she—she got one for him. Used somebody's." Kitty's glance flashed at Jim. "Yes! Gave him your blouse and somebody's pass. The sentries—" She ran onto the obvious snag, blinked at Harry and said, "Well—maybe they didn't look closely. Something—"

Jim said slowly, "Either he lives in the Row or he's got a pass. There's never been any question of that. If whoever murdered Parly had to get out of the Row, he had to get past the gates at a time when the sentry would remember him. He could have come into the Row through the gates at almost any time during the evening, or even during the afternoon. But if he left that late at night one of the sentries would remember him. So he gets into the administration building and knocks out Smith—"

Obviously they had been over it many times. Harry said, "Don't forget he'd have to know Smith was there. Smith or somebody. He'd have to know our setup. He'd have to be familiar with the whole organization, orders—"

Kitty flashed, "But he does, Harry! He's somebody who can come and go whenever he likes. He knows the hospital; he knows the base; he knows the Row—" She glanced out toward the blackness beyond the area of lamp light and gave

156

a kind of shiver. "For all we know he's out there now, watching us."

"Kitty—" Harry went to sit beside her on the porch swing. Kitty said, "He was out there last night! Nobody knew it! But he was there!"

Jim said slowly, "Kitty, I don't want to make you talk about it if you don't want to. It was a horrible shock to you last night—"

"No, it's all right. We've got to talk about it." But there was again a kind of drawn, gray line around her mouth.

Jim said, "I know you've told Harry everything there was to tell about it. But—but did you see anybody at all? Anybody—"

"No." Kitty's voice was unsteady. She took Harry's hand hard and looked at Jim. "Nothing. Just the lights along the road and in the hospital and in some of the houses, and in B.O.Q. Before I turned into the hospital, I could see the gate and there were two sentries there, just standing there. I could see them—not their faces, I was too far away, but there are the lights over the gate and I saw two men in uniform. Then I turned to walk along the road that goes into the hospital and—and then I waited and—and then," Kitty said, "I found him."

There was a long pause. All of us, I think, could see too plainly the half-obscured, half-lighted thing that Kitty had seen, there in the heavy shadows of the bank shrubbery. Her coral sweater touching it as Kitty in terror looked, and knelt there on the grass, and looked. And then in blind panic hurried home to burn the sweater, to yield to the frantic impulse of terror.

Harry said gently, "It's all right, Kitty. It's all right—"

It was very far from all right, but we knew what Harry meant.

Jim lighted a cigarette and walked up and down the porch and I said, "Jenson knew something. That's clear enough. And I can't help thinking that—if Jenson knew something, then I know it too. And I don't know what it is."

Jim's feet made quick, hard thuds along the grass rugs. Kitty put her curly head close to Harry's shoulder. Nobody seemed to be listening to me. I said, "When I got on duty that night, everything was all right. Sally was there, of course, but I didn't know it. The lights went out and—"

Jim stopped with a jerk beside me. "See here, could anybody have got into the west wing while the lights were out? Sally left then, and neither you nor Jenson saw her. If somebody came in at the same time and hid somewhere—"

It could—it just could have happened like that. I said, thinking back, "It was only for a few minutes. And he couldn't have known that the lights would go out just then. That was an accident. The electrician was working on the electric grill, there in the diet kitchen—" I stopped. Jim said, "The electrician! Did you see him leave?"

Harry was rising, going to the door. I think I said no, and then I said, "He was here last night, too. I saw him. He was fixing the radio in B.O.Q. He—"

Jim said, "You're right. We'd burned out some tubes—"

The door into the house slammed as Jim ran after Harry.

Kitty's eyes were bright black pools in her white face. "It's Johnny! Johnny Wilson—"

I tried to remember that shadowy figure, coming out of the lighted doorway at B.O.Q., shouting back something about radio tubes as he got into his car. A car which had rattled away toward the gates, much as Dave Winters' car had rattled and wheezed.

We could hear Harry's voice, crisp and rapid at the telephone in the study. I suppose Kitty breathed and so did I, but I only remember her eyes on the door, waiting for Harry and Jim, and the way we both listened and the blackness of the night beyond the screens.

Harry and Jim came back. "Fellow by the name of Jack Lewis. Civilian employee," Harry said. "Does the repair work on the Row and in the barracks across the road. He'll be here."

"I didn't see him leave the hospital! I'm sure I didn't. The grill was still wrong when I went to make some coffee. And—" Another little scrap of fact which still *was* fact and might be important, floated back to me from the few moments in Buffalo Bill's room before we found Parly murdered. I cried, "He—the electrician—this Jack Lewis was in Parly's room that afternoon! He was fixing the electric fan. Buffalo said that—" I groped back for Buffalo Bill's exact words. "He said Parly gave him hell."

Nobody said anything and all at once I felt deflated, for Parly would have given him hell, Lewis, or me, or anybody, if he'd felt like it. It didn't mean that—well, to put it in words, it didn't mean that Jack Lewis was Johnny Wilson.

Kitty, perhaps all three of them, had followed my thought. Kitty said, "Sally can identify him. If he's Johnny Wilson—"

But Sally wouldn't. It flashed like a current between Jim and me. Jim said, "The photograph of Wilson has arrived. It should be here tomorrow."

"And tomorrow," Kitty said, "the men from the District Office will be here. They're on their way now."

I thought of them—how many? What would they look like? Perhaps at that moment they were preparing to leave; trained, skilled men—yawning a little, preparing to sleep while they crossed mountains and desert. Talking among themselves, perhaps. Putting information together; planning. No, they wouldn't make plans; it wasn't necessary. Each knew exactly what his duties were; the grooves made by long training were already exact and inexorable.

There were too many—and too few suspects. Too many if they included the entire base personnel; far too many. Too few if it remained a question only of motive.

And that, of course, was what it was. The only possible method by which to eliminate anybody—or to convict him. Motive. As old as murder. Its stubborn, terrible seed. Motive and murder, an indissoluble secret twinship.

I said, "What will they do first, Harry?"

"We'll turn over things to them. We don't have many suspects. Dave Winters and his sister are out of it, if his alibi checks, and somehow I think it will. Besides, there's no evidence against Dave except his fight with Parly—"

"Buffalo Bill!" Kitty cried. "Buffalo Bill! Or Smith! He *could* have knocked himself out; he ran around with Parly; he'd borrowed money from him. He says somebody hit him but—"

Harry said, "If Johnny Wilson's alive and on the base, they'll find him."

Kitty leaned forward. "They'll question Sally first! Sally—" Suddenly she put both hands on Harry's arm. "Harry, what do they do when they arrest somebody? I mean, if Sally still won't talk. If she—"

Jim said in a queer, harsh voice, "If they arrest anybody, Kitty, it's likely to be me. Don't forget the blood on my blouse. And Parly was going to get even with me!"

Perhaps the plane was lifting then, the lights of the airport sinking away below it. I could almost hear the thud of the engines, as if they were the distant pulse of an approaching fate. I shifted uncomfortably and the wicker chair creaked.

Harry said mildly, "Don't forget, Jim, I didn't feel exactly friendly toward Parly myself."

Kitty took a sharp breath. And after that none of us said anything and a sense of time began to press upon me, as if there wasn't enough time. As if something urgently required to be done then, at that moment.

We heard the telephone in the study and Jim said, "That's

159

Lewis," and went to answer it. He came back and none of us had moved. "He's at the gate. Told the sentry you sent for him."

So we waited and listened again and heard a car rattling along the road. It stopped. Harry rose and Jim went to the top of the steps and called into the darkness. "Lewis? Captain Somers is here—"

Footsteps came along the driveway. Johnny, I thought, Johnny Wilson.

20

A civilian employee, lying about his name, forging what papers he had to have, following Sally to the base. Johnny, who had stolen money from the wrecked plane. Johnny, who had been for Sally the boy next door, the boy she'd known all her life and married. Johnny Wilson, who had had a good record until he'd taken the wrong turning. Johnny Wilson, who had made a deal with Parly so both of them would extract money from Sally. Only Parly had been double-crossed.

All that went through my mind as those footsteps drew nearer and, strangely, I wouldn't look. Even when the footsteps came up on the porch and Jim said, "Lewis? I'm Commander Warring. This is the Captain—"

"Want to see me?" said a flat, colorless voice.

I looked up.

It wasn't Johnny Wilson.

I was as sure of that as I have ever been sure of anything in my life. Later, if I questioned my own certainty, I could have said that perhaps he was older than I thought Johnny Wilson could have been. But mainly I only knew that this was not the boy next door who had grown up with Sally; this was not the man Sally could have married, or mourned, or fought authority, fought all of us, fought even Jim with all her loyal, stubborn strength, to shield.

There are things like that that you know without being able to say in so many words how you know it. But I think the others shared my instantaneous conviction, for there was an odd kind of silence that savored of both anticlimax and, which was rather dreadful but comprehensible, of disappointment.

Lewis' face was familiar to me although in a rather vague way; I knew that I had seen him from time to time going on his work about the Row. He was lanky, yet somehow flabby as if such muscles as he had hadn't known much in the way of exercise. He had reddish hair and the hazy reddish-brown eyes that sometimes go with that coloring; he had a long, lantern face with deep creases down his cheeks and almost no eyelashes and eyebrows, so his face looked both strangely bare and open, and at the same time perfectly self-possessed. He was dressed in a khaki shirt, open at the throat, and khaki trousers, a universally adopted garb for the civilian employees, I suppose because it approximated a uniform and gave a kind of status to their military employment, and was also practical. He was perfectly at ease.

Indeed his ease and his self-possession, I think, rather disconcerted both Harry and Jim; they had been braced for something difficult and even dramatic and suddenly perceived that there was to be nothing of the kind.

Harry said, "Well, yes I do want to talk to you. You were at the hospital the night Lieutenant Parly was murdered?"

"Sure. Repaired an electric grill."

"How long were you there?"

If the question surprised Lewis, there was no evidence of it. "I don't know. Maybe an hour. Had to give it up. It needed some new parts; came back the next day and fixed it."

There was a short pause. Kitty's pretty face was perfectly blank and flat with disappointment. Harry's fingers began to beat on the arm of his chair. Jim said, "When did you arrive and when did you leave?"

Everybody waited for the reply.

Lewis' composed gaze went to Jim. "I must have got there a little before 10; somebody had phoned to say the grill wasn't working. So it was probably a little before 11 when I went away." He paused and then added as if as an afterthought, "Had a little bad luck on the job. Blew a fuse. Took me a little while to get it fixed up, maybe a couple of minutes. The nurse and the corpsman—the one that was stabbed last night—got some flashlights. They didn't like it. But I got that fixed up, all right. Worked over the grill awhile and had to give it up for the night."

"Did you talk to Jenson?"

"Sure. Told him I couldn't repair the grill till I got a new part for it. He said it didn't matter, as nobody used it but the nurse—" His eyes drifted to me. "She liked to make coffee on it. Then I went away."

"What door?"

161

If he had had eyebrows, I felt they would have lifted. "Nearest one. West door at the end of the corridor."

I said, "I didn't see you."

He looked at me incuriously. "Didn't you?"

"You were in Parly's room that afternoon, weren't you?" I asked.

"Sure." His reply was still completely devoid of interest. "Fixed his electric fan." He paused and then volunteered a scrap of comment. "He didn't like the way I did it. Thought he knew more about it than I did. I told him I knew my job and he could keep his mouth shut." His eyes went to Jim and the bare eyelids lowered a little. "No young one-and-a-half striper can pull any rank with me. I'm not in the Navy."

Harry said, "Let me see your union card."

"Sure." He dove into a pocket, pulled out a billfold, opened it and gave it to Harry. Harry glanced at it and handed it back. "All in order. You've been on the base for about three months?"

"Nine weeks," Lewis said, "and three days."

Jim said, "Did you see anybody in the wing that night besides Miss Keate and Jenson? Any of the sick patients, I mean or—anyone else?"

"Saw the other nurse—the day nurse—when I came to the hospital. I don't know whether she saw me or not."

"What about last night? You must have come into the Row at about the time Jenson came to the hospital. You were at B.O.Q."

"Sure. Fixing their radio. I didn't want to, either. It could have waited till morning. I don't mind coming out at night when it's like something at the hospital. But a radio—I work all day and I don't like to do any jobs at night too."

"Why did you do it then?" Jim asked shortly.

Again the invisible eyebrows seemed to lift. "Because one of the guys over there said he'd give me ten dollars. And he did. The radio only needed new tubes," Lewis interjected dispassionately. "They run the thing night and day." He looked at nothing and said to nobody, "You'd think they'd have something else to do."

Jim let that pass. "Did you see Jenson when you passed the gates or—anywhere?"

"No. I stopped for the sentries. Saw the men in B.O.Q." He glanced covertly at me. "Saw her. She was walking along the road. Seemed to want to get out of the way of my car lights."

Harry said quickly, "Yes, I know about that. What time

162

was it when you stopped at the gate and what time did you leave?"

He thought for a moment. "I don't know. I left around 10, a little after."

"Would you say then you passed the gates about—when? Nine-thirty? Quarter to 10?"

"Maybe. I checked the radio; it takes a beating over there. Didn't take long, though. Guys at B.O.Q. can tell you."

"That was about the time Jenson was murdered."

"So I hear."

There was a pause. Then Jim said, "All right. You've seen the order requesting information. Is there anything at all that you saw or remember that the Captain ought to know?"

"About Jenson? Or Parly?"

"If you know anything about Parly," Jim snapped, "you'd better speak up."

Lewis eyed Jim for a moment. "If I'd known who murdered Parly, I'd have reported it. I follow orders. If I had seen Jenson or any sort of funny business, I'd have reported that. But—I'll tell you one thing. When I left the hospital the night Parly was murdered, somebody with three stripes on his shoulder was in the room with him. . . . Maybe," Lewis said, his gaze upon Jim's left shoulder board, "the doctor."

Harry rose as if his wiry muscles had pulled him upward without his own will. Jim made a quick movement forward. Lewis seemed to back against the door. But he said, with something that wasn't quite a grin, "Wasn't the doctor supposed to be there?"

The doctor hadn't been there; he'd said he wasn't there; I hadn't seen him and neither had Jenson.

Jim said, "You'd better tell us how you happened to see that."

"Sure. I'll tell you." It was very simple and very definite. He'd gone out the west door ("The nurse," he said with a glance at me, "was in that little room where they keep medicines. I don't know where Jenson was"), and walked across the lawn to his car, which was parked in the road leading into the hospital from the gate. The windows were low; Parly's room had been lighted. A man had been standing in Parly's room, apparently talking to Parly. "I couldn't see his face. He was about—" his eyes measured Jim—"about your height. Dark hair." He paused and added, "Only thing funny was his feet."

"*Feet!*" Harry cried.

"Sure. I could see the whole room. Coat was a uniform with three stripes. Hair was black. Man about—six feet maybe. Wearing sort of funny shoes. Not . . ." His gaze shifted to Harry's neatly polished black oxfords and to Jim's. "You fellows wear black shoes. I guess it's some more of your regulations. He had on sort of—like tennis shoes." Again he didn't quite grin. "Maybe he was resting his feet."

There was a long silence. Somewhere off in the night two men were walking evenly, as if they were marching along the road. Lewis heard it, we all heard it and after a moment as the marching feet came nearer and then turned into another road, Lewis said, "You've sure got patrols out tonight. Not expecting some more trouble, are you, Captain?"

Harry said, "What time was that?"

"I told you. Probably a little before 11. I went on to my car and went home. There was a dance going on in your little—I should say the officers' club. I met some cars, people coming back to the Row." He waited a moment and said, "Anything else?"

Jim said, "Where were you before you came to the base?"

"Oh, here and there. It's on my application. I was in San Francisco when I heard there were some jobs going here."

There was another pause. Harry glanced at Jim, and said finally, "All right, Lewis, thanks for coming to see me. That's all."

"Okay. Sorry I can't help you."

His lanky figure vanished, once it got beyond the area of light from the porch, as suddenly as if he had exerted some magic trick of dissolution.

I was both let down and irritated. "There's a man that needs a dressing down!"

"Oh, well," Harry said equably, "he's independent and knows it. Likes his job and the pay. Does his job all right or he wouldn't be here."

"Most of them," Jim said wryly, "are a little more co-operative."

"But he says he saw somebody in Parly's room before 11. Jenson went to Parly's room at about 11. There wasn't anybody there then. He talked to Parly—"

Kitty interrupted me. "There's that clothes closet! Somebody could have hidden there! The man that took Jim's blouse—"

There was an obvious flaw in that. "If it was anybody Parly was afraid of he'd have told Jenson. He'd have—"

"Maybe," Jim said, "he *wasn't* afraid of him. If he was in a deal with the man that murdered him and didn't have any reason to think he was going to be double-crossed—no, he wouldn't have told Jenson."

That was right, too. And I thought of the shoes—tennis shoes with rubber soles which would have made no sound along that corridor. No sound at all along the road the night before.

The marching, steady footsteps of the patrol came back again, growing gradually louder, passed the house, turned around with a brisk martial rhythm and marched off again.

Jim said suddenly to Harry, "Harry, they did stop that telegram of Sally's, didn't they? It was never sent."

Harry looked surprised. "Why, yes. It had gone before I got a copy of it. The boy at the Western Union office sent it off right away. It was after he'd sent it that he got to thinking it was an odd sort of telegram and turned it over to the O.D. The Security Officers have drummed it into them, you know; anything that seems fishy ought to be reported and . . . What's wrong, Jim?"

Jim couldn't turn white; he was too deeply tanned, but his face was an ashy gray. "When was that? Day before yesterday—"

"Tuesday. Yes—"

Jim didn't say anything. He crossed the porch and took the steps at one motion and vanished as Lewis had done into the blackness. We heard him running along the driveway, his feet pounding hard. I cried, "Harry, I thought— You said— But I thought they'd stopped it— *Harry!* There's been time—" It was incoherent; neither of them heard me. And I'd blundered; I knew it then, and how serious a blunder it was. I hadn't asked Harry whether or not the telegram had gone. I had assumed that it had been stopped. I had told Jim—yes, and Buffalo Bill—at least I had implied, that the telegram had never been sent and that consequently Sally hadn't yet received any money.

Kitty was at the steps. Harry called, "*Jim*—" His voice was blotted out by the black, heavy silence. Then a car door slammed. The car started up with a roar and shot away.

Kitty whirled around to Harry. "What's he going to do? If he knows anything about this he ought to tell you! Permission to act on it himself! How *could* you let him! It's only Sally Jim's thinking of—"

"Kitty—"

"I won't stop! Harry, you've *got* to make a stand! You've got to . . . He's in love with that girl! He doesn't know what he's doing. He—"

Harry caught her rebellious hands. "He knows what he's doing. Leave it to him. Besides," Harry said quietly. "Sally's

165

in love with him. Remember that. He can get the truth out of her, if anybody can."

"I think you're wrong," she said. "I think it's a mistake—"

But I knew where Jim was going and I knew why. If the telegram had gone Tuesday, then Sally could have received the money that day, by the afternoon mail. She could have already given it to Johnny.

If she had the money, if she'd handed it over to the murderer, then he had no more use for Sally.

She knew who he was and where he was. She was now a danger to him.

21

Kitty said sharply, "*Sarah!*"

I was at the door, yet I didn't know where I was going or what I intended to do.

Perhaps Harry, all along, had seen and understood more than I knew he had seen. Suddenly he was beside me, his thin face intent. He said quietly, "What do you want us to do?"

I didn't know. I sank down into a chair again. "Wait a minute—"

I had to find a way through wildly zigzagging paths of thought with not the faintest glimmer of light to show the right course to take. "Harry, can you find out whether or not Sally got that money today?"

"Why, yes, I think so." He went into the house.

Kitty said, "What is it, Sarah? What do you mean?"

The thing to do, first, was make sure that Sally was safely at home in the Waves barracks and tell her to stay there. I followed Harry into the study and Kitty followed me.

Harry was holding the telephone at his ear. We could hear a repeated and unanswered buzz in the receiver. He looked at us. "I'm calling Commander Gary. Sally's mail would be delivered at his office and—" He spoke into the telephone: "Yes, keep on ringing."

I'd forgotten, if I ever knew, the fact that mail was delivered directly at the various offices. And then as the buzz repeated and repeated itself and was still unanswered, I remembered the scrap of conversation between Marie and Ruth Gary that had floated toward me as they were leaving the Somers house, and Jim and I met them in the path. "Harry, try the Sinclairs. I think they're there at dinner—"

"Give me Colonel Sinclair."

This time the buzz was answered; we could hear the Colonel's booming voice and we listened while Harry asked for Commander Gary. When he put down the telephone we already knew the answer. "She got it this afternoon. She was in my office, so Gary signed for it himself. Says it was a sort of package; remembers it was from Virginia. Put it on Sally's desk. It must have been the money, Sarah." Harry got up.

"Where are you going?" Kitty demanded. *"Harry—"*

He looked at me. "Shall I leave it to Jim?"

He knew—or what he didn't know he guessed in a general but accurate way. And I didn't answer because a new and appalling conjecture really stifled me. If it had dimly crossed my mind that perhaps—just perhaps—Johnny had demanded certain information from Sally (information from Gary's records or papers that he might have in his house), then I had automatically rejected it. That was shocking enough. But the ugly juxtaposition of certain facts that struck me then was even more appalling. Sally had received the money. Gary had known it, and Sally had gone to the Gary house while Ruth and Commander Gary were out of it. Could she—*could* she have left the money there? Secretly, in some hiding place which Commander Gary would know? Which had been arranged between them?

Commander Gary—besides Harry himself—would know any secret undertakings, any important and classified information, any telling and significant results of testing or proving, that might be under way on the base.

And men have been bought.

Indeed it had always seemed to me that secret enemy activities played more upon venal and self-seeking motives on the part of their instruments than upon anything like personal conviction. Somewhere, somehow, money slides from one furtive hand to another. And Commander Gary had a charming and attractive wife—who liked smart clothes and might have wanted money, and he adored her.

The study seemed to waver around me. It was as if a black abyss had opened at my feet and it was one that I couldn't just then warn Kitty and Harry against, because I must be wrong—I had to be wrong.

Yet why had Sally gone so secretly to the Gary house? Why had she left it with that air of furtive haste? In spite of myself, with a hideous swiftness, other facts began to array themselves together. A man who could come and go at will on the base, a man who lived in the Row itself. A man who knew the ins and outs of routine. A man who was trusted by other men.

A man who could have taken Jim's blouse and yet, if anyone saw him, he would be wearing the insignia of his own rank. Six feet or thereabouts, the electrician had said; dark hair. It all fitted Commander Gary.

Kitty and Harry both were looking at me queerly, rather as if I'd taken leave of my senses, and perhaps for a moment or two I had.

I must say something. I had to think of Sally. Jim had gone to her. I knew that. But suppose he didn't find her. Suppose it was too late. No, Commander Gary was still at the Sinclairs'; there was time.

But I had to be wrong about that; I must be wrong. I said as if the words had weights on them, too heavy for my pulling them into intelligible sounds, "Sally had the money. If she gave it to Johnny, then she's in danger."

"Danger—" Harry said. Kitty put her hand on the telephone and took it away.

"She's of no use to him now. He's got the money. But she knows who he is, where he is—" It was Buffalo Bill's argument and mine; it was Jim's argument and he'd seen it before I pointed it out to him. He'd been guarding Sally, trying to protect her from a distance since she wouldn't let him help her. She tried to evade him, she'd refused even to see him.

But if it was Commander Gary she'd got that money for, then of course it wasn't Johnny. Johnny wasn't alive; he wasn't anywhere. Parly—well, Parly had invented his story; he'd only tried to get money from Sally for himself. No! No, that wasn't logical. Nothing was clear except that I had to make sure that Sally was safe. Then, that moment.

Harry said, "Do you want to bring Sally here—" Kitty cried, "bring her here?"

Harry gave Kitty an odd, half-stern, half-loving look, lifted the telephone and called the Waves barracks, which was of course the obvious and sensible thing to do.

"This is Captain Somers. Is Ensign Wilson there?—Oh, Oh, I see. When was that? . . . Right . . . Thanks." He put down the telephone. "She's all right, Sarah. She's gone out with Jim. That was Lieutenant Hagshaw."

My knees quite oddly dissolved, fortunately beside the sofa.

"Well, then she's all right," Kitty said. "The question is whether Jim's all right or not." All at once she pounded her

168

little fist on the desk. "Don't you see it all comes back to Sally! It was *Sally* Parly threatened! *Sally* who promised him money! *Sally* who won't tell the truth! *Sally*—"

The telephone rang. I jumped. Harry reached it first. I could hear a man's voice, rapid and excited. The muscles tightened around Harry's mouth. "All right. I'll be there—"

"What?" Kitty cried, leaning over the desk. Harry was opening a drawer. A revolver lay there.

"*Harry*—"

He closed the drawer, leaving the gun inside it. "It's loaded," he told Kitty. "Better lock the doors."

"Harry—"

"It was the O.D. Buffalo Bill's got out of the hospital. He's got away—"

I ran after him. "Buffalo Bill is as sane as I am! He didn't murder anybody!"

"They've alerted the M.P.'s. They'll find him—"

Military police, Marines with agile trigger fingers! I cried, "Harry, they mustn't shoot him! Tell them—"

He gave me a hurried—yet a queerly forebearing glance, as he did sometimes when I displayed my ignorance of service custom. "Good God, no Marine's going to shoot another marine. They won't hurt a hair of his head. It's the Row—the base—hysteria—"

But he'd made sure Kitty knew where the revolver was, all the same; he'd told her it was loaded.

The porch door banged after him. By the time we reached the porch he had disappeared into the darkness. We could hear only his running feet along the driveway and then nothing.

Kitty whirled around to me. Her eyes were glassy in her white face. I don't think she saw me. "He could be anywhere. Anywhere at all—" Her eyes focused on me. "He's so strong. Look what he did to you! Lock the doors! Lock the doors!"

She turned the little latch on the porch door. She snatched my wrist and pulled me after her into the house and bolted that door. She ran toward the kitchen and I could hear her back there closing windows, slamming doors. We ought to warn Suli and the cook; they had rooms in a kind of ell back of the kitchen, shut off from the house by a breezeway. I thought that. But then I thought, no; that's wrong. It can't be Buffalo Bill. Besides, there's the money. Commander Gary. Johnny. Somewhere, Johnny was in it.

My pulses were making a kind of beat in my ears like warning drums, saying, hurry. Hurry. Hurry.

Kitty was moving about in the back of the house. The

169

telephone stood on the desk. I called the Waves barracks and Lieutenant Hagshaw answered again. "Miss Hagshaw, this is Sarah Keate."

"Yes, yes—"

"Did Commander Warring come for Sally? Did you see him?"

"Sally— Oh, Sally Wilson! Yes, yes. Miss Keate, I can't talk now. He's escaped—they say he's a homicidal maniac. I've got to see to—"

"Are you sure? Did you talk to Commander Warring?"

"Miss Keate, I can't talk now. All these girls. They say he's the murderer. I've got to check in—"

"*Miss Hagshaw, please answer me. Did you see Commander Warring?*"

"Yes, yes. I—that is, no, of course I didn't! I think he phoned. Yes, yes, he phoned but then Sally went right out to meet him. I saw her. I've got to go—"

"*He phoned!*"

"I tell you it's that marine sergeant. The one that attacked you. The one that—" She banged down the receiver.

But Jim hadn't telephoned. There hadn't been time. We'd heard him, running toward B.O.Q.; we'd heard the car door slam; we'd heard him start away at top speed, grinding the gears. He hadn't stopped to telephone.

The telephone was making metallic and irritable sounds. I still had it in my hand. I said into it, not knowing I was going to say it, really, "Send Captain Somers' car. Send it here, to the house. Hurry—" Somebody said something which sounded affirmative and I put down the telephone.

It was Johnny who had telephoned for Sally. Johnny, saying, meet me. I'm here. Tell them it's somebody else. But come to meet me.

My handbag was on the table and I snatched it up automatically. I must remember to see that the door was locked. Kitty would be safe. Buffalo wouldn't hurt anybody. But I made sure the night lock was turned so as to lock the door when I closed it after me. My hands were clumsy, fumbling at the little button. I tried the door once I was out on the porch and it wouldn't open. Then I waited on the porch. There was a kind of remote hum, like the mingled faraway voices of men, yet nothing clear and distinct. I could see the lights of the hospitals. I couldn't hear anything of the measured, comforting tread of the marine patrols. I hoped Kitty wouldn't realize that I had left the house; that was all I could think of while I listened and little drums beat all through me. Hurry, hurry, hurry.

The car came; I heard it hurtling along. I waited till a sailor in white emerged running from the darkness and then I unlocked the porch door and ran to meet him.

"The car's here for Captain Somers—"

"It's for me. I've got to—I'm going to Wanaha City."

In the glow from the headlights I saw that it was the same young sailor who had taken me twice to Wanaha City—where Sally had gone, searching for somebody. Searching, searching for Johnny. It was my only clue to their possible meeting place.

I got into the car and the sailor said doubtfully, "You sure you want to go there tonight, Miss Keate? I mean, they say it was this marine sergeant. The one they call Buffalo Bill. He's a homicidal maniac, and he's got away and—"

"Hurry! It's—it's the Captain's orders." It wasn't, but I didn't care.

His white shoulders lifted. "Okay. Okay, I guess you know what you're doing."

We shot away, leaving the lighted Somers house where Kitty still was locking up doors, bolting windows.

How would Sally go to meet him? Would she take the bus? How long ago had she left? Why hadn't I asked that?

Well, I hadn't. B.O.Q. was lighted but empty-looking. There were lights all over the hospital, running figures crossing the lawns, clustering around the shrubbery. All the houses were lighted, too, except the Gary house as we passed it. A marine snapped out under a street lamp and stopped the car. "It's the nurse," the sailor said. "She's got a pass—"

"Have you seen Sergeant Brown?" snapped the marine.

Sergeant Brown? I thought. Oh, yes, Buffalo Bill!

"Haven't seen anybody—" the sailor replied.

"Okay. Go ahead. Except—" The marine looked at me through the dim light. "You ought to stay home, lady. Till we get this poor guy—"

We left him standing there. The administration building was lighted too and a couple of marines came running down the steps and around toward the road leading to the hospital. We reached the gate and one of the sentries stopped us. He had a gun in his hand. The sailor leaned out. "It's okay, buddy. Captain's orders—" He added under his breath, "I hope."

I fumbled in my handbag. "Here's my pass."

Another sentry opened the door and looked into the car as if he expected to find Buffalo there. "It's the lady that stays at the Captain's house," the sailor said.

The sentries looked at me, looked at each other and finally one of them shrugged. "I guess it's all right—"

"Hurry," I said to the sailor. We shot out of the gates and turned into the long highway leading to Wanaha City. Across the road the barracks were lighted. A squad of marines jogged swiftly toward the gates, at what I believe is called the double.

The sailor speeded on, but said over his shoulder, "It's none of my business, Nurse, but the base is secured, you know. Nobody can leave it except under orders."

I didn't say shut up—stop—I've got to think. I said, "Go on." The car leaped ahead as if it had been shot out of a gun.

The lights around the base dropped away behind us. Away ahead there was the faintest rosy glow in the sky above the lights of Wanaha City. The road was deserted. Hadn't they said that the entire base personnel were confined to quarters that night; the entire base secured, no leaves or passes granted? I remember thinking, oddly, that it would be a dull night at El Rico's.

The lights of the car sped ahead of us, spreading out across the pavement, touching the clumps of sagebrush and spiky yucca at each side to bright, sharp outlines and then leaving them in obscurity again.

We passed the road that turned into the Area, with its brightly lettered sign. "Restricted Area. Keep Out. Naval Reservation." I had a glimpse of the road, paved and wide enough for heavy trucks and traffic, winding off into the sandy, hummocky desert.

From there I couldn't see the first, guarded barrier; it lay perhaps half a mile beyond the entrance from the highway. Two miles on into that darkness the great loading plants stood, guarded night and day; igloos humped themselves up like sleeping prehistoric monsters, dangerous, not to be disturbed. The marine guard in the Area and trained and savage dogs were waiting somewhere off in that darkness.

We turned into the brilliantly lighted street at Wanaha City; it was strangely empty as if a blight had fallen upon the little town. As if it had received some lightning stroke which at one blow sent it on its way to join that ghostly parade of forgotten towns. I felt as if dust would gather, the lights would slowly burn out, sometimes a straggling figure might pass along its crumbling walks, striking long dead echoes.

Yet, of course, there were a few stragglers, here and there. One lonely figure, walking in a rather disconsolate way along the street, paused, seeing us, and jerked a tentative thumb at

172

us as if asking for a lift, a barely sketched gesture, withdrawn as if he sensed its futility.

The sailor said, "Where do you want to stop, Miss Keate?"

And it was exactly then that I knew who had murdered Parly. I knew who had murdered Jenson. I knew why Sally had gone to the Gary house. I even knew that the description of the man in Parly's room which the electrician had given us was in its essentials all too accurate. And I knew why.

I said, "El Rico's."

So I went into El Rico's again. It seems odd in a way that it should have been El Rico's. But I didn't look for Dave Winters; I didn't look for Bonny. There was a pay telephone booth near the door. I closed the little door of the booth and the nickels I dropped into the telephone sounded like a knell. I got the Gary house and Ruth, out of breath, answered. "Oh, Sarah! I've just got back from the Sinclairs and heard the phone ringing—"

I asked her one question. When she'd answered that I hung up.

Then I gave the number of the base again and asked for the sentry box at the gate. I knew there was a telephone there, but it rang and rang and nobody answered. There were people at the tables outside the booth, not many, and a complete absence of uniforms. Somebody put a nickel in the juke box and it roared out dance music. The air in the little booth was suffocating and the thud of the drums in the orchestra—and the warning drums in my ears—were so loud that I could barely hear the sentry's faraway voice when, at last, he spoke into the telephone. I asked him one question, too, and then had to wait while he consulted the other sentry and at last came back. "No—" he said. "No. Who is this?"

I hung up again.

When I came out of the booth I don't remember moving or walking. I don't remember approaching the car, or the sailor standing beside it. I don't even remember telling him where I wanted to go, but I was in the car, he was turning at the intersection and we were shooting back toward the base. Brilliant orange and red and green neon lights made a moving, checkered pattern across my light skirt and upon the sailor's white-clad shoulders. It was like a fair, some gay and lighted celebration, except it was played silently for all but empty grandstands. We turned and the road stretched ahead of us, with again the spiky shadows of the tall yuccas, the bitter, acrid scent of sagebrush, the rolling shadow of a tumbleweed taking on for an instant an eerie semblance of life.

But I knew who had murdered Parly and who had murdered Jenson. And I knew that Sally was in the most frightful danger. She had to be put out of the way; she had to be silenced. There was no other way of escape.

What I didn't think, what never entered that strangely clear and urgent process that had been thrust (but so clearly, so convincingly) into my mind, was that I might be in danger, too.

22

There was only one road which turned off from the highway and that was the road to the Area and the ammunition plants and igloos. It marked a kind of halfway point, so I was looking for it and thankful when we passed. I knew exactly what I would do. I'd stop at the gate. I'd have the sentry get Harry. The Row was alive by now with marines, with officers, all of them searching. In seconds after I reached the gate they'd know what to look for. I might—I might not be too late. I leaned forward. "Oh, hurry—"

"Going as fast as I can, miss. This road's—"

The car slithered off to one side, rocked perilously in the sand, righted itself.

The headlights of an approaching car from the base shot into view ahead of us, racing toward us. We shot past each other.

I ought to have told the sentry! I ought to have told him to get Harry, told him what to do. Well, I hadn't. But in a matter of moments we'd reach the gate. I thought that and then only the car that had flashed past us made its picture on my mind.

"Stop! Stop! Turn around—"

The sailor jerked his face toward me and the car swerved off into the sandy edge again; he jerked it back and slid to a stop. "What do you mean, for gosh sake?"

"Turn around. Hurry. Follow that car—"

"But miss—"

"It's the Captain's orders! Hurry—"

Undoubtedly this time he questioned my authority, and rightly. "Okay," he said, "but I don't like it." He backed and turned and backed again. By the time we had reversed ourselves the speeding car was so far ahead that we could see only its red rear lights and the fanlike glow of its headlights across the road. The sailor, muttering, put on more speed.

The driver of the car ahead was aware of our pursuit. The distance between us increased. Then the lights ahead swerved suddenly, shot off the road and across sandy hummocks and went out.

"Where is he?" I shouted. "Where did he go?" Why hadn't I told the sentry what car to stop! I'd only made certain that it hadn't passed the gates, that it was in the Row. I'd only made sure, or thought I'd made sure that Sally was in the Row.

Why hadn't I told the sentry to stop that car no matter whose pass was presented at the gate!

The sailor yelled, *"He's turned into the Area. It's one of the officers!"*

"Where's the road into the Area?"

"Damn near," the sailor flung back at me, but he had his foot on the gas, too. "We can't enter it. I'm not going to take this car—"

"Go on! No, wait, there's the sign. Turn into the road."

The sailor said something extremely emphatic but also rather scared about orders, but he did swerve into the road leading straight into the Area, past the sign forbidding it. There was no car ahead of us, no car lights, nothing but a winding road and night-dark desert, hummocky and uneven and black, stretching out on both sides of us into nothing. Away off ahead there was a barely visible glow which I knew marked the lights around the loading plants. But they were nearly two miles from the entrance.

Where were the guards? Where was the barrier? I had never visited the Area before; visitors were not encouraged; it was off limits. But I knew that there was a kind of buffer of space, a long strip of land which provided a safety factor, between the ammunition storage igloos and the manufacturing and loading plants, and the highway. Suddenly the sailor braked to a stop. "He's gone out there—" he pointed. "See the tracks. He's left the road."

I could see heavy tracks in the sand, leading away from the road. Deep tracks, as if the car we were following had swerved wildly as it plunged off the road and into the sand. We could follow the marks to the rim of the light from our headlights; beyond that they vanished into the hummocky, uneven black space.

The sailor turned off the engine. There wasn't a sound anywhere; there is no silence like that of night in the desert.

The car somewhere off there in the darkness couldn't have

gone far; it would have bogged down in sand and brush.

The sailor said, "What do we do now?"

There was only one thing to do. I got out of the car and plunged into the deep, freshly made tracks of the other car. The sailor ran after me and caught my arm. "We've got to get out of this. My God, there's marines on guard. They'll shoot—"

I jerked my arm away from him. Sand was clogging my feet, dragging at me when I tried to run. A tall yucca plant loomed up ahead of me and tore at my skirt as if to stop me. Suddenly a solid object was beside me. Solid, dimly lighter, than the surrounding darkness, and it was the car. The driver's seat was empty.

If only Sally would cry out, scream, anything!

Suppose she couldn't. Suppose there was a quiet, huddled bundle, covered over with something, in the car. I stumbled and went to my knees and then dragged myself up again, holding to the door of the car which was open. I remembered my fingers scrabbling frantically over the seat and the floor. There was nothing there.

I groped my way past the car and up a little rise which the car had failed to climb. It was rough going, sand and tough, spiky growth. I struggled to the top of the hillock and plunged down into the shadow on the other side, down and down and stumbled again and fell. The sailor had followed me.

I hadn't known that he was there. In my plunging rush I hadn't heard him. But I felt his presence then and heard his heavy breathing near me. I cried, "She's here—somewhere. She's here—"

Somewhere behind me, away off toward the highway, I heard another car.

The sailor didn't move. I could feel him, standing there behind me, but he didn't speak or move. I thrust at the sand and sagebrush and got myself to my knees and turned. "Hurry! Stop that car out there on the highway! We've got to have help—"

I stopped, because the sailor looked different. There was the dim outline of his figure—but it was dark. No white uniform. No white gob cap. Different—then I saw an arm rise, savagely, against the black sky.

I didn't see the savage downward thrust, half begun.

An animal moves swiftly and instinctively from danger and so did I. Without plan or purpose I simply rolled down that little incline, rolled and squirmed and rolled again. Brush caught at me and I squirmed away and at the same time, somewhere, the thud of that approaching car was louder, roaring into the Area road, covering the sound of my escape—covering the sound of pursuit and the sound of flight, covering everything.

The car stopped. I came up against a great growth of yucca which sent swordlike thrusts at me. I crawled on my hands and knees around it and I couldn't go any farther. My heart was pounding in my throat. I couldn't breathe; I couldn't hear.

But I did hear Jim, back toward the road. "Sarah—Sarah—"

I couldn't believe it. It couldn't be Jim. It was somebody else.

"Sarah—"

My light dress loomed up in the darkness so he found me huddled behind the yucca. I felt his hands on my shoulders.

"Jim!" I made a desperate move and caught his hands. "Sally's here. I don't know where. He was here too—he tried to kill me—he got away and Sally—"

A car started with a roar on the Area road. Jim plunged away from me toward it, shouted something and stopped as the thuds of the racing engine dwindled rapidly away.

He plunged back toward me. "He's got your car. He's headed straight for the barrier. They'll get him . . ." He was helping me to my feet.

"Sally," I gasped and spit sand.

"Sally's all right. She's okay. She's all right—"

There were shots off in the black desert night.

Loud, sharp, quick. There was a pause and I think I heard voices, shouting. And then there was a rapid volley of shots and all at once a heavy, smashing crash.

Jim flung me back down into the sand. He flung himself down beside me, his arms over my head, holding me down, my face in the sand. And the sand simply heaved itself all around us and a kind of shudder passed over the night and then I heard the blast.

The sand under my face quivered. The earth seemed to unbalance in its steady course, shake itself, rock around us.

Jim pressed me down so I couldn't breathe but I rather fancied I wasn't going to do much in the way of breathing ever again, in any case. "Wait," he shouted hoarsely, "wait—"

I waited, needless to say.

The night seemed to shudder back into quiet.

If the blast set off what they called a chain detonation, the whole base would go up. But we'd go up first and more energetically. I tried to burrow into the sand.

Then through the shocked and shuddering stillness I heard a long terrible wail off in the distance. It was the disaster whistle.

Jim's hold of me relaxed but I only dug deeper into the sand, or tried to—not very successfully. But after a long time I raised my head cautiously like an ostrich out of the sand. Jim was on his feet, staring into the darkness. He turned and gave me his hands and pulled me to my feet. "I think it's all right. God knows what happened but—come on. We'll get back to the road."

We struggled up the sliding, humpy rise and down again. We passed the empty car, which curiously had slewed around and was tilted over drunkenly. "Blast," Jim said. "Come on."

We got to the road. I felt its hard surface under my feet. My car—or rather Harry's—was still there. No; it wasn't. It was Jim's car he helped me into. A white figure staggered, running, into the glow of the headlights. It was the sailor and he looked as if he'd been through the wars. Not exactly shredded but with that effect. His eyes were wild, his gob cap was gone and there were sandy smudges on his white uniform. "He got the Captain's car!" He shouted. "He got past me and into the car and shot away. I couldn't stop him. I ran after him and—" he skidded to a halt beside Jim. "My God, did you hear that, sir?"

We'd heard it, all right. The sailor shouted above the din of sirens, "I hit the deck. I thought the whole works was going up. My God, what happened? What did he hit?"

"I've got to find out. Get in this car and take Miss Keate back to the Row. Snap into it."

The sailor gulped, leaped into the car beside me, and began a frenzy of reversing and turning. Then we left Jim behind us and were shooting toward the highway again and all I wanted was to get out of there.

The sailor was most heartily in sympathy with me. We were emphatically two minds of a single thought. Cars from the highway swerved into the Area road and shot past us. We gave a wild swerve ourselves and got onto the highway and met a wild array of headlights and passed them, too.

Nobody stopped us although there were shouted, indeed violent, imprecations hurled at us as we missed the Fire Department by inches. But the sailor bent over the wheel and drove as if the devil were in him. But he was listening too, so hard that his young ears seemed to flap backward. I wiped sand and listened too. But aside from the racing cars, there wasn't anything.

The sailor began to sit more easily when we reached the

gates; we stopped and both sentries jumped at us and the sailor then wiped his own face with his once-white sleeve, and I think got more sand in his mouth for he sputtered and coughed. The sentry shouted, "The ambulance went out. How many hurt?"

"Don't know—" the sailor shouted back at them. "Don't stop me—"

We shot along the road toward the Somers house. The Row was alive with lights and clusters of people on the lighted porches. The squad of marines was drawn up in front of the hospital and looked remarkably belligerent, as if ready to fight the world, the flesh, the devil and the tons of ammunition out there in the Area. All of it, it seemed to me just then, to be brooding over whether or not it was satisfied with one explosion, but just might, if the fit took it, give itself another heave and shoot the whole base and everything around it into the sky and have done with it.

We whirled to a stop in the Somers driveway. The sailor helped me out, dislodging sand over both of us.

Then he took a long breath. "Miss, I'm not going to drive for you again. Not anywhere. Not—" he said passionately, "if they put me in irons."

With that he got back into the car and the door slammed; he didn't waste any time in leaving.

The porch was dark except for lights streaming out from the windows. My eyes felt as if I had scooped up most of the desert in them. The house door flung open and Kitty stood there. She gave me a blank look, said, "Oh, it's you," and went straight back along the hall, and she had a revolver in her hand. I started after her, a little taken aback by the coolness of her reception considering the recent, I might even say shaking, events. And Sally said, "*Miss Keate—*"

She was on the porch, in the porch swing, for it was still moving. She ran toward me. "There's been a blow. Out in the Area—"

I told her that I knew it.

"Where's Jim? He went to find you! He—"

"Jim's all right. Unless the place blows up," I said crossly and sank into the nearest chair and wiped sand out of my eyes. There was no sound at all from the Area. The porch didn't rock, the house remained quite steady on its foundation, so I didn't run upstairs and dig in under my bed and pull pillows around me as had been my intention.

Sally said something, turned on a lamp, and gave me a horrified look. "Miss Keate! Where have you been! Mrs. Somers said you'd gone for a drive."

"Oh, yes, certainly," I said bitterly. "A nice, quiet little drive."

"Your hands!" Sally squealed. "Your stockings!"

Well, there wasn't anything left that could be called stockings. Sally gave another squeal and flashed into the house.

I wiped away at sand and then Sally was flying out the door again, her arms full of bottles and bandages.

The Navy missed acquiring an excellent nurse when they made Sally an ensign in the Waves; she went straight to work and she didn't ask me a thing. It was while I was holding the little blue eyecup to one eye and Sally was rolling off what was left of my stockings that I became aware of a subdued but determined pounding inside the house. It sounded as if somebody had a chair and was quite simply and resolutely battering in a door. I jerked the eyecup from my eye and the liquid ran down my face. *"What is that?"*

"Oh, that," Sally tipped alcohol on some cotton and swabbed a scratch with it and I resisted an impulse to utter a sharp howl. "That's Buffalo Bill. He's locked in the study. Mrs. Somers is sitting in the hall with a gun in her hand, keeping him there till the Captain gets back."

23

The pounding reached a wild crescendo and I was sure I heard the door splinter, and then it stopped, doubtless to permit Buffalo to take a breath, and I heard Kitty from the hall. "Stop that or I'll shoot straight through the door."

There was a reply, somewhat breathless and muffled; I couldn't hear the words.

But I thought things could remain, so to speak, in status quo; Kitty wouldn't really shoot. At least I didn't think so. And I had to talk to Sally.

I also felt a rather urgent need for getting myself abreast of recent events on the Row. Sally's little hands were working methodically, her bent face serious.

"Sally," I said, "somebody phoned and said you could see Johnny, didn't he? He said he'd arrange it so you could meet Johnny. So you told Miss Hagshaw you were going to meet Jim—"

I waited. She ripped off the cellophane covering for a

bandage. I went on, "But you were really going to see Johnny. You were going to tell him he must give himself up tomorrow. And then—"

She said, "Buffalo Bill was waiting for me. Outside the Waves barracks. He said I must come with him."

"What did you do? Where did you go?"

"Buffalo wanted me to come here. He said you and Mrs. Somers would let me stay. But I couldn't. I had to—" she stopped. I said gently, "You had to see Johnny. Of course. Then what—"

"Well—Buffalo said that—" She kept right on working at my scratches, but her voice was unsteady. "He said that I—that Parly and Jenson had been murdered and that the murderer—" she stopped.

"He said you were in danger. He said the murderer had to—"

She still didn't, wouldn't believe it. "Johnny wouldn't hurt me. He *wouldn't*— "

Buffalo had not resumed his battering of the door. I said slowly, "Then what happened?"

"Buffalo said that the whole base would be looking for him. He'd got out of the hospital and he was limping so and I could see it hurt him to walk so I—I said we'd come here. There were some patrols so it took us a long time because we had to hide and wait. But finally we got here and Buffalo knocked and knocked and Mrs. Somers opened the door and she had a gun and she made Buffalo go into the study and she locked him in there and said I was to wait till the Captain got back. She wanted to phone for him but of course Buffalo was in the study where there's the telephone and she wouldn't open the door. She wouldn't let me phone from the extension upstairs. She said I had to stay out here. She—I think she's a little upset. I don't think she'd really shoot anybody but I—I wasn't sure."

I wasn't sure either. But Buffalo had dodged guns before then and he had good sense. "And then what?"

"Well, then Jim came. He came running up to the porch. He saw me." A little pink came into her cheeks. She bent her head over the bandages. "He'd been looking for me. He—he was glad to see me," she said. Which I felt was a truly remarkable understatement. "And then Mrs. Somers heard him and came to the door and he asked where you were and she told him you'd gone for a ride and she had Buffalo in the study and he was to get the Captain. But Jim just shouted at me to stay here, not to go any place or see anybody, and then he ran for his car and—and since then," Sally said with a kind of gulp, "I've been waiting here. Jim—the way he shouted at me—I decided to wait until—I decided to stay here."

So Jim (and Buffalo) had put the fear of something or someone into her. And saved her life. She said, "Then there was the explosion and the whistle blew. I ran into the house and Buffalo was shouting through the door and Mrs. Somers waved her gun, so I came back here to wait for Jim."

Buffalo began to batter at the door again and the revolver went off. I ran into the hall, knocking over various bottles, and Sally ran after me and Kitty was standing in the middle of the hall, just outside the study door, firing straight into the floor. She said coolly, "Get to the telephone upstairs, Sarah. Tell them I've got him here—don't let Sally get away—" and fired again.

I took her revolver. I don't really know how I did it, having a firm conviction that firearms are highly dangerous and mysterious in their mechanics. I suppose I didn't stop to think. And just then somebody came running across the porch, several people, and I whirled around and in spite of what I knew—or had rather conclusive reason for thinking I knew—I whirled around and leveled the gun at the doorway.

Straight at Jim. Harry was behind him. And at that instant Buffalo launched a furious attack at the door—made, we found later, with the end of the sofa employed for a battering ram.

It was Jim who took the gun from me. "For gosh sake, Sarah," he snapped, "always point a gun downward." He put his hand over his stomach in an odd, exploring gesture as if to make sure it was still complete. Kitty ran to Harry, flung herself into his arms and burst into tears. Buffalo rammed at the door, which gave a quivering groan. And since it had to be said, I said it—not the right moment, perhaps, but there's never a right moment.

"Sally, it's no use trying to protect Johnny, dear, Johnny's dead."

She moved back a little, her eyes wide and darkly blue.

Kitty sobbed, "Harry, I heard the explosion. I was afraid you—"

Harry was patting her heaving shoulders. "It's all right, Kitty. It's all right. There was a truck loaded with some dynamite and some caps. A car swerved into it, past the flares, and it went up."

"I was afraid," Kitty sobbed and cried. "A car ran into it! Who?"

"Man was trying to get away. Marines tried to stop him; he

182

wouldn't stop; they shot at him. May have been wounded. Anyway the car got out of control apparently and shot straight into the truck at top speed."

Kitty cried again, wildly, "Who?"

Jim went to Sally and put his arm around her. Buffalo yelled, "Let me out of here." I went to Kitty, undid one of her hands, which was clenched together, and took the key and unlocked the study door.

Buffalo edged his way around the sofa.

"Miss Keate," Sally said, "tell me . . ." But she couldn't ask the anguished question in her eyes. I said gently, "Johnny didn't murder Parly. Or Jenson. It wasn't Johnny who wanted the money. It was Parly—"

"Parly was killed!" Jim said.

"He was double-crossed. He had a deal. They knew Sally had some money or could get it. Johnny's been dead, all this time, Sally. It *was* his body in the plane."

Sally turned blindly, as if she didn't know what she was doing, and put her head against Jim's shoulder as if it were a wall of refuge. Buffalo shifted his leg a little and I said, "You'd better get back to the hospital."

"Oh, they know where I am," he said. "I telephoned as soon as Mrs. Somers locked me in there. Told 'em where I was. Then I tried to get hold of the Captain but the blow came and I couldn't get the switchboard. It went wild." He was looking at Sally with a wistful expression in his blue eyes.

Sally lifted her head. "Oh, Jim, he said Johnny was alive. He said Johnny had stolen the money from the plane. He said it was somebody else they found in the wreckage. He said Johnny was sorry, he'd used up the money or most of it so he couldn't replace it, but he said that if I'd send Johnny some money, he'd give it to him. Then Johnny could give himself up and give them the money for—for restitution. He said Johnny sent him to me. I didn't have enough to pay it all back but he said thirty thousand would make it easier for Johnny."

"*Who* said that?" Harry demanded.

"Parly first," I began, but Sally swept on as if, now, she couldn't stop. "I couldn't give Johnny away! I had to give him a chance to give himself up. I could see that it would be better that way. I was sure Johnny must be here somewhere and I tried to find him but I couldn't. Parly had sent for me and told me Johnny was alive and had to have money, but then he was killed and I knew Johnny hadn't killed him. Not Johnny! So I thought it was somebody else, somebody Parly had quarreled with. It had nothing to do with Johnny. I was

183

sure of that. I only knew I had to get the money and find Johnny. And that night—I'd tried to find him in Wanaha City and when I got home a man was outside the Waves barracks. So I went out, I thought it was Johnny but it wasn't, only he said that Johnny had sent him, and I was to give him the money instead of Parly. He said that Johnny had heard that Parly was dead. So—I—*I had to*," Sally said. "I couldn't understand Johnny—taking money and letting me think he was dead and—Johnny wasn't like that. But Parly had a letter; he said Johnny had written it but he wouldn't let me see it. I had to believe him. I had to help Johnny if he needed me."

"*Who*—" Harry tried to ask again, but Sally went on swiftly, "I tried to get the letter after Parly was killed. You'd have found out about Johnny and arrested him and if he was sorry and wanted to give himself up—I had to help him."

"*Who* came to you after Parly's murder?" Harry said tersely. "*Who* told you all that? Did you give him the money? *Who was it?*"

Somebody was running up onto the porch; several people. The door banged and Commander Gary cried, "Harry! Are you here? Everything's under control. Nobody hurt but the guy in the car and there's not much left of him—"

I started for the porch along with the others and once there sank down into a chair. I heard Kitty cry, "*Who?*" in a voice like tearing silk.

Nobody answered so I snapped, "You know as well as I do. It couldn't be anybody else."

Harry said into a rather frozen stillness, in a voice that was cold as ice, too, but very slow and distinct, "What in hell do you mean?"

I reached for the bottle of alcohol. "The hitchhiker. The electrician. Jack Lewis."

I dabbed at a scratch on my ankle. Nobody spoke. So I said, "It had to be somebody who could come and go on the Row—somebody nobody would notice. Like the—the postman. Lewis was in the west wing, that night. The lights went out; I think he turned them out and it was during that time while Jenson and I were rummaging in the storage room for flashlights, that he took the ether from the drug room. The lights were out for three or four minutes. I think Lewis ran down to Parly's room, and in the dark, so Parly didn't know what he was doing, he unlatched the screen at the window and left the ether somewhere in the room, the closet maybe. Then (Jenson and I were busy and had only flashlights, so

184

Lewis didn't run much risk) Lewis went back to the diet kitchen, turned on the lights again, took his bag and left. Simply walked out the west door as he said he did, and I was busy somewhere and didn't see him. Then Lewis waited outside until things were quiet, and he was sure Parly was asleep, got back into Parly's room by the window, pressed a towel or something over Parly's face—and killed him."

Somebody said, "Go on," and, nothing loath, I did.

"Lewis locked the screen, then, from the inside. That was dangerous, because he then had to leave by way of the corridor but in another way it might serve to divert suspicion from himself. Two other ways, in fact; first it would seem to show that somebody in the west wing, and he'd been gone for some time, had killed Parly. Second, if anybody did get a glimpse of him leaving, he was wearing Jim's blouse. It was easy enough for him to steal that; he came and went everywhere in the Row. So if anybody did get a glimpse of him, they'd think it was an officer. Which of course is what happened. He even described himself to us, in case he had been seen or to divert suspicion. It was accurate, too, except he said the man he saw in Parly's room had black hair."

I think Jim said, "Then Lewis took the money from the plane and—"

I interrupted, "Yes. Lewis followed Sally here. He'd run out of money and thought up this scheme to get money out of her. He got himself taken on as an employee, probably he used a name that didn't belong to him and forged his union card, but he knew enough about electrical repairs to get by. But I don't think he knew Parly had been transferred from San Diego here until he went to Parly's room that afternoon to fix the electric fan and Parly recognized him. Buffalo heard them talking—"

"Parly was giving him hell about something, I couldn't hear what," Buffalo said. "But then their voices quieted down—"

"Parly knew that he was the man who had wanted Johnny to give him a lift in the plane. Parly must have jumped to the conclusion that Lewis had gone with Johnny and that Lewis knew something about the missing money. Lewis had to keep Parly's mouth shut, so he told him his plan to get money out of Sally and said he'd take Parly in on it. Parly, obviously, agreed and sent for Sally. Bonny saw Parly late in the afternoon; he was then boastful about the money and he was going to get even with Jim. So, I—yes, I think it happened that way."

185

Somebody said, "Uhh," in a rather startled manner. I went on. "But in fact Lewis didn't intend to share the money with Parly. He let Parly write a note to Sally, asking her to come to see him and I imagine left it at the Waves barracks himself. Sometime that evening Parly composed the letter he read to Sally and wouldn't let her see. Later, of course, after he'd killed Parly, Lewis took the letter."

"That was why I believed him," Sally said slowly. "He knew about the letter and Parly said that Johnny had written it."

Jim said, "Then Lewis made his plans, then and there. Probably jammed the electric grill so someone would be sure to call him to the hospital that night. Took my blouse—"

I said, "He carried a little bag for his tools. The blouse was in it. Then he left the note for Sally at the barracks and—and came back to the hospital when the day nurse reported the electric grill."

That was all, wasn't it. Oh, yes. "But then he had to get out of the gates if possible without being seen or remembered. It was late by then, so he knocked out Smith and touched off the disaster whistle and in the rush of people coming and going managed it so the sentries passed him along with the others. He dropped the blouse at the dry cleaner's; he had to get rid of it somehow and when it was found it would undoubtedly arouse suspicion. As it did. But Jenson—we never know what it was he remembered or was curious about, but I think he may have seen Lewis in the corridor while the lights were out. And of course Lewis ought to have been trying to fix the fuse, not wandering around the corridor. I don't think Jenson suspected him, not really; he'd have reported it. He was only curious. When Lewis came to the Row to fix the radio at B.O.Q. Jenson must have stopped him only to ask what seemed to Jenson a safe question—"

"A dumb little guy," Buffalo said, softly.

Commander Gary got up and sat down again and said, "Oh, my God. He was in our house this afternoon! While we were here. Fixing the electric stove—"

"Yes," I said. "I telephoned to Ruth and asked her why she'd gone to the Sinclairs for dinner. I'd heard Marie tell you and Ruth to come there and have a hot dinner. So naturally I wondered why Ruth had expected to have a cold dinner. So—but then I knew it was the hitchhiker. You see—" It was so clear that I couldn't understand why we hadn't seen it from the beginning. "You see, none of us had ever said, well, if it *was* Johnny's body they found, as they believed it

186

to be, and if there *was* a hitchhiker, then what became of the hitchhiker? And there was a man, just strolling along the street there in Wanaha City and he put up his thumb to get a ride and—well, there it was. The hitchhiker. Lewis. Sally gave him the money this afternoon, there in the Gary house. He phoned to you, didn't he, Sally, and told you to meet him there and bring the money?"

Her eyes were blue and shining with tears. "Yes. I had to trust him. There wasn't anything else I could do. He promised to arrange it so I could meet Johnny."

I said, "And after that, of course, he had to murder Sally." Buffalo had stopped that. Jim had stopped that. But he'd almost murdered me. Because he was in mortal terror. Because I was following him and he knew it and he knew why.

It was then only that they began to talk. In fact, as I remember it, they all talked at once. Much of it was, of course, sheer surmise. As Commander Gary said tersely, "It's too late to question Lewis. Your car's gone to blazes, too, Harry."

"He couldn't get his own car out of the sand," Jim said. "The sailor had lost Sarah in the darkness and didn't know what to do. Then I came up and stopped and he told me you'd been with him and—I got there."

And saved my life. I thought that and he went on quickly, "Lewis must have heard my car stop and seen me, running toward you both. He ducked me, got to Harry's car and jumped in it. The sailor tried to stop him but he drove as fast as he could toward the Area—I suppose he intended to stop the car before he reached the marine guard. Leave it and make a run for it back to the highway and get away. But the marines got him. Probably he was already hit when he swerved into the truck."

Harry came to me. "Look here, Sarah. That plane with Johnny in it did crash—"

"It did," I said, "and it crashed because Lewis . . ." It had to be said sometime. Jim knew it was coming, for he took Sally's hand, hard. I said, "I think that when they investigate they'll find that Lewis, in San Diego, maybe under another name, knew Johnny. And found out somehow that Johnny was carrying money."

Everybody knew what was coming. Sally put her white little face against Jim's shoulder again. And, still, it had to be said. "Lewis induced Johnny to take him along. Then he—hit him, knocked him out, and—there was a parachute in the plane and Lewis got it and jumped." I looked at Harry with perhaps a certain defiance. "And you can't say he didn't."

187

"No," Harry said after a moment. "No. I can't say he didn't. In fact I don't see any other way it could have happened."

Commander Gary was the first to leave and I remember shaking hands with him so fervently that he gave me a surprised look, but he didn't know that I was apologizing to him even more fervently for something I would never tell him or anybody. We got Buffalo back to the hospital after Kitty put her hands on his great shoulders and cried a little and said she wouldn't—she really wouldn't have shot him.

Harry disappeared into the study to get on the telephone. When I limped into the house and turned at the door to say good night to Sally and Jim neither of them heard me because Jim had Sally in his arms so tight and close that I could barely see the top of her head and they were kissing as if the earth had stopped whirling and the stars had checked themselves in their courses and the whole universe held its breath. I must say I held my breath a little too and then I tottered upstairs, shedding sand at every step.

I don't mind admitting that I spent the next day in bed and thus missed most of the commotion on the base, with men in uniform coming and going, telephones humming and some of the quite remarkable yardage of reports already getting under way. I only knew that in a remarkably short time they traced Lewis through several different names and a rather ugly career of money-spending and money-losing which included some underworld connections, back to San Diego and an acquaintance with young Johnny Wilson. Who, like Sally, had never before in his young life had occasion not to trust anybody.

I might add that before I concluded my visit on the base I arranged for Buffalo to visit El Rico's with me. I introduced him to Bonny and I was rather pleased to note, when we left, that a certain gleam had replaced the wistfulness in his blue eyes.

I might add, too, that when I returned in the fall to attend a quiet little wedding there in the ivy-covered church, with the padre performing it in a beaming way which all but undid its solemnity because he would keep smiling even while uttering the sternest admonitions, I also attended the subsequent party at the officers' club. I watched Sally, now Mrs. Jim Warring, waltzing in white chiffon and her husband's arms. And then I went to speak to Buffalo, brave in marine blues and white gloves, with Bonny sitting beside him and both of them smiling at each other. Sally cut the wedding cake with Harry's dress sword.

The first toast, however, wasn't to the bride. Indeed I wouldn't have had the sense to get to my feet, if Buffalo hadn't pushed me and Bonny put out her sturdy little hand. "Get up, Miss Keate! It's you he means!"

I couldn't say anything so somebody kindly made a signal toward the marine band and they burst at once into the Marine Hymn, "From the Halls of Montezuma to the Shores of Tripoli." It was like a decoration.

There's an epidemic with 27 million victims. And no visible symptoms.

It's an epidemic of people who can't read.

Believe it or not, 27 million Americans are functionally illiterate, about one adult in five.

The solution to this problem is you...when you join the fight against illiteracy. So call the Coalition for Literacy at toll-free **1-800-228-8813** and volunteer.

Volunteer Against Illiteracy. The only degree you need is a degree of caring.

Ad Council Coalition for Literacy

Warner Books is proud to be an active supporter of the Coalition for Literacy.

"AN EXCITING SPECTACLE"
The New York Times

Presented by C. C. Flanagan—The flamboyant showman who pulls off the impossible and puts on the longest-running show on earth!

Doc Cole—The ex-Olympian who's run all over the world...but never 3,000 miles across America!

Lord Peter Thurleigh—He rides in a Rolls and runs in silk—for a side bet of 1000 pounds.

Hugh McPhail—The stubborn Scotsman who won't stop running until he's left the Glasgow slums behind him forever.

Kate Sheridan—The gorgeous showgirl who figures she can hoof it on the road as well as on the stage.

Mike Morgan—The tough steelworker with rockhard fighting fists—and a heart gone soft on Kate.

...ANT NOVEL...
...LOUSY
...AINING"
...day

FLANAGAN'S RUN

TOM McNAB

AVON
PUBLISHERS OF BARD, CAMELOT, DISCUS AND FLARE BOOKS

AVON BOOKS
A division of
The Hearst Corporation
959 Eighth Avenue
New York, New York 10019

The William Morrow and Company, Inc. edition contains
the following Library of Congress Cataloging in Publication Data:

McNab, Tom.
  Flanagan's run.

  I. Title.
PR6063.C6F5   1982   823'.914   81-22574
                                            AACR2

First Avon Printing, June, 1983

To Pat

CONTENTS

16 ...
17 THE GHOST ...
18 ...
19 ST. LOUIS, MAN WAITS HERE ...
20 THE BIG FIGHT ...
21 SHOWDOWN WITH TOFT ...
22 MEETING MR CAPONE ...
23 END OF THE ROAD ...
24 MANHATTAN ...
25 NEW YORK ...

1   LOS ANGELES 13
2   FLANAGAN MEETS THE PRESS 21
3   THE BROO PARK 36
4   THE PRESS MEETS DOC COLE 54
5   THE START 66
6   THE GIRL FROM MINSKY'S 80
7   MORGAN'S STORY 91
8   ACROSS THE MOJAVE 102
9   INTO THE DEVIL'S PLAYGROUND . . . 114
10 CROSS-COUNTRY TO LAS VEGAS . . . 132
11 THE MEADOW WITH MANY STREAMS . . 148
12 THE PICNIC GAMES 172
13 MOMENT OF TRUTH 199
14 ACROSS THE ROCKIES 220
15 DENVER: A THOUSAND MILES ON . . . 242

16 KING OF THE WHARF 260

17 THE GAMBLE 277

18 DOC IN TROUBLE 294

19 ST. LOUIS: MAN VERSUS HORSE 315

20 THE BIG FIGHT 348

21 SHOWDOWN WITH TOFFLER 368

22 MEETING MR. CAPONE 382

23 END OF THE ROAD 400

24 MARATHON 422

POSTSCRIPT 444

FLANAGAN'S RUN

1

LOS ANGELES

Hugh McPhail dropped his trousers, stuffed them into his knapsack and started to run.

As his feet settled into a rhythm he saw ahead of him the train clicking away into the distance, its smoke whorling black behind it. The old Superchief had carried him halfway across America. It had been the first time he had ever ridden boxcar, carrying a ticket free of fear, and it had given him a sense of security. Just before leaving the train he had tossed his ticket to the old man who had sat unseeing in the corner for the whole thousand-mile journey. "Save yourself a beating, old timer," he had said. Then he had jumped.

Above him the road sign read: LOS ANGELES SIX MILES. That meant forty minutes. McPhail ran easily, on his heels, with low frugal strides, his feet hardly leaving the ground. He wore a knapsack with thick padded straps to protect his shoulders, and a flat plaid cap. His upper body was not that of a runner, for he was heavily muscled, particularly in the shoulders and back, but months of distance training had scoured his body of every scrap of fat. As he ran, trickles of sweat started to roll like tears down his brown cheeks and joined with others to form streams on his back and chest. The salt sweat seeped into his eyes and made them smart. He brushed it away with the back of his hand and looked up at the sun. Midday: a bad time for running.

For a mile there was nothing but the soft dirt road, spun out before him across the brown plain, like a ribbon casually cast off by a child. The surface was pockmarked with holes, destroying his rhythm but nevertheless keeping his mind in focus.

This was rich country, its earth quite unlike that of the sour, bleak land from which he had come: in the north, moor and heather, in the center, coal and shipbuilding, in the south, moor again. But here everything had hot, vital life, and the land seethed with movement. It was strange, but generous too, and McPhail felt no fear of the many miles he would soon have to trek across its surface.

His eyes took in the cultivated groves on either side. After a moment's thought he grinned. He had never thought of oranges actually growing: they were simply something which arrived at the grocery store at the end of the street, and he had never considered what their source might be. But here they were, planted in row after neat row, stretching all about him far into the heat-haze. The plant life and the heat gave the air a taste, and McPhail drank in its perfume through his lungs, while his ears absorbed the steady purr and buzz of insects.

Old men in blue dungarees rested on their hoes as he ran past, chewing on straws, their eyes unblinking in brown, lined faces. They showed no emotion, as if it were for them a daily occurrence to see a man in plaid shorts striding past their homes. Perhaps McPhail was not the first; perhaps they had already seen a steady stream of runners from "C. C. Flanagan's Great Trans-America Race," men striding in from all over the world, soon to become part of a two-thousand-man surge across the state of California.

McPhail, fed by the glossy dreams of Glasgow's Electric Picture Palace, had thought that all Americans lived in ease and luxury. These people inhabited mean wooden shacks, fronted by small fenced-in vegetable patches. No ease or luxury here. But somehow their poverty was softened by the heat and the richness of the land. True, the children ran barefoot, but they ran on warm ground, their bodies massaged by sun, not on the frozen lunar landscapes of a winter Glasgow.

As he ran through the shanty town mongrel dogs snapped for

a moment at his heels before being shouted off by the men seated on the sidewalks. They were replaced by children who accompanied him, prancing with knees kept high in a grotesque parody of his running action. The men of the town looked on benignly, smiling as the children surrounded McPhail. "Hup! Two-three-four!" they screamed.

McPhail looked around him and again he grinned. These children were no different from those he had encountered six thousand miles away. Somehow the lone runner always had to be a figure of fun. He was an intruder, a man whose lonely and inexorable rhythms destroyed the daily patterns of those around him, whether they were those of the street life of Glasgow tenements or of a shanty town in Southern California. The runner must always be challenged—challenged and harried. It was harmless fun, but McPhail always felt behind it a note of menace. Every runner, whatever his abilities, was making a personal statement every time he ran. *Here I am*, he was saying. *This is what I do. I run. This is what makes me different.*

He was beginning to flow now as muscles, stiff from days on the hard floor of the swaying train, began to drink in the oxygen from the rich blood flowing through them. The sun was a welcome lubricant, although McPhail knew that in the long run it was also his enemy. However, there were no dangers in a short stint of six miles, and he relished the loose, fluid feeling which the heat lent to his limbs.

At the crossroads he was suddenly joined by another runner, coming in sharply from the south. He was a small brown man, running fully clothed and with a bulging cardboard suitcase strapped to his back. He made a sharp left turn and joined McPhail without speaking, running on his left side. The little man was wearing white flannel trousers which stopped abruptly about six inches from the ground, and heavy black leather boots, but no socks. His upper body was covered by a formal black pin-striped jacket, while on his head he wore a military-style cap. McPhail noticed that he had a thin black moustache below his nose, and could only be in his late teens.

There were only three miles to Los Angeles. McPhail moved the pace up slightly to test the little man, who showed no sign of recognizing the increase in speed, and stayed pinned to his left shoulder. McPhail injected more speed and moved up to six-minute-mile pace, but his companion did not flag, moving in a high-trotting-pony style in complete contrast to McPhail's low, economic scuttle. With a mile to go the Scot pressed again, but still he could feel his companion on his left side, still hear his light unhurried breathing. They ran for another half-mile, locked in silent struggle.

The little man looked over his right shoulder at McPhail. "Martinez," he said, lifting his cap. "Juan Martinez, Mexico."

Then he spurted. McPhail was shocked by the suddenness of the acceleration. The little Mexican pranced off down the dusty road and was soon over twenty yards away, dust spurting behind him. McPhail let him go. He had come to America to race, but not just yet. Soon all he could see was Martinez's little cap bobbing in the distance.

A Model T Ford chugged toward him, spluttering and groaning. He remembered that he should always run on the left, facing the traffic, and switched to the other side of the road. The driver stopped and looked out of his window. It was a young farmer. "Buddy," he said, grinning. "You're losing real bad. Saw a little feller, legs going like a fiddler's elbow, way up that-a-way."

McPhail smiled and nodded. The road had changed from a thin dirt track to two lanes of hard road, and cars threw up clouds of dust as they passed. He was coming into the outskirts of Los Angeles and now the houses too were of a different character: white adobe walls, palms, close-cropped lawns, gardeners. To McPhail, the houses of Los Angeles looked more Spanish than American.

About a hundred yards ahead was a banner straddling the road: LOS ANGELES WELCOMES THE TRANS-AMERICA RUNNERS. Just beyond it on the left side of the road was a small booth. TAKE COCA-COLA ACROSS AMERICA, said the notice above it.

McPhail pulled up and fumbled in his knapsack.

"Have a Coca-Cola, buddy?" asked the white-coated attendant.

"Free?" the Scotsman asked.

"If you're in the Trans-America."

Without thinking, McPhail pushed the lip of the bottle to his lips and gulped it down. The drink was cold and sweet. He had forgotten that, in America, warm drinks did not exist. He coughed, wiped the tears and sweat from his eyes and sipped the rest.

"Must be a thousand men here already," said the attendant.

"From all over. Japs, Turks, Injuns. Even saw a feller in a skirt."
He eyed McPhail's plaid shorts with interest. "If some of them
guys are runners then I'm Alice Craig McAllister."

The evangelist's name meant nothing to McPhail. He sipped
the last of his drink, then placed the empty bottle back on the
stand. "Thanks. Where do we report?"

"Five hotels close by: the Grand, the Imperial, the Ambassador,
the Gateway and the Eldorado. C. C. Flanagan has sure done you
fellers proud."

McPhail trotted on into central Los Angeles, the drink slopping
around in his stomach as he ran. The town was indeed packed.
Runners of all nationalities strode the sidewalks in small groups,
chatting and gesticulating ferociously. Some jogged in packs in
the broad main street, and were narrowly missed by honking
cars. Others sat in deck chairs, outside cafés, while their bodies
were pummeled and massaged by their managers. The town fairly
seethed with runners

Hugh had felt a stranger in America for three thousand miles
by rail, and even during the six miles into town, but no longer:
this was a runner's town. For the moment Los Angeles was the
Trans-America, the Trans-America Los Angeles. Even the streetcars,
clanging and clacketing along the streets, stopped to allow the
passage of the runners who pattered between them. Beefy policemen ignored traffic signals to allow athletes to run unchecked.
Runners stood signing autographs for children or elderly matrons
before trotting off to continue their solitary preparations.

He felt a familiar sick feeling at the pit of his stomach. Did he
really have a place here, in Los Angeles, now swarming with the
greatest long-distance runners in the world? Perhaps in a handful
of miles he would be revealed for what he was, a gambler, with
little enough chance of even finishing the race, let alone winning
it. He thought back to the little Mexican in his white flannel trousers,
scurrying on ahead of him.

What he experienced now was the same feeling that he had felt
each winter before the beginning of an athletic season—a lack of
belief in his body, in its powers of development, in its ability to
return each summer not only as good as before, but even better.
It was the uncertainty of a farmer who has planted his seed, and
stood before it, unsure of the harvest. It was the doubt he had
always faced, and, so far at least, always beaten.

True, they were the greatest runners in the world, but no one in history had run three thousand miles, fifty miles a day, day in, day out. There was no means of knowing what that daily pounding would do even to a well-trained body. The Trans-America was a lottery.

He decided to make for the Grand, a white pillar-fronted hotel which had seen better days. Outside on the road was a row of wooden trestle tables, behind which were women taking details from lines of men in front of them.

"Your name, mister?" asked an attractive blond girl, looking up at him from a table with a sign saying "Miss Dixie Williams." She looked in her late teens, and had a skin of a stretched, full quality that was the bounty of the sun. Her hair was in the classic curled Mary Pickford style, her full lips sharply etched in bright lipstick.

She sensed his attention.

"Your name?" she said again.

"Hugh McPhail."

"Country?"

"Scotland."

Miss Williams glanced at his plaid shorts and his strong, lean legs.

"You've sure come a long way."

"Yes. Six thousand miles."

She smiled. "Is it cold in Scotland?"

"Freezing."

The pressure of the men behind him in the line was building up.

The girl handed him a number on a white card. "Well, here's your racing number and your room number." She handed him two cloth patches and eight safety pins. "You have to be numbered back *and* front at all times during the race. Mr. Flanagan will explain all the rules at six o'clock this evening here at the Grand. Meantime, report to the dining room for lunch. Here's your lunch ticket. And good luck."

McPhail walked slowly up the steps into the hotel lobby. It was chock full with runners and their trainers. On his left was a row of telephones, into which journalists were babbling in myriad tongues.

"Yes, Doc Cole's here," said one. "Just try keeping him away. Yes, in great shape, giving a press conference in a couple of days. The Germans? Just arrived. What the Sam Hill *are* Nazis? Sure, that's what they call themselves, *Nazis* . . ." McPhail stopped still, intrigued. "Lord *who*? Oh, Thurleigh. If he's here it'll make a *great* story. Good pictures, too. How the hell do I know if he wears a monocle? No, no word yet of a Mexican. M-A-R-T-I-N-E-Z. Okay, I'll check it out. Yes, I'll get a quote from Flanagan—never any problem there . . ." The journalist stopped to scribble something in his notebook before setting off again.

"Morgan? Mike Morgan. Involved in some union trouble in Pennsylvania? Yep, there's a Mike Morgan entered. Don't know if it's the same man, but again I'll check it out. No news of Paavo Nurmi. But Hugo Quist, his manager, he's out here. Calls himself a 'technical adviser,' but no sign of Nurmi himself. Make a great story if he comes!"

McPhail felt he had heard enough and sauntered idly on. To his right was the hotel reception desk where an elderly and bespectacled female receptionist was being besieged by athletes. Straight ahead was the restaurant. He was just deciding to go in when the decision was taken out of his hands by a rush of runners who swept him up and into the room.

Inside was Babel. Not far from the entrance sat a group dressed in immaculate blue-silk track suits with stars-and-stripes badges. This was the first time McPhail had ever seen a track suit, and at first he thought they were pajamas. On the back of each suit was emblazoned the words "Williams' All-Americans." At the end of the table stood their team leader, a burly bronzed man with a crew cut, who had both hands on the table and was bellowing. In one corner of the room a man was running in place on a table. In another a sunburned old man appeared to be selling a patent medicine, babbling as he did so. Yet another table featured a man who was displaying his brown leathery feet to an admiring audience. But everywhere, above all things, men were eating. Most devoured rather than ate their food, shoveling it in with mouths close to their plates, pausing only to gulp down great mugfuls of coffee.

Perspiring waitresses in black uniforms shuttled endlessly back and forth, slamming down the food in front of the runners, who dug in immediately, some consuming helping after helping. Hugh sat down eagerly, and in a moment found a full plate in front of him. It was better than anything that he had eaten for months—great fat hamburgers and beans, followed by a wedge of apple pie and as much coffee as he could drink. Hugh had taken a liking to hamburgers. The Scottish equivalent was mince, but he had never eaten it in the form of hamburgers till his arrival in America. He ate slowly, his pulse throbbing from the effects of the run, sweat still trickling down his cheeks and neck. What a place!

There were at least two hundred athletes in the dining room, and just two basic activities, talking and eating. Most did one or the other but some, mouths bulging, attempted both, spraying hamburger and apple pie in every direction. McPhail glanced over at the little bald man in the corner, who was holding aloft a bottle of what appeared to be medicine, declaiming all the while to an audience of about a dozen, most of whom were Chinese. McPhail could not hear what he was saying, but the word "Chickamauga" recurred. The little man seemed undeterred by the lack of response from his audience. He ranted on, his gestures becoming progressively wilder and wilder. He ended by pouring the medicine down his throat and standing on his hands. The Chinese applauded politely.

His apple pie had arrived. So had his coffee. McPhail was reassured by the familiar food, for he still did not feel totally at home. Looking up he noted Martinez, his Mexican rival, leaving the room, his jacket pockets bulging with rolls and apples. It was not long before he himself felt uncomfortably full, and he squeezed his way through the crowds toward the stairs.

There were two beds in Room 262. On one lay little Martinez, fully clothed, his hands folded across his stomach, surrounded by rolls and apples. His eyes were shut and he was snoring loudly. Hugh put down his knapsack, stood at the washbasin and watched it fill with yellow, tepid water.

He washed himself down, dried himself and lay on his bed for some time, hands behind his neck, staring at the ceiling. If this was a taste of Flanagan's Trans-America race, then so far so good. He lay back, his head cupped in his hands, and closed his eyes.

2

FLANAGAN MEETS THE PRESS

Three telephones rang at once. Charles C. Flanagan picked up the one nearest him and jammed it to his ear. "Ham on rye!" he shouted. "I said *two* ham on rye!" He slammed the phone back on its rest and flopped back into his armchair.

The bedroom was a wilderness of telephones, press clippings, ticker tapes, half-eaten sandwiches and cold cups of coffee. Flanagan stood in his flowery blue-silk dressing gown, his long, knobbly hands on his hips, his great thin toes poking out of open slippers. He was in his mid-forties, with lank hair, already prematurely gray, that constantly sprayed across his forehead; yet it was his teeth, great broad tombstones, white and shining, that dominated his face.

He picked up another phone on its first ring. "Willard!" he roared, turning toward the bathroom. "*Willard!* No, not you, ma'am," he cooed back into the telephone.

There was the flutter of a female voice in the earpiece. Flanagan's voice continued in low key. "Yes, ma'am. *Milwaukee Ladies Home Journal*? Yes, we have"—he thumbed through a hash of papers on the floor—"at the last count, one hundred and twenty-one ladies in the Trans-America race . . . *Chaperones*?" He put his hand over the phone and whirled around on Willard Clay, a small, plump, bespectacled man who had just emerged from the toilet in red-striped pajamas, and who was brushing his face with shaving soap.

"She's asking for chaperones for the girls," hissed Flanagan.

He removed his hand and again spoke into the phone, his great white teeth flashing.

"Of course, Miss . . . Miss McGregor." He grimaced at Willard, who was now unconcernedly scraping his chin with an open razor. "Three ladies from the San Francisco Ladies Seminary have kindly donated their services as chaperones. Yes, San Francisco Ladies Seminary."

He slowly spelled the title out, nodding the while and smiling into the telephone. "Yes, I can guarantee that strictly nondenominational services will be held every Sunday. Thank you kindly, ma'am."

He put down the phone and glared at his assistant. "Why didn't *you* think of chaperones?" he snapped.

Willard began to scrape soap from beneath his chin, rinsed the razor in his shaving mug and shook his head, soap dripping to the floor. "We didn't even know some of them *were* women till they started to arrive a couple of days back," said Willard plaintively. "Anyhow, they sure as hell won't last long."

Flanagan threw himself back onto an armchair swathed in ticker tape, a pile of which he immediately hurled on to the carpet. "How do you know? Could be there's some female Nurmi lurking out there among all those fat broads."

"Sure make a good story if there were," chuckled Willard, turning back into the bathroom to lay down his shaving bowl, at the same time announcing over his shoulder, "Miss America—she challenges the greatest footracers in the world."

Flanagan stroked his unshaven chin. "Willard, baby, you are one hundred per cent right." He lifted both hands to frame an imaginary headline. "Miss America in the Trans-America. We could dress her up in the Stars and Stripes, tour her across the whole country after the race." He sat back, pondering, his eyes distant.

Two phones rang. Flanagan pulled himself away from his reverie and picked up the one balanced precariously on the edge of his armchair. "Charles C. Flanagan," he said cautiously, then, on hearing who his caller was, exclaimed, "Paramount Pictures!" He sat bolt upright and beckoned the half-shaven Willard close to the telephone. He cupped his hand over the mouthpiece and listened for several minutes. "Paramount," he whispered. "They want us to move the start of the race into the Coliseum Stadium."

His voice dropped an octave as he resumed his conversation. "You must realize the difficulties, Mr. Schenck. We have two thousand runners here, the largest field in the history of professional sport. A quarter-mile running track is hardly an appropriate starting place for a race of such magnitude."

Some of Willard's shaving soap had smeared the mouthpiece of the telephone. Flanagan brushed it off and scowled at Willard.

"What *sort* of financial compensation?" he asked, his eyes lighting up. Willard, undeterred, again pressed close.

"Ten thousand dollars? Absolutely impossible. Fifteen? No, there is no way in which I could possibly compromise the start of the Trans-America . . ." his voice trailed off, and he again covered the mouthpiece as Willard pulled at his sleeve.

"Take it, boss," whispered Willard. "For Christ's sake, *take* it."

Flanagan returned to the phone, his face impassive. "Yes, I *know* we have an agreement, but *not*, sir, to start the race from the Coliseum. Twenty-five thousand? Make it thirty and I think we may have ourselves a deal." Willard could hear the raised tones of the voice at the other end of the line. Flanagan paused dramatically.

"Thirty thousand? Have it in writing in a contract here by noon at the Plaza Hotel and it's a deal. Yes, indeed, a pleasure and privilege to do business with you, Mr. Schenck."

He put down the phone and leaned back in his chair, his hands linked across his stomach.

"Willard," he said. "I truly think we're sitting on a pot of gold."

"But the Coliseum, boss? Two thousand men on a quarter-mile track?"

"No real problem," said Flanagan. "We can start some from outside the stadium, have them all run a couple of laps inside the Coliseum, then off they go into the boondocks toward Pomona. Look at it this way. It's *better* than starting out on the road. We can charge *admission*. And think of the catering concessions—hot dogs, Coke, popcorn . . . Why didn't I think of that before? And Willard, why didn't you?"

Willard shrugged and waddled off into the bathroom.

The phone rang again. "City police?" Flanagan's face dropped. He listened intently for a few moments, then said, "Let me get this quite clear, Commissioner Flaherty. Are you seriously telling me that my Chinese runners are urinating in your streets? Any particular streets? Oh, I see. *Any* street. Commissioner, I promise you that I *will* speak strongly to them. Confidentially, I think it may be some kind of religious observance, so I must be careful not to offend. While you are with me, I would consider it a great honor if you and your good wife would be with us at the opening ceremony. I might mention that Miss Mary Pickford and Mr. Douglas Fairbanks have made a particular request to meet you both. Delighted you can make it, sir."

He put down the phone. "Like hell they have," he said as Willard shambled through the ticker tape, patting after-shave on his smooth round face. "That mick had fifty of our boys in the can in the first week for infesting the public highways. Took me a hundred dollars to sweeten him."

Flanagan looked around him wearily, picked up a pile of ticker tape and held it out in front of him. "Willard, must we live in this squalor? Mother of Mary, we're paying fifty dollars a day." He grabbed the phone. "Room service? For God's sake send someone to clean up this place. Pronto!"

Another phone rang. This time Willard picked it up. He listened for a few moments, then put the phone down with a dazed expression.

"Boss," he said. "A Mr. Seidlitz said to tell you, the midgets are booked. A hundred midgets. What are we doing with a hundred midgets?"

Flanagan looked at his assistant with scorn. "Didn't I tell you? We finish the race indoors in Madison Square Garden on June 16. Before the runners arrive we have a little floor show. You know, some acrobats, a strong man. I've got a Turk who can lift an elephant. Not much of an elephant, but hell, an elephant's an elephant. The big finale, before the runners arrive, is midgets racing around the track on ponies. It's never been done before. First time in the history of sport."

Before the speech could develop further there was a knock on the door and a bellboy's head appeared.

"Mr. Flanagan, sir. Your press conference in the Coolidge Room—in an hour."

Flanagan waved over his shoulder. "I'll be ready. Willard," he said. "Let me have another look at the press list before you set it all up. In an hour we meet the gentlemen of the world's press."

Flanagan scanned the list Willard gave him and scowled. One hundred and eighty journalists from all over the world, many of whom had been at every Olympics since Athens, every World Series since the beginning of the century. From the moment in 1930 when he had first proposed the Trans-America the press had ranged through the whole gamut of opinion, from incredulity to derision. There would, of course, be those dear, innocent souls who took the Trans-America at face value, seeing it as a means of padding out expense accounts for three months or more; those he would take in his stride. But there would be others, case-hardened journalists who were not sports reporters at all, who would see the race as simply another junk sport of the thirties, in the same class as Bronx bullfighting or underwater baseball. Such men would require careful handling.

The press were essential to the Trans-America. They must be used, they must be amused, all the way from Los Angeles to New York. He crumpled the press list into a ball, aimed it at the wastepaper basket and flipped it across the room. It hit the outside of the basket and bounced off into a corner.

At two-thirty precisely Charles C. Flanagan adjusted his pearl tie pin, straightened the handkerchief in the jacket pocket of his immaculate gray double-breasted suit and looked at the journalists buzzing and scribbling below him. The Calvin Coolidge Room was a veritable League of Nations of the world of sports journalism. For the Trans-America had brought together reporters from all over the world, men who rarely met between Olympics. Now they jostled and hailed each other, scribbled and chattered, all waiting for the moment when the Trans-America would spring into life. The room itself had a sober, imposing quality: chairs topped with brown leather, the oak-lined walls hung with the oil portraits of past Presidents. On the wall behind the platform on which he stood hung a portrait of Calvin Coolidge himself, poring over a massive tome which, on closer inspection, revealed itself to be a telephone directory.

On Flanagan's left sat Willard and the pretty young blonde, Dixie Williams, poised with pencil and pad. On his right was a tanned bald man in a pin-striped suit.

Flanagan knew many of these journalists well, and they knew him. He placed both hands in a splayed tripod on the table in front of him, then stood back and stretched himself to his full height. Flashbulbs exploded and cameras whirred around him. "This way, Mr. Flanagan," shouted a group of photographers, and Flanagan turned to the right and flashed his white teeth in a frozen grin. In response to a request from the left he turned and, for variety, lifted his arms to the side, palms up—Flanagan the human cornucopia, the source of all good things.

"Gentlemen, gentlemen," he said, beckoning away the photographers and sitting down. "We must proceed with the business of the day." He banged a heavy wooden gavel on the table in front of him, but it was fully a minute before the babble was stilled. "Could I have the first question, please?"

"How far is the race?" shouted a journalist toward the front of the room.

"Three thousand, one hundred and forty-six miles, two hundred and twenty yards," replied Flanagan smoothly.

"You dead sure about those yards?" shouted a man whom Flanagan recognized as Frank Pollard of the *St. Louis Star*, a veteran of American sports journalism.

"Not dead certain, Frank. But we'll get our consultant surveyor to check it out, every yard of it if you have any doubts, first thing in the morning." Through the laughter Flanagan pointed to another questioner in the middle of the room.

"Charles Rae, *Washington Post*. What's the money for first prize?"

"One hundred and fifty thousand golden dollars, guaranteed by the Trans-America Bank," said Flanagan.

"And the other prizes?" asked Rae, staying on his feet.

"Fifty thousand dollars for second, going down to two hundred dollars for hundredth place. The total is three hundred and sixty thousand dollars. Fancy pickings."

There was an immediate babble of discussion as the prize money was translated into pounds, marks and francs by the foreign press.

Flanagan again hammered on the table for silence.

"Can we say that this is the richest footrace of all time?" pursued Rae.

"You sure as hell can," said Flanagan, grinning. "Indeed, I insist on it."

"What is the entry fee?" asked Pollard.

"Two hundred dollars per man."

Pollard poked his pencil at Flanagan. "Isn't that a little high in the present economic conditions?"

Flanagan put both hands flat on the table. "These are hard times, gentlemen. You must realize that we provide three square meals a day for nearly three months. Boys, you'll soon find out it's worth coming just for the food!"

He raised his hand to silence the hubbub.

"Seriously, gentlemen, I had to have some evidence of good faith on the part of each competitor, most of whom are sponsored by states or nations, and the two-hundred-dollar entry fee provided the best evidence of that. Next question, please."

He pointed into the forest of raised hands.

"How many miles will they cover each day?" shouted an unidentified voice from the back of the hall.

"An average of fifty, usually divided into two stages. The minimum is thirty, the maximum sixty-one. May I ask you to identify yourselves, gentlemen? Let's keep it formal."

"James Ferris, *The Times* of London. Has any man ever covered such distances daily?"

Flanagan had been expecting the question, and promptly stood up. "I think that there's a man sitting beside me who is better qualified than I am to answer that. Doc Cole, the father of American distance running, is with us on the platform. All of you who have followed track over the years will know Doc. He ran marathon for Uncle Sam in the Olympics of 1904 and 1908 and has run pro ever since. Could you deal with that question, Doc?"

"Doc" Cole slowly got to his feet. The arc lights reflected on his bald brown head. In his neat pin-striped suit he looked more like a clerk than an athlete. "Could you repeat the question?" he asked in a light midwestern voice.

"Has anyone ever covered fifty miles a day, Doc?"

"Not for long," said Doc. There was a ripple of laughter. "My pap told me of a fellow, a Yankee called Edmund Payson Weston, round about 1880. He could walk five miles an hour from here till Judgment Day. Couldn't walk any faster, mind. He walked about three thousand miles across America once, about forty miles a day, back about 1885. Then there were the old six-day walkers when I was a boy. The best of them walked about a hundred miles a day, indoors in armories back east for six days at a time."

"A hundred miles a day?" asked a reporter, scribbling furiously.

"Yep. They called the six-day races 'wobbles,' on account of most of the boys spent a lot of the time wobbling around the track."

"But it would be true to say that no one has ever *raced* fifty miles a day across America?" the journalist persisted.

"Not to my knowledge or recollection," replied Doc.

There was a babble of discussion and a rustling of paper as the journalists compared notes.

"Thank you, Doc," said Flanagan, taking advantage of the pause in the questioning. "May I say at this point that Doc, because of his unique knowledge of distance running, will hold his own press conference tomorrow. Next question, please."

"Forrest, *Chicago Tribune*." The man who had asked the earlier, unidentified question stood up at the back of the crowded room. "What medical provision will there be for the runners?"

"Ten fully qualified doctors headed by Dr. Maurice Falconer of Los Angeles City Hospital, plus twenty masseurs. You must also remember, gentlemen, that many competitors will have their own doctors and masseurs with them."

"What happens if someone drops out? How does he make it home?" pursued Forrest.

"The best way he can," said Flanagan. "Gentlemen, this is the land of opportunity. There are no handouts in the Trans-America. These athletes have come from sixty-one nations, from all over the world, to get here. Some are unemployed, some have sold their houses, some have left wives and sweethearts to compete in this race. These are *men*, gentlemen. They know it's a gamble, because no man in history has covered three thousand miles across these here United States of America. These men are athletes— they are also gamblers. They're gambling that their bodies can hold out for three months at fifty miles a day."

"But are *you* gambling, Flanagan?" asked a voice from the middle of the room.

"I'm gambling, yes—that there'll be at least someone still on his feet at the end!"

"Campbell, *Glasgow Herald*. We have considerable knowledge of professional running in my country and our experience is that it is usually corrupt. How do you prevent cheating?"

Flanagan pursed his lips. "A dozen officials will follow each stage of the race. Anyone caught hopping on trucks or cars will be immediately disqualified."

"Clare Marsh, *Woman's Home Journal*. How many women are in the race, Mr. Flanagan?"

"One hundred and twenty-one."

"Are there any separate prizes for women?"

"No," said Flanagan. "I reckon women are always trying to prove they're man's equal. Here's their chance to prove it."

"What is the longest distance a woman has ever covered, Mr. Flanagan?"

Flanagan looked down at his notes. "The longest Olympic distance is eight hundred meters. About half a mile."

"And weren't there protests after the Amsterdam Olympics about the dreadful finishing condition of the female competitors in the eight hundred meters?"

Flanagan looked nonplussed and whispered for a moment with Willard. Then he said, "It is our view that the ladies in the race will have prepared themselves thoroughly for the Trans-America. Only time will tell if their preparations have been thorough enough. Next question."

"Are the ladies being provided with chaperones?" asked Miss Marsh.

"Five ladies from a well-known seminary are acting as chaperones, led by Miss Dixie Williams." He nodded to his left to the girl whom Hugh McPhail had earlier met at the reception area.

"Who's chaperoning *her*, Flanagan?" asked a voice.

"I will treat that question with the contempt it deserves, Mr. Grose," said Flanagan with a smile, scanning the room for further questions.

"Howard, *Chicago Star*." The top baseball reporter of the Eastern Seaboard stood up at the front of the hall, sucking his pencil. "I have reviewed the route, Mr. Flanagan. There seems to me to be no rhyme or reason to much of it. Why have you failed to choose a direct route across the continent?"

"Two reasons, sir. One is that I wished competitors to see every aspect of our beautiful nation. The second is that several cities have expressed a particular desire to host the runners of the Trans-America."

"Isn't there another reason, Flanagan?" asked Howard. "Isn't it true that each major town on the route has to pay what you call an 'assessment'?"

Flanagan flushed. "If you mean that certain cities are paying sums to have the Trans-America pass through, then that's perfectly true. Their mayors believe that the Trans-America will be good for business, and I have given them the complete franchise on race programs. That *has* meant that the race is sometimes less than direct, but it puts more money into the pot for stage prizes."

"Tell us a little more about the stage prizes, Flanagan," said Howard.

Flanagan visibly relaxed. For the moment he was off the hook. "Stage prizes of between three hundred dollars and one thousand dollars have been offered at certain points along the route. For instance, Coca-Cola is offering a three-hundred-dollar stage prize in the Mojave and General Motors a prize of one thousand dollars for the King of the Mountains, in the Rockies. But remember, gentlemen, that the Trans-America winner will be the man—or woman—with the lowest aggregate time over the full distance, like your Tour de France bike race."

Carl Liebnitz, of the *New York Times*, rose to his feet. Liebnitz, lean, tanned and white-haired, had earned his reputation as the seeker out of all that was false or phony. He was not, strictly speaking, a sports reporter, enjoying the rare freedom to comment on what he pleased in his weekly column of national and international gossip. "Is it true that you are also featuring a circus, involving"—he picked up a press release—"Madame La Zonga, the Samoan snake woman, Fritz the talking donkey, and the mummified head of the Mexican bandit, Emiliano Zapata?"

"Correct," said Flanagan. "And you might also note the Jungle Dodgers, the first baseball-playing chimpanzees."

Liebnitz could not completely mask a grimace. "May I respectfully ask you what in the name of tarnation a troupe of freaks has got to do with a serious footrace?"

"What we are taking from here to New York is entertainment," said Flanagan. "Everywhere we go, every minute of the way, I aim to put on a show. When the runners are tired, then it's up to Madame La Zonga to do her stuff. This isn't college track and field, gentlemen; this is the world of entertainment."

Liebnitz resumed his seat, shaking his head.

Albert Kowalski, of the *Philadelphia Globe*, burly and crew-cut, stood up. "Sir, in a year Los Angeles will host the 1932 Olympic Games, which is an amateur meet. Won't your professional Trans-America race therefore deprive the United States of possible Olympic gold medals?"

Flanagan placed the knuckles of both hands on the table and the cameras exploded. "A good question," he said evenly, flashing his great teeth. "First, it's a free world. Olympic medals pay no rent, and if an American boy chooses to take a chance on setting himself up for life by running in the Trans-America rather than going for an Olympic gold medal, then surely that is up to him. Second, when did America last win gold in a marathon Olympic event?"

There was no answer.

"I'll tell you: 1908 when Johnny Hayes beat Dorando in the London Olympics. That's one helluva long time to wait, gentlemen. Let's face it. Here in the USA we're sprinters and jumpers and throwers, not marathon runners. I don't see a three-thousand-mile race losing us any goddam sprinters or shot putters. Do you?"

There was silence; Flanagan had made his point.

Liebnitz was on his feet again. "Carl Liebnitz. I see you have a nineteen-year-old Mexican, Juan Martinez, entered. We have no athletic record for Mr. Martinez. Have you any background on him?"

Flanagan leaned to his right to whisper to Willard.

"I'm afraid I can't help you there, Carl. We know that he is the only Mexican entered and that he has been sponsored by his village, Quanto."

"Pollard here. I can help you there, Flanagan, though"—he turned to face the reporters behind him—"I ain't certain I should be helping my learned colleagues. Quanto is right in the middle of a famine area. I've talked with young Martinez. My information is that he is running in the Trans-America to save his village from starvation."

Flanagan glanced quickly around the room. "There's your story, gentlemen," he smiled.

"Kowalski again. What are the living facilities for the athletes like?"

"For the next couple of days they're living high on the hog in hotels. En route they live in twenty specially constructed tents, a hundred bunks to a tent."

"And press facilities?" queried Kowalski.

"Six thirty-seater press buses are being provided, courtesy of Ford Motors. I know that you fellas are making your own accommodation arrangements at each town." He sensed that questions were slowing up, and a few reporters were drifting toward the back of the packed hall as deadlines approached.

"Rae. What provision is being made for food for the competitors?"

Flanagan riffled through a file of papers and selected one. "The culinary arrangements are in the hands of international chefs specially brought over from Europe," he said. "Dr. Maurice Falconer, our medical director, one of America's leading nutritionists, is also acting as our nutritional adviser."

"What about drinks?" asked Liebnitz.

"No question that adequate supplies of fluids will be essential, particularly in the desert areas," said Flanagan. "Maxwell House is supplying all the hot drinks and will follow us all the way to New York in a specially constructed refreshment trailer, the Maxwell House Coffee Pot. Cold drinks will be supplied by Sport Ade, the sensational new sports drink."

"Do you have any knowledge of the Williams' All-Americans?"

Flanagan held up a sheet of paper and read from it. "The All-Americans are one of fifteen teams, most of which are company or state teams. For instance, Oklahoma and Arizona both have strong teams entered."

"What's the *point* of teams, Mr. Flanagan? You've got no team competition," Ferris, *The Times* reporter, asked belligerently.

"That is correct," replied Flanagan. "The object of the teams is to gain prestige for the organizations which sponsor them. Each man earns a wage, with bonuses if they finish in leading positions."

"What do you know about the German team?" It was Liebnitz again.

One further time Flanagan filed through his pile of notes.

"The team is a young one," he said finally. "From a group which calls itself the Hitler Youth Movement. It's a five-man team of boys aged nineteen to twenty-one, headed by a team manager, Herr von Moltke, and a team doctor, Eric Nett."

"Have they any track record?" asked Ferris.

"Only the one-hundred-kilometer trial—that's about sixty-two miles—they held to choose the team."

"Can this be called a German national team, Flanagan?"

"Strictly speaking, no. Herr Hitler is an aspiring politician. His Youth Movement is part of his political push."

"Rae again. How many Olympic medalists do you have entered?"

Flanagan made a show of shuffling his papers.

"At the last count, twenty."

"Fair enough, but how many can you guarantee will start?" asked Howard from the back of the room.

"As many as are willing to take a chance," said Flanagan, leaning forward.

For a moment his mask of geniality dropped. "Let's face it. This amateur setup is a can of worms. The reason why some of these so-called amateurs are afraid to run in the Trans-America is because they can pick up two or three thousand bucks a year, steady money, no tax, year in, year out, as amateurs. They get that not for winning but just, for God's sake, for *appearing*! With me, they'll have to run hard for every buck they earn. No play, no pay."

"Munaur, *Paris Match*. Is there any truth in the rumor that Paavo Nurmi, the Flying Finn, will run in the Trans-America?"

Flanagan pursed his lips. "Fellas, all I can say is that Mr. Nurmi is at present in San Francisco with his manager, Mr. Quist, considering the possibility of entering. He has just finished an exhausting American tour and is also embarking upon his preparation for the 1932 Olympics. All that can be said for the moment is that he's giving the matter considerable thought."

"Are you saying, Flanagan, that as an amateur Nurmi might not be able to *afford* to enter the Trans-America?" shouted a reporter.

Flanagan grinned. "No comment."

"Kevin Maguire, *Irish Times*." A thick-set, tweed-suited man stood up. The strong Irish brogue made many of the departing journalists turn around to listen. "Mr. Flanagan, is it true that Lord Peter Thurleigh, the British Olympic athlete, has entered the Trans-America?"

There was a hush in the room. Flanagan took his time, teasing out every moment.

"Yesterday," he said, "it was my pleasure to meet for the first time Lord Peter Thurleigh, British Olympian in 1924 and 1928. Lord Peter has been given special dispensation to stay with the British Consul, rather than being exposed to the publicity which he would have to endure at our final training camp."

Liebnitz stood up. "Flanagan, can you give us any good reason why an English aristocrat should lose his amateur status and spend three months plodding across America with a couple of thousand tramps and a freak show?"

Flanagan paused. "It is my understanding," he said, putting

on what he imagined to be an English accent, "that Lord Peter has wagered a hundred thousand pounds with a group of English aristocrats that he will finish in the first six places."

"A hundred thousand pounds? What's that in U.S. dollars?" asked Kowalski.

"At yesterday's rate of exchange, I reckon about four hundred thousand dollars," answered Flanagan. "The biggest wager in the history of footracing."

The reporters at last had their lead story. There was a general rush for the lobby telephones, leaving a trail of upturned chairs in their wake. The conference was at an end.

Flanagan bit off the end of his cigar and spat it toward the wastebasket. This time it landed in the basket, plumb center. He leaned forward, surveyed the chaos of upturned chairs and discarded papers, and beamed. The first hurdle had been cleared and cleared in some style.

Carl Liebnitz sat on his bed, propped against his pillows. He wore red-silk polka-dot pajamas and sat, legs crossed, his Trans-America report on a clipboard on his knees. He was sucking the tip of his pencil.

Liebnitz had been with Clarence Darrow at the Scopes "monkey" trial, with Lindbergh in Paris, and in Washington when Douglas MacArthur had scattered the Hooverville rioters. His assignment from his editor was to treat the Trans-America for the carnival that it was, and that meant three hundred words, crisp and sharp, twice weekly. Flanagan he couldn't yet place. That the Irishman was a flimflam man he had little doubt; what the chances were of his getting his ragged crew across America Liebnitz did not know, but the odds were against it. And that was exactly what he was going to tell the American public. He adjusted his pillow, bent his knees, and slowly started to write.

AMERICANA DATELINE MARCH 19, 1931 LOS ANGELES

Your columnist has known of Charles C. Flanagan for some time, but his qualifications for running an enterprise of the complexity of the Trans-America footrace are unknown to him. Flanagan is a forty-five-year-old Irish-American whose father, for thirty years, pounded the beat on New York's East Side. Mr. Flanagan first came to our attention in 1919, at the time of the Black Sox scandal, when he tried, as he put it at the time, "to bring some dignity back to baseball" by starting a women's baseball team, the Tallahassee Tigerbelles. Alas, many of the Tigerbelles showed more talent for maternity than for the baseball diamond and the team folded in 1921, with Mr. Flanagan saddled with at least two paternity suits.

Mr. Flanagan surfaced again in New Orleans in 1923, with a team of midget mud-wrestlers, which he eventually sold to a circus. For a time he managed a boxer rejoicing in the name of the "Young John L. Sullivan," but not, alas, also rejoicing in Sullivan's talents. The "Young John L." went down to the first firm blow which he received from a Milwaukee bank clerk and was last heard of in the chorus of a male burlesque show called "Swain Lake."

Mr. Flanagan's fortunes took a turn for the better in 1927 when he briefly managed the delightful tennis player, Miss Suzanne Lamarr, but plummeted again when he attempted to import the European game of soccer to the American continent. Soccer, indeed! Undaunted by the disasters of the past, Charles C. Flanagan has now bobbed up again, with his Trans-America footrace, in which two thousand runners will attempt to cover on foot the distance between Los Angeles and New York for prize money of $360,000.

He has certainly gathered about him a motley crew. His band of two thousand athletes does, it is true, contain some of the finest long-distance runners in the world. It also contains one hundred twenty-one women, a Hindu fakir, sixteen blind men, three men without arms, twenty grandfathers, sixty-one vegetarians, and a spiritualist who claims to be advised by the long-dead Indian runner, Deerfoot. And this is to say nothing of Madame La Zonga, Fritz the talking mule and a baseball team composed, we are told, entirely of chimpanzees, all of whom are to accompany the runners on their trek to New York.

It would therefore be true to say that nothing of its like has been seen since Peter the Hermit and his Children's Crusade. Let us hope that Mr. Flanagan proves to be better qualified than his illustrious predecessor.

—CARL C. LIEBNITZ—

3

THE BROO PARK

Hugh McPhail had first heard about the Trans-America at half-time in a sixpence-a-man soccer match on Glasgow Green, a rough stretch of land known locally as the "Broo Park." "Broo" was a colloquialism for the unemployment bureau which all the twenty-two players dutifully attended each Thursday. There they collected the few shillings which the government supplied to sustain them and their families for another week.

There were few recreations available for the unemployed in the bleak winter Glasgow of 1930. The public library, the park bench, the street corner, the betting shop, the pub: there was little else to do.

The library was one of the few warm places in the city, and in its antiseptic silence lived the unemployed from 9 A.M. when the doors opened till 7 P.M. when the library was cleared. There were three activities. The first was the study of racing forms in the pages of the sporting press. On such earnest studies rested the long-odds "doubles" and "trebles" designed to bring the unemployed if not to riches then to slightly better rags. Alas, the library did not house the specialized racing papers beloved of gamblers, such as the *Sporting Life*. Hugh's father, down to his last sixpence, had once sent his son to the news dealer in search of the newspaper. Finding none available, the boy had purchased a copy of the comic paper, *Comic Cuts*, which featured his favorites, Wearie Willie and Tired Tim. His father, enraged, had given him a sound thrashing. However, later that evening Hugh had been treated to a massive bag of candy; his father's Aintree double of "Wearie Willie" and "Tired Tim" had come in at one hundred to one.

The second activity at the library was sleep. All day long men who had exhausted the possibilities of the daily press and the *Encyclopaedia Britannica* sat with their heads resting on the backs of their hands on the glass tables in front of them. This was a dangerous practice, for it gave the assistants an excuse to move them out. Better by far, therefore, to pretend to pore over a vast medical dictionary, snatching a few moments of furtive sleep behind it when one could.

The final activity was study—random study of anything and everything the reference library had to offer—and many men became experts on subjects as diverse as astrology and bee-keeping from those long empty hours in the silent libraries of Glasgow.

The park bench provided no such solace. The west of Scotland, warmed by the sea, is rarely bitterly cold, but its winter wetness chills the bones. Similarly, there was comradeship but little solace for those small groups who would stand hunched at street corners all over the grimy city, moving their weight from foot to foot.

The betting shop, like the pub, offered warmth, companionship and hope: when you are at the bottom of the heap the only way is up. That at least was the theory, as men placed their sixpences and shillings on drugged greyhounds at massive odds, or on long-odds horses from lush stables somewhere in southern England. The regularity of their losses did not deter them, for there was always the hope of the "big one" that would change their luck.

Glasgow was a wasteland. Its main industry, shipbuilding, had virtually closed down, and with it the small industries which supported it. The cranes lay still, like frozen prehistoric animals waiting for a breath of life. The great steel mills at Dixons Blazes were silent.

Hugh McPhail was simply one of thousands, a legion of the lost containing some of the world's most skilled craftsmen, men denied the opportunity to express their unique and subtle skills.

At first it was believed that the layoffs would be short, but as time wore on men began to rot. Deprived of work, the spine of their life had vanished, and with it the core of their belief in themselves. These men *were* what they worked at. Nothing in their recreation or their family life could ever make up for that loss.

Hugh had started as a shipyard riveter, ten hours a day on a narrow scaffold, his arms shuddering as he drilled five thousand holes a day; even at weekends his hands still shook. Laid off in 1927, he had spent two hard years in the mines at Shotts, south of Glasgow.

There even his fitness had not saved him. Each day, after stumbling through the early morning mists, he and the others had crawled two miles underground to the coal face. For most of the time he had been in agony, for his thighs, unused to the cramped movements imposed by the narrow tunnels, were in constant spasm. Even his best friend, Stevie McFarlane, who had hardly taken exercise in his life, had found it easier. The other miners were sympathetic, waiting for Hugh and massaging his legs until he was ready to continue.

Then there was the work itself, ten hours in semidarkness, hacking at the coal face. Much of the time the men worked naked, the sweat streaming in white rivulets down their black bodies. It was no wonder that miners were lean-waisted; all day long they pumped into the face with bellies of steel. Food was taken on the job—sandwiches and cold tea, with the men crouching together in crevices, mice scuttling between their legs. Then the return, two agonizing miles bent double, back to the elevator.

Hugh dreaded each morning. The only saving grace was the miners themselves. They had been born to it, to accept scarred backs, skins veined like Stilton cheese, crippling injury and death. However, they accepted him, knowing that it was barely possible that he could condition himself to the work, and respecting his painful attempts to do so. To begin with his work rate was dismal, but eventually he came to accept the pain. It took him longer to adapt to the walks.

It was not only Hugh who was cheered by the presence of wee Stevie. The miners had taken to the little man instantly. Even in the worst times his quick and ready wit had lifted their spirits. A product of the worst slums of Glasgow, he had somehow managed to rise above the stinking squalor of the "single end" which had been his home and the rickets which had put his legs in irons until his early teens. Working at the coal face was particularly hard for him, for he was not built for such toil. But Stevie McFarlane was invincible. He had already seen the worst, and it had not been that bad.

Then, after two years at the mine, came "the visit." In the winter of 1928 the Shotts mine was visited by Lord Featherstone, M.P., and a member of the British Olympic team soon to travel to Amsterdam. McPhail was immediately sought out by the mine's manager, Fallon.

"We hear you've done a bit of running in your time," opened Fallon.

"A bit," Hugh replied guardedly.

"Then you've heard tell of Lord Featherstone?"

"The Olympic athlete?"

"The pit's due for a visit to open the new pithead baths. The usual thing—Lord Featherstone, a fella from the Scottish Amateur Athletic Association and a clanjamfray of local bigwigs. The Tories have heard you've run at the big professional races at Powderhall and they think it might make a nice touch if you and Lord Featherstone had a wee race. What d'you think?"

For a moment Hugh looked straight ahead. Then he said:

"Featherstone's a quarter-miler. My top distance is what we run at the Powderhall handicap. One hundred and thirty yards."

"Oh?"

"I'll race him, all right, but over a hundred yards."

Fallon nodded, and went off to convey Hugh's views to his masters. Two days later news came through that the race was on.

It soon became the talk of Shotts, but even Lord Featherstone had to secure clearance from the SAAA to run against McPhail, for three years a "pro." The race was therefore required to be billed as an "exhibition," to avoid breaching amateur rules.

That night, Lang, the shop steward, broached Hugh in the Miner's Arms, nodding to the barman to set up two pints.

Lang was direct. "What are your chances?"

Hugh shrugged. "Six weeks to go. I reckon the mining has taken about six yards out of my legs. That puts me back around ten point six. Featherstone runs about ten point one. So I've got just six weeks to find six yards."

"Jesus Christ! Some of the boys are laying their wages on you already. They're getting terrific odds."

"I'm not surprised. The bookies've got it right as usual. As things stand, I haven't got a snowball in hell's chance. Man, Featherstone eats steaks seven days a week! He's got his own track in his father's grounds, his personal professional trainer. His running shoes are handmade by some guy in Bond Street. Me, I spend all week doubled up two miles underground, drinking cold tea and eating bread and butter. Who the hell's the amateur?"

Lang put both hands on Hugh's shoulders. "There's a bit more to it than that, son," he said. "There's an election coming up soon. Featherstone only has a couple of thousand votes in hand. McNair, the Labour agent, says that a win in the sprint could come in very handy. Man, the national press is coming up to cover it."

Hugh exploded. "What is this, a bloody three-ring circus? I agreed to run this little race; okay. But I didn't think it was going to be built up into the bloody Olympics."

"Calm down, lad," said Lang. He puckered his lips in thought, then sipped his beer. "You said six yards. Jesus, we know here what professional runners have to do if anybody does. You said steaks. Then you'll get steaks, the best. We don't have a trainer, but Dad McPherson's got the best hands in the business. We don't have a track, but there's the hundred and fifty yards of cinders down by the railroad track. We'll get it rolled as flat and hard as Powderhall. What d'ye say?"

"It's no good," said Hugh. "Four miles walking underground and ten hours a day at the face is no way to prepare for a sprint match."

"We'll get you work above ground," said Lang. "The lads'll club together to make up your wages."

"Then you're on," said Hugh, nodding.

The next night, after work, Hugh and Stevie met at the pub for a council of war.

"Six yards," said the wee man, gulping down his McEwans, the foam staying on his lips.

"Six weeks," said Hugh.

They took physical inventory.

"How's your weight?"

"About a hundred and fifty-five pounds."

"Too light."

"Lost a hell of a lot of muscle underground," Hugh explained.

"Your legs?"

Hugh grimaced. "The mines again—all that walking doubled up. I'll pull a muscle just thinking about sprinting."

Stevie made some notes. "The steaks'll take care of your weight. As for your legs, Dad McPherson can get to work on them, and you'll have to stretch daily. Now that you're to be moved above ground the muscles should start to lengthen anyway."

"So who made you the expert?"

"I can read," answered Stevie, holding up a thick red book. "It's all in *The Complete Athletic Trainer* by Sam Mussabini. He coaches some university guy named Abrahams. I've read it from cover to cover. And now it's all in here." He tapped his head.

"Well, just make sure it all comes out," said Hugh sourly.

But Stevie was as good as his word and conducted every detail of Hugh's preparation. And every day old McPherson massaged Hugh's legs.

"Tight," he said, on the first day. "Don't run hard on these yet."

McPherson had been blinded in a pit accident, but the old man had supple hands smoothed by years of massage, most of it on racing whippets.

"Stiff," he said, when he came to knead Hugh's calves. "But it's all there—just wants bringing out."

Others did their part with equal dedication. As he had promised, Lang smoothed and flattened one hundred and fifty yards of cinder track by the side of the railroad, the area earmarked for the "exhibition." It had taken ten miners most of two days to take the wrinkles and bumps out of the surface, but in the end it was sharp and fast. "A Powderhall indeed," Hugh said admiringly when he saw it.

For a few weeks this bleak anonymous strip of track in the middle of a grimy coal mine in central Scotland would be the focus of his life. Six weeks from now it would be transformed into an arena in which he would face a man from another class—indeed, another world. Hugh felt the hair on the back of his neck rise, and he shivered. He had only run once with real money on his back, at the New Year handicap at Powderhall, and he knew the agonies of self-doubt which grew day by day as fitness becomes increasingly sharp and the mind trembles on a fine edge. He looked again down the dead, silent strip of cinder, and thought of the life which his feet would bring to it, and in turn drain from its surface.

Training—or "prep," as the specialized preparation was called, in the time-honored traditions of Scottish professional running—went well. Prep was the method of pedestrians who ever since the great clashes of professional sprinters in the nineteenth century had honed their bodies to a knife edge for two-man "matches," or for those twelve burning seconds which formed the annual New Year's Day Powderhall sprint in Edinburgh.

The method itself was a ritual whose secrets were as closely guarded as those of any ancient priesthood. After a big breakfast Hugh would be massaged lightly by Dad McPherson, then off to the track for six scores—twenty-yard sprints with great attention to relaxed running technique. Next would follow an hour's sleep, in turn followed at one o'clock by a steak dinner; there was no such meal as lunch to the miners at Shotts.

After another hour's sleep it was back to the track for six runs over one hundred and twenty yards, at half speed, every run watched by the meticulous Stevie, who would again stress relaxation and running form. Then, in a disused hut beside the track, where Stevie had created a primitive gymnasium, Hugh practiced for half an hour on the punchball, the sweat drenching his thick jersey as he rhythmically pummeled the springy leather ball. The next half hour was spent on hundreds of repetitions of abdominal exercises, performed until his stomach went into spasms.

"Mussabini says the secret of sprinting is in the abdominals," Stevie would comment earnestly, tapping the spine of *The Complete Athletic Trainer*, as Hugh lay writhing on the floor of the hut. Sometimes Hugh wished Mussabini had kept his secret to himself.

The day's ritual ended with a walk back through gathering gloom to McPherson's cottage for a final massage and high tea. Hugh would then put in a light shift on the mine's surface before retiring to bed at nine-thirty.

There was no doubt that the training was working. Every day Hugh's recovery from runs became quicker, and gradually the running began to flow into him and from him. Under Dad's skillful, searching fingers his muscles became soft and supple, the hardness of the months at the pit face teased gently from them.

More important, Hugh again began to feel like an athlete. With the hardening and stretching of the muscles he could feel that his mind became daily quicker and sharper, like some delicate, hunted animal learning to tread its way in a world of danger.

Nor was there a day when a miner did not approach him to ask how he was feeling. "How's it going, then?" they would ask. "The training. Getting enough steaks, are you?"

There was no envy in their questions. Hugh was their man, on whom they had placed their hopes, and it was right and just that he should be given special treatment. The miners' experience with whippets and pigeons had taught them that you did not treat diamonds like quartz. They knew that a professional sprinter, a "ped," had to be treated with care, like the greyhound he undoubtedly was.

However, each question, each query about his health and well-being increased the weight of responsibility Hugh felt resting upon him. What had begun as a "wee race" was, whatever Lord Featherstone felt, going to be a race to the death for Hugh. Men had staked their wages, some their entire savings on him, for the initial odds offered by the bookmakers had been generous. Featherstone was after all an Olympian, having run 47.8 seconds for four hundred meters, one of the fastest times in the world. Hugh realized that it was not only the money, though God knew that was reason enough for concern. It was "Them" against "Us," Tory against Labour, workers against management.

Final training went well. With two weeks to go Hugh clocked 10.3 seconds in a trial run, two yards off target time. For all that, Stevie could feel his man becoming more and more tense in the week before the race.

"Let's go to the pictures," he said one afternoon, over tea.

The Roxy in Shotts was a fleapit, but a warm and pleasant place. The Charlie Chaplin film *The Gold Rush* was ideally suited to the occasion, and Stevie knew he had made the right decision.

Then came Pathé News. A couple of items, then "Oxford versus Cambridge, Queen's Club, London" read the titles. The annual athletics match. There on the screen was Featherstone, clad in slacks and white sweater with a woolen scarf wrapped carelessly around his neck.

"Lord Featherstone, a triple winner," said the titles. "Four hundred forty yards—forty-eight point two seconds. Two hundred twenty yards—twenty-one point nine seconds."

"Wait for it," said Hugh, gripping his seat.

"One hundred yards—nine point nine seconds."

"Jesus Christ!" Hugh exclaimed.

They could both feel the change in the atmosphere as the lights went on. All around the movie house miners were arguing.

"I think they know the score now," said Hugh quietly, as they made their way to the exit.

"It was probably wind-assisted," growled Stevie on the way home. "Amateur timekeepers."

It did not take the people of Shotts long to hear that their man would have to find four extra yards by race day. The atmosphere at the mine on Monday was sepulchral.

"What do you think?" asked Lang that evening at Dad Mc-Pherson's.

Hugh shook his head.

"I'll not run nine point nine if you took a red-hot poker to my arse," he said, then added, "still, we've got two weeks, and that railroad track isn't Queen's Club."

Lang's eyebrows lifted. "How d'you mean?"

"I mean nine point nine at Queen's Club might only be worth ten point one here. I'm running ten point three now, with two weeks to go. I've got to find two-tenths. Anyhow, for Featherstone, it's just an 'exhibition.' For me it's shit or bust."

In his final trial, two days before the race, he ran ten point two. Everyone at the mine knew, for there were at least ten watches on him when the trial was run. Still two yards to find, perhaps three.

"I'd like you to see someone," said Stevie as they talked together at Dad McPherson's one night after training. "It might help."

"Help!" exclaimed Hugh. "I've had help enough. Steaks, massage, my own track, handmade spikes from London. I'll tell you the help I need. I need a bloody miracle."

"Calm down," said his friend sharply, as there was a knock at the door. "Here," he added. "I'd like you to meet Jock Wallace."

He ushered into the living room a big, heavy gray-haired man in his mid-fifties, cap in hand. The man looked uneasy and immediately sensed Hugh's antagonism as he lay on the bed on his stomach with Dad's smooth fingers kneading his calves.

"Sorry to trouble you . . . at this time," he said apologetically, as Hugh looked up.

Gathering himself he blurted: "Just some advice. You forget

about Featherstone. You're not running against him. You run against yourself when you've got big money on your back. Run in four feet of space. That's all. Just run in four feet of space."

He picked up his cap, nodded at Stevie, and was led out of the room by McPherson.

Hugh scowled and looked at Stevie.

"What did he mean, four feet of space?"

"He meant run *your* race. If it's good enough you'll win, if not you lose. So just drill through your four feet of space. That's what sprinting's all about. You run in blinkers."

"What does *he* know about it?"

"You know who that was? That's Wallace of Perth. He won the Powderhall sprint in 1888. That old man ran with five thousand pounds on his back. He's been there. He's been through it. He *knows*."

Wallace of Perth. Hugh had heard of him. Twelve point seven seconds off two yards handicap on crushed snow. Wallace had been a legend in his time, a Scot who had taken on and beaten some of the best professional sprinters in the world. And now there he was, a big, soft old man telling Hugh to run in four feet of space. As Hugh pondered he realized the old man was right. You ran a hundred yards in separate tunnels, the winner being the man first out of his tunnel at the end. That tunnel was four feet wide and that was the space he had to penetrate oblivious of Featherstone.

He couldn't sleep the night before the race. In his dreams he ran and reran the race, each time wallowing with leaden legs up endless tracks. Each time he woke up sweating.

Management tried to play down the exhibition, treating it as just a minor part of a day of handshakes, junketing and grand speeches. But there was no doubt about how the miners saw it. All morning long the pit seethed with anticipation.

Hugh could eat virtually nothing and had only tea and toast. Stevie, as was the custom, had given him a good dose of laxatives the night before, and Hugh spent most of the morning in the toilet. By noon he felt he could not run one yard, let alone a hundred.

"Relax," said Stevie, as Hugh lay in the cottage on the massage table. "For God's sake." But Hugh could feel the tension in Stevie's voice and knew that the little man had invested as much as anyone in him, not merely in money but in the meticulous and purposeful training program he had devised. For the past six weeks the bandy-legged little man had lived his sporting life through Hugh. They both knew how fragile a sprint performance was. The slightest overtraining and a muscle could go like a violin string. Undertrain, and one came to the start sluggish and heavy. In the race itself the slightest mistake was lethal: over a hundred yards there was no time to recover from error.

That afternoon, an hour before the race, even Dad McPherson sweated as he lightly caressed the muscles of Hugh's hamstrings. The old man had put his life savings on Hugh—fifty pounds, ten shillings and sixpence, at ten to one. For him the race meant the difference between five more cramped years at the pit and a life of ease with his beloved pigeons and whippets. McPherson knew how greyhounds sprang from the traps to seek their whirling prey. He prayed that his fingers could breathe something of that quality into Hugh McPhail.

Half an hour later, a black-silk dressing gown, which had been purchased by the miners, draped around his shoulders, Hugh walked down through the packed pit toward the competition area, flanked by Stevie, engulfed by the crowd who lined every yard of the cinder route. Hugh felt weak in the stomach. This was not what he had expected; no fragile sprint was meant to bear such pressure, and certainly no man. He felt like a pit prop, bending and groaning under the black earth above. These miners were burying him beneath their hopes.

He warmed up, feeling tired and breathless. Everything poured into ten brief seconds. His mouth dried as he thought of it.

Featherstone was a tall blond man, his lightly tanned skin a product of Cannes in summer, Chamonix in winter. He had a soft handshake.

"Pleased to meet you, McPhail," he said.

Despite his manner Featherstone was under no illusions about what was at stake. Row upon row of grimy-collared men in flat caps and pit boots, straining at the ropes which enclosed the track, made it only too clear. He checked his lane. Those fellows had certainly done a good job: it was quite the equal of Queen's Club. He looked across at Hugh. The man had the look of a sprinter. Thick, powerful thighs, light calves, strong shoulders. Well, they would soon see.

They stripped down. Featherstone wore long silk Oxford shorts, rimmed in dark blue, as was his half-sleeved shirt. A whisper ran through the crowd. The man had a superb physique, yet as unlike McPhail's as could be imagined. It was completely balanced, with no obvious rippling muscularity. Featherstone looked like an animal born to run.

Hugh did not even glance at him, focusing rather on his strip of track. Four feet of space, old Wallace had said . . . Gradually the area outside of his lane was narrowing, and with it the babble of the crowd faded.

"Take to your marks!" The starter stood only ten yards behind them, but his voice seemed to come from a long way off.

Hugh looked up the track again. His lane was like a beam of light, with nothing but darkness on either side. He screwed his feet into his holes, feeling the light pressure of his right knee upon the cinders as he lowered it to the ground. All was still.

"Get set!"

He lifted his hips, feeling the pressure on his fingertips.

The gun was a release. He surged out like water bursting through a hole in a dam, piercing the space, his legs eating the ground beneath him. Then, suddenly, it was slow, but not sluggish, for this was the slowness of ease, the slowness induced by a feeling that there was ample time for every movement, time enough for the high pickup of the thigh, time enough for the strong drive-back of the elbows. Hugh knew that his running was pouring out of him, gushing along that narrow four-foot strip which had been made for his movements and his alone. He ran in a sweet dream, only dimly aware of the noise which raged on each side of his lane. He wanted it to last for ever. Then it was over.

Hugh's legs burnt the final yards of the track. He had no need for the "dip" finish with which his chest snapped the tape.

Featherstone proffered his hand, this time with a firm shake.

"Congratulations," he said. "You ran as if you were on your own."

"I was," replied Hugh.

When the official announcement came it was almost drowned in the shouts of the crowd. "First, McPhail, Shotts. Ten seconds even." Many of the miners started to dance up and down, gripping each other by the shoulders. Children ran onto the track to touch him. Stevie and McPherson stood by the finish, tears streaming down their faces. On the special dais constructed for management and guests there was silence.

Although a reporter from every national newspaper was there the "exhibition" was reported in none of them. It was as if a race watched by six thousand people had never happened. A week later Hugh and Stevie were fired. No reason was given, none required. It was not simply that Hugh had beaten Featherstone. His mistake had been in taking it too seriously—in having the miners formally invest in him in a way which Featherstone's class had done since birth as a matter of course. Worst of all they had won for Lang, the union man, and for the people. For Featherstone the race had merely been a ripple in what was to be a successful campaign, and he was not told of Hugh's leaving.

But Lang did not let them down. Through contacts in Glasgow the union man had arranged work for Hugh and Stevie as dishwashers in a central hotel. Ten hours a day with hands in hot greasy water was a far cry from the pampered life of a professional athlete, but Hugh was content. Those ten seconds of the Shotts sprint had taught him much about himself. He had been tried and had not been found wanting. The work in the hotel was, however, only a short step from the unemployment of 1930, and for Hugh and Stevie it was soon back to the pleasures of the library, the street corner and the Broo Park.

McPhail had tried them all, these pleasures of the poor, and, being physically active, had found the "tanner-a-man" matches on Glasgow Green most to his liking. The rules were simple enough: if you won, your opponent gave you sixpence; if you lost, you gave him the same sum.

The name Glasgow Green was misleading, for there was little green about its soccer fields. The area around the Green had once, long past, been elegant enough, with pillared Georgian houses, homes of the eighteenth-century tobacco barons, but had long since gone to seed as successive generations of the working class had pressed in and on, and the rich had moved south or west to avoid both the smoke and the workers who created it. The remaining "green" lay in the well-cut lawns provided by thoughtful Victorian councillors, but the soccer fields themselves were made of rough, black industrial cinders. Now, in winter, corrugated, gripped by frost, they could rip a man's flesh to shreds.

The "tanner-a-man" matches were desperate affairs, for few of the men could afford to lose even sixpence. It was one-all at halftime and McPhail and his team were squatting at the side of the field when wee Stevie let slip that he had read in a newspaper about the Trans-America race. "Ninety thousand pounds," said Stevie. "But the bastards'll earn it. Three thousand miles across America. Poor sods." Stevie had read the news in a paper in which he had bought his staple diet of fish and chips, so for all McPhail knew the race had already been run. But he made a mental note before returning his attention to the game.

One of the players, McGowan, had in his early years been a professional with Partick Thistle. He had been a beautiful player, a nimble dribbler who could lay off streams of goal-scoring passes, but a leg injury had stopped short his career. Now in his midforties, tubercular, he hardly appeared to run a step but dominated the middle of the field, rarely having to make a tackle, always reading each situation early, making interceptions and still pushing out accurate passes. The game was tied at two-all when McGowan fell to the ground coughing. He put his hand to his mouth and dark blood seeped through his fingers. McPhail went to him.

"Off you go, old man," he said. "I'll pay if we lose."

The old player was helped, protesting, from the field, still spluttering blood. Ten minutes later McPhail laid on a pass for another team member to score in the top right-hand corner. "You've earned a pint," said McGowan, as McPhail trudged from the field.

The game had been over for two hours. Hugh, after a brief excursion to the public library, had settled in a corner of the pub to drink his pint with McGowan and look at the page of the newspaper which he had ripped off from the library copy, the same page he had seen beneath Stevie's fish and chips. No, there was time: the Trans-America race was still several months away in March 1931. But where in God's name was California? He finished his drink, and after making his farewells to McGowan returned to the library to seek out a map. California was on the west coast, and could not have been farther away. He could see no way of getting there.

"You're not using the head," said Stevie, when he told him.

"What d'you mean?" Hugh replied testily.

"Look," said Stevie. "First you're a sprinter. You've never run a hundred miles, let alone three thousand. Second, you've no money to get there. Why not kill two birds with one stone?" Hugh did not reply, so he went on. "Get somebody to organize a Scottish Trial, for God's sake. Some newspaper like *The Times* or the *Citizen*. That way if you are good enough you'll find out. If not, you won't have wasted your own or anybody else's money, going all the way out to California."

Hugh thought for a moment. "You're right, Stevie. But the man for this is Jimmy G. Miller."

"Jimmy G.," as he was commonly known, a Bridgeton bookmaker of doubtful reputation, was not immediately taken with the idea of putting up five hundred pounds in prize money for an unheard-of event. "What do I get out of it?" he asked Hugh suspiciously.

"First," said Hugh, "the prestige. You've put up the cash so that a Scot can go to America and take on the best in the world. Second, the betting. You'll take a big book on the result of the race. And third, me."

"You?" exploded Jimmy G. "God in heaven, you're a bloody sprinter. Where's the money in you?"

"Give me six months' preparation. Take me off with a good trainer and some steaks and I'll *win* you that trial. You'll get big odds on me, and clean up a packet."

Jimmy G. took the wet stub of the cigar from his mouth and looked across the table at him. "Can you guarantee to win?"

"I can't. That's *your* gamble. That's what you are anyway, a gambler, isn't it?"

"Not really," replied Jimmy G. "I'm a bookmaker." But he was smiling.

After that events moved quickly. The five-hundred-pounds prize money that James G. Miller of Bridgeton put up for the Scottish Trans-America trial caused a sensation, and the bookmaker and his race became a national talking point, just as McPhail had prophesied. Jimmy G. was happy with the result, for overnight, for a mere five hundred pounds, he had been elevated from the relative obscurity of a Bridgeton bookmaker to the status of a national figure. Times were hard, the winter was bleak, Scotland had just lost in the annual soccer match against England. Jimmy G. had given the country something to talk about, something to which people could look forward. The only problem was that he had never organized a race in his life. He decided to seek the advice of someone who had—Murdoch, the organizer of the 1909 Powderhall marathon.

"No problem," said the old man, and set to planning a course from Aberdeen to Glasgow.

Meanwhile Jimmy G. had kept the final part of his agreement and had sent McPhail to the Highlands under the stern eye of the professional trainer "Ducky" Duckworth. The bookmaker saw little hope of any return on his investment on McPhail, but reckoned he would soon know from Duckworth's trials if the Glasgow man had any chance of surviving the Trans-America race, let alone winning it. Duckworth was not so optimistic, for though the trials run by professional sprinters were good guides to eventual racing form, there was no real way of testing whether or not a man could run a hundred miles without exposing him to massive fatigue, from which there might not be time to recover. There was no real precedent for training for this length of race, and there was a real danger of running your man into the ground before the contest. He therefore resolved to make the final trial at least two weeks before the race, and for it to consist of two fifty-mile runs, with three hours' rest in between.

McPhail's stay in the central highlands was an exhausting one. First, Duckworth boiled him down to "racing weight" from his normal weight of one hundred and seventy pounds by having him lose eight pounds in the first two weeks. During that time McPhail ran and walked only about eight miles a day, mostly on soft grass, in stints of three to five miles. At first he found this hard, particularly as Duckworth made him run part of the distance in boots and heavy clothing. Gradually, however, he felt his thighs harden again, his breathing become easier.

After a month Duckworth gave him a trial over a hilly ten-mile course. "Run it in inside an hour," he said, "or the preparation's over."

Hugh got through the first five miles in well inside the half hour, with Duckworth behind him on a bicycle. Even at seven and a half miles he was inside his schedule, and feeling pleased with himself. Then, at eight miles, he cracked. Suddenly, as if someone inside his body had turned off a faucet, his legs tightened and his stride dropped to a crippled trot. Duckworth immediately saw what had happened, slowed, and sat back to watch.

Hugh had never experienced anything like this before. True,

he had tightened up in sprints, but that had been painless, over in a flash. Now his thighs and the inside of his groin were screaming. Yet he did not drop to a walk. He did not dare, for he knew that if he did he would never be able to restart.

Just as the chemistry of his body had changed, so had that of his mind. Perhaps a scientist could analyze and measure it in terms of molecules whirling desperately toward some mad collision. To Hugh it took the form of a blur of images: on the one hand, the cinders of tanner-a-man soccer on Glasgow Green, endless cups of kitchen tea on endless winter afternoons, standing in line at the Broo. On the other, a chance—not much of a chance, perhaps—of a money prize and a trip to the sun on the other side of the world. Above all, a chance to break clear, to start again. On the one hand, the pain, and the certainty of at least another quarter of an hour of it; on the other, his hopes and his dreams.

Hugh started to groan. It was not a conscious groan, but one which came from deep inside and pulsed in rhythm with his now short and shattered strides. In a way it helped, acting as a sort of metronome against which his strides could be placed, his pain measured. Every now and then his groans would be interrupted by a sound which came from even deeper within him, a little scream which pierced the groans and then died away.

In the central highlands of Scotland, silhouetted against the gray winter sky, a man staggered, groaning, followed by a little man on a bicycle. Fiercer battles had been fought on stranger ground, but none more severe.

It took Duckworth more than half an hour to bring his charge around. Hugh jerked his head away from the sharp smell of the smelling salts.

"Did I make it?" he asked, propping himself up.

"Yes," said Duckworth. "Ye ran ten miles."

"But the time? Did I make it in the hour?"

"No. One hour and two minutes."

McPhail wept, the salt tears dropping onto a shirt already sodden with sweat. He wept like a child, in deep sobs.

Duckworth bent down, so that his eyes were in line with Hugh's. "Ye didn't make it in the hour, but ye've satisfied *me*. Ma faither, when he telt me of great runners, used tae call it 'bottom'. A' the great yins had it. Ye can call it whit ye like—courage, stamina, endurance. He called it 'bottom.' You've got it, lad."

"You mean we go on with the prep?"

"Aye. Now it's just a matter of getting miles under yer belt. Now we know ye'll stay when trouble comes."

Three months later, his body toned and hardened by Duckworth's training, Hugh found no difficulty in winning the Scottish Trans-America trial. He had been virtually the only trained man in the trial, a race in which he had faced the gaunt men of the Scottish Broo Parks. He led them easily through the black, slimy streets of Glasgow, and finished before forty thousand spectators at Ibrox stadium.

Throughout that day broken men stumbled around the sodden cinder track, all hope of the Trans-America gone. Hugh watched them from the comfort of the stands and asked himself why they kept going. Months later, thousands of miles from home, he was to receive the answer.

4

THE PRESS
MEETS DOC COLE

Doc stood up and propped himself on both arms, knuckles down, on the table in front of him. "Okay fellas," he said. "Shoot."

Wearing a faded 1908 Olympic blazer, Alexander Doc Cole looked even smaller, older, less athletic than he had at Flanagan's press conference the day before. Bald and brown, he looked more gnome than man as he stood at a table on the dais facing the assembled press.

In fact, Doc could almost have been tailored for the Trans-America. He had set out from his home in Montgomery, Alabama, and had hitched the first two thousand miles, run the last five hundred. The long run-in into Los Angeles had got his legs and feet in shape, for he knew that the Trans-America would be a test even for someone with his background. He reckoned he would be the most experienced runner in the race, with a heart rate of thirty-four beats per minute and with over a hundred thousand miles of running in the fibers of his lean, hard legs. But he would also, at fifty-four, be one of the oldest men in the Trans-America.

On the other hand, age in a race such as this would be no disadvantage. True, the young would have tough, adaptable bodies, and the Trans-America might indeed allow some time for adaptation. But they had never been where he had been, in sour lands where the body dragged itself from one stride to the next, while the mind, still fresh but desperate, fought its own battles. It was in that dark battleground that races were won or lost; and he had lost a few, but won many.

He had made good use of his thousand miles of travel. The first four days had seen the sale of a hundred bottles of Chief Chickamauga's snake bite remedy. The first two days, in farmer's country, he had sold it as a liniment, because farmers were always good for anything that would cure their aches and pains. He had also managed to unload ten of Dr. Pulvermacher's magnetic belts, the first he had sold for many years. The glamor and mystery of electricity and magnetism had by 1931 worn thin. He had seen the time when he could not sell enough of the magnetic belts, the answer to every ill from constipation to impotence. The odd thing was that they *did* occasionally work. On more than one occasion a constipation-gripped cowboy had had to make a sprint to the john only seconds after Dr. Pulvermacher's belt had started to fizz and flash around his belly. Doc's information on the belt's effects on impotence were less easily come by, but this had never prevented large sales to the lovelorn.

The next two days he had sold the remedy as a tonic, with equally good results. This change of tack also involved a slight change in formula with the alcohol content lifted to thirty percent. This form of the remedy had always gone down well in temperance towns, and many a stern Baptist maiden aunt who had solemnly taken the pledge swore by the Chief's answer to all ills, from the vapors to morning sickness. The remedy had an equal appeal to men, particularly when Doc described its "virilizing" qualities. Doc's audiences therefore went off with a dollar's worth of hope in their pocket. They had also been royally entertained.

Alas, it had not been quite like the old days. Then, Doc Cole could have swept toward Los Angeles like an avenging fury, littering the area behind him with thousands of dollars' worth of Chief Chickamauga's remedy and Dr. Pulvermacher's magnetic belts, to say nothing of Simmon's liver regulator, Dr. Kilmer's swamp root and Perry Davis's painkiller. Alas, federal drug controls had seen the disappearance of Dr. Hercules Sanche, Doc McBride (the Great King of Pain), Doc Ennis and his universal balm . . . Dear God, they had swept through the West like a plague of locusts. No state fair had been complete without them, dressed in their fancy vests and black bowler hats, their "wives" jabbering beside them as Queen Nookamookee, their sons as Prince Achmed lately rescued from cannibals in the Trobriand Islands. Still, if they had been rogues they had been damn funny ones, and no one had come to much harm because of them.

Those days had gone for good, and Doc had spent the last ten years behind the counter at Bernstein's Drug Store in Montgomery, Alabama, dispensing milkshakes and homespun homilies to college kids for five bucks a week. He had, however, never stopped running. The 1908 Olympics had resulted in a four-year boom in professional marathon running, with the magic twenty-six mile three hundred and eighty-five-yard race being held for money everywhere from Cairo to the Yukon. It had been short-lived, but Doc had been one of the better contenders, though never a match for the Indian Longboat, the Englishman Shrubb, or the stocky little Italian Dorando Pietri, whose running in the London Olympics had triggered off the whole mad marathon craze in the first place. They had run anything up to ten marathons a year, and this had been too much for even the best of them, who had met with illness and injury, leaving good pickings for the second rank of runners, of whom Doc had been one. By 1913 the bubble had burst. Back they had gone to their respective countries, many to surrender their fit, hard bodies to the sniper's bullets and shrapnel of the French trenches, others simply to bland domesticity. The world of amateur athletics was closed to them, while that of professional athletics existed only in the industrial towns of Northern England and parts of rural Scotland. Thus some of the greatest running machines the world had ever seen had been broken, dismantled or simply rusted away.

After the war there had been a delay in the revival of amateur athletics, and many state fairs and local carnivals, knowing nothing of the amateur rules, had put on "picnic" meetings for money prizes. The longest distance run had been three miles, a mere sprint to Doc, and he had won such races easily, trotting around the rough grass tracks in about sixteen minutes, far ahead of the college boys and farmers who had been his challengers. Occasionally, echoing the old days, a town would hold a marathon, usually over only ten or twelve miles, and again Doc was back in his element, slaughtering the ill-trained locals.

In the early twenties, as amateur athletics picked up the traces, Doc had found fewer and fewer meetings in which to race, but in some ways this had been his golden period. He had gone bald early in middle age and in his road shows, as part of his Chickamauga spiel, he would issue a challenge to race the fastest runner in town. "Who's your best runner?" he would shout, tearing off his jacket and pulling out the cork from a bottle of Chickamauga with his teeth. "Dear Lord, I'm fifty-five (he was then ten years younger) but give me a slug of Chickamauga and I'll take him on." Every town had its star athlete, sometimes a college boy gone to seed, sometimes a fit young farmer. The lad would be thrust forward, blushing and uncertain at first, but encouraged by the back slaps and shouts of the crowd, becoming progressively more confident as he reached Doc on the stage. "If this young feller here will give me a start . . ." Doc would begin, to be drowned in jeers and catcalls. "All right," he would say. "We'll start even. But first let's see some money down." In a matter of minutes the farmers were raining dollars on the stakeholder, Doc's "daughter," Alice, betting five to one on their champion.

"One moment," Doc would then shout above the furor. "If— if anything should happen to me, I hope you'll see me in a Christian grave." Satisfied by the raucous assurances of the crowd, Doc would arrange a course of at least three miles and would then give a lengthy lecture on the values of the remedy. If it was being sold as liniment he would massage himself vigorously, giving little groans if it went close to his private parts. On the other hand, if it was being sold as a tonic Doc would savor the remedy in sips, like a fine wine, before allowing it to slide down his throat.

Then the race would start. Doc usually let his challenger stay with him for the first couple of miles, always keeping a close check on his opponent's rate of breathing. If the local boy was gasping Doc would slow down, so that the lad could finish the course in style, making a race of it. On the other hand, if the local champion was going easily, Doc would step up the pace, for he had no wish to face the sprint finish of a younger man.

Every now and then as he ran through the crowded town Doc would give a groan and hold his side, as if suffering from a stitch.

The crowd loved this, for here was their champion running this smart-aleck medicine man into the ground. With half a mile to go Doc, rolling around, would obviously be in great pain. Then his "daughter" would rush to his side with a bottle of Chickamauga. Revived, Doc would sprint the last half mile and win easily. He always, however, seemed to have enough breath left to harangue his doting audience for another hour on the benefits of Chickamauga and of a life of exercise and moderation.

The last years of the twenties had seen a revival in all marathon-type activity, excluding marathons themselves. Marathon dancing, pole-sitting, skipping and cycling had become popular, but this had not resulted in a revival of the marathon-madness of 1908. Professional distance races did revive, however, and Doc, although now in his early fifties, had found no trouble in dealing with another generation of challengers.

This was a new and different group of men from the "circus" of prewar days. Unemployment was growing rapidly, and baseball, football and boxing were the only sports which offered outlets for the working class. The ghettos of New York had spawned endless Negro boxers, but football and baseball were open to whites only. Not so running, but few Negroes had any background in distance running and most of them were helpless after a few miles. For different reasons, it was the same for most of the unemployed white men who, in desperation, entered for local races, for they had neither the training nor the feeding to enable them to complete the distances, let alone race them.

In this mini-boom Doc thrived. With thirty years of running behind him the competition presented few problems. His only difficulties arose whenever an amateur distance runner turned professional. These were young men, running as fast as Doc had done twenty years before, and there was no way he could contain them at distances less than ten miles. The mini-boom of the late twenties did not, however, provide for Doc the economic basis for a second career as a full-time athlete, as races were spread unevenly across the continent. Doc had stayed behind the counter at Bernstein's, happy with a steady five bucks a week, occasionally picking up races in nearby states.

As soon as he heard of Flanagan's Trans-America race he had known that this was what he had been waiting for, his last chance to set up Doc Cole's Drug Store or Sports Emporium and live the remainder of his life in style. The other competitors did not worry him; he knew that if he could stay healthy over the distance he would be in the frame at the finish. That hundred and fifty thousand dollars was a lot of money and anyway, he was going nowhere in particular. He had therefore given in his notice at Bernstein's and trotted off toward Los Angeles.

Doc had reached the bustling city two days before the required assembly time, at Flanagan's request, and had met Flanagan in his headquarters at the Imperial Hotel a couple of hours after his arrival.

"You don't know me, but I sure as hell know you," said Flanagan. "When I was a boy I followed all the pro marathon runners—Longboat, Johnny Hayes, Dorando. I even saw you run a marathon indoors at the Garden once."

"That was in 1911," said Doc.

"That's right. You got beat by Shrubb and Dorando."

"Right again," said Doc, accepting a glass of orange juice.

"Well, Doc, I need your help," said Flanagan. "I've set this race up, got all the organization planned down to the last tent peg. In a couple of days I'll hold my first press conference. But hell, I never ran marathons and the press boys will want something more than a press release for what I'm going to hand them. That's where I need someone of your weight."

"How?"

"By you having your own conference a day later," said Flanagan. "That way you can fill them in on all the hard technical stuff. Those press boys don't know a marathon from a fortune cookie—you can give 'em the real McCoy."

Doc was silent for a moment.

"Well, what do you say?" asked Flanagan.

"Won't the other runners think I'm getting the star treatment?"

"Doc, you *are* a star—hell, you've run more marathons than most of 'em have had hot breakfasts. So I'm certainly not going to be apologizing to anyone and neither should you. What do you say?" asked Flanagan.

"Yes," said Doc, quietly.

"Carl Liebnitz." The thin panama-hatted journalist rose, took off his glasses and polished them with his handkerchief. "Doc, you may recall that we first met in 1904 at the St. Louis Olympics marathon. Was that your first full marathon?"

"Yep," said Doc, smiling in recognition of Liebnitz. "The first and the worst. I had already been two months selling snakeroot at the St. Louis Expedition. So I wasn't in too good shape for that one."

"I seem to remember that it was pretty hot in St. Louis," said Liebnitz.

Doc puffed out his cheeks. "Hot as hell! It must have been over ninety in the sun, and men dropped out like flies."

"Did you know the Cuban, Felix Carjaval?" asked Liebnitz.

"Felix?" Doc laughed. "Yes, I knew Felix quite well. He was a mailman, had never run a marathon before. He raised the money for St. Louis by running around the town square in Havana for a couple of hours. When he collected enough pesos he hightailed it to St. Louis. But Felix lost all his money in a crap game and ended up bumming his way to the Olympics. Yes, I knew Felix. What a joker! But he finished fourth, a full ten minutes up on me."

"Rae here, *Washington Post*. Didn't you go on to run for Uncle Sam at the London Olympics in 1908?"

Doc wrinkled his nose. "Yes, in the Dorando Marathon. Boy! I hit the wall at twenty miles and ended up watching the finish from the bleachers."

"Forrest, *Chicago Tribune*. Do you think the Trans-America field is too large?"

Doc slowly brought his little brown hands together. "It'll soon trim down. By my reckoning the field will halve in the first week and halve again two weeks later. I don't see more'n five hundred men making New York."

"And women?"

Doc chuckled. "Any lady who makes the final five hundred to New York will receive a chilled bottle of vintage French champagne, compliments of Alexander Cole."

"What about a bottle of Chickamauga remedy, Doc?" chuckled Forrest.

"She'll have taken that already just to help her get there."

There was laughter. This was copy, what they had come to hear.

James Ferris of *The Times* stood up. "Doc, how did you come to acquire your medical degree?"

Cole grinned, wrinkling his leathery face. "I freely confess that I never actually picked up a *college* degree. But you fellers know the way it was. There wasn't much in the way of Harvard doctors and hospitals back where I came from. So any coot like me who came around in pin-striped trousers with a few bottles of horse liniment, swinging a two-dollar watch was elevated to the ranks of the medical profession. Me, I always looked upon it as a sort of honorary degree."

Albert Kowalski rose. "Doc," he said, after identifying himself, "you seem to have been around a coon's age. Do you mind telling us how old you are?"

Doc smiled. "A hundred thousand miles old," he replied. "Seriously, fellas, I'm fifty-four."

"Do you think the Trans-America may have come too late for you?" pursued Kowalski.

The smile faded from Doc's face. "Perhaps," he said. "But I can't allow myself to think that way. Anyhow, in a race of this distance age can be an asset. Age means experience. That means experience of pain, of injury, of days when your legs won't move. That sort of experience is money in the bank."

"In the Trans-America bank?" flashed Kowalski.

"For the moment, yes," said Doc, smiling.

"What's the farthest distance you've ever run?" asked Forrest.

"In a race, nonstop, one hundred miles, back in 1912 in Berlin. Two years back I ran a hundred and eighty miles in three days at sixty miles a day, in snowshoes, in Alaska."

"So the Trans-America represents a completely unique challenge even for someone like you?" asked Kowalski.

"I should say so. Fifty miles a day for three months, over all kinds of country. No runner has ever raced such distances before."

"What is the most you have run in training?" asked Forrest.

"In a week, two hundred miles."

"So even in the first week you will be in unknown territory?" asked Forrest, scribbling furiously.

"Any way you look at it it's unique," said Doc. "That's the challenge. Even old-timers like me are novices in the Trans-America. That's what makes it a lottery. That's why it's pulled in two thousand runners from all over."

"Trevor Grove, *New York Herald*. Doc, would it be true to say that you are the most experienced runner in the race?"

Doc shrugged. "Yes and no. Yes, I've run more long-distance races than most of the men here, except possibly the Englishman Charles Fox. No, because no one here is experienced at running three thousand-odd miles across America."

"Pollard, *St. Louis Star*. Doc, will you have any special diet for the race?"

"The secret is to carry on as usual—never take anything you wouldn't normally eat," answered Doc. He held up a glass of water. "The big problem will be drink, particularly in the desert heat. When you run out of water you overheat. Next thing, it's curtains."

Forrest was the next on his feet. "What about race walkers? How do you see their chances?"

Doc pursed his lips. "Not good," he replied. "Over distances in the twenty- to twenty-five-mile range, walkers can't pump out much better than ten- or twelve-minute miles. By my reckoning it will take an average pace of inside ten minutes a mile to take the Trans-America. And I believe Mr. Flanagan proposes some qualifying times in the early stages, to cut down the field. So I can't see many of the walkers making it through the first cuts."

"Doc, three thousand miles is one helluva long way to race. How are you going to keep mentally sharp?" asked Grove.

Doc's lower lip pouted. "For me it won't be a race till about five hundred miles out from New York. Any guy who goes out to race hard every day will blow a gasket in the first month. My aim is to run as if there's no one else in the race. The moment I start *racing* against people at each stage I'll be finished, 'cause I'll be racing at their pace and not mine."

"What do you mean by only racing the last five hundred miles?" queried Ferris.

"I mean that by that time the Trans-America will have shaken out the men from the boys. By then we'll know who can run what. The race will probably divide itself into three kinds of runner. First, the guys who are sprinters—these guys will win short stages up to fifteen miles. At the other end of the scale will be the sloggers, coots who can chug forever at ten minutes a mile over fifty miles. In the middle will be the marathon men. They'll run inside ten minutes per mile. By five hundred miles out I'll know what has to be done. I reckon if I'm within an hour of the leaders at that point then I can make up the gap in the remaining distance."

"Doc, what in your estimation will be the qualities required of the Trans-America winner?"

Doc paused for a moment. "The Trans-America winner," he said, "should be a pair of legs with a head on top. The man must have a tough heart to pump enough blood to let him average ten-minute miles, day in day out. That heart will knock along at a hundred beats a minute over road, over country, on rough track, on flat plains and high sierras."

He sat on the edge of the table, his legs dangling.

"The winner will have tough, hard feet, feet that won't cut up and blister. In the end a Trans-America runner is only as good as his contact point. Six million contacts from here to New York; remember that."

"But what about the mind, Doc?" Ferris asked.

Doc stood up and tapped his forehead. "That's where the real battles will be won and lost," he said. "The winner has to keep going every one of the thousand times his body will beg him to stop between here and New York. The winner mustn't think of *three thousand* miles, only of the next one. He must live in his own mind, defeating only one man every day. Always. The same man—himself."

"Martin Howard, *Chicago Star*. Are there any other factors?"

"Health," said Doc. "If he feels ill or has tendon and muscle pains he must be brave enough to ease off and walk. Otherwise a pain becomes an injury, and an injury soon becomes crippling. In a race of this distance there is time for injuries to heal up—but only if you give your body a chance."

"Will you wear any special clothing?" asked Howard.

Doc grinned. "You'll make me give away my secrets," he said. "The main thing is to let the body *breathe*. That's why I run in this string vest kinda shirt." He lifted from the table a shirt punctured with holes. "This lets the body get rid of heat. That apart, you must avoid chafing—and that means wide-legged shorts, six pairs of well-worn shoes—and protection from the sun. These are the essentials. Sunburn can make you raw meat in a few hours."

"Doc, Mr. Flanagan tells us that Paavo Nurmi might be a competitor. What are your thoughts on that?" asked Pollard.

Doc wrinkled his nose. "Heck," he said, "I'm surprised Paavo can even *afford* to turn professional." There was more laughter. "Seriously, Nurmi is the greatest runner of all time, and if he enters, then he must be a strong contender. My philosophy is this. You don't win races by worrying about other competitors. You respect them, yes. You keep an eye on them, yes. But worry, hell no. So if Nurmi throws his hat in the ring, so be it."

"What about sex, Doc?" shouted a sweating reporter toward the back of the hall.

"Well," said Doc. "What about it?"

There was laughter.

"I get your drift," he continued as the laughter subsided. "Sex is like food—you shouldn't change your habits even during competition. I don't propose to change mine—but I'm sure as hell not telling you fellas what they are!"

"Pop Warner won't let any of his players near women close to a game and Dempsey stays away from his wife for three months before fights," observed Ferris.

"Hell, Mr. Ferris, we won't be playing much football or doing much fistfighting in the Trans-America," said Doc, his eyes twinkling.

"Do you know much about the form of the other runners?" Ferris countered.

Doc shook his head. "Not really. Kohlemainen I know something about—I ran against him a heap after the 1908 marathon—even beat him once in Mexico. The Englishman, Charles Fox, he's one of the all-time greats, but Charles is now close to seventy."

"Campbell, *Glasgow Herald*. Do you know anything about the Scot, Hugh McPhail?"

Doc's eyebrows lifted. "I've been told he was a *sprinter*! Well, the Trans-America sure ain't no sprint."

"Maguire, *Irish Times*. What do you know of Lord Thurleigh?"

"Heard tell he ran in the five thousand meters in the Amsterdam Games." Doc smiled. "I don't have to tell you that there's one helluva difference between three miles and three thousand."

"Ferris again. What about the organized teams, like the Germans and the All-Americans? Won't they have a big advantage over lone individuals like yourself?"

"Yep," said Doc, nodding. "They'll have coaches and managers with them every step of the way, thinking ahead all the time. The rest of us will have to think for ourselves. Sure, they'll have an advantage, all things being equal."

"Liebnitz. Doc, don't you think that there's something wrong when there are men on the bread line all over the States and here we have a thousand guys footracing across America for a total of three hundred and fifty thousand dollars?"

Doc shook his head. "I'm with you on the first point. It's bad that there are working men on the bread line all over the States, all over the world. But there's no way I see anything wrong with a couple of thousand men running their balls off for a money prize, any more than it's wrong for Doug Fairbanks to get paid for showing off his muscles in the movies. Sure, I'm sorry for the poor stiffs who're only running for the three meals a day. I'm sorry for the ones who'll run themselves into the side of the road for stage prizes when they haven't a hope in hell of winning them. Still, at least they'll go down *trying*, which is more than they can do in soup kitchens."

"How many miles do you reckon you've run in training, Doc?" asked Rae.

"About a hundred thousand," said Doc. "About a mile for every dollar I hope to win. Still, let's get things clear. Training's physical, racing is emotional. Tomorrow there'll be a couple of·thousand guys out there, ready to run their hearts out. Some of those men will discover themselves between here and New York. They'll find that they have physical and mental qualities they never even dreamed of when they started out. Those guys will get fit *on* the run—and they're men to fear."

Carl Liebnitz rose again. "Correct me if I'm wrong, Doc. You ran in the 1904 and 1908 Olympics without getting into the medals. Then, as I recall, you ran pro until the war, but you never won any really big money. Is this your last chance? The big one?"

Doc bit his upper lip. "I think you put your finger right on it, Carl. This is the big one for me."

5

THE START

"Ladies and gentlemen!" Charles C. Flanagan cleared his throat and boomed into the microphone. The sound set a flock of pigeons fluttering above the Roman pillars of the Los Angeles Coliseum. He was standing on a wooden dais in the center of the stand in the home stretch. Beneath him, in the bright spring sun, were over two thousand runners circling the track and stretching far out into the stadium parking lot. The Coliseum, which for the past hour had been entertained by an endless succession of acrobats, clowns, and brass bands, was full to the brim.

"Ladies and gentlemen," Flanagan roared again. "This is indeed a historic moment." He looked across at the stadium clock. "In ten minutes there will be set in motion the greatest professional long-distance race in the history of mankind, a race in which the cream of the world's athletes will set out to cross the great continent of America. Each man is a Columbus, for he steps into the unknown, attempting to achieve a conquest that has never before been attempted by any athlete. I wish all of you, each man and woman among you, good fortune. My task is to ensure a fair and honest race. This I will endeavor to do."

Flanagan half turned toward the celebrities seated behind him on the dais. "Some of you will already have recognized the distinguished celebrities who have consented to grace this occasion . . .

"Mr. Buster Keaton!" All eyes focused on a glum little man on Flanagan's right.

"Miss Mary Pickford!" There was a ripple of applause as Flanagan moved to one side to reveal America's darling.

"That great athlete, the fastest man in the world, Charley Paddock!" Paddock, now a plump, moon-faced man, stood up and nodded to the runners.

"The former world's heavyweight boxing champion, Mr. Jack Dempsey!" Dempsey, lean and bronzed, stood up and clasped both hands above his head, boxing-style, turning to left and right.

"And finally, a man I am privileged to count as a friend, a man who is both great actor and great athlete, the man who is today going to set you all on your way across America . . . Mr. Douglas Fairbanks!"

Waves of applause broke out on all sides. Fairbanks was well known as a fitness fanatic, an actor who insisted on performing his own stunts. Though the advent of the talkies had caused his star to wane he was still immensely popular: the world's Mr. America.

Looking up, Hugh McPhail thought Fairbanks much smaller than he had expected. Plumper too; Fairbanks was already showing a second chin, and his double-breasted suit strained at its pearl buttons. However, as he stood with both arms out, his teeth flashing in a wide smile, Fairbanks exuded glowing animal fitness.

"My friends," he said, stilling the applause with raised hands. "When I first heard about Mr. Flanagan's race my first thought was to enter *myself*." There was laughter. Fairbanks waited until the stadium was again silent. "Happily, wiser counsels prevailed. Sure, I'm an athlete, I love athletics, but long-distance running was never my strong suit. Jumping, vaulting, capturing pirate ships, rescuing maidens in distress"—he gave a sidelong glance at Mary Pickford—"that's my bag. Even now I'm just off the set of *Around the World in Eighty Minutes*. I guess you fellas will take just a little longer to reach New York!" Again there was laughter, and again Fairbanks raised his hands and shook his head. "Seriously, I feel deeply honored to be here. I suppose in some way this race represents the Great American Dream. Sure, many of you guys and gals have seen hard times. But now, with one throw of the dice, you can change it all, here in the Trans-America.

"As Mr. Flanagan has just said, this is the greatest footrace of all time and it is both my pleasure and my privilege to start the competition." He lifted from a table a massive double-barreled shotgun. "So: ladies and gentlemen, get to your marks . . ."

Every muscle in the throng before him was tense, the Coliseum quiet but for the shrill cries of wheeling Pacific gulls skimming through its Roman pillars. Fairbanks looked down at the cinder track below him, at the runners coiled in row upon row around the green infield. They reminded him of some still, vital creature waiting to be unleashed.

On the track below, Doc Cole likewise looked around him. Two thousand men and women waiting, poised, to rush across a continent . . . Just behind him were the swarthy Scot, McPhail, the strange limey, Lord Thurleigh, and the lean, impassive Finn, Eskola. A few rows farther back stood four of Williams' All-Americans, dressed in white silk stars-and-stripes shirts, and in front of them four crew-cut, sun-blackened young Germans. In the same row crouched the British veteran, Charles Fox, wrinkled and white, eyes almost closed, waiting for the start.

Standing beside him was a slim, attractive young woman, wearing a white shirt with the words NEW YORK printed in black front and back. The girl looked poised and confident, and Doc wondered how many other women were sprinkled throughout the field. Whatever the number, he could not see any of them making it as far as Las Vegas, let alone New York.

"Get set . . ." Fairbanks played the moment to the hilt, sensing the tension. His finger tightened on the trigger of the Winchester.

". . . Go!" The explosion of the gun, the roar of the crowd and the din of the massed infield bands seemed to come as one. Immediately the runners started to move, like lava pouring down a mountainside. Some runners, excited by the dramatic preliminaries, sprinted through the crowds, skidding, stumbling and falling as they bumped into slower, more cautious runners ahead of them. Others simply stood still waiting for space to open up in front of them. Yet others set off in a jaunty, hip-wobbling walk which drew raucous jeers from the crowd. For thirty minutes the mob streamed around the stadium waving and shouting to spectators as they covered two miles of the track before leaving for the open road. Then they moved out into the parking lot, through the noisy jangle of Flanagan's carnival, out into the crowded car-lined streets of Los Angeles.

Doc waited till the group ahead of him had departed, then launched into a bandy-legged jog trot. He looked at his watch. Twenty-nine miles to go: that meant about five hours of running. He wore no socks and his shorts were brief and wide. On his head he wore a sweatband and a peaked white cap. In his right hand he carried a white handkerchief, which he had knotted around his wrist. Hooked to his waist was a small water bottle. It was a long, long way to New York, and it would be a long time before he would give any thought to racing. For the present it was a matter of getting out of L.A., and of running at steady ten-minute miles today and every day. If he could keep doing that he would be around somewhere at the finish.

Ahead and around him Finns, Scots, Americans and English mingled and jostled with Turks, Africans, Chinese and Samoans. Bearded, long-legged Sikhs strode beside tiny, pattering Japanese; slim, brown Californian women beside men from the industrial towns of northern England. On their shirts were advertised the wares of Hull, Calcutta, San Francisco, Budapest and Edinburgh. Some ran in modern shorts and shirts, others in equipment that had not seen the light of day since the turn of the century. Others ran in track suits, walked in ordinary daytime clothes, or even carried sticks. Doc saw at least one blind man and two men without arms.

The variation in speed was remarkable, ranging from fully dressed walkers striding out at a sedate 4 M.P.H. through to trained athletes running over twice as fast. There was no way that could be kept up, thought Doc; not for sixteen miles, let alone twenty-nine.

He hardly seemed to be moving, pegging along at a steady chugging gait, heel first, his nut-brown bandy legs gobbling up the rutted, dusty road. Yet all around him runners were already falling back, some dropping to a jog trot, others to a walk. Some, having completed less than five miles, stopped and simply sat by the roadside, sobbing with fatigue, gaping at the stream of runners that poured through the crowded sidewalks east out of the city.

Doc had anticipated neither the dense traffic nor the crowds. For the first ten miles cars were parked two or three deep, and thousands of clapping, cheering spectators lined the route, leaving only a narrow channel for the runners. Ahead, forging a path for them, were Flanagan's Trans-America bus, the Maxwell House Coffee Pot—a grotesque jug-shaped refreshment van—and a train of press buses.

Hugh McPhail had been sucked in by the early pace, and had gone eight miles through the channel of cheering crowds, also running in the wake of the Coffee Pot, before he realized that he was running much too fast. He dropped back and joined a lean, tanned runner, attired in silk shirt and shorts.

"How goes it?" he asked.

There was no reply.

"Suit yourself," said Hugh, continuing to run at the same even pace, and the two men pressed on in silent tandem. Behind him the four young German runners flowed on like so many smoothly oiled pieces of machinery. None was much older than twenty-one. All were burned black with the sun. At their side, on a motorcycle, cruised their team coach, a bull-necked German with a stopwatch looped on a cord round his neck. "*Langsam*," he shouted. "*Langsam!*" and the young Germans obediently slowed.

Not far behind were the Williams' All-Americans. Like the Germans, they ran as a team, their fat coach behind them in the back of an open Ford, shouting out instructions on a megaphone. "Relax," he bellowed, as they made their way up a slight incline. "Stay loose."

Close on the heels of the All-Americans was little Martinez, clad in close-cut shorts and white shirt, flowing along with light, springy strides. He was hardly breathing. Just ahead of him was the Pennsylvanian, Mike Morgan.

At a hundred and fifty-five pounds, Morgan was heavy for a distance runner. He had a dark, copper-colored body, with clearly defined musculature. Martinez watched the muscles of Morgan's back flutter and ripple as he ran, flexing and relaxing on each stride: the Pennsylvanian ran impassively, no sign of effort on his face, its only hint showing in the tiny streams of sweat which ran in rivulets down the muscles of his chest and back. Morgan checked his wristwatch. Twenty miles to go. No problems.

They were out in the country now, between Montebello and La Puente. The crowds had thinned and the only immediate problem was the exhaust fumes of the surrounding cars. Doc wiped his handkerchief across his face. All around him men were fading. On the side of the road a man sat whimpering, his bare feet ripped and bloody.

The race had already divided into four identifiable groups. First, there were the trained athletes, men with thousands of miles in their legs, running to their trainers' orders or to the metronome of past experience, steadily making their way through the twenty-nine miles to Pomona. Behind and among them ran fit, hard men who had little experience of competitive racing, men who hoped to flower into athletes in the weeks to come. At the back of the field two other groups emerged. Both were novices, but the members of the first, driven by desperation and strength of will, somehow dragged themselves through the long miles of the first stage. Those in the second group, mind and body shocked even by the efforts of the first five miles, were broken before the field had even pierced the suburbs of Los Angeles.

The Trans-America was thus already spreadeagled along the road east from Los Angeles. From above, in the buzzing Pathé and March of Time newsplanes, the field could be seen, even after only fifteen miles, to stretch over a distance of six miles, snakelike, hardly seeming to move.

For Doc it was an easy run. Twenty-nine miles, no big hills, no real problems. Ten miles from home he cruised past the Germans and the All-Americans, dragging with him Morgan, the broad-shouldered, flat-nosed man he had noted the day before in the hotel. With a mile to go, Doc had passed all but a runner in tartan shorts and his companion, Lord Peter Thurleigh. Together Doc and Morgan pressed on toward the finish of the first stage.

From the brow of the hill they could see laid out on the dry, broken plain the vast tented camp that Flanagan had built for the race: twenty separate dwellings, each capable of holding one hundred runners, and in the center a giant food tent. Doc and Morgan trotted down the hill, happy to come in half a minute or so behind the two leaders.

Doc checked his wristwatch as they passed the finish.

"I reckon we made around five hours," he said, easing down as he approached the rows of notice boards which detailed the accommodation arrangements. Doc and Morgan together scanned the boards and finally located their tent.

"Looks as though we're bunking down together," said Doc.

Together they walked through the rows of tents, finally picking out the one allocated to them. Beside it, in a separate tent, the washing facilities were primitive. There were only a dozen buckets of cold water and a number of rough blue towels. However, Doc had earlier noticed a river a few hundred yards beyond the camp.

"Looks like there's a creek nearby," he said to Morgan, picking up his towel. Morgan nodded, and a moment later had joined Doc on the walk across the rocky plain toward the creek. Once there, Doc sat down on a rock, put his towel round his neck and let the water splash over his feet. He put out his hand to Morgan. "Name's Alexander Cole," he said formally, then added: "Most folks call me Doc."

Morgan responded with a firm grip. "Mike Morgan," he said, kneeling down and cupping the clear water in his hands and lapping it like a dog.

Their bodies streamed with sweat, and the taste of the water from the stream came as a pleasant shock.

"You run long distances before?" asked Doc.

"Not much."

"Me, I been running most of my life, one way or t'other," said Doc. He took hold of one of his feet, rotating it so that the sole was upwards. "Reckon these feet have done one hundred thousand miles. Time for a new pair."

They sat in silence, relishing the cool water flowing over their feet and legs. Then they walked back from the creek together, their towels draped over their shoulders. The elder man felt uneasy in Morgan's company. Morgan was not exactly unfriendly, yet he made no positive response. Doc always felt uncomfortable during silences, feeling obliged to fill them with speech, however inconsequential.

He looked up the hill, now dotted with runners descending on the camp.

"Poor devils," he said. "First day, last day, for most of 'em."

As the two men came nearer to the camp they were able to view more closely the condition of the latest arrivals. Some, the trained athletes, had experienced no problems and mostly stood drinking and chatting at the Maxwell House Coffee Pot, the sweat streaming from their lean bodies. Others sat on the ground, propped on their hands and knees, gasping, while others lay on all fours, like dying animals, groaning and sobbing. Some were carried off on stretchers by the waiting medical staff. Others simply limped off to their tents.

"Like Bull Run," said Doc. Indeed, the scene was much like a battleground. Runners continued to trickle from the hill above, but these were no longer competitors, no longer even runners. They either walked, limped or staggered. Some came in by truck or car, to be immediately disqualified.

"One thousand eight hundred and twenty-three," boomed Flanagan through his megaphone. "One hundred and eighty-nine to come!"

Flanagan's bellowed instructions continued to fill the evening air. The area beyond the bannered finish was now littered with men and women, the broken remnants of the first thirty miles of C. C. Flanagan's Trans-America. Doc threaded his way between the sobbing casualties toward the tent marked "Fizz," the name of the root beer company which had supplied it.

On reaching it he pointed toward a roped-off area fronted by a notice board bearing a list of names. He squinted at the list.

"Cole, Morgan—that's us. McPhail, Martinez, Lord Thurleigh," he read. He paused, bringing his face closer to the paper. "Jesus, what in God's name's a Lord Thurleigh?"

From inside the tent an arm rose languidly from a bed. "Peter Thurleigh. I don't believe we've been formally introduced."

A man in silk shorts and shirt rose and offered his hand. He was blond and tanned and had piercing blue eyes.

"Alexander Augustus Cole," said Doc, introducing himself yet again.

Thurleigh's grip was weak. He did not shake hands, rather he allowed his hand to be shaken. He ignored Morgan altogether and resumed his seat, lying back with his head pillowed in his hands.

"You spoke last week to the press," he said. "Aren't you some sort of doctor?"

Doc nodded sourly. "Some sort of."

"Good," drawled Thurleigh. "Might come in handy later."

The British runner turned over in his bed with his back to Doc, the interview over. Doc shook his head and moved on to his bunk, a rough camp bed. On the bed next to him lay Martinez, mouth open, snoring. On the other side Hugh McPhail was peeling off his shoes.

"Evening," said Doc. "Name's Cole, Alexander Cole." McPhail

looked around, lifting his hand to grasp that of his companion. "Hugh McPhail." He stood to greet Morgan.

The Pennsylvanian introduced himself, shook hands, and moved over to his bed.

Doc looked around him. "Looks like this is going to be our little family for the next three thousand miles. God willing."

"What's God got to do with it?" asked Morgan tersely.

"God sure as hell didn't intend the human foot to hit the ground six million times in two months," Doc replied. "Stands to reason we'll all need His help if we're going to reach New York."

There was no reply.

"Time for the trough," said Doc at last, rising. Morgan and McPhail rose with him, and Martinez, jerking himself to the vertical as if being snapped out of an hypnotic trance, scampered behind. Peter Thurleigh lay still, as though he had not heard.

The tent stank, as the men divested themselves of shirts and shorts. It was an exotic aroma, compounded of sweat, feces, urine and grass, with just a hint of vomit. It was the air they were going to breathe for the next three months.

In the vast refreshment tent about a thousand men and women ate, their utensils clinking noisily on tin plates. They sat on benches, eating from wooden trestle tables set in long rows.

"Sure ain't the Ritz, but it'll serve," said Doc, sitting down with his food, and flanked by Morgan and McPhail.

True, the fare was not princely. Hamburger and beans, followed by the obligatory apple pie, washed down by hot coffee.

Morgan said nothing, eating his food with almost a cold fury. McPhail gobbled his, hardly pausing between one gulp and the next. Martinez held his face close to his plate, using his fork as a shovel. In the middle of mouthfuls he gulped down his coffee, sloshing both food and liquid into his mouth before swallowing it all like a seal.

Doc watched his companions without comment. It was clear to him that for them even such a meal was rare. He wiped his mouth with the back of his hand. "Looks like that's dinner," he said, looking around him. The men finished their meal and walked to the tent exit.

They blinked as they came from the gloom of the tent into the thin evening sun. "Jesus H. Christ," said Doc, stopping, hands on hips. "I'll be damned."

On an open patch of grass stood a black Rolls-Royce. Beside it was a wooden table. On the table stood a gleaming silver salver, plates and silverware, while in an ice bucket stood a bottle of champagne. At the side of the table a butler stood stiffly, impeccable in black evening dress, a white towel across his right arm. On a wood camp chair sat Lord Thurleigh, dressed in a dark business suit, sipping wine and calmly dissecting what appeared to be roast turkey.

Dixie Williams stood by Flanagan's massive, gaudy Trans-America trailer and watched the runners come in. She had been watching for almost two hours. Never had she imagined it would be anything like this. Indeed, she had given no thought to the nature of the Trans-America when she had won first prize in a "Miss Trans-America" competition and found that it constituted an "advisory" position in the footrace. If she had imagined anything at all it was that the Trans-America would be a form of high school dash, with the competitors coming in at the end of each stage breathing heavily, but a few minutes later sipping Coke with the girls at the soda fountain. But never this.

True, some runners came in fresh after the thirty-mile stint, and it surprised her how old many of these men were. They were almost skeletal, the muscles of their thighs standing out like those in drawings from an anatomical chart. She wondered how such sinewy bodies even managed to exude sweat, for they seemed to be entirely composed of muscle and bone. Yet sweat they did, and in profusion, as they stood talking together at the Coffee Pot, drinking endless containers of iced coffee.

Oddly enough, they did not act like competitors, but more like friends who had simply been out together for a long run on the road. There they stood in the thin evening sun, chatting easily, stripped to the waist, their abdominals rippling like washboards, their bodies still winter-white, while the remaining competitors continued to stream down the hill into Flanaganville.

As her gaze wandered she could see too that the condition of many of the competitors was desperate. Some staggered or walked in, their shirts clotted with sweat, jackets and jerseys draped over their shoulders or around their necks. Some had taken off their shoes and had walked or limped the last miles, their bare feet or stockinged soles now caked with blood. Littered across the vast field competitors lay on their backs, knees bent and chests heaving, or, like animals, propped themselves on knees and hands, coughing and spitting. Dixie felt tears well in her eyes, and then, turning, was surprised to find the journalist Carl Liebnitz standing beside her. He took off his steel-rimmed glasses, polished them and finally replaced them on his nose.

"I wonder if your boss Charles Flanagan really knows what he's gotten himself into," he said. "Some of these poor souls have come straight from the soup kitchens. They won't make it as far as Barstow, let alone New York."

Dixie did not know how to respond. "At least they'll be better fed here," she said defensively, wiping her eyes with her handkerchief.

"Yes," said Liebnitz. "Perhaps they will." He gazed for a moment without speaking, then excused himself and walked off, picking his way between the prostrate bodies of exhausted runners until he had reached the press tent.

Dixie looked across the vast field. On her right were the twenty massive white tents that housed the Trans-America athletes. She walked idly between them and half glimpsed, in the dim gloom, naked men sponging themselves down from buckets of cold water.

She passed two hysterical, weeping women, supported by attendants, and a moment later saw she had reached the circus trailers. Madame La Zonga, standing outside her trailer, was slowly unwrapping a snake from her neck. She paid no attention to the runners limping in and out of the first-aid tent. She had spent her life in the company of the strange and stricken, and Flanagan's runners came as no surprise to her. Close by, Fritz, the talking mule, was silently munching grass.

"Hi," said Dixie.

Fritz looked up, bared his teeth, and returned to his meal. It was evidently not talking time.

Just beyond Fritz's paddock an elderly man in white tights was juggling with five golden Indian clubs, while behind him two young men trembled delicately in a hand-to-hand balance. To their right a great bull of a man, dressed as a Roman gladiator, grunted as he heaved aloft massive barbells.

A small, middle-aged man—the one who had spoken at Flanagan's press conference—passed her in the company of a lean, somber companion. They both had towels over their shoulders, and had obviously come from washing in the river. The elder man nodded cheerfully to her as they passed, but the younger runner gave no sign that he had noticed her.

She watched them both pass. The young man's body was bronzed and hard and looked as if it had been sculpted: hard defined shoulders, sharp horizontal slivers of muscle across his chest, the flesh of his ribs flickering like tiny fish. Dixie could not understand how a little old man like Doc Cole could possibly challenge such an athlete. And yet she knew from what she had read and heard that Cole was the most experienced runner in the race. She shook her head and made her way back to her trailer.

Carl Liebnitz sat on a camp chair in the press tent, engulfed in the clatter of typewriters.

"Great day," said Frank Pollard, tapping out his report on two fingers at the desk beside him.

"Sure," growled Liebnitz. "Stupendous." In truth, he did not know quite how to respond to what he had seen.

True, he had seen the Dorando Marathon at the 1908 London Olympics and had endured the stupefying boredom of the first dance marathons of the twenties. But the former had been controlled within the limits of a sports stadium and the latter had been a harmless, if sickly, flower of the period. But the human debris now scattered on the edge of the Mojave as a result of Flanagan's call to arms—that was a human tragedy of a different dimension.

Most of the people littering the ground outside the press tent were not athletes. Liebnitz had seen their like at strikes, soup kitchens and Salvation Army shelters all over the nation. They had no more chance of making it on foot to New York than he had. No, the Trans-America looked to him like just another sad, seamy story of the twenties, to be filed away with pole-sitting, marathon dancing and all the other sports mutations of the period.

"Great day," Pollard growled again, engaging a fresh sheet of paper on his machine. "Bring on Madame La Zonga and the talking mule."

AMERICANA DATELINE FLANAGANVILLE MARCH 21, 1931

Charles C. Flanagan's two-thousand-man caravan is now making its broken way toward San Bernardino.

A crowded Coliseum, after a couple of hours of carnival high-jinks, saw Douglas Fairbanks, the increasingly portly spring-heeled jack of the silver screen, fire the Winchester that set Flanagan's hordes surging toward New York. Sadly there were falls, sprained ankles and bruises for many competitors even before the Coliseum exit was reached, as hundreds of Trans-Americans, clearly misjudging the distance between Los Angeles and New York by an odd three thousand miles, bolted from the stadium. On and over the bodies of their prostrate comrades they surged; on, ever on, toward their distant goal.

As early as ten miles out, around San Gabriel, the sidewalks were littered with the flotsam of Mr. Flanagan's enterprise. Your correspondent counted at least forty women sitting distraught by the road by the time the press bus had reached Montebello, coughing as they inhaled the exhaust fumes of passing cars. Others staggered on for another six miles or so toward Pomona before collapsing into Mr. Flanagan's following trucks. Close on two hundred failed to complete the first stage to Pomona Hill, just outside Pomona, where a camp, immediately dubbed "Flanaganville" by its weary residents, has been set up.

There was little in the way of competition over the first stage. The Scots runner Hugh McPhail trotted in first, with the English aristocrat Lord Thurleigh, followed by Alexander Doc Cole, the fifty-four-year-old former fairground huckster, and the Pennsylvanian Michael Morgan, in that order. Close behind them came the German and All-American teams.

Flanaganville more closely resembles a Gettysburg casualty station than the finish of a footrace, with its medical tents choked with injured competitors. It remains to be seen if Mr. Flanagan's Trans-America footrace is a genuine athletics competition or merely another mad little, sad little sports saga of our times. So far, the only person in the money is Mr. Flanagan, who is $40,000 the richer from the failure of two-hundred-odd competitors to finish the course.

—CARL C. LIEBNITZ—

Pomona Hill (29 miles)

			Hrs.	Mins.	Secs.
1 = { H. McPhail P. Thurleigh	(Great Britain)		4	43	12
3 = { A. Cole M. Morgan	(USA)		4	46	50
5 = Williams' All-Americans (Brix, Hall, Capaldi, Flynn)	(USA)		4	48	10
9 = Hitler Youth Team (Muller, Stock, Woellke, Stratt- mann)	(Germany)		4	49	30
13 = J. Martinez	(Mexico)		4	51	35
14 = P. Eskola	(Finland)		4	51	55
15 = J. Bouin	(France)		4	51	56
16 = { P. Dasriaux P. O'Grady	(France) (Ireland)		4	52	10
18 = C. Charles	(Australia)		4	52	30
19 = K. Lutz	(USA)		4	54	10
20 = L. Svoboda	(Austria)		4	54	20
21 = C. Montes	(Cuba)		4	55	40
22 = P. Maffei	(Italy)		5	06	05
23 = R. Desruelles	(Belgium)		5	07	01
24 = P. Coghlan	(New Zealand)		5	08	40
25 = J. Schmidt	(Poland)		5	09	01

1st Lady: (729) K. Sheridan (USA)   6   41   08
Number of finishers: 1821
Average speed (leader): 9 mins. 46 secs. per mile

6

THE GIRL
FROM MINSKY'S

From the window of his trailer, Flanagan had watched the finish with mixed feelings. True, every tramp out of the race made him two hundred dollars richer, but it was essential that none of his "stars" be injured, and also vital that he keep his numbers reasonably high. He was delighted to see Cole and Morgan trot in together, and to see Lord Thurleigh and Hugh McPhail come in ahead of the Williams' All-Americans and the German team. Thurleigh was both a pleasure and a problem: a pleasure, because Thurleigh's presence gave the race unique news value, and a problem because Flanagan had no real idea how to deal with an English lord. For days he had practiced what he imagined to be an English accent, based on a Noel Coward play which he had seen on Broadway and on a slight knowledge of the New England bourgeoisie. But it was no use. Flanagan was New York Irish through and through.

He also had no notion how to address Thurleigh. "Your highness" or "your worship" sounded too formal. He settled for "your lordship," though he hoped he would not have to say it too often.

The question of Thurleigh's feeding and accommodation was more complex. Thurleigh had asked for separate feeding and accommodation arrangements to be made for him, and indeed had offered to provide his own trailer. Flanagan had agreed to Thurleigh's having separate food; diet was, after all, a personal matter. He had, however, refused to allow Thurleigh separate living quarters, for if the Englishman had a trailer to himself so would dozens of other sponsored athletes, and the Trans-America would soon begin to resemble a vast, sluggish wagon train, moving at the speed of the slowest vehicle.

He turned away from the window. His own trailer had been sumptuously furnished by the Ford Corporation and contained bath and shower, radio and telephone communication systems, and a superb Bechstein piano, which Flanagan could not play. In a corner, on the right of the refrigerator, stood three large black tin drums marked "molasses." These contained the nine gallons of bootleg whiskey which would sustain Flanagan and Willard Clay through the long miles ahead. It had come by fishing boat from Cuba, via Hennessey's warehouse, New York, to join the millions of gallons of bootleg booze in which the country had been illicitly wallowing since 1921. The Cuban stuff was the real McCoy, vastly superior to the Japanese brew, Queen James Scotch Whiskey, which they had been uneasily drinking in Los Angeles.

Willard Clay was typing furiously. He stopped and looked up at his employer.

"It's a great start," he said. "Paramount will have the finished film to use by the time we reach Vegas. Doc Cole, that Scots guy McPhail, Lord Thurleigh, Eskola the Finn, the little Mex Martinez, the Kraut team, the All-Americans—they all finished well up. And that little doll, Sheridan, was a real bonus . . ."

"Doll?" asked Flanagan.

Willard ran his finger down the list of finishers. "Kate Sheridan from New York. She came in at seven hundred and twenty-nine, fresh as paint and pretty as a picture."

"Pretty?" asked Flanagan. "Real good-looking?"

"See for yourself," said Willard, pointing out of the trailer window. A barefoot brunette was coming out of the press tent accompanied by Pollard and Kowalski.

Flanagan eyed the girl carefully. Like most athletic women, she had small breasts, but the nipples showed up sharp and clear beneath her shirt. The girl's main physical quality lay in her lean-hipped athleticism, thighs long, toned and muscular, ankles neat and well shaped. However, these qualities alone did not add up to Kate Sheridan. The runner exuded a vital, glowing sexuality that derived from a complete certainty of who and what she was. Flanagan turned to face Willard.

"Ask Miss Sheridan to come and see me," he ordered.

He watched Kate Sheridan for a few more moments as she stood chatting to a journalist just outside his trailer. She smiled as Willard approached her, and Flanagan noted that it was a warm, womanly smile. He had seen a few female athletes in his time, most of them hairy, thick-thighed viragos. But Sheridan was a woman all right—perhaps even a star? Together she and Willard walked toward the trailer.

When Kate Sheridan entered, Flanagan beckoned Willard to leave, but his deputy stayed by the door, fascinated.

"Sit down, Miss . . ?" said Flanagan.

"Sheridan," said Kate. "Kate Sheridan."

"Care for some refreshment?"

Kate nodded and looked around her at the lush furnishings. Finally she sank into a soft armchair. Flanagan passed her a glass of lemonade.

"What do you think?" he asked, turning toward the back of the trailer. "Classy, eh?"

The girl looked around her and nodded. Flanagan flushed as he caught sight of her tiny feet and her neatly painted toenails, wondering how such perfect feet had survived the first stage. She trapped his glance.

"Your feet . . ." said Flanagan.

"They're fine," said the girl, enjoying his embarrassment. "I've trained for a year for this race. They can take it."

"Were you a track and field athlete at college?"

"No," said Kate. "Never even went to college. Never ran track either. That's for serious female athletes." She returned to her lemonade.

"Then—then how come you're here?"

"Simple: money. This time last year I was in burlesque at Minsky's. Three shows a night, twenty bucks a week. Then I read about the Trans-America, and about you putting up two hundred and fifty thousand dollars for staying on my feet for three months—"

"But only if you get in the frame," interrupted Flanagan.

"Yes. Only if I win," said Kate, crossing her legs. "At first I couldn't run the length of the block, but after a month's practice I could run eight miles without stopping. Not fast, mind you, but then the Trans-America isn't a dash either. At the end of nine months I could cover over fifteen miles in two hours. So here's the way I see it. No man runs much more than fifteen miles in training or more than twenty-six miles in competition, so why shouldn't I have a chance?"

"But . . ." Flanagan began.

"But what?" asked Kate. "But I'm only a girl. That's what you're really trying to say, Mr. Flanagan, isn't it? Well, let me put you straight, sir. I've taken a little trouble to set myself up for this race. I've been to the library and I've checked all the anatomy books and there's no physical reason why a woman shouldn't be as good as most men over three thousand miles. Mr. Flanagan, when it comes to taking pain we women have had plenty of practice."

"No offense meant, Miss Sheridan," interjected Willard. "It's just that we ain't ever heard of no lady running in long-distance races."

"Well, you sure got one now," said Kate, standing up and turning to the door. "Anything more, Mr. Flanagan?" Flanagan shook his head. Kate winked at Willard and went out.

Flanagan flopped back in his red-velvet rocking chair, and reached to his desk for a cigar.

"What the hell do you make of that?" he asked, spitting the plug into the wastebasket.

"I'll tell you what I think," replied Willard. "I think we got a star, boss. If she can just stay on her feet."

"We got to make *sure* she stays on her feet, Willard," said Flanagan, lighting his Havana. "She's money in the bank, man, money in the bank: so is any good-looking broad. Just make sure you take real good care of those ladies."

"Okay, boss," said Willard. "Back to business. The marshals have completed the first day's count."

"How many finishers?"

Willard sucked on his pencil. "At the last count, one thousand eight hundred and twenty-one," he said. "One hundred and eighty-one picked up in the trucks or disqualified, thirty still out there somewhere."

"Jesus!" said Flanagan, looking out of the window into the gathering gloom.

"It might not be so bad," said Willard. "They might have flunked out way back in L.A. Hell, some guys gave up after about three miles. Our first pickup trucks lay five miles out from the Coliseum, so anyone dropping out before that . . ." He shook his head.

"Jesus," said Flanagan again, chewing on his cigar.

"But what about those guys, the ones who can't go on?" asked Willard.

"How do you mean?"

"I mean, what do we do with them? How do they get back?"

"How the hell do I know?" exploded Flanagan, throwing out his arms. "They all knew the rules when they started out. Sink or swim, kill or be killed, that's what it's all about. If you drop out of a track meet you don't expect the referee to see you back home."

"But this ain't no track meet," Willard persisted. "Some of these people are hurt bad. Some are back with the medics, sick as dogs."

"No!" said Flanagan. "I don't want to hear about it. They got here, they can find their way back, and there's an end of it."

There was a knock at the trailer door. Willard opened it. One of the runners, a balding man in late middle age, timidly entered.

Flanagan swore under his breath.

The man's feet were a mess, one toenail ripped off and another dangling. He had obviously fallen more than once, for both elbows and chest were badly grazed. His right temple bled and his right cheek looked as if it had been rubbed with sandpaper. He looked more like a losing prizefighter than a runner.

"My name's McCoy," he said. "County Limerick. The guys who were picked up in the trucks, they've asked me to speak for them."

"Yes, Mr. McCoy," said Flanagan quietly.

"Some of the boys back in the tent are in a pretty bad way. We was wondering how we'd get back to Los Angeles."

"Where do you hail from, Mr. McCoy?" said Flanagan, beckoning the uncertain athlete to a seat and uncorking a bottle of whiskey with his teeth.

"You probably never heard of it, Mr. Flanagan," said McCoy. "A little place name of Kilmoy, County Limerick."

"Yes," said Flanagan. "I've heard of it." He handed the Irishman a glass of whiskey. "And how did you get all the way out here to Los Angeles?"

McCoy's face relaxed and he gulped down the whiskey, its rawness bringing tears to his eyes.

He sniffed. "Back in March last year. The Limerick *Star* set up a trial race over fifteen miles." He sniffed again and laid down his glass. "The winner got the trip out here to the Trans-America."

Flanagan slowly poured out two further glasses of whiskey and drew one to his lips.

"So you traveled out all this way, and now it's all over for you in the first day?"

McCoy nodded, picking up his glass again and looking down into its contents, before swallowing the remainder. "Still," he said, "we didn't have much back in Kilmoy. At least I got to see California. Man, in this life you've got to take a chance, haven't you?"

"Yes, Mr. McCoy," said Flanagan. "You've got to take a chance."

Flanagan sipped his own drink slowly. "How many people do you reckon need transportation back to Los Angeles?"

McCoy shook his head. "Difficult to say, Mr. Flanagan. Must be over a hundred. The rest have had friends and relatives pick them up and take them back."

Flanagan nodded, detaching a loose flake of cigar from his tongue.

"Let me ask you one final question, Mr. McCoy," he said, looking the Irishman straight in the eye. "Coming all this way, then out of the race on the first day—was it all worth it?"

"Definitely," said McCoy, standing up as he drained the last of his drink. "If I had my chance, I'd do it again, only better." Flanagan smiled and looked at Willard, who looked back blankly.

"The trucks will take you back to L.A. in the morning," said Flanagan. "Anyone requiring hospital treatment will be treated for the first seven days entirely at my expense. Does that answer your question?"

McCoy finally lost his shyness and smiled. "I told the boys you wouldn't let us down, Mr. Flanagan."

"But . . ." said Willard. "You just said—"

"Willard," said Flanagan. "You just *heard* what I said. See to it!"

* * *

Next morning the first casualties of the Trans-America were taken by truck back to Los Angeles, while the remaining runners made their way past San Bernardino in two twenty-four-mile stages, out on to the edge of the Mojave Desert, leaving one hundred and ten competitors to be returned to Los Angeles. The Trans-America was shedding fat.

7:30 A.M., March 24, 1931. One hundred and twenty-six miles on; the town that Flanagan had built was being dismantled for the third time.

The athletes' tents had come down at seven o'clock and only the massive refreshment tent still stood erect. The last of the trucks taking the sick and disabled back to Los Angeles was disappearing over the brow of the hill. Madame La Zonga and her colleagues had left early and were now ten miles up the road, nearing the Mojave, moving toward Barstow. The runners were either finishing breakfast, washing at the river or chatting in small groups.

The German team stood away from the others in a tight semicircle, listening to their coach, Volkner.

A couple of hundred yards away the Williams' All-Americans sat on an upturned log. Their irate coach's admonitions could be heard all the way across the flat, cactus-stubbled field.

At the river a number of runners, clad only in their underpants, were washing themselves down.

"Hell," said Doc, pulling open the top of his pants and pouring water down onto his genitals. "No profit in being Caspar Milquetoast here."

Kate Sheridan came over by Doc's group and McPhail and Morgan made desperate attempts to retreat across the pebbled brook to their shirts. Doc stood his ground, holding open his shorts and continuing to splash water down between his legs.

"Don't fret on my account," said Kate, hands on hips. "You boys aren't going to give me any big surprises." Her eyes settled for a moment on Morgan, his body wet and shining in the weak morning sun.

"My name's Doc Cole," said Doc, offering his hand. He gestured toward the others. "That's Hugh McPhail, a Scotsman. The little un's Juan Martinez—he's Mexican. The gabby one," he wryly noted her interest in Morgan, "he's called Morgan."

The girl nodded, then introduced herself.

"You the last lady in the race?" asked Doc.

"No. Some came in after me last night. I don't know if they'll stay with it, though."

"Sponsored?"

"Nope. New York City backed two men but wouldn't put a cent on a woman. The pair of them finished up in the truck yesterday, so maybe I got the last laugh."

"How far've you ever run at one time?" Doc persisted, drying his chest vigorously with a rough towel.

"Fifteen miles."

"We reckon two and a half times your training distance, then it's Goodnight Vienna," said Doc.

"How do you mean?" asked Hugh, finally stepping out of the brook and pulling his towel from the top of a yucca tree.

"It's just a rule-of-thumb guide we use in marathon running," said Doc. "If your normal training mileage is, say, twelve miles, then you should just be able to handle a twenty-six-mile marathon. It'll be tough over the last six miles, but you should make it if you take it steady. If you've run fifteen miles regularly, then you might be able to handle thirty miles, with an outside range of forty-five miles. Whether or not you can do it day in, day out for three months—well, that's another ball game."

"Are any of you really sure of that?" asked Kate, glancing from Doc to the others.

"A good question," said Doc, rubbing the back of his neck. "And the answer is 'no'—sure as heck we ain't. That's what makes it all so interesting. What do you think, Juan?"

The little Mexican spread out both hands and showed his white teeth in a childlike smile. "You right, Mr. Doc. I sure never run no fifty miles in a day, not six days a week."

"Well, that's reassuring," said Kate, feeling suddenly embarrassed. The men found it difficult to avoid staring at her, a slim feminine intruder in an all-male group of runners.

"Well," said Doc at last. "You certainly do have the legs for it." He was using the cloak of his age to put words to what the other men were feeling. Morgan and McPhail stood by uneasily, toweling themselves down.

"Yes," she said. "Six hours a day at Minsky's burlesque."

"You really danced at *Minsky's*?" asked Doc, as he accompanied her back toward the Trans-America center, the three other men following.

"If you can call it dancing," said Kate. "Running fifty miles a day can't be much worse."

"It can," said Doc quietly. "You can lay bets on it."

"You mean you don't think I can do it?" asked Kate sharply.

"Don't get me wrong, lady," said Doc, raising his hands to placate her. "You made nearly thirty miles in under seven hours on the first day. Ma'am, that's fancy running in my book. Every day completed in a race like this is some kind of victory. But, lady, it's early days yet. None of us knows who's going to see Madison Square Garden in June."

"Sorry I barked at you," said Kate, conscious of her quick temper.

"No offense taken," said Doc, smiling. "Looks as though we may travel together quite a piece. We all swim in the same water. May as well get to like each other."

They were now some yards ahead of Morgan and the others. Kate nodded back toward the Pennsylvanian.

"Where does that guy Morgan come from?" she asked, trying to appear indifferent.

Doc simply shrugged. "Don't rightly know," he said. "He can run some, though. Back at training camp the other guys called him the 'Iron Man.' Not an ounce of fat on him. Morgan's made for running. He'll take some beating."

"Not much of a talker, though, is he?" asked Kate.

"Not much," said Doc. "But then this ain't no debating competition. Still, we've got over ten weeks on the road together. One way or the other, we'll all get closer in the next three thousand miles."

Kate hoped so. She looked back and saw McPhail and Martinez in earnest conversation, with Morgan walking a few yards behind them. She wondered if these men felt as she did. They all looked so lean, so strong. For her even the first hundred and twenty miles had been tough, and now she faced the start of the fourth stage, on the fringe of over two hundred miles of desert: endless stretches of sandy road, hills, cacti, Joshua trees and brown dust. Already she seemed to be among the last women in the race, for she could not see many of the whimpering, broken ladies from her tent reappearing to take on another forty miles of punishment. Earlier that morning she had looked beyond the hill out into the desert. It was almost completely flat, stretching endlessly toward distant brown hills. She felt the same flutter in her stomach as she had that first night at Minsky's when she had danced, spangled and half naked, exposing herself to a thousand strangers. Kate bit her lip. She had beaten that. She could beat this.

Men were being slowly sucked toward the Trans-America center, drawn by Willard's amplified voice. Before long most of the eighteen-hundred-odd survivors had seated themselves on the rough broken ground in front of the loudspeakers.

"Can you all hear?" shouted Willard.

"Yeah, but I'm sure willing to move somewhere where I can't," shouted back a thin white-bearded man. There was scattered laughter.

Flanagan stood at a microphone beside Willard and in front of the Trans-America trailer, dressed in his favorite Tom Mix cowboy outfit.

"This is Charles C. Flanagan again. My congratulations to all of you for qualifying for the next stage." He paused and scanned the crowd. "May I offer my particular compliments to our leading lady competitor, Miss Kate Sheridan, from New York. Could you please stand up, Miss Sheridan?"

Kate Sheridan stood up and was greeted by scattered applause and wolf whistles.

Flanagan raised his hands for silence, and continued. "I'd like also to mention Miss Jane Connolly from Nebraska, Miss Kathy McGuire from Kansas City and Mrs. Patricia Paish from San Francisco, all of whom figure in the first-half-of-the-race finishers. Could you stand up, ladies?"

One by one the ladies rose to their feet, to be met with similar cheers, shouts and catcalls.

"And now to our youngest competitor," said Flanagan. "Seventeen-year-old Jim Pierce from San Bernardino High School, now in seven hundredth place. To my recollection, no high school boy has ever achieved such performances over these distances. So show yourself, Jim." A slim, blond youth shyly stood up to further cheers and clapping.

"And finally," said Flanagan, "to our oldest competitor all the way from Southampton, England, Mr. Charles C. Fox now in four hundred and first place. Sixty-six years old tomorrow." The white-bearded old man stood up, to be greeted with unreserved applause, and several of the more mature runners stood up in appreciation. The cheers lasted for over a minute.

"Okay, gentlemen, quiet down." Flanagan raised his hands. "Now to the main business. Today we have two separate stages of twenty miles. The Coca-Cola company has generously put up prizes of five hundred, three hundred, one hundred, and fifty dollars for the first stage; Ford Motors the same prizes for the second stage. Today we will have the first 'cut.' Any competitor running outside eight hours total time for the complete forty miles is out of the race. That means an average speed of about twelve-minute miles. Any questions?"

"If you please, Mr. Flanagan," said Volkner, the German trainer, getting to his feet. "You have rests between the two stages?"

"Yes, four hours, so that we miss the noon sun."

"And what of water and feeding points?"

"Ten per stage."

A gray-bearded Texan, McGraw, was next to his feet. "We camping out again?" he asked.

"Yes," said Flanagan.

"Well, kin I have another blanket?"

For the first time Flanagan was lost for words, and he turned away from the microphone to Willard, smiling. Regaining his composure, he turned back to his laughing audience. "My assistant, Mr. Clay, will deal with your request, Mr. McGraw," he said. "I appreciate you Texans have mighty thin skins."

There was a cluster of questions relating to feeding and medical matters and the meeting broke up fifteen minutes later.

Morgan walked away from the crowd out to the fringe of the camp and sat down on a rock. Five hundred dollars: it *had* to be his.

After only one twenty-mile stint he could send back six months' money to his son Michael in Elmira. Back there lay the focus of his life, gurgling happily in his crib, oblivious of his father three thousand miles away in the Mojave Desert . . .

7

MORGAN'S STORY

The winter of 1929 in Bethel had been a hard time. For three months the sullen black mills had been still, the roaring furnaces silent. The great dark town had been gripped with frost, powdered with black snow, its grimy streets as sullen as the striking steelworkers who lived there.

It had been unanimous. Italians, Scots, Poles, Irishmen: all had been part of the forest of arms that had stabbed the winter air when Morgan had finally put the strike to the vote. They had asked for just five cents more an hour, yet they had been refused outright. Morgan had been there at the negotiations, among the plump, soft-handed men who had never in their lives sweated behind a shovel feeding greedy, belching furnaces.

He had repeated his arguments about sick pay, about insurance, about the injuries suffered in the mills, the appalling infant mortality in the town; but it was no use. These men were not concerned. They listened, but Morgan felt his helplessness even as he spoke. The only answer had been to strike.

Morgan had planned the men's protest like a battle campaign. Food supplies had been bought months before and were stored in the Mission Hall. A strike fund had been set up in good time and families with special needs had been satisfied. A communications system of telephones and relays of children kept three thousand families in constant touch.

But they had not planned for such a fierce winter, and the owners knew it. By January many children had become sick; by February six of them had died, and by March mothers who had denied themselves food were also beginning to fade.

Morgan watched his men wither, first in their muscles, finally in their minds. Daily he would look in the mirror and see a physique fashioned by years of hard work losing not fat but solid tissue. His body was consuming itself, drawing upon its last reserves, and he could feel his own resolve weaken. After all, even without the five cents extra pay they had *lived*: perhaps not well, but it had been a life.

Ruth, his wife, though in her early months of pregnancy, had stood with him. The dark days bound them more closely together than all the happy times they had known. When the owners' strikebreakers—a hundred men drafted in from the slums of New York's East Side—had finally attacked the Mission she had been there, as had all the women. The men had stood four deep in the frozen, corrugated mud with nothing but fists and fence posts. Facing them, a hundred yards away, in front of the buses which had brought them, stood the owners' men. Each was armed with a nightstick.

The battle had been brief and bloody. The first rush on the union lines left twenty thugs stranded on the iron ground between the strikers and the buses. But the union line had been broken, and many of the steelworkers lay unconscious or groaning on the hard ground.

Morgan looked around him and sucked his bloody knuckles. Up the road the owners' men had regrouped and had taken three heavy wooden boxes from the trucks. It was impossible at first to see what was in them, but Morgan felt a sickness in the pit of his stomach. This was going to be no stand-up fight to Marquis of Queensberry rules.

A massive Scot, Cameron, his red beard streaked with blood, came up behind him. "Man, we fair bloodied their noses."

The words had scarcely left his lips when he fell back, his right shoulder shattered by a rifle bullet. The women screamed, begging their men to retreat. At a distance of one hundred yards, a line of the thugs knelt and began to fire a second volley. Morgan's men started to drop around him, and the strikers' ordered ranks were pocked by broken, wounded men.

He shouted his men back, away from the line of fire, and he and the survivors dragged their wounded away across the frozen ground, out of the path of the oncoming owners' men.

The steelworkers wept, the tears freezing on their ridged, stubbled faces, as the thugs strode on past them on to the Mission Hall. It took them only a matter of minutes to burn it down, destroying the remainder of the strikers' food supplies.

The strike was over, and Morgan knew it. The rest of the strike fund was soon wiped out by hospital bills, and in two weeks the walkout was over and the men back at work—at five cents an hour less than their previous rate.

The owners had the muscle, and even without it they could always afford to wait. For them, time meant loss of money, but no hardship, while for the steelworkers it meant hunger and loss of life. It had all been for nothing.

No, Ruth had said. It is never for nothing. Even when you are beaten. Every time you fight you become stronger, even in defeat. But there must surely be better ways.

Naturally, there was no work for Morgan now at the mill. Every day he had stood hands in jacket pockets at the black iron gates and every day been turned away.

Then, one winter morning, as he turned away from the gates he felt a hand on his shoulder. It belonged to a small, foxy-faced man in an expensive fur coat.

"Sharpe," he introduced himself, offering Morgan a gloved hand, which Morgan reluctantly accepted. "Saw you in a few tight spots, my friend. You're real quick. I like the way you handle yourself."

Sharpe saw that Morgan did not understand. "Cut a long story short, how would you like to earn some real money—folding money?"

"What do I have to do?" said Morgan suspiciously.

"Hit—like you did in that line couple of weeks back."

"Keep talking," said Morgan, putting both hands in the pockets of his jacket. They started to walk away from the gates, their breath steaming around them in the sharp, still air.

"Fights," explained the smaller man, flipping a cigarette into his mouth. "Bareknuckle fights. Anything goes, except feet."

Morgan shook his head. "I've never fought to hurt," he said. "Just for what we had coming to us."

"What you get for it?" said Sharpe, lighting his cigarette. "Your buddies—you fought for them. Now they got work while you freeze your butt off. So what you got now, union man?"

"Keep talking," said Morgan again, without animosity.

"McGrath's warehouse, Salem. We have three fights a night, big money in side bets. You come up good, we move around the state circuit. Fancy pickings."

"How much?"

"Ten bucks, win or lose. A hundred bucks a win. Either way it's money in the bank." Sharpe blew smoke into the icy air.

"But what makes you think I can do it?" asked Morgan, uncertainly.

"I've *seen* you," said Sharpe, pressing his arm. "You hit crisp, you hit neat. This ain't no Golden Gloves, mind."

"How do I start?"

"First we see Clancy," said the little man. "Back at Milligan's speakeasy."

Morgan knew Milligan's well, but nothing of Clancy.

"This Clancy—where does he figure?"

"Clancy makes fighters," said Sharpe in explanation. "Used to work legit at Stillman's in New York. If he likes you, you got it made."

They walked slowly through the morning mist to Milligan's.

Eamonn Clancy hit the seven ball into the middle pocket, put down his cue, and removed a cigarette from his mouth. Like Sharpe, he was a short and squat man, but with a flat, fleshy boxer's nose.

"Gimme your hands," he said.

He pressed Morgan's hands in his and turned them around, looking closely at each knuckle in turn as if they were pieces of fine china. The knuckles were flat, the hands hard and firm.

"Make a fist," he said. He looked up quickly at Morgan. "Ever bust these on some Polack's head?"

"No," said Morgan sharply.

Clancy turned away and picked up his cue. "No bones sticking out—okay, so his hands are made for hitting. But does he have with his right and closed in for the kill. But Morgan's right now came over like a whip to land plumb on Fogarty's nose. There was a small cracking noise and Fogarty went down spurting blood and groaning, his chin furrowing the dirt floor. He slowly raised himself on one knee and then collapsed. The fight was over. Clancy threw a ten-dollar bill to the ground beside the fallen streetfighter and moved toward the door.

"Thanks, champ," he said. "I'll buzz you when I got me another likely boy." He put a thick jersey over Morgan's shoulders and dabbed his charge's nose and mouth with a towel. They walked back together through the snow and mud to the car. Once in the Ford, Clancy put the car into gear and looked ahead at the glassy frozen road. "Sharpe told me you could hit. And you proved you could dig deep running out in the hills. But the big yes/no is always what happens when you *get* hit. That's where Fogarty always comes in."

He moved into high gear, then looked to his side. "You see, this is the way it usually pans out. Nine outa ten guys go back when they get hit. It shocks the hell outa them when they get sight of their own blood. So they wanta get the hell out. Don't get me wrong: they ain't cowards. No guy who works twelve hours a day in mills or down a mine is yellow. It's just they ain't fighters, that's all. You are. How do I know? Item one, you came up off the floor. Item two, you came up fighting. Item three, you came up thinking. And item four, you can hit."

He took his right hand from the wheel and put it around Morgan's shoulders. "Let that mouth heal up, Morgan. Two weeks from now, next stop Salem warehouse."

They stayed a final week at the cabin in the mountains to allow Morgan's mouth to heal. It was only then that Clancy started to open up, to deal with the real meat of streetfighting. This related directly to the game of combat chess which would enable Morgan to survive. Clancy drew upon fighting lore that had been known since the eighteenth century, when the Englishman Jack Broughton had created the first rules of prizefighting. Morgan absorbed every word of Clancy's advice and committed it to memory, and the week in the lonely cabin passed quickly. Soon it was time to travel back to Bethel, to prepare for his first fight.

Starr's warehouse, Clairton, had not been used for years. Even the rats, which had fed on the rotted fruit that had been stored there, had long since scuttled off to other feeding places. As Morgan looked around him he shivered. The warehouse was vast, still and cold. In the darkness, in the center of its concrete floor under a pool of light, was a dense square of men, the mist from their breath hanging in a cloud above them as they shouted odds at each other.

In the corner opposite Morgan, stripped to the waist, his back to him, hands on the shoulders of his handlers, was Morgan's first opponent. He wore black shorts over a pair of black woolen training tights. As his opponent turned to face him Morgan saw that he had a tough, flat-nosed face similar to Fogarty's. He was glad. Now there would be no room for pity. The man's white muscular body steamed in the chill, dank air of the warehouse. He pressed his fists together as if sharpening them for battle, turned and sank down on his stool. Above him, his handlers stroked and kneaded his neck and pectorals and whispered advice from the corners of their mouths.

The referee, dressed in fur cap, gloves and thick plaid jacket, bellowed for silence, his voice echoing in the high steel rafters. The babble stilled, to be replaced by an expectant hush.

The referee turned toward Morgan's opponent. "McGuin, Chicago, versus . . ." He turned to Morgan. ". . . Chuck Petrack, the Bronx." It was the first time that Morgan had heard his ring-name spoken in public. It helped distance him from what he was about to do.

He looked around a further time at the taut, expectant faces in the crowd. He had never before seen such expressions. True, these men had come to bet, but their real desire was to see strong men hit, punished, better men than themselves broken and humiliated.

He was now deep in the underworld of sport, light years from the Olympics, distanced by law even from the seamy but legal world of professional boxing.

Clancy massaged the muscles at the top of Morgan's neck as he sat on his stool.

"Easy," said Clancy. "Easy."

Morgan looked across at his opponent. He felt a still coldness come over him.

There was no gong, but someone in a neutral corner blew a whistle. Morgan got to his feet and came out slow, crouching, as did McGuin. For fully a minute they circled each other, only the sound of their breathing breaking the stillness.

One hit settled it. As with Fogarty, Morgan made a feint with his left, then hit his man on the side of the nose with his right. McGuin went down like a stone and lay for a moment, blood flowing from his nose on to the concrete floor. Like Fogarty before him, he raised himself painfully on both arms, then sank to the cold warehouse floor. It was all over.

A hush fell upon the crowd. Morgan turned to Clancy, taking his dressing gown from him.

"Let's get out of here," he said, trembling.

He felt sick as he was driven home, a hundred dollars burning in his pocket. When he reached his own house he spread the money he had earned on the table in front of Ruth. "There you are, honey," he said.

He saw her amazement.

"Want to know how I got it?" He lifted his right fist and spat on it, then hammered it on the table.

"Hitting a guy," he said, the tears trickling down his face. "Hitting some poor bum. That's how I earned it. That's how I aim to keep you and the baby from now on."

When he had finished his story of the evening, and what had led up to it, Ruth lifted his head with her hands and looked into his eyes. "Morg," she said, "you're the bravest man I ever knew. If streetfighting's what you got to do, then do it. But do it well."

He did. Under the name of Petrack, the Bronx Bomber, he had six more fights at Salem warehouse. Then, two months later, it was time to move on to the main East Coast circuit, a streetfighting network spanning the industrial centers of the area.

The world of streetfighting was a subterranean one of empty warehouses, ancient armories and midnight railyards. Of blood and darkness.

Sometimes the fights went longer, but not once did Morgan lose. Clancy helped him develop tactics, taught him how to hit to the body. "Kill the stomach and the head will die," he explained. And as Morgan won so the greenbacks poured in from the ringside.

During the year that followed the bond between Morgan and Clancy became strong, though both men knew it would not survive for a moment in the world outside. It was a bond created by mutual respect for each other's skill and knowledge. Clancy's eyes could pierce the smoke of the tiny cockpits in which the battles were fought, picking out that single flaw in an opponent which might be the difference between success and failure. Morgan's task was to translate these instincts and insights into explosive action, to live violently through Clancy's eyes.

But while as a team they prospered, Clancy sensed that Morgan had no real love of streetfighting.

"So it ain't Madison Square Garden," he would say. "But then we ain't beating up any old ladies and we don't throw no fights, so who loses? A few guys get bust noses—ribs even—but they could do a lot worse. Say an accident at the mill or in a rock fall down the mines. So who loses?"

Morgan would not answer. He could never grow to love what he did, but—he felt himself echo Ruth's phrase—it was better to do it well than badly. As Clancy would say, "Everyone wants to win, or says they do. But what it's all about is not wanting to *lose*."

Then came the night when his man lay still and had to be carried from the ringside. Morgan was dragged away, looking over his right shoulder at the fallen fighter as Clancy hustled him out of the warehouse and into the Ford. A week later, Morgan learned that his opponent had died. He drifted about the Eastern Seaboard, aching and silent, occasionally sneaking back to Bethel to see Ruth and his son. He took on any work he could, but he knew that his days of streetfighting were over.

He was in New York, working on the docks, when news came of Ruth's death. She had died over a week before, but the letter had taken six days to reach him. He had never really thought of dying, though always at the back of his mind had been a dim, childlike idea that he and Ruth would walk off toward death hand in hand.

He could stay in Bethel only for a day, after four hours by train from New York. To have stayed any longer might have been dangerous. He stood in front of the grave, while down in the town the mill whistles blared to signal the end of a day's work. The town had killed her. The mill had killed her. In a way, in his dogged determination to fight on, he too had been an accomplice. And yet he knew that, were she alive, she would do it again, with him and all the other losers. All he had ever won had been with his body. The day he had left New York he had heard of a

"Then run with old Charles Fox. Greatest pro in the world up to the war. He'll run inside four hours for this stage. Stay with him as long as you can, and you'll make it through. And, remember, keep low—and drink at all the water points."

Before she could answer Doc tipped his cap and started to thread his way up through the field. He was not going to race hard, but he still wanted to be in the first twenty finishers, to keep his aggregate time close to the leaders.

It was like the League of Nations. He passed a trio of Chinese, trotting easily in their strange-looking shoes, the same men to whom he had sold some Chickamauga remedy back at the hotel. The Frenchman, Bouin, was running with the Finnish Olympian, Eskola, and the two chatted to each other in German. Both men were fine runners, with many miles behind them. They would have to be watched.

The three remaining Germans ran as if on parade, moving as one, but why had Muller gone so far ahead? True, the German lacked experience, but he was undoubtedly running to orders. Perhaps the Germans had trained a new breed of runners, men capable of running better than nine-minute miles over such distances . . . ?

A couple of hundred yards later, at the ten-mile mark, Doc came abreast of the All-American team, now in about fiftieth position. They were running at a good even pace so he stayed with them, drinking on the run at the second water point, twelve miles out from the start. He checked his watch: one hour forty-eight minutes. About right.

Two miles behind Doc Cole, Kate Sheridan now ran with Charles Fox. The old man said nothing, but shuffled along on mottled, varicosed legs at a steady five miles an hour. Twenty years before no one in the field could have lasted over such distances with Fox. He had been the first professional athlete to run twelve miles in the hour, to cover thirty miles in three hours, to break twelve hours for a hundred miles; but the Trans-America had come too late.

Now, at the age of sixty-six, he was reduced to running alongside a slip of a girl.

Kate ran oblivious to the old man's feelings, her mind reverting to her days at Minsky's. No one who watched the smiling, spangled girls nightly kicking in military precision could possibly have imagined the fatigue involved in six shows daily. The ache never really left her legs; but she had learned to tolerate it, accepting it as part of the price that had to be paid. In the Trans-America it was different. Hour upon hour of running, no music to drive her on, none of the challenge of new steps to be learned and none of the occasional adrenaline of an excited audience. Simply mile upon mile of desert, with hundreds of lean, seemingly inexhaustible men stretching out in front of her and driving her from behind. It was a world as far from vaudeville as it was possible to imagine.

Doc had been right, she thought, as she picked up water at the eight-mile point, in thirty-three minutes past the hour. She was going well; it was coming easily. But she could no longer see the leaders, now well over two miles away.

From the very first mile it had felt fast to Morgan. He had followed Muller on to the hard, bumpy road, out on to the fringe of the desert, but the young German would not let up. He covered the first three miles in twenty-four and a half minutes, the first six in just under fifty-two minutes; he did not stop at the first water point but picked up a drink from his trainer a mile later. Yet Morgan stayed with him, pinning himself to the German's left shoulder.

In the leading press bus Pollard wiped the dusty back window with his handkerchief and shook his head. "Can't really figure out what's happening out there, Carl," he said, turning to Liebnitz. "That Kraut's running as if the race finishes up at Barstow, not at New York."

Liebnitz joined Pollard at the back of the bus, and peered through the window at the leading group of runners a couple of hundred yards behind.

"Beats me," he said. "Still, I can see why some of the others might want to stay in the frame on a money stage like this. Five hundred bucks in the hand now might look better than a hundred and fifty thousand in the bank in New York. These goddam stage prizes may kill off some good men before we even get to Vegas."

"I don't see Doc Cole out there," observed Pollard.

"No," said Liebnitz, returning to his seat. "Doc's a cagey old bird. He said he would run at around ten-minute miles back in

L.A., and it's my guess he'll stick to his plan. But he'll be keeping Muller and the others in sight, mark my words."

"What about the girl?"

"Sheridan?" said Liebnitz. "She's quite an impressive young lady, but it's my bet that she's going to find this a whole heap harder than high kicking at Minsky's. The next two stages should tell us if she's going to figure anywhere in the race. Flanagan's times are tough—I reckon he'll wipe out most of the walkers today, and the field should be down to closer to a thousand by sundown. I wouldn't bet my shirt on Miss Sheridan being among that thousand—or any other woman, for that matter."

"Pity," said Pollard, reaching for his glass of beer. "She makes a great story."

"Well," said Liebnitz, adjusting his glasses, "don't be too surprised if it turns out to be a short story."

They were now deep into the Mojave, into the dry, brown broken plain, the only watchers the twisted Joshua trees, standing like crippled spectators as the leaders wound their way into the desert, preceded by the press buses, the noisy, jug-shaped Maxwell House Coffee Pot and Flanagan's Trans-America bus.

Sixty years before, the desert had taken its toll of settlers struggling with wagons and handcarts through sun, rock and sand, constantly harassed by marauding Indians. Now the Indians had gone, but nature was enemy enough for the men daily battling with each other and with themselves.

Ten miles on, six men were still there with Muller, including Thurleigh, Martinez and Morgan. The bronzed young German had begun to sweat, but there was no break in his driving rhythm. At twelve miles he went clear, breaking away from the field.

In the Trans-America officials' bus, Charles Flanagan sucked on his cigar, realized it had gone out, and fumbled in his pocket for a box of matches. "How's it going out there?" he asked, turning to Willard, who was peering out of the window.

"Difficult to see, boss. Too much dust. But it looks to me like that young German, Muller, is burning up the road."

"Great," said Flanagan, "that'll keep Pollard and the press boys happy. A story a day makes the journalist's day, eh?"

"Yeah," Willard agreed. "But Muller's burned off some good runners today."

Flanagan drew on his cigar.

"Perhaps that's what he's there for," he said darkly.

Five hundred bucks or three hundred? It took Morgan only a moment to decide. He stretched out after Muller, dragging Martinez and Thurleigh with him. The leading four were soon locked together, all beginning to breathe heavily, a sign that intake no longer matched demand.

Morgan had been in this condition before, two years ago, in the Tuscarora mountains. It was no harder now, for this was flat land, but there was another twenty-mile stage ahead, and over three thousand miles ahead of that. Perhaps he had made the wrong decision; perhaps. But he had committed himself; there was no going back.

Beside him, on his right, Martinez ran like a willful child, his breathing clean and fast, his white, shining teeth bared. Thurleigh pushed back a lock of hair and pressed on, ignoring the runners to either side.

"Five miles to go," roared Willard from the loudspeaker atop the Trans-America bus, a couple of hundred yards ahead of the leaders.

Muller, sweating profusely, spurted again. Morgan followed with Martinez, but this time Peter Thurleigh hung back.

Morgan's breathing was coming hard and it was a comfort to him that he could hear both Muller and Martinez breathing in the same rhythm. He did not stop at the final water point. Nor did the others. Five hundred bucks. Five miles to go.

Doc had left the Americans at ten miles and, eight miles from the finish, had moved steadily through to sixteenth position. A mile later he was joined by McPhail and together they picked up the debris of Muller's first rush, broken runners who had dropped to a shambling trot or even a walk. Doc was running at just under seven miles an hour. He and McPhail could see Muller and the others about a mile up, and in front of them the buses. A mile was over nine minutes, thought Doc, wiping his wrist handkerchief across his brow. He would prefer to be closer at the finish, if it was not too much effort.

* * *

Almost two miles behind Doc and McPhail, Kate Sheridan had passed the ten-mile mark. She was still with Fox. They passed the fifteen-mile mark at comfortably inside three hours, but then Fox started slowly to move away. Kate realized it was not that the old man was accelerating but that she was beginning to slow up. She felt her legs becoming steadily heavier, her hips begin to sink. She was also on her own now, in a limbo between groups. Five miles to go; to be safe, she would have to run them inside sixty-five minutes . . .

Half a mile to go. The three leaders could see Flanagan's stage camp in the bright desert sun, set out on the hilly scrub beside the road. They ran almost in line, with Muller's brown shoulders only slightly ahead, the trio held in a strange, fragile balance. Then Morgan made his decision and broke the spell that bound them. He pressed ahead. Neither Martinez nor Muller responded. He was clear!

A hundred yards later he heard Muller's tortured breathing again at his right side. As the German pulled level with him he felt a momentary wave of despair. They ran clamped together, their breath rasping in their throats, every fiber at its limit, oblivious to the shouts of the waiting crowd and the tooting of the cars and buses at the lonely desert finish. But all either of them could hear was the scraping of their breath in the tunnels of their lungs. They ran low, legs bent and buckling, barely able to support their body weight.

Five hundred bucks. Five hundred bucks . . . Morgan felt as if his lungs had taken over his whole body. He was simply one heaving lung, sucking oxygen in great desperate gulps. Five hundred bucks, a hundred yards to go . . . He squeezed his body for one last effort, but it was not there. He could go no faster. Then, as Morgan felt himself wither and fade, the menacing brown shoulder on his left side disappeared, as Muller gave a deep sob and dropped back. Morgan passed the Trans-America bus a good ten yards up.

Half a mile behind, Doc and McPhail picked up a broken, exhausted Martinez, who summoned a tired smile, the sweat dripping from his face.

He pointed his finger to the side of his head as they passed. "They mad," he said. "They mad."

Flanagan had erected only six main tents for this intermediate camp, five as rest tents, in which a supply of blankets had been placed, upon which the runners could lie for four hours. The other was the medical tent, within which Dr. Falconer and his staff dealt with a diminishing number of casualties.

Doc watched the first hundred-odd finishers, noting each man's condition. The race was already hardening up, with a solid core of experienced distance runners dominating the first three hundred places. The All-Americans and the German team looked solid and well-organized and Eskola looked strong, as did the Frenchmen Dasriaux and Bouin. Doc was surprised how relaxed Thurleigh looked, despite his following Muller's mad rush. The Englishman had trotted in a couple of minutes behind Martinez, looking as if he had been out for little more than a stroll along the Thames.

The runners continued to stream past the finish toward the Maxwell House Coffee Pot, just one hundred yards beyond. After a while Doc walked down from the road to the camp area and entered the first rest tent. Martinez, Morgan and McPhail stood together, bodies streaming sweat, unrolling their blankets.

"Why?" said Doc, hands on hips. "*Why*?"

All three men knew what Doc was talking about.

Morgan held up five fingers, the sweat streaming down his face and neck. "Five hundred bucks, that's why."

Martinez sat peeling off his shoes. He shook his head. "Five hundred is a lot of money where I come from. We plant new crop with five hundred."

Doc looked down at Morgan, who had pulled his shirt over his shoulders.

"You need it that much?"

"Yes."

Doc shrugged. "You know your business best," he said, finding a space on the floor to the right of Martinez. "But there's one helluva long way still to run. A few more sprints like that could bust your balls."

For the first time Morgan's face cracked into a smile.

"What the hell do you care, Doc? We're competing, ain't we?"

Doc returned his smile. "Yes and no," he said. "I've been racing for about thirty-odd years now. Most races you see your men before the start of your race, then it's good-bye, Charlie, till next time. Sure, you get to know the guys you race against—you become friends—but this caper's a whole new world. Here what you're up against isn't each other, it's the desert, the hills, the cold, the wind, the sun, the snow. We're *all* up against them, kinda like a team. Even those Krauts, those crazy Chinamen, the whole nutty League of Nations out there. By the end of the next leg we'll have sorted out the jokers and we'll be down to the real runners. And every time one of those guys drops out you'll suffer a little. You can bank on it."

Morgan thought back to his own past. He knew what Doc meant. In the line at Bethel he had seen his friends fall around him; in the first fights he had felt pain every time he knocked down his man. Pain inside.

Hugh moved around and sat on Doc's left, so that the four men now formed a tight semicircle.

"Why do you think Muller hit it so hard?"

Doc shook his head and slowly unlaced his shoes. "I can't figure it out. He musta gone through the first eight miles in close to an hour. Crazy."

He dropped onto his back. "Still, no point in letting it bother us. Four hours. That means four hours' shuteye."

He unrolled his blanket and laid it on the floor. Then he took two rolled-up blankets, placed both at the bottom of his "bed," and put his feet on top of the bottom roll.

"The circulation," he explained. "Having my feet above my head means that the waste can get pumped back to the heart easier. Try it."

He leaned back on to his mat and within minutes was snoring loudly.

"You the only girl left?" asked Dixie. She was standing with Kate Sheridan outside her trailer on the edge of the camp.

"No girls passed me," said Kate, "but I think we got about ten left. Say, they only seem to have a tent for the men. Could I use your trailer to clean up?"

"Sure," said Dixie. "We've got showers. You want one?"

Kate nodded gratefully, peeled off her running shoes and climbed up the trailer steps.

"Three of us sleep here," said Dixie, following her. "Myself, and Mr. Flanagan's and Mr. Willard's secretaries; but I don't see much of them. They seem to spend most of their time at the Trans-America bus."

Kate nodded. "With Flanagan? That figures." She pointed to the end of the trailer. "That's the shower over there?"

Dixie nodded and opened a cupboard behind her to take out a rough white towel. The trailer was sparsely furnished: three beds, a chair, a simple stove, a shower and sink.

Kate quickly peeled off her shirt and brassiere, and walked over to the crude, makeshift shower. She unbuttoned her shorts and slid off the dark silk briefs below them.

Dixie had never seen an adult woman naked before, and she had never imagined that anyone would ever strip down with such impunity. But there Kate stood, legs, face and shoulders brown with the California sun, and the fluffy pubic "V" which Dixie could scarcely bear to look at.

Kate sensed her embarrassment.

"When you've been in a burlesque a few years you've seen one helluva lot of naked women. No place for modesty there."

The shower was a rough, improvised affair, little more than a punctured bucket served by tepid, brackish desert water, which was released by pulling a chain.

Kate stepped into the shower and let the dark, lukewarm water flow over her. The Trans-America was skimming every ounce of surplus flesh from her. Even as a dancer her body had been hard, but this was a new and different hardness. Her thighs had become lean and rocklike, her stomach flat, her shoulders muscular and firm. But the real hardness was inside. There she was beginning to feel the growth of a powerful engine: a heart and lungs capable of pumping out enough oxygen for fifty miles a day was beginning to develop. She hoped it would develop in time.

Kate had never realized that there were men like this, hundreds of men who could run at nearly seven miles an hour, seemingly for ever. At least there was a rest day after the "cut" which would give her time to recover.

Even as the water flowed over her and she massaged her thighs with soap, Kate felt tired. Doc had given her good advice, but the first twenty miles had been hard and the next twenty would be even harder. She had run the first stage in fifteen minutes inside four hours; that gave her fifteen minutes' grace for the next twenty miles, in order to beat the cut. But she was now running with tired, heavy legs, and beginning to realize, too, the enormity of the task which would face her over the next three months.

"Everything all right?" shouted Dixie above the hiss and splatter of the shower.

"Great," said Kate, stepping out of the shower to pick up the towel which Dixie had laid out for her.

Dixie ventured a closer look. She had always thought of women athletes as masculine creatures, akin to the big-buttocked "hockey hags" she had seen play in college matches. True, Kate Sheridan's body lacked the softness of her own, but she was just as much a woman. Her femininity simply expressed itself in vibrant, glowing athleticism.

"How do you feel?" asked Dixie.

"I'd feel a lot better if I didn't have another twenty miles ahead of me," said Kate, toweling her black hair. "Jesus, my legs are stiff." She kneaded her calves.

"D'you . . . d'you want me to rub them?" asked Dixie nervously.

"Would you? I don't want to ask any of those guys—they might get the wrong idea!"

Dixie laughed. "How do I do it?"

"I've been watching those fellas. They always push upward, toward the heart."

Kate pulled on her pants and stretched herself out slowly and painfully on the couch.

Dixie started on Kate's right calf, gently pressing upward toward the back of the knee. She had expected to find Kate's muscles hard, and was surprised to find them soft, even flabby to the touch.

She was, in fact, finding that high-quality muscle is loose and supple when relaxed; it is untrained muscle that is stiff and rigid.

Kate groaned, her arms dangling over the side of the couch.

"Am I hurting you?" asked Dixie.

Kate raised her head. "Hell, no. Just that they're so stiff. Don't be afraid to press hard."

When Dixie had finished on her calves Kate sat up and pointed to her thighs. "I've watched those guys working on each other.

They roll the muscles around from side to side, with the knees bent. Then they work on the backs, the hamstrings, and finish off on the front of the thighs, with the legs straight."

Dixie turned to Kate's thighs, using both hands. The muscles moved through about forty-five degrees, then recoiled, the muscles at the front of the thighs flickering subtly beneath the girl's smooth, hairless skin. Then Dixie turned them in the other direction and watched the muscles flutter back into position.

As she pressed upward on the thick muscles at the back of Kate's thighs she could feel tension in the bulging belly of the hamstrings.

"Ow!" yelped Kate.

Then to the front of Kate's thighs, working with both hands, pressing upward toward the inside of her groin. Again she could both feel and see the muscles flowing beneath her hands. She could also feel herself begin to flush and glow as her hands moved into areas which she had never explored, even in her own body.

"Thanks a million," said Kate, sitting up. "Now maybe these legs'll carry me twenty miles to get inside the cut."

"What time do you have to reach?" asked Dixie.

"Got to go for about four hours five minutes, just for safety," said Kate, pulling her shirt over her head. "That would give me a total of seven hours fifty minutes and qualify me for the next stage into the Mojave."

"Do you think you can do it?"

"A year ago I couldn't make it around the block. Sure I can do it. There's thousands of girls out there who could do it if they just got off their butts and tried. But forget about me. Are you Flanagan's girl?"

"No," said Dixie, blushing.

"I've seen the way he looks at you. I know that look. He giving you trouble?"

"No," she said awkwardly.

"Just you let me know if he does. I've met plenty of guys like him."

"Leave me to deal with Mr. Flanagan—you've got over a thousand men to cope with." Dixie was surprised to hear the words rush from her mouth, and she blushed again.

Kate smiled and draped Dixie's towel across a chair.

"I don't see that as much of a problem," she said. "Fifty miles a day would kill off any Valentino."

Kate ruffled her hands through her still-damp black hair and walked toward the trailer door.

"No," she said. "A couple of thousand men are no sweat. Three thousand miles . . ." She sighed, shook her head and opened the door.

"Do you think you can do it?" asked Dixie.

"I've got to," said Kate, looking out into the desert. "Nowhere else to go."

She turned to Dixie and smiled.

"Anyhow, can you think of anything better to do?"

Dixie sat at the door of the trailer, looking out over the baked scrubland, and watched as the other girl made her way back to camp. Kate seemed so sure, so confident, so hard. Yet it was not the same as her own hardness. Kate's was the hardness of cynicism, hers of fear and doubt. Perhaps they could help each other over the long miles between here and New York; though she could not see what she herself could offer.

9

INTO THE
DEVIL'S PLAYGROUND

3:45 P.M., *March 24, 1931*. One thousand four hundred and eighty-three men and women sat silently in front of the Trans-America center, awaiting the afternoon briefing for the second money stage. It was sixty-five degrees Fahrenheit, but the sun was hidden behind light cloud, as thankfully it had been all morning. They were now deep into the Mojave, and the first days of running had taken their toll. At least three hundred of the competitors would have difficulty surviving the six-hour, ten-minute "cut."

"Gentlemen," said Flanagan, then—"sorry, and ladies," as he motioned to Kate and the small group of women of which she was a part. "The second part of the day's final stage will be twenty miles into Shot Gun Camp, five miles ahead of the Mojave Indian village. It's rough country, with a few long hills."

He pointed behind him to a line of Ford trucks, some of which were already rolling up the desert road.

"Six of the trucks will start half an hour behind the field and pick up those who aren't able to finish. The lead trucks are moving off now to set up camp ahead of us, but the Maxwell House Coffee Pot and a first-aid truck will stop three miles out from the start, and there'll be another first-aid point at fifteen miles. This time there'll be three further food and water stations—at five, ten and fifteen miles. Any questions?"

"Yes," shouted out the swarthy little Frenchman, Bouin, standing up, "M'sieur Flanagan: no more of your peanut butter sandwiches at the feeding stations, I beg of you." There was the customary barrage of jeers and catcalls from the athletes.

"Point taken, and accepted," said Flanagan, smiling, looking over his right shoulder at Willard, who nodded. "And remember, everyone—tomorrow's your first rest day. I reckon you've earned it." He checked his watch, then looked up. "You have thirty minutes before the start."

The Trans-Americans broke up and settled themselves into small groups as Flanagan's crews finished the dismantling of the midday camp. The German team moved away from the central area in front of the Trans-America bus to sit apart on the sand in an arc around their team coach, Volkner, who spoke to them quietly and earnestly. A couple of hundred yards away, not far from the road, O'Rourke, the plump American coach, could be heard haranguing his team. To their left, the Finns, Pentti Eskola and Juouko Maki, sat beside each other on a rock, neither saying a word, while the Frenchmen, Dasriaux and Bouin, jabbered and gesticulated to each other only a few yards away. The Trans-America trucks continued to roll off across the desert, the Maxwell House Coffee Pot wafting Rudy Vallee's "Whiffenpoof Song" out through its loudspeaker system into the dry desert air, to no one in particular.

The start was an exact replica of the morning stage. Muller strode into the lead immediately, this time sucking in Bouin, Eskola, Martinez and the Mojave Indian, Quomawahu, was well as four other unknown runners. Doc shook his head as he padded off with Thurleigh, Morgan and McPhail, and they spent the first three miles together, running evenly through the stretched field, in the mid-fifties.

"That guy Muller must have Montezuma's Revenge," Doc growled, moving up behind the All-Americans who were in the first fifty places, for their early running had been more cautious than that of the morning.

Muller started to sweat early, but the German's rhythm was

still relentless, and the first five miles were accomplished in a swift forty-five minutes. As before, Martinez pranced alongside the German, this time on his left, seemingly untroubled by the fast pace. Quomawahu, who had finished twenty-first in the morning leg, was a tiny nut-brown figure in a white headband who had dominated local Mojave desert runs for many years. The Indian's stride was unusually short, but low and economical, and he scuttled across the sandy desert like a frightened beetle.

Bouin was another of the front-runners. Hirsute and mustachioed, he ran with the fluidity and certainty of a three-time Olympian, occasionally looking to his side over his left shoulder to check on Muller. The four other runners who had stayed with the leaders for the first part of the stage faded after only five miles and sank back into the heart of the field.

Eight miles in just over an hour and ten minutes, and of the leaders only Bouin stopped for water. Muller was still pressing hard, his only sign of effort being a muscular twitch at his right temple. Bouin looked at the German's back, shrugged, then trotted on. Surely, he thought, Muller's pace would drop.

Behind them, in thirtieth position, Doc could see the leaders three quarters of a mile up, on a curving incline ahead.

"Look," he said to Hugh, pointing ahead. "They must be five minutes up on us and still going away."

The All-Americans had also noted the position of the leading runners and had slowly started to ease away from Doc's group and from the Germans. Doc let them go. He would have to make a decision on whether or not to pull Muller in within the next three miles.

Some way back, Kate Sheridan had early in the stage sought out Charles Fox and settled in on the right side of the old man.

"Afternoon, ma'am," said the veteran, raising his right hand to his forehead. "Might you be looking for me to get you to Shot Gun inside three hours?"

Kate nodded.

"If you don't mind me tagging along, Mr. Fox."

"Not at all," said her companion. "Let's see what we can do for you, at least for the first part."

Fox turned out to be as good as his word, and took Kate through the first six miles in just over the hour. Surprisingly, the old man became garrulous, and during that first hour Kate was treated to the story of his life in professional footracing in the last part of the nineteenth century.

Fox told her of the six-day "wobbles" on the wooden indoor track at London's Agricultural Hall, Islington, where Victorian runners had staggered around a two-hundred-and-twenty-yard track for six days on end. Fox had been the first to average a hundred miles a day in the "wobbles," running six hundred and one miles in 1899.

"I still have the old Astley Belt for that 'un," he said, wiping his watering eyes with the back of his hand.

And then there had been the big matches, against time, and in these Fox had been the first man, amateur or professional, to run twelve miles in the hour, at the old Hackney Wick ground, the home of nineteenth-century London professional footracing.

There had also been the "man against man" matches, often for massive side bets. Twenty thousand or more Victorians would crowd into dank stadiums to watch George versus Myers, Hutchens versus Gent. Or Charles Fox versus Cannon, Watkins, Shrubb or any one of a dozen other great pedestrians.

"I won my manager plenty," said Fox. "I was the best there was, in my day, when the money was on."

Kate forgot her growing fatigue. "But where did all your money go, Mr. Fox?" she asked.

Fox shrugged. "Training expenses. Gambling. Pubs. Ladies. Always had a lot of friends back in them days."

He eased up as they approached the second feeding station.

"Feeding time," he said, pointing ahead. "Make sure you have a drink, miss. And eat. But don't you take none of Mr. Flanagan's peanut sandwiches." They both smiled.

As he moved slightly ahead, she looked down at his white legs, still surprisingly muscular but now heavily varicosed. The back of his shirt had a dark patch of sweat and his red wrinkled neck ran with perspiration. Kate felt no pity for him, for the old man had no pity for himself. He was simply doing what he had done for forty years; what he had always done best.

Two miles ahead, Doc decided it was time to get closer to the leaders. Otherwise he could see himself nearly twenty minutes down on aggregate at the end of the third stage. There were something like five hundred hours of running ahead and only about twenty hours would be completed by the end of the day, but he could not afford to throw away time.

Morgan and Hugh sensed the change in pace, though neither said so to Doc. Gradually they moved away from the All-Americans, putting yard after yard between them.

Running beside them, Peter Thurleigh felt like an alien. He had never before met athletes like this; only dimly imagined the nature of such men and their lives, men who had spent every day since youth fighting toward the next day. It was a long way from Cambridge; from March 20, 1930, when it had all begun . . .

The Oxford versus Cambridge athletics match. March mists had been closing in on the stadium at Queen's Club, and already some of the massive crowd were beginning to drift away as Peter Thurleigh had stood studying the first announcement in *The Times* of the Trans-America race. Peter had thrust his hands deep into his blazer pockets and wrapped his woolen scarf even more tightly around his neck. It had never been the best time of the year for a track and field meeting for the best athletes of Britain's leading universities to compete, as a prelude to the summer track and field season. This was, however, tradition, just as Eton and Shrewsbury and the other public schools had pressed untrained boys into athletics in the bleak winter months before King Cricket took his throne.

Eton! Lord, in April 1920 he had run close to two minutes for a half mile on its sodden turf. It had been half an hour before he had fully recovered consciousness and he had suffered blackouts for the rest of the day. This was not surprising, for he had come from the rugby season into half-miling without a yard of training. Peter Thurleigh had always had the ability to run himself to oblivion, a quality later to stand him in good stead.

As he had stood in the empty stadium he had seen in his mind's eye the trainer, old Sam White, shepherding the last of the Cambridge runners from the darkening field. Thirty years of students had, literally, passed through the hands of the gnarled old trainer. When he had first arrived at Cambridge in 1920, and had won the Freshers Mile, Peter had been massaged by Sam. "I do think you may have the makings, sir," the old man had said then, gently kneading the undergraduate's calves.

The makings: for the next three years Sam White had carefully threaded through the fabric of the young undergraduate's mind years of running lore. These were ideas and attitudes passed on to Sam from a sepia world deep in the nineteenth century, from matches run by men in faded photographs standing forever frozen on their marks. At first, names like W.G. George, William Cummings and Charles Fox had meant nothing to Peter and when Sam went deeper into the nineteenth century and spoke of Deerfoot, of "The Gateshead Clipper" and of "Crowcatcher" Lang, it was as if the old man were describing a lost world.

It was in this world that Sam White had survived and triumphed, and from it that he drew the knowledge that was his strength, long after the spring and suppleness of his limbs had left him.

Three years with Sam had brought Peter Thurleigh from a staggering, goggle-eyed four-minutes-forty-seconds novice in the Freshman Mile to the Stade Colombes in the 1924 Paris Olympics. Hundreds of miles on winter tracks, hour upon hour under those old hands smoothed by years of massage . . . and yet despite this intimacy they had never been close, and their discussions had dealt only with running. Peter had no idea if Sam White was married, had children, or even exactly where he lived. Sam was simply *there*. To him, White was part of that seamless continuum that existed only to serve. At home, the servants and gardeners, in autumn the ghillies on sour Scottish moors; their lives outside of service were of no concern to him.

In his final year, after his return from the Paris Olympics, he had arrived at the university track to find that Sam was not there, and had been directed by the groundkeeper to the old man's home, a cottage a mile or so from the track. When he arrived at the cottage the door was unlocked, but Sam was not at home. He had pushed open the door and ventured into the dark cottage. The smell was appalling, a mixture of rotting food, excreta and stale sweat.

In the center of the dank, stone-floored main room stood a rough wooden table on which lay a tin mug and a chipped plate containing the greasy remains of a meal. Sunk into the wall was a smoldering wood fire, in front of which stood a tin bath. On Peter's right was a bed, its ruptured canvas mattress leaking straw onto the floor of the cottage. The place was a slum.

Peter moved uncertainly forward. On his left stood a sideboard which he found contained the fruits of Sam White's professional career: the 1890 All Round Championship Belt, a discolored brass belt composed of championship medals for one, three and six miles, linked by rotting, fading colored braid; a yellowing cup for the World's Ten Miles Championship, 1895; a few rusting and indecipherable medals. That was all, a lifetime of running. Peter Thurleigh stood for a moment fingering the tattered championship belt, trying to trace in the gloom of the cottage the lettering on some of the more obscure medals.

Something, a muffled sound perhaps—he wasn't sure—made him turn around.

Sam White was standing behind him. He saw anger in Sam's eyes, anger that vanished as the old man's voice gave out its customary deferential tones. After that, relations between them had never been quite the same. Somehow he had crossed the line into another, forbidden world, a world in which Sam wished to live alone.

Six years later, after he had decided to compete in the Trans-America, Peter Thurleigh went back to Cambridge to the old trainer to seek his advice. Sam was not at the track and Peter walked to his cottage; but the building was no more than a pile of rubble. Neighbors told him that the old trainer had died a few months before. No, there was no gravestone; Sam White had been buried in a pauper's grave. For some reason, Peter Thurleigh had wept.

In certain ways, Doc was like Old Sam. But Doc Cole had a strength and confidence, even in some odd way a culture, that Sam had never possessed. Doc had spoken to him as an equal, but Peter did not yet know how to respond.

And Morgan. Morgan did not appear to acknowledge his existence. The American drove himself through each stage as if pushed on by some strong inner passion, sweat welling from the pores of his lean body like blood from a thousand wounds.

The Scot, McPhail, he could place, for he had met men like him before. His father had called them "Reds," thus damning any man who had dared to challenge pay, working conditions, or the way society was run. McPhail's resentment was almost palpable. Yes, undoubtedly a "Red." Peter did not know how he could bear to live in the company of such men as these for the next three months.

Gradually they were sucking in the leading group, running easily and evenly over the baked and broken ground. Peter, too, had felt the change in pace, but decided to trust Doc, for he still had no idea of the speed that would be required to get from Los Angeles to New York. He would live from mile to mile, stage to stage, relying on his body to tell him what had to be done.

In front, Muller showed no signs of letting up, and took his drink at the final feeding station, at fifteen miles, on the run, the water spilling as he ran. Eskola and Bouin stopped to drink, found difficulty in regaining their running rhythm, and were soon a couple of hundred yards down. The Finn shook his head and eased to a trot. Bouin kept going, the sweat glistening on his swarthy legs, but he could make no impression on the three leaders and found himself in a limbo between them and the trotting Pentti Eskola behind him.

Three miles back Charles Fox had done his work well, and had talked Kate through to twelve miles in just over two hours, twenty minutes. Even so, he could sense the American girl weakening. Kate's breathing was no problem to her, but she could feel her legs becoming heavier, her hips dropping, her muscles become less and less capable of absorbing the broken contours of the soft road.

"You all right, miss?" he asked, increasingly aware that runner after runner was now passing him.

Kate nodded weakly, sweat breaking over her brow and biting her eyes.

"No problem," she said. "Go on, Mr. Fox."

"See you at Shot Gun Camp then," said Fox. "Just you keep it steady, mind, miss. Run through it."

Even through her fatigue Kate was surprised to note, as Fox moved away from her, how slowly he appeared to be running. God only knew what she must look like! She stopped at the fifteen-mile feeding point and stood for a moment among a dozen runners standing at the table, splashing a cup of water over her face and neck, and drinking two more cups. Kate looked desperately at her watch. Three hours two minutes: it had taken her nearly thirty-nine minutes to run the last three miles, an average of thirteen minutes a mile. This time she was finished. Done. It was all over.

In the lead, Muller, Martinez and Quomawahu now ran as one

to the rhythmic chant of hundreds of Mojave Indians who had lined the final miles of the route to cheer on their champion.

Muller progressed grimly now, his face and shoulders streaming sweat, but still breathing evenly, if deeply. In contrast, Juan Martinez took in air in great sobbing gulps, his eyes wide and staring, while Quomawahu crawled his way ahead, occasionally grunting with fatigue. All ran at the same speed, and yet the outward expression of its cost was peculiar to each man.

Half a mile to go, and the chanting of the Mojaves by the side of the road became ever more insistent. As soon as he sighted the waiting buses at the finish Quomawahu responded by surging away, setting up a ten-yard lead. Soon it had stretched to thirty. The finish was now only a quarter of a mile away.

With a furlong to go, Martinez made a final desperate effort to catch the Indian, the rasping sound of his breathing drowned by the screaming of the massed Mojaves. But Quomawahu was too strong. Martinez could come in only second. Muller finished third, vomiting only seconds after he staggered past the line.

Doc and his group cruised in five minutes later, followed closely by the German and American teams.

Over three miles back Kate Sheridan was dying on her feet. She had never stopped running and her will was still strong, but somehow her body would no longer respond. She was empty. Her legs, sapped of life, had lost all rhythm. As each new runner passed her, Kate clung to him desperately, hanging on his shoulder, sucking a temporary strength and momentum from him, only to sink back into a broken struggle as she was dropped. Nothing in her past life provided her with the reference point to demand a reply from muscles seemingly drained of energy.

She looked up ahead at a long, slight incline which had assumed the proportions of a mountain. Kate Sheridan's feet were now barely clearing the ground, and she saw through the heat-haze, as in a mirage, a billowing stream of runners seemingly jogging on the spot, on the crest of the rise, moving away from her.

"Run, Kate, run!" said a voice in her head, and she labored up the incline, spraying small stones to the sides of the road, her feet shuffling through the brown dust. "Run, Kate, run!" She heard herself answering through dry, split lips, her hips continuing to drop.

She groaned as she reached the top of the rise, stopping for a moment with hands on hips. When she tried to start again her legs would no longer support her. She fell, grazing both shoulders and elbows as she rolled down into the rough ditch. She turned onto her back, spitting dust from bleeding lips, and lay still. For a moment she thought she had lost her sight, for she was quite unable to focus and the salt sweat stung her eyes and seeped into her mouth. Then she saw two men above her. Two men with the same sweating face, looking down at her.

Both faces smiled and leaned over her.

"Get up," said a single voice.

Kate pushed herself up onto her elbows, shook her head, and continued to spit sand and dirt.

"Get up," repeated the voice, this time more urgently.

Kate shook her head again.

Morgan slapped her hard across the face. The two images coalesced into one.

"You son of a bitch," she shouted, pushing herself up on one arm and rising unsteadily to her feet.

"Run, lady," said Morgan. "You've got thirty-five minutes to run the next three miles. You can do it. *Go!*"

Kate Sheridan forced a crooked, wan smile, walked back up onto the road and started to move. They ran together, slowly at first, Kate adjusting her stride to Morgan's rhythm. Out of the corner of her right eye she could just see his left shoulder, feel it suck her in toward their common goal, feel him as a magnet drawing her toward the finish.

Above them, a Pathé newsplane saw only a male runner and a young woman staggering uncertainly across the gathering gloom of the Mojave. As it made its way back to Los Angeles with film of the day's dramatic finish the pilot closed in on the two runners and the cameraman finished his day's film on the scene. Kate heard the noise of the plane's engines above her, looked up and smiled, a broken smile. Perhaps, after all, she was going to make it.

An hour later Flanagan looked out of his trailer window as the last runners limped into camp.

"So how many beat the cut, Willard?" he asked.

"At the last count, twelve hundred and eighty," said Willard, rising from his desk and consulting his clipboard.

Flanagan swore loudly. "Nearly a thousand gone in four days! This race is more like a massacre than a competition. What about the girl?"

"You mean Sheridan?" Willard flipped through the result sheets. "She made it okay. All the other gals flunked out."

"A pity," said Flanagan. "The feminine interest sells a lot of papers. That means we got to find some new angle on the Sheridan girl to keep it alive. Make sure the press boys know Sheridan's the only gal left. Maybe they'll come up with something."

"Done," said Willard.

There was a knock at the door. Willard opened it to reveal the German team manager, Hans von Moltke. For a moment the German stood stiffly, as if on parade, then made a formal bow.

"Herr Flanagan, I regret to have to make protest."

"Say your piece, Mr. von Moltke."

"What I have to say concerns Miss Sheridan," said the German. "The American girl. Over the final part of the race she was—how do you say?—illegally assisted by another runner."

"Illegally assisted?" said Flanagan. "Explain yourself, please."

His visitor set his lips. "An American runner, Morgan, went back and ran with her to the finish. We therefore demand that both runners be disqualified."

"Demand?" exploded Flanagan. "Did I understand you to say 'demand'?"

"Perhaps I use the wrong term," said the German defensively. "Let me therefore say 'request.' "

Flanagan beckoned to Willard to take some notes.

"Let me get this clear, Mr. von Moltke," he said. "Did Mr. Morgan lift or carry Miss Sheridan?"

The German winced. "No. I am saying that he assisted her by—how do you say?—pacing her over the last miles."

"And that's all you claim he did?" said Flanagan.

"Yes."

Flanagan looked at Willard.

"Got that all down?" he asked. Willard nodded.

Flanagan rose. "Thank you, Herr von Moltke. I think I have all the essential details now. Rest assured I will let you know my decision in due course."

The German opened his mouth as if to interject but decided against it. He bowed his cropped gray head and left the trailer.

"Go get me Doc Cole," said Flanagan to Willard.

Five minutes later Cole was comfortably settled in front of a tall glass of iced orange juice in Flanagan's trailer.

"How can I help you, Flanagan?" he asked, the sweat still visible on his forehead.

Flanagan gulped down his coffee.

"I think we face a little technical problem, Doc. I suppose you already know Morgan went out and brought Kate Sheridan in?"

"Yes," said Doc. "What of it?"

"The Germans have demanded I disqualify them both."

"On what grounds?"

"That he assisted her in finishing the stage."

Doc took a final gulp of his orange juice, sucking on the cube of ice he had taken with it. He looked up.

"Did he pick her up, drag her along, carry her?"

"No. Not as far as I know."

"Flanagan, you probably know that I ran in the Dorando Olympic Marathon of 1908. Perhaps you heard of it? Dorando arrived in the White City Stadium first but in a state of rigor mortis. Hell, he didn't know if he was in London, England, or Gary, Indiana. He fell, was picked up by some officials, fell again, and in the end was practically carried over the line by the judges."

"And was he disqualified?"

"Yep, but remember that he was lifted and carried across the line. Could I have another peek at your race rules?"

Willard handed the slim rule book across the trailer to Doc, who ran his finger slowly down each page in turn.

The runner shook his head.

"I can see that you've pretty much followed the amateur rules, but there's nothing here to cover Morgan's situation. Hell, what do you think those Germans and All-Americans are doing if it isn't pacing each other every day of the goddam week?"

"What would you say if I disqualified both of them?" asked Flanagan.

"I'd say you were disqualifying her for something in which she played no active part, and him for sheer decency and kindness."

Flanagan put down his cup.

"Thanks, Doc. You've helped me make up my mind."

The older man rose to go. "And do you mind telling me what you've decided?"

Flanagan gave him a toothy smile. "That they both run," he said.

"Coffee?" asked Dixie.

For a moment Kate did not know where she was. She looked sleepily around her, at the plain white ceiling above, her black hair tumbling over her sunburned face. She felt the coolness of silk on her arms and realized that she was wearing a pair of pink silk pajamas, and was covered by a thin white cotton sheet. She was in bed in Dixie's trailer.

"How . . . ?"

Dixie anticipated her question. "How did you get here?"

Kate nodded sleepily, shaking her tousled hair.

Dixie poured out a steaming cup of black coffee, asked about sugar and cream, then explained. "It was Morgan and McPhail who brought you in. Them and Doc Cole. But don't worry—it was me who cleaned you up and undressed you. You weren't really capable of much last night. How do you feel now?"

Kate rubbed her calves. "Stiff. Feels like someone's been banging my legs with jackhammers." She sipped her drink. "Did anyone ever tell you you make great coffee?"

Dixie smiled.

Kate put down her cup thoughtfully. "I just can't figure out that guy Morgan. Jesus, the first time he spoke to me was only yesterday—and then he bopped me one."

Dixie stared at her.

"Morgan hit you?"

Kate cupped her jaw in her hands and gingerly moved it from side to side.

"No complaints. I had it coming to me. Anyhow, I made it. The only thing I can remember is the time. Seven hours fifty-four."

"So you beat the cut?" said Dixie, pouring herself a second cup.

"Yes, by over five minutes. I sure hope Flanagan doesn't have any more of these cuts for a few days."

Dixie picked up her clipboard and shook her head.

Kate smiled. "That's all I need. A couple of days' rest and some easy running and I'll be right as rain. You just watch me."

Dixie looked out of the window at the rows of tents on the

desert plain. She could see Hugh McPhail walking not far from the trailer, and waved.

He looked over toward her and smiled in response. Within two minutes he was seated in the small traveling home sampling her prize brew. Their hands touched as she held his cup, and for a moment he wondered if her hand had lingered a moment on his.

"How are you feeling?" he asked Kate, who sat in her running outfit on Dixie's bed.

"All the better for this coffee," she replied. "I'd sure like to thank you guys for getting me here last night."

Hugh blushed. "It was mainly Morgan," he said, looking down at his cup. He was still thinking of Dixie's hand.

There was a moment's silence, then another voice joined in the conversation. "What the hell is this, a coffee klatch?"

They looked around to see Flanagan at the door. He was dressed in his Tom Mix outfit and carrying a sheaf of papers on a clipboard.

He pointed to Kate.

"I've got some news you won't like," he said. "The German manager Moltke has put in a protest—about Morgan helping you. He wants you both disqualified."

Kate flushed and started to speak. "You can tell Moltke, whoever he is . . ."

"Don't get yourself in a tizzy," Flanagan said quickly. "I threw his protest out cold. Anyhow, it was Morgan he was really after, not you. Morgan's the one who might cream his blue-eyed boys, they must reckon. But I've got some good news for you, too. The *Woman's Home Journal* has offered a ten-thousand-dollar prize if you can finish in the first two hundred places. Does that get to you?"

"I'll say," said Kate, grinning. "What place am I in?"

"Seven hundred and eighty-ninth," he said. "So you'll have to kill off over five hundred guys to get to that ten grand. Even the famous Miss Lily Langtry herself couldn't have done that."

"No," replied Kate. "But then Lily Langtry hadn't hoofed for six shows a day!"

Close on two hundred miles east of Los Angeles, the Trans-America had ceased to become a race purely between individuals. Rather, it was between teams, between groups of men drawn together by friendship and the desire for success, and the certain knowledge that it was going to be difficult for any individual runner to win on his own. The fifteen state teams, the All-Americans, the Germans, the various company-sponsored teams—these groupings had been known at the start of the race, but now the social chemistry of the Trans-America had changed, and the race was composed of dozens of less formal alliances. Some of these had in common age, others experience, yet others race, religion or color; but most of them cut across all these boundaries. Just as men had traveled in families from the East fifty years before, so the Trans-America was dividing up into families to make the return journey, only this time families of athletes.

Kate Sheridan was aware of this, aware of the daily need to go beyond individual ambitions. She knew herself to be in a unique position. She was now the only woman left in the race, with no female group to which she could adhere.

C. C. Flanagan had not been the only man to show interest in her. The two-hundred-odd miles of the Trans-America did not appear to have depleted the sexual energies of some of the competitors, which seemed to be fueled by quite a different source from their running.

Chance, however, had led her toward Doc's group, which, though its members had reached no formal agreements, moved about the camp as one. At the center of the group was Doc himself, the fountainhead of running knowledge, even more than that— someone with whom she and the others felt entirely comfortable.

After tea on the rest day Kate had made her way to Doc's tent to find him sitting outside with Martinez, Morgan and McPhail.

As she approached she saw Doc fish deep into his knapsack and pull out a small piece of sandpaper. Then he pulled off his shoes and inspected his feet closely. Hugh, Morgan and Kate looked at each other in wonder.

" 'Spect you're wondering what I'm about," said Doc. He rubbed the paper across the side of his left foot. "Friction," he said. "We got to run on ball bearings. Have any of you any idea how many times our feet will hit the road on any one day? Then I'll tell you. About seventy thousand. So we don't want roughness on the feet or in the shoes. That's why I polish my feet smooth. I do it every day."

Disregarding Kate, Doc went quickly over both feet, then clipped his toenails close, so that there were no protrusions. Next he powdered his armpits with talcum and then smeared Vaseline on the front of his chest and his nipples. "Friction again," he said. "Used to get sore nipples. Same with the crotch." He opened the top of his shorts and poured some more powder down inside, then shook his shorts around with both hands. "You don't just run with your legs," he explained. "You run with everything you've got. The Ford Automobile people call it 'testing to destruction.' That's what we're doing out here. Testing ourselves to destruction. Only I don't figure to get destroyed."

Hugh looked on dumbly. There was so much he had to learn, and quickly, or he would soon be out of the race, stranded on the roadside on some vast American desert. Luckily, his feet had so far held out, though he had done no more than powder the inside of his shoes.

Doc next drew out from his knapsack a long-sleeved football shirt. "It's going to be sunny tomorrow. Every part of your skin below neck level should be covered, otherwise that sun'll flay you alive. Sure I'll sweat in this, but my arms and shoulders won't burn." He pulled out his white peaked cap. "This'll protect my face," he said. "Reckon my legs are brown enough to take the sun, so I'll leave them free."

He looked up at his three companions.

"I don't know why I'm telling you guys all this, 'cause one of these days one of you is going to have me whole for breakfast."

He stood up. "Look out there," he said, pointing into the desert. "The devil's playground; it's the meanest, dryest land God ever made. A fossil wasteland of yucca, Joshua trees and dry lake beds. Jesus, sixty years back they brought out camels from Arabia, and even they didn't last long."

He returned to examining his feet, but the respite only lasted a moment.

"Any of you think you're going to run easy across that in seventy-five degrees or more, then think again," he said, looking up. "No, just you treat the Mojave with respect and run out quiet on tiptoe and maybe you might just make it across."

He pointed out into the distance. "Tomorrow I intend to shuffle across that desert at just over six miles an hour at best. And if that mad young Kraut wants to run wild again then let him. Anyone who goes with him every day will be a total wreck by Vegas."

"And what about me, Doc?" It was Kate who spoke.

Doc finally nodded his recognition, picked up a broken branch and traced a line on the ground.

"This is where we are now," he said, making a mark on the sandy soil. "About a hundred-odd miles south of Vegas. Then more desert, then the Rockies. If you can make it over the Rockies, Miss Sheridan, then I reckon you just might've run your body in. Depends how quickly you can adapt."

"You were talking about clothing, Doc. Does that go for me too?"

"Exactly the same. Cover up all light colored skin. Get a floppy hat in Barstow to keep out the sun and keep your face cool. You mayn't look much, but this ain't no beauty competition."

"What about face creams?"

"Hell, no," said Doc, "Unless you're figuring to fry like an egg." He looked at her, sensing her uncertainty.

"Look, Kate, you can make it. You showed your stuff at the last cut. But just you take it slow, and stop at all water points. And don't be too proud to walk."

"Walk?" said Kate.

"Walk. At seventy-five degrees and above your body can't keep its temperature in balance, even with all the sweating in the world. In that heat the body chemistry goes crazy. So listen to your body; do what it tells you. Nothing chicken in that."

"You've really got it worked out," said Kate admiringly.

"Well, I've had thirty years to think about it," said Doc. "I don't know much else."

She turned to the rest of the group, reddening. "I'd . . . I'd like to thank you guys for yesterday."

"Heck," said Doc. "It was Morgan here who went back. The rest of us, we just did a peck of stretcher bearing. Morgan here did all the real work. Thank him."

He stood up, patting his belly. "Anyhow, my stomach tells me it's dinner time." He gave a quick sidelong grin at Morgan, and walked off toward the refreshment tent, followed by McPhail and Martinez, the little Mexican gabbling excitedly away to Hugh about his earnings. Kate watched them move off, then sat down on the rock which Doc had vacated. She looked steadily down at the sand at her feet.

"I'd like to thank you, Morgan." She realized suddenly that she didn't even know his first name.

There was no reply.

"Why did you come back for me?"

Mike Morgan looked at her steadily, chewing on a straw. At last he spoke. "Maybe it's because I once trained with a pug called Clancy up in the Tuscarora mountains, back in Pennsylvania. It was the hardest time of my life. Back there Clancy said I had 'bottom.' He said it to me like it was some sort of compliment. Bottom. Well, you got it, Miss Sheridan."

"Bottom?" said Kate, reddening again.

She looked across at her companion, his body only partly visible in the gathering dusk. For a moment she felt again the tug of that invisible thread that had bound them in those last desperate miles, even though the need for the link had now gone.

"Yes," said Morgan. "And don't think for one moment that if I hadn't got to you that you would have just lain there and given up. No, you would've got up and finished, because that's the kind of person you are, ma'am. Lady, you ain't got a single ounce of give-up in you."

With that Morgan got to his feet and ambled off toward the others.

Bottom. That was all the man could say, and then just walk away. Kate normally had a flow of smart repartee to hold a man long enough to keep his interest; but not this time. She sat dumb, letting Morgan amble off into the dusk. Surely there had to be more than this? Perhaps hundreds of miles on, far beyond these sour, arid wastes. But not now. Sometime, maybe.

10

CROSS-COUNTRY TO LAS VEGAS

6 P.M., *March 26, 1931. Silver Lake, Nevada.* "Testing, testing . . . one, two, three," bellowed Willard into the microphone. In front of the Trans-America trailer sat one thousand two hundred and fifty-five men and one woman, all that remained of the Trans-America after just two hundred and thirty miles. Five days in the California sun had tanned their complexions a golden brown, and a day's rest had given their skins an added glow and vitality.

Willard Clay was in his element. All his life he had been a fixer, an organizer. At five foot four inches and one hundred and seventy pounds, he knew that there was no athletic event for which he was suited, except possibly sumo wrestling, and he had been born in the wrong country for that. However, even as early as the fifth grade he had been the one who had arranged the basketball matches between local street teams, raised money for Father Murphy's church funds, even organized track and field meets on a sixty-by-forty-yard strip of dirt sunk in a canyon of tenements.

Willard loved the challenge of organizing people. The more the better.

Flanagan: he was the dreamer, and in the ten years since they had first met it had been Willard's job to put flesh and bones on Flanagan's dreams. Flanagan was, in the best sense of the word, a "con" man, in that he had the capacity to gain people's confidence, and Willard knew that it was something that he himself could never do. However, once Flanagan had launched himself into a project, it was Willard's job to place brick on brick, and this he did superbly. Willard made certain that there was a man for every task, that each man knew his role, and, however humble it was, that each man was recognized. Flanagan could well strut about in his Hollywood gear, but it was Willard who would get things done.

He had known that the Trans-America would be his most difficult task. Organizing a race across a continent was difficult enough, but handling two thousand runners, plus a circus and the attendant press corps—that was a job in the loaves and fishes category, and Willard did not anticipate the same level of divine support. Yet he reveled in his work. What was more, from the beginning he had taken to the runners. They were honest, decent men. He respected them, and in time they would grow to respect him.

"Testing . . . one, two three," he shouted again. Hands were raised to indicate that he was being heard.

Flanagan took over the microphone.

"Thank you, Willard," he said, looking at the throng seated in front of him. Under his breath he added, "Hell, I feel like Moses leading the Israelites."

A Trans-American standing close to Flanagan stood up, his voice ringing out in the dry air.

"Mr. Flanagan, if you *are* Moses, for pity's sake gimme some of them tablets of the Lord—I haven't been to the john for days!"

The athletes roared, their laughter lost in the dry desert.

Flanagan in turn grinned good-naturedly then held up his hands for silence.

"Okay, fellas, quiet down. Just want to let you know the program for the next few days. Tomorrow, just over forty miles through the desert across the McCullough range taking us into Las Vegas . . ."

Jeers and laughter interrupted Flanagan as the stocky Frenchman,

Bouin, got to his feet. For Bouin, in the Great War a sergeant in the French army, had already become known as the barrack-room lawyer of the European group. "Mr. Flanagan, what manner of place is your Las Vegas?"

Flanagan's eyes twinkled in response. "I think that you'll find it entirely to your liking, Mr. Bouin," he said. "Around here they call Las Vegas the Monte Carlo of the USA. They've got everything there any man could want, and perhaps a few things more."

Doc was the next to shout out. "What's the weather forecast?" he asked, already on his feet.

Flanagan looked sideways at Willard, who duly leaned forward to the microphone. "Hot," he said. "At least seventy-five degrees in the shade, eighty-five degrees or more in the sun."

Doc stayed standing.

"Then we'll need to double up on water points," he said. He turned to the desert behind him. "Out there's the meanest land in the world," he said. "They call it the devil's playground. People dried out in droves back in the Gold Rush days. Their bones are still out there somewhere. The speed we're moving at, we burn up fluid like a racing car burns up gas."

Flanagan looked sideways again at Willard, who nodded.

"It'll be done," Flanagan said. "Any other points?"

"Yes," said Doc. "No cuts till we get out of this graveyard. Else some of us won't be having good times in Las Vegas or anywhere else."

There was a rumble of support. Flanagan immediately sensed the mood of the runners and nodded. "Agreed."

Pentti Eskola stood up. "What sort of country is it ahead, Mr. Flanagan?" he asked. "In more detail, please."

"Well, very similar to what you have already passed through. Like Doc said, it's hot and it's dry. It's a land of wastes, dry river beds and salt flats. We call it a desert, but it's full of saguaro, yucca, mescal and palo verde—and rattlesnakes. Further on, there's mountains going up to about five thousand feet."

"Any Indians, Mr. Flanagan?" shouted a Cockney voice.

"Plenty," said Flanagan. "But you'll find them selling sand paintings and blankets at the roadside or pushing gas at the gas stations. So don't look for any Tom Mix action around here."

Eskola stood up. "What are the starting times?"

Flanagan looked at his timetable. "Tomorrow's leg starts at eight so we can get the first twenty miles under our belts before noon. We break till three, then run the second leg till six."

"What about prizes?" asked another voice. Flanagan smiled. "I thought that might come up sooner or later." He picked up his clipboard. "The biggest money yet. The Six Companies, who are building America's biggest dam at Boulder just south of Vegas, have put up prizes of two thousand dollars for first place down to a hundred dollars for sixth. That makes the Vegas stage our richest so far."

Jean Bouin got to his feet. "M'sieu Flanagan, the finish—is it in the center of Las Vegas?"

"Good question," said Flanagan. "Yes, plumb in the middle of the main street, right by the Golden Nugget Casino. The whole goddam town is going to be there—the mayor, the city council, the whole circus. Tomorrow night, you guys are going to be the toast of Vegas."

"And what about these?" Doc Cole stood up, holding a yellow running shirt with the letters "IWW" emblazoned on the front and "Vegas" on the back. "We've been told that we've all got to wear these shirts on the way into Vegas. Why?"

Flanagan smiled uneasily. "Courtesy. Courtesy. We show a little respect for Vegas, they're gonna show some respect for the Trans-America."

"Now Las Vegas I can understand," rejoined Doc. "But what in tarnation does IWW stand for?"

"I don't care if it stands for International Widow Women," shouted a gruff voice from the back of the crowd. "They're clean and they sure beat that ole YMCA shirt you've been wearing for the past week."

Doc tried to reply, but his answer was drowned in jeers and laughter. He sat down, shaking his head uncertainly and a few moments later the meeting drew to a close, and Doc's group followed him back to his tent.

"A real ball buster," said Doc, kneeling on all fours, spreading a map evenly over the rough sandy ground. "Begging your pardon, ma'am," he added, looking over his shoulder at Kate.

She grinned and shook her head.

He jabbed his finger at a point in the map. "I reckon we're about here, just beyond the Soda Mountains, about two hundred and thirty-odd miles out from Los Angeles. We've been climbing for the past three days of running, though it's been gradual, for the most part."

"How high are we now?" asked Kate, joining Doc on her knees.

"Must be over three thousand feet—even those goddam Germans are dropping close to nine-minute miles. The air gets real stingy at these heights."

His finger traced a short line on the map. "We have about forty-odd miles to Vegas. The first fifteen or so see us clear of the desert. Then it's hard climbing all the way into Vegas, through the McCullough range."

"What height do they go to?" asked Hugh.

"Over five thousand feet. At that height, even a ten-minute pace is tough, 'specially on the steep climbs. Your legs go, your breathing goes, everything goes."

"You ever run that high before, Doc?" asked Morgan, kneeling on one knee beside Kate and looking intently at the map.

"Once," said Doc. "Mexico City in 1912. Some fancy Mexican general had put up a couple of thousand dollars for a marathon there. That was real big money in those days, and we came clambering from all over to get at it. Kohlemainen, Shrubb, Appleby, Fox—all the great professionals turned up."

"How high was Mexico City?" asked Kate.

"Something over seven thousand feet. The boys didn't pay it much attention, though. They all went bounding off at the usual six-minute-mile pace, while I chugged along at the back of the field about half a minute a mile slower. They went through ten in the hour all right, but then at fifteen miles it all went haywire. They started coming back to me like I was pulling them in on a string. All the greats fell apart. There was Kohlemainen, dying on his feet, and even Alf Shrubb ended up in a pushcart. Old Charles Fox over there finished up walking."

"Did you win?" asked Kate.

"I didn't win it—they lost it. I just kept plugging along, staying loose, taking it easy, while they were dropping around me like drowned men. It was one of the slowest marathons I ever ran— it took me over three hours. I spent two weeks recovering too, much longer than usual. Kohlemainen and Shrubb were in a Mexican hospital for weeks, and so were a dozen others. Meanwhile, there I was traveling back first-class in the S.S. *Marianna* with two thousand bucks in my pocket. Happy days."

"So we have to keep the pace low?" said Hugh.

"Exactly," said Doc. "It's always the pace that kills, never the distance."

Flanagan put down the telephone, his face fixed in a scowl, and slumped back into his armchair. He took his revolver from its holster, opened it and flicked its cylinder around.

"Trouble in New York," he said looking up. "Trouble for Mayor Jimmy Walker, and if Jimmy goes hungry then we starve."

Willard waited for an explanation.

"That Sir Galahad Franklin Roosevelt, the state governor, has got a petition from the public affairs committee asking for Jimmy Walker's removal. 'Malfeasance of office' they call it." Flanagan got up and poured out a full measure of whiskey and gulped it down in one.

"So what?" said Willard. "Walker's signed up to us tight for twenty grand."

"If this charge sticks, Walker could be on his way to the Tombs a full month before we hit New York. Twenty grand—we won't see twenty cents! Jesus H. Christ, it's all happening at once."

Willard picked up a sheaf of papers. "I know this may not be the best time, but could you look at these bills? All of a sudden they've started pouring in."

"Strange," said Flanagan, pouring himself another drink and leafing through the bills.

"Most of these people offered us long-term credit," said Willard. "Now they all seem to want their money yesterday. The toughest one is the catering contract with De Luxe. They want twenty thousand dollars advance by the end of next week or they pull out the cooks."

"How much have we got in the kitty?"

"About thirty grand."

"Pay it," said Flanagan, pointing out of the window. "We run out of food, they run out of legs. They run out of legs, we run out of business."

He lay back on the trailer couch and closed his eyes. "Excite me, Willard," he said. "Go over the figures again. You know what I mean."

Willard recited the accounts in a low monotone.

"Costs: salaries and services till New York total six hundred forty thousand dollars. Equipment costs twenty-five thousand dollars. Publicity costs fifteen thousand five hundred dollars. Sundries twenty-five thousand five hundred dollars. Prize money to be met by Trans-America Bank. Grand total seven hundred six thousand dollars.

"Income: entry fees four hundred thousand dollars. Films fifty thousand dollars. Appropriations from towns three hundred thousand dollars. Sundry income one hundred forty thousand dollars. Total eight hundred ninety thousand dollars."

Flanagan kept his eyes closed. "Now to the best bit," he said. "The profit."

Willard's voice rose from its monotone.

"Even excluding post-race contracts, there will be a profit of one hundred eighty-five thousand dollars."

Flanagan stood up and stretched. "I feel better already."

"But what about the bills?"

"Burn them," said Flanagan. "The whole damn lot."

Unaware of Flanagan's problems, Rae, Kowalski and Liebnitz were busy comparing notes in the press tent.

"How do you think it's going so far, Carl?" asked Rae.

Liebnitz took off his horn-rimmed glasses and polished them.

"You guys know I'm no sports reporter. Still, Flanagan has surprised me. First, he somehow got two thousand men and women from all over the world to run in this crazy race of his."

He paused to replace his glasses on his lean, peeling nose. "Perhaps, in the circumstances, that wasn't too surprising, considering the present state of the nation. What *is* surprising is that up till now the whole goddam jamboree has been so well organized. When I first met Flanagan, it wasn't that he didn't know the next step ahead—he didn't know the step he had just taken!"

"Yep," said Kowalski. "You've got to hand it to him, Carl. And he's done well by the press corps too. Every day, a pack of good stories."

Liebnitz nodded.

"And who have you got your two bits on, Mr. Liebnitz?" It was Kevin Maguire of the *Irish Times*. Liebnitz smiled and continued polishing his glasses.

"When I first hit Los Angeles I would have bet my last buck on Doc Cole," he said, investigating the lens by holding it up to the light. "But that young German Muller . . ."

"He's going to take some beating," interjected Kowalski.

"And his pal Stock is still running easy," observed Rae.

"Perhaps Muller's just the stalking horse," said Liebnitz. "Put out there just to burn off likely contenders, to set the race up for Stock."

"He sure burned me off yesterday," growled Kowalski. "I couldn't get a word out of him after the finish."

"And then there's young McPhail and the Yankee boy Morgan," said Maguire.

"And your Lord Thurleigh's no slouch, even if he has left his butler back at Barstow," said Kowalski.

"Don't call him *my* Lord," replied Maguire. "I hate the bloody English."

Liebnitz replaced his glasses and rubbed his nose, removing a surface layer of dried, sunburned skin.

"I'll take a chance," he said cautiously, "and pick McPhail, with Cole second choice."

"Banana oil," said Kowalski. "It's got to be Muller and Stock. What about you, Kevin?"

Maguire tipped back his hat and mopped his brow.

"I'm going to use the Irish method," he said. "Cole, Muller, Stock, Morgan, Thurleigh, Eskola, McPhail. It's going to be one of them . . . I think."

7 A.M., March 27, 1931. The runners stood massed on the road to Las Vegas, a few miles north of the Soda Mountains. The desert air was sharp and clear. Behind them, Flanagan's workers were clearing away the remains of the night's stay. Ahead of them were Flanagan's Trans-America trailer, six press buses, the Maxwell House Coffee Pot and a collection of over a hundred cars and motorcycles. Around them, still and silent on the cool desert surface, the cottonwood, cactus and yucca, which grew at between three thousand five hundred and five thousand feet.

As Doc had predicted back in Los Angeles, the cranks, the dreamers and the optimists had now gone, and the Trans-America was composed either of athletes or men rapidly becoming athletes. Luckily, the weather had been kind; they had been favored by a succession of unusually mild spring days, days in which the desert was unable to impose its full vigor upon them. At present, only mileage was a problem, before they reached Las Vegas—"the meadow with many streams."

Again it was the German, Muller, who took the lead, this time after a mile of easy running with the main pack of thirty, in which Doc, Hugh, Morgan, Martinez and Peter Thurleigh were securely tucked, together with Eskola, Bouin and Dasriaux, the All-Americans and the remainder of the German team.

The leading groups slipped into a reflex rhythm, running between six and seven miles an hour, for they had now accepted the reality both of their bodies and the nature of the Trans-America. They ran like clockwork toys, daily insinuating themselves into rather than piercing the desert, as they had tried to do in their first springier, more optimistic days.

For Hugh, the road had become a dream, and as in a dream there was no pain. For he in turn had become a machine, through which oxygen and blood flowed endlessly, the oxygen exactly matching his needs. The stumbling, staggering days of his early training were long past him; he was no longer a sprinter, but a roadrunner.

In the early days, the air had sometimes ripped through him, rasping in his throat like sandpaper. Now the easy in-and-out of his breathing was balanced, his strides were never an inch longer or shorter than necessary, regardless of the surface. He ran as if the road and its contours had been made for his legs and his alone. And, like a confession, the run somehow purged and cleansed him, bringing a daily flow of memories unchecked and without order.

Hugh remembered that he had been drawn two nights before across to the circus camp by the mournful wail of bagpipes coming from somewhere on its perimeter. It had taken him some time to locate them in the cluster of tents, trailers and cages that formed the circus camp, but eventually he found that the pipes were being played by Albert Koch, the fat, balding owner of Fritz the talking mule.

Koch stood in front of Fritz, his sweating face reddening as he played "The MacRimmon's Lament" a few feet from the donkey, who silently munched from the trough in front of him. Albert Koch looked up apologetically as Hugh approached.

"I'm trying to teach him some new words," he explained. "These bagpipes—they gets him in the right mood—at least it always has done before. Goddam beast."

"Don't you know any other tunes?" asked Hugh.

"Hell no," replied Koch. "I had enough trouble learning this one from the Scotsman who sold me this damn donkey."

"Did he sell you the pipes too?"

"You bet your sweet life he did. Ten dollars extra, and a buck fifty for teaching me the tune."

Hugh put out his hands to Koch. "Care to let me try?"

"My pleasure," said Koch, handing him the pipes.

Hugh cleaned the mouthpiece and filled the bag. They were poor pipes, probably made in Aberdeen, Idaho, rather than Aberdeen, Scotland, but he would squeeze a tune out of them. As he looked up at Koch he saw that Dixie Williams had strolled by, and was watching the scene, chewing on a blade of grass. Hugh reddened, but placed his fingers automatically in place on the chanter and swung into "Flora McDonald's Jig."

At the sound of the jaunty melody Fritz lifted his head from the trough and viewed McPhail intently.

"Dooog," he brayed.

"Great!" said Koch. "Keep at it."

Hugh continued to play, walking rhythmically, Highland style, in front of the now attentive donkey.

"Caaat," brayed Fritz again in a high nasal whine.

"You got yourself a friend for life," whooped Koch. "I been saying 'Cat' to him all goddam night."

Hugh continued to play for about ten more minutes, during which Fritz made several other additions to his vocabulary, none of them intelligible to Hugh or Dixie but evoking immediate response from Koch.

Hugh handed the pipes back to Koch, who shook him vigorously by the hand.

"What you think I should do, Scotsman? I'm moving up to Vegas tomorrow to set up camp."

"I think you should learn some new tunes, Mr. Koch," said Hugh. "And stay away from the sad stuff. That donkey's got a sense of humor."

"So have you," said a voice behind him. It was Dixie. Hugh blushed again.

Leaving Koch with his pipes and his donkey, the two of them strolled back through the camp, through the tents and trailers as dogs scampered between the evening fires.

"Where did you learn to play the bagpipes?" Dixie asked.

"With the Boys Brigade," answered Hugh.

"Brigade? Is that the army?" asked Dixie, kicking a pebble along the dry ground.

Hugh smiled. "Not quite," he answered. "More like the Boy Scouts. All drill and marching up and down the church hall. I joined for the soccer. But they did teach me the pipes."

"Whatever happens you can always get a job with Mr. Koch," said Dixie.

They had now reached the edge of the circus encampment.

"It's always a possibility," he replied. "Well, we'll see in Las Vegas if Flora McDonald's jig will help Fritz learn a few more words. I think I'll have a look at this circus—I've never seen one in action."

"You'll have to wait a bit," said Dixie. "They only work the big towns. Mr. Flanagan has got them booked ahead in all the towns from here to New York." She paused. "Anyway, who was this Flora McDonald?"

Hugh beckoned her to sit down on a rock, then sat down beside her.

"Back in 1745," he said, "Bonnie Prince Charlie led a Jacobite uprising against the King. He was beaten in battle and hunted the length and breadth of Scotland."

"These Jacobites," said Dixie. "They like Democrats?"

"Something like," said Hugh, smiling. "The King offered a big reward for his capture. But not a single Highlander betrayed the Prince. Flora McDonald was one of the main people who took care of him, helping him to escape back to France."

"All over the country, protected by a woman even though he was a prince?" mused Dixie.

"Yes. But he made it eventually," said Hugh. "He escaped to France."

"Did they ever meet again?"

"No. Not as far as I know."

"That's often the way of it," said Dixie, standing up. "People come from far off, get together. Then they never see each other again."

Hugh looked down at the ground. "Yes," he said. "That's often the way of it." He watched her move slowly off in front of him toward her quarters.

"*But it doesn't have to be,*" he said, under his breath.

* * *

A fat globule of warm rain hit Hugh on the forehead, bringing him back to the present. Within seconds the rain was rushing down, as if from a celestial faucet, hissing through the still desert air. The pace dropped to a crawl as runners, blinded by the warm torrent, slowed in order to focus clearly on the slippery, muddy road ahead. Packs which had been glued together for the first ten miles were pried apart by the blinding rush of water. Hugh's shirt and shorts clung stickily to his body.

The runners, who had up till that point run sparingly, output exactly balancing input, now found their breathing rhythms broken as they breathed in rain through nose and mouth. Worse still, the road had already started to break up, as the rain gouged and cut across the softer portions of its surface, creating networks of tiny streams. It was really no longer a road but a mixture of mud and stream, and what had started as a road run had become a cross-country.

As the rain lashed down, Kate was glad that she had tied back her hair, though the rest of her was wet through, and her nipples were already showing clearly through her wet bra. At least, she thought, she was wearing dark briefs underneath her shorts. It was amazing how her concern for modesty remained, she thought, even in the lashing rain on a desert road with a thousand sweating sodden athletes. Beside her, Charles Fox was now struggling, for his old legs simply could not take the changing contours of the increasingly slimy road. His rhythm broken, he was beginning to breathe heavily and his short regular stride had dropped to an erratic, choppy pecking action.

"On you go, lass," gasped Fox. "I'll catch you up later."

Kate nodded and Fox dropped back.

At the front of the field, Muller had built up a half-mile lead at fifteen miles, but it was now impossible to see him: they were now running through solid walls of rain. Suddenly they heard Willard Clay's voice through the loudspeaker system.

"Flash flood!" he shouted. "Flash flood ahead, two miles on. The road is down. Repeat, the road is down. Cut south at the point of breakdown. Repeat. Cut south at the point of breakdown, five miles to bridge, and make your own way north back to the main Vegas road."

The information was swiftly passed back down the field by

word of mouth until it reached Doc and his group.

"Hell," said Doc, the rain streaming down his face. "That means another two hours' running."

Soon Doc, McPhail, Morgan and the rest of their group had reached the point of the flood. The rains had etched a thirty-foot wide, six-foot deep chasm, ripping away the road. Doc stopped, took off his cap and from inside it took out what looked like a watch. He replaced his cap and looked sideways at Morgan, Hugh and Martinez, then back at the watch.

"You know what this is?" he said.

There was no answer.

"Then I'll tell you. This is a compass. This might mean a mile, and maybe a thousand dollars to us."

They slithered right, south into the desert, the mud turning their once-tight shoes into brown, slimy clogs. Cactus and yucca ripped at their legs as they stumbled and staggered through the lashing rain. They ran parallel to the roaring flash flood on their left, which had broken through the road east to Las Vegas, and they had traveled about half a mile downstream before Doc shouted to them through the noise of the rain.

"There!" he shouted, gesturing to the narrowest point in the brown rush of water, only about twelve yards across. They stopped and gathered around him.

"Here's how I see it," gasped Doc, the rain rolling down his cheeks and into his mouth. "We make a chain across the stream with Mike leading, Juan and I next, and Hugh as anchor holding on to that yucca." He pointed to a stout twisted yucca on their side of the flood whose roots had not yet been loosened by the flood. "When Mike manages to get a firm grip on that yucca on the far side, Hugh lets go and we pull each other across. I reckon it's about a four-man-span—just over ten yards."

There was no reply from the others, only the hiss and splatter of the rain as following runners began to slither south past them.

"Well?" yelled Doc. "What the hell is this? A staring competition? Jesus, we can pick up a couple of hours on that Kraut!" Doc walked forward a few yards and then looked back expectantly at the others.

They moved off toward the stream's edge and linked hands, with Hugh mooring himself firmly to the yucca. He nodded to Doc, who tapped Morgan on the shoulder.

"Here goes nothing," said Morgan, stepping first into the brown torrent, with Martinez and Doc following, holding each other firmly at the wrist. Morgan trod cautiously, feeling with his feet for broad stones on which to balance. He was lucky, for on his first tentative steps he at once made contact with firm, gritty surfaces, and the chain of runners made its way painfully across the stream, constantly buffeted by the warm, gushing water.

"Right!" shouted Morgan through the roar of rain and river. "Got it!" He had made contact with the tree branch on the far side of the stream. As Morgan shouted, the yucca tree on which Hugh was holding himself firm, its roots at last eroded by the flood, tumbled into the stream, taking Hugh with it. Doc, caught between stones, hung on tight to Hugh, but was ripped from Martinez's grasp and tumbled helplessly downstream, still clasped in the Scotsman's firm grip.

"Jesus!" said Morgan, dragging Martinez onto the muddy bank, where he lay gasping like a stranded fish. "Jesus."

Morgan looked desperately around him. He stood up and pulled savagely at a yucca tree at his side, but the twisted, wiry branch would not break.

"Come on, you bastard," he snarled, continuing to heave.

At last the branch broke, throwing Morgan backward. He got to his feet and half slithered, half ran down the side of the stream, which fortunately curved, cutting down the distance between Morgan and the two in the water.

Meanwhile Doc and Hugh tumbled crazily downstream, swallowing rainwater from the heavens as well as gritty mouthfuls of the muddy flash flood. Doc had been submerged several times but still Hugh held grimly on, attempting to swim with his free right arm. Doc, however, a nonswimmer, had become a dead weight. Hugh felt himself weakening.

Then above the brown swell he saw a blurred Morgan at the stream's edge, about ten yards downstream.

"Here!" shouted Morgan, reaching out into the stream with the yucca branch. Hugh was still on the right side of Doc, who had gone under yet again, and had to spin in the water over Doc onto his back to get closer to the branch.

At last he reached out, only to miss it completely, and rolled further downstream, still clinging leechlike to Doc's wrist with his left hand. Morgan cursed and dashed on a further twenty yards downstream to the next curve and again held out the branch.

Hugh managed to get his fingers firmly around the branch, but the force of the flood and Doc's pull on him were too great; he lost his grip and again the two men tumbled downstream, the skin of their backs ripping as they hit the gravelly bottom of the stream.

Hugh surfaced again, pulling Doc with him and saw, almost above him, the yucca branch and Morgan's face. He clawed for the branch and this time his grip held firm, though their bodies were swung downstream by the force of the current. Morgan grabbed the Scotsman's other arm and pulled slowly; Hugh, still holding Doc, was dragged onto the bank.

The young Scot sat gasping against a rock; but Doc lay still, on his back, on the bank. Immediately Morgan pushed Doc onto his front, placing his head to the left and started to pump his upper back, forcing water and grit to erupt in great spurts from his mouth. Only moments later Doc started to groan. Then he coughed, and Morgan pulled him roughly into an upright position.

"You all right?" he asked. Doc spat out a stream of muddy water and stood up uncertainly, leaning on both Hugh and Morgan.

"Of course I'm all right," he growled, shaking his head. "Take more than that to finish me."

"You never died a winter yet," said Hugh.

Doc grinned and spat out more water. "How much time d'you reckon we lost?"

"I reckon about twenty minutes," said Morgan.

Doc coughed again. "Then we still got plenty of time in hand." He gave a wheezy cough and started to hop from foot to foot. "Then we got 'em. We goddam got 'em!" he chuckled. "Muller and his boys will run a good ten miles before they can get back on the Vegas road."

They walked back slowly to Martinez, who was standing a couple of hundred yards upstream. Doc had almost fully recovered, though he still spat out grit and water as he walked along.

"You said we'd save two hours, coming across the flood," said Morgan mockingly.

"Okay, okay," said Doc, "so I'm no Johnny Weissmuller. Five'll get you ten that none of the others will try to make it across."

Doc was right. No other runner ventured across the flood, choosing instead to stumble and slide almost five miles downstream to a stout bridge, there to turn to run north five miles back across the desert to the main Las Vegas road. Doc and his friends had gained well over an hour's lead, and all within the race rules.

"Right," said Doc, as they stood shivering in the warm rain. "We've got more than twenty miles to go into Vegas. So we can do one of three things. First, we can race our nuts off all the way for the prize money. A couple of us will pick up the big money, but we'll all be pooped for the next desert stages past Las Vegas."

"What else can we do?" asked Hugh.

"We can take it easy for, say, fifteen miles, staying close, then run for the money over the last five miles."

"And what's your last option?" asked Morgan cautiously.

"For us to make it into Vegas real easy, and split the prize money between us."

"A lot of people have come into Vegas to see a race," said Hugh. "Not a fix."

"You got a point," said Doc. "But this ain't the United States Senate. We've got to decide—now."

Martinez shrugged his shoulders while Hugh looked back at Doc uncertainly.

"You know a kid's game?" asked Morgan suddenly.

No one spoke.

"You know," said Morgan. "We all put one hand behind our back. We got a choice of showing one, two or three fingers. Majority takes it."

"So if we want to race all the way it's one finger, two fingers for the last five miles, three fingers for a share-out?" asked Doc.

"That's it," said Morgan. "Game?"

This time they all nodded.

Each man put his right hand behind his back. There was a moment's pause.

"Now!" shouted Morgan.

All four men thrust out their right hands. Each one showed two fingers.

They laughed. Then they trotted together up toward the main road, the road to Las Vegas.

11

THE MEADOW
WITH MANY STREAMS

As the Trans-America ended its first week on the road to New York Flanagan had some reason for satisfaction. True, the two-thousand-man field had almost been halved, but though unexpected this had in many ways been a blessing. He had no desire to carry the halt, the lame and the weary all the way across the Mojave to Las Vegas and beyond. He had realized from the outset that in Doc Cole he had a star performer, but Morgan and McPhail had been unexpected bonuses. Muller, though lacking charisma, had also provided journalists with plenty of copy, as had Martinez. Kate Sheridan had been a complete surprise to him; he had not expected any female competitor to survive the initial stages, but now, by chance, he had his first female star, an athlete who would keep the Trans-America on the front pages of newspapers the world over as long as she stayed in the race.

Flanagan would have been less happy had he known of an occurrence almost three thousand miles away in Washington, D.C., just a few days before.

There, in a still, high-ceilinged office, the tranquillity of presidential aide Gerald H. Gruber's Monday morning had been rudely disturbed. As was his custom, he was busy at work on the crossword in that day's *Post*. The clue for ten down ran, "Festival initiated by a French nobleman," and was eight letters. Gruber, sitting in an office only a few feet away from the Oval Room, had been struggling with it for over ten minutes when the telephone rang. Gruber put down his pencil and picked up the White House telephone.

"Toffler here," a voice announced at the other end, without explanation.

For a moment Gerald Gruber was at a loss. "Mr. Martin P. Toffler," repeated the caller, slowly stressing the "P." Gruber's neat mind finally produced the required information. The caller was one of the party's biggest supporters in the Midwest. Gerald Gruber listened with attention, sharpened pencil poised over his pad.

Toffler was for some unknown reason talking about a race. Gruber could not tell if it was a horse race, a car race or for that matter the human race. He listened patiently, hoping that Toffler would somehow explain himself.

Eventually Toffler did—at least to a degree. The race was called the Trans-America, so it could hardly be a horse race. So far, so good. Strangely the race's very existence concerned Mr. Toffler, though for the moment Gruber could not see why.

"Let me write this down, Mr. Toffler," he said, scribbling on his pad. "The Trans-America. Exactly what nature of race is this?"

Toffler bellowed his answer over the phone.

"I see," said Gruber patiently, writing on his pad. "A professional footrace from Los Angeles to New York. Quite an undertaking. Now what exactly do you wish the President to do about it? Are you telling me that these athletes are breaking certain federal laws?"

No, it did not appear that they were. Mr. Toffler, it further appeared, was speaking (and very loudly) as a member of the United States Olympic Committee responsible for the staging of the 1932 Los Angeles Summer Olympics. This Trans-America race, if successful, would, he said, both seriously damage the world of Olympic track and field in general and next year's Olympic Games in Los Angeles in particular.

For Gerald Gruber the mists were beginning to clear.

"And precisely what action do you wish the President to take?" he asked politely.

Mr. Toffler's request was not one which Gerald Gruber could put to the President without considerable modification. In short, it was that if he wanted any further goddam contributions to party funds, that he would have to put every possible barrier in the way of those Bunion Derby sonofabitches.

Gruber finished his notes, crossing out certain words and underlining others.

"Thank you, Mr. Toffler. I think I have the full picture now. I will give your message to President Hoover and am sure that he will give it every consideration."

Gruber put down the telephone he had been using and immediately picked up one to its right.

"Carter, find out everything you can about the Los Angeles to New York Trans-America footrace. And have its precise route on my desk by this afternoon. I want to know every town, every village, through which the race passes."

Gruber then put down the internal telephone, sucked his pencil, and resumed his crossword. He smiled, and slowly penciled in the word, "Olympics."

After that things had happened quickly. Within a week the President's office was in touch with FBI Director J. Edgar Hoover, and for the first time the Trans-America came under the scrutiny of the Federal Bureau of Investigation.

Two days before Flanagan's men had even reached Las Vegas the immediate fruits of Toffler's work began to show. Federal Agent Ernest Bullard, a lean, swarthy man in his late thirties, faced his superior, Charles Finley, across the heavy brown oak table of Finley's sparsely furnished office.

Bullard opened the bulky gray file on his knee marked "Trans-America." "I knew most of this before, sir," he said. "I'm a track fan. I've been following the race since that guy Flanagan announced it. The papers and the radio have been full of it."

Finley nodded, his face expressionless.

"But it's a pretty thin lead, sir," complained Ernest Bullard, pulling his belt in a notch. "Over a thousand runners, and one of them just might be a killer."

Charles Finley, a thin, humorless department head of the Federal

Bureau of Investigation, looked at his agent across the table and frowned.

"There's more to it than that, Bullard," he said. "But first let's have a look at what we've got on file." He riffled through a pile of papers in front of him, selected one, then stood up, holding it in both hands.

"March 28, 1929, Clairton, Pennsylvania. Money fight with fists, Starr's Warehouse. Nick Wieck versus Chuck Petrack, the Bronx Bomber; Wieck goes down in the first round, dies a week later. Petrack blows town. Manslaughter, possibly more. Either way, we want Petrack."

"But what do we have to go on, sir?" said Bullard. "One anonymous call—which didn't even give us any real details. So Petrack just *might* be in this race—but how do we know Petrack is his real name?"

"It isn't. Sure as hell Petrack was fighting under a false name; all these goddam streetfighters do. It's not altogether certain that Wieck even died from the fight. We know that he walked home that night, after all, and we also know he had pneumonia. But the director has *personally* asked me to pursue this matter."

"All the way across America for two months to find a guy who *might* be in the race and who *might* have killed Wieck? Have a heart, sir."

Finley smiled, and lifted a bulky green file from the desk. "I told you there was more to it than that. Much more." He replaced the file on the table.

"This has come right from the top. The director believes that the Trans-America footrace may be the breeding ground for Reds and anarchists. He thinks that there're bound to be strikes and riots in depressed cities all along the route because of these runners. That's the real reason for your trip: to keep an eye on potentially disruptive elements."

Finley looked up at the map immediately above him and placed his finger a couple of inches east of Los Angeles.

"Last reports say that they're on their way to Las Vegas. Now, you may recall that our agents cleaned Vegas up a couple of months ago—cleaned it right out." He chuckled drily. "So by about now Vegas should be just about back to normal. So have yourself a good time—and watch your expense account."

Bullard sighed, stood up and shook his head.

"One more thing, Bullard," said Finley.

"Yes, sir?"

"How often do you shave each day?"

Ernest Bullard tried not to show his surprise, but simply stroked his chin.

"Same as most people, sir. Once, before breakfast."

"Then take my advice. Make it twice, eight A.M. and six P.M. Mr. Hoover likes clean-shaven agents. And another thing."

"Yes, sir?"

"Open or safety?"

"Safety razor," said Bullard, blinking.

Finley took out a leather wallet from his inside pocket, peeled off a dollar and threw it down on to the table.

"Then go treat yourself to an open razor. Mr. Hoover is of the opinion that Gillettes are a sissy way to shave. Know what I mean?"

Bullard did not reply.

Finley picked up the dollar bill and held it out to Bullard. "Have it on the agency. Just to please Mr. Hoover."

Bullard forced a smile, accepted the bill and left, closing the heavy door quietly behind him. Two months in a footrace, looking for a killer and some Reds all the way across the face of the continent. His wife was never going to believe him. But he was damned if he was going to shave twice a day, J. Edgar Hoover or no J. Edgar Hoover. For a moment, he stood with his back to the door, looking at the dollar bill Finley had given him. He smiled. The dollar would buy enough Hershey bars for the kids to keep them happy till he returned.

Las Vegas, March 27, 1931. Only a month before, Bullard's federal colleagues had swooped down upon the desert city, arresting two hundred citizens, including many public officials. The ragged rabble had been herded into the backyard of the Brown Derby hotel, as the local jail could not deal with more than ten occupants.

While this was happening the majority of the populace devoted itself to drinking as much of the liquid evidence as it reasonably could within the time available. Others, in desperation, set fire to their liquor, and as a result the fire department's engines clanged throughout the night. The streets were alive with fire engines and people scampering about to find lawyers or someone to set bail.

But within two weeks the federal agents had departed to root out evil elsewhere and Las Vegas had indeed returned to normal. The first large casino, the Meadows, had opened: a Moorish-style building of buff stucco, designed and built by the fashionable architect Paul Wagner. The gambling casino was run by a former Goldfield gambler, H. H. Switzer, and featured celebrities like the Mormon Kid, Jimmy Lewis, W. H. Mitchel and Frank Morey. The Meadows was an immediate success, and at weekends was jammed with workers from the Boulder Dam project, forty miles to the south.

The Boulder men had always flocked to such clubs as the Bull Pen Inn, the Black Cat and the Blue Heaven. For five days a week, twelve hundred men slaved on one of the most dangerous public projects since the first railroads west. The enterprise was held in an iron grip by the Six Companies, which resisted even the power of state mining inspectors. Gasoline trucks had been used in narrow underground tunnels and there had been many explosions. There was only one doctor for the entire project and the men did not possess either rudimentary sanitary facilities or even sufficient water.

Two months before, eight hundred of the dam workers, led by International Workers of the World leader Eamon Flaherty, had gone on strike for better working conditions. The Six Companies had been forced to shut down and the men had set up a ramshackle camp just south of the city. The Boulder men called it "Camp Stand," and there they held out, money and food dwindling.

In an attempt to gain favor in the town, the Six Companies had put up a two-thousand-dollar first prize for the first Trans-American into Las Vegas, with one thousand dollars for second, five hundred dollars for third and two hundred fifty dollars for fourth. The men of Camp Stand were enraged. For that rage there was but one focus, and that was the Trans-Americans soon to slog their weary way across the sodden desert into their town. Nevertheless, as Flanagan sat himself down at the crowded speakeasy in the Blue Heaven two hours after his Trans-Americans had set out on their final stage to Las Vegas, there was no sign of any trouble on the horizon. The town now seethed with gamblers, sucked in by the lure of the Trans-America, and almost a quarter of a million dollars had already been laid on the stage, most of it on Muller, who now stood firm favorite at two to one on.

"You really think that young Kraut can take it again?" said the barman to Flanagan, uncorking a bottle of whiskey and pouring the brown fluid into a tumbler.

Flanagan, dressed in an immaculate white tropical suit, watched the whiskey surround the ice in his glass and listened with satisfaction to the crack of the cubes as they melted. He gulped down his drink, took out a cigar and struck a match with a flick of his thumb. He lit the cigar and took a long pull.

"The smart money says so," he said. "That young German's got an hour's lead on race aggregate already."

"But what about Doc Cole?" asked the barman. "My old man brought me up on stories about Doc Cole, so why ain't he out there tanning the hide off that young whippersnapper?"

Flanagan was enjoying his new role as athletics expert. He pulled again on his cigar.

"Doc's sneaky," he said. "He probably reckons young Muller'll blow a gasket by the Rockies. So Doc just sits back and lets him do it."

"Sounds smart thinking to me," said the barman, nodding as he topped up Flanagan's drink. "So you reckon my fifty bucks on Doc Cole winning the Trans-America is safe?"

"I think you've put your money on a good man," said Flanagan guardedly. "But it's early days yet."

Hearing a noise behind him, he began to turn and realized with a start that he was not alone. On his left side stood a small, red-haired, ruddy-faced man wearing a rumpled gray herringbone suit and a bowler hat.

"You C. C. Flanagan, manager of the Trans-America?" asked the little man.

"Sure am," said Flanagan, putting out his hand and swiveling on his bar stool. "What can I do for you, sir?" He settled back on his stool, only to become aware that there were now two other men directly behind him.

The little red-haired man had ignored Flanagan's hand and stood staring at him. "My name's Eamon Flaherty—I'm the head man of the IWW union here."

Flanagan felt himself flush; there was trouble brewing. "Then have a glass with me, Mr. Flaherty." He grinned and nodded to the barman.

Flaherty shook his head. "I ain't drinking with no goddam Six Companies man," he growled.

"What do you mean?" asked Flanagan.

"You know exactly what I mean," said Flaherty. "The Six Companies are putting up over five grand for the race—the papers are full of it. Those horsecocks need all the good publicity they can get in this town. Buying up your race has put a quarter of a million bucks into Vegas. Even my own boys have been laying money on it."

"Look," said Flanagan, picking up a glass, increasingly aware of the two men behind him. "Why don't you and your colleagues have a drink on me and we can sit down and talk this over like gentlemen?"

" 'Cause we ain't no gentlemen," said Flaherty. "All we want is that your boys don't come into Vegas."

"But that's impossible," protested Flanagan. "They're on their way here now—there's no way they could run around Las Vegas. I couldn't stop them if I wanted to. We've got camp set up for them. These guys will have run nearly fifty miles—there's no way I can reroute them now."

"Then you better find some goddam way," said Flaherty. Despite his size, he suddenly reached up, grabbing Flanagan by his lapels. Flanagan did not respond immediately, for his first reaction was to consider the ludicrous nature of the scene, with the tiny union leader suspended on his jacket like a man hanging on the edge of a cliff. Then Flanagan slowly felt the hot flush of Irish bile rise and he picked Flaherty up and dumped him on the bar stool beside him.

"Now see here, Mr. Flaherty," he said. "You're starting to get me riled." But the union leader was looking over the Irishman's shoulder at the men behind him. Flanagan felt himself grabbed from the back by one of the thick-fingered henchmen. The man's fingers were in his mouth, so Flanagan bit down hard and tasted the salt taste of skin and felt the soft crunch of bone. The man screamed and dropped back, clutching his injured hand.

Flanagan turned to face him, only to receive a glancing blow on his right cheek from the second of the two men. He fell back awkwardly, his shoulders scattering glasses from the bar behind him onto the floor. He could taste the salt blood from his cheek and threw himself in fury at the burly IWW man who had hit him, butting him in the chest and throwing him to the ground.

"Can it, you guys!" shouted the barman, picking up his nightstick from a ledge behind the bar.

But Flanagan was beyond restraint. He again lunged forward, his right eye closing fast. Flaherty, who had so far kept out of the fight, leaped like a monkey onto his back. Flanagan tried to shake him off as the two henchmen, having recovered, closed in.

"Three against one!" shouted the barman. "That ain't fair!" He reached forward over the bar and directed a well-aimed blow with his nightstick, not at Flaherty, but at the back of Flanagan's neck. Flanagan went down like a log, falling onto his knee with a glazed, sickly look before slumping to the floor.

The barman came around from the bar and looked down at his prostrate customer.

"Like I said, Mr. Flanagan," he said. "Three on to one just ain't fair." He looked up at Flaherty's men.

"Less'n you boys want to continue the argument you better get outa here. I keep a nice place. And don't forget—I got fifty bucks riding on Mr. Flanagan's race, so no funny business." Flaherty and his men looked at each other, said nothing, and left.

The barman took Flanagan under the arms and dragged him slowly into a back room where he settled him on a couch. There Flanagan lay throughout the afternoon, ignorant of the preparations being made at Camp Stand for the evening arrival of the Trans-Americans.

Eamon Flaherty was a first-class organizer, and had made sure that his best weapons, one hundred and twenty-five pickaxe handles, went to his top muscle. Eighty-five fence posts, also courtesy of the Six Companies, went to the youngest, most agile of his men. For the rest, it would have to be business as usual, with judicious use of knuckle and boot. Twenty banners, ranging from "Trans-Americans Out!" to "No to Blackleg Runners," were distributed to women and children and completed Flaherty's party. At five o'clock Flaherty's welcome committee poured out of Camp Stand by car, mule cart and foot, and by six o'clock had taken their positions in the main street, as news passed along the crowd that Flanagan's runners had crossed the McCullough Range and would soon be within the city limits.

Since the destruction of the Vegas road by the flash flood Willard Clay had excelled himself; he had established an emergency feeding station at the bridge, five miles south, and had clearly flagged the route from the bridge back north across the drying desert to the main Las Vegas road. At last, just as suddenly and dramatically as it had begun, the rain stopped, and the runners made their way diagonally back northwest to the road. Muller, not knowing that Doc and the others had crossed the flood ahead of him, drilled slowly and steadily across the desert toward the main route, again confident of victory, trailed by Bouin, Dasriaux, Thurleigh and a group of a dozen others.

The flood had broken the race into two distinct groups. The first was Doc's group of four, who, with well over an hour to spare, were making their way north toward the main road to Las Vegas. The second was a stretched line of a thousand runners, its subgroups shattered by the desert downpour, its leaders now reaching the bridge five miles south of the point at which the flash flood had broken the road.

At the front Doc and his group could afford to take it easy. They trotted along at about six miles an hour, aware of the gradual climb to the thin atmosphere above four thousand feet as they passed through the McCullough Range.

For some time Willard feared that he had lost Doc's group, but at the improvised feeding station other runners told him that they had crossed the flood, and Willard's Trans-America bus churned its way painfully across the desert in pursuit. Willard picked up Doc's group just outside the village of Jean, where he supplied them with food and drink.

"Where's Flanagan, Willard?" asked Doc, sipping an orange juice.

"Up in Vegas, setting up camp," said Willard confidently.

Like the others, Kate Sheridan had slithered south through the lashing rain, across the slimy desert, taken refreshment at the feeding station, then made her way back north to the main Las Vegas road. To her, the rain came as a welcome relief and she used the drop in pace to pass a dozen men before her return to the main road.

Around the runners churned the press buses, support cars and motorcycles, struggling through the desert mud, occasionally becoming marooned, to be pushed out of muddy ruts by journalists and runners.

Five miles out from Las Vegas Doc's group began their drive into town. No one made any decisive break; rather, the pace quietly increased from a steady seven minutes per mile to a crisp six.

Normally Doc felt no trouble at such a pace, and could cover close to twenty miles at that speed. However, the residual effects of the week's running, the altitude, the struggle across the muddy desert and his experience in the flood stream—all had combined to sap him, and for a moment he felt again the doubt that all runners feel when the pace rises and the body makes its protest.

They ran four abreast, like soldiers in line, cutting through the steep, stony passes which carved through the mountains to Las Vegas. Luckily there were few really steep hills; but when such hills were encountered the pace dropped to a heavy-legged crawl and all four men struggled for oxygen in the thin air.

"Vegas," said Doc at last, as they reached the crest of a hill.

Below them, twinkling in the early evening gloom, was "the meadow," just four miles away: "the meadow with many streams," as the Indians had originally baptized it. The first sight of the town charged Doc with a fresh surge of energy, but he knew that he could not risk a sprint finish, not with such young men. He would have to squeeze them, but squeeze them ever so slowly. Gently he started to inch up the pace. The others felt it, but held on through the next half mile. Again Doc pressed, smiling inside himself as he heard the labored breathing in response. He was getting to them; he kept pressing.

Juan Martinez was the first to succumb, easing off with a sob with little over a mile to go. But Hugh and Morgan held on, both gulping now rather than breathing hard. But Doc Cole could not be withstood. By the time they had entered the suburbs of Las Vegas he had set up a twenty-yard lead and was pulling away steadily. By this time the route was lined with thousands of Las Vegans cheering them on, but there was still half a mile to the finish—in the center of town, at the Silver Dollar.

The runners moved through a blur of lights, every casino and speakeasy empty as its customers crowded the rapidly narrowing road into the town center. Through the roar and cheering of the crowds Doc Cole plodded, the sweat streaming down his lined, gnomelike face, the blood from cactus scratches showing red scars on his legs. He could see the finish now, the banners, the waiting tables only a few hundred yards ahead.

But then, with only three hundred yards to go, the cheers were drowned by angry, menacing boos. Through his fatigue Doc sensed the change and looked around him in bewilderment. It was the IWW strikers from Boulder, pressing in on the tunnel of spectators, pinned back by a thin line of straining policemen.

Doc could see the Golden Nugget Casino sign on his right and the Trocadero on his left as he entered the final furlong; a band in front of the casino broke into an overture from *The Pirates of Penzance*. On each side hands strained and reached out to make contact with him, and he could feel their fingers touch him as he trotted the final yards. In one stage he had made up the deficit on Muller. Blocking out the jeers, he put all his concentration into completing the last two hundred yards . . .

But suddenly he was down, forced to the ground by a burly IWW man who had squeezed himself through the police barrier. For a second Doc did not respond, the fatigue of the day's running having finally sapped his energy. The two men rolled over untidily on the rough ground, as the boos grew to a crescendo, and even in his fatigue Doc could smell the whiskey on the man's breath. Then Doc became aware of another runner—McPhail, he realized—pulling his attacker off, leaving Doc gasping on hands and knees, blood seeping from a cut lip.

Hugh McPhail and the IWW man grunted and wrestled scrappily with each other on the ground and were joined by another IWW man, who grabbed Hugh by the throat from behind. Then Morgan, twenty yards behind Hugh, joined the fray, and the four men grappled clumsily to the boos and roar of the crowd and the din of the brass band. Doc pulled himself glassily to his knees, as a man pushed through the crowd, both hands raised. It was Eamon Flaherty, the strike leader.

"For Christ's sake, stop!" he shouted, pulling one of the men from Morgan.

"What the hell do these boys have on their chests?"

He dragged Doc to his feet, followed by Morgan and Hugh. On each of their sweaty yellow shirts were the letters "IWW."

Flaherty raised his hands.

"IWW," he shouted. "IWW! Our boys! Our boys! They're with us!" The message quickly passed through the crowd. Silence fell, to be replaced, not by jeers, but by mounting applause.

Morgan pushed at Doc's shoulder, pointing to the finish. "On you go, Doc. It's your money."

Doc rubbed his lip and smiled. He realized now why Flanagan had insisted on the IWW shirts. A moment later he was trotting toward the finish, through waves of applause, up the narrow channel in the crowd. He passed the finish line as the applause reached a crescendo. Flanagan was standing just beyond the massed band, his face swollen and bruised.

Doc winked at him.

"Looks like you've seen a little trouble, Flanagan," he said. "You should have worn one of your own shirts."

Flanagan fingered his eye and grinned wryly.

Eamon Flaherty entered the Trans-America trailer, slowly peeled the paper from a large red steak and slapped the meat on the table.

"It's the least I can do," he said. "Slap it on that eye of yours. The bruise'll be out in a couple of days, with luck."

Willard gingerly picked up the limp steak, took it over to the refrigerator and put it on the top shelf. Flanagan beckoned the IWW leader to sit down.

"Beer?" he asked.

"Thanks," said Flaherty. "I'm real glad you're taking it so well. I told you there was nothing personal."

"There's *always* something very personal about a black eye," said Flanagan, pouring out a foaming beer for his guest. "Still, I can see your beef. Your IWW boys are out on strike. The Six Companies sponsored the Trans-America. I took their money, so I've got to be the bad guy."

Flaherty wiped the tears from his eyes as the cold drink hit the back of his throat.

"Christ, you don't know the half of it," he said. "Sure, the boys was fired up when they heard those fat-arses had backed your race. Hell, we've been out for over two months now. Two months of nothing but mulligan stew and sourdough biscuits."

"Why are you out, Flaherty? Is it the money?" asked Willard.

Flaherty took another pull at his beer and shook his head. "No, the money's okay," he said. "Good for these times. But my guys are losing blood at the dam. Three men dead in the last six months, fifty-two more busted up bad. No safety rules, no insurance, no sick pay. That's all the IWW is out for."

"Aren't there state safety rules?" asked Flanagan.

Flaherty laughed and gave him a veteran's look. "You're damned right there are. A whole stack of them, a mile high. The state inspector, Malloy, has warned the Six time and time again, but they've got pull up at the state capital, so they just laugh and spit in his eye. Malloy's been beaten up twice himself. Goddamit, we got gas trucks working underground against state laws, we got guys doubling up on hours, we got unsupervised blasting; you name it, here at Boulder we got it. It's like a butcher's shop in the tunnel when there's a blow-back. The walls are red with blood."

Flanagan swore loudly, shaking his head.

"Don't ask God for help. God's a rascal," interpreted Flaherty. "If He were any good He'd have seen off those Six Companies a long way back."

"You said there was more to it," said Flanagan beckoning Willard to refill Flaherty's glass. "What did you mean?"

"I mean that somebody up there doesn't like you," said Flaherty. "Up at the state capital. I know; some of my boys were slipped five-spots to make things tough for you."

"Where did the money come from?" asked Flanagan thoughtfully.

"The cops," said Flaherty. "You noticed they didn't do nothing when those drunks hit your boys? The money came straight from the mayor's office. Our drift is that it came from someone big back at the state capital."

"But the mayor himself invited us here," interjected Willard.

Flaherty shrugged. "He couldn't come out in the open earlier, on account you pulled so many gambling men into Vegas. But he was leaned on from upstairs to make it hard for you. You can take it from me. Lucky your boys was wearing them IWW shirts, otherwise it could have been real messy for you."

"Luck had nothing to do with it," said Flanagan, pulling on his nose.

Flaherty blinked questioningly, but receiving no response he gulped down the last of his beer, wiped the foam from his stubbled chin and stood up. "My boys would like to make it up to you, Flanagan; have some of your men down to Camp Stand. Can't promise you no fancy food, mind, but we do make a real sweet line in bootleg booze."

"Accepted gratefully," said Flanagan, standing up. "Just give us a couple of hours to organize things."

When Flaherty had left, Flanagan closed the door behind him and stood with his back pressed against it.

"Well," he said. "What do you make of that, Willard?"

Willard Clay shrugged. "Don't make no sense to me," he said. "Who would want to stop *us*?"

Flanagan sat down and opened another bottle of beer.

"No one I can think of," he said. "But it all begins to add up. All those goddam bills that are piling up, the towns ahead making no-no noises . . . Still, let's face each problem as it comes. And let's see what friend Flaherty's fixed up for us."

Flanagan looked up at the map and traced with his finger the route east from Las Vegas. More desert, then up into and across the Rockies. It was going to be hard going, even without the hassle. For the moment, however, he was simply going to enjoy himself.

Four miles south of Las Vegas stood Camp Stand, a tattered collection of tents and lean-tos, housing seven hundred and sixty-three Boulder Dam workers and their families. As Flanagan and his runners picked their way through the muddy ground toward Flaherty's command center, barefoot children ran between the tents, followed by thin, yapping dogs. Ragged women boiled clothes in black iron cauldrons at Flaherty's "camp laundries" or poked brown bubbling messes of mulligan stew.

"How do you like my center?" asked Flaherty, after Flanagan, Willard, Dixie, a dozen of Flanagan's Trans-Americans and a handful of journalists—now including Agent Ernest Bullard—had pushed their way under the flap of the main tent. "This is where we put it all together."

For all the signs of hardship, the atmosphere within the tent was very far from being one of despair. Flaherty had transformed his primitive command center into a buffet area, with trestle tables spread with chicken, salami and hot pizza. On another table sat glass jugs of frothy bootleg beer.

Flanagan shook his head. "Beats me how you do it," he said. "You can't have left a chicken alive for a hundred miles around."

"It ain't often we entertain fellers running all the way to New York," grinned Flaherty. "Usually it's horse and rabbit stew here."

"I know that recipe of old," smiled Flanagan. "One horse to one rabbit."

Certainly Flaherty's fare was a welcome change from the monotonous diet of the Trans-America. The runners dug in with vigor.

Hugh had never actually tasted chicken. He saw Dixie look at him as he gingerly picked up a chicken bone, and blushed.

"Never eaten chicken before," he said.

"Don't they have chickens back in Scotland?" asked Dixie, smiling.

"Yes, but not for people like me. I hadn't even tasted coffee before I came here."

In mock disbelief Dixie shook her head, then nibbled at her chicken. "You ought to taste it Southern style," she said. "That's really something."

In another corner of the tent Flaherty was in conversation with Doc.

"I'd like to introduce you again to someone," he said, drawing to him a rugged, bearded man. "You met him yesterday, only in different circumstances."

Doc had indeed. It was the man who had put him down the day before. Flaherty's companion stood towering above him, grinning sheepishly. Then he stuck out a great paw.

"Kovak," he said. "Mike Kovak. Want to say sorry about yesterday. Nothing—"

"I know," Doc interjected, smiling wryly. "Nothing personal." He shaped up to hit the big Pole but instead tapped him lightly on the chin. "Even up," he said. "Have a beer."

Flaherty smiled and moved over to Flanagan, who was standing talking to Willard. "Who the Sam Hill are those guys?" he said, pointing over to the Germans, who stood in an orderly group in a corner of the tent, sipping root beer.

"Krauts," said Flanagan. "But they keep themselves strictly to themselves. Surprised they even joined us here. But they won't trouble anyone."

"I checked them out," said Willard. "They're from the National Socialist Party in Germany."

"Socialists?" said Flaherty, smiling broadly. "Then they're my kind of people." He walked briskly over to Moltke, the German manager, and immediately started to engage him and his group in earnest conversation. They looked at him blankly through cold blue eyes and responded politely but without enthusiasm, while Eamon Flaherty jabbered on regardless.

"I've got a feeling they aren't exactly his kind of socialists," chuckled Flanagan.

"They're sure cold fish," agreed Willard, gnawing on a chicken bone. He looked around the vast crowded tent as the IWW men mingled freely with the Trans-Americans.

"What exactly to Flaherty and his IWW lot hope to get out of striking?"

Morgan, standing nearby with Kate, answered his question. "A fair deal. That's all any man asks."

"Has he got a chance?" asked Flanagan.

"Not much," said Morgan. "All he's got going for him is the fact that it's public money going down the Swanee each day the dam is delayed. They say it's going to be called the 'Hoover Dam.' So perhaps the President will put in his two cents."

"Hoover?" snorted Flanagan. "A marshmallow in a bag of marshmallows. He'll just sit back and watch."

Flaherty had left the Germans and now stood on the fringe of Doc's group. "You're right," he said, reentering the conversation unabashed. "We don't expect no Washington cavalry riding in to the rescue. We're on our own here, and we know it. If we lose we go back to more of the same. We just got to stay out as long as we can and keep out any scabs."

"Irishmen like you have made losing an art form," said Flanagan, smiling.

"But we can't lose," insisted Flaherty. "Not in the long run. You can take all your managers, your salesmen, your members of the board and dump them in the middle of the ocean, and we could still build this dam, but take away the workers, the muscle, and you've got nothing."

"Let's hope that's the way the Six see it," said Flanagan.

"It's simple endurance," said Morgan. "Who can last out longest. But you tell me, Flaherty, how many times have the workers won?"

For a moment Flaherty was at a loss, his ruddy Irish face displaying a mixture of good nature, aggression and doubt.

"You've got to keep trying, just like we do." It was Hugh, standing behind Flaherty, who spoke. "The moment you give up, you're lost. The moment you give up, other men behind you die a little too. When you kill hope, you kill life."

The words rushed from Hugh's lips, surprising him with their passion. He blushed, ending lamely, "Well, that's the way I see it."

The group was silent. They knew he was right. Right about the Trans-America, right about Camp Stand.

It had been more an order from Flanagan rather than a request that led to Mike Morgan and Kate Sheridan finding themselves driven by Willard Clay to the Blessed Mary Orphanage, on the outskirts of Las Vegas, on their rest day. Flanagan's massive white Buick convertible threw up little whirlwinds of dust as Willard drove the car up the hill toward their destination.

Willard glanced over his shoulder at Morgan and Kate as they sat in the bright morning sun on the seat behind him.

"I suppose you're trying to work out why Mr. Flanagan picked you out?"

"It had occurred to me," said Kate drily. "I'm sure no Sunday-school teacher."

"Because they asked for you—that's why," said Willard, his eyes now fixed on the road ahead. "You may not know it, but you two are well on the way to being celebrities. The older kids up at the Blessed Mary know all about you—they get it all on the radio every day."

Willard downshifted expertly as they approached a steep curve.

"Anyhow, Flanagan reckoned you two would do a good job. And so did I."

The Buick slowly drew to a halt in front of a massive brown oak doorway. The Blessed Mary had an unexpected atmosphere of stillness and calm. Kate and Morgan got out of the car and stood below its tall stone walls, occasionally glimpsing a child peering at them from the windows above, before he was pulled away by some unseen hand.

A tall, slim young nun, dressed in a black habit and white surplice, emerged from the darkness of the entrance doorway and walked over to them, smiling.

"Sister Eileen O'Rourke," she introduced herself, proffering a hand to Kate. "You'll be Miss Sheridan, I take it? We've heard so much about you."

She shook hands with the two men and beckoned all three to follow her into the orphanage.

It was like being in church. Morgan could hear the hollow sound of his sandaled feet on the gray stone floors as Sister Eileen led them along a long, oak-paneled corridor. There was no sight or sound of a child.

At the end of the corridor Sister Eileen knocked gently at the door of the principal's office and entered.

In the center of the room sat an elderly nun in a high-backed leather chair behind an enormous desk. She rose, smiling, as they entered. Mother Theresa McEwan was at least sixty, but wore her years well, her face still retaining its strong, handsome features.

"Sit down," she said, indicating three chairs in front of her desk. Sister Eileen placed herself behind Mother Theresa's chair.

"God bless you for finding the time to come," Mother Theresa continued. "You see it was only yesterday that we asked Mr. Flanagan to send you up to meet the children, but we never for a moment thought that it might be possible."

She sat down.

"You must be very tired," she said. "Would you like something to drink?" There was silence as Morgan and Kate looked uncertainly at each other.

"Orange juice?" volunteered Sister Theresa.

"Great," said Willard. "I never drink anything else."

Kate thought she saw the flicker of a smile in Mother Theresa's eyes, but she could not be certain.

"Then orange juice it is," said Mother Theresa, and nodded to Sister Eileen, who excused herself and left the room.

The principal put her sun-tanned hands on the desk in front of her.

"Well," she said. "We have over a hundred children here, aged between eight and fourteen. What would you like to do? Give them a lecture about the Trans-America?"

There was a further silence, again broken by Willard.

"If I might make a suggestion, ma'am . . ." he began uneasily.

"Yes?"

"Most kids don't really want to listen to people talking at them, you know what I mean? They want to *do* something—run, jump, throw—let off some steam."

Mother Theresa nodded. "That sounds like a good idea," she said. "I know that's what I would have wanted at their age—I was always an active girl." She smiled. "You know I always had an idea of myself as a great long jumper."

She looked to her left as Sister Eileen entered with a tray on which stood a jug of iced orange juice and five glasses.

"What are your present sports facilities, Sister?" she asked.

Sister Eileen laid the tray on the desk and poured the juice slowly into the glasses.

"A field, a hundred yards by sixty, and two sand pits. That's about all."

"What exactly do you intend, Mr. Clay?" asked Mother Theresa.

"A track meet," replied Willard promptly.

"A track meet?" exploded Morgan, almost spilling the contents of his glass as it was handed to him.

"Sure," said Willard. "I've organized meets for a thousand athletes in the Bronx in half this space. Here's the way we play it—begging your pardon, Mother Theresa," he said, nodding in deference to the principal.

Willard sipped his juice, then laid his glass down on the desk.

"We have three groups of thirty-odd children. I take runs, you take throws, Morgan, Kate takes jumps."

"Throws?" asked Morgan. "What do they throw?"

"A rock, a baseball, a medicine ball, anything. It doesn't have to be no Olympics."

"What kinds of jumps?" asked Kate.

"Make 'em up," said Willard, gulping the remains of his drink. "Long jump for starters, hop, step and jump, standing long jump—when you run out of ideas, come over and see me, and we'll make up some more."

He looked at Kate and Morgan, then at the two nuns.

"Can some of your staff help?" he asked.

Mother Theresa nodded. "Just one question, Mr. Clay," she said.

"Yes?" said Willard.

Mother Theresa smiled. "Can I judge the long jump? I fancy I'd be rather good at that."

An hour later Carl Liebnitz pushed back his Panama hat and stood, hands on hips, on the rim of the natural bowl in which lay the primitive playing fields of the Blessed Mary Orphanage. Below him, the rough, sandy scrub grass of the playing field was covered by children running, jumping and throwing. That morning he had sought out Willard Clay to get the full story of the previous day's fracas with the IWW workers, but had discovered that Willard, together with Kate and Morgan, had been given the orphanage assignment.

Liebnitz's lean face cracked into a grin as he gingerly descended the steep slope to the field. A baseball rolled to a stop a few feet to his left, pursued by a tiny, red-haired boy. Liebnitz stopped, picked up the ball and lobbed it underarm to the boy.

The boy grinned and rushed back to Mike Morgan who was surrounded by a dozen excited children. Liebnitz nodded at Morgan as he passed, raising both hands.

"Don't let me stop you, Morgan," he said. "Looks like you're doing a great job."

Morgan feigned a scowl, as Liebnitz moved on and passed a sister vigorously engaged in conducting a javelin competition—which consisted of throwing a wooden broomstick for distance. Just beyond, another group of children were throwing stones for accuracy at squares of paper imbedded in the slope, this time organized by a white-haired sister.

In the center of the arena, Willard was conducting handicap races around a vaguely circular two-hundred-yard track. Liebnitz winced as a tiny boy, legs in steel braces, struggled past the tape to win a race, then fell to his knees. He rushed to the boy, placing his hands under the boy's armpits, to heave him to his feet. Sweat streamed down the little boy's face as he stood hands on hips, chest heaving.

"You all right, sonny?" asked Liebnitz, bending down to brush dust from the boy's shorts with his hands.

"Did I win?" the boy asked. "I got it, didn't I?"

Liebnitz gripped the boy by both shoulders and looked into his eyes.

"You sure did, son," he said. "You won it clean."

He got to his feet as Willard Clay, a whistle between his teeth, walked over.

Willard blew a blast on his whistle and gesticulated at a group of children moving to their marks for the next heat of the handicap race.

"On your marks," he shouted.

He waited till they all stood poised on their marks, strung around the rough, uneven track.

"Get set!"

A moment later Willard blew a blast on his whistle and ten children scampered around the track, the older children at the back, giving massive starts to scurrying infants at the front. Willard let his whistle drop from his mouth to dangle at his plump waist and grinned as a dozen children ran past him and lunged at the finishing tape.

"Great handicaps," he crowed, turning up both thumbs to Sister Eileen, who held one end of the broken finishing tape. "Who's the handicapper?"

"You are, Mr. Clay," said Sister Eileen, smiling primly, as she noted the result of the heat.

"What on earth is this, Willard?" asked Liebnitz, taking off his hat and fanning his face with it. "The kindergarten Olympics?"

"That's about it, Mr. Liebnitz," said Willard, walking with Liebnitz toward the far corner of the ground, where Kate Sheridan, Mother Theresa and three other nuns were conducting a variety of jumping competitions.

"How did you find us here?"

Liebnitz grinned. "I weaseled that out of Flanagan," he said. "He's a strange guy, your boss. Thinks he's some kind of a sissy if someone sees him doing a good deed."

Willard and Liebnitz stopped at the long-jump pit, where Mother Theresa was measuring the jump of a large long-legged girl who stood over the principal, her skirt tucked into her bloomers.

Mother Theresa looked up at the girl standing above her.

"Fourteen foot six inches exactly," she said, smiling. The girl ran shrieking back to her friends assembled at the end of the approach run, informing them of the distance she had achieved.

A few feet away, at another sand pit, Kate Sheridan was reaching the final stages of an absorbing high-jump competition. The high-jump stands were makeshift, being broomsticks stuck into the ground with nails inserted all the way up, on which a strip of wood rested.

Two competitors remained, and the other children surrounding the sand pit became silent as the first, a leggy Mexican fourteen-year-old, approached the crossbar, which stood at four foot eight inches. It was a fine, high "scissors" jump, but the Mexican grazed the bar with his rear leg. It quivered for a moment, then fell to the ground, to groans from the audience.

Then the last jump of his rival, a tiny, freckled Irish boy of about twelve. The Irish lad sprinted at the bar from the front and hurled himself into the air, bunching himself into a ball. Like the Mexican, he touched the bar and as he landed in the soft sand

he turned around toward the trembling bar to see if he had dislodged
it. It stayed on. The boy bounded from the pit, to be engulfed by
the other children. Kate smiled and looked at Liebnitz.

"You know the most popular kid here?" she asked. "That little
fat guy over there. He got himself over three foot six inches. You
should have heard the other kids when the little guy made it."

Liebnitz looked around the field, hands on hips, as the sports
drew to a close.

"You seem to have given these kids here a real nice time," he
said. "Most people who'd just run fifty miles through the desert
would be putting their feet up today, not holding kids' sports."

"I wasn't sure when Flanagan asked me," said Kate. "But he
was right. It's been great here. I wouldn't have missed it."

They walked together toward a table in the center of the arena
around which the children and staff were now gathering.

"It's so obvious, plain as the nose on your face," said Liebnitz.
"But we always tend to forget it. When you recognize effort, and
achievement, then everyone's a winner. And when you've got
no losers, then everyone's with you."

The hundred children squatted expectantly in a semicircle in
front of the table in the middle of the field in the setting sun.
Behind the table stood Mother Theresa and her staff, to be joined
by Morgan, Kate and Liebnitz, and a few moments later by a
sweating Willard and the school caretaker, both carrying large
cardboard boxes.

"Back to your groups," shouted Morgan and in a moment the
children had obediently divided into their original three divisions.

Willard dipped into the large cardboard box below him, pulled
out two chocolate bars and held them above him, to the whoops
of the children.

"Prizes," he shouted. "Compliments of Mr. Flanagan."

Friday, March 27, 1931

Las Vegas, Nevada (270 miles)

			Hrs.	Mins.	Secs.
1 = A. Cole	(USA)		41	37	30
2 = C. Muller	(Germany)		42	13	15
3 = P. Stock	(Germany)		42	17	20
4 = H. McPhail	(Great Britain)		42	26	16
5 = M. Morgan	(USA)		42	28	18
6 = J. Martinez	(Mexico)		42	42	22
7 = P. Eskola	(Finland)		42	50	04
8 = A. Capaldi	(USA)		42	52	06
9 = J. Bouin	(France)		42	54	21
10 = P. Thurleigh	(Great Britain)		42	58	23
11 = F. Woellke	(Germany)		43	09	55
12 = D. Quomawahu	(USA)		43	21	57
13 = L. Hary	(Germany)		43	24	01
14 = P. Dasriaux	(France)		43	38	04
15 = L. Svoboda	(Austria)		43	40	20
16 = P. Flynn	(USA)		43	45	20
17 = R. Mullins	(Australia)		43	48	01
18 = P. Maki	(Finland)		43	52	06
19 = S. Hall	(USA)		44	01	07
20 = P. Brix	(USA)		44	06	09

1st Lady: (701) K. Sheridan (USA)   54   01   06

Number of finishers: 1201

Average speed (leader): 9 mins. 15 secs. per mile

12

THE PICNIC GAMES

"Goddamit!" shouted Flanagan, ramming down the telephone. Willard Clay did not respond immediately, but sat opposite his employer in the Trans-America trailer, patiently waiting for him to explain himself.

Flanagan began chewing on his unlit cigar. "Those horsecocks up in Cedar City won't come up with their ten grand," he said finally. "They want the runners for free."

He shook his head and looked to his right at a map of the United States, on which the Trans-America route had been charted, each fee-paying town marked with an American flag. He pulled out the Cedar City flag and hurled it to the floor.

"How come?" asked Willard, carefully picking up the flag and placing it on the desk.

Flanagan shrugged and lit his cigar. "They must have got it on the grapevine that the mayor back in Vegas wouldn't pay up because of our boys wearing the IWW shirts. Who knows? Who cares?"

He stood up and continued to scan the map, using his finger to trace the route northeast between Las Vegas and Cedar City.

"Another town, another ten grand," he mused. "That's what

we need. There's not much but desert and mountains between here and Cedar City."

"What about McPhee?" asked Willard, poking the map with a stubby finger.

"McPhee? That ghost town? It died about the same time as Dodge City. No one's lived there since Wild Bill Hickock and Calamity Jane."

Flanagan stubbed out his smoldering cigar on the oak tabletop and hurled it at the wastebasket, missing by a foot.

"Not so, boss," corrected Willard, gingerly picking up the soft, wet stub with his fingertips and dropping it into the basket. "Last year they struck another big seam of silver up at McPhee. It's no Klondike, but the town's booming again. It's all here in the Vegas *News*. They've got over five thousand people up there, half of them in tents. Try them: sure no harm in *trying*."

Flanagan pulled on his nose and looked again at the map. "McPhee? Hell, where *is* it? I can't even find it on the map."

Willard looked at the map for a moment. "It's about here"— he jabbed with his finger—"twenty-five miles off Route 15, just north of Cedar City right on the edge of the Escalante Desert."

"That means about forty miles extra running for the boys," sighed Flanagan. Nevertheless he returned to his desk and picked up the telephone.

"Get me the mayor of McPhee, Utah. MC-P-H-E-E. Of *course* it exists—five thousand people there, biggest mining town in the whole goddam state." The earpiece was again rammed down on its hook, after which Flanagan lay back in his chair and lit another Havana.

It was a full ten minutes before the phone rang. Flanagan snatched it up at once.

"Could I please speak to the mayor? Mayor McPhee? This is Charles C. Flanagan here, director of the Trans-America footrace. Perhaps you've heard of me? No?"

Flanagan scowled and switched the phone to his right ear.

"Mayor McPhee, I have this Los Angeles to New York footrace, the greatest professional running competition in the history of man. Over a thousand runners. We'll be passing through Cedar City next Thursday . . ."

Flanagan was silent for a moment, then covered the mouthpiece with his hand.

"He's a Scot for sure. Wants to know how much we're asking." He returned to the telephone.

"I suggest fifteen thousand dollars," he said. "Sir, we have some of the greatest professional athletes in the world; Alexander Cole, Lord Peter Thurleigh . . . We could put your town right back on the map."

He covered the mouthpiece again. "He's only offering three grand," he growled. "Says McPhee's already on the map. Says he doesn't give a docken for Lord Peter Thurleigh."

"A docken—what the Sam Hill is a docken?" asked Willard abstractedly.

"I'm afraid the line's rather bad, Mr. Mayor," said Flanagan, in his Noel Coward voice, shaking the telephone. "I didn't quite catch your reply. Just something about a docken. Exactly what *is* a docken, Mr. Mayor?" He covered the telephone again and scowled at Willard.

"Says it's some sort of goddam weed," he hissed. Back in the mouthpiece he continued, "No, Mr. Mayor. I'm afraid three thousand dollars is completely out of the question. Sir, I don't think you quite realize that I have national and Olympic champions on my team—indeed, one of my athletes won your own Powderhall sprint championship."

He stopped abruptly and screened the phone with a cupped left hand.

"*That's* got to him," he said gleefully. He returned to the telephone. "Yes, Hugh McPhail, Powderhall professional champion a few years back."

He listened again, intently. "Yes, Mr. Mayor, ten thousand dollars would be acceptable," he said. "Payable to me immediately on arrival."

He listened again for a few moments. "Yes, sir," he said. "The Trans-America will arrive next Friday evening. My assistant, Mr. Willard Clay, will be with you tomorrow afternoon to arrange all the practical details."

Flanagan listened for several moments more, during which his gleeful expression gradually changed to one of bewilderment. He slowly replaced the telephone, his brow furrowed.

"We've got the money?" asked Willard anxiously.

"Of course," said Flanagan. "No problem there. And he says that the people of the town will take care of most of the runners in their homes. That'll save us nearly five thousand bucks. But he's got one condition. He wants us all to compete in something called Highland Games. Now what in tarnation are Highland Games?"

Half an hour later Flanagan was to find out, as Hugh McPhail and Doc Cole joined him at his request in the Trans-America trailer.

"McPhail, you're Scotch—" he began.

"Scots, Mr. Flanagan," corrected Hugh quietly. "Scotch is something you drink."

"Then I'll start again," said Flanagan. "Scots. We've all been invited to something called Highland Games, at a town called McPhee about two hundred miles northeast of here. These Games, what sort of meet are they?"

"It's a sports gathering," said Hugh. "Folks come in from all around to run, jump, throw and wrestle. There'd be dancing and piping competitions too."

"A sort of glorified track and field meet?" asked Flanagan.

"I suppose that's what you'd call it here in America," said Hugh. "But it's a wee bit more than that. It's a big social occasion, a chance for people to get together for a crack and a dram."

"A crack and a dram?" asked Willard, eyebrows raised.

Hugh grinned. "To talk and have a drink together."

"So it'll be like a day's holiday for our boys," said Flanagan, smiling. "What do you think, Doc?"

Doc leaned forward in his chair. "My paw took me to my first Highland Games back in 1890 in New York. They called them the Caledonian Games then back East. They were real big money meets—most of the throws and jumps were won by the Scots and Irish, with us Yankees left to pick up what we could in the dashes and distance races. They were big business in those days—twenty or thirty thousand used to pay a buck a time to watch."

"Did you ever run in them?" asked Willard.

"And lose my amateur status? Hell, no." Doc leaned back in his armchair. "But when I turned pro in 1908 I ran in some and picked up a few bucks. But they were going downhill fast by then—the big Scots immigration was over and the sons of the first immigrants were running amateur at college by that time. No, I guess you can say that the Scotch Games"—he winked at

Hugh—"that's another name we had for them back East—they were on the way out by the War. By 1920 it was all over."

"So what are we getting into there up at McPhee?" asked Flanagan, pointing at the map. "The Ghost Town Games?"

"I guess you can call the McPhee Games a reminder of times past," said Doc. "Hell, folk out in country districts never gave a hoot about amateur or professional—they just wanted to have themselves a good time. Those Scots miners up at McPhee don't give a goddam about the Olympics—they've probably never heard of Baron de Coubertin."

Flanagan laughed, as Doc continued.

"In the old days, out in the boondocks, they used to call the Highland Games 'picnic' games. So I guess that's what we'll find when we get to McPhee."

Two days later, on Willard Clay's return from McPhee, Flanagan assembled his Trans-Americans in the refreshment tent and informed them of his intention to take them to the town.

Dasriaux was the first to get to his feet.

"Mr. Flanagan," he said. "We do not *have* to compete in these—these 'ighland Games?"

"No," answered Flanagan. "You don't *have* to, but it's compulsory."

There was derisive laughter and Flanagan smiled.

"Seriously, gentlemen, I want you to think of the McPhee Games as a *rest* day. I want everyone to go along to McPhee next Saturday and have themselves a real good time."

"But these *are* athletic competitions," persisted Dasriaux

"Handicap competitions," corrected Flanagan.

"And who decides these handicaps?" shouted Eskola, from the back of the tent.

Flanagan looked uneasily at Willard, who shrugged. "A good point," he said. "That's something I've got to negotiate with their mayor. But have no fear, I'll make sure that all you guys get a fair shake."

"Are there money prizes?" asked Dasriaux.

Flanagan chuckled, then picked up a sheet of paper from the table beside him.

"Yes," he said. "And some real fancy pickings, too. Just listen to this. Three hundred bucks first prize for the handicap sprint, two hundred for the three miles, and all the other races a hundred bucks each."

There was an immediate buzz of discussion among the Trans-Americans. This was good money in hard times.

Flanagan held up his hand for silence. "And don't forget there's big money right down to fourth place," he said. "But there's more. Shot, hammer, weight for height, caber, all three hundred dollars apiece. There's even a hundred bucks for a goddam sack race!"

There was laughter and a mood of anticipation as Flanagan's sales pitch gathered momentum. "High jump; long jump; hop, step and jump; pole vault; hitch-and-kick." He raised his eyebrows and looked at Willard. "Anyone here know what's a hitch-and-kick?" he shouted. No one answered. " Well, whatever it is, they're giving two hundred bucks first prize for it *and* for all the other jumps."

Flanagan handed Willard the program of events. He then turned to his Trans-Americans and signaled for quiet.

"Boys," he shouted. "It's payday. Payday! Hell, what are you going to be up against at McPhee? Guys who spend twelve hours a day grubbing about in the hills like goddam gophers. McPhail here tells me some of 'em even wear *skirts*! If you guys can't come away next Saturday with a couple of thousand bucks then I'm Daniel Boone."

There were whistles and applause.

The tall Texan, Kane, stood up.

"One thing, Mr. Flanagan," he drawled. "You got anything on that there schedule for our Miss Sheridan here?"

Willard Clay pored through the list of events and shook his head.

"You ever done any Highland dancing, Miss Sheridan?" he asked.

Kate, squatting in the front row, shook her head. Kane looked down at her.

"No sweat, honey," he said. "You've still got a whole goddam week to learn."

Kate smiled as the Trans-Americans hooted and laughed around her.

"Okay," said Flanagan, as the laughter died down. "So here's our program. We've got about two hundred miles to McPhee, which we'll take in four easy stages. We arrive there on Friday night and put up with the people there overnight. The Games start at nine sharp on Saturday morning. The morning's mostly peewee sports and novelty events. The main events are the real big money, and they're in the afternoon with a finish at around six o'clock. Then we clean up and we have a —" he looked down at the sheet in front of him—"damned if I can work this out . . . a KEELID."

"*Ceilidh*," shouted Hugh from the front row.

"Thanks," said Flanagan. "From what I can gather, it's a sort of hootenanny, clambake kind of affair. You know, singing and dancing and hollering. We stay the night at McPhee, then it's fifty miles next day to Sevier, toward Route 70, east of Richfield, Utah. Any questions?"

There was silence; the Trans-Americans had decided that a day at McPhee would suit them very nicely.

"Fine," said Flanagan. "Now, I'd like to get some idea of the number of entries we're going to get for the various events." He retrieved the program from Willard and peered at it.

"First the three dashes, hundred yards, two-twenty and quarter-mile."

About fifty runners, including Hugh McPhail, raised their hands.

"What about the half-mile and the mile?" Flanagan asked.

Over two hundred, including Thurleigh and Morgan, put up their hands. These middle-distance events were much closer to the running talents of the Trans-Americans.

"Let's see it for the three miles and six miles," shouted Flanagan.

Over two hundred and fifty runners now raised their hands, including Doc, Bouin, Dasriaux and Martinez. Willard whispered to Flanagan that the German team were standing still and silent beside their manager, Moltke. They had as yet entered for none of the events. Flanagan shrugged and pressed on.

"Now—the jumps," he shouted. Six hands went up.

"C'mon fellas, have a heart," pleaded Flanagan. "It's only a picnic games. So let's see it real big for the jumps." Three more hands were raised. Flanagan shook his head wearily in resignation. "Have it your way," he said. "Now we come to the big money, the throws. Three hundred smackers for first, two hundred for second, one hundred for third. It's taking candy from a baby."

No one moved.

Flanagan spread out his hands in mock disgust. "You mean to say that you guys are passing up over a thousand bucks? There's people where I come from who'd throw their own grandmothers for that kind of dough."

He looked down at Morgan in the front row.

"What about you, Morgan?" he begged. "You look a well set up young fella."

Morgan stood, shaking his head.

"Flanagan, I once saw some Scots picnic games up in the mountains in Pennsylvania. I couldn't pick up one of those weights, let alone throw them." He shook his head again and sat down.

The stringy Texan, Kane, in the same row, stood up again. "C'mon Mike," he shouted, looking down at Morgan. "You enter and so will I." There were shouts and grunts of agreement. Kate flashed a glance sideways at Morgan, who grinned sheepishly, and got to his feet.

"All right," he said. "Put me down for a couple of throws . . . But on one condition."

"Yes?" asked Flanagan.

"That *you* enter for a throw, Mr. Flanagan," replied Morgan. There was an immediate roar of approval and many of the Trans-Americans rose to their feet shouting and clapping. It was the first time that any of them had seen Flanagan blush.

He motioned for silence.

"Okay, okay," he said. "So you got a deal." He turned to Willard and winked.

He turned back to face his athletes and flexed his lean right biceps.

"So exactly what throw have you got in mind, boys?"

Many of the events advanced by the Trans-Americans were not in the program, nor had they ever featured in any Highland Games schedule—events such as catching the javelin or heading the shot. Flanagan had to shout several times for silence.

"Easy, boys. Remember there's a lady present," he shouted. "Let's ask the Scotsman." He turned his head toward Hugh. "So, what do you suggest, Mr. McPhail?"

Hugh stood up and looked around him solemnly. "The caber, Mr. Flanagan," he said. "I think the caber."

Flanagan pointed dramatically to the east. "Boys," he said, "in four days, we hit McPhee. We're going to give 'em the goddamdest Highland Games they ever did see."

The two hundred miles into the town were uneventful. Doc's

narrow lead over Muller was quickly whittled down by the young German and, by the time they reached the town's outskirts, Muller was only just behind Doc, closely followed by Morgan, Thurleigh, Martinez and McPhail, with Bouin, Eskola and Dasriaux also in contention. Muller was still running at a remarkable average of over six miles an hour, and few runners now attempted to stay with him as they had in the early stages of the race.

The Trans-Americans entered McPhee on the Friday evening at seven o'clock, the race finish having been set half a mile out of town. The town looked just as it had forty years before, its single dirt street bustling with miners, mules, wagons and hand-carts. To Hugh it was like something out of a Western movie, complete with saloon, barber shop and sheriff's office. Indeed, he half expected William S. Hart or Tom Mix to come galloping up the street in a ten-gallon hat astride a white horse. The town was made almost entirely of wood, and above its one main street glowered the brown, pockmarked mountain of silver which was now being reworked. A new seam had been opened on the eastern side of the mountain, and it was here that most of the prospectors had gathered, but others later on the scene were reworking old mines, burrowing even deeper into holes made over forty years before by men long dead. Outside the town a camp city had been built to accommodate the overflow, and to this population had been added visitors, sleeping in cars or tents, who were in town because of the coming Games.

Flanagan's runners settled in for the night with the good people of McPhee. Mayor McPhee, son of the town's founder, with whom Flanagan was staying, had never left the town when the original seam had petered out in 1902. Together with his father and a dozen other Scots, he had made a bare living scraping silver from thin seams for almost thirty years and only the discovery of bauxite in 1928 had enabled him to secure sufficient financing to drill again for silver. This had resulted early in 1930 in the discovery of a rich fresh seam, and prospectors had once again rushed to the town. The place was now completely owned by McPhee and his durable Scots friends, and the cost of land and water to prospectors was high. Every store was owned by McPhee and his cronies; every truckload of goods brought to town had to pay a toll to them.

Mayor McPhee had, of course, known of the Trans-America

and had been aware that it was to pass McPhee forty miles away on the road east between Cedar City and Beaver. Thus, though Flanagan's willingness to change the route had come as a surprise to him, he was fully aware of the potential of the rerouting of the Trans-America to McPhee. Another five thousand cars into town at three dollars per car came to fifteen thousand dollars. Ten thousand extra spectators at one dollar a man came to ten thousand dollars, and the refreshment tent was liable to be about another ten thousand dollars the richer, to say nothing of the town's stores. And then there was Flanagan's circus. Nothing like Madame La Zonga and Fritz the talking mule had been seen in McPhee since the turn of the century. At ten thousand dollars the Trans-America was dirt cheap, and McPhee was generous with the measure of whiskey he poured into Flanagan's glass as he entertained him in his living room.

"Thanks, Mr. Mayor," said Flanagan, as he looked around the lushly furnished room. "First time I've ever set eyes on tartan curtains."

"McPhee tartan," said the little mayor proudly.

"How many years have you had these Games?" asked Flanagan.

"From 1888 to 1903," said McPhee. "I was only a bit of a lad in 1888—I won the boys' race then. We had three thousand people here then, nearly all from the auld country. Aye, some of the best athletes used to come here, some all the way from Scotland. Y'see, we always gave big prize money."

He sipped his own whiskey slowly. "I remember one year, we had a big Irishman called McGrath—1898 I think it was. He even brought his own hammer, with a shaft made of vines."

"Vines?" said Flanagan.

"Yes," said McPhee. "Wrapped round and round like a rope. Ver-ry strong. We measured it to see how long it was, but it was only four foot six, regulation size. My father, God bless him, was chief judge, and he checked it himself. Well, first throw McGrath puts it out to a hundred and thirty feet, ten feet beyond the Games record. That meant a bonus of a hundred dollars for the record. But my dad wasn't happy."

"Why not?"

"Well, y'see, when McGrath swung the hammer the vines stretched, and the longer the hammer shaft the farther it'd go. So my dad goes up to this big Irish whale standing up his whole five foot three, and says, 'Mr. McGrath, I think that hammer shaft looks about six feet long when you start swinging it.' And you know what that big Irishman said?"

"No," said Flanagan, smiling in anticipation.

"He said, 'Well, Mr. McPhee, I suggest you measure it while I'm a-swinging it.' " The little Scot exploded with mirth, and the tears flowed from his eyes. He reached for the bottle at his side.

"Here, Flanagan, have another dram," he said.

"Thank you, Mr. Mayor," said Flanagan, grinning. Then his face became serious. "But let's get down to business. My assistant has given you our entries?"

"Yes," said McPhee. "And a real fine turnout you've given us."

"The only problem my runners envisage is the handicaps," said Flanagan. "You see, the handicapper surely has to know each runner's form before he can set fair handicaps. After all, there's a lot of money at stake here."

"True, true," said McPhee, nodding.

"For instance, I've looked at the hundred-yards handicap," said Flanagan. "There's a man there with a start of fifty yards. All he has to do to win is to fall forward."

The mayor's face became stern. "Mr. Flanagan, you're talking about my father."

"Oh," said Flanagan, reddening. "And could I ask who is handicapping the running events?"

"Here's the program," said McPhee, handing a sheaf of papers to Flanagan.

Flanagan checked the front page of the Games program. "It says here that the handicapper is a Mr. McPhee," he said.

"That's me," said the mayor.

Elsewhere in McPhee things were going more smoothly for the Trans-Americans. At Mrs. McDonald's, Hugh McPhail was tucking into his first dish of oatcakes in over a month, while Juan Martinez was making his first acquaintance with black pudding. Two blocks away with the McLeods, Peter Thurleigh and Mike Morgan were making an uncertain assault upon a haggis, and at the Moncrieffs, Kate Sheridan was being taken through the rudiments of Highland dancing, watched by a bemused Dixie.

The German team had camped outside the town, aloof from the social life of McPhee, while the All-Americans had based themselves in the Caledonian Hotel. Also in the Caledonian were most of the press corps, including Liebnitz, who was busy absorbing the history of the McPhee Games from Mayor McPhee's father, a tiny seventy-five-year-old sprinter. It was well past midnight before the last lights went out in McPhee.

At 9 A.M. precisely the Games commenced. The bagpipes began their solemn drone, and on the dancing platform tiny girl dancers pranced three at a time to endless music. Their toes picked out precise and delicate patterns, their medals jingling on their velvet tunics as they competed before impassive, pipe-smoking judges. Children of all ages sprinted down and around the rough grass track in an endless series of handicap races and novelty events, while on the infield men slithered up and down greasy poles or, straddling logs, swiped fiercely at each other with feather pillows. Others, strapped together at the ankles, half limped, half ran in grotesque three-legged races or crawled and stumbled over benches and hoops.

Flanagan had never seen anything quite like it. Already, by 9:30 A.M., there were at least five thousand spectators in the natural bowl below the town, as cars continued to pour from Colorado and Utah into the parking lot adjacent to the area. On the bumpy desert crabgrass surface a rough running track had been marked off, five laps to the mile, while on the infield a six-lane sprint track, each lane separated by strings, had been created. In the center of the home stretch was the dancing platform. On the infield were tree trunks, jumping stands, hammers and ring-weights of all shapes, even bamboo vaulting poles. In the center of the field was a tiny tent, which Flanagan rightly assumed was for the officials. What he did not know was that this tent was also the exact alcoholic center of gravity of the McPhee Games.

As the Games progressed into the heat of the Utah day, so more and more they took on a dreamlike quality. At the center of that dream was Games chieftain Mayor McPhee, bestriding the field like a kilted, bandy-legged colossus. He seemed everywhere, egging on vanquished three-legged competitors, laughing helplessly at pillow-fighters or growling unheeded advice to wrestlers locked in solemn conflict.

And pervading all was the skirl of the pipes. Even at lunch, the morning's sport over and the Games at a pause, Flanagan imagined he could still hear their mournful wail singing in his ears.

"I reckon yer lads have brought us in a few hundred extra

spectators," said McPhee, contentedly watching the incoming cars continue to grind up the dusty hill below, as he and Flanagan stood outside the refreshment tent.

"A few thousand, more likely," growled Flanagan. "Just tell me, when did you last have a crowd like this?"

"Nineteen-three," replied McPhee. "We haven't had the Games since then."

A few moments later the little Scotsman went to the microphone in the center of the games field.

"I would like formally to declare," he said, "the 1931 McPhee Games open." There was applause from the crowds massed on the slopes surrounding the arena. "We have great pleasure welcoming to our fair city Mr. Flanagan's famous Trans-America footracers, brought here by our committee at great expense"—he glanced sidelong at Flanagan—"to our historic Games." McPhee paused. "Among others, we welcome Doctor Alexander Cole . . . a leading member of the British aristocracy, Lord Peter Thurleigh . . . and finally, from Glasgow, Powderhall professional sprint champion—Hugh McPhail." The crowd, composed mainly of Americans, had no idea what or where Glasgow or Powderhall were, but applauded dutifully.

Hugh McPhail managed to give the elder McPhee, a skeletal athlete clad in long black Victorian running shorts, a fifty-yard start and a beating in the hundred-yards handicap. Indeed, old McPhee, hard of hearing, had only just got up into the "set" position when McPhail passed him, on his way to a narrow victory over the other four finalists.

"Winner, hundred yards, world's professional champion, Hugh McPhail, Glasgow, Scotland," intoned the Chieftain, to a roar of applause.

Mike Morgan was not so fortunate. In the throws, he faced miners with years of hard muscular work in their bodies and events which he had never dreamed of, let alone experienced. The shafted hammer weighed sixteen pounds and was a round iron ball, into which a flexible bamboo shaft had been inserted. The throw was made from a standing position, from behind a wooden backstop, and Morgan almost strangled himself in his preliminary swings before hurling the hammer sixty feet, a full forty feet behind the leaders. "We go for distance here at McPhee, laddie, not depth," growled McPhee as he passed Morgan.

Throwing the fifty-six-pound ring-weight for height proved to be even more of a nightmare. Five hundred miles of running had boiled Morgan from a chunky one hundred and seventy pounds down to a lean one hundred and fifty pounds, and in an event where muscle mass was essential he was at a great disadvantage. Indeed, he could hardly lift the weight from the ground, let alone toss it high over a crossbar set nine feet above him. He had smashed three crossbars in practice before McPhee, shaking his head, drew him aside. "Laddie, you know you're costing us a fortune in crossbars," he said. "Here," he added, drawing a hip flask from his sporran, "have a dram."

Doc Cole, in contrast, was in his element and set to make the three-mile handicap the opportunity to sell his Chickamauga Indian remedy, which he had labored hard to prepare till three that morning with the Chinese, Ni Chi Chin. This time, because of the heat, Doc decided to use the remedy as a drink rather than a liniment and modified the formula accordingly. He therefore made a great show of swallowing the mixture before the race, surrounded by a wondering crowd, to whom he resolutely refused to sell a single bottle.

He was not worried about the miners, but he was concerned about experienced runners like Dasriaux, Bouin, Eskola and Martinez, all of whom had already shown a fair turn of speed. Luckily, all four had been given a start of only forty yards on him, with the miners receiving starts of up to a quarter of a mile. In the first mile, covered in five and a half minutes, Doc, billed by McPhee as the "Olympic marathon champion," duly picked up the four closest Trans-Americans, twenty miners and almost all of the other Trans-Americans.

Half a mile later there were only ten plodding miners, spread over a hundred and fifty yards, in front of him, and he was gaining on them with every stride. He eased off, playing out the drama to the end. At the end of two miles with a mile to go, he was only forty yards from the leader and in second position, with Bouin and Martinez forty yards behind. Suddenly Doc gave a desperate groan and fell to the ground. Morgan, suitably primed beforehand, rushed to his side with a bottle of Chickamauga. Doc crawled along the track to Morgan as Bouin and Martinez passed him, groped desperately for the bottle and gulped down its contents. In a moment he was on his feet, sprinting. The massive crowd roared, for Doc was now fifth, over one hundred and fifty yards behind the leaders.

The old man played the situation beautifully. Slowly, painfully, he pulled in the leaders, groaning on every stride, passing man after man. Men shouted him on, women begged him to stop. The arena was in a turmoil. With only a lap to go, Doc was a full ten yards behind the two leaders, Martinez and Bouin, and looking bad. "Cole—Cole—Cole!" screamed the crowd. Somehow Doc dragged himself to just a yard behind the leaders with a furlong to go. To the crowd it was clear that Doc was finished, for he was now making no further impression on the runners ahead of him. But with a hundred yards to the finish Doc sprinted forward again, and snapped the tape five yards ahead of Martinez, with Bouin third.

Outside the athletes' tent Morgan was besieged by miners, desperate to relieve themselves of two dollars for the privilege of purchasing Chickamauga's magic draught. Within half an hour he had sold out.

Things were going well for the Trans-Americans. In fact, Peter Thurleigh, starting from scratch in the mile and giving away starts of up to two hundred yards, caught the front-runners after three quarters of a mile, only to fight a battle with Mike Morgan, to whom he had given a start of twenty yards, over the final lap. The crowd of twenty thousand roared the two leg-weary Trans-Americans around the last lap, with Thurleigh winning at the tape by less than a yard. At the afternoon break, Kate Sheridan, benefiting from her previous evening's coaching at Highland dancing, gave a burlesque display of the art, entitled "Caledonian Capers," which went down well with her American audience, if not with Scottish Highland Games purists. The Trans-Americans were less happy with the jumps, where McPhee had declined to offer normal sand pits, and they gained only a comprehensive range of bruises. The hitch-and-kick event, involving kicking a suspended sheep's bladder with one's jumping foot, almost resulted in a victory for the lanky Kane. The Texan, alas, though touching the bladder with his foot, forgot that the same foot had to touch the ground first, landed on his backside, and had to be taken by stretcher to the refreshment tent.

The final event of the meeting was the caber. For this event McPhee had found Flanagan a Royal Stewart kilt. But it had obviously been intended for a much larger man, and Flanagan was forced to wrap it around his waist twice. Beneath it his white, skinny legs hung like vines from a garden wall. The entrepreneur emerged from the darkness of the dressing tent blinking in the bright sunshine and was led to the massive log, and to the other competitors, seated elbows on knees on a bench beside the caber.

The caber itself weighed about a hundred and twenty pounds and was about sixteen feet long. The two largest competitors, the Scots McCluskey and Anderson, stood over it, looking down at the log.

"Too big," growled McCluskey, a massive chunky man, hands on hips.

"Right, Angus. Too big for the length," said his compatriot.

Flanagan, mystified, was inclined to agree.

McCluskey lifted the caber by its thick end and let it drop with a thud to the ground.

"Never get this beast over to twelve o'clock. Not in a million years."

"Right, Angus. Absolutely impossible," agreed Anderson, standing, massive arms folded.

McPhee was summoned to the spot.

"What's the problem, lads?" he asked genially.

The two Scotsmen explained.

"What d'ye mean, too big?" said McPhee, indignantly. "Back in Scotland, they throw cabers twice this size."

"Perhaps, but not here," replied McCluskey.

"And exactly what do you expect me to do?" asked McPhee, still straining to be polite.

"Only one thing we can do," said Anderson, looking around the other throwers. "Saw a lump off."

McPhee almost danced with impotent rage.

"You know your problem?" he hissed, looking up at McCluskey.

"No," growled the giant, arms folded.

"You're a damn weakling!" said McPhee, stamping off toward the judges' tent for further sustenance.

Twenty minutes later, after a sizable chunk had been sawn from the offending caber, the competition began. There were twelve competitors and Flanagan, sitting on a bench with the others in the middle of the sun-baked arena, was not surprised to see that Anderson and McCluskey, far from being weaklings, looked like the only really proficient caber-tossers there. The other competitors were lean miners or local farm boys and looked just as apprehensive as Flanagan. McCluskey, the first to throw, easily hoisted the caber to his left shoulder, balanced it there for a moment, then commenced on his run, followed from behind by the chief judge. Then McCluskey stopped suddenly, both feet in line, and drove down hard with legs and back as the caber tilted forward, finishing with a high flourish with both hands as the caber finally left his grasp.

It was not a perfect "twelve o'clock" throw, the caber falling slightly to the left at "five to twelve," but McCluskey strutted back to the bench, evidently satisfied. His fellow Scot, Anderson, achieved a similar result, his caber falling to the right, at five past twelve, so the two Scots shared the lead.

Flanagan had difficulty keeping his face straight as he watched the other competitors. Some did not know which end of the caber to lift and had to be directed to the thin end. Even then, their problems had only begun, as they had no idea how to set the caber up onto their shoulders. When they did manage to lift the caber to the correct throwing position, having been allowed help from other competitors, they either allowed it to fall back behind them, or performed a desperate bandy-legged dance before dropping the caber and leaving it to its own devices. The arena was a sea of laughter and little McPhee scowled from the gloom of the judges' tent as he watched.

Flanagan's first throw maintained the carnival spirit. With help, he got the caber into the throwing position on his first attempt but found that the bark of the tree trunk grated on his left collarbone and he felt his knees buckle under the caber's weight. By the time he had balanced himself and it, his energies had been totally exhausted, and all he could do was to drop the caber and run, to hoots of derision from the crowd.

The second round of the competition saw perfect twelve o'clock throws from Anderson and McCluskey, but Flanagan's second-round attempt was as disastrous as his first, and he only narrowly avoided decapitating the following caber judge. He returned to the bench flushed and sullen, his blood slowly coming to the boil.

"Flanagan, last throw!" shouted the recorder, a few moments later.

Centuries of Irish bile and resentment were pouring through Flanagan's thin frame. This time he needed no help to raise the caber to the throwing position, and McCluskey and Anderson looked at each other in surprise. He moved off quickly, suddenly possessed by a surge of strength. The caber threatened to fall sideways. As he tried to maintain balance he started to zigzag, and in front of him other competitors began to move hurriedly to one side. First, Flanagan staggered toward the dancing platform; the dancers leaped off in alarm. Then he changed direction and teetered drunkenly toward the wrestlers who, glancing up, hurriedly broke their holds and fled for safety.

Flanagan felt himself weaken. He was totally out of control and now thought only of survival. All pride gone, he summoned one last desperate burst of energy and launched the hated caber. It was the third twelve o'clock toss of the day—and went straight through the side of the judges' tent, stripping it of its canvas to reveal Chieftain McPhee standing alone drinking whiskey straight from the bottle.

The Highland Games of Scotland were first called "gatherings" because they were occasions when country people, who had through the winter lived remote from each other, came together in spring or summer for a day of sport and social communion. When the gatherings were over there were no real losers, and thus it was at the conclusion of the 1931 McPhee Games held far from Scotland in a dry, dusty bowl north of Cedar City, Utah.

There were over three thousand people in the vast sweaty refreshment tents. Most of them were not Scots, and yet the main tent was ablaze with plaid and filled with piping and Scots songs. Somehow everyone within a hundred miles of McPhee had found in his family some trace of Scots ancestry, and from lofts and cupboards the ancient garb of Gaul had been extracted.

"I've got to give credit where credit is due," said Mayor McPhee, beckoning the barman to him. "Ye brought some bonny lads with ye, Flanagan. That Doc Cole's a wonder—he sold me ten bottles of his remedy."

"Thanks, Mr. Mayor," said Flanagan. "Yes, I think my boys did do themselves proud. Now, about the ten thousand dollars we agreed on the telephone . . ."

"Plenty of time for business," said McPhee. "Here, just you have a half and a half."

Flanagan was puzzled.

"A half and a half, man," repeated McPhee, pouring out a generous half-tumbler of whiskey and beckoning the barman to pour out Flanagan a half-pint of beer.

McPhee dropped his head back and slipped down his own "half" of whiskey and lifted his half-pint of beer.

"The beer's the chaser," he explained, gulping it down. He slapped Flanagan on the back. "Get it down ye, man! It's the real Mackay, all the way from Scotland. None of yer bootleg rubbish."

Flanagan did as he was told.

"Set them up again, Angus," said McPhee. McCluskey the caber-tosser was now acting as barman, his customary role in the town. "Mr. Flanagan here's just warming up."

"About our fee . . ." started Flanagan.

"Fee?" snorted McPhee. "Man, this is no time to talk of money. Get that whiskey down!"

On a wooden platform in the center of the tent a *ceilidh* was beginning, and a young woman was singing a Gaelic song. In one corner the Finns, Eskola and Maki, were being introduced to the rudiments of sword dancing. In another Bouin and Dasriaux were making their first tentative attempts to master the bagpipes. At the bar Carl Liebnitz was deep in discussion with a weary Peter Thurleigh, while behind them Agent Ernest Bullard was recovering some of the liquid lost during the afternoon. Bullard had finally surrendered his amateur status at the age of thirty-eight, though he felt no regret at the loss. He had run in the half-mile handicap, receiving a twenty-eight-yard start from Peter Thurleigh. Though he had not competed for fifteen years Bullard was still in good condition, and had clocked just over two minutes five seconds in finishing second to the Texan, Kane, picking up seventy-five dollars in the process.

A few yards away, Flanagan's world was becoming increasingly blurred, as McPhee continued to ply him with "half and halves." He had already consumed six, and his legs had the rubbery quality which the Trans-Americans, for different reasons, knew only too well.

He began to realize that McPhee was dragging him toward the center of the crowded tent.

"Look," said Hugh, pointing. "It looks as though Flanagan's going to make a speech."

And so it appeared. Even the German team, who had for most of the evening stayed aloof from the surrounding revelry, looked up as McPhee dragged Flanagan toward the platform in the center of the tent.

"My lords, ladies and gentlemen," said the little Scot, pulling the microphone down. "This has truly been a great day for McPhee, a great day of manly sport and endeavor. Your Games committee has been delighted by the attendance of twenty-one thousand three hundred and twenty spectators"—there was cheering and applause—"and the Games' takings which must exceed forty thousand dollars.

"It has indeed been an honor to welcome Mr. Flanagan's famous Trans-Americans, men who have become household names in the last few weeks. If I may mention one athlete in particular it must be our own Powderhall champion, Hugh McPhail, a true son of old Gaul, who won the handicap sprint, against great odds. Less successful, but more spectacular, was Mr. Flanagan's performance in the caber."

There were cheers and laughter.

"The Trans-Americans will, alas, be on their way east tomorrow, but I think that everyone here will agree that each one of them will be welcome back here again at any time."

There were cheers, applause, shouts of assent.

"I therefore think it appropriate," he continued, "that at this stage in the proceedings Mr. Flanagan himself should say a few words."

Flanagan gathered himself, loosened his tie and bent down to the microphone.

"On behalf of the Trans-America footrace," he began, "I thank the people of McPhee for their truly generous hospitality. When I was asked last week to have my men compete at your Games I had little idea of what I was getting them into. I now realize that what you have here in McPhee is a sports festival unpolluted by modern times: a small part of America that is forever Scotland."

His head swam.

"Stop blethering, Flanagan, and give us a song," came a voice from deep in the throng.

"A song, yes, a song." Flanagan fumbled in the mists of his mind. Even in his stupor he could think of songs, but none suitable for a mixed audience. "A song," he said again. Suddenly it came to him.

"I have great pleasure in inviting to the microphone our star performer of today, our Powderhall champion, Hugh McPhail, to sing a traditional Scottish ballad," he blurted.

Hugh's name was immediately taken up and, before he knew what was happening, the day's hero was pushed and nudged forward toward the microphone.

He stood on the platform and the tent gradually became silent.

Hugh flushed. They were waiting for him. He cleared his throat. Only one song seemed appropriate.

> Scots, wha hae wi' Wallace bled,
> Scots, wham Bruce has aften led,
> Welcome to your gory bed,
> Or to victorie.
>
> Now's the day, and now's the hour:
> See the front o' battle lour!
> See approach proud Edward's power—
> Chains and slaverie!
>
> Wha will be a traitor knave?
> Wha can fill a coward's grave?
> Wha sae base as be a slave?
> Let him turn and flee!

The tent was still, not even the clink of a glass. Hugh surged on through the last verse, his voice strengthening as he was joined by Scots all over the tent.

> Lay the proud usurpers low!
> Tyrants fall in every foe!
> Liberty's in every blow,
> Let us do or die!

When Hugh had ended the tent erupted with Scots, would-be Scots, and plain old Americans.

"Lovely voice, lovely voice," said McPhee, drawing Flanagan with him to the crowded bar. "Same again, Angus," said the mayor to Flanagan's massive tormentor of the afternoon. Flanagan started to refuse, but McPhee ignored him.

"Flanagan," he said, eyeing him up and down, "I reckon you for a gambling man. Am I right?"

The mayor gulped down a massive measure of whiskey and pushed his empty glass toward Angus with a nod.

Flanagan did not reply and McPhee went on. "I see you as a gentleman willing to take a chance. Know what I mean?" McPhee opened his sporran and withdrew a thick wad of money.

"Here's your ten thousand dollars," he said, placing the bundle on the wet surface of the bar. "It's yours. You've earned it."

Flanagan, his cash reflex still intact, put his hand on the money, but McPhee placed his own hand on top of Flanagan's.

"So how do you fancy a gamble?" he said. "A wee flutter? Double or quits?"

Willard Clay had now joined Flanagan at the bar and looked anxiously at his employer. "Boss," he hissed, pulling at Flanagan's sleeve.

Flanagan shrugged him off. "Double or quits?" he asked. "What do you mean?"

"I mean a little side bet. Nothing for you if you lose, twenty thousand dollars in your hand if you win."

"A side bet?" asked Flanagan. "What the hell do we bet on? The Games are over."

"The Games are over when I say so," said McPhee firmly. "So what d'ye say?"

"What's the deal?" asked Flanagan.

"Tug-o'-war," said McPhee.

"Tug-o'-war?" exploded Flanagan. "My boys are runners, not goddam weight lifters."

"Tug-o'-war," repeated the mayor patiently. "Best of three pulls. Against a team of lassies."

"Lassies?" asked Flanagan.

"Gurlls, ladies," explained McPhee. "A team of young lassies from Powder Valley against your strapping lads."

Flanagan's mind, though blurred, sensed danger, though he knew not why. He tried to remove his money from the bar, but the mayor kept his hand firmly on top of his.

"Double or quits," he repeated. "And, win or lose, we'll forget about payment for the damage you did to the judges' tent. So what d'ye say?"

"Boss, can I have a word with you?" interrupted Willard.

"Angus," said McPhee, sensing danger. "Give Mr. Clay here a drink, will you?" The big barman was immediately with Willard, sliding a glass along the bar toward him.

"Double or quits, you say?" asked Flanagan slowly.

"That's the bet," said McPhee. "The best of three straight pulls wins."

"When?" asked Flanagan.

"Now," said McPhee, looking out into the gloom outside the tent. "We'll get some cars to put on their headlights so that we get some light." For the first time he took his hand from on top of Flanagan's and held it out toward Flanagan.

"Well?"

Flanagan hesitated for a moment, then clasped the mayor's hand. "You got yourself a deal," he said.

Willard groaned.

McPhee made his way quickly to the platform in the middle of the tent, interrupting the Gaelic chant of an elderly Scot.

"Ladies and gentlemen," he bellowed. "Here is a special announcement. The committee is pleased to announce a final challenge competition. Mr. Flanagan's Trans-America team has decided to challenge the ladies of Powder Valley to a three-pull tug-of-war competition."

There was uproar and McPhee bellowed for silence.

"The competition will take place in half an hour, directly outside the refreshment tent. I would ask that all car owners willing to use their headlights to provide light for the competition report to me immediately. Let me repeat, the competition will commence in half an hour."

The tent emptied, and within a matter of minutes at least twenty had made book on the competition. But Flanagan was surprised at the odds.

"Five to one against my boys," he gasped. "Against broads?"

"You haven't seen these broads, boss," said Willard. "They really are broad." Willard was right. He had seen the ladies of Powder Valley demolish every male team previously that morning. The "ladies" were strapping frontier women of whom Flanagan had had no experience. Indeed, their anchor, Martha, was not so much a person as a place. Martha soon assembled her Amazons in a corner of the tent to prepare for battle.

Flanagan's head began to clear. He had been taken, no doubt of it. "Get me Doc and Morgan," he croaked to Willard. "We've got to work something out."

Willard duly made his way through the seething crowds and returned with the two men.

Doc was not optimistic. "You've been had this time, Flanagan," he said. "Those broads must average over a hundred and sixty pounds. We'll do well to get within ten pounds of that." He shook his head, looking over at the Powder Valley team. "First women I've ever seen who make me feel effeminate."

"But there *must* be some way," said Flanagan desperately.

Doc stroked his chin. "There's always a way," he said. "But let's first see what we've got. Morgan at anchor, McPhail, Bouin,

Thurleigh, Eskola, Casey. These look to be the strongest, heaviest boys around. It's a nothing team, but sometimes nothing's the best you've got."

Flanagan nodded to Willard, who went off to tell the Trans-Americans concerned. "I sure hope that our boys haven't mopped up as much booze as you have, Flanagan," said Doc. "Or we're done for."

"Let's hope those broads have," said Morgan, scowling.

The Trans-America team was soon gathered around Doc and Flanagan. They crowded in a tight circle, crouching.

"Two hundred bucks a man if we win," hissed Flanagan.

"I didn't hear you clear," said Doc.

"Three hundred," said Flanagan.

"Still not hearing you too clear," said Doc, putting his right hand to his ear.

"I'm a fool to myself," said Flanagan. "Make it five hundred."

Doc looked around the circle at his men. There was no dissent.

"You've got a deal," he said. "So let's get ourselves a game plan."

Doc talked to the team for five minutes in a low whisper. Then they stood up and Doc turned to Flanagan.

"We're as ready as we'll ever be," he said.

"So what's your plan?" asked Flanagan, his hand on Doc's left shoulder.

"All we got going for us is endurance and competitiveness," said Doc. "So we dig in and lay right back on the rope on the first pull and let those ladies pull their hearts out. We stretch it out as long as possible, so even if they win the first pull they'll be pooped. Then we give 'em no rest between trials and go eyeballs out in the second pull. If we win that we're still in business."

"And after that?" said Flanagan.

"Let's get to that third pull, then I can put on the miracle hat," said Doc. "And don't touch another drop of that hooch, Flanagan. You'll need a clear head in the next half hour."

He turned to Willard.

"Get us some running spikes," he said. "That could make all the difference."

Twenty minutes later all was ready. Fifty cars spread a bright pool in the inky darkness outside the tent. Behind the cars stood a thousand spectators, still betting heavily among themselves in the warm, buzzing Utah night. McPhee and Flanagan had agreed that the elder McPhee would act as chief judge, with Liebnitz and Bullard as jury of appeal.

"Are you ready, ladies and gentlemen?" asked old McPhee, tying a knot of red ribbon in the center of the competition rope and laying the thick hemp carefully on the ground.

"Then pick up the rope!"

Both teams picked up the hemp and dug in, the chunky Powder Valley team in incongruous blouses, tights and black thick-heeled leather boots and the Trans-Americans in shirts, shorts and running spikes. Martha and her adversary, Mike Morgan, tied the rope around their waists in the anchor positions and Morgan nodded to Doc. They were ready.

"Take the strain!" shouted McPhee, and waited till the red ribbon was directly above the center line. There was silence, with only the whirr of insects to be heard.

"Pull!"

The sturdy ladies of Powder Valley pulled indeed and in seconds the Trans-Americans had given away six inches. But they held and lay back on the rope, setting their heels in firmly. Then, aided by the grip of their spikes, they too pulled and regained the grooves they had first created as a platform for themselves. Again stable, they lay back almost horizontally as the Powder Valley team set and reset their feet in an attempt to unbalance them. But the Trans-Americans held and used body weight rather than muscle to retain their position. The pull lasted five minutes and the sweat streamed as the gasping ladies gradually pulled the Trans-Americans toward them. Then it was over—the pull had gone to the girls of Powder Valley, who collapsed like stranded whales on the rough scrub grass.

Doc was quick to seize the advantage. "Pick up that rope," he hissed. "They've had it."

The rope was soon reset and this time Flanagan's Trans-Americans pulled viciously from the first moment. Their gasping opponents, never allowed to regain their balance, slithered and slid on the thin dry grass as Doc screamed his men onward.

"Pull, goddamit, pull!" he raved. Suddenly it was over. The red ribbon was in Trans-America territory, and the second pull was theirs. It was now even at one-all, and everything rested on the final pull.

McPhee was not slow to realize what had happened, and saw

his twenty thousand dollars slipping through his fingers. He took from his sporran a large pocket watch.

"I call ten minutes' rest before the final pull," he shouted above the din. "Only fair," he said to Flanagan. "After all, they're only gurlls."

Flanagan, now almost sober, shook his head. The old mayor had got the better of him. He walked over to the girls' team and a few moments later he was seen in smiling conversation with the massive Martha. Flanagan nodded to her, returned to the Trans-Americans and stood hands on hips in front of Doc.

"Well," he said. "What's the master plan this time?"

"Master plan?" said Doc. "Goddamit, Flanagan, have a look at our boys." He pointed to the Trans-Americans lying face down on the grass parallel to the rope. "A little prayer might help." He smiled. "Only one plan now. No more tricks. Just pull on that rope until we drop."

The rope was set for the final pull and again a hush descended on the crowd. The Powder Valley team had by now recovered completely, and their plump, round faces were set in a look of grim determination.

"Pull!" screamed McPhee.

The pull was by far the longest of the three, and lasted almost ten minutes. It was a pull that ebbed and flowed to the roar of the crowd, with Mayor McPhee now losing all pretense of impartiality, dancing up and down beside the Powder Valley team like a demented leprechaun. But after nine minutes the Trans-Americans were drained. Hugh McPhail could feel the strength ebbing from him and Morgan's upper body had gone into spasm. Peter Thurleigh's eyes were glazed and he felt his grip weakening as Bouin, Casey and Eskola started to slide in front of him. Ever so slowly, the pull was slipping from them and every Trans-American knew it. Doc stopped shouting and turned away, not daring to look.

Then there was a thud as Martha, the Powder Valley anchor, slipped to the ground with a dull thump and in an instant her team had lost balance and had started to slide.

The crowd gasped with surprise.

Doc heard the gasps and turned. "Pull!" he bellowed. "Pull, you weaklings!" Dixie and Kate rushed from the crowd and joined him, screaming at his side, tears streaming down their faces.

The Trans-Americans, feeling the resistance against them slacken, dug deep and found from somewhere fresh reserves of strength. Bathed in an ocean of roaring sound, their bodies awash with muscular waste, they pulled like men possessed. Nothing or no one could stop them now, as they found new rhythm, new fire, and in less than a minute they had pulled their broken opponents over. They had won!

Trans-Americans poured from behind the parked cars, through the roar of the crowd, to engulf their team, who knelt on bent knees, sobbing with fatigue. Doc looked around at Flanagan and shook his head.

"You got to her, didn't you?" he asked, nodding over to the prostrate, heaving Martha, who lay on the ground, her great bosom heaving.

"In a manner of speaking," said Flanagan, adjusting his tie.

"I know your manner of speaking," growled Doc, leaning forward with Flanagan to pull Martha to her feet. "Just what did you say to her?"

"Nothing much," said Flanagan, turning away from Martha. "I just made her an offer she couldn't refuse."

"Jesus," said Doc. "What was that?"

"You," said Flanagan.

13

MOMENT OF TRUTH

Two hundred miles beyond McPhee and its Games, the Trans-America had settled back into a daily routine of forty- to fifty-mile stages, usually divided into morning and afternoon sections, as they made their way toward Colorado. Muller and Stock had wiped out the advantage that Doc and his group had established at Las Vegas, and again led the field, if only narrowly. Other runners such as Williams' All-Americans' hope, Capaldi, the Australian, "Digger" Mullins, and the Japanese, Son, had begun to feature in the top ten at the end of each stage, and were now in the top twenty on aggregate time.

The McPhee Highland Games provided a welcome respite for journalists hard-pressed for copy, and pushed the Trans-America into the columns of the weeklies for the first time. But the impact of Carl Liebnitz's article did not hit the Trans-America until two days after its publication, when it came into the hands of Flanagan's medical director, Maurice Falconer.

By this time, the Trans-America lay just short of the Utah-Colorado border, near Green River, having crossed forty miles of steep mountains by Richfield and Salina. The article read:

"There will be those that will die." Those were the words of leading physiologist Dr. Myron Bernstein, Professor of Physiology at the University of Stanford. Dr. Bernstein was commenting on reports of C. C. Flanagan's Trans-America race, now sweating its way toward the Utah-Colorado border.

Dr. Bernstein's prediction is based on the massive daily calorific requirements of Flanagan's Bunion Derby runners. The Stanford physiologist estimates that the running itself consumes about 5,000 calories a day, and added to this another 1,000–2,000 calories a day for normal basic body functions. Professor Bernstein sees no way in which the runners can consume the necessary 6,000–7,000 calories a day to enable them to avoid cannibalizing their own bodies. "These men," he said, "are literally eating themselves up. First, they will burn up all available body fat, then they will start to consume muscle. Mr. Flanagan's men are heading in only one direction—into the hospital."

I put it to Professor Bernstein that the runners might have enough excess fat and muscle to burn up, but the professor was emphatic. "These men are distance runners. Double their height and you have their weight in pounds. They carry only about 5% fat, in comparison with the normal 20% you and I carry around. And remember that these are hard times and many of them may already be inside the 5%, in which case they are undoubtedly on the brink of disaster."

When I put this to the race organizer C. C. Flanagan, his response was immediate. "Scientists said the bee couldn't fly—but it did. They said no man could run a mile inside 4.10, but it has been done, and mark my words, one day some college boy will put up two fingers to the scientists and run it in four minutes flat. We're talking about men, not machines."

So we have the classic case of the expert versus the dreamers, our dreamers in this case being the thousand-odd men and one woman plodding East across the desert beyond Las Vegas. As Mr. Flanagan says, men are not machines, for there is a ghost in these machines that may make all scientific discussion about calorific input and output not worth the paper either the experts (or me for that matter) write upon.

It was Dr. Maurice Falconer who spoke first, brandishing Liebnitz's article as he pushed open the Trans-America trailer door.

"Just what does this mean, Flanagan?" he shouted. "Who the hell runs the medical department here, you or me?"

Flanagan did not respond, but pulled out the cork on a bottle of whiskey with his teeth and poured out a large glass, pushing it along his desk toward Falconer.

"Have a snort, Maurice," he said, and sank onto his rocking chair.

Falconer frowned and snatched the glass from the desk and gulped it back. Flanagan poured him another drink, gave himself one, then replaced the cork in the bottle.

"Now, what's the big problem, Maurice?"

Falconer gulped the first half of the fresh glass and sat back, visibly more controlled.

"You've seen this article?" he said, putting it down on the desk on his left.

"Naturally."

"Then why didn't you refer Liebnitz to me?" asked Falconer.

Flanagan glanced across the trailer at Willard Clay.

"Willard, when did Carl Liebnitz come to me with Bernstein's statement?"

"First day, at Flanaganville, at the end of the first stage," replied Willard.

"And where was Dr. Falconer at the time?"

"Up to his neck in cripples back in the medical tent."

"So what was I to do?" asked Flanagan, raising his arms. "There was no way I could interrupt you, was there?"

"No," admitted Falconer grudgingly.

"More to the point," said Flanagan. "Is this guy Bernstein right?"

Falconer took another pull at his drink. "In strict theory, yes," he said. "These runners should be burning up about seven thousand calories a day. So they need that number of calories simply to maintain their body weight."

"But in practice?" pursued Flanagan.

"In practice, who the hell knows?" growled Falconer, drawing a damp white handkerchief across his brow and pushing back a mane of white hair. "Payson Weston walked across the USA about fifty years ago and he was only a little runt. Okay, so he lost some weight, but it didn't kill him. He sure didn't vanish into thin air in the middle of the Rockies."

"So what's your opinion of the physical condition of our men?" asked Flanagan.

Falconer shrugged. "About a quarter of them should never have been within a thousand miles of this race," he replied. "Even at their fittest they could never have made it, and after two years on the bread line . . . well, most of that bunch are out of the race anyway. Another quarter are fit men, not athletes perhaps, and in better times they might have made it, but only a handful should even get as far as Nebraska. The third quarter are low-caliber athletes in the conventional long distances, or men from other sports who have licked themselves in shape especially for the Trans-America. Some of them will make it."

Falconer closed his eyes for a moment, then opened them. "The final twenty-five per cent, men like Cole and Eskola, are fine long-distance athletes, but even for them the Trans-America is a gamble: no one since Weston has ever covered such distances daily and even then it wasn't in a race."

"So how many do you reckon will make it to New York, Maurice?" Flanagan went on.

Dr. Falconer wrinkled his nose.

"My guess is between four and five hundred," he said. "But remember, we're dealing with human beings, and there's three hundred and sixty thousand dollars at stake. For many of these men that's the difference between life and death, so there's no real way of knowing how many will finish."

"So, this smart-ass Bernstein is just pissing in the wind?" said Flanagan.

"Perhaps; but we've still got to keep up the calories. Myself, I think that milk may be the answer to the problem. It's virtually a complete food and very high in calories. So we'll have to get iced milk in daily."

Flanagan looked at Willard, who nodded.

Falconer loosened his collar and sighed. "Bernstein's a nutritional specialist and he's looking in a narrow mirror. The real problems for these men lie in three places. The first is in the ability of their muscles and tendons to take the daily pounding. So the answer to this race may lie in the few millimeters of Achilles tendon rather than in calorific intake."

The medic picked up his glass. "Got any ice?" he asked before continuing. Willard placed two cubes in his glass. "The second is in the various body systems. By this I mean general health, things like stomachaches, throat infections, the normal run-of-the-mill ailments that most men work through every day without giving them much thought."

Flanagan nodded.

"The problem is that the athlete is a living contradiction, for he's both tough and delicate. Sure, he can take hours of pain and discomfort that the ordinary man couldn't handle for five minutes. But the other side of the coin is that trivial complaints that Mr. Joe Average would shrug off and ignore are disasters to a highly tuned athlete. What's a molehill to the average guy is a mountain to him. So it's essential that the general health of the runner is good."

"And the third?" asked Flanagan.

"The third place is in the mind." Falconer tapped his forehead. "This is where the daily battles will be lost and won. The Chinese have a saying, 'A tiger's picture is outside, a man's picture is inside.' The Trans-American's picture is inside, and that's a picture we haven't seen completely yet."

"So what should we do about Bernstein?"

"Nothing," said Falconer, standing up and placing his empty glass on the table. "Carl Liebnitz has his story and he'll soon be on to something else for his next piece. Journalists are sprinters, not marathon men. If our friend Bernstein were really interested he'd be down here like a shot with a team of experts—Jesus, this race is a ready-made thesis for a man like him. No, I don't think we shall hear much more from Professor Bernstein."

He opened the trailer door and started to leave.

"Sorry I blasted off at you like that," he said, turning. "It's been a hard day."

"Forget it, Maurice," said Flanagan. "Just get yourself a good night's sleep."

Flanagan poured himself out a long drink and then filled Willard's glass. He shook his head. "How many crates of booze do we get through every week here?" he asked. Willard realized that he did not have to reply. "Wow," Flanagan went on, "I never saw Maurice riled up like that before."

"Still, he had a good point," said Willard, gulping down his drink. "The way Bernstein put it, most of our guys would have vanished down cracks in the road by Cedar City."

"So we take Maurice's advice and put in an order for two pints of milk per man per day," said Flanagan. "They got that many cows in Utah?"

Willard scribbled the details on a pad. "And another thing," said Flanagan. "Get a crate of booze over to Maurice Falconer's tent. We've got a good man there. So let's keep him sweet."

In every race, whatever the distance, there is a moment of truth, when one man imposes his will upon the field and stamps his authority upon it, or when he realizes forces within himself whose existence he has not expected. For Hugh, the final twenty miles toward Grand Junction was that moment. It was a long "moment," lasting for almost three hours, much of it in the harsh Utah sun, and it was a struggle that had nothing to do with the other competitors, though it had everything to do with the eventual outcome of the Trans-America.

As before, a German had surged into the lead, though this time it was not Muller but his compatriot, the stocky, bronzed Woellke. The initial speed was nothing like Muller's cracking seven miles an hour of two weeks before, but it was sufficient to leave the field, after just half an hour, stretched for over a mile on the narrow road. He pulled with him a dozen optimists, including the Mojave Indian, Quomawahu.

Hugh wore a soccer shirt and a trimmed sombrero, the latter a purchase from an Indian back in the Mojave. He had sandpapered his feet, cut his toenails and talcumed his armpits and chest, as he had seen Doc do, and around his wrist he now wore a handkerchief as a sweatband. If only Stevie and the boys back in the Broo Park could see him now!

A light breeze blew little whirls of dust in the road ahead as the runners pierced the central desert. Hugh had always thought of the desert as a dead thing. But this was alive and watching. All around the tall saquaro cacti stood like silent spectators, with hedgehog cacti crouching like dogs at their feet. In the distance he could see the soft chocolate brown of the hills through which they would soon have to pass. Everything was bright, sharp, alive.

Again he was running with Doc, the little man having added sunglasses to his desert equipment. Doc looked at his watch and eased off as the five-mile point was reached. "Forty-five minutes," he said. "Let's drink."

Hugh drank the warm, bitter desert water, then poured a container over his face and neck.

"Heating up," said Doc, pointing to the rising sun. It was, and all around the pace continued to slow as the heat made its impact.

By the next water point, at ten miles, they were passing sweat-drenched runners who had dropped to a walk. Behind them, Flanagan's trucks had already begun to pick up nonfinishers.

"I reckon we're the first people to come here by foot since the eighteen-eighties," said Doc. "About three thousand came out here from back East with pushcarts—they could move twice as fast as oxen."

Hugh pulled down his sombrero and drew his kerchief across his brow. He could feel the sweat build up again on his forehead even as he brushed it off. It poured in rivers down his cheeks and neck and soon he could feel it coursing down the valley between his abdominal muscles.

At first the sweat was a relief, acting as it was intended to do, as a means of cooling the skin. Slowly, however, the sweat started to encroach upon him. It tickled his temples, drenched his eyebrows, poured its salty tears into his eyes, making them smart and sting. Then he began to sniff the salt sweat up into his nose, making him cough. His light jersey absorbed all the sweat it could, then stuck to his body like a leech. The sweat ran down the inside of his crotch, down his legs, into his feet.

He looked sideways at Doc. Sweat was running down the channels in the older man's lined face. Doc shook himself like a dog, spraying out showers.

"Time for more water," he said, nodding to the attendant at the water point, who was serving Bouin, Dasriaux and a half dozen others.

Hugh's thirst had started to rage. He had gulped back two containers of water when Doc laid a hand on his arm. "Easy," he said. "Let it go down slow. Let the mouth enjoy it."

Half-past ten, and five miles to go to the first half of the day's stage. The road shimmered with heat, and Hugh felt as if they were running through a corridor of warm air. He noticed he had stopped sweating. The sun was evaporating his sweat and his skin was hot.

They completed the twenty miles in just under three hours forty minutes, finishing in tenth and eleventh positions. Flanagan had set the midpoint of the stage by a dried-up river bed, where there was plenty of shade under gnarled and twisted Joshua trees, and had set up two great central refreshment tents as places both for food and for respite from the heat.

By midday the sun was so hot that the Trans-Americans were

confined to tents and trailers. For the moment the Trans-America lay still and dead, twenty miles out from Grand Junction.

"Can't figure it," said Doc, sipping his tenth orange juice in the gloom of the tent. "The way those two Krauts have been burning up the road. Something's wrong."

"What can be wrong?" asked Hugh.

"For starters"—Doc put down his drink—"those guys are too young to be running these big distances. Hardly out of their teens. It ain't natural. They haven't got the miles under their belts. No. Something's wrong, though I can't yet figure it out."

He turned onto his back and pulled his cap over his eyes.

"By the way," he said. "You're doing good out there. Real good."

The runners lay like dead men, like the debris of some great battle. They lay in rows, naked on their backs on their blankets, their hands across their chests, bodies gleaming even in the gloom. Now that they were out of the sun the sweat streamed from each pore; the tent stank of the sweat of forty-thousand miles of running.

Outside, the sun hit the tent relentlessly and its surface was impossible to touch. Inside, in the cathedral of the great tent, the Trans-Americans dedicated themselves to the next stage of their race.

For Hugh it had been his first experience of running under hot conditions. His only flicker of fear had been when he had stopped sweating, for this had been a new experience. The feeling of the body burning itself up stride by stride was an uncomfortable one, and one which he would have to face until they had cleared the desert. Since it had not been accompanied by any noticeable muscular fatigue he was content, but he had become increasingly aware of how little he knew about covering such massive distances daily.

In his researches back in Glasgow's sepulchral Mitchell Library he had devoured every book he could find on distance running. Good God, even marathon runners were not advised to run much more than twenty miles a week in training! And now he was trying to cover twice that distance and more a day, six times a week for three months on end, across some of the toughest country in the world. The settlers had had enough on their hands getting across these dry wastes even without the Indians, he thought.

Barstow, Los Angeles, Las Vegas, Boulder—places he had never even heard of, or if at all only in the darkness of the Carlton Cinema, Townhead, Glasgow, fumbling with some unwilling lass in the back row of the balcony. Hugh had no fear of failure, for somehow he sensed that even getting as far as Las Vegas had been a kind of victory, and that every day since then had been a fresh achievement. In each day's running he had found, and hoped he would continue to find, new depths and qualities in himself, and that was a victory whatever the outcome of the race.

His thoughts strayed to Dixie. He had often dreamed of girls like her, but now that he had met her he had not the first idea of how to approach her. She seemed so controlled, so sure of herself. Even the thought of laying his hand on hers made him shiver, not because he did not want to touch her, but out of fear of rejection. What could they talk about? They had so little in common. He would ask Doc to organize something for one of the rest days, he decided, something that would bring them together and spare him the embarrassment of her saying no . . .

Doc lay back, head cupped in hands, chewing on a straw, and allowed his thoughts to slip back to his first day as a traveling man. He had ranged the Midwest in summer, the Deep South in fall, for only at harvest time was there money in a farmer's pockets.

He would set up a platform near the river and at night, as twilight came, set the kerosene torches ablaze. When, drawn by the lights, the banging of drums and the blare of trumpets, a sufficiently large crowd had drawn around, he would put McGinty the comedian on stage.

"Why do old maids go to church on Sunday?" McGinty would ask. "So they can be there when the hymns are given out!" Or, "Why did the chicken cross the road?" "So he could get to the other seed!"

All good stuff, plundered from Jackson's *On a Slow Train Through Arkansas*.

Then to the pie-eating contest.

Pies, liberally coated with molasses, were suspended from a beam and the boys of the town, hands behind their backs, would make idiots of themselves trying to consume them.

Then to the real business of the evening. Doc, in goatee and Prince Albert coat, sporting on his chest a jangle of medals, would stand on stage for some moments, his back to the crowd, silently studying an anatomical chart.

Then he would turn to face his audience.

"In life there are only two certainties, ladies and gentlemen," he would say, grasping his lapels. "Death and the taxman. I cannot do anything about the Department of Internal Revenue, but, ladies and gentlemen, I *can* change your life."

He would then dramatically reveal a bottle of Pinkham's remedy.

His spiel would last anything between half an hour and an hour, depending on how the mood took him, and would end with a clamor of hands grasping for Mrs. Pinkham's elixir.

Lydia Pinkham. Even twenty years after her death she was still offering advice to women by mail—before the government stepped in and stopped it.

Doc lay cradling his head in his hands. Yes, it had been a great life. But this, the Trans-America, was what he had waited for . . .

Morgan looked around him. They were certainly a strange bunch. Gabby old Doc, who seemed to have lived ten lives, all of them on the run. That dark, hard Scotsman, McPhail—a decent enough guy, but somehow young for his age. Martinez: Martinez was like a child, springing along gaily and happily, but with an immense responsibility, the life of his village, resting on his slim shoulders. Morgan was glad that the little Mexican had won a few bucks on the second stage, back in the Mojave.

And Thurleigh. The Englishman was like something out of a school picture book, delicate and remote. Thurleigh had come from some other world, a world of assumptions that Morgan instinctively disliked. Still, as long as he kept out of his way.

And what of the girl, of Kate? He still had no idea why he had gone out after her. She was as unlike Ruth as it was possible to be. Just the thought of Ruth made him wince. This race was for her, for their child. He had dedicated himself to it completely; no woman must be allowed to divert him.

Juan Martinez lay on the floor in a corner of the tent, rolled up in a tight ball, engulfed in the folds of his blanket. Already he had won more money than he had dreamed possible and had arranged with Flanagan that it should be forwarded to his village through the agency of the Bank of Mexico. Juan Martinez lived from day to day. In any case, for him New York was simply a dream. He could not conceive of it, could no more imagine its crowded streets and its skyscrapers than a deaf man could imagine a Wagner opera. The Trans-America was proving tougher than he had expected, harder even than his daily runs with the Tarahumares had been. But a thousand-odd miles away in his village life was immeasurably harder, and he daily dedicated himself anew to grinding out fifty more miles on the endless dirt roads, the memory of his people firmly in his mind . . .

Only a few feet away from him Peter Thurleigh, his brown feet poking beyond the foot of his blanket, started to snore, realized he was doing so, gulped, and settled back again into silent sleep. Though he had still not discarded his blue-lined Oxford shorts he had adopted more practical long-sleeved clothing for his upper body and was now—his body burned almost black by the desert sun—indistinguishable from the other Trans-Americans, and was still in the top twenty places on every stage. Though his view of the world was incomparably broader than that of Martinez, like Martinez he had never conceived that the Trans-America would be like this. He had never imagined men who could notch up fifty miles a day, day in, day out, over nightmare deserts and crippling hills, in temperatures that would fry an egg.

He lay on his bed, listening to the scuffles and snores of the thousand men around him. His Rolls-Royce had ended up in a ditch back in Barstow and now his chauffeur-butler, Hargreaves, was in the Barstow hospital with appendicitis. Thurleigh was on his own, with well over two thousand miles still to go. Peter Thurleigh smiled. The butler and the Rolls had really been rather juvenile; a piece of undergraduate showing off. Hargreaves, an out-of-work American actor, had never been closer to England than Sunset Boulevard, his only experience as a butler having been in Erich von Stroheim's *Foolish Wives* in 1921.

No, thought Peter Thurleigh, a titled parentage counted for little out here. All that mattered was the ability to hold body and mind together for fifty miles a day, six days a week, over country that made even the torrid Paris Olympics cross-country race look like a Sunday-school picnic.

For the dirt roads of Utah absorbed titles and professions just as they had absorbed settlers half a century before. In any case, even back in England his peerage had counted for little. For his father, Albert Swindells, had made his money in Luton in the 1880s in the hat trade. It had been his financial support for the Liberals in difficult times that nad secured Swindells his peerage. But the "man of straw," as Swindells the milliner had been called, had never secured the hoped-for respect from the class which he so admired. And neither had his son.

Thurleigh imagined he was back in the "dorm" at school. The same groans, the same fetid smells, the same creaks as men turned from side to side, or sought furtive sexual relief. For a moment Peter felt that cold shiver of fear and uncertainty he had known as a twelve-year-old on his first night at Eton.

At school, sports had been the key, for there sports were a religion. Individual sports like track and field athletics or cross-country running could, however, only be tolerated if linked with success in team sports, and his ability on the rugby field provided that essential balance, that team involvement, which made individual prowess in athletics acceptable. It also made almost acceptable the fact that his father, though a peer, was in trade.

At Cambridge he had never felt at ease, and even his title and his affluence did not allow him to relax. Not for him the spinning of idle days at Fenners, of training that consisted merely of a trot and a massage. While others dined on tea and crumpets, watching him through rainy pavilion windows, he plodded dourly around the Fenners track. Long after they had gone at night and long before they had risen in the morning, he ran mile after mile.

But they did not care. Indeed, they despised him for it. It was simply not right to show such seriousness, such commitment, for everything had to be accomplished with ease and grace. He was acting like a tradesman, not a gentleman. No, young Thurleigh simply would not do.

He had tried everything to be accepted. Indeed, he even became an anonymous sports correspondent to *The Times*, sometimes commenting at length on his own performances in an attempt to make his fellow undergraduates understand his commitment. But it was no good. Always they, the charmed ones, danced the night with the gossamer girls he so feared while he stood in the shadows, expensively and impeccably dressed, invariably alone.

At both the Paris and the Amsterdam Olympics he had met another kind of athlete, the harriers, working-class men steeped in road and cross-country running. But Peter could no more relate to them than he could to his contemporaries at Cambridge. He was stuck in a sort of limbo, aware all the time of a nagging inadequacy which athletic success seemed unable to assuage.

It had never occurred to him to enter the Trans-America until that night at the Reform Club. Some members had been discussing the Trans-America race earlier, but now they had moved on to the subject of the sprinter compared with the distance runner . . .

"Sprinting," said Lord Farne loudly. "Nothing to it. Like a bloody greyhound. No guts, no heart."

Peter Thurleigh had swung around in his chair immediately.

"And how, Farne, would you define a sprint?" he asked.

It was Aubrey Flacke who answered. "How far did you run in Paris at the Olympics?"

"Fifteen hundred meters, just short of a mile," said Peter. "That was my main race."

"Then my answer is fifteen hundred meters." Grinning, Farne pulled lightly on a Havana. "Yes, that's my idea of a sprint— fifteen hundred meters. Happy?"

"So what's your idea of a real test of an athlete?" asked Peter through clenched teeth.

"The long distances," said Flacke, scenting blood. He picked up a copy of *The Times*. "Like this damn race in the States." He put down his drink and riffled through the newspaper until he reached the sports pages.

"Here we are, my lad," he said. "C. C. Flanagan's Trans-America next March. Three thousand one hundred and forty-six miles. Take a bloody Irishman to think up a race like that, says I."

Peter Thurleigh looked at Farne.

"Is that your opinion too?"

"I should say so," said Farne. "Three thousand miles—that's my idea of a bit of sport."

"Does it say how many have entered for the race?" asked Peter.

Flacke sipped his brandy, then returned to *The Times*.

"At the present date one thousand one hundred and twenty," he replied.

"And what would you lay against an English runner finishing in the top six?"

Flacke looked across at Farne.

"I would say that depends on which Englishman we're talking about."

"Me," said Peter Thurleigh.

"Ten to one," said Flacke. Farne nodded.

"Then I lay ten thousand pounds," said Peter Thurleigh, standing up. "No need to shake hands on it."

On the other side of the tent Hugh McPhail could not sleep and instead sat writing a letter to his friend Stevie. How could he explain what it was like to be here, somewhere in the middle of a desert north of Las Vegas, to little Stevie, back in a dark Bridgeton slum? How could he explain the endless daily stream of men pouring themselves into the landscape, crawling painfully east, driven on by a crazy Irishman in a cowboy suit? It was like something out of a Hollywood movie; certainly it was the same terrain, and all that it lacked to make it complete was the menace of Indians lurking behind rocks. He put down his pencil, only the first paragraph of his letter complete, and shook his head.

A hundred yards away, in the luxury of Dixie's trailer, Kate Sheridan slept soundly. Now that Flanagan had ended his "cuts" she was able to run at a pace which allowed her body to adapt daily. Daily, however, she still managed to pass a few more men, moving slowly toward her target of a place in the first two hundred and a prize of ten thousand dollars. The national press was already speaking of her as the first of a new breed: a superwoman capable of taking on men at their own sports. Only she knew how weak, how uncertain she really felt, never sure that her body or will could stand up to the searching daily tests.

But while some newspapers had taken her up as a symbol of the "new woman" of the thirties, and the Isadora Duncan of sports, some had ignored her altogether, while still others had denounced her as a muscular strumpet—although they changed their minds as photographs of a vibrant, attractive woman started to arrive at their offices. The ladies section of the Amateur Athletic Union of the United States refused to comment on "Miss Sheridan," beyond observing that she had undoubtedly lost her amateur status. Kate had retorted by saying that she had lost that years ago; a comment which was not reported in the national press. Meanwhile she was enjoying herself immensely. Her body now stripped of fat, her pulse down to a regular fifty beats a minute, she had never felt more alive. The running, far from taking something from her, made her feel stronger. It would all be perfect if only Morgan would touch her. Every day, after the stage was over, they met with Doc and the others in unspoken but understood union. But unspoken and unacted upon it remained.

Two-thirty. The tent was beginning to stir. Half an hour to the next stage, twenty miles across hot, dry, rising ground.

Doc kneaded olive oil lightly into his calves and thighs. They were climbing up to over five thousand feet in the next twenty miles in unseasonable heat, and he would feel it. They would all feel it, particularly those who had not at least a few hundred miles' training under their feet.

Mean air. The air thinned at these heights—not to the degree that it would later in the Rockies, but, with the heat, enough to stretch them, even at a modest six miles an hour or inside.

He patted Hugh on the knee.

"Take it easy," he said. "We're running to over five thousand feet again. Thin air. Slows you down."

He looked over at Morgan. "Tell the girl too," he said. "Tell her to take it slow."

The gun cracked and one thousand and twenty runners trundled out onto the soft broken road. The sun had not yet lost its sting and Hugh could feel it on the surface of his soccer shirt.

Although they were now moving into mountain country the road itself did not rise steeply. These were quite unlike the mountains of the Scottish Highlands. These mountains were brown and scabby like slag heaps, nature imitating not art but industry. The sandy-colored hills were cracked and lined, split by endless sun and occasional flash floods. Farther off, Hugh thought he could see the white of snow, but surely that could not be.

Even on this stage the German Muller took the lead, flowing easily out into the still bright desert. This time no one attempted to keep up with him.

Doc, Martinez, Morgan and McPhail joined the leading group, behind the All-Americans and the German team, forty runners strung out over a hundred yards. Kate settled in at the back of the field, her running stride modified to a low, neat, heel-first action.

This time Hugh did not sweat at all. Rather he felt his body begin to burn early on, and he craved water long before the first refreshment point. He looked to his right at Doc. The older man's body was like that of an insect. He crawled across the broken road, taking up each rut and ripple easily.

On reaching the first water point Hugh drank in great gulps, but this time there was no satisfaction, no matter how much he took: his body absorbed the water just as the greedy road was absorbing him.

Five miles on, at the next water point, the heat had not diminished.

The leading group had telescoped to a huddle of men running at a steady nine and a half minutes per mile, with Muller and Stock over half a mile ahead. Hugh could not stop drinking, and even when he splashed cooling water on his face and body it dried immediately. There seemed not enough water on earth to satisfy him.

Between ten to fifteen miles it happened. The field split. Hugh could feel himself become detached, gradually dropped by the leading group, and there was nothing he could do. Doc, Martinez, Thurleigh and Morgan and half a dozen others slowly eased away from him, and Hugh found himself with the Indian, Quomawahu, and a dozen others, struggling, his breathing becoming increasingly labored.

They were still climbing and the thin air was beginning to take its toll. It was like running in an airless furnace. Soon Hugh was no longer racing; he was simply surviving, moving from one stride to the next.

The telegraph poles. They looked more like crucifixes strung across the brown plain. Hugh thought only from one crucifix to the next. By these painful steps he made his way to the final water point, five miles from the finish. He drank until his throat ached. Five miles to go. He poured some water on the front of his thighs and gulped down the remainder. He was on his own now, no Doc to pull him through. His legs were heavy, and even after several minutes at the water point his breathing had not fully recovered.

He had been in this situation before, back in the sour mosses of the Highlands with Duckworth, but never at altitude and never in such heat. Every message from his body told him to stop. After all, it was all pointless. There was always the next stage, and over two thousand miles to go. What did it matter that he stopped and walked for a few miles? But it mattered to him. Back in Scotland he had made a vow that he would never walk. He would *run* across the United States of America.

Pole to pole, crucifix to crucifix, endlessly spanning the plain. About him lay the crumbling hills over which shadows now slid like sleek cats, but Hugh no longer knew nor cared. His mouth had completely dried out and hard white foam began to form on the outer edges of his lips. Somehow he was still aware of his hands moving in front of him, his toes below him just passing within vision. Somehow his mind was still working, fighting its own battle, as if there were two selves in senseless debate.

He was dying, for there were miles to go, weren't there? Miles which his legs could not possibly penetrate. He was alive, for he was moving. He was dead, for the air itself seemed to be poison, destroying his throat and lungs. He was alive, for the blood still pulsed through him, serving his onward legs. He was alive. He was dead. Alive, dead, alive, dead, alive, dead . . .

Hugh fell forward into a dark pit, spent, arms out to his sides, helpless.

"Fifty-fifth," shouted Willard Clay. "McPhail, Great Britain."

When Hugh recovered consciousness he was in the hospital tent with Doc Cole and Dr. Falconer standing over him. Falconer flicked his thermometer and put it back in his pocket. "A hundred and four point five degrees," he said. "His blood's been on the boil."

Doc looked anxiously at Falconer. "He going to be all right?"

"A week ago I would have said no," said Falconer. "Doc, do you realize McPhail's pulse was two hundred and five beats a minute when we brought him in? He must have run the last five miles with a pulse close to two hundred and a temperature of over one hundred and five degrees. Crazy!"

He took his stethoscope from his ears to let it rest on his shoulders and pulled his fingers through his yellow-white hair.

"Have you any idea what you men are?" he said. He did not wait for an answer. "Living laboratories. In these three thousand miles you could provide enough information about the human body to keep physiologists at work for a hundred years. But no, they'll be sitting back in their labs in their clean white coats, dissecting frogs and rats, when the real stuff is out on the road here. Hell, they could find out more about heat tolerance here than they'll discover in a million years back in their universities.

"A week or so from now, in the Rockies, they'll find out more about the heart, local muscular endurance, and the way the body responds to altitude than they'll get in a mountain of books. Jesus, each runner's heart will beat fifty-four thousand times a day, every single day of this race! Our scientists have got over a thousand living experiments out there, and none of them gives a damn!"

He looked down at Hugh.

"All of this doesn't help you much, son. Sure, you'll be all right. Anyhow, the forecast for tomorrow is cool, perhaps even a touch of rain."

Doc pulled Hugh to his feet, and, after thanking Falconer, the two men walked out of the tent into the gathering gloom.

"You sure had us worried out there," said Doc. "Muller blew up, but still made first, Stock just behind, myself fourth. What you didn't know back there is that the guys in front of you were running even worse than you, so you didn't lose much time. As things stand, just over an hour covers the first twenty men so far. It's a real tight race."

Hugh shook his head. "I can't face heat like that every day, Doc. It's not possible."

"You won't have to," said Doc. "The forecast is cool for the next few days. Today's heat was way out of line for the time of the year. Anyhow, give me your shirt."

Bewildered, Hugh did as he was told. Doc opened the bag he was carrying and withdrew a thin knife.

"You know all your body needed today?" he said, stabbing the knife through Hugh's jersey. "Air." He stabbed Hugh's shirt again. "Your body couldn't get rid of its heat. No wonder you couldn't run."

He sat down on a rock and continued to pierce Hugh's shirt with his knife.

"This lets the air get to you and cool the skin. Then you can stay cool." Doc handed him back his punctured shirt. "Heat," he said. "It near finished the whole field at the St. Louis Olympics back in 1904. The only thing that kept Hicks, the guy who won it, on his feet was the slugs of strychnine his manager kept fixing him.

"Then, in 1908, in London in the Dorando race, it was just the same. The sun hit us like a stone and guys were reeling about like drunken sailors. Johnny Hayes, one of our boys, won that one. Funny thing, no one remembers Johnny, 'cept his mother. No, next day the papers were all full of Dorando, Dorando Pietri. They said his heart had moved *two inches*. Anyhow, Princess Alexandra gives him a cup for bravery a few days later and off we all went on the great professional marathon merry-go-round. We ran *everywhere*—the Nile, Berlin, Edinburgh; we even ran indoors at Madison Square Garden."

"Indoors?"

"Anywhere, just so long as it was twenty-six miles three hundred and eighty-five yards. I ran in some good ones too. The best was the last, a two-hour twenty-nine-minute run by the Finn, Kohlemainen, in 1912. I ran two thirty-four, the fastest I ever did. Then a few years later it was all over: the marathon bubble was bust. All of us, Dorando, Hayes, Shrubb, were pros—no way back to the Olympics. Still, we had a few laughs and made a few bucks."

"Why did you keep running?"

"Just couldn't stop. Funny thing—when I got drafted in 1917 the army wouldn't take me—flat feet!"

Doc saw that Hugh had not yet taken his point.

"Hell," he said. "I know running isn't a team sport. The biggest load of crap I ever heard was at the 1908 Olympics. We were on the boat to London, first day out. The team manager, an East Coast Irishman, name of Gustavus P. Quinn, gets us all together in the ship's lounge. There we are, big Irish shot-putters like whales, bean-pole high jumpers, quarter milers, just a pair of legs with head on top, and marathon-runners like skeletons on diets. 'First thing I want you men to realize,' said Quinn, standing to his full five foot four, 'is that you are a *team*, the United States team. Therefore, gentlemen, you must *help* each other. So I want to see the shot-putters out there putting up the bar for the high jumpers. Middle-distance boys, get yourselves our there and run beside the walkers. All the time, remember, men, you are a *team*.' All the fat-arsed noodles around him nodded and filed off into the bar."

"And what happened?" asked Hugh.

"Nothing much," said Doc. "The putters threw, ate and drank. The runners ran around and around the boat, the jumpers jumped, and the walkers heeled and toed it around the ship. In track and field you are alone, 'cause this is sure as hell no team sport. Don't get me wrong. It's not that I'm not happy when I see the Stars and Stripes go up there on the masthead. Just that it's only by running for *yourself* that you can do the best for your country. Hell, what's a country anyhow? Just a collection of people who live in the same place, most of whom don't care a dime whether you're on your way to the Olympics or the moon. But this, the Trans-America, it's different."

"How?"

"First, because there's money at stake, enough money to split with a partner if you win one of the big prizes. Second, because here men can team up and help each other through bad patches all the way to New York. It's already happening, every day. You see what I'm getting at? How we could work together?"

"But what chance do we have against teams like the Germans and the All-Americans?" asked Hugh.

"The way those Germans are going, not much," said Doc. "They've got a manager, doctor, masseurs. But that's my point. We've got to form teams. That means groups of guys who will split whatever prize money comes their way, guys who trust and respect each other and who'll back each other up over the next two and a half thousand miles. That's the only hope for people like us."

Hugh nodded. "It's happened already. I've heard that Bouin and Eskola have teamed up, and so have Quomawahu and Son."

"Jesus," said Doc. "A Frenchman ties up with a Finn, an Indian with a Jap. We're doing better here than the League of Nations."

"It makes sense though," said Hugh, opening the flap of their tent and holding it for Doc to enter.

They sat down on their blankets, facing each other.

"So here's my offer," said Doc, drawing a circle on the dirt floor with his index finger. He cut the circle in half.

"A fifty-fifty split all the way, no matter what. Say, for argument's sake, one of us gets hurt, and the other takes the race, it's still a fifty-fifty split."

Hugh nodded. "What if anyone else wants to join the team?" he asked.

"Then we both have to agree to their joining. No point in teaming up with someone one of us doesn't like. Hell, it's a big enough pot, and I'm sure we can both think of guys we'd like to team up with. But let's cross that bridge when we come to it. What do you say? Partners?"

Hugh pulled his punctured shirt over his head and tugged it down over his waist. He stuck out his hand.

"Partners," he said. "Though God knows why you chose me."

14

ACROSS THE ROCKIES

The Trans-Americans had been the first men to cross Colorado by foot since the Mormons had traveled west, toward Utah, eighty years before, although they were passing through three times faster than ever the Mormons, with their creaking pushcarts, had done. They were pioneers, too, not in the geographical sense, but in a different way, moving daily into uncharted territories of their own bodies and spirits.

Many of the press began to realize this, sensing the difference between the Trans-Americans and the marathon-dancers, pole-squatters and tree-sitters who daily competed for headlines along-side Flanagan's men. Every state in the union had individuals or teams in the race, and daily the results made the front pages of local papers, or, where none existed, in the windows of Western Union offices.

The nation's political leaders had not been slow to take advantage of the Trans-America. The national mine workers' leader, John L. Lewis, proclaimed that Flanagan's Bunioneers proved beyond doubt that if all Americans were given a fair day's work for a fair day's wage they could bring the nation's economy back to life. Vallone of the Federal Inter-State Truckers was even more blunt. "Has anyone ever thought of the energy, the sheer horsepower, these men are putting into the roads of the United States?" he asked at a union meeting. "And we're supposed to be in a worldwide Depression. If we could put a tenth of that energy into something worthwhile we could cure this whole sick world." In New York Governor Franklin D. Roosevelt, now deeply involved in the investigation of the administration of Flanagan-supporter Mayor Jimmy Walker, observed that, while applauding the achievements of the Trans-Americans, he would review Mayor Walker's pledges to Mr. Flanagan within the week. Avery Brundage, then making his dogmatic way through the American Olympic Committee, was still more outspoken. "The Trans-America footrace," he said, "represents the apotheosis of professional sport, the crass exploitation of athletes by unscrupulous promotion."

The public reaction to Brundage's statement was swift, comprehensive and in some cases unprintable. Letters supporting Flanagan and his Trans-Americans poured into newspapers and radio stations throughout the land. There was no doubt where the nation's sympathies lay.

The race had also come to the notice of the country's religious leaders, and the evangelist Alice Craig McAllister had composed a stirring radio sermon on the "Athletes of the Bible." Samson, not surprisingly, was "the world's strongest man," while Jacob had become "the greatest wrestler" and Enoch "the long-distance runner." Miss McAllister then moved on to baseball to describe David as "the pinch hitter," and Saul, more critically, as "the man who fumbled the ball." At the top of Miss McAllister's list came Jesus as "the World Champion," no event specified.

In Europe, every nation with runners in the race now followed the Trans-America avidly. Even the London *Times* covered the race, although its society columns made occasional slighting reference to Lord Peter Thurleigh's athletic aberrations on the American continent. In Scotland, Hugh had become a national hero, just as had little Juan Martinez in Mexico, and Hugh's friend Stevie McFarlane was belatedly sent to cover the race for the *Glasgow Citizen*. In Germany, Dr. Goebbels, though now under indictment for both libel and slander against the government, made certain that the daily victories of Muller and Stock were well publicized in the party paper *Der Angriff*, while regular bribes to sports correspondents ensured that the rest of the national press covered the victories of Hitler's youth squad in full. After Las Vegas, Goebbels also featured a cartoon of Flanagan as "a Communist lackey," groveling to a heavily moustached Joseph Stalin.

Yet if Flanagan, Willard and the Trans-America Bank had good reason to be pleased with the gentlemen of the world's press, elsewhere things were not going nearly as well.

In New York the investigations into Mayor Jimmy Walker's conduct in office had lifted a few stones, and some exotic insects had been uncovered. Rollin C. Battrass, chief inspector of the Manhattan Building Bureau, had been arrested and taken to the Tombs on a charge of accepting bribes, and everywhere Walker's men were running for shelter. Similarly, in Chicago, Mayor "Big Bill" Thompson, Flanagan's one-time friend, had just been ejected from office by a massive 191,916 majority and was now on vacation somewhere on the Mississippi; so no longer of use to Flanagan. Now in mid-April Chicago and New York were still three weeks or more away; Flanagan had more immediate problems. De Luxe Catering, the company he had employed to deal with his feeding arrangements, were asking for more money in advance, and had told him curtly that if he could not come up with fifty thousand dollars by Denver the Trans-America would simply stop short in its tracks.

Whichever way Flanagan looked at it, with close to a thousand miles gone things were beginning to look pretty dark. Nevertheless, as usual Will Rogers, America's favorite comedian, had some words of hope; "The great thing C. C. Flanagan's runners demonstrate is that a fellow can still get onto the front page without murdering anyone."

Charles Finley read in a firm clear voice, sitting stiffly and uncomfortably in a high, leather-backed chair in front of the vast, neat desk in the director's office.

" 'April 10, 1931. Initial Report by Agent Ernest Bullard.' " He cleared his throat.

" 'My surveillance of the Trans-America race has lasted two weeks, during which time the runners have traveled from Las Vegas, through Utah, to Grand Junction, Colorado. The Las Vegas stage resulted in an affray at the finish, involving the three race leaders, Cole (USA), Michael Morgan (USA), and Hugh McPhail (Great Britain), and striking IWW workers from the Boulder Dam project. On the discovery that the leaders were wearing IWW shirts the affray was brought to a summary halt by IWW leader Eamon Flaherty.' "

"A known Communist," interjected J. Edgar Hoover in a low flat voice.

"Indeed, sir," said Finley. He went on. " 'There were no further untoward incidents. Rather, the remainder of the race was cheered loudly by both IWW workers and public alike. I noted that, despite clear evidence of assault, no arrests were made, though there were Las Vegas police close at hand.' "

"That figures," said Hoover, doodling on a pad on his desk.

" 'After the race I made myself known to Charles C. Flanagan, the race organizer. I asked him why he had provided his leading runners with IWW shirts. He replied that he had received wind of trouble ahead in Las Vegas and took out insurance (as he called it) by having his runners wear the shirts. It is my belief that Flanagan, rather than trying to identify himself politically with striking IWW workers, was trying to avoid trouble. Later, however, at a party at IWW headquarters at Camp Stand, several of the athletes made what can only be called radical or left-wing statements.' "

"Any details?" asked Hoover.

Finley scanned Bullard's report.

"No, sir," he said.

Hoover grunted and beckoned Finley to continue.

" 'Since then, in the guise of a newspaper reporter, I have moved freely among the competitors. These men have come from thirty-one different nations, and many are ex-Olympic athletes. Most are unemployed or have come from low-paid jobs in depressed areas. The Trans-America represents for them an opportunity to achieve a new life—if they can win one of the major prizes. As yet I can find no evidence of organized left-wing political groups among the competitors.' "

Finley laid down the first sheet. "Sir, this is the end of the first section relating to political factors. The second part concerns Agent Bullard's mission on the Clairton killing."

"Forget about it," said Hoover. "That's not why Bullard's out there." He stood up, and turned to look at a massive oilcloth map of the United States hanging on the wall behind his desk.

"Where are they now, Finley?" he asked, scanning the map. Finley joined him behind the desk. "About here—around Gypsum, in the Rockies," he said. "They get out of the Rockies next week, so they'll soon be on the edge of the Great Plains."

"Tough country. But it's a long way to go yet," said Hoover. "It's early days for Bullard, too. Remember, Finley, this information about radicals came straight from the White House itself."

"Yes, sir," said Finley, dutifully. "Right from the top."

"Bullard," Hoover mused. "What manner of man is he?"

"One of our best agents, Director. You know he worked with the New York Prohibition Squad from 1920 to 1924 under Captain Dan Chapin."

"That goddam Dan Chapin," chuckled Hoover. "What a ramrod! You know, one day he got all his agents in his office. 'Gentlemen,' he said, 'all hands on the table. Now every one of you sonofabitches with diamond rings is fired.' That day he canned half his staff."

Finley permitted himself a thin smile. "Captain Chapin gave Bullard an excellent reference, Director."

"No diamond rings, eh?" growled Hoover. "Is Bullard a family man?"

Finley did not look at his files.

"Two children, aged eight and ten, sir."

"No horsing around?"

"Not to my knowledge, sir."

"Politics?"

"Republican."

"Church?"

"A Presbyterian, sir. Regular churchgoer, when bureau duties permit. What the Presbyterians call an elder of the church."

"Height and weight?"

"Five foot ten, one hundred and sixty-eight pounds," said Finley. "Used to play quarterback for UCLA, ran first in the NCAAA half-mile in 1914. Bullard still keeps himself in pretty good shape."

"Good," said Hoover. "I like a man to keep himself in good physical condition. One final point . . ."

"Yes?" Finley looked up.

"You checked on Bullard's shaving?"

Finley covered his confusion well, then regained his composure.

"Of course, sir . . ." he said.

"I mean twice a day, eight and five? Open razor?"

"I'll check on it again, sir, to make completely certain."

"Do that," said Hoover. "Bullard sounds like a good man, but details like that tell me more than you might imagine. That's been my experience, anyway."

Hoover returned to his chair and bit on his pencil. "This fellow Flanagan," he said. "Do we have anything on him?"

Finley picked up a thin file and opened it. "Charles C. Flanagan, born New York, April 22, 1884. Left school in fourth grade, 1901–08, working part-time in Mott Street YMCA with track and field and basketball teams, 1908–12, sold insurance, 1914–19, journalist with *Chicago Tribune*, 1919–21, manager of women's basketball team."

"You said *women's* basketball?" said Hoover, stroking his chin.

"Yes, sir," said Finley. He looked up again before continuing: "Nineteen twenty-three, made abortive attempt to introduce indoor horse racing to New York, 1924, attempted to organize major indoor international track and field meets at Madison Square Garden; vetoed by AAU; 1925–28, managed international tennis player, Suzanne Lamarr."

"Nothing much there," said Hoover.

"Except perhaps the women's basketball team," said Finley.

"Yes," said Hoover, making a triangle with his hands over his lips. "What about the Trans-America athletes?"

"Not much," said Finley, picking up and opening another slim file. "Some of the American boys are ex-college athletes—no political affiliations. Lots of farmers, again no clear political links. The most likely politicals are the industrial workers—the race has quite a few of them—but it would take us months to check them all out. As for the non-Americans, it's impossible for us to check back."

"So we've got to wait for some overt political activity?"

"It seems so, sir," said Finley. "The papers report that, since Las Vegas, every tramp in the areas through which they've passed has somehow got to the route to shout them on. They went through the Mojave alone, but they won't be alone now for a single yard all the way into New York."

Hoover jerked up his cropped, bullet head.

"So it's your opinion that they *do* represent a radical threat?"

"I didn't say that, sir," said Finley patiently. "They have—

probably unwittingly—become a focal point for people who are out of work, perhaps even for radicals and left-wing elements. There's no lack of them these days, sir, and the race has become . . . well, a sort of symbol, a rallying point, for many such malcontents."

"And what have Reuther and Lewis and those other union sonofabitches said?"

Finley picked up a pile of newspapers and laid them on Hoover's desk.

"They're all solidly behind the runners, sir, but then again so is Carl Liebnitz of the *New York Times*, so is Alice Craig McAllister, so is Cardinal O'Rourke."

"Reuther, Lewis, Liebnitz, McAllister, O'Rourke," rasped Hoover. "What a helluva mixture."

"And don't forget Will Rogers, Director," added Finley. "He has expressed his support on several occasions."

Hoover permitted a smile to flicker across his featureless face. "Ol' Will Rogers," he said. "Well, don't that just beat the band."

As Doc had predicted, the weather cooled as they moved on to the fringe of the Rockies, though it was to be another hundred and fifty miles beyond St. George before Hugh had fully recovered the quality of his earlier running. He and Doc were now a team, and Doc, still up with the Germans since Las Vegas, stayed back in the earlier parts of each stage and talked Hugh through the days succeeding his collapse, before threading through the field to catch up with the leaders.

Through Doc, Hugh made his first acquaintance with Mark Twain's *Huckleberry Finn*. Doc knew most of Twain's book by heart, and rattled through the "Cole version" on the flatter parts of the route. Thus Hugh entered the world of Tom Sawyer and Huckleberry Finn, of the Negro slave Jim, and the hucksters The Duke and The Prince. He had never taken much interest in reading at school, but through the long miles Doc made the Mississippi world of Twain live for him.

Muller and Stock, after a fruitless appeal by their manager Moltke against Doc's shortcut into Las Vegas, ruthlessly cut down his lead, and by Grand Junction, Colorado, on the fringe of the Rockies, they were a few minutes ahead.

The daily quality of the young Germans' running was beyond even Doc's experience. After every marathon he had always needed time to forget the pain before he could face the next race. Yet these lean Teutonic youths were running two marathons a day, five days a week, at close to nine-minute miles.

Doc knew that worrying about Stock and Muller was going to serve no purpose. If the Germans were running at the winning pace, so be it. But if Doc and Hugh were ever going to catch them then they must run at their own speed, in a cocoon of their own making. This cocoon was not only physical but psychological and so, every morning, Doc would take Hugh out into the Rockies and there they would talk to themselves, reciting the same strange litany: *"I am a distance runner. My bones are light, my muscles lean. My heart will pump blood forever, flushing my muscles with oxygen."*

Their voices would echo through the mountains, for Doc insisted that the litany be occasionally shouted, as if it were not merely an affirmation of their nature but a gesture of defiance.

"I am a runner. I live as a runner. I eat as a runner. I see the weather, the road, the world as a runner. I have come to run fifty miles a day, six days a week."

At first Hugh had felt foolish, and had kept his voice low until they were well out of earshot of the camp. At first, too, the words seemed trite, and he mumbled them without conviction or understanding, just as he had the Lord's Prayer years before at school. Gradually, however, like the Lord's Prayer, Doc's litany began to assume a strength that it had not at first possessed. Hugh was, in truth, becoming a runner. What they were describing was him as he now was—distance runner, part of the seamless live continuum that was snaking its way painfully through and over the Rockies.

"Know what I think?" said Doc one day in Green River. "We can't lose. 'Cos we came here with nothing, we came here beat. Hugh, what did you have in Glasgow in your Broo Park? Nothing! And Morgan? Martinez? Nothing.

"The way I see it, every single mile we put in, every foot of ground we cover, that's a victory. Every time we think of stopping and keep going, that's another victory. Every goddam moment on that road is too. Out here we grow every day. We *grow*, don't you see? What's more, we thumb our noses at the bastards all over the world who forced us out here."

Hugh's response was less philosophical. "The way you tell it, Doc, we've scored one helluva lot of victories this last month. But who knows about them? Who really gives a damn?"

"I'll tell you," said Doc. "There're millions of middle-aged guys out there wondering how ol' Doc Cole's getting on, thousands of braceros listening to people reading the newspapers aloud to each other so they can hear about Juan Martinez. Back in your Broo Park in bonnie Scotland I bet you're some kind of god! But most important, do you know who knows? *You* know. *You* know what you've done out here, day after day, win or lose, sink or swim. Hell, Hugh, it's part of you and you'll never forget it."

Hugh had grudgingly to admit that his running partner was right. Day after day he felt himself grow stronger, more confident. The rotten decay of Broo Park was being burned out of him by the endless miles, the daily challenges faced and met. Even so, the early days in the Rockies were like those first days in the Highlands, for pain and stiffness never left his legs. The steep climbs and descents brought into play small remote groups of muscle-fibers which were not used on the flat plains or on gentler inclines. Thus every day it took at least half an hour's walking and trotting with Doc before he became sufficiently loose to face that day's running.

In the coal mines Hugh knew that men went only one of two ways, to "bull" or to "wire." Those who went to "bull" developed massive shoulders, arms and thighs, while those who went to "wire" became lean, spare, stringy. The Trans-America caused everyone in it to go to wire. Before the race Hugh had been one hundred and fifty-four pounds of what he had thought was solid bone and muscle. Now he was one hundred and forty-five pounds. The hills made his thighs rock hard, an anatomical chart fit for medical students, the separate heads of the quadriceps showing fine and clear like rivers seen from above, with the diagonal sartorius etching its way across his thighs to the inside of his knees. Behind the thigh, when he stretched his legs, his hamstrings stood out like bowstrings, and on recovery bulged like soft, muscular breasts.

Daily he had chugged up the hills with Doc, the mountains pumping pain into them like a bicycle pump. They ran as if driven by one heart and one will, and occasionally, when their strides matched, like one man.

Though a few runners already wore long johns and jerseys and gloves—bought during their rest days—they were never really warm as they faced close to zero temperatures, sharpened by cutting winds. Even Muller slowed up, though, with each stage, he continued to add minutes to his narrow lead.

Daily, the mountain's icy tableaux had been repeated, with Doc, Hugh, Morgan and Martinez hanging on grimly at the Germans' heels. Behind, Bouin and Capaldi closed in, with Thurleigh also up with the leaders, but behind them new faces began to appear, with the lanky Australian, Mullins, the squat Japanese, Son, and the skinny Pole, Komar, now featuring in the top dozen at each stage. The field was telescoping, as the specialist hill runners, men with legs of steel, sucked in the leaders.

It was at Gypsum that they began to run into the really high country, and forty miles later they labored painfully in dropping temperatures through the Shrine Pass, eleven thousand feet above sea level. They camped just beyond the Pass, on the central spine of the Rockies, some sixty-odd miles short of Denver.

Willard Clay had excelled himself in these testing conditions, and each of the athletes' tents was, every night, warmed by dozens of paraffin stoves. The atmosphere was muggy and smelly but it was also warm, and Doc and Hugh listened contentedly as the winds swept by outside, screaming through the mountain passes.

"Cross my heart, he used to run *backwards*," Doc was saying, as he squatted with Hugh and Morgan on the dirt floor of the tent.

"His name was Edmund Payson Weston," he went on, "and he walked from New York to Los Angeles about fifty years ago, covering about the same daily mileages we do. He traveled the world in a velvet jacket and pants, walking fifty-five miles in twelve hours around running tracks for big money. For the last mile or so he would play a trumpet, or walk backwards. Then afterwards, for good measure, he would talk for an hour on the value of walking and exercise for good health."

"But what has this to do with hill running?" asked Hugh.

"I'll tell you what," said Doc. "We're coming to some really steep ones now . . ."

"You can say that again!" said Hugh. "They can't come any tougher than what we've been through."

"Well, Payson Weston had this theory that going down steep hills was best done by running backwards, so that the fronts of the thighs weren't damaged."

"Your Weston guy may not have been too far out," said Morgan. "The long downhill stretches are tough. All that paying out of muscles to keep you from falling forward."

"Exactly," said Doc.

"Well, why don't you follow his theory?" asked Hugh.

"The way I reckon it, if I'm going to run three thousand-odd miles I sure as hell want to see where I'm going," grinned Doc. "Still, one thing we do need from now on is a few pairs of these." He turned to his knapsack and drew out a pair of red long johns.

"The forecast for tomorrow is snow. What with snow and winds, we're going to be running uphill into subzero temperatures for the next few days. Your legs never get warm, no matter how far you run. Tomorrow morning we get you both a pair of long johns in Leadville. I reckon the stores at Leadville will be sold out of warm clothing soon, so we'd best be up early."

"Wow," said Willard Clay to Dixie, both hands on the wheel of the Ford pickup. "It's colder than Alaska out there." Willard's plump face creased into a frown as he tried to focus through the slow snow-clogged windshield wipers. They drove south toward Leadville, Colorado, their mission—to purchase warm clothing for over eight hundred ill-equipped Trans-Americans, huddled five miles back in tents whipped by wind and snow.

"Will Mr. Flanagan cancel tomorrow's stage, do you think?" asked Dixie, face close to the misty windshield.

"Impossible," said Willard, shifting down a gear to negotiate a steep incline.

"Mr. Flanagan and me, we got a tight schedule to keep. Sure, we've got a little slack, but come hell or high water, tomorrow we got to run."

Dixie peered out into the thick, fluffy snow at the towering white mountains through which the Trans-Americans would tomorrow have to pass. Up till now, the weather in the Rockies had been unusually mild, and the runners' main problem had been running up the steep, uneven roads in the oxygen-starved atmosphere. Now they were to face snow and subzero temperatures.

Dixie looked to her left at Willard. She had now been with Clay for almost two months, yet she knew virtually nothing about him. But in the first days of the Trans-America, when she had faced the problem of logging the positions of two thousand finishers in the heat of the Mojave, it had been little Willard who had found the time to stand for a moment by her side and point out more effective ways of completing the task. Willard was everywhere, yet it was difficult to imagine him as a person with a life independent of the Trans-America and its needs.

Certainly he was no ladies' man, and generally presented a complete contrast to his employer. It was the first time that they had been alone together, and Dixie decided to seize the initiative, in the only way she knew how, by asking questions.

"How did you first come to meet Mr. Flanagan?" she asked.

Willard's eyes remained fixed on the road ahead.

"Back in New York, in 1923. Me, I was a smart nobody selling bootleg in Hell's Kitchen. Mr. Flanagan, well, I had known him from way back in his old YMCA days. But he sure had to do some sweet talking to drag me away from my bootleg business!"

"Were you making a lot of money?"

"I'll say," smiled Willard, sweat beginning to roll down his bulbous neck. "Three hundred bucks a week. Then Mr. Flanagan comes to me with this crazy idea for indoor horse racing. The scheme was to bring in horses and cowboys from out west and race them around a dirt track in armories in New York and New Jersey."

"And did it all work out?"

Willard grinned and shook his head.

"I went in with Mr. Flanagan, and gave up my bootlegging. Don't ask me why—I even had to grubstake him five hundred bucks just to get him started. A week later the cops busted my old bootleg operation and my buddies all spent two years in the pen."

"And the horse racing?"

"Mr. Flanagan paid out a couple of thousand bucks to some operator out west for a herd of wild horses. We waited for two months for those horses. That was the last Flanagan ever saw of his two grand—so our horse-racing business never ever got to first base."

"So what did you do then?"

"Me and Mr. Flanagan picked up some loose change scouting for the Brooklyn Dodgers, out in the bush leagues. In between we set up poker games for guys looking for some action. Then, in 1925, Mr. Flanagan started to manage a pro tennis player, a French girl name of Suzanne Lamarr. I worked as her road manager. Mr. Flanagan and Miss Lamarr spent most of their time fogging up windshields from the inside. Then she beat it to Brazil with an Italian waiter in 1928 and in 1929 Mr. Flanagan got the idea for the Trans-America."

Dixie fumbled in her handbag for her cosmetic bag.

"And what did you think of the idea?"

"At first, not much. Then I thought to myself—when is a little guy like me ever going to get the chance to get two thousand guys across America? It was the chance of a lifetime. Heck, I'd spent most of my life grafting in toytown—here I could do something real big, something nobody had ever done."

"And can you and Mr. Flanagan do it?"

Willard's smile faded.

"Ma'am, we've got to do it. I came from nowhere—no family, no education, half way to the pen—when Mr. Flanagan picked me up. Now I'm fixing the greatest footrace in the world."

Dixie withdrew a lipstick from her bag, looked into her compact mirror and carefully etched her lips.

"But what about all the towns that won't pay, or are pulling out?"

Willard reached for a pack of cigarettes and flipped one of them into his mouth.

"I leave all that to Mr. Flanagan," he said, flicking his lighter into life. "He fixes that part of the operation. I just get us from one place to the next." He lit his cigarette. "Mr. Flanagan's half Houdini, half Holy Ghost. With that kind of combination we could get these guys to the moon."

Dixie was silent. They were approaching the outskirts of Leadville. Together, Flanagan and this plump, rumpled little man were dragging a thousand runners, a circus, a press corps and a hundred-odd staff across the winding roads of America, through every possible adversity. And somehow she was involved, and daily grew more involved, as she came to understand and become directly concerned with the logistics which were a matter of instinct to Willard Clay. From being a passive spectator, a decoration, she was becoming a part of the Trans-America, part not only of its administrative machinery, but also of its heart and will.

Willard drew the pickup into the brown slush of the sidewalk, alongside the general store.

"Leadville, Colorado," he said, pulling on the hand brake. "And by the way, Miss Williams, Mr. Flanagan says to tell you you're doing a good job. Thought you'd like to know."

It had been Hugh's idea that they take a trip to the movies, and he who had prompted Doc to put it to the rest of the group, in the hope that Dixie could be persuaded to join them. To his relief she had accepted, and he had sat uneasily beside her on the rough floor of the truck, their bodies occasionally touching as the vehicle made its bumpy way into town.

That night they crowded into the Electric Picture Palace, Main Street, Leadville. The movie house was undoubtedly electric, but with its patched screen and dingy mock-velvet seats it was equally no palace: hard to believe that the Douglas Fairbanks that they were watching leap across the screen as Sinbad the Sailor was the same stocky little man who had sent them on their way from Los Angeles only four weeks before.

Kate and Morgan, Hugh and Dixie, Doc and Martinez blinked and looked around them as the lights came on for the intermission. The theater was crammed with Trans-Americans, munching popcorn and gulping down root beer, their sun-blackened faces setting them apart from the rest of the audience.

Soon the lights dimmed again, and the previews for the next week's show filled the screen. It was *The Public Enemy*, starring James Cagney and Jean Harlow. For a few moments the theater resounded with the blarney of the preview—"her kiss was as deadly as his gun"—before it was replaced by a Laurel and Hardy one-reeler.

Despite the roars of laughter around him, Hugh was aware only of Dixie's presence just a few inches away, of her brown arms against her light cotton dress. He imagined her smooth brown body glowing beneath the coolness of the dress, and wondered if she was even remotely aware of him and of his longing. Slowly he placed his left arm on the armrest closest to her. To his right Morgan and Kate sat, fingers entwined, their eyes streaming with laughter. On his left Dixie seemed similarly caught up in the picture, as on the screen Stan Laurel settled down in bed for the night with a gorilla. Hugh felt totally alone, burning helplessly in a sea of laughter. He could feel himself trembling, just as he had years before when he had raced against Lord Featherstone.

Then he had prepared for months for the race. Now there was no knowing. In a second, total failure, complete rejection and the longing of two months and countless dreams would count for nothing. Why should she have anything to do with him, a nobody from the black bowels of Glasgow?

The distance between the left armrest and Dixie's slim right hand could not have been more than eight inches. It could have been the Grand Canyon. In Hugh's imagination he saw himself not merely touching her but grasping her hand in his, and her firm and passionate response. He ached to bridge those few dark inches, but felt paralyzed. In only a few minutes the lights would return and the moment would be lost forever.

He moved his arm a few inches. It felt as if he had stretched it several feet, but there was still no contact. Hugh's whole body was wet with sweat. He moved his left hand farther. Still no contact. Perhaps Dixie was aware of his movement. Perhaps she was even moving away from him. He dared not look to find out.

He stretched the little finger of his left hand. Still no contact. Farther. Suddenly, it touched hers. For a moment he froze as he felt the warm, moist flesh of Dixie's little finger. Then slowly, but with purpose, it overlapped his.

Hugh prayed that the darkness would never end. When the lights finally came on they stood up, looked at each other and smiled.

At 10 A.M. next morning, April 15, 1931, one thousand one hundred and eleven runners jogged in place in the biting wind in front of the Trans-America trailer, the snow matting and freezing in their hair and eyebrows. The athletes were dwarfed by the sharp, snow-topped mountains that surrounded them, etched against the cold blue sky. The wind shrieked across the flat, icebound field to which their tented camp had clung precariously throughout the night. Behind them, Flanagan's tent crew struggled with numb fingers against stiff icebound canvas and frozen tent pegs, as the camp was again dismantled.

"Today's stage . . . forty-two miles to Silver Plume." Flanagan's words were lost in the screaming wind. He repeated his announcement, to no greater effect. "Food stop at twenty miles for two hours," he continued, bellowing into the microphone. He felt ice form in his nostrils as he sniffed in the sharp mountain air. He raised aloft his pearl-handled six gun and the report of the gun sent the Trans-Americans trundling slowly through the snow toward Silver Plume.

Doc, Hugh McPhail and Morgan all wore gloves, balaclavas and red long johns, and Morgan noted that Kate now wore black dancing tights. Of the others, only the Finns, the Germans, the All-Americans and perhaps six hundred others wore any leg covering. Many of the runners had no covering at all, and their brown legs were goose-pimpled by the subzero temperature.

Luckily the first sixteen miles were relatively flat, and Doc and Hugh settled into a steady six-miles-an-hour trot, in twentieth position, with Muller and Stock leading a pack of a dozen others about half a mile ahead. It provided Hugh with time to look around.

What he saw was a land of granite cliffs dropping thousands of feet into blue-water lakes, of snow peaks and clinging glaciers. As they began to climb he spied below, through the light snow, lakes of green water with tiny icebergs bobbing on their surface. Above and ahead lay dense pine forest and high flower meadows.

"Mother of Mercy," said Doc, pointing ahead. About half a mile in front the road rose steeply, winding around the mountains like a ribbon. It was Caribou Pass, elevation 11,050 feet.

The runners dropped to a crawl and Hugh again felt the pounding of his heart and the quickening of his breathing which had come on their earlier, more gradual climbs at altitude. Ahead, Stock and Muller had already dropped the leading group of a dozen, now strung out behind them on the white mountain road, and Hugh caught a glimpse of Stock driving steadily on upward, alone, about a hundred yards ahead of Muller.

The snow became steadily more dense, swirling down in thick, fluffy flakes, landing on their hair and eyebrows and freezing immediately, while, in contrast, the heat of their bodies melted it on contact.

For Kate Sheridan, back in four hundred and twentieth position in a pack of eight runners, the race had again become a nightmare as legs, tuned to the sidewalks of New York, met steep, winding gradients at seven thousand feet, often in driving snow. On the toughest hills she was forced to drop to an inside fourteen-minutes-per-mile walk, moving up to over ten-minute miles downhill. At first she had wept at the pain in her thighs, her sobs echoing through the mountains, her tears freezing on her cheeks. But now she no longer cried. Kate had become two persons. In the first person was the meek, weak Kate Sheridan who got tired and breathless, the Kate Sheridan who kept wanting to stop. The other was a tough, vicious Kate Sheridan, constantly driving "Kate the meek" to keep moving, keep running, keep passing broken men, for fifty miles every day. And every hour the two Kates did battle, the fierce keeping the meek at bay.

Up near the leaders, in eighth and ninth places, Doc and Hugh ran as if driven by a common heart, their strides exactly matched, their breathing synchronized—heavy, but controlled. After only two miles up the mountain they had come upon the first broken stragglers of the leading group, walking or plodding desperately through the snow.

Their own stride length had now dropped, their breathing changed to a metronomic groan. Hugh could feel his thighs become steadily heavier and more painful—first the flickering muscles of the front and side of his thighs, then the hamstrings and groin, finally the whole of his buttocks.

"Lean in," Doc urged. "Put your hands on your legs, like this."

He put his hands on the front of his thighs, the way he had seen English hill-runners do. Hugh did as he was told and soon felt his leg muscles relax. Thankfully they were almost at a crest of the mountain, with half a mile or so of white, flat, winding road ahead of them, giving them a chance to recover.

They grunted and sobbed their way on passing another four runners. A few hundred yards later they picked up Martinez and Morgan running in unison, just before the next climb began, and they ran together. Again it was a steep, winding slope, into the slap of wind-driven snow, hitting their red, sweating faces, sodden jerseys and long johns.

Caribou Pass had shattered the Trans-America as even the deserts had previously failed to do. The desert had been hot, but there had been no hills, no lack of the oxygen essential to running. The mountains demanded more of the runners, but gave back less.

The mountain road, thick with powdery new snow had become slippery and soon all four were reduced to a broken, gasping slither up the treacherous slope. For a few hundred yards Doc and Hugh repeated their hill-running technique, but even that was of little use. Fluid running was impossible and they were all forced to adopt a walking version of the same technique, pressing on their thighs as they struggled upward.

Eventually the snow started to thin, and as they reached the brow of the next hill a thin, bleak sun broke through. It revealed a white tableland four thousand feet below, and above the sharp snow cap of Mount Teat, set against a turquoise-blue sky.

They stopped at the brow of the hill, brows and hair furred with ice and snow.

"Look," said Doc, pointing ahead. A runner was lying face down in the snowy road, about a hundred yards ahead. When they got closer they saw that it was Muller. The young German lay inert, face down on the road, arms by his side, a thin trickle of blood from his mouth staining the snow.

"Get him up," said Doc.

Martinez and Doc pulled the German into a sitting position.

He was not breathing and his eyes were closed.

Doc put his fingers at the side of Muller's neck.

"Hell," he groaned. "No pulse."

He stood up and peeled off his top jersey.

"Lay him on this," he said. They laid Muller down on his back on the jersey.

Doc knelt and hit the German hard on the left side of his chest with the side of his fist. There was no response.

"What the hell are you doing, Doc?" asked Morgan, kneeling to join him.

The older man did not reply, but instead hit the German hard again, then put his ear to Muller's chest.

He cursed. "Still nothing."

He hit a third time—harder—thumping as if hammering on a table, and again placed his ear to Muller's chest.

Doc let out a sigh. "It's beating." He stood up. "How far ahead is the truck?"

"About a couple of miles at most," bellowed Morgan, raising his voice against the screaming wind.

"Get ahead—and get Doc Falconer back here pronto."

"What about you?" asked Hugh.

"I'll stay till Falconer gets here. I'll catch up, never fear." He bent down again over Muller. Seeing their uncertainty, he added, "Get a move on, you bastards, or this guy'll die!"

It was enough. The three runners trotted off down the slope, leaving Doc with his ear still to Muller's chest.

The old runner watched them go. He looked down the mountain at the six-mile-long stream of runners laboring through the thinning snow toward him and felt his own spirits sink. Doc sniffed and brushed the crusty snow from his eyebrows. He had no idea what he would do if Muller's heart stopped again. He put his arms under Muller's shoulders and dragged the German across the road into a recess in the vertical rock face and propped him up against the side of the rock. Then he sat beside Muller, pulled the limp young German over and hugged him close to his steamy, sweating little body. He pulled the runner's cheek to his. "*Live*, you bastard," he whispered into the young German's ear.

He sat watching other competitors pass and make their way down the mountain as the snow thinned, sat and felt his body lose heat as he pressed it closer still to Muller's. He could see Hugh, Morgan and Martinez close in on the finish, with the Trans-America truck standing beside the road, see the quickening of activity as Dr. Falconer hastily assembled his equipment and set off by ambulance toward him up the mountain.

In a matter of minutes Maurice Falconer was with Doc and Muller and had his stethoscope pinned to the German's chest.

"You're sure his heart had stopped beating?" he asked.

"Certain," said Doc.

"Well, it's going at a hundred and forty beats to the minute now, so what the hell did you do?" Falconer took his stethoscope from his ears.

Doc removed his jersey from around Muller and pulled it back over his head.

"I just gave it a little encouragement," he said, and began to trot down the snowy road toward the finish. Doc ended up in ninety-fifth position, twelve minutes later.

Six hours later, as the weary Trans-Americans ate dinner or rested in their tents at the end of the day's second stage, Flanagan, Willard and Dr. Falconer sat drinking hot coffee in the Trans-America trailer at Silver Plume.

There was a knock at the door.

"Come in," shouted Flanagan, lighting a cigar for Falconer, who sat at his side, scanning a result sheet.

It was Doc Cole, now dressed in his day clothes and jacket, his face still red from the day's exertions.

"Thanks for coming, Doc. Sit down," said Flanagan. He drew from a cabinet a brown stone jug and pulled out the cork.

"Brandy?"

Doc shook his head. "No thanks. I leave that to the St. Bernards. An orange juice will suit me just fine."

Flanagan beckoned to Willard, who located a container of juice in the icebox and poured Doc out a tall glass.

"A tough day," said Flanagan, nodding over his shoulder at the window as the mountain winds whistled outside, the snow again matted on the windowpane of the trailer.

"About the toughest yet," said Doc, sipping his drink. "Be glad to get to Denver."

"The press boys have been badgering me for an interview with you," said Flanagan. "Any objections?"

"Nope," said Doc. "No objections. I'm rested up now."

"Before you talk to them there's one thing I'd like to ask you. Why did you stay back for Muller? That young pup's been showing you his rear end for the last nine hundred-odd miles."

"It was the only thing to do," said Doc. "Up there on the mountain Muller wasn't a competitor any more, just a sick young guy in one hell of a lot of trouble. I think anyone would have done the same."

"Some wouldn't. Not back where I come from," said Willard.

Doc continued to sip his juice. "One thing you'll learn, Willard, as this race goes on, is that though athletes are the most selfish guys on earth, there's no way they'd let a guy like Muller die if they could help it."

"But I hear he was dead anyway," said Flanagan. "His heart had stopped beating."

"That's not always the same thing," said Doc.

"No," agreed Falconer, tapping his cigar on the ashtray. "Doc's right. It isn't always the same thing. But how in God's name did you get his heart started again?"

Doc handed his empty glass back to Willard.

"Back in the Mexico City marathon in 1912 a guy's heart stopped beating after the race. We had an Indian there, Tom Longboat. I'll never forget what he did as long as I live. He thumped that guy half a dozen times on the chest until his heart started beating again. Longboat said it was an old Injun treatment. So that's what I did with young Muller."

Falconer shook his head, smiling.

"Folk medicine," he said.

Doc spread his hands. "But it worked. That's all that matters. So what else did you want to see me about, Flanagan?"

Flanagan lifted a list of race results. "How far down do you reckon you finished on Morgan, McPhail and Martinez on that first stage?"

"I reckon maybe about fifteen minutes," said Doc.

"We put it closer to eighteen," said Flanagan, looking at Willard, who nodded. "Willard and I have talked it over with all the leading runners, including the Germans. We've decided to take eighteen minutes off your time today. Are you happy with that?"

Doc's lined face creased into a smile. He stood up. "Delighted. As far as I know that's never happened in any race before."

"But then," said Flanagan, "we don't see many competitions with runners stopping to bring other guys back from the dead."

"I suppose not," said Doc. "Look, I don't want to seem ungrateful, Flanagan, but could I see those press boys right now? I'm beginning to feel bushed." He reached the door, then turned.

"One point, Dr. Falconer. Next time you see him, have a look at Muller's eyes."

"How do you mean?" asked Falconer, drawing on his cigar.

"Last time I saw eyes like that was in New York."

"What caused it?"

"Cocaine," said Doc, and closed the door quietly behind him.

Friday, April 10, 1931

Grand Junction, Colorado (721 miles)

		Hrs.	*Mins.*	*Secs.*
1 = C. Muller	(Germany)	114	09	36
2 = P. Stock	(Germany)	114	12	12
3 = A. Cole	(USA)	114	16	14
4 = M. Morgan	(USA)	114	25	06
5 = J. Martinez	(Mexico)	114	40	12
6 = H. McPhail	(Great Britain)	114	45	15
7 = F. Woellke	(Germany)	114	50	20
8 = P. Eskola	(Finland)	115	02	08
9 = A. Capaldi	(USA)	115	05	10
10 = P. Thurleigh	(Great Britain)	115	10	12
11 = J. Bouin	(France)	115	12	43
12 = P. Dasriaux	(France)	115	15	51
13 = P. O'Grady	(Ireland)	115	20	30
14 = R. Mullins	(Australia)	115	20	41
15 = L. Son	(Japan)	115	45	40
16 = P. Flynn	(USA)	116	01	10
17 = C. Charles	(Australia)	116	06	10
18 = L. Hary	(Germany)	116	10	12
19 = P. Komar	(Poland)	116	12	15
20 = P. Tajuma	(Japan)	116	18	20

1st Lady: (661) K. Sheridan (USA)		145	12	20

Number of finishers: 1141
Average speed (leader): 9 mins. 30 secs. per mile

15

DENVER:
A THOUSAND MILES ON

Doc Cole's rescue of Claus Muller in the Rockies made headlines throughout the United States, was briefly reported on in the sports pages of the London *Times*, and Flanagan even secured a further mention, albeit an unfavorable one, from Dr. Goebbels in *Der Angriff*. The incident turned a slow, snowbound stage through the Rockies into a front-page story, while in the daily reports on the sports pages column inches grew immediately. Newspapers which had, up till then, merely taken agency reports of the race at once dispatched journalists to Colorado to catch up with the Trans-America. The press corps had soon swelled to over three hundred and Flanagan hurriedly had to commission another press bus.

The crowd surging and jostling through the lushly carpeted halls of the Cow Palace, Denver, toward Flanagan's "Thousand Mile" press conference, was composed of athletes, journalists, coaches, team managers, politicians and show-business celebrities—anyone, indeed, who felt he could profit from the Trans-America's growing fame.

Flanagan himself sat on an improvised dais, flanked by Willard, Dixie and Falconer, and the leading runners, while in the audience their coaches and managers sat among the press, which included a sprinkling of local journalists from Colorado and Nebraska.

Flanagan was still playing his part in style. Every one of the three hundred and twenty journalists had been provided with an initialed leather briefcase, and inside each case was a Trans-America fountain pen. The conference room, which frequently housed Republican caucuses, was lushly furnished: red velvet curtains, black leather chairs, Persian carpets. If the Trans-America was in financial difficulties, there was no sign of it in the hospitality that Flanagan was providing.

Willard banged hard three times with a gavel, and the buzz of conversation slowly died. The conference was under way.

The first journalist to get to his feet was Carl Liebnitz. Liebnitz had become, by general assent, the press's unofficial spokesman, and they looked to him to lead the way.

"First, a general question. How do you see the race so far?"

Flanagan stood up, smiling. "Well, Carl, in return I'll give you a general answer. For the past year or so, ever since I first announced the Trans-America race, every smartass in the track and field world has been telling me it couldn't be done. First, they told me that I would never get two thousand of the world's best runners to pick up stakes and travel all the way to California to run. Well, I got 'em. Then they told me that no one would sponsor the race: I got the Trans-America Bank to put up two hundred and fifty thousand dollars. They said next that we would never get the runners across the Mojave Desert. We got over a thousand across, even though they did get stopped for a while by a million gallons of desert rain. Now look at us, over a thousand miles east, with half my runners still in the ball game. Carl, you ask me how do I see the race so far? I'd say we've done a pretty good job."

Liebnitz took off his glasses and began to polish them. "Thank you. I'd next like to ask Dr. Falconer a question. What have been your main medical problems?"

Maurice Falconer rose and pushed back his hair.

"The main problems," he said, "came in the early few days after Los Angeles when we had the first shakeout of the really unfit. These were men and women who should never have been in the race to start with. They were shipped back to Los Angeles before they could get into the Mojave and come to any real harm."

"Is it true that Flanagan paid out twenty thousand dollars in medical bills?" continued Liebnitz.

Falconer turned to look at Flanagan, who nodded.

"The exact figure was twenty-one thousand two hundred and fifty-one, mainly for sprains, blisters, stress fractures and heat exhaustion," said Falconer, consulting a small notebook in front of him.

"You're telling me that there have been no heart attacks?" pursued Liebnitz.

Falconer smiled and also removed his glasses, lightly rubbing the bridge of his nose as he did so.

"I am," he said. "Mr. Liebnitz, I'm afraid that even the medical profession doesn't have much idea of what the human heart can handle." He rapped the table in front of him. "The heart is tough," he said. "And immensely adaptable. Even in the past month men who started out with normal resting pulse rates of sixty-eight beats per minute have come down to close to fifty. Gentlemen, I have seen, in the past month, soft, flabby men of a hundred and sixty pounds change to lean, fit animals of a hundred and forty pounds, capable of running over mountain and desert at over six miles an hour for six hours a day."

"Are you saying that the medical profession should be learning something from what's happening out here?" pursued Liebnitz.

"I sure as hell am, Carl, if the ladies here will forgive the phrase," said Falconer. "Our Trans-Americans are showing what Americans were like back in the old frontier days—what men could be again if they regularly pushed their bodies hard. Remember, gentlemen, that the human body is above all a *running* body. That's what it was intended for, not for sitting behind the wheel of a Buick, or smoking a pack of cigarettes. These men are an example of what we can be at our best."

Liebnitz nodded and scribbled on his pad before sitting down again.

"Could you be just a bit more specific about the main injuries, Doctor?" asked Frank Pollard, the old hand from the *St. Louis Star*.

Falconer picked up a sheet of paper at his side.

"Thirty-five per cent are foot-blisters. Twenty-five per cent are Achilles' tendon injuries. Thirty per cent are cramps, sprains and muscle strains. Ten per cent were such ailments as sunburn, stomach complaints, and the like."

"No heart strains at all? You can be categoric?"

"No. As I think I indicated before, to damage these men's hearts you'd have to extract them and beat them with a club."

"What about the German, Claus Muller?" asked Pollard, his pencil pointed toward Falconer.

The physician flushed and looked down at the German team manager, Moltke, whose face also colored. The German official showed no other signs of even having heard the question. "Herr Muller," Falconer said slowly, "is now in the Denver City Hospital, and at the last report was responding excellently to treatment. Furthermore, it is not my view that he suffered a conventional heart attack."

"But his heart *did* stop beating?" said Pollard.

"I believe so," said Falconer. "But it is also my belief that there may have been other contributory factors which the Denver medical staff are now checking out. Next question, please." To his relief, there was no further follow-up.

"Kowalski, *Philadelphia Globe*. How many men will make New York, do you reckon?"

Falconer replaced his notes on the table in front of him. "It's difficult to say," he said. "A month ago, before we set out, I wouldn't have put the figure at much more than a couple of hundred. Now I think that well over six hundred will make it."

"What about Miss Sheridan?"

Falconer motioned to his left. "Miss Sheridan is here on the platform," he said. "Why not address your question to her?"

Kate Sheridan stood up and looked down nervously at Mike Morgan, who was sitting beside her on her left. She was dressed in a neat blue running outfit, and a number of the reporters stood up to get a better view of her. Some of the Colorado and Nebraska reporters, who had not seen her before, whistled.

"How many miles have we covered so far, Mr. Flanagan?" she asked.

Willard answered for Flanagan. "One thousand and twenty."

"Well, up till the date we started, I had covered only five hundred miles in my whole life," said Kate.

"And how long would that be?" shouted a young reporter from the back of the hall.

"Gentlemen, that would be telling," said Kate, her eyes flashing. There was laughter as she continued. "So if someone had told me then that I would be in Denver a month later, with a thousand miles of running under my belt and about one thousand men in pieces behind me, I would have said they were nuts. But I made it here and a thousand miles from now I aim to be with you at Mr. Flanagan's next press conference."

"Have the male competitors been helpful to you?" asked a female journalist.

Kate nodded. "Without Doc Cole, Charles Fox and Mike Morgan I wouldn't be here. Doc told me how to run, what to wear, who to run with. Charles Fox dragged me through the first days in the Mojave, before he had to give up in the Rockies. Mike Morgan— well, he bopped me back in the Mojave."

"You say that Morgan struck you?"

Kate smiled. "Only in the cause of sport. I was lying in a ditch, feeling sorry for myself. Mike came back, knocked some sense into me and paced me in to the finish. Yes, you can say that the male competitors have helped me a lot."

"Clare Marsh, *Woman's Home Journal*." A severe, angular lady, her graying hair set in a tight bun, stood up. "I would like to ask: have you experienced any . . . social problems?"

Kate smiled. "I think you really have another word in mind, Miss Marsh. No, when a guy has run fifty miles he doesn't have much energy left for romance."

Clare Marsh's lips tightened, but she managed a bleak smile. "You misunderstood me, Miss Sheridan. I was thinking of—specifically female problems." She sat down, blushing.

Kate shook her head. "No, ma'am," she said. "When you've got fifty miles a day to get under your feet female problems are something you've got to live with. One thing I've learned in this race—there are pains that stop you and pains you can run with. What you call 'female problems,' Miss Marsh, come under the second category."

Clare Marsh again smiled thinly and took to her feet once more. The other journalists settled in their chairs, expectant.

"Millions of women all over the world are anxious for you to win the ten thousand dollars offered by my magazine if you can finish in the first two hundred places. You've become, Miss Sheridan, something of a symbol for women the world over. How does that make you feel?"

"It makes me feel great," said Kate quietly. "A couple of months ago I was just a dancer no one had ever heard of. Now you tell me that women all over the world are following my every step.

You should read some of the letters they send me! If what I'm doing helps girls to get out from under and tackle sports—not only sports, but the other things that women have been kept out of—then it'll have served some purpose, whether I win the money or not."

"Do you feel you have become less feminine?" asked Clare Marsh. "I'm sure that's what worries many women about sports."

"Heck, no," said Kate. "When you feel more alive then every part of you enjoys everything more. Perhaps I'm not making sense; I think that running brings you to life."

"You still have well over four hundred men in front of you, Miss Sheridan. The question our readers are asking is: can you make it to the pot of gold?"

"That's a question I never ask," said Kate. "All I aim to do is to cover fifty miles a day and to pass a few more guys each day. We have something like forty days of running left; that's five men a day I have to pass on aggregate, and make sure I keep them behind me. It's going to be fun trying."

At that Kate and her questioner both sat down, to scattered applause.

Bill Campbell of the *Glasgow Herald* took their place. A middle-aged man, he was himself running three miles a day with the Trans-Americans, and had lost fourteen pounds in weight, and now he looked ten years younger than his forty-nine years. He spoke in a rich Scottish brogue. "One of the surprises from a sports journalist's point of view has been the success of unknowns—runners like Hugh McPhail, Mike Morgan, Juan Martinez and the German team . . ."

"I suggest that you direct your questions to them personally, Bill," interrupted Flanagan.

"Fair enough. First, Hugh McPhail. You were a Powderhall sprinter, weren't you?"

"Yes," said Hugh. "I've been a sprinter since I was a lad."

"Didn't you find it a little hard to make the change from sprinting to ultra-long-distance running?"

Hugh looked below him to Doc, seated at his side. "Doc here's a great educator," he said. "He's got a phrase he's drummed into my head. It goes something like this. 'When a man knows he's going to be hanged in the morning, it concentrates his mind wonderfully.' Running for a prize of a hundred and fifty thousand dollars concentrates my mind wonderfully."

"But what lessons have you learned from the race?"

"Well," said Hugh. "You learn that your body can take far more discomfort and pain than you ever thought. Back in Scotland, in training, I thought I had taken the lot. But out there, beyond Las Vegas in the stage to Grand Junction, I ran my eyeballs out for over twenty miles in close to a hundred degrees. In the Rockies I ran in snow at seven thousand feet up mountains like the side of a Gorbals tenement, where there wasn't enough air for a bird. I've learned a lot since Los Angeles. I'm still learning."

Campbell nodded before sitting down.

Albert Kowalski was next on his feet. "I'd like to speak to Mr. Eskola. Mr. Eskola, you're placed ninth at the moment. It's still early days, but how do you see the race so far?"

Eskola's gaunt tanned face was impassive. "Very close indeed. Just over three hours separates the first forty runners after one thousand miles. For such a distance, that is what you call shoulder to shoulder."

"Who do you fear most?" asked Kowalski.

The Finn looked around him. "I fear no one. I respect Alexander Cole, Jean Bouin and Paul Dasriaux—their records speak for themselves. The young German, Stock, is still strong—so are McPhail, Morgan, Thurleigh and Martinez. But there are others, ten places or so back, who may be dangerous later, when we are close to New York. It is, as you say, early days."

Kowalski sucked his pencil. "How do you think Paavo Nurmi, the famous Finn, would have done in the Trans-America?"

Eskola's expression did not change. "Mr. Nurmi is not here," he said, and sat down.

There was an embarrassed silence, but soon another reporter was on his feet.

"Charles Rae, *Washington Post*. I'd like to ask Lord Thurleigh some questions, if he would be so kind."

Peter Thurleigh stood up and nodded. He was dressed in a blue blazer and slacks, his bronze skin constrasting strongly with his white shirt and white silk muffler.

"Lord Thurleigh, you have competed in an Olympic Games, and England is famous for its traditions of fair play. How have you found the standard of sportsmanship here?"

There was another short silence.

"Until I competed in this race," Thurleigh said in a clear voice, unperturbed by the implications of the question, "I had been told that the 'pros' were cads—you might call them shady customers. But this has not proved to be the case. Indeed, if Baron de Coubertin were to come here as an observer I think he would find that his Olympic ideals were being completely met."

"Are you finding the race difficult?" Rae went on.

"That, sir, would be an understatement. In the Mojave Desert I thought I was going to die. In the Rockies I was *certain* of it. But somehow, by some miracle, I reached Utah."

"Colorado," corrected a journalist.

"Colorado," Thurleigh repeated, smiling self-deprecatingly. "My apologies."

"Some journalists have tried to compare you with Phileas Fogg of Jules Verne's *Around the World in Eighty Days*. Do you see yourself in that light?" asked Kowalski.

"In that I entered the race for a substantial wager there is indeed a valid comparison," agreed Thurleigh, picking his words with care. "But the difference is that I also entered the race for personal reasons. You see, I have enjoyed a very privileged existence and, indeed, even my 1924 Olympic selection owed a great deal to that background. But here in the Trans-America that is of no value to me. I am alone. I find that very challenging. And exciting." He sat down.

The Scottish journalist, Bill Campbell, stood up again and turned to Morgan.

"Mr. Morgan, I've been checking on your background." He picked up some papers at his side. "Correct me if I'm wrong, but you led the '28 strike up at Bethel, Pennsylvania, didn't you?"

"Yes," said Morgan. Kate noted that both his fists were clenched.

"The strike folded and you were shut out. A year later you had the misfortune to lose your wife."

Kate raised her hand to grasp Morgan's. He held it firm.

"After that, from 1929 to 1930, we seem to lose track of you."

"I was around," said Morgan flatly. "Newark, New Jersey, New York."

Campbell extracted a single sheet of paper from the sheaf which he held in his left hand and studied it for a moment. "How have you found the race?"

Kate felt Morgan's hand relax, though it still held hers.

"Sure beats working," said Morgan drily.

There was laughter, and the crisis passed.

Ernest Bullard decided that it was time for him to become a reporter. "I would like to ask Mr. Martinez a question," he said.

Martinez, dressed in shorts and running shirt, stood up and made a tentative bow.

"How did you train for the race?"

"My people send me far into the mountains, to the Tarahumares. They are running people. They run sixty, maybe eighty miles a day over rough ground, sometimes playing a ball game called 'rarajipari.' It was hard, for me, from the plains. I run and walk only twenty miles a day at first. Soon I get fit, I stay with best runners. Then I am ready for my village. I come here."

"Is it true as stated in Los Angeles that your village is dependent on your success here for its survival?" asked Bullard.

"Yes," Martinez said simply, and sat down.

There was a hush in the room. It was broken by Carl Liebnitz.

"Flanagan," said Liebnitz. "One of the surprises of the Trans-America has been the success of the young German team. I would like to address my comments to their team manager, Mr. von Moltke. Herr von Moltke, have you been pleased with the performance of your team so far?"

Moltke stood up and adjusted his monocle. Hard, lean and military, he looked as fit as any of his athletes. His voice was similarly vigorous. "Before we came to the United States, German scientists said that it was impossible for any human being, much less young men like ours, to cover seventy kilometers a day, five days a week, for three months on end. They had studied in detail human physiology, the mechanics of running and nutrition. In Germany we have a phrase—*Das Wissenschaft des nicht Wissewerten.*" He permitted himself a thin smile. " 'The science of that which is not worth knowing.' Our men have *proved* that their science was 'not worth knowing.' "

"What about Claus Muller?" asked Liebnitz.

Moltke paused again to adjust his monocle. He glanced uneasily around the crowded conference room. "Muller's condition arose from a bad fall," he said. "That, combined with the cold and the altitude, resulted in his present illness."

Liebnitz stayed on his feet. "I've been doing a little research into your Party, the National Socialists," he said. "As I see it, you are not, strictly speaking, socialists—in fact you are in conflict with German Communists. Is that correct?"

Moltke nodded, his face again expressionless.

"I've been reading about your leader—Herr Hitler's writings. He talks of the Aryans, of a master race. Would it be true to say that your team is the first of this master race?"

Moltke nodded, and the room buzzed with discussion. He waited for silence. "Correct. Soon, when we come to power, Germany will bid for the 1936 Olympic Games. You may remember that the 1916 Games were originally planned for Germany. In Berlin in 1936 the fruits of our labors will be seen."

He smiled stiffly and sat down, indicating that his part in the conference was over.

"Forrest, *Chicago Tribune*. I'd like to address Mr. Corbett, the manager of the All-Americans."

Corbett, a burly, thick-set man, stood up, laying down a Havana cigar in an ashtray on the arm of his chair.

"Mr. Corbett, there is only one All-American in the top twelve—Capaldi. Do you think that your boys still have a chance?"

Corbett held out a race-results sheet in front of him. "I suggest that you check the top twenty places, Mr. Forrest. You'll find that my other three boys are placed fifteen, eighteen and twenty-two. There's a long way to go yet, and my coach reckons an average of about six miles an hour will win it."

"So you think that the others will burn themselves out?"

"No, I'm not saying that. I'm just saying that our boys are running to orders, moseying along real easy, staying loose, always finishing with a little in hand. It's our view that anyone at present in the top thirty has a good chance. I've noted the Australian Mullins coming through, the Japanese—Son—the Pole, Komar. They've hardly ever figured in the top twelve at any time, but they're all dangerous."

"Ferris, *The Times* of London. Mr. Flanagan, a Mr. Avery Brundage of the American Olympic Committee has said that the Trans-America represents a crass commercial exploitation of athletes. Would you care to comment?"

Flanagan laughed. "We have upwards of fifty athletes in the room. Let's ask some of them. Any of you guys who feel exploited, stand up and say your piece." No one moved. "There's your answer," said Flanagan flatly.

"Not exactly," persisted Ferris. "You had your boys wear IWW shirts in Las Vegas and you sold them for ten thousand dollars at a Highland Games at McPhee. Rumor has it you've hawked them to a couple of carnivals in Kansas and three in Nebraska, and that you take a substantial slice out of any post-race contracts that any of them may secure."

Doc Cole stood up, preempting Flanagan. "Could I answer for the athletes?" he said. "Sure, we might have to jazz it up a little in Kansas and Nebraska. But when Mr. Flanagan put out the word a year back, what was I doing? Serving milkshakes for five bucks a week. McPhail here was on the bread line. So was Morgan. Martinez was starving, Bouin was selling matches in Boulogne. Eskola was unemployed in Helsinki. So who's being exploited? Who's losing out? What alternatives were Mr. Brundage's buddies of the American Olympic Committee offering us? If I'm being exploited then, Mr. Ferris, let me tell you this: I'm *loving* it."

There was a rumble of approval from the athletes, and many stood up to applaud. Flanagan grinned and folded his arms.

"Kowalski, *Philadelphia Globe*. Several members of the United States Senate have expressed concern that the Trans-America has become a focal point for industrial and social unrest. Can you comment on this?"

Flanagan pushed aside a lock of gray hair which had settled on his forehead.

"If you mean that the union boys, Reuther and Lewis, have supported us, then I admit it's true. But we can't choose our friends any more than we can choose our parents. Heck, I've got a letter here from Mr. George Bernard Shaw in England. Anyone here want to hold that against me?"

"You might like to know that the Russian Communist premier, a Mr. Molotov, has called you a capitalist exploiter of the workers." It was Liebnitz again.

"Doesn't make much difference to the price of cotton," said Flanagan. "The Trans-America goes on no matter what Stalin or Brundage says. People see the race the way they want to see it. Me, I see it as a race where the runners make a few bucks and so do I. If other people want to latch on to it for their own purposes, then that's their problem."

A young man, still in his early twenties, stood up. He was a new face, one of the journalists to have arrived in the wake of Muller's rescue in the Rockies.

"William Nicholson, *Montreal Star*. Flanagan, we notice that you are providing hundreds of gallons of milk. Is there any reason for this?"

Flanagan smiled. "Goat's milk," he said. "To help them over the Rockies. Our medical adviser, Doc Falconer, has tried to beef up the calories by increasing milk intake. Remember, our boys have to put in five to six thousand calories a day, and many of them couldn't eat that much in solid food. Milk is almost a complete food, and it's easy to take in. That's the reason, gentlemen."

"Pierre Mimoun, *Paris Match*. Mr. Flanagan, it is strongly rumored that several towns and cities ahead of us have refused to pay their financial appropriations. Is there any truth in this?"

Flanagan made a show of riffling through a wad of papers in front of him, then cleared his throat noisily.

"Yes," he said. "It is true that we have had some difficulties along the route. It would, however, be wrong to prejudge issues which, we hope, may not come to court, by discussing them at this point."

"Come on, Flanagan, level with us," shouted Kowalski. "We *know* the names of at least six major towns in the next thousand miles who won't come up with the cash, and at least six more are making rude noises. If these monies aren't available, just how long can you keep your show on the road?"

Flanagan reddened. "We'll keep it there, you have my word on that. Next question, please."

Martin Howard of the *Chicago Star* stood up. "Mr. Flanagan," he said, holding in his right hand a piece of paper, "I have here a carbon copy of a letter to you of March 29 from De Luxe Catering of Minneapolis demanding payment of fifty thousand dollars for food, equipment and staff. Their manager, Michael Poliakoff, said to me this morning that he intends to withdraw his staff immediately if payment is not made."

Flanagan had not expected the question, but his reply was immediate.

"The letter comes as no surprise to me," he said. "It caught up with us a few days ago. My verbal agreement with Mike Poliakoff was for a stage-payment of thirty thousand dollars on April 18— and I still intend to honor that commitment. Poliakoff and I shook hands on that over a game of pool in Los Angeles way back in January."

"But what happens if your catering services stop? What are you going to do?"

"First," said Flanagan firmly, "I'm going ahead to Kansas City to speak to Poliakoff. I'm certain there's been some misunderstanding. But if I have to find fifty grand then I'll find it."

Howard remained on his feet. "I believe that your friend and supporter in Chicago, Mayor 'Big Bill' Thompson, has lost the election. Where does that leave you as far as Chicago is concerned?"

"I have every confidence in the newly elected Mayor Cermak's standing behind ex-Mayor Bill Thompson's commitment to the Trans-America."

"How much did Thompson agree to?" asked Howard.

"Twenty thousand dollars."

"How will Mayor Jimmy Walker's position in New York affect the Trans-America? It looks to many people as if Walker may end up in the can."

"I haven't been able to keep up with the news from New York," said Flanagan. "But the state governor, Roosevelt, has indicated his support for the race. So I think that we can safely count on New York."

"Flanagan, are you as optimistic as you were a month ago back in L.A.?" pursued Kowalski, smelling blood. But Flanagan's reply came in even, confident tones.

"If anything, more optimistic. Sure, we've had some problems I couldn't have predicted. Two inches of rain in an hour outside Vegas, for one. The hottest March for thirty years after Vegas, for another, and the coldest April for fifty years in the Rockies. No way these natural catastrophes could have been prevented, but only one man ended up seriously ill as a result. That's not a bad batting average.

"As for the man-made problems, they keep coming up and we meet them as they come. In a year we've created and adapted an organization to meet the problems of the world's first transcontinental race. They all said it couldn't be done. Every day we're doing it."

Flanagan closed the file on the table in front of him and hugged it to his chest.

"Gentlemen: I've set aside a couple of hours for informal interviews with myself and my staff, the athletes and their managers and coaches. I suggest that we end the formalities now and allow you to conduct any interviews. Thank you."

As the conference broke up, Carl Liebnitz buttonholed Doc. "Doc, you're a sensible man. The doors are slamming shut on Flanagan all the way up the line. Do you think that he can still make it?"

The veteran's lips tightened. "If anyone can do it he can. Flanagan's like a boxer: he thinks on his feet. The problem is, he's got to hump about one thousand athletes and staff another two thousand miles across a continent—it must be costing about four thousand dollars a day just to stay alive."

"I reckon well over five thousand," said Liebnitz quietly.

"From the runners' point of view, all we need is food and shelter," said Doc. "That, and to be pointed in the right direction every day. So far Flanagan's delivered. The moment that stops, so do we."

Liebnitz nodded. "Keep this information between us for the moment, Doc. My sources indicate that pressure to stop the Trans-America is coming right from the top."

"Just how high is 'the top'?"

"Certainly state level, maybe even higher. If you want to know the truth, check it out with the gambling boys. They're already giving two to one against the Trans-America making it to Chicago, four to one against it making New York. Those boys don't lay odds like that without solid information."

"Well," said Doc, frowning. "That's real bad news. But there isn't much we can do about it. We just keep running."

"One other thing, Doc," said Liebnitz. "I trust that you won't take this personally, but what was a smart guy like you doing selling milkshakes for five bucks a week at a soda fountain?"

Doc blinked. "No offense taken," he said. "But I really can't answer that question." He chuckled. "I don't know, perhaps I grew up too late. By the time I woke up, the carnival was over and everyone had settled down in comfortable jobs. I suppose that's why the Trans-America is so important to me. It's what you might call a second chance—another bite at the cherry. That's why the Trans-America's got to stay on its feet."

"A three-thousand-mile cherry," said Liebnitz. "That's one helluva piece of fruit."

Doc smiled. "Carl, perhaps I like life better as a dream—the down payments are lower." His smiled faded. "Seriously, running's what I do best, and the Trans-America's my last chance."

"But do you think you *can* do it?" asked Liebnitz sharply. "Don't you ever think you might be too old?"

"Off the record?" said Doc.

Liebnitz nodded, and put his pencil away in his breast pocket. The two men walked to a corner of the conference room and sat down.

"The toughest thing for a athlete," said Doc, "is competing in life when there's no more clapping. That happened to me in 1913, when the pro marathon boom went bust."

Liebnitz nodded.

"But I kept running—God knows why. I must be psychic, because up comes Flanagan last year with his Trans-America race. And do you know my first feeling?"

Liebnitz shook his head.

"Fear. Know why? Carl, if you took an X ray of my skeleton it would look like a junkyard. Years of running, years of injury. The only thing I haven't broken is my concentration."

He bent and unbent his right knee. "Listen to that," he said. "Sounds as if it's full of gravel."

Doc sat back in his chair.

"You asked me if I think I can win it," he said. "Does a fish shit in the sea? Of course I can win it."

"Thanks, Doc," said Liebnitz. "A pity I can't use any of this."

In another corner of the room Ernest Bullard had engaged Hugh.

"Glasgow, Scotland," he said. "You've come a long way, Mr. McPhail. Do you miss it?"

"I miss my parents. I miss my friends," said Hugh. "But it was like living in a rotten tooth in Glasgow. Here everything's clean and bright. Fifty miles a day, three good meals. When you've been on the Broo for two years—man, that's paradise."

"The Broo?" queried Bullard.

"The unemployment bureau," explained Hugh. "Every Thursday I lined up with a thousand others to pick up my money. Then it was down to the park, the pub or the library."

"Not much of a life," said Bullard.

"No," said Hugh. "Not much of a life."

Bullard thanked him and scribbled a single hyphenated word at the bottom of his notes. It read: "non-political."

Hugh stood alone in the noisy, crowded room, his eyes idly scanning the milling throng around him.

For a moment he could not believe his eyes. He walked forward a couple of steps and looked again. But there was no doubt who it was. There, at the entrance to the room, dressed in an outrageous white summer suit, sunglasses, a straw hat and white patent-leather shoes stood Stevie McFarlane.

"Over here!" Hugh shouted.

The little Scot recognized Hugh and immediately pushed his way through the crowds to him, losing his straw hat on the way. The two men hugged each other excitedly.

"Easy on the suit," said Stevie, brushing off imaginary dust. "This put me back all of five pounds, courtesy of the *Glasgow Citizen*."

Hugh stood back and gazed at his friend in mock admiration. "Stevie McFarlane, ace reporter," he said.

"None other," said Stevie. "The *Glasgow Times* started sending back reports of the Trans-America race and people in Glasgow had only got one paper to find out how McPhail the Flying Scot was getting on . . . So next thing the *Glasgow Citizen* sent me and a reporter called McLeod out here, post haste."

"And where's McLeod now?" asked Hugh.

"Propping up a bar in town somewhere," replied Stevie. "The poor fella nearly lost his mind when they confiscated all his whiskey as he got off the ship at New York."

At the same time as the two Scotsmen were talking to each other a Western Union messenger was making his way over to Carl Liebnitz, finally handing him a slip of paper. Liebnitz scanned the telegram and walked over to Flanagan at the dais, threading his way through the mass of journalists and athletes.

"Just received this from Reuters, Flanagan. Topeka, Bloomington and Peoria have formally withdrawn their financial support for the race." He handed over the telegram. "Have you any immediate comment?"

Flanagan glanced at the telegram, then looked up at Liebnitz.

"Only a strictly off-the-record one, Carl, so don't mention this, even to your mirror. This whole thing is beginning to look like a fix." He walked away, rolling the telegram into a ball as he did so.

Liebnitz smiled wryly. Two good stories, both "off the record." Still, the thousand-mile conference had given him plenty to write about.

AMERICANA DATELINE APRIL 20, 1931

Despite claims to the contrary Charles C. Flanagan is alive and well and somewhere on the dusty road to Salina, Kansas.

The race is in a strange position. On the one hand, all indications are that it has now captured the attention of America, even the world. Despite this its catering company, De Luxe, may withdraw its services within a matter of days, and such cities as Hays, Salina, Junction City and Topeka have already announced their withdrawal from the race schedule.

If, as Napoleon said, an army marches on its stomach, certainly Flanagan's army does, and any stoppage of its food supplies will bring the Trans-America to an abrupt halt somewhere around Hays, Kansas.

The financing of Flanagan's Trans-America is unclear. His prize monies, guaranteed by the Trans-America Bank, are secure; but, by most informed reckoning, the Trans-America requires some $5,000 to $6,000 a day simply to stay on its feet. By now, what with the refusal of such towns as Las Vegas and Grand Junction to pay their "appropriations," massive hospital bills in the early California days, equipment repairs in Burlington and mounting legal costs, Mr. Flanagan must be deeply in the red.

As a journalist it is my task to report rather than serve as advocate. I must say, however, that it would be a tragedy if the Trans-America were to wither away somewhere in the green cornfields of central Kansas. These men, the cream of the world's long-distance athletes, have gambled not only on Charles Flanagan but on themselves, on their capacity to grind out fifty miles a day, day in, day out. The Trans-America athletes represent human beings trembling on the tightrope of the ultimate—both in their physical and mental potential. As such they represent the human race at its best, and it is my hope that the towns and cities spread ahead of us on the way to New York will stand firmly by their obligations. It is not too much to say that they owe it, not simply to Mr. Flanagan, but to themselves and to all of us.

—CARL C. LIEBNITZ—

Friday, April 17, 1931

Denver, Colorado (1080 miles)

			Hrs.	Mins.	Secs.
1 =	P. Stock	(Germany)	172	42	04
2 =	A. Cole	(USA)	173	10	03
3 =	H. McPhail	(Great Britain)	173	20	12
4 =	M. Morgan	(USA)	173	25	24
5 =	J. Bouin	(France)	174	02	04
6 =	J. Martinez	(Mexico)	174	04	08
7 =	A. Capaldi	(USA)	174	10	10
8 =	P. Thurleigh	(Great Britain)	174	12	12
9 =	P. Eskola	(Finland)	174	18	14
10 =	F. Woellke	(Germany)	174	18	16
11 =	R. Mullins	(Australia)	174	21	18
12 =	L. Son	(Japan)	174	22	20
13 =	P. Dasriaux	(France)	175	12	15
14 =	P. Clarke	(New Zealand)	175	24	20
15 =	P. Flynn	(USA)	175	28	01
16 =	C. Charles	(Australia)	175	32	06
17 =	P. O'Grady	(Ireland)	175	34	07
18 =	P. Brix	(USA)	175	34	08
19 =	P. Coghlan	(New Zealand)	175	38	09
20 =	P. Komar	(Poland)	176	04	02

1st Lady: (491) K. Sheridan (USA)   216   01   02
Number of finishers: 1095
Average speed (leader): 9 mins. 35 secs. per mile

16

KING OF THE WHARF

The Roosevelt Suite, the Green Davison Hotel, Kansas City. Charles Flanagan had always rather relished the sound of the word "suite." It smacked of opulence, of heavy drapes and spongy carpets and the discreet clink of cut glass. He settled back in the soft green velvet cushions of the sofa, placed a thick pile of newspapers on the glass-topped table to his left and sipped his coffee.

He picked up the first newspaper, the *Detroit Star*. A full half-page was devoted to the Trans-America, much of it dedicated to the hopes of a local hero, a gnarled veteran called O'Brien, now struggling in eightieth position. Flanagan eagerly leafed through the other newspapers. Yes, the press boys had come around: even Carl Liebnitz was begining to melt as Flanagan's men slowly made their way across the nation.

And yet Kansas City might be the end, with bills piling up, his catering staff threatening to pull out and towns from Burlington to St. Louis likely to withdraw their sponsorships. It didn't make sense, now that things were beginning to go so well.

Flanagan leaned forward, fingered his cup and grimaced. Hell, that's how he was going to earn his keep, by holding it all together. He sat back and allowed his mind to drift back over the years . . .

His father had arrived dirt poor in New York from Ireland in

260

1877, all the way from MacGillicuddy Reeks to 10 Baxter Street. Ten years later Flanagan had been born, and within five years the stones of the streets of the neighborhood had become as familiar to his bare feet as the fields of MacGillicuddy Reeks had been to those of his father.

He was nine when he made his first business deal, selling newspapers. Dazzled by the stories of older boys who had given glowing accounts of the profits to be made, he pleaded with his parents nonstop for three days until they funded him. Daily he ran all the way to City Hall, two miles distant. There he battled with two hundred other tough, barefoot urchins, elbowing, pushing and struggling to get first to the tables where the newspapers were handed out. He had kept his money in his mouth, under his tongue, and did not take it out until the precise moment of delivery.

His bundle secured, he had fought his way out of the crowd without losing a single paper and rushed back through the streets to secure his corner. Young Charles Flanagan became the Tarzan of the tenements, leaping up flights of stairs, sliding down bannisters or darting over roofs and serving customers on the way down.

But a day's work was never complete without a fight for a corner with another boy; and there was never time to think about a bloody nose, a thick lip or a loose tooth. The evening crowd moved thick and fast, and if young Flanagan was not quick enough they would buy from another boy farther on. In certain districts of the city, from five to six-thirty, the sidewalks seethed with people returning from work. From this mass young Flanagan received valuable training in concentration, the quick reading of faces, discrimination and judgment of human character. Bread and butter was on the line; decisions had to be made quickly.

Flanagan did well, for he had two advantages. First, when he was forced to fight, he fought with all he had, without reserve, and this total commitment caused fear—even in older, stronger boys. Second, he could think on his feet, juggling with mental arithmetic while planning his next move.

Flanagan's territory was from City Hall to Grand Street and from Broadway to the Bowery. In his seven years on the street he sold to prostitutes, gamblers, crooks, drunkards and dope fiends, to priests, policemen, truck drivers and bankers. It was an education no college or university could ever have provided.

Yet even in those early days it had been sports first, always sports. He had first learned to swim—in thirty-foot-deep murky water at the Fulton Street Fish Market wharves—simply by wallowing from one fish box to another. There was no room for error in such deep waters; one either sank or swam. A boy who went down was scarcely missed until the following day. There young Charles Flanagan soon learned to swim and dive, to plunge underwater for clam shells and coins.

High and fancy diving was also popular, and the boy who could dive from the greatest height was the King of the Wharf. The greatest challenge came from diving from the masts of visiting ships. Half the thrill lay in avoiding the rattan canes of the ship's officers as one scrambled up the mizzenmast before diving into the dark water to the cheers of one's friends.

The wharf was the Olympic arena for the children of the area. Once Flanagan had even swum from the Battery to Bedloe's Island, across strong tides and treacherous currents, to the newly built Statue of Liberty.

Baseball in the streets, handstands against walls, somersaults into water—every day had presented some new form of physical challenge. And now Charles Flanagan of Baxter Street was directing the greatest long-distance race in the history of mankind. And still, thirty years later, thinking on his feet—or rather on *their* feet.

Flanagan's mind traveled back to the present. He pulled back his shirt cuff and checked his watch. Just over an hour to go before he confronted Mike Poliakoff of De Luxe Catering. Surely it had to be some misunderstanding: he and Mike Poliakoff went too far back, to Baxter Street and the brown waters of Fulton Street Wharf. No, old Mike Poliakoff would not pull out on him now. An hour to go, so time for a little more shut-eye. Flanagan swiveled around, lifted both feet up onto the sofa, put his hands in his lap, and closed his eyes . . .

It was only a little over an hour later that he faced Mike Poliakoff, manager of De Luxe Catering, in the speakeasy in the basement of the hotel. All around them he could hear the clink of glasses. And the quiet hum of talk in the small, dimly lit room as the romances and business details of Kansas City were discussed and resolved in alcoves across glass-topped tables.

"Whiskey, Charles?" asked Poliakoff, smiling uneasily as he looked up at the waiter.

"Thanks," said Flanagan, watching the brown liquid pour into his glass. He thought for a moment of his Trans-Americans, running across the plains of Colorado toward their camp at Agate.

"You've come a long way, Mike," said Flanagan, thinking back to his musings in his room.

"Yeah," said Poliakoff, smiling, "we've both come a long way, Charles."

Michael Poliakoff was fat and Polish. As he sat in front of Flanagan, his massive stomach spilling out over the waist of his expensive slacks, it was inconceivable that he had once been the undisputed King of the Fulton Street Wharf.

"You were the first to swim it to Brooklyn, Mike," said Flanagan.

"Yeah, and the cops wouldn't let me land there and I had to swim a mile back till you came and picked me up in the rowboat." He smiled. "Them was real good days."

"They were, Mike," said Flanagan. "They sure as hell were. But we both know that we're not here just to jaw over old times." He paused. "Mike, you've put me in a real fix." The smile left Poliakoff's round, indulgent face and his left eye started to twitch. "We have an agreement," Flanagan continued. "Thirty grand when we reach Kansas City, the final payment in New York. Now I get a letter saying you want fifty grand now, or you pull out your catering staff as of this week. So how do we stand?"

Poliakoff fingered his glass uneasily, and avoided looking Flanagan directly in the eye. "We got nothing down on paper, Charles," he said. "You know we got nothing down on paper. Nothing legal."

"Jesus Christ, Mike," exploded Flanagan. "Come on, you tell me, when did we *ever* have anything on paper?"

Poliakoff looked nervously around him. "Keep your voice down," he whispered. "People know me around here."

"Shit," said Flanagan, settling back in his chair, visibly controlling his feelings. He dropped his voice. "Mike, I've got the biggest thing since the Charge of the Light Brigade back there in Colorado. When we get to New York I'm going to bust this whole amateur thing wide open. We'll have a goddam *Trans-Europe* next year! And you'll be right up there with me, Mike, De Luxe Catering, all the way from London to goddam Red Square Moscow."

Poliakoff continued to peer down into his glass.

"Great, Charles," he said. "So I'm happy for ya; but I got no way round it. I got to have my fifty grand right now."

Flanagan shook his head. The Trans-America was money in the bank for De Luxe, so there was no rhyme or reason for Poliakoff's attitude. Unless someone was pressuring him. His voice dropped.

"Level with me, Mike," he said.

Poliakoff lifted his eyes from his glass.

"Has someone got to you?"

"What do you mean?"

"You *know* what I mean. Is someone leaning on you?" It was almost a shout.

"Keep your voice down," said Poliakoff, his own voice quavering. "No one got to me. No one's leaning on me." He moved to the bottle of whiskey on the table in front of him and poured himself a large measure. He again turned to Flanagan, withdrew a white silk handkerchief from his breast pocket and wiped his brow.

"You know the Los Angeles Olympics are next year," he said. "Well, this time they got something new, called an Olympic village. Just for the guys—the gals are stashed safe in hotels in L.A. Well, the catering contract's up for grabs, for the village, the Coliseum stadium and all the other arenas. Charles, this is going to beat all the other Olympics into a cocked hat. It's got to be worth over a quarter of a million clear to the guy who gets it."

"So what's that got to do with the Trans-America?" asked Flanagan, gulping at his drink.

Poliakoff grimaced.

"That's what I'm trying to tell ya. I got it on the grapevine that there's no way they'll even look at my bid if I stay with the Trans-America. Those Olympic guys have got me by the balls."

"I see," said Flanagan. "I see now what we're talking about. Either you play ball with those Olympic assholes or you stay with me." He took another swig from his glass before placing it on the table in front of him. "You know damn well I can't raise fifty grand, Mike. Not just like that. How long can you give me?"

Poliakoff scowled and bared his teeth. "I can give ya two weeks more, then I pull my boys out. Try to see it my way, Charles. The Olympics is forever—but nobody knows if you can even get your guys to New York. Not even you. So if I stick with you I gamble. If I go with the Olympics then it's hot coffee all the way for me from now on."

Flanagan rose, shaking his head. "You know, Mike, back on Fulton Street Wharf we were rich. Those days, a guy gave his word to a buddy, he kept it. I didn't know it then, but I do now. We were rich."

Poliakoff bowed his head, looking down, and mopped his brow. He looked up and forced a thin smile, which froze as he caught Flanagan's eyes.

"No hard feelings, Charles," he mumbled, extending a moist hand.

Flanagan ignored the outstretched hand, gulped down what little remained of his drink and returned the glass to the table.

He leaned forward till his face was close to that of Poliakoff.

"You asshole," he hissed. "I shoulda let you drown back in Brooklyn." He pushed on the table abruptly and got to his feet, scattering the glasses across the tabletop. Without looking back he strode through the speakeasy and ascended the stairs, out into the afternoon sunlight. As he stumbled blindly out of the Green Davison Hotel there was a tap on his left shoulder. He had taken a couple of extra steps before he reacted, turning to see behind him a burly figure waiting patiently at the hotel door.

"Ernest Bullard," said the man. "Just happened to be in Kansas City. You look a little down, Mr. Flanagan. Perhaps I can be of some help. Let's you and me have a drink." For a moment Flanagan had difficulty in gathering his wits.

Then he pulled himself together.

"Yes, I remember," he said. "Bullard. Can't remember your paper, though. I'm afraid you may have wasted your time trailing me to Kansas City. All the news is back apiece in Colorado."

Bullard smiled.

"I know that," he said, gently guiding Flanagan along the crowded sunlit street. He pointed to a barber's striped pole about a hundred yards ahead.

"Mulligan's," he said.

Ten minutes later Bullard and a sullen, depressed Charles C. Flanagan sat in an alcove in the bowels of Mulligan's speakeasy. Mulligan's was as unlike the Green Davison Hotel as it was possible to imagine. With its sawdust-covered floors and roughhewn wooden tables, it was a place for serious drinkers. Flanagan loosened his tie, soberly sipped a glass of iced water and looked across the table at Bullard. The plainly dressed agent exuded an air of strength and confidence, and Flanagan, against his will, felt the better for his company.

"Scotch on the rocks for my guest, and orange juice for me," said Bullard, taking off his hat and placing it on the seat beside him. "Better make it a double for Mr. Flanagan," he said, smiling.

The waiter returned a few minutes later with the drinks. Flanagan swallowed his in a single gulp and Bullard at once signaled for another.

"Shoot," said Flanagan. "Surprise me."

Bullard looked the Irishman in the eye and smiled.

"Let me hazard a guess as to what Mr. Poliakoff said to you back there," he said, sitting back.

"Who the hell are you, anyway? The Wizard of Oz?" asked Flanagan, making a weak attempt at a scowl.

Bullard smiled. "No. But it just happens to be my business to know such things. First let me level with you. My name *is* Bullard, but I'm no reporter. I work for the Federal Bureau of Investigation."

"The FBI?" exploded Flanagan. "Who we got running in the race? Baby Face Nelson?"

Bullard grinned. "No. Though we do have information that a homicide suspect is in the Trans-America." He paused to let the information sink in.

"The real reason for my presence is that someone up top thinks that the Trans-America may be a breeding ground for industrial unrest. You know what I mean—communists, anarchists."

Flanagan shook his head. "You're on the wrong track there," he said. "If it's anything at all the Trans-America's one helluva piece of capitalist get up and go. It's about as communist as Mom's apple pie."

Bullard nodded. "You don't have to sell me a bill of goods," he said. "But let's get back to your meeting back there with Poliakoff. I suggest that he told you that he wanted his fifty grand now. He knows full well that you can't pay. Even if you did cough up he'd soon find some other reason for pulling his staff out."

"He said it was on account of the Los Angeles Olympic contract," said Flanagan, gloomily.

Bullard sipped his fruit juice. "Yes," he said. "That's true. But it's only part of the truth. You see, your Mr. Poliakoff has political ambitions—wants to run for mayor here. If he dumps you he'll get the necessary political support. You can lay short odds on that."

"But why?" asked Flanagan. "Who's behind it all?"

Bullard's lips puckered. "Perhaps it might help if I tell you a little fairy story," he said.

"Jesus," said Flanagan, scowling. "Now you're Hans Christian Andersen."

"The year is 1912," said Bullard, disregarding his companion's look. "I was running good at college—ran one fifty-nine indoors for half a mile. But my college had no interest in the AAU indoor championships in New York, and they wouldn't grubstake me. So I bummed and grafted my way to New York, got there a couple of days before the meet. I had lost about ten pounds in weight and was in pretty bad shape.

"I turned up at the Garden the night before and met up with one of the officials, a bright young guy from the YMCA who was helping the AAU run the meet. I told him where I'd come from, what I'd done. He took me out and gave me the biggest porterhouse steak I'd ever seen. Then he slipped me a five spot for a hotel."

"And did you win?" asked Flanagan.

"No," said Bullard. "I came in third. But I ran one fifty-six point eight—best I ever ran, indoors or out."

"Great," said Flanagan. "But why are you telling me all this?"

"That guy who gave me the five spot was you," said Bullard.

"Jesus, now I remember," said Flanagan, shaking his head in disbelief. "You must have been twenty pounds lighter then."

Bullard looked down at his stomach and grinned. "Don't let's get too personal," he said. "Now let me tell you another fairy story," he added. "A year later, in 1913, a college boy called Martin La Verne is making all the front pages in the East Coast papers. He's running miles in four sixteen, four eighteen easy. He's good-looking, rich, and he goes to Harvard. So one of the AAU bigwigs decides young La Verne should try to beat the world record for the mile. You know, they even started talking about a four-minute mile."

"The four-minute mile," said Flanagan derisively. "Might as well talk about the seven-foot high jump."

"You know that, I know that," said Bullard. "But you know how it goes; newspaper talk. It sells papers. So it's all a fix. They decide to run it on a straight boardwalk track at Atlantic City."

"I know that track," said Flanagan. "The goddam wind blows in straight off the sea."

"You got it," said Bullard. "A straight, wind-assisted mile. Flanagan, those guys didn't care *how* they got their record. So they set it all up. I have to take them poodling through the first quarter in around sixty-two seconds, then go through the half to around two minutes five, then peel off and leave the rest to La Verne."

"Had you ever run a mile before?" asked Flanagan.

"Yes, in relays, around four twenty-four," said Bullard, sipping his drink. "But I had never really hurt myself, never really found out how fast I could run."

"So what happened?" said Flanagan.

"Well, there we all are in Atlantic City, and there's something like a forty-mile-an-hour gale coming behind us right off the sea. We have half a dozen real milers and half a dozen hares like me. Bang goes the gun and I stroll off, feeling real good. The quarter is sixty-one point five seconds and I'm running sharp and tall. Jesus, the wind is just about *carrying* us along. At the half mile it's two minutes three and I'm still hardly breathing."

"So you peel off," said Flanagan, downing his drink. "You'd done your piece."

"No," said Bullard. "I figure I'm feeling good, so I'll pull La Verne through the three-quarter mark and then bug off. We get to the three-quarter and I hear them shout out three minutes seven seconds. Well, my legs are beginning to go and I'm tiring now, but I look around and there's only La Verne a couple of yards behind me—all the other guys are twenty yards or more back. I wait for him to take the lead, but now he's breathing real heavy too. So I keep chugging along and hit the mile tape in four fourteen—just outside the world record."

"And where was our Mr. La Verne?" asked Flanagan.

"A few yards back. He ran four minutes sixteen point five seconds," said Bullard. "But wait, the story isn't over yet, not by a long shot. So we all get taken by limousine to the City Hall for the big prize ceremony. You know, the usual bit—the mayor, the congressman, the pink champagne. And they've got a silver cup you could live in. Next thing, one of the AAU officials takes me into a side room for expenses and slips me twenty bucks. When I get out they've given the cup to La Verne!"

"And what the hell did *you* get?" asked Flanagan.

"A dime-store medal saying 'Atlantic City Boardwalk Pacemaker 1913,' " said Bullard, bitterly.

Flanagan whistled. "What sort of crook would do a thing like that?" he asked.

"Only a gentleman of the AAU by the name of Martin P. Toffler," said Bullard.

There was a moment's silence.

"Okay," said Flanagan. "So we've had your two fairy stories, and I'm ready to be tucked in. Where does that take us?"

"To Poliakoff, to Kansas City," continued Bullard. "Flanagan, you've lived out of the top of your head since way before I met you at the Garden, but as far as our records go you've never done anything crooked. All the same, it's none of the FBI's concern if the Trans-America stops in its tracks and everyone packs up his bags and goes home. So even if Toffler's leaning on Poliakoff with an offer of an Olympic contract—well, that's business. On the other hand, if I can find a direct link between Toffler and that Las Vegas assault that's a horse of a very different color. Incitement to assault."

Flanagan held up his glass as the drinks arrived and shook his head. "You'd better let me get another one of these," he said wearily. "I can't take all this in. Why should a big shot like Toffler be trying to stop me?" He turned to signal to the barman.

"I don't know, but I'll try to make an intelligent guess," said Bullard. "The last time the USA had the Olympics, in St. Louis in 1904, it was a goddam farce. It lasted three months and hardly any of the athletes came from outside the USA. The whole meet was linked up with the St. Louis World's Fair and they even spiced things up with an Anthropological Games."

"Yeah," laughed Flanagan, "I remember. They brought a bunch of savages from all over the world, didn't they?"

"Most of those 'savages' came from the World's Fair," corrected Bullard.

"Yeah, I knew a midget called Charlie Satz who blacked up and competed as a pygmy," mused Flanagan. "Entered the shot put. Only got it just beyond his left foot."

His companion smiled. "They had mud-throwing competitions, pole climbing for speed; it was a crazy carnival," said Bullard. "Well, this time they want to do it right, put the USA on the map as a sports nation. But one big cloud has just appeared on the horizon."

"What?" asked Flanagan.

"You," said Bullard. "If you hit pay dirt with the Trans-America, Nurmi, Zabala and all the world's top distance runners will be falling over themselves to compete for you in 1932—in Olympic year. And every American runner from five thousand meters up will be with you. Let's face it, Flanagan, no athlete has any objection to earning an honest buck, certainly not Nurmi. The Trans-America can kick the Los Angeles Olympics straight in the teeth."

"And that's where Toffler comes in?" said Flanagan, leaning over the table toward Bullard.

"Exactly. He's put his reputation right on the line on the Los Angeles Olympics. He wants to be the next International Olympic Committee chairman—sit at the head table with all the Olympic top brass. If the Olympics goes down the Swanee, so does Toffler."

"So what's his program?"

"I can only guess," said Bullard. "This Poliakoff business, I would put that directly at his door. The towns that are pulling out, I reckon it's maybe fifty-fifty. He's leaning on a few people who owe him favors—he's a big Republican—and for the rest it's a sort of domino process."

Flanagan bit his lip. "The trouble is, we've got to keep moving. You see, Bullard, it's like an army, and it costs the same amount to keep them on their feet doing nothing as it does to keep them on the move. Second, some of these towns we're scheduled to get to want us on certain days—the day before or the day after's no damn good."

"You got any political pull?" asked Bullard.

"Maybe," said Flanagan thoughtfully.

"Well, use it—and quick. Buy yourself some time."

"Two weeks I got, before the food runs out," said Flanagan. "Even if I *can* rustle up food, in a week I hit the first town that's giving me trouble. So I only got a week before I start to bleed. Hell, I'm in deep enough as it is. Tomorrow morning I've got to be back in Burlington trying to talk Mayor Tweed into staying with the race. If I don't I'm another ten grand in the hole."

"As I see it, you've only got one choice," said Bullard. "Stop Toffler. I can't say kill him, but stop him, somehow, or there'll be no payday in New York."

Flanagan rose slowly to his feet and reached down to shake Bullard's hand. He forced a smile. "Thanks," he said. "That steak I bought you back at Madison Square Garden has sure paid off!" He lightly knuckled Bullard on the shoulder before wearily making his way through the crowded bar.

Tomorrow morning he would travel back to Burlington to try

to seal up another hole in the dam. He trudged slowly up the steps which took him from the depths of Mulligan's speakeasy to the weak spring sunshine in the street above.

That night he was on the train speeding back west toward Burlington, Colorado.

Mayor Tweed, mayor of Burlington, stretched a plump hand out across his desk as Flanagan approached him, and dropped back into his black leather chair.

"Sit down, Mr. Flanagan," he said. He pressed a buzzer on the right of his desk and his secretary entered the room. "Coffee for two," he said. "Cream and sugar?" he asked next, turning his head toward his visitor.

Flanagan nodded, his eyes wandering around the somber, oak-paneled room. He pulled the sleeve of his black pin-striped suit over his white shirt cuff.

"How many miles are your runners from Burlington now, Mr. Flanagan?"

"About two hundred. That's four days' running."

Tweed stood up and placed both hands behind his back.

"Let me be frank with you, Mr. Flanagan," he said, repeating Flanagan's surname as if to commit it to memory. "I have recently been in receipt of some disturbing reports about your Trans-America race. That nasty business in Las Vegas, for instance."

Flanagan started to reply, but Tweed stilled him with a short movement of his hand. He took out of a drawer a sheaf of press clippings and placed them on the desk in front of him.

"I have the reports here," he said. "Some of the Vegas press seem to think your runners are Reds, some sort of Bolsheviks, Mr. Flanagan. What's your answer to that?"

"Can *I* be frank with *you*, Mayor Tweed?" asked Flanagan. Tweed nodded. "Someone set us up in Las Vegas. They got ahead of us and riled up the IWW boys. I got wind of it and had my men wear IWW shirts. It saved the race. That was all there was to it."

Tweed puckered his lips. "I'm inclined to believe you, Mr. Flanagan. And let me tell you why. In the last month, considerable pressure—let me put it no higher than that—has been put upon me, and upon the mayors of other towns on your route, to renege on their commitments to your Trans-America race. All manner of reasons have been given, the main one being that the Trans-America would cause local labor troubles."

Flanagan again started to interrupt.

"Please allow me to finish, Mr. Flanagan. Two days ago I spoke to your assistant, Mr. Willard Clay, telling him that it was unlikely that we would welcome the Trans-America in Burlington. Only a few hours later, I received a call from a Federal Bureau agent, a Mr. Ernest Bullard. Agent Bullard was very enlightening. In any case, I owe J. Edgar Hoover a favor; his agents did a good job for me out here a year or so back.

"And let me tell you something else, Mr. Flanagan. I believe that your Miss Sheridan and Mr. Morgan visited a children's home back in Las Vegas. It didn't make the front pages, but the news got to me all the same. And one of my brother Elks tells me that your Doc Cole gave a most entertaining talk back in Denver at our Elks luncheon. As a result, the long and short of it is that Burlington stays with the Trans-America."

Flanagan beamed and gulped down his coffee. The first breach in the dam had been sealed.

Four hours later Flanagan got out of his car and stood on the hot roadside outside Agate, Colorado. It was one o'clock in the afternoon and his road gang was setting up evening camp for the approaching Trans-Americans. All looked well, but only Flanagan knew the tightrope upon which the Trans-America was now trembling. He pushed back a lock of hair and stood, hands on hips, surveying the bustle of the camp in the field below the road. Thank God, he thought, those poor devils sweating toward him on the rutted road were innocent of that knowledge.

"Am I glad to see you," said Willard Clay, shaking his head as he walked toward his employer.

"What's the problem now?" asked Flanagan, contentedly looking around the busy campsite.

Willard pointed back to the trucks. "We stopped the road crew at a diner ten miles back for a couple of hours this morning. When we got out half the tents had been slashed clean through. We've lost sleeping quarters for over two hundred guys."

Flanagan threw his Panama hat to the ground. He looked up at the sky and raised both hands, palms up, imploringly.

"Why me? Why me, Lord? What have I done?" he groaned.

17

THE GAMBLE

The Trans-America was holding together. Perhaps only by a strip of adhesive tape, but it was holding. In the space of twenty-four hours Flanagan had regained Burlington, Colorado, and brought Alice Craig McAllister to the rescue of his stricken camp. But he could not rely on an unholy alliance of the FBI and the Almighty all the way to New York. And as he faced the staff of De Luxe Catering, crammed into the small, sticky conference room of the Capitol Hotel in Hays, Kansas, the clock above striking twelve, it looked like the end of the line.

The staff's position was desperate. Poliakoff had not paid them for two weeks and had now served them notice to return immediately to their Kansas City base. Had it been possible for a room to sweat, then the committee room would have done so as thirty angry De Luxe employees babbled and argued with each other in half a dozen different languages. It was an ugly situation. Flanagan beckoned to a white-jacketed waiter who squeezed through the crowd toward him. "Whiskey all around," he said. He pulled on the waiter's sleeve. "Best make it doubles."

Before the waiter had turned toward the door a burly man with a red beard at the front of the crowd had stood up. It was McGregor, the head cook, and he was vigorously shaking his head.

"Bide a wee, Flanagan," he said. He turned to the men behind him. "Now you lads know I like a dram as well as the next man, but I want a clear head to look at this problem." He scratched his shock of flaming red hair and put his hands on his hips.

"Here's the way I see it," he said, pointing a finger at Flanagan. "We've had no pay for two weeks. No blame on you, Flanagan— that's the Polack's fault. But he wants us back in Kansas City in a hurry. The way I see it Poliakoff's the piper, and he plays the tune."

"So you're going to pull out?" Flanagan said, head down.

McGregor spread his hands. "I don't see there's much else we can do, Flanagan. Look at it from our point of view. We've all got wives and families. If Poliakoff shows us the door we're on the bread line, and that's the plain truth of it."

Flanagan looked at the tense, anxious faces in front of him. "Is that how you all feel?"

The plump French cook, Lemaitre, stood up, sweating profusely in the heat of the room.

"Mr. Flanagan, France has several runners in this race —Bouin, Dasriaux, men like them. Me, I want to see them reach New York. But you must understand our position. Mr. Poliakoff, he is our employer. Before the Trans-America I was three months in the soup kitchens. If it is a choice between the Trans-America and— how you say?—the can . . ." He spread his hands and shrugged.

The little New York-Irish pastry cook, O'Rourke, took over. "Flanagan," he said. "There can't be a man here that hasn't made good friends among your runners." There was a rumble of agreement. "They're the salt of the earth—there ain't much we wouldn't do for them. But you got to see it our way. Here we are, no pay for weeks, and we'll be back on the streets if we stay with you. You got no way of knowing if the towns ahead are going to ante up; a coupla hundred miles from now we could end up on our butts somewhere in Nebraska with no job, no money, no nothing."

A small group of runners had slipped in quietly at the back of the room while O'Rourke was talking, and now they edged toward the table at which Flanagan stood.

Meanwhile McGregor stood up again, stilling the noisy hubbub with his hands. "Let's have some quiet, lads, and hear what Mr. Flanagan has to say for himself," he said.

Flanagan mopped his brow. "I'll give it to you straight, boys," he said. "We're up shit creek without a paddle. Someone—I can't say who—is leaning on us heavy from upstairs—someone who wants the Trans-America to fall on its butt. That's the real reason why Poliakoff is pulling you all out. And I can tell you we've got some pretty fancy enemies."

He picked up a sheet of paper. "I have food supplies guaranteed all the way to New York. But they're no good to me without skilled catering staff like you, men capable of working under tough camp conditions the way you guys have done so far. No, you pull out now, and the Trans-America ends right here, in Hays, Kansas."

O'Rourke stood up again. "You say some Mr. Big is leaning on you? Then I say to hell with him! I say we stay on!"

McGregor shook his head vigorously. "No, Sean; that just won't do. I know how you feel. But we've got to use our heads here, not our hearts. We've got our kin to think of. We've got no choice, man."

"Gentlemen, I think you have."

It was Doc Cole, speaking from the middle of the packed room, where he stood with Morgan, Kate, Eskola, Martinez and McPhail.

"My apologies, Flanagan," he said. "I know I've got no real business here. But if the Trans-America folds we *all* go bust."

McGregor flushed and started to speak, but stopped himself.

Doc Cole moved up to the front of the room, followed by Morgan and McPhail. Within seconds he was at the desk, looking like a sun-blackened gnome, waiting for silence, sensing the mixture of uncertainty and hostility of the men below him.

"Do you fellas know what odds the smart money is giving against the Trans-America reaching New York?" he asked. "Have any of you the slightest idea?"

There was no reply from the now silent staff.

"Two to one? No. Three to one?" He shook his head. "Wrong again. I'll tell you, gentlemen." Doc's voice rose to a shout. "Anything up to ten to one against! Ten to one!"

Doc placed both palms flat on the table in front of him and leaned on them, weighing every word. His voice dropped.

"Now, my friends, those sort of odds don't get laid if the information on which they're based doesn't come from the very best sources. So it looks as if the smart money is against us, and they know something that we don't."

"So what, Doc?" bellowed a voice from the back of the room.

"I'll tell you so what," Doc shouted back. "We runners came here from all over the world. We gambled, we all sure as hell gambled. Some guys sold all they had just to get here. Most of those guys never made it beyond the Mojave. But they *tried*—you all saw them. And, as I said, they gambled. Now I'll give you guys your chance to gamble. Ten to one against us making New York: those are sweet odds. So pull out, all of you, pull out now and announce it to the press today."

Flanagan's face dropped, and he slumped back into his chair.

McGregor stood up, shaking his head. "Let me get this clear, Doc. You're telling us to pull out. Where does that leave you?"

"Still in the ball park, ready to hit a homer," said Doc, grinning. "An hour after you announce you boys are pulling out, the odds will go up to twenty to one, perhaps even more. And that's when we lay five grand on the nose on our making it to New York. When the money's safely on, you guys have a change of heart and stay with the race."

"Five grand? *Whose* five grand?" asked McGregor, his voice no longer hiding his suspicion.

"Ours," said Doc firmly, taking a thin bundle of bills from his back pocket and laying it on the table. "My team has picked up five grand so far in stage prizes. We're willing to give it to you boys to bet on the Trans-America. If we make New York that might be sixty grand, and that means over two G's apiece for each one of you. With that sort of money you can each buy your own hamburger joint."

McGregor stroked his red beard. "No saying you're not a cool customer, Doc," he said finally. "I've seen a few stunts in my life, but this one fair beats the band. But are you sure them boys in New York are going to buy it?"

Eskola stood up and slowly looked around the rest of the men.

"It could just work," he said. "It is true, the moment the press hear that you men say that you will withdraw, then the odds *must* rise. It is a gamble; but the rewards are high."

Flanagan sensed the change in climate and seized the initiative. "High?" he said, pulling a gold watch from his wrist and a diamond ring from his finger and putting them both on the table in front of him. "These must be worth at least another two grand. Here," he said, pulling off his diamond cuff links. "There's another five hundred dollars in the pot. Take it all."

"What about your mink jockstrap, Flanagan?" came a voice from the middle of the group.

"Must protect the family jewels," said Flanagan, loosening his tie. "Gentlemen, what do you say?"

McGregor looked around him, again stroking his beard. "You men are laying a lot on the line," he said. "But it's real fancy pickings in New York."

"Nearly four grand apiece for every one of you now if we make it," hissed Flanagan. "Four grand each. Just think of it."

McGregor again looked at the men nodding around him.

"Done," he said, putting out his hand. "Done, and God help us all."

Twelve hours and close to eighty telephone calls later, Charles Flanagan was, despite his success of the morning, totally drained. True, Poliakoff had been cut off at the pass, but the road to New York was still beset with troubles. Sometimes, in a weak moment, he wondered if he had not taken on too much, and it was then that he felt the sick lump of uncertainty in his throat, the acid taste in his mouth. He felt it now.

He plodded wearily up the thick-carpeted stairs of the Capitol Hotel, toward the blissful anonymity of Room 209. The key turned easily in the lock, and he opened the door, turned to close it behind him, and switched on the light.

"Evening, Flanagan," said a soft, husky voice behind him. He turned around to face the bed.

It was Alice Craig McAllister. She lay in his bed under the crisp white sheet, the outline of her trim little body just visible beneath it. She held the top of the sheet demurely over her breasts and reached out a delicately manicured right hand toward him.

"Jesus H. Christ," said Flanagan quietly, putting his hands on his hips as he took in the scene before him.

"No, Charles," replied Alice. "For once the Lord had nothing to do with it."

Flanagan looked across the room at his bureau. There, on top of his Trans-America files and results sheets, Alice had carefully folded her severe blue denim dress known everywhere throughout the Bible Belt. On top of his Gideon Bible she had placed her slip and panties, again neatly folded. At the side of his bed lay her plain black shoes, her black stockings tucked inside.

"Champagne?" she queried, allowing the sheet to drop as she

reached across the bed to the bedside table on her left on which a fat bottle nestled in an ice bucket. Flanagan now saw that she was wearing a thin negligee, over which her soft blond hair tumbled loosely. She picked up the bottle and poured Flanagan a foaming glass.

He approached the bed and took the proffered drink. He stole a glance at her feet, which peeped out beyond the bottom of the sheet. Each toe was delicately painted with pink polish, matching the nails of her fingers. Her feet had always had a particular attraction for him. His reverie was broken by her soft voice.

"Pay-off time, Charles," she said, slurring her words as she poured herself a glass and lifted it to her lips, spilling it slightly. She laid the glass down on the table to her left and beckoned him to the side of the bed. She placed a warm, white hand on his and he felt the bed give as he sat at her side.

"You know," she said, "I'll never forget the first time you spread me—back in New York. Must have been seven years ago. You were trying to sell some idea with midgets riding Shetland ponies, something like that."

"Not quite," said Flanagan, laughing, "but something like that."

"That was my very first time," she said. "You know that? The very first time."

Flanagan smiled, gulping the remains of the champagne. He could feel the life begin to flow back into him.

"I never lie," she said, picking up her glass. "It was, and I was scared out of my skin. But you, Flanagan, you made it something to remember."

She had obviously been drinking for some time. He noted an empty bottle beneath the bedside table.

"They say," she said, "that it's always pretty rough first time. That's what they all say. But not with you."

She placed her left hand on his. "So I always reckoned I owed you something, Flanagan."

"You sure paid off good," said Flanagan, refreshing both their glasses. "You got my boys to Burlington, so I'm still in the frame. I was finished without you, Alice."

"Burlington?" she said, sipping her champagne. "With my connections, I could see you and your runners through the Bible Belt free. But forget about that, Flanagan. You won't need much more of my help."

She emptied her glass, took Flanagan's from him and placed them both on the table. Then she pulled on the straps of her negligee, allowing the brown tops of her nipples to be exposed.

"You know," she said. "I've spent most of my life telling people to fear the wrath of the Lord, to be good, to be virtuous. And, Flanagan, I believe it—I swear to God, I do believe it. Then, suddenly from the darkness of my soul, I remember that night in New York. Do you often think of it, Flanagan?"

"Yes," he lied.

"And even now my knees tremble, and I feel it right here, like an ache." She slipped her hand beneath the sheet.

"So here we are again," said Flanagan, loosening his tie and prying off his left shoe with the toe of his right.

"Yes," she said. "Here we are again." Slowly she pulled her negligee over her head. "This cost me all of fifty bucks, Flanagan, and I seem to recall that you were a pretty powerful lover. Don't see why I should risk fifty bucks. Not even on your account."

Flanagan took the negligee from her, folded it neatly, and placed it on top of a folder on the bureau. The file was headed "Advance Planning."

The rhythmic tapping of Dixie's typewriter faded into the background and Kate Sheridan lay back, eyes closed, on the couch in the trailer which she now shared with Dixie. It was dusk, and in the field outside the kerosene lamps in the Trans-America tents had gone out. Tomorrow, forty miles on dirt roads to Dorrance. Her mind went back, as it now did constantly, to the Denver Cow Palace at the conclusion of Flanagan's press conference, to the whirring and exploding cameras and the babble of reporters in a dozen different languages.

Neither she nor Mike Morgan would ever be quite certain whether he took her hand or she his as they made their way from the seething conference room. There was, however, no doubting the strength and urgency of his grip as he drew her swiftly along the hallways of the Palace, on past cameramen and autograph hunters, upstairs into the carpeted quietness of the second floor of the hotel. Kate walked beside Morgan as if in a dream, her feet making no sound on the thick lush carpets of the hallways.

Morgan had stopped suddenly at the end of the hall, in front of a velvet-curtained window. He drew her behind the curtains and swiftly closed them. The softness of his kiss was a shock to her. She felt her hard muscular legs quiver and soften, hardly able to support her as her body seemed to dissolve into his. She felt close to collapse and Morgan had had to support her with both arms.

"You all right?" he had asked anxiously.

"Never felt better," she quavered.

"Then just wait here," he had said, jogging off down the hallway.

Five minutes later he returned, pushing back the heavy folds of the curtain. He held up a hotel room key.

"Room five hundred."

"My lucky number," she whispered.

"Sure?" he had said taking her hand as they walked along the hall.

"Certain," she had replied, tightening her grip on his hand . . .

Back in her trailer, Kate smiled to herself. Dorrance would be no trouble at all.

Topeka, Kansas, May 1: It had been a miserable day, and Flanagan's attempted salvage operation in Topeka had been a total failure. There was no question that Mayor Matson had been well and truly sewn up by Toffler, and there would be no ten thousand dollars' appropriation forthcoming from Topeka, Kansas, when the Trans-America reached it the next day. Worse, they were not going to be allowed to run through the town in daylight, but would be forced to pass through unlit streets at the unearthly time of two o'clock in the morning.

Flanagan ordered another double whiskey and put it down in a single gulp. "Set 'em up again," he growled, placing both elbows on the bar.

On the other side of the dark bar a small, plump man in a well-cut suit was speaking loudly to a rapt assembly. "Drinks all around, barman," he bellowed. "And have one yourself, my friend."

Flanagan smiled grimly. One man up, another down. That was always the way of it.

"One minute fifty-six seconds," the fat man kept howling. "One minute fifty-six! Nothing on four legs can touch my beauty."

Flanagan was slowly sinking into a drunken sourness. The little man was beginning to annoy him. No one should be allowed to be that happy, at least not when he, Flanagan, was in the cellar.

"One minute fifty-six," bellowed the little man again. "Even

Dan Patch himself couldn't have touched her. Silver Star—fastest thing on four legs, no question. Silver Star!"

Flanagan put down his whiskey and blinked. He did not like the little man, or Silver Star, or even, for that matter, one minute fifty-six.

"Sir, if you will forgive me," he shouted, lifting his glass in mock politeness across the semicircular bar, "balls to Silver Star."

The voice at the other side of the bar cut off abruptly. The little man drew himself to his full height—about five foot four inches—and said, "Did I hear you correctly, sir?"

"You surely did," said Flanagan. "I said balls to Silver Star. Jesus, I've got some fellas a hundred miles back who could run her into the ground."

The man walked slowly around the bar, followed by his companions. He smiled and nodded to the barman, who set up another round of drinks.

"Be my guest," he said to Flanagan, who nodded and downed yet another whiskey. "You have the advantage of me, sir. My name is Leonard Levy. Perhaps you may have heard of me. Levy of St. Louis." From his pocket he drew a crisp white business card edged in black, and handed it to Flanagan.

"No," said Flanagan. "Can't say I have." He peered into his empty glass.

"That is not altogether surprising, sir. I am an undertaker." His friends laughed. "But perhaps I misunderstood you. You said that you had *men* who could outrun my champion trotter? You know that she broke the state record today? Ran one minute fifty-six seconds?"

"Couldn't help knowing, the noise you were making about it," mumbled Flanagan, again looking into his glass.

"I am sorry, sir. I did not catch your name," said Levy more tightly, but nodding again to the bartender.

"Charles C. Flanagan, director of the Trans-America footrace," said Flanagan.

Levy's eyes gave a glint of recognition. "Ah!" he said. "The Trans-America. Yes, of course, it's in all the papers. But let me ask you to make yourself perfectly clear, Mr. Flanagan. You really think that your runners can beat Silver Star?"

"Yep," said Flanagan, putting down another whiskey in a single gulp. "No question of it."

"Over what distances?"

"Any distance you goddam choose," said Flanagan.

Levy pursed his lips. "A sprint?" he asked.

"Yep," said Flanagan. "A hundred yards."

"A long distance?"

"Five miles, ten miles, any distance you want," said Flanagan.

"You are prepared to put money up?" said Levy, his eyes narrowing.

"Any amount you say," grunted Flanagan.

"At what odds?"

Despite his alcoholic gloom Flanagan still retained his ability to think on his feet.

"Jesus," he said. "Four legs against two! You got to give me twenty to one on that sort of race."

"Ten," said Levy.

The barman, his interest aroused, intervened. "What speed does your horse Silver Star run at, Mr. Levy?"

Levy pouted, his puffy cheeks bulging.

"About thirty miles an hour."

The barman put both meaty hands on the bar.

"And what about your fellas, Mr. Flanagan?"

"About ten, at best."

"I take your point, Mr. Flanagan," said Levy grudgingly. "Now let me put it to you this way. If I let your two best men run in a *relay*—say, a mile each—for ten miles, would you take ten to one?"

There was silence. Flanagan desperately tried to clear his mind, but failed.

"Make it twelve to one," he said dourly.

"Done," said Levy, slapping his hands together and looking about him at his friends. "And now to your sprinter. One hundred yards, you said. Will you take the same odds?"

"Why not?" said Flanagan.

Levy took a notebook and pencil from his pocket.

"What figures are we discussing, Mr. Flanagan?"

"Four grand on each race," said Flanagan without pause.

Levy pouted his lips and shook his head from side to side. "A trivial sum, but acceptable. After all, it's only sport," he winked at his smiling companions. "And the date?"

"We arrive in St. Louis on May 9," said Flanagan. "Make it May 10. That's our rest day."

Levy scribbled the date in his diary and replaced his pencil in his inside pocket.

"You already have my card, Mr. Flanagan. Telephone me tomorrow and we'll arrange the contract. I rather think that May 10 is going to be a day to remember in St. Louis."

May 2, 1931: Nine hundred and seventy-eight men and one woman sat in the open in the early morning sun on a field outside Paxico, Kansas, fifty miles from Topeka. Flanagan took the microphone to his lips.

"You've got a free day," he said. "We start at six for Topeka. Camp is three miles on the other side of the town."

"But why do we run at midnight, Mr. Flanagan?" asked Bouin, standing up, hands on hips.

"Some sort of local ordinance," lied Flanagan. "It won't allow us to go through the town during the day. They say it would cause public congestion."

There was a general rumble of discontent as the meeting broke up.

Flanagan went back with Willard to the Trans-America trailer.

"Get Doc Cole, could you? Pronto," he asked Willard as soon as they were inside.

A few minutes later Doc was comfortably seated opposite Flanagan.

"What can I do for you?" he asked, shaking his head as Flanagan produced himself a drink from yet another bottle of whiskey.

Flanagan watched the brown liquid gurgle into his glass. He gulped it down and grimaced.

"Doc," he said. "We're in real trouble. Back in Topeka a few days ago, when I was trying to patch things up"—he reached for his glass—"I did something foolish."

"Yes?" said Doc wanly.

Flanagan closed his eyes. "I got you boys into a money race in St. Louis."

"So?"

"With a horse."

"A horse!" Doc laughed. "I think I'll have that whiskey now."

Flanagan blinked. "You mean you aren't mad at me?"

"You haven't told me yet what the terms are."

"Well, first the good news," said Flanagan, pouring out the whiskey and handing it to Doc. "We've got twelve to one. I've put four grand on each race."

"Those are great odds," said Doc. "But it all depends what we've got to do to win the money."

"First, a sprint."

"I hope to hell it's damn short," said Doc, frowning.

"A hundred yards," said Flanagan.

"Short enough," said Doc.

"The next race is tougher," said Flanagan. "Ten miles."

"Jesus wept!" Doc put down his drink and stood up.

Flanagan placed his hands on Doc's shoulders and gently pressed him back into his chair.

"Take it easy, Doc. We're allowed a sort of two-man relay."

The old runner shook his head. "That's better," he said. "But still not good."

He finished his drink and sat back, his fingers to his lips as if in prayer.

"Let's get down to some details," he said. "What kind of horse is it?"

"A trotter," said Flanagan. "Called Silver Star. Ran one minute fifty-six for a mile last week."

"One minute fifty-six. That's good," said Doc, his brows furrowed. "Not many trotters can break two minutes. That's a fancy piece of horseflesh we're running against, Flanagan."

"So you're saying that we're beat?" groaned Willard.

"No, not exactly. But first let me put a question to both of you. If we put a racing pigeon against a greyhound over a hundred yards, which would win?"

"The greyhound," said Willard and Flanagan simultaneously.

"No," said Doc. "Never. I've seen it done many times, sometimes for big money. First problem is that the greyhound doesn't react quickly enough—there's no rabbit to run after. Second is that the pigeon's owner holds its mate in his hands at the finish of the race. Sex is a strong impulse—you should know that, Flanagan. That bird is winging its way toward its lady friend before the greyhound has even twitched. So I'd put my wallet on the bird every time."

"But what has this to do with this St. Louis deal?" asked Flanagan. "We aren't running against any pigeon."

"No," said Doc. "I only put it up as an example, where common sense would put the money on the greyhound. But it doesn't always work that way. I'll have coffee now, Flanagan, if you don't mind. I need a clear head for this. So will you." He stood up. "What detailed terms have you got drawn up?"

"None, as yet," said Flanagan.

"Thank God for that," said Doc. "And what sort of man are we up against?"

"A loudmouth called Levy," said Flanagan. "But no man's fool."

Doc leaned back in his chair and allowed his eyes to close for a moment.

"Okay," he said. "So let him shoot off his mouth to the press for a couple of days. By then he'll be in so deep he'll have to take what we say. The important thing is to race on our terms."

"What should the terms be?" asked Flanagan.

"First, the sprint. The only man who could win this for us is Hugh McPhail. By St. Louis he won't be as nimble as he was back at the Highland Games, but he must be our fastest man by quite a few yards. Sprinting's not really my territory, so I suggest that you bring him in right away."

Flanagan nodded to Willard, who left the trailer.

"While we're waiting, what about this two-man relay?" asked Flanagan.

"Thank God you made it a two-man race," said Doc, accepting a cup of black coffee from Flanagan. "Our boys can keep up better than twelve miles an hour that way."

"But the horse can go at thirty."

"Not for long," said Doc. "But then, you should have thought of that when you laid your money."

"But that makes us about half a lap behind on each lap," groaned Flanagan.

"Not so," said Doc. "But first, we don't want any professional jockeys. What weight is this guy Levy?"

"About one hundred and ninety pounds," said Flanagan. "He's a real greaseball."

"Then he's got to be the jockey. If you've sized this guy Levy up right he'll jump at the chance to ride. That doubles the weight his horse has to pull. What track are we running on?"

"Still to be arranged."

"Levy will be sure to want it to be on some sort of trotting track, 'cause that's what trotters compete on," mused Doc. "More of a crowd, too, to see his big day."

Doc paced back and forth across the trailer, then stopped and turned to Flanagan. "We must get Silver Star out into rough country."

"Why?"

"You see, Flanagan, a trotter's delicate, like a piece of bone china. It can't trot fast over rough country—sometimes it can't even trot at all. The sulky it pulls is pretty delicate too, really made for a smooth dirt track, not for rough ground. So you must arrange to run some of the race over country."

"But who'll run the distance relay for us? You and Stock?"

"No. I'm too long in the tooth for that sort of running," said Doc, shaking his head. "I could run around four minutes thirty for a mile at best, and that was way back in 1904. No, we need speed here. Now Thurleigh ran the fifteen hundred and five thousand in the 1928 Olympics. He's got the pace for this sort of operation. I'd have him."

"And Stock?"

Doc shook his head again.

"We've no idea what his speed is like over short distances. And if you'll forgive the pun, Flanagan, it's a question of horses for courses. Anyhow, I don't see the Germans letting their golden boy put himself in this kind of a three-ring circus on a rest day. You can try them, though. He looks like a handy athlete."

"And if Stock isn't available?"

"Morgan," said Doc. "Mike will run till he drops. And he may have to."

"Anything else?"

"Not for the moment," said Doc. "But let's get someone impartial, some federal judge, someone like that to act as arbiter. No contract could possibly cover all the possibilities in a race like this."

"Would Clarence Darrow be all right?" asked Flanagan, grinning.

Doc smiled. "If he's available, he'll serve." He looked up as Hugh McPhail entered the trailer.

"Hugh, Mr. Flanagan's got us fixed up with a couple of races against a horse," he said, expressionless.

"A horse?" exploded Hugh.

"Calm down," said Doc, laughing. "It's not a proper racehorse, just a trotter. The first race is over a hundred yards, and you look to be our best man. Do you reckon you can handle it?"

Hugh shook his head doubtfully.

"What speed can this horse run?"

"About thirty miles an hour," said Flanagan.

"My top speed over a hundred yards is about twenty-five miles an hour," said Hugh, sitting down. "Though God knows what I could run now, with over a thousand miles in my legs."

He bit his lip. "The real question is how quickly a horse and rider can get to top speed. My guess is that I can take them the first sixty yards. The crunch comes in the last forty yards, when the horse is still accelerating and I'm slowing up."

"But it's possible?" begged Flanagan.

Hugh did not answer. "What odds are you getting?" he asked finally.

"Four grand at twelve to one," said Flanagan. "And you all get twenty-five per cent of the action."

"Then it's possible," said Hugh, smiling. "Just you have Dixie twenty yards from the finish, holding a white handkerchief."

Flanagan looked at Doc. "Just like the pigeon," he said.

Hugh looked at them both uncertainly.

"Just a private joke," said Flanagan, smiling again.

AMERICANA DATELINE MONDAY MAY 4, 1931

A leading English journal once conducted a short-story competition, requiring entrants to complete a story in which the hero, up to his neck in rising water, gas seeping into the room from above, lies bound and gagged. The journal's editor received thousands of entries, some running into volumes, but the winning entry consisted of just one line: "with a bound he was free."

That line might well have been coined specifically for Mr. Charles C. Flanagan. In the past month, the towns ahead of him have been pulling out of the Trans-America as if its runners had the bubonic plague. His tents have been sabotaged, his runners have wallowed through floods in Nevada and snow in the Rockies. This week, his catering staff threatened to resign, yet somehow, I know not how, Flanagan persuaded them to stay with him to New York. So, with a bound, Mr. Flanagan has extricated himself and he and his pilgrims now make their way to St. Louis and a series of races with, of all things, a horse.

One of the likely competitors in this man versus beast contest is a certain Lord Peter Thurleigh, who has shown an aristocratic back to most competitors for the past thousand miles or so. Lord Peter's fortunes have, however, taken a distinct turn for the worse in the last few days. Just outside Hays, Kansas, Lord Peter received the following cable from England. It read: "Shares collapse. All money gone. Run for your life. Father."

The true significance of this cryptic letter became clearer the following day, when my investigations revealed that the Thurleigh family fortunes had indeed vanished in a stock-exchange collapse, yet another victim of the times we live in. Lord Peter Thurleigh is indeed running for his life. It may take quite a bound to set him free.

—CARL C. LIEBNITZ—

Monday, April 27, 1931

Hays, Kansas (1413 miles)

			Hrs.	Mins.	Secs.
1 = P. Stock	(Germany)		226	47	12
2 = A. Cole	(USA)		227	10	02
3 = H. McPhail	(Great Britain)		227	16	04
4 = M. Morgan	(USA)		227	22	06
5 = A. Capaldi	(USA)		228	10	07
6 = J. Bouin	(France)		228	20	00
7 = P. Eskola	(Finland)		228	43	01
8 = F. Woellke	(Germany)		228	47	06
9 = P. Thurleigh	(Great Britain)		229	01	07
10 = R. Mullins	(Australia)		229	20	18
11 = L. Son	(Japan)		229	21	18
12 = J. Martinez	(Mexico)		229	24	16
13 = P. Dasriaux	(France)		229	43	12
14 = P. Brix	(USA)		229	52	10
15 = P. Coghlan	(New Zealand)		229	58	06
16 = P. Komar	(Poland)		230	10	07
17 = J. Schmidt	(Poland)		230	20	08
18 = C. O'Connor	(Ireland)		230	40	09
19 = K. Lundberg	(Sweden)		231	10	06
20 = P. Maffei	(Italy)		231	15	20

1st Lady: (521) K. Sheridan (USA)   282   36   08
Number of finishers: 1054
Average speed (leader): 9 mins. 38 secs. per mile

18

DOC IN TROUBLE

Suddenly, one morning in 1920, in a dingy hotel room in Carson City, Nevada, Doc had realized that, were he to grow a beard, it would be gray. At forty-three he was not old, but he was aging, and even the daily running, though it gave him a physical capacity far beyond a man half his age, could not stop the clock. Soon after, his hair had started to thin rapidly, and by his late forties he had been almost completely bald.

For some years later Doc had made a pathetic attempt to wrap the remaining hairs on the left side of his head in a wet flap across his bald pate, but after a while he gave up, instead contenting himself with the rest of his body's continuing efficiency.

It is never easy for an athlete, uniquely sensitive to his physical capacities, to accept the gradual fade into middle age. In many ways the athlete is far more aware of this decline than the ordinary man, for the stopwatch is neutral and merciless. Thus it was with Doc Cole. By forty-six he could no longer run twelve miles within the hour; by the age of forty-eight even running ten miles in fifty minutes had become difficult. He saw that his running was slowly slipping away from him, despite a mind and a will that were as sharp and determined as they had been when he had met the challenges of Dorando and Longboat twenty years before.

It therefore seemed to Doc that his one talent was going to vanish into the mists of sporting legend, to be classed with the feats of the hill-runners of England or the speedy Ute Indian, Candiras de Foya, who had run nine seconds for a hundred yards in 1901. Doc Cole would simply become a footnote in a Ripley "Believe It or Not" ragbag of sports history, unfit even to be mentioned in the same breath as a Nurmi or a Kohlemainen.

Doc scraped the last of the soap from his chin and peered into the broken mirror suspended on the side of the tent. The sun surely made you look younger even if you were as bald as a coot, he thought.

He doused his face with cold water and dried off with a rough towel. Still half an hour behind Stock, he was now half an hour ahead of Hugh McPhail and Morgan, with Eskola, Mullins and Son closing in fast, and Capaldi every day a danger. The fact that he and Hugh had an agreement made no difference to Doc, for the money meant nothing to him. If his life was to possess any meaning, then he must get into New York first. After all, what else was there? A thousand carnivals, a hundred thousand bottles of Chickamauga remedy sold—that could hardly add up to a life. But winning the Trans-America, the greatest test of an endurance athlete—that would be something.

Doc had over the years devised a variety of techniques to take his mind off the fatigue and boredom of running. First there was the "physical" method. In this he went through a detailed inventory of his body's movements, checking their efficiency as a mechanic might check the parts of a car.

Wrists: relaxed, thumbs up, fingers lightly pinched. That would take him through a few more minutes. Head: still, relaxed, sitting on a vertical spine. That would take him a few yards farther. Jaw: loose, lower lip relaxed, would take him farther yet. Then to his feet. He would check on their alignment as they hit the ground: there had to be the minimum splay, and a solid heel-first landing on each stride.

Thus Doc would reduce the monotony of the miles, the dull pain of the flat dirt road daily spinning endlessly into the distance. The checklist method had the added advantage of refining and making more efficient his running technique; even a fraction of a per cent improvement in each stride meant a lot when he was taking over eighty thousand strides a day.

Inventory complete, Doc would go back over it again and again before he moved on to another device, the "inner method." He had learned it from Fu Li, an old Chinese with whom he had traveled the carnivals in the 1912–20 period. Fu Li, though no athlete, had shown an immediate sympathy for Doc's desire to run, even when there was no longer professional competition. "In running," he said, "every day you conquer yourself anew." Fu Li's method was to have Doc move *inside*, to forget both technical detail and fatigue. "Think of your body as a still, hollow tube, through which air passes endlessly. Move back into that stillness, into that peace." And so Doc would move away from the pain, the road, the crowds of well-wishers, his rivals, into just such a cool inner world.

Sometimes, however, these methods simply would not work, and Doc found that chatting with other runners or taking note of the surrounding geography was the only way to pass the boredom and leaden fatigue of the miles. Thus on each stage he plucked from his past experience some device, some trick, some mechanism of the mind that would drag his body toward the next checkpoint.

But it was going well. All the experience of the past was enabling him at fifty-four years of age to run stride for stride with a tireless young German. Daily he checked his inventory and found it complete: all parts in working order.

It came so suddenly, the pain, that Doc recognized it immediately: the old enemy, those few millimeters of tendon tissue that had so often in the past denied him victory. And there it was again, in the same old place, at the bottom of his right calf, in the Achilles tendon. It was not yet desperately sore but it was undoubtedly a warning. Luckily, it came at the end of a stage, just as they were closing in on Salina, Kansas, about four hundred miles east of Denver, at the end of the day's second section of twenty-three miles.

Hugh felt the break in his companion's rhythm, sensed that Doc was slowing down, and looked to his left.

"Nothing," said Doc. "You go on ahead."

Hugh paused for a moment, but Doc pushed him on, putting the flat of his hand on Hugh's shoulder blades. The cars of local sightseers blew dust into the runners' eyes as they padded toward Salina, and a couple of hundred yards ahead they could hear the inevitable "Whiffenpoof Song." Hugh moved through the field over the last couple of miles to finish in sixth place, with Doc six places behind him.

Hugh noted that Doc was limping slightly as he finished. "How are you?" he asked anxiously.

"Just been visited by an old friend," said Doc, scowling. He peeled off his tattered shoes, bending down to gently pinch the top of his right ankle. "Bum Achilles. Beat me in Baghdad in 1910, again in Rome in 1912. It's no big surprise. I've been waiting for it—it was bound to come at these distances, on these surfaces, running day in, day out."

They walked together toward the main tent, now both in their bare feet. When they reached the tent Doc fished deep in his knapsack and pulled out a pair of worn leather boots. "Here's the answer to the problem," he said. "Boots."

He pulled them on over his leathery brown feet and started gingerly to walk around the tent.

"The next two days I walk and run in these," he said, pulling his sweat-sodden shirt over his head. "The high heel keeps tension off the Achilles; rests it up good."

"Walk?" said Hugh. "But you'll lose hours!"

Doc bared his teeth and bit his lip. "Perhaps. I reckon I can walk at a steady five miles an hour. If now and then I run a little maybe I can bring that up some. In two days that means a loss of about one and a half hours on Stock."

Doc unlaced the boots and replaced them carefully in his knapsack.

"I've no choice, Hugh," he said. "If I keep running on this Achilles in sneakers I'll end up in the hospital by Topeka. Two days' rest, plus . . . this." He broke off to pull out a bottle of Chickamauga remedy, carefully poured some of the fluid into his left hand and kneaded it gently into his right Achilles tendon. "Whatever else it does, one thing Chickamauga sure as hell *is* good for is tendon injuries. Meanwhile you'll have to carry the flag for us for the next couple of days, hang in with Stock, and hold off all those outlaws closing in from the back."

He smiled ruefully and continued to knead the Chickamauga into his ankle. He was in deep trouble, and no one knew it better than he. Now almost an hour behind Stock, even at best he would be two and a half hours, almost thirteen miles, behind by the end of the next two days. By that time Capaldi, Morgan, Eskola and Bouin, already close, would be an hour or more ahead of him.

And that was at the very best. If the Achilles tendon took another couple of days more to mend, then by the end of the week he would be four hours behind Stock. Until now Doc had run easily, but such a deficit would mean daily stints on the edge of exhaustion for the next half of the race to catch up. Doc grinned painfully as he lay back on his bunk, head cupped in his hands, the sweat of the day's run glistening on his lean little body.

If it had to be done, if he had to walk the tightrope all the way to New York, then so be it. He had trained for thirty years for the Trans-America and no Achilles tendon was going to stop him now.

Next morning Doc watched Hugh and the leaders stream off far in front of him at a steady six and a half miles an hour. Ahead of him were at least seven hundred runners, their feet throwing up clouds of dust from the dry Kansas field on which they had camped. He was alone, plodding in thick, heavy boots, for the first time in the bottom half of the field, among the stragglers, the trotters and walkers, eating their dust on the soft dirt ribbon of road toward Abilene.

As the runners slowly unraveled themselves, Doc saw Kate Sheridan only twenty yards ahead look back and pick him out.

"Want some company, Doc?" asked Kate, dropping her pace to run beside him.

"Glad of it," said Doc gratefully. "But won't I slow you up?"

Kate shook her head. "I'm down to about five miles an hour for the next couple of hours anyway," she said. "The curse. I'll pick up tomorrow. I can do with the company."

She glanced down at his heavy brown boots but said nothing. Doc realized that she had noticed his footwear and pointed down at his feet.

"An old Doc Cole remedy," he said, smiling. "For the ancient Achilles."

Kate nodded. "Are you hurt bad?"

Doc shook his head.

"Nothing I can't handle," he said. "An old enemy. I've beaten it before. I'll do it again. Just you watch me."

He tapped his sweating scalp. "One thing I've learned," he said, "is to listen to my body. All that Achilles of mine is asking for is a couple of days' rest. Then I'll be up there with Stock and the others, burning up the road to Kansas City. Just you mark my words, lady."

Doc walked the next six miles in silence. He had no idea if his leg would heal in time. If it did not, then the Trans-America would be irretrievably lost, here on the flat fields of Kansas, the easiest running ground of the race. He was glad that Kate had remained equally quiet, for there was nothing she could say to comfort him. He would just have to pray that, after all these years, his body would not let him down.

Even in boots Doc, who had race-walked many times, could just make a steady five miles an hour, and Kate trotted easily beside him.

Even after five miles, he knew it. He had been right. The tendon, only slightly inflamed, responded well to the raised heel and the walking pace, and at the second feeding station at ten miles he stopped to cool his foot in a rocky stream by the roadside. Cold running water had always eased it in the past. He enjoyed the feeling of the icy water lapping over his feet as he sat on a rock beside Kate and noted that at least a score of runners had also stopped to cool themselves.

He cupped some water in his hands and lapped it like a dog, pouring the residue over his head. He scowled. Only ten miles run, and already the leaders were over three miles ahead, and going away from him. He had dropped a couple of places on aggregate time and the lead he had established on everyone but Stock was melting away.

He looked up at the morning sun and shielded his eyes. The sun was his friend. It would slow down even Stock to well inside six and a half miles an hour and lessen the effect of his enforced walk.

Thank God, the Trans-America was slowing down in the hot plains of Kansas. If only he could keep the deficit down . . .

It was the strange, twisted paradox of super fitness. The fitter you were, the closer you were to injury, the closer to tearing or inflaming that microscopic area of tissue that would stop you as surely as any bullet. Thus, from being a running machine, capable of churning out nine-minute miles an hour, day after day, he was now a near cripple.

Doc felt a deep sick feeling in his stomach. One hundred thousand miles of running, a heart pumping at a steady thirty-three beats a minute, a body made for traveling long distances. But all of it counted for nothing here on a hot, dusty dirt road to Abilene, plodding along at a miserable five miles an hour.

Yet beneath the sick-heart feeling Doc knew that thirty years of running had prepared him for just this crisis, not the moment of triumph but a challenge even greater than the covering of three thousand miles across America. For it was the manner in which he faced failure which was going to be his sternest test.

He had, of course, failed before. In 1908, in the blinding heat of the London Olympics, he had succumbed to hypothermia at twenty miles and had ground to a halt. Afterward, when he had traveled north immediately following the Games, to compete in professional hill races, though there had been failure there had been no dishonor. At rural games at Grasmere and Burnsall Doc had faced specialist hill-runners, iron-legged shepherds, who, hands on knees, had chugged remorselessly up crippling crags, and, on the way down, leaped like stags through the bracken in massive bounds toward the finish. Those hill races had produced local muscular agonies which he had not previously experienced and which he was not to face again till twenty-odd years later in the Rockies. But he had faced the hills of the Lake District, and if he had not exactly conquered them certainly it had been an honorable draw.

Doc wiped the sweat from his face, looked up at the sun and checked his watch. Kate was now far in the distance out of sight and he was alone, now in about four hundredth position. Again his thoughts drifted back . . .

Dorando, Longboat, Shrubb, Appleby, all those great runners of the past, where were they now? Jesus, he must have trotted through three generations of runners. They had come, taken their share of notoriety and applause, made their mark on the history of athletics, and vanished. But who would ever remember Doc Cole? Perhaps the Trans-America was the last opportunity to prove himself. Perhaps now was the real test. The next couple of days would tell. Doc ended the day's stint in the crowded, dusty main street of Abilene, having preserved a sturdy five miles an hour over the two twenty-mile stages. His hips were stiff from the unaccustomed action of walking, but he was still in the race.

Topeka Chief of Police Wilbur T. Fiske took off his silver badge and placed it on the table in front of him. Forty years on the force, thirty of them under that amiable shamrock, O'Brien, and ten of them free and clear on his own as chief.

Free and clear. For there had not been a single major decision that he had made for himself in all those ten years. When a businessman's son had been found drink-sodden, having driven a car through Stacey's Department Store window, it was Chief Fiske who had smoothed things over and arranged the payoff. After all, he and Stacey were both Masons. When the order had come for the department to stay out when the meat packers brought in hoodlums to break the strike of 1929, he had let his men stand idly by, while thugs made bloody gargoyles out of decent, hard-working men.

Free and clear. In only three days he would indeed be free and clear, his pension assured. And now the order had come from Mayor Matson to keep the Trans-Americans out of the city until way after midnight, to allow them only to run through dark, unlit streets. He had checked on the race, and he could see no reason for the mayor's decision. Knowing Mayor Matson, it was bound to be something political, something rotten. Still, it was no skin off his nose, not after ten years of cleaning up Matson's dirt.

And then the call had come. At first he could not believe it, that Miss McAllister herself had actually telephoned *him*, addressed him by his first name, was asking his help, in the doing of God's work. He had listened dumbstruck as she had told him what she wanted of him, of what his brothers and sisters all over America, indeed all over the world, required of him, of Wilbur T. Fiske. He dimly remembered kneeling by the telephone, sobbing, begging that his sins be washed away. Yes, she had said, do only this and your sins will indeed be washed away, as if in the River Jordan.

Free and clear. Free and clear and clean on the evening of May 2, the stroke of midnight. For the call had come, and this time Wilbur T. Fiske was not going to be found wanting.

May 1, 1931: It was getting better. Slowly, but it was getting better. Doc had long since become aware of every nuance of his muscular system, every good and bad message it sent him. This third day would therefore be the last day of walking and trotting in boots across the soft Kansas roads, the thin veins that crisscrossed the waving seas of supple May wheat.

Even five miles an hour was hard walking, but Doc went back to the vigorous hip swivel which he had used as a race walker, pumping his arms across his lean body. After he had warmed up he moved to a faster jog trot, his speed limited only by his boots, and this took him cutting through the middle of the sluggish field. He was again on the move.

Now, back at two hundred and twentieth position and still holding twenty-sixth place on aggregate time, Doc had time to study the men with whom he was running. Kovak, the gimpy Czech, carrying one leg shorter than the other, because of a polio infection in his youth. The Czech had limped and hobbled nearly two thousand miles on a leg not fit to support a chair, let alone 140 pounds, hitting the ground ten thousand times a day, six days a week. But Kovak had never stopped running, and was now closing in on Topeka, the state capital of Kansas, groaning every step of his lopsided way. With him was Carl Blake, the young Kansas farmer, whose land had blown away in one week in 1930, and who was running only a few miles from the same stricken fields which he had once tilled and cherished. Blake, bowed, skeletal, black with sun, his feet hardly leaving the ground, shuffled through Kansas at a steady five miles an hour. Every stride looked to be his last, but still somehow he kept on going, sweat streaming from a body that looked drained of all fluid.

Just ahead of Doc was the little Irishman, Matt O'Carrol, his sweat-sodden green shirt sticking to his back. O'Carrol ran with teeth tightly clenched, foaming slightly at the mouth. For him, too, every stride looked an agony as he and Blake ran side by side, the gaunt Kansan and the tiny, bandy-legged Irishman.

Blake, Kovak, O'Carrol and at least a thousand others, none of whom had the slightest chance of being in the money in New York: why did they keep running? Doc was surprised that the question had ever even occurred to him. They ran because this was the moment which no landlord, no employer, no politician, could take from them. They had stood in bread lines, taken handouts and pay cuts, watched while plump politicians had pursued their round of conferences. They had watched, impotent. It had not taken them long to realize that others were going to win the Trans-America, nor had it taken them long to reach their personal decisions to continue. They had come to run across America and no one on earth was going to stop them. No, there was no need to ask why these men kept running.

The fields were endless, rolling seas of green wheat, billowing and flowing into the horizon. Occasionally the houses of rich farmers would rise up above the wheat like crusaders' castles:

gaunt, white-clapboard wooden houses, cool and still as they had been in that hot autumn of 1914 when Doc and his road-show assistant Lily Hudson had worked in the Kansas harvest. He remembered the chanting, white-robed priests and the smell of incense before they had started the harvesting. The harvesters were horse-drawn and Lily and the women had scampered behind them, throwing the bales to the side for the men to stack. Then came the back-breaking job of pitchforking the wheat onto the carts. Doc had watched the fluid movements of men twice his age forking high and easy and had tried to copy them—fruitlessly. Within minutes the pain in his arms and shoulders forced him to rest on his pitchfork. He was soon abruptly reminded by the foreman that no work meant no pay.

Doc's distance training had served him well in those first painful days. True, distance running had done nothing to prepare the specific muscles required for this type of work. What it had taught him was that he could suffer almost any amount of muscular discomfort. He had run through it, so he could harvest through it.

Each night Lily had rubbed Chickamauga into his stiff arms and shoulders, as they listened to the strains of a crazy fiddle or peasant campfire songs from all over the world. In the mornings, before work, he had talked to the gnarled peasants who had been brought by cattle truck from Chicago to bring in the Kansas harvest. They had shown him how to place the bales relative to his legs, how to keep the pitchfork close to the body, how to swing the bales upward in a single, economical, flowing movement. They had taught him the rhythm of rural labor.

Doc had been a quick learner. Within a day he was keeping up with the best of them, feeding the greedy trucks with their supply of wheat. In the evenings he lay with Lily out of the light of the campfires, exploring her firm sunburned body beneath the coolness of her cotton dress.

Concordia, autumn 1914. It had been hard; but those had been good days. Lily was now in far-off Chicago, the owner of her very own hairdressing parlor. And he was running through that same land, with the same kind of men as those with whom he had harvested in those far-off days.

Two miles ahead, at the front of the pack, where Doc longed to be, Lord Peter Thurleigh was racing for real. He now daily ran stride for stride with Stock; but he ran in a panic. In the past, whatever the stress of studies or athletic competition, there had always been in the background the certainty, the comfort of his wealth. He had not realized how much he had depended on that background.

Until he had arrived in Los Angeles he had been unable to take the Trans-America completely seriously. Indeed, until he had seen the Los Angeles hotels and boardinghouses choked with Trans-Americans and journalists and had read newspaper reports of Flanagan's first press conference he had half suspected that the Trans-America might be some gigantic hoax and that Flanagan, whoever he was, was safely established with the competition entry fees in some far-off Mexican hacienda.

The reality of the first days on the road had ended all such thoughts. This was indeed real. The disappearance of his butler and Rolls-Royce in the Mojave had only underlined the fact that he was going to have to tap every resource if he was to take the smiles from the faces of his adversaries back at the club in London; the disappearance of his family fortunes even more so.

Thurleigh had soon realized, too, that the world of Oxford and of genteel amateur athletics had done nothing to prepare him for the Trans-America. For this was not a race of a few minutes of pain or discomfort like the Olympic five thousand meters. Here, in the Trans-America, it hurt all day and every day. And each day there was some new problem, a blister to be lanced, a stomach upset to be treated, a tendon to be nursed, sunburned ankles to be salved. Peter Thurleigh had got used to calves and thighs from which a dull soreness never retreated, but had never become accustomed to the permanent pain in his joints and bones.

After only two hundred miles he had thought he would have to give up, that there was no way he could stand three months of pounding on the dirt roads of America, living nightly in the reek of liniment, sweat and human excrement. But slowly the Trans-America had both infected and absorbed him. It was nothing to do with the wager he had made, even though now his financial future depended on it. Rather, like Kate Sheridan and the others, Thurleigh had become engaged in a battle with himself. It was a battle which he was never quite certain of winning, but one which he grew to relish.

The receipt of his father's telegram informing him of the loss

of the family fortunes in some strange way freed Peter Thurleigh.
Now there were no buffers, no cozy retreat if things went wrong.
Like all the other competitors he was on his own, with no safety
net to catch him if he failed. That knowledge gave him the daily
jolt of adrenaline which took him through the hard miles.

He had asked to join Doc's group, not out of any sense of
weakness but rather because he could sense the camaraderie which
had developed between Doc, Hugh, Morgan and Martinez; even
the frail childlike Martinez seemed to have drawn strength from
the group. He felt, too, that in their company he could only learn
and grow and absorb something of a world which, up till then,
had been as remote to him as the surface of the moon. But Doc
had procrastinated and had asked Thurleigh to wait till the conclusion of the race against Silver Star in St. Louis.

Behind him, Martinez, Morgan and McPhail ran as a unit. Martinez
and Morgan had joined Doc and Hugh's "cooperative" back in
Abilene. Henceforth they all would share whatever the Trans-
America brought them, working under Doc's guidance. Their orders
were to keep Stock in sight, but not to become involved in racing
with him. For the first ten miles they had run behind Stock and
Thurleigh, and watched the back of Thurleigh's silk shirt gradually
darken as it absorbed his sweat.

Directly behind them pressed Eskola, Bouin and Capaldi, themselves tracked by the Japanese, Son, and the sinewy Australian,
Mullins. The race was telescoping, as the end of the first two
thousand miles loomed ahead in St. Louis, now only four hundred
miles away.

Kate was finding it difficult to think of anything but Morgan, of
his body pressed against hers in the darkness of the strange room.
Daily, as she cut through the green Kansas fields, she recalled
each moment, from the first tentative touch to her final cry. She
found it impossible to believe that he felt as she did; so much of
Morgan was hidden from view. Gradually, however, she had
learned about his past. She sensed his guilt, his feeling that in
being with her he had betrayed his dead wife.

"Look, Mike," she had said, "from what you say I think I would
have loved her too. I haven't taken you over from her. I've taken
you on. So don't ever forget her."

Morgan looked straight at her. "You would have liked each other," he said.

Her running had become automatic, freeing her mind to think of him as she continued to pass man after man. With the Rockies behind her, she at least was relishing the flat roads of Kansas.

Doc picked up and passed Kate early that morning, and started to cut easily through the field. By the end of the day, at Wamego, he would be two hours down on Stock, an hour down on the others. That would mean that he would have to battle with Stock for at least a week even to regain his second position. Beyond that he could not think, for he could see no way of actually catching Stock if the young German maintained his present form. Such a performance by a young athlete was outside Doc's experience, for distance running had always been the province of men in their thirties and forties, men race-hardened with thousands of miles of running.

Doc took his food on the run now, thus gaining half a minute at each feeding station. Flanagan had, mercifully, given up the peanut butter sandwiches back in the Mojave, providing instead light, easily digestible snacks of fruit, chocolate and water, milk and saline lemon drinks.

Doc poured the remains of his drinking water over his head as he trotted down the main street of McFarland, and waved at the cheering crowds as he picked up another container of water from the feeding station. As he did so a little boy in brown corduroys pushed his way out of the crowds and stood in front of him. The boy, who could not have been more than nine or ten, held in his hands a grubby school notebook and a short, stubby pencil.

He looked back anxiously at what Doc guessed were his classmates in the crowd. "Could I have your autograph, sir?" he asked, finally.

It was the first time Doc had been asked for his autograph by a child since the London Olympics.

"Have you any idea of my name, sonny?" he asked, wiping the sweat from his hands.

"Yes, sir," replied the boy. "We see movies of the race at the Roxy every week. You're Doc Cole the runner, and me and my buddies have a dollar on you getting first to New York."

"Doc Cole the runner," whispered Doc under his breath. To the boy he said, "I'll try to help you hang on to that dollar."

He laid down the container of water on the table beside him and slowly wrote on the first page of the boy's notebook.

"Alexander (Doc) Cole, with best wishes to . . ." he wrote, then looked at the boy.

"Just put 'the boys of McFarland,' sir," said the boy, standing on tiptoe to look over Doc's shoulder as Doc completed the autograph.

Doc closed the notebook and handed it back to the boy. He leaned down and kissed him on the cheek, to the applause of the crowd. A tear trickled down his own cheek. Doc drew the back of his hand across his eyes and trotted down the main street, waving at the crowds as he did so. Tomorrow he would start to catch up, all the way to St. Louis. Doc Cole would show them some fancy running.

As usual, Peter Stock had led all the way, and now, at one in the morning, three miles outside Topeka he chugged behind the brightly lit Trans-America truck, which blared Rudy Vallee and the "Whiffenpoof Song" from its loudspeaker system. A quarter of a mile behind followed Eskola, Thurleigh, McPhail, Martinez and Morgan, followed in turn by Mullins and Son. The rest of the field was strung out for six miles along the road, with a rejuvenated Doc moving up into the low thirties now, well ahead of Kate, who was running close to three hundredth position.

Peter Stock trotted wearily across the unlit Kansas Avenue in the residential area of the town, followed by the purring black Mercedes containing the German team staff. There was not a streetlight in town, for the mayor had acted on his instructions from Toffler.

Flanagan turned on all the Trans-America trailer lights and beamed the searchlight on top of the trailer on Stock.

The Trans-America trundled quietly into the darkness of Main Street, passing the Capitol Building on its right. The shopping area was completely still.

"Like a graveyard," Flanagan said, chewing on his cigar at the window of his trailer.

Suddenly there was the shrill hoot of a policeman's whistle. The lights of every shop in the street flooded on, blinding Stock and the stream of runners behind him. At the same time the headlights of hundreds of cars, lined for half a mile on each side of the street, sprang to life. It was like daytime, and the runners cruised through the street bathed in a sea of light.

The whistle shrilled again and the street reverberated to the noise of a thousand car horns, working in unison. A third whistle brought waves of sustained applause, for there were at least five thousand people lining the main street. A fourth whistle signaled a brass band at the finish to start up with "See the Conquering Hero Comes."

Once again Flanagan's men were among friends as men, women and children from the crowd came out to shake their hands and give them candy and drinks. The runners were engulfed in a sea of Topekans.

Willard Clay stopped the Trans-America trailer beyond the finish. A portly figure in dress uniform stood facing Flanagan as he left the trailer. The man pumped Flanagan's hand warmly.

"I'm chief of police, Wilbur T. Fiske," he said. "You'll be Mr. Flanagan. My apologies for the lack of streetlights, but I hope our little welcome made up for it. Our ladies are along at your camp now fixing up some special vittles for your boys. Miss McAllister can't be here herself but she asks to be reminded to you kindly."

"Miss McAllister's a very kindly lady," said Flanagan.

"All the Lord's work," said Fiske. "All the Lord's work."

"Then praise the Lord," said Flanagan. "Sure praise the Lord."

Alice Craig McAllister had done her work well. And it was as well that May 3 was a rest day, for Wilbur Fiske's religious convictions had not prevented the provision of copious quantities of bootleg liquor.

"God," said Hugh, "I should have stuck with the orange juice."

"Don't expect any sympathy," Doc laughed. "Be like me," he said, putting on his boots. "Live clean. Come on, let's walk some of that moonshine out of your system."

They strolled out in the bright morning sunshine onto the dirt road leading to Lawrence.

"There won't be any Huck Finn for the next week or so," said Doc. "I'm healed up now, but I'm placed about sixtieth on aggregate. Maybe I'm wrong, but I want to pick up an hour or so on Stock in the next four hundred miles. Won't feel comfortable otherwise. That means that I'm going to have to beat the pants off that splendid young Kraut every day next week."

"Isn't that taking a risk?" said Hugh. "Couldn't you bust your Achilles again, or simply exhaust yourself catching up with him?"

"That's a risk I've got to take," replied Doc. "At least the roads up ahead are mainly soft dirt-track, easy on the Achilles. And I've been running inside myself till now, apart from the Rockies. No, I'm going to have to show Mr. Stock some sweet running, run the legs off him, every stage. I've got to get back up in the main pack, and that means gaining a half an hour a day for the next week or so."

"Reckon you can catch Stock?" asked Hugh, chewing on a straw.

For a moment Doc was tempted to tell Hugh of his suspicions of Stock. He had seen other runners on drugs like cocaine and strychnine. Hell, in 1912 a Frenchman had tried arsenic before a marathon in Cairo. It had worked well, helping him to a second place a few minutes ahead of Doc, but most of his prize money had later been absorbed in hospital bills. No, it was best to keep his suspicions about Peter Stock to himself.

He shook his head.

"Not if he keeps going the way he's been doing so far. Eskola, Mullins, Son, Bouin—these guys I can understand, even someone like you, but this boy Stock is running out of his skull. Where does it come from? We'd never heard of him, or his buddy, Muller, before he ended up in a basket in Denver. And what about the rest of those cold, blue-eyed beauties? Jesus, they're like something from another planet."

"And what about this race Flanagan's fixed us up with once we get to St. Louis?" asked Hugh.

"All part of life's rich pattern," said Doc. "If we get the contract right then we just might give this Levy guy a run for his money. If not, then it will be a farce. Sure as hell Thurleigh will run his guts out for us. He's asked to team up with us, but I haven't thought it through yet. So I'll tell him that we're using it as a trial to see if he can join the group. And you know what Morgan is like."

"But a horse—" Hugh began.

"A trotting horse, a sprinter," said Doc. "Pulling a two-hundred-pound bag of lard cross-country for ten miles. Do you remember how long it took you to condition yourself for distance running?"

Hugh nodded.

"Well, that horse has got just one week," said Doc. "It couldn't condition itself for a cold shower in that time."

He picked up a stone and threw it along the road.

"The long road to St. Louis," he said. "Four hundred miles. I'm going to hurt some in the next week. But sure as hell so is Mr. Stock. You can count on it."

Doc was as good as his word. The pace had dropped to inside six miles an hour across the flat roads of Kansas, but Doc, now running with heel supports in his shoes, lifted it to just over eight-minute-mile pace. Even so, Stock would not give way, and daily the little bald man and the blond youth ran stride for stride, spinning the rest of the field out behind them. Doc was putting to use thirty years of experience, thirty years of knowing exactly what pace he could sustain over a day's running. But Stock hung on, silent, impassive, never giving a yard.

They reached Lawrence together, he and Stock, half an hour ahead of the field, bringing Doc up to twenty-first position on aggregate. Then on into Kansas City, running together through the scrapwood shanties of the town, the settling point of the "Exodusters," freed Negroes from the south, into the city, past Wyandot Park, where rested the bones of the chiefs of the Wyandot Indians. Doc burned off the young German and another lost fifteen minutes were picked up on the stage which finished in the roaring crowds of Kansas City, bringing him up to fourteenth position. It was going well: he was closing in. But he was still a long way from Stock on aggregate time.

Then another dusty fifty miles to Concordia, Missouri, again locked with Stock all the way. Doc moved up to twelfth position.

It was on the road between Concordia and Columbia that at last Stock started to wilt. It was almost perceptible. Doc felt the young German suddenly weaken and lose his rhythm, and in a matter of seconds he had dropped back and had eased to a shambling trot.

Doc pressed home his advantage and ended up twenty minutes ahead of the next finisher "Digger" Mullins. He was now eighth on aggregate, back up among the race leaders.

An hour later Doc stood in a field outside Columbia with a hundred others below the primitive showers which Willard Clay had constructed, enjoying the lukewarm water as it dripped unevenly from above and streamed down his body. He rubbed the red carbolic soap which he was holding with both hands and wiped the foam beneath his armpits.

"All I want is all there is, and then some," he crooned.

Dimly, through the steam of the shower and the gathering gloom, he could see Willard Clay hastening toward the washing area. It was the first time he had ever seen Willard run.

Doc stepped out of his cubicle and was stretching for his towel as Willard finally reached him, blowing heavily. Flanagan's lieutenant paused for a moment to regain his breath. Then—

"It's Peter Stock," he said. "We think he's dying."

Maurice Falconer was the first to speak. "He's in the emergency ward of the City Hospital," he said, pulling his fingers through his gray hair.

"The doctors are doing all that they can. He collapsed after finishing," explained Flanagan.

"What do the medics say?" asked Doc.

"They've never seen anything like it," rejoined Falconer. "His rectal temperature was a hundred and four point seven degrees Fahrenheit, while his heart was going at one hundred and eighty beats for half an hour."

"And what do you think?" asked Doc, turning to Falconer.

"Drugs—just like you thought. Maybe not cocaine, but something like it. See this?" Falconer held up a small unmarked bottle of pills. "I picked it up when I visited the German team quarters. Five will get you ten that it's some sort of depressant, some dope which dulls the inhibitory centers."

"You mean that it blocks the natural feelings of pain that you experience in fatigue?" asked Doc.

"Exactly," said Falconer. "But it's probably more complicated than that. God knows what else they've been pumping into him— some goddam crazy cocktail of drugs. No one knows what happens to the body when you put it into a stress situation like the Trans-America, but when you start adding some godawful mix of drugs into a man, who knows the end of it?"

He put his head in his hands. "It's a mess. One hell of a mess."

The telephone rang.

"It's the hospital," said Willard, answering it. "For you." He handed the telephone to Flanagan.

Flanagan listened for a moment.

"Thank you, Doctor," he said. "We'll call back in the morning."

He dropped the telephone on to its rest, but his hand remained on the receiver. "He'll make it," he said. "He's out of danger."

"Thank God," said Falconer.

Flanagan stood up.

"Well, what do we do?"

"What do you mean?" asked Doc.

"I mean, how do we get the Krauts out of the race?"

"I see," said Doc. "Do you have anything in the rules to cover it?"

"We used the IAAF amateur rules," said Flanagan. "Nothing much there about drugs."

"So, technically, they've done nothing wrong?" asked Falconer.

"The hell they have!" shouted Flanagan. "Goddam cheats. All you guys running your balls off twice a day while those blue-eyed superior Aryans, or whatever the hell they call themselves, are running up front like something out of Wagner. Goddam—"

"Don't blame Muller or Stock," said Doc. "Those young guys probably had no idea what was being pumped into them. Probably thought it was some sort of vitamins."

"Doc's right," said Falconer. "It's Moltke and his gang of coaches you should tear into. They're the real culprits."

"But how?" asked Flanagan. "They haven't broken any race rules. More to the point, there's no means of proving they took drugs."

Doc stood up.

"When I'm not running I read newspapers," he said. "In fact it's like a drug: I can't do without them. Now I read in the papers that these National Socialists made it big in the elections last December, but they've had a lot of internal splits. And they're not in power yet—so the last thing they want is bad publicity. It's not much good saying that the master race has to take drugs to win the Trans-America!"

Flanagan's eyes narrowed.

"So what are you telling me to do?"

"Get Moltke in here. Tell him that if he doesn't withdraw his team you'll make it all known to the press. See what he says then."

Flanagan looked at Willard. Willard nodded.

"Okay," Flanagan said. "Willard, wheel in the master race . . ."

The Germans withdrew from the Trans-America the next morning. The official announcement was that the team management wished to return Muller and Stock for specialized medical treatment in Germany, and were, therefore, forced to withdraw the remainder of their runners.

For the first time Hugh McPhail was now in the lead, with a hundred miles to go to St. Louis. And his battle with a horse called Silver Star.

Sunday, May 3, 1931

Kansas City (1627 miles)

			Hrs.	Mins.	Secs.
1 = H. McPhail	(Great Britain)		263	10	12
2 = M. Morgan	(USA)		263	20	10
3 = A. Capaldi	(USA)		263	22	10
4 = J. Bouin	(France)		263	24	12
5 = P. Eskola	(Finland)		263	26	10
6 = R. Mullins	(Australia)		263	30	12
7 = P. Thurleigh	(Great Britain)		263	35	21
8 = A. Cole	(USA)		264	01	12
9 = J. Martinez	(Mexico)		264	20	10
10 = L. Son	(Japan)		264	35	12
11 = P. Dasriaux	(France)		264	45	10
12 = P. Komar	(Poland)		265	10	10
13 = P. Coghlan	(New Zealand)		265	11	12
14 = P. Brix	(USA)		265	12	20
15 = C. O'Connor	(Ireland)		265	20	10
16 = J. Schmidt	(Poland)		265	25	17
17 = P. Maffei	(Italy)		266	50	12
18 = K. Lundberg	(Sweden)		267	10	14
19 = R. Brady	(Ireland)		267	30	12
20 = P. O'Grady	(Ireland)		267	45	06

1st Lady: (550) K. Sheridan (USA)   325   24   01
Number of finishers: 1042
Average speed (leader): 9 mins. 41 secs. per mile

19

ST. LOUIS: MAN VERSUS HORSE

Carl Liebnitz sat in the press tent, fingers poised on the typewriter keys. Man versus horses! What next? He smiled, scratched his ear, arranged his notes, then quickly began to type . . .

AMERICANA DATELINE MAY 9, 1931

Archaeologists have found evidence of trotting races in the Middle East dating back to as early as 1350 B.C. Modern American trotting dates from 1788 which was when the English trotter, Messenger, was exported to the United States. Messenger was a classic trotter who never infringed the rules, using the high-knee diagonal gait which separates the trotter from the pacer, who uses the legs on one side of its body at the same time.

Messenger appeared three times in the pedigree of another horse, Hambletonian, the most famous of all stud trotters. Hambletonian, who had never himself run better than a modest 3 minutes 15 seconds for the mile, foaled such champions as Dexter, Robert Fillingham, Shark and Goldsmith Maid. By the time of his death Hambletonian had sired 1,300 foals, 40 of whom trotted the mile in better than 2 minutes 30 seconds. By the end of the nineteenth century all but three of the 138 trotters who had run 2 minutes 10 seconds could be traced directly back to Hambletonian, who had richly deserved the $288,000 he had earned at stud for his owner, Rysdyk.

It was 1806 before the 3-minute barrier for the mile was broken—by a horse named Yankee—and almost a hundred years later before Lou Dillon was to break the magic 2 minutes in running 1 minute 58.5 seconds. The essential difference between Yankee and Lou Dillon's performance lay not so much in the horses themselves but in the nature of the sulkies they pulled behind them. The sulky was made in two sections: first, two long shafts running along either side of the horse, and attached at its shoulders and withers; then the bridge, joining the shafts behind the horse and on which there was a seat for the driver. In 1806 Yankee had pulled a clumsy, ponderous sulky of 125 lb., plus its rider, while in 1903 Lou Dillon was pulling a rider and a light, flexible sulky of only 25 lb. By the turn of the century an arched axle had been invented, to prevent the trotter from striking into the axle with its rear leg; earlier, in 1855, a roller-bearing axle had been introduced, while in 1892 the cycle maker, Elliott, had invented a bicycle wheel which had reduced vibration, checked the tendency of the sulky to slew at bends, and reduced air resistance.

Thus in Coolidge Stadium Flanagan's runners tomorrow face, in Silver Star, a direct descendant of the great Hambletonian, a standard-bred stallion pulling a flexible, feather-light, 22 lb. sulky. Luckily for them it will also pull, not a 100 lb. professional jockey, but the solid 202 lb. of the undertaker Leonard Levy, and Silver Star, after facing McPhail in the sprint, will then have to haul its Falstaffian master over ten miles of rough country.

The two races take us right back to the roots of American sport, when men wagered on the jumping powers of a frog, when John L. Sullivan battled against a French foot-boxing champion, or when little "Sure Shot" Annie Oakley took on the world with a rifle. Thus for a few moments the world of the stopwatch, the world of certainty will be suspended, as Flanagan's men pit themselves against one of the world's fastest trotters. A distinguished colleague of mine, H. L. Mencken, once said that all life is six to four against. The odds against Flanagan's runners are pitched a little higher, but I reckon that there will be more than a few long-shot bets on Messrs. McPhail, Morgan and Thurleigh when they toe the line at Coolidge Stadium tomorrow.

—CARL C. LIEBNITZ—

The heart of the city of St. Louis, Olive Street Canyon, bristled with bookies from throughout the Union. At first came the men who normally made book on fighters, horses and greyhounds, but soon they were joined by ordinary God-fearing citizens, men who had never in their lives bet on anything more than horse races like the Kentucky Derby or the Preakness. Even barber-shop bookies were offering ten to one against Flanagan's runners in each of the races, a hundred to one against Flanagan's men making the "double." At first, no one knew who Flanagan's runners were to be, but what did it matter? Goddamit, runners could no more beat horses than horses could outrun cars, or cars whip planes. Might as well say that Babe Ruth could chin Jack Dempsey. Still, at a hundred to one they were tempting odds, a good blind-shot bet . . . By the time—May 8—that Flanagan's runners reached Denville, about forty miles short of St. Louis, St. Louis seethed with excitement and anticipation.

Since Topeka Leonard H. Levy had not been idle. He had hired Coolidge Stadium, a trotting park just outside the city, holding forty thousand spectators, for a mere five thousand dollars, and was charging spectators three dollars each for admission. Since most of the race was over country he had also rented a hilly area adjacent to the stadium and planned to charge spectators two dollars a man for the privilege of watching the cross-country section. Popcorn, hamburger and drinks concessions had pulled in a further five thousand dollars, and he had hired General Fosdike's Wild West Show to support Flanagan's ragged circus. Financially, Leonard H. Levy could not lose; but his obsession still lay with his beloved trotter, Silver Star.

Men who themselves lack physical ability are prone to project their hopes and desires upon those who have that quality, be they animals or men. Thus they buy themselves a fighter, a baseball team, a horse, and live their fantasies through the successes of their purchases. Thus it was with the plump, balding Leonard Levy, a man who had, all his life, made up for his lack of physical prowess by the use of his wits. Levy would bargain for anything, from a Buick to a bag of popcorn, getting his kicks not from saving a few dollars or cents from the purchase, but simply from the pleasure of the hassle. So no smart-aleck Flanagan from New York was going to make him look a jackass. Anyhow, it was nothing to do with money—Levy had plenty of that. No, out there at the Coolidge Stadium Leonard H. Levy was going to show them all that he was an *athlete*.

"Charles H. Lindbergh," exclaimed Flanagan. He, together with

Doc, Willard and Kate, were standing with the runners in Coolidge Stadium, in the cathedral-like silence of an empty arena, the evening before the competition. Levy had indeed done them proud. The six-hundred-yard trotting track had been sifted, brushed and rolled to perfection, and the assorted flags of the nations of the world, which had lain unused in St. Louis since the Olympics, fluttered around the stadium. Silver Star's races against Flanagan's men might well have originated in a Topeka speakeasy, but come May 10 all of St. Louis, and spectators from nearly every state in the Union, would flood the Coolidge Stadium.

"This track doesn't interest me," said Doc, as he was joined there by Morgan, Thurleigh and McPhail. "We lose time in here. It's the country stretch *I* want to see."

"Spoken like a true distance man," said Hugh, bending down to pick up a handful of the dirt track. "Me, I'm interested in *this*."

He rubbed the gritty brown dirt, then let it pass through his fingers and looked at Flanagan. "Soft for sprinting," he said. "I'll have to use my long spikes, the ones I used back at McPhee in the Highland Games."

"Don't talk to me about McPhee," said Flanagan, kneeling to touch the surface of the track. "Those Scotch half-and-half pints of yours nearly did me in back there. But remember, Levy got me to agree to a three-race sprint series to give the crowd more for their money. You'll have to be in top shape."

Hugh looked up at the flapping flags and took a white hand-kerchief out of his pocket and watched it flutter.

"Get them to run the races into the breeze," he said. "A horse and sulky has more wind resistance than a man. And get them to put me down a sprint lane, Mr. Flanagan. Four feet of space. Something I can focus on."

Flanagan jotted down some notes on the back of an envelope and nodded at Willard.

"Got it," he said. "Now let's have a look at the country." They walked to the stadium exit, which led through the parking lot for fifty yards to a rough, rocky stretch leading up a hill into bumpy grassland, on which Levy had already pegged out a three-quarter-mile course. Levy's workmen were hammering in fence posts and stretching rolls of fence wire as Doc and his men began their walk.

"This is where we've really got to make it count, out here in the country," said Doc, turning to Thurleigh and Morgan as they walked up the hill. "You see, a trotting horse is a rhythm animal—take it out of its rhythm and it wastes energy, gets pooped."

"What about our boys' rhythm?" shouted Flanagan, raising his voice over the noise of hammering workmen.

Peter Thurleigh answered. "I've trotted horses," he said, walking away from the noise. "And run cross-country. Doc's right. We can keep rhythm over broken ground much better than any horse, particularly a trotter."

"Okay, I suppose you guys know your business best," sighed Flanagan. "So will you run a mile each in turn all the way?"

Thurleigh looked at Doc.

"Yep," said Doc, nodding. "I reckon Mike and Peter here can run inside five-minute-mile pace all the way, given five-minute rests between. Perhaps even better."

"Jesus," groaned Flanagan. "Levy's horse can run inside *two* minutes. Back in Topeka, Levy prattled on about one minute fifty-six till the time rattled around in my head like a pea in a can!"

"Yeah," said Doc. "But not one minute fifty-six seconds over rough, uneven ground like this. I reckon that Levy's horse could run full speed, carrying a one-hundred-pound jockey, about three and a half minutes around this course."

"And remember that Silver Star is a sprinter not a distance runner," said Thurleigh. "Tomorrow it's got to keep up that pace for ten miles, nonstop."

"I reckon that brings it up to over four minutes a mile," said Doc. "If not more. So we're getting closer."

"But it still leaves you a minute a mile to find," observed Kate.

"Not really," said Doc. "Kate, just imagine you had to run ten miles with an extra hundred-odd pounds around your waist."

"I'd die," said Kate, laughing.

"Well then," said Doc, "that's precisely what Silver Star has to do, with our friend Levy providing that extra hundred pounds of lard. Our friendly undertaker may not know it, but he's our first ace in the hole."

"And do we have another?" asked Kate.

Doc winked and looked up at the blue, cloudless sky. "That, lady, is in the lap of the gods."

The races were scheduled for two in the afternoon, with Hugh McPhail's sprint series first on the program, but by 10 A.M. the gates were closed, Coolidge Stadium was already packed and General Fosdike's Wild West Show and Flanagan's circus were already in full and noisy flow in a field adjacent to the stadium. Even out in the country, before noon, families had set up picnics at the edge of Levy's pegged out track, and impromptu books were being made and bets laid. Betting was now down to nine to one against Thurleigh and Morgan, six to one against McPhail in his "best of three runs" competition. Over a million dollars had been laid on the race in the St. Louis area alone.

With just over an hour to go Peter Thurleigh had never felt so nervous, not even at his first Olympics in 1914, when he had run against Nurmi in Paris. The Finn had run him ragged in the five thousand meters, lapping at a steady seventy-two seconds, at the end of each lap coolly checking his pace on the stopwatch he carried in his right hand. But the watch was superfluous. Nurmi ran to a deep inner clock set and held in motion by his cold Finnish will.

Even so it was in the cross-country event, run in the dry, torrid heat of a hundred and five degrees Fahrenheit, that had showed Nurmi at the peak of his powers. The Finn flowed over the parched, dusty course as if he were still on the track at the Stade Colombes, while the greatest cross-country runners in the world gasped and wobbled behind him. Peter had run himself into glassy-eyed delirium, and it was only in the hospital in Paris the next day that he learned that he had finished a creditable fifteenth and that Nurmi had been holding interviews with journalists by the time the second runner had entered the stadium.

One o'clock, only an hour to go. Morgan lay parallel to Thurleigh as they were being rubbed down, on black, leather-topped massage tables in the still, dark stone-floored dressing room. Above them, a naked bulb provided the only light. The room itself stank of horse liniment. Thurleigh smiled wryly and looked sideways at Morgan. Only a few yards away, they were probably rubbing the same stuff into Silver Star's supple flanks.

Morgan lay with eyes closed, while Doc gently teased the belly of his bulging hamstrings. He had faced worse challenges: running against a horse was nothing compared with facing the bare fists of another man in an ice-cold warehouse. Morgan knew it was going to be tough, for running five-minute miles on his own, over rough country, was quite different from slogging across America in company some two minutes a mile slower. This would be a world of heaving lungs and oxygen-debt, with legs which already had in them two thousand miles of running. He looked above him at Kate, standing beside Doc.

"Nervous?" she asked, attempting to conceal her own anxiety.

"No." He took her hand in his. "Perhaps a mite scared."

"No problem, Mike," said Doc, tapping him on the right knee as a signal to turn over onto his stomach. "You're in great shape."

"Sure," growled Morgan. "But who's rubbing the horse, and what the hell are they saying to *it?*"

Hugh McPhail stood in the tunnel below the main stand. At the end of the tunnel, the glare of the afternoon sun. Hugh could hear the babble of the crowd, even here, deep beneath the stand. It was just like Powderhall again, like that bitter January day eight years ago. The crowd outside reminded him of the miners who had watched him run against Featherstone. They had laid their bets; now they waited to see the outcome. Three runs against a horse, with forty thousand people looking on . . . Stevie walked down the tunnel toward him, dressed in an over-large summer suit and a ludicrous Panama hat. Hugh still found difficulty in accepting that the little man from Glasgow was really here in America.

"Jist like the old days," said Stevie, nodding behind him.

Hugh could not prevent a yawn, a sure sign of tension.

"Aye," he said. "But back at the pit I hadn't run two thousand miles for a warm-up."

"How fast do you think you can run now?" asked Stevie.

"Now . . . about ten point six for a hundred yards, eyeballs out."

"That might be enough."

"Against a horse?"

"Maybe," Stevie went on. "The big thing is that you've got three runs—you can learn. I don't think the horse will, and this man Levy, he's no Olympic athlete, is he?"

"No," said Hugh. "But I've been told he's no fool, either."

"You know the odds the Glasgow bookies were giving on you?"

"Ten to one against?" suggested Hugh.

"No," said Stevie, walking up the dark tunnel with him toward the bright sunshine of the trotting track. "Four. And that's because of old Wallace of Perth. Remember how he talked to you, back at the mine, before you ran against Featherstone? Well, he once ran against a horse himself, way back in 1901. Old Wallace's been talking to the Glasgow bookies. More to the point, he's been talking to me. This race will be won or lost at the start. So pin back your ears, my friend . . ."

1:30 P.M., May 10, 1931. In the gloom of the officials' dressing room at the Coolidge Stadium, Colonel Alan Carlsen bent over the dressing-room table and carefully loaded a clip of blanks into his Winchester. There was going to be no hanky-panky this afternoon, not if he had anything to do with it. After all, he had his reputation to consider. He had ridden with Teddy Roosevelt and the Rough-riders in the war against Mexico, and had been mentioned in dispatches. Not long after, in 1912, he had finished only one place behind that arrogant upstart, George C. Patton, in the Olympic modern pentathlon in Stockholm. In France, in the Great War, he had served with distinction with the fighting fifty-first, America's most distinguished regiment.

Alan P. Carlsen still considered himself an athlete even at the age of fifty-two. Every morning he took a cold shower, exercised rigorously to Bernarr McFadden's calisthenics program, then further purged and punished his body with a three-mile run. Carlsen was not only a career soldier: he was a public figure. And when he had been approached by Levy to act as arbiter between himself and Flanagan in their crazy "man against horse race" his first impulse had been to refuse.

Then he had thought again. Carlsen soon realized that this was going to be a big affair, discussed nationally, perhaps even internationally. Flanagan's Trans-Americans were already household names. Dammit, his grandson had even asked him for "Iron Man" Morgan's autograph, and his wife had begged to be introduced to the Sheridan girl after the race. Whoever acted as arbiter in the St. Louis races would have to be someone of repute, of strong character; men against horses wasn't like football or baseball—it was uncharted territory.

In short, he had accepted.

Now he yawned and stretched to his full six-foot four. He laid his Winchester down gently on the dressing-room table, then turned and faced Flanagan and Levy.

Pressing back his neat, crinkly gray hair with both hands, he began his prepared speech. "Gentlemen," he said. "Let's first establish some ground rules. Let me make it clear to both of you that I didn't take on this job in order to look like a damn jackass in the eyes of the world. I remember all too well what befell General Douglas MacArthur when he managed the 1920 Olympic team. So first let me make it clear that I must be the final arbiter on all matters pertaining to these races. Otherwise, I open that door over there"—he pointed to the dressing-room door—"and leave you two to fight it out between you."

The imperious Carlsen, impeccably dressed in his khaki ceremonial army uniform, brooked no dissent. Levy, already bursting at the seams of his silk jockey pants, nodded. Flanagan followed suit.

"Now both of you know as well as I do that, though there are clearly prescribed rules for races between men and for that matter for races between horses, there is nothing in writing to cover the present situation in any of the rule books of either harness racing or track and field. Nothing beyond what you have written here in your contract."

Carlsen picked up a sheet of paper, perched his glasses on his lean nose and held it in front of him. "Here are the rules to which both of you agreed. They're mostly common sense, but there is one which appears to me to be critical. Mr. Levy, your horse Silver Star is a trotter. Trotter means exactly that—trotting. Any 'break' into a gallop during the sprint will mean automatic loss of that heat. And that decision must be mine and mine alone . . . Agreed?"

Levy again nodded.

"Now I fully realize that the sprint finish may be tight," continued Carlsen. "I have therefore asked Eastman Kodak to provide cameras at the finish. Film can be developed in ten minutes for scrutiny. These films, if required, will be the final arbiter."

Carlsen hoisted himself up to sit on the dressing-room table, allowing his booted legs to dangle loosely. "However," he said, "the distance race presents greater problems. After all, I can hardly disqualify the horse during a ten-mile run for a single break in its trotting action on rough ground."

"No question, Colonel," said Flanagan, obediently, looking at Levy.

"So I propose the following," said Carlsen. "For a foul during a lap we immediately stop the horse for half a minute. These penalties will be signaled by the sound of a bugle, so that both the stadium crowd and Mr. Flanagan's helpers back at the track can be kept fully informed."

"How many fouls are allowed before disqualification, Colonel?" asked Flanagan.

"Eight," said the Colonel. "Agreed?"

Levy made to speak, but stopped himself. He had never even considered the possibility of Silver Star fouling.

Carlsen raised both eyebrows. "You have something to say, Mr. Levy?"

"No," said Levy, fingering his whip. It was a negligible handicap: he would put such distance between Silver Star and the runners that even a few fouls would not matter.

"But how are you going to check for fouls, Colonel?" asked Flanagan. "After all, it's a one-mile course, most of it out in the country."

"I intend to have six judges, all army officers, posted at intervals around the course," said Carlsen. "Each one is a qualified trotting judge. Take my word for it, gentlemen, they'll miss nothing." He picked up a whistle and a clip of blanks and stuffed them into his top jacket pocket, then finally he looked down at his watch.

"Any further questions, gentlemen?"

"I think that we can both safely leave matters in your capable hands, sir," said Flanagan. Levy nodded in agreement.

"That settles it then," said Carlsen, reaching over to shake Flanagan's hand in a strong grip before doing the same to Levy.

"Gentlemen," he said. "It's a beautiful day out there. I think we're going to see some fine sport. Teddy Roosevelt sums it up perfectly for me: a fair field and no favor, that's what he always used to say. And that's exactly how I see it too."

Colonel Alan Carlsen turned, picked up his Winchester, opened the door, and straightened himself to his full height, pulling down on his jacket and adjusting his tie. It was now 1:42 P.M. At the end of the dark tunnel he could hear the expectant crowd. Yes, it was going to be a great day.

One forty-five P.M. Thurleigh, Morgan and McPhail sat on the dressing-room bench in front of Doc. It was nearly time.

Doc was sweating hard, having just completed his massage of all three men.

"Right," he said, clasping both hands in front of him and interlocking his fingers. "Up till now, most of the time we haven't been racing in the Trans-America, we've simply been running, getting fifty miles under our belts every day. Running's physical. But racing—that's emotional. So you guys have got to dig real deep out there. The whole Trans-America's riding on you. Win, and Flanagan can take about a hundred grand from here, enough to pay off most of his debts and take us beyond Chicago."

He paced up and down restlessly in front of them.

"Hugh, in the sprint you know your business best, so there's no point in me telling you what to do. You're a pro. Dixie will be standing in the crowd twenty yards from the finish with a white handkerchief. Just sprint as if the devil's behind you with a poker at your ass."

Hugh nodded, smiling nervously, feeling the dampness of his palms, the thin trickle of sweat on his flushed right cheek.

Doc looked at Thurleigh and Morgan.

"In the distance run, the main thing is not to go crazy in the first couple of miles. By my reckoning you will be close on two minutes down on Silver Star by that time. You should be running steady at five minutes a mile or inside for the first six miles. Doc Falconer will be taking your pulse at the end of each mile to give us a guide on your condition, to let us know if we can safely push you harder."

He turned his back, took a deep breath, then turned to face them again.

"God knows how many words coaches have wasted at times like this. You'll have a thousand Trans-Americans out there rooting for you every yard of the way, guys who know exactly how it feels to dig into your guts when your whole body is begging you to stop. In the end all that counts is that, win or lose, you don't let them down."

Hugh felt like a gladiator going out to face hungry lions. He blinked as he stepped out into the sunshine onto the soft dirt track, his body still glowing from Doc's rubdown.

On the infield cheerleaders were still at work. Levy had trained a hundred plump-thighed High School majorettes to prance about in the center of the arena, singing his "Levy can't lose" jingle to the off-key strains of John Philip Sousa. To this sheer volume of noise Flanagan had no real answer, but he had scattered a dozen Hawaiian dancers around the arena, to dole out kisses and Trans-America badges to the crowd, and had paid two hundred dollars to Rickenbecker's Flying Daredevils to pull a Trans-America streamer a thousand feet above Coolidge Stadium. A thousand lean, sun-blackened Trans-Americans had posted themselves in groups in each quarter of the stadium and throughout the crowd on the cross-country course. Already their self-appointed cheerleaders were warming them up, to the amusement of the good-natured St. Louis crowd.

Hugh stepped gingerly onto the trotting track.

"The world's champion sprinter, five foot ten inches, one hundred and fifty pounds, Hugh McPhail from Glasgow, Bonnie Scotland!" boomed the announcer. There was sustained shouting, scattered applause, and rhythmic chanting from the Trans-Americans.

Hugh looked around him. He felt engulfed. The arena was packed to capacity, with children resting on the shoulders of sweating fathers, and popcorn and drink vendors finding it difficult to find channels in the vast, sticky, expectant crowd. Beyond the bleachers some intrepid youths had even settled in the trees. In the backstretch he could see massive improvised Trans-America banners: "Hugh, Hugh, we're with you!" and "Go Morgan, go Lord, go!" they said. In the packed stand to his right the Trans-Americans had somehow devised a yellow Scottish flag, featuring the red lion rampant, and he could hear the wail of pipes, abominably played. He became aware of the whirr and click of cameras.

Again the crowd roared, drowning the announcer's next statement. The cause was Levy, who had just entered, sitting on a light sulky behind a superb black stallion. Silver Star's glossy coat radiated the precise, controlled fitness of a champion trotter. His movements were light, supple and rhythmic, and Hugh immediately recognized in the horse another sprinter, as he was. Or had been. For two thousand miles of running had taken more out of his legs than Doc's probing fingers could ever replace. His throat was dry and again he felt the overwhelming desire to yawn. He wished himself ten thousand miles away.

Silver Star pranced fluidly around the six-hundred-yard circuit, dimpling the track with his tiny hooves. The town loved this horse: Silver Star was St. Louis, and they showed it in their applause. Hugh strode at half speed in his spikes up the track, feeling smooth but ponderous. It was just as he had feared; the speed, the snap, the cadence, had vanished. His legs felt hollow. "Think fast"—those had been Stevie's last words. He attempted a faster stride. It felt better, but worlds away from the real, blazing power which had once been his.

The roar of the crowd swelled as Silver Star slipped into full speed, pulsing down the back stretch. Hugh looked left across the track. The animal could certainly shift, and he could see no way in which he could conceivably stay with him—short of holding onto the back of the sulky.

One fifty-eight P.M. Colonel Carlsen blew his whistle for the first time. "Please prepare yourselves, gentlemen," he said. Within seconds the crowd had stilled, the last sounds being the cries of peanut vendors echoing across the arena. Hugh felt his legs tremble as he walked toward the start. He handed his dressing gown to Doc, then looked up the track at the single roped lane. *Focus in.* Silver Star trotted in on his left, snorting lightly, supple shanks quivering.

"Get on your marks!" shouted Carlsen.

Hugh's world had slowed down now, the crowd reduced to a soft blur. He again felt a thin trickle of sweat on his right temple. His breath seemed to come from far off. He blinked. Yards away, down his lane, he could see the sharp white of Dixie's handkerchief. Suddenly he was back in childhood, at the mine with Stevie, at winter Powderhall in four feet of space. As then, the space around his lane melted, as his lane became sharp and clear. *Focus in.*

He felt the roughness of the grit of the track on his right knee and through the tips of his fingers. Why in God's name was the starter so slow?

"Get set . . ."

Hugh came up late, to lessen the pressure on his arms and shoulders. When the gun cracked he drove off with range and power, eating up the track with long surging strides. Levy was slow to react and Hugh was five yards down the track before his opponent had even put the whip to Silver Star and another two yards down before the horse reacted. Somehow, miraculously, Hugh's body had remembered the thousand sprint drills of the past. He burned through the space toward the white handkerchief, oblivious to the throbbing hooves behind him.

The trotter rushed up the track, his supple legs flowing underneath him. But the late reaction of his rider, coupled with the problem of moving from rest two hundred pounds of rider and sulky, had in all lost Silver Star nearly twelve yards over the first fifty. The horse was closing fast, but not quickly enough. Hugh snapped the tape a good three yards ahead.

At the end of the stretch he slowed down to a trot, his gaze fixed on the beaming Dixie, bobbing delightedly beside a radiant Juan Martinez. Above him the Trans-America banners were swirling crazily as the runners danced up and down with delight. Children were restrained from running onto the track to greet McPhail by burly, smiling policemen. For a moment there was chaos, as the announcer repeatedly tried to declare the result. He gave up, as wave upon wave of cheering and applause drowned his attempts. The St. Louis crowd roared and kept on roaring. Although most of their money was on Silver Star somehow irrationally and against their own interests they wanted this Scot to win.

Levy glumly drew Silver Star to a halt, shaking his head, but was soon in close discussion with his trainers who had watched the race from the infield. He listened to them intently, nodded, then started to smile. Hugh walked back through the applause, down the home stretch toward Doc, who put his dressing gown back around his shoulders. "Great," he said. "But keep warm, inside and outside. We ain't home yet, not by a long way."

A few moments later Hugh lay on his stomach on the massage table, as Doc lightly stroked his calves. He felt a great stillness, and could hardly believe that only a few minutes before he had exploded down the track before forty thousand spectators. He wiped his forehead with his right hand, put his fingers to his lips and savored the salt taste of his own sweat.

He heard a click as the dressing-room door opened behind him. It was Flanagan. Doc shook his head and put a finger to his lips. Flanagan nodded and closed the door gently, leaving Doc and Hugh alone together. Doc tapped Hugh on the back of his neck and the sprinter turned to sit, supported on the heels of both hands. Doc then gently drew a white hand towel across Hugh's forehead, as if he were drying a baby.

"You did good out there," he said, then looked at his watch, which showed two-twenty. "Ten minutes to go. Plenty of time. Just do the same again and our money's in the bank."

Ten minutes later, at exactly 2:30 P.M. the crowd was again hushed. The second race was about to begin. Now only the cries of children and wheeling birds broke the silence. Colonel Carlsen loaded his Winchester with two blanks. Hugh could hear the greased cartridges click into the gun's barrels.

"Please prepare yourselves, gentlemen."

Silver Star was already at his mark by the time Hugh reached the starting line. This time there was no need for Hugh to focus in, for his lane was etched sharp and clear. He was ready. But now so was Levy, his whip poised only a foot or so from Silver Star's flickering withers.

"Get set . . ."

The gun cracked and this time Levy smacked Silver Star's rump at once, bringing the trotter into immediate movement. The horse still had yards to pick up at fifty yards, but he pulled Hugh in as if with a lasso, his prancing legs snapping underneath him like whips. The horse clawed back yard after yard in the last fifty as Hugh drove in desperately on the tape.

Hugh could feel Silver Star at his shoulder at ninety yards, knew instinctively that the horse was surging past him. Still, he did what he had always been trained to do—to drive remorselessly in on that tiny white handkerchief. But even as he dipped for the tape he could see out of the corner of his eyes that he was beaten, that the prancing trotter had taken him by at least a yard.

This time the Trans-America banners in the back stretch were limp, but the roars from the crowd were the same, though they were now for Levy. The smartass had come back punching, and the St. Louis crowd recognized it in their applause for him. Levy's trainers rushed to his side and he leaned over grinning, the sweat streaming from his plump face, nodding as they pumped his hands. Hugh dared not look at Dixie, as she stood at the end of the stretch, head down, Juan Martinez's arm around her shoulder. He walked slowly back down the track toward Doc, who stood at the mouth of the tunnel holding Hugh's dressing gown in front of him. Doc's face was grim, but he summoned a smile.

"One to go," he said. "Still got a chance." He put his hand around Hugh's shoulders as the announcer boomed out the result over the babble of the crowd, and they walked together into the gloom of the tunnel.

"Result of second trial. First, Silver Star." The announcement was drowned in cheers. "Time, ten point five seconds. Second, McPhail, ten point six seconds. The final trial will take place in twenty-five minutes, at three o'clock."

Back in the darkness of the dressing room Hugh sat upon the massage table, weight on his hands, while Doc lightly rubbed his calves.

"How do you see it?" asked Doc, the anxiety showing in his voice. The Scotsman sat up, resting on his elbows, and shook his head as Flanagan entered the room. "Levy's got the start taped," sobbed Hugh. "I can't find another yard, Doc. I don't have an inch left in me. I can't go any faster."

"But the bloody horse can get slower," came another Scots voice—from the door. It was Stevie, coming in behind Flanagan.

"Rules say that you've both got to be still on the mark, don't they?"

Hugh nodded, and Doc stopped his massage.

"So just look at the bloody horse at the start—he's moving all the time, particularly his head. I've been checking on trotters. They move their heads from left to right—that's their natural action. So we've got to protest to Carlsen—get Silver Star's head held at the start, with his head to the right. That means that he will have to move his head left–right before it gets going. That'll take time—it might even be worth that extra yard to you."

Flanagan withdrew a pad from his pocket and scribbled down some notes. He looked up.

"I can't see that Carlsen can object to Silver Star being still at the start," he said. "But a yard only puts us level at best. We need more. Anything else?"

Stevie reached into his pocket, drew out two pieces of cotton, and gave them to Hugh.

"We always used to talk about running in silence, in four feet of space, didn't we?"

Hugh nodded.

"Well, one thing you don't want to hear is that bloody horse thudding up behind you," he said. "You've got to make this last run a *pure* run, with nothing distracting you. So stuff these in your ears and you can run in a world of your own. You'll hear the start, 'cause Carlsen's right next to you with his ruddy Winchester. After that it's just you and a hundred yards to be gobbled up."

Doc looked at Flanagan, who nodded, then gulped, feeling tears come to his eyes. He lightly jabbed Hugh on the left shoulder.

"Do what you do best," he said gruffly, pulling Stevie with him toward the dressing-room door.

"Finished," said Doc a moment later, and tapped Hugh on the thigh.

Hugh stood up and together the two men walked through the tunnel. At the mouth of the tunnel leading out to the track stood Thurleigh and Morgan. Neither spoke, but both put a hand on Hugh's shoulder as if trying to transfer some of their own strength and energy to him. Hugh barely acknowledged them as he walked past out into the sharp sunlight of the arena.

This time the crowd was immediately silent when they glimpsed Hugh's lean, slight figure at the entrance to the stadium. Even when Levy and Silver Star reappeared there was no applause—simply silence. Only the sharp flapping of the flags around the stadium could be heard as Colonel Alan Carlsen summoned the contestants to their marks for the last time.

"Gentlemen, prepare yourselves." Carlsen's voice broke slightly on the final word, his feelings reflected in the vast, still crowd that now hung on his next words of command. Hugh stuffed Stevie's plugs of cotton into his ears and trotted to the start, followed by Levy and Silver Star.

Carlsen had readily agreed to Silver Star's bridle being held, and Levy, certain of victory, had made no attempt to protest.

Forty thousand people focused hearts and minds on the hundred yards through which Hugh and Silver Star would travel. Flanagan hardly dared look, and in the crowd Martinez and Dixie covered their eyes.

"On your marks . . ."

Hugh could hear Carlsen's command clearly, and knew that the thunder of Carlsen's Winchester would set him off, even if muffled by the earplugs. He settled himself in as Silver Star's handler gripped the trotter's bridle, holding the horse's head to the right.

"Get set . . ."

Then it all happened with a rush. The gun released Hugh from his prison and he drove up the soft dirt track like a man possessed. Behind him Silver Star jerked his head to release himself from the pressure on his mouth, swept it to the right and moved late to Levy's sharp and urgent whip.

Hugh, in an eight-yard lead by forty yards, was solidly in the present, yet in the past, back in a perfect muscular memory of even-time sprinting. He rippled—flowed—legs sweeping under him in a blur. He could hear nothing, see nothing, but the white reality of the handkerchief out ahead of him. He was again a machine, a sprint-machine. Though he automatically threw his chest in on the tape as he had been taught he knew that he had won.

He pulled the cotton from his ears. But the roar of the crowd almost deafened him and, smiling, he put his hands to the sides of his head. Then children in the crowd broke the barrier created by the police and engulfed him, thrusting programs and grubby scraps of paper up to him. He bent down to them, grinning, and had completed a dozen autographs by the time the St. Louis police had regained control. He looked into the crowd for Dixie, who was weeping unashamedly on Juan Martinez's shoulder. The Mexican raised his eyebrows and shrugged as Hugh caught his eye.

Above the din the Trans-Americans in the crowd took up the chant "McPhail, McPhail," soon picked up by their colleagues dancing excitedly on the cross-country course above the stadium. The commentator attempted to announce the result, but again it was impossible, for the crowd would not permit him. A man had outrun a horse, and they knew that the three ten-second snatches of conflict they had seen would remain with them for the rest of their lives. So the St. Louis crowd cheered until they were hoarse and when they were too hoarse to cheer they started to applaud. Then, at the end of the home stretch, a piper appeared, dressed in immaculate Black Watch plaid, and with Hugh jogging beside him they performed a lap of honor to the applause of the crowd.

"Third and final trial," said the announcer, at last audible above the rantings of the crowd. "First, Hugh McPhail, ten point five seconds."

Hugh finally reached the entrance of the tunnel where Doc, Dixie, Stevie and Flanagan awaited him.

"Give us a kiss," said Doc, hugging him.

"Nae fear," said Hugh, grinning. "Not until you've shaved, anyway."

He looked at Dixie, standing in front of him, still weeping.

"Woman," said Hugh, "I'm glad I won. God knows what you would ha' done if I'd lost."

Dixie smiled through her tears.

"And Stevie?"

"Yes?" responded the little Scot.

"Remember you told me before the race about Wallace of Perth running against a horse all those years back. Did he win?"

"Of course not," said Stevie, unbowed.

Half an hour later the Coolidge Stadium was again hushed in expectation. Out in the country another forty thousand spectators had gathered, pressing in on the pegged out, bumpy, roped circuit, which, when added to the four-forty-yard track, made the course one mile, to be covered ten times.

Down in the dressing room beneath the single light bulb the Trans-Americans had regained their composure.

"Remember," said Doc, flicking Thurleigh's thighs from side to side with practiced hands, "don't get panicked when the horse picks up an early lead. It's bound to happen. Think of Nurmi. Keep to your pace."

A hundred yards away, in a dressing room at the opposite end of the stadium, Leonard Levy still smarted from his defeat in the sprint. He lay on his stomach as his masseur desperately tried to make contact with muscle under the layers of fat which covered the flabby back.

"Sulky checked?" he said, looking up at his trainer, Rafferty, standing above him.

"Yes, Mr. Levy," replied Rafferty obediently. "In perfect condition. Ready to start anytime you say."

"And Silver Star?"

"No problems, sir. That sprint has warmed him up nicely for the big race."

"The big race," repeated Levy. "Yes, I reckon this is the big one. That sprint—no real test of a trotter."

"Just so, sir," replied Rafferty obediently. "In a sprint you blink an eyelid and it's all over. No, Mr. Levy, this is the real race. We'll get our money back on this one. You can bank on it, sir."

The masseur tapped Levy on the back and Levy turned around and lay, head cupped in hands, then checked his wristwatch. Fifteen minutes to go.

At 3:30 P.M. the contenders had assembled at the start. On the infield stood Doc, Flanagan, Willard, Dr. Falconer, Kate and the two runners, Thurleigh and Morgan. On the track Levy sat on Silver Star, adjusting the reins as his trainers and grooms put the finishing touches to the stallion and the sulky. Levy looked across at Flanagan. "The best of luck to you, Mr. Flanagan," he said, smiling.

"Yes," replied Flanagan. "May the best man win."

The smile left Levy's face. He would put so much space between Flanagan's men and himself in the first few miles that they would simply concede defeat.

"Prepare yourselves, gentlemen." Carlsen was quietly pleased at the way things had gone. He had come out well so far and he was going to see that the cross-country race was conducted in a similar sporting fashion. A fair field and no favor.

Peter Thurleigh took off his dressing gown to reveal his now-familiar, if faded, Oxford silk shirt and shorts. He had never run before in a continuous relay of this type and had no idea how his body would respond to five separate miles over country, each broken by a five-minute rest. He was, however, a horseman, and could see little likelihood of himself and Morgan dealing with a stallion of Silver Star's caliber. He glanced to his left at Silver Star and Levy, poised, whip in hand.

"Get set . . ."

The gun cracked and Silver Star snapped off around the track, prancing with neat powerful action and leaving Thurleigh plodding behind. The crowd roared: this is what they had come to see. By the time Silver Star had passed the stadium exit at the beginning of the back stretch Levy was already over a furlong in the lead.

But the cross-country course was bumpy and uneven and Silver Star slowed as even the supple sulky creaked and skidded on the rugged ground. By contrast Thurleigh moved smoothly and easily over the course, passing the three-quarter-mile mark in three minutes forty seconds. Even so, Silver Star reentered the stadium almost a quarter of a mile in front. Thurleigh had covered the first mile in four minutes fifty seconds; Silver Star in four minutes ten seconds.

"Great," said Doc, as Morgan set off to start the second mile. "What's his pulse?"

"One hundred and thirty-five beats a minute," said Falconer. "Should be down well inside one hundred by the time Morgan comes in. That means he'll be well recovered."

Morgan knew no other way than to push himself hard, and came in at four minutes forty-eight seconds. Silver Star was one minute ten seconds ahead by now, already well into the country by the time Morgan had finished.

"Same again, Peter," said Doc, tapping Thurleigh on the thigh as Morgan raced in. Thurleigh ran a fast four minutes forty-five seconds for the third mile, with Silver Star now one minute thirty-five seconds ahead.

"It's no race," said Flanagan, raking his hands through his hair.

"You think so?" said Doc. "Take a look at the horse." He pointed to the end of the track. Silver Star was still running well, but was lathered with sweat and beginning to foam at the mouth. "That horse is tiring. Look at the watch. We lost forty seconds in the first lap, thirty seconds in the second, and only twenty-five in the third. Man, we're catching up!"

"But is there time?" said Flanagan.

Doc looked at the panting Thurleigh, who shook his head.

"Step it up, Peter," he said, then turned to Falconer. "What was his pulse this time?"

"One hundred and fifty at the finish," said Falconer. "Now, with a minute to go, one hundred and fifteen. It's staying high, but he's still in pretty good shape."

Doc looked at his watch again and then across at Flanagan.

"Flanagan," he said, "we can still do it. Silver Star is tiring, and a tired horse makes mistakes. And every time Silver Star breaks into a gallop we pick up half a minute."

Flanagan shook his head. "I hope you're right," he said.

Morgan cut another five seconds from Silver Star's lead on the fourth mile, running four minutes forty-three seconds, but it was clear that even the Iron Man was in trouble. Falconer checked his pulse at one hundred and eighty on arrival: close to maximum. The sweat gushed from Morgan's body as he sat, gasping, at the finish.

Silver Star's first foul, signaled by a bugle blast, came as Thurleigh left the stadium for the fifth mile, and a minute later there was a second bugle. Carlsen strode over to Flanagan's retinue.

"Two fouls by Silver Star," he reported. "That means Silver Star has been stopped for a minute."

Doc whistled. "That keeps us right in the ball park," he said. "How does that place us?"

This time Dixie answered. "We were two minutes behind at the fourth mile. We should have come in a total of two and a half minutes down at the end of the fifth. Take off a minute and that leaves us about a minute and a half to find in five miles."

"And the horse is getting more tired by the minute," said Doc.

"Just as I thought it would. That animal is bushed."

Doc was right. Out in the country Levy was having difficulty even in keeping Silver Star moving. His horse was essentially a sprinter, and sustained running over hilly, bumpy ground, dragging twice its normal load, was foreign to it. Soon Silver Star had dropped to a slow canter, occasionally breaking, under Levy's whip, into a desperate, slow-motion version of his superb trotting action. During the fifth mile Peter Thurleigh seemed to be pulling him in on a long rope, eating up the three-quarters of a mile or so that lay between them. When Carlsen's bugle for a further foul sounded halfway through the sixth mile, Silver Star was just over a minute ahead.

In the sixth mile Morgan ran like a machine, every stride eroding the gap between him and the now faltering trotter, and the runner's breath seared through stretched lungs. The crowd sensed what was happening and were torn between concern for their beloved horse and admiration for the bravery of the men who had dared challenge it.

Then came tragedy. As Morgan bounded down the hill toward the race track at the end of the sixth mile a boulder slipped from under his foot. He struggled to regain balance, but his momentum was too great and he fell, hitting the rough ground with a dull thud. For a moment he lay still. When he rose he looked around like a prizefighter after a knockdown, blood gushing down the left side of his face from a gash high in his scalp, just above his ear. Morgan looked down the hill, saw Silver Star entering the stadium, and started on his way again, his bleeding legs buckling on each stride.

"Jesus wept," said Doc, handing his binoculars to Falconer, who took one look and handed them back.

"Get my bag," snapped Falconer to Willard Clay.

Doc looked at Peter Thurleigh as Morgan staggered down into the arena. "You said you wanted to prove yourself," he said. "Nothing in the rules says you can't run twice." He walked over to Colonel Carlsen, who listened for a few moments, then nodded agreement. "I want two five-minute laps out of you, college boy," he said. "Meantime Doc here can patch up Mike. So you got your orders. Now get ready to run your nuts off."

Thurleigh said nothing, but nodded, gulping.

Silver Star had passed the Trans-Americans at the exchange

point and was into his seventh mile, slowing slightly as Levy, checking on Morgan's position, saw that for some reason the Pennsylvanian had dropped back. Now was the time to regain control, decided Levy, to get Silver Star back into his immaculate trotting rhythm, show a bit of class. The Trans-Americans were beaten. He would finish the race in style, show the crowd Silver Star at his best.

Morgan had now entered the stadium dripping blood, the groans and sighs of the crowd running ahead of him as they realized his condition. For a moment he almost ran in the wrong direction, into Silver Star's path, then checked himself and set off around the track toward Thurleigh. He had somehow regained his rhythm, but he was down to a trot, holding his left hand to his forehead in an attempt to staunch the flow of blood.

As he reached the final stretch and saw Doc and the others, and Peter Thurleigh crouched waiting for the touch that would set him off, he dropped his hand from his brow and broke into a desperate sprint, blood spattering onto his shirt and shorts. To Thurleigh, coiled at the end of the stretch, it seemed as if Morgan was running in a dream, in some private world of his own. Finally, Morgan reached Thurleigh and for a moment they touched hands, setting Thurleigh off. Immediately Morgan collapsed into Doc's arms, both eyes closed, limp.

Another bugle from the hillside indicated that Thurleigh had gained a further thirty seconds, so at the beginning of his seventh mile the Trans-Americans were only just over a minute down. However, they were bound to drop back, as Thurleigh had to cover two laps on his own without the normal lap rest.

As he left the stadium Thurleigh could see Levy's sulky only a quarter of a mile away at the base of the hill, about sixty seconds from him. At best he could only hope to keep the gap from widening. His mind returned yet again to Paris 1924. That was how he must run, steadily, evenly, preserving exactly the balance between input and output.

He completed the first lap in just under five minutes, running straight past the Trans-Americans, his breath coming from him in deep gasps.

"*Go*, Peter!" screamed Doc, dancing on the grass as he receded from them, on his way up the hill into the country section.

Falconer looked up from stitching Morgan's head and pointed

to Thurleigh, now attacking the hill. "His pulse must be over one hundred and eighty now, just about maximum," he said. "He'll be lucky if he comes back in one piece."

Morgan looked up at Falconer expectantly, as the doctor fumbled in his bag for a cleansing swab.

"Give me time, man," Falconer snapped, cleaning around the spiky stitches. "I've just put eight stitches into you."

"Have you patched him up?" asked Flanagan, missing the comment and impatiently standing over them.

"Yes," said Falconer, testily. "But in my professional opinion he shouldn't run. His pulse is still one hundred and fifty beats a minute and he must have lost nearly half a pint of blood. What kind of a man are you, anyway? These men have run two thousand miles, and now just because of a boozy bet you've got them killing themselves against a horse. Throw in the towel, Flanagan. These men have had enough."

Doc ignored him and grabbed Morgan's face in both hands, putting his face within a few inches of the Pennsylvanian's. "Do you think you can make it, Mike?" he asked. "If you say no, then we give up now."

For a moment Morgan said nothing. Then he nodded and got to his feet, the sweat dropping from his face onto the grass, his eyes on Kate Sheridan, who stood directly behind Doc, her eyes glistening.

Doc turned to Falconer.

"Falconer, you told me long ago that for you the Trans-America was like going back to school. Well, let me tell you, sir, today's graduation day. I'm telling you that out there in the country the lord of the manor is pulling in that horse with every yard he runs. And I'm telling you that five minutes from now this patchwork quilt called Mike Morgan will get up and take another chunk out of that animal's lead."

Falconer said nothing but closed his bag, shaking his head.

"I can see Silver Star," screamed Kate. The trotter had appeared on the brow of the hill above Coolidge Stadium, trotting slowly, but with increased control, his body flecked with foam and gleaming with sweat.

"Check the second hand on your watch, Kate," said Doc. The seconds flickered painfully away as they waited for Peter Thurleigh to appear.

Exactly fifty seconds later Thurleigh appeared on the crest of the hill. He had narrowed the gap, but at terrible cost. His breath came from him in deep groans and his body was drenched in sweat. His legs wobbled as he ran down the hill into the stadium and along the stretch, but at last he ran over to Morgan, to hit the ground beside Doc with a thump, his breath coming from him in deep, harsh wheezes.

Falconer checked his watch as he held Thurleigh's wrist. "Two hundred and ten beats a minute," he said. "The highest I've ever taken." He turned again to Doc. "Thurleigh's done," he whispered. "His body's full of waste—you could sell it by the barrel. He could lie here for another hour for all that it matters. He'll never make that last lap for you. He's finished."

"Finished?" shouted Doc. "Finished? Maurice, he's just *started*." He pulled Peter Thurleigh to an upright position. The runner's face streamed with sweat and his eyes were glassy and unfocused. Doc smacked him lightly on the cheeks.

"You said you wanted to join my team," he said. "Well, sir, here's your chance to pay your dues." He pointed up the hill. "Mike Morgan's out there, running his heart out for you after a tiring horse. And I'm telling you, we can *take* it. Peter, I can feel it in my water. I can *taste* it."

Thurleigh nodded and got to his feet but immediately fell to the ground. He got up again, nodded, still gasping, and leaned forward, his hands on his knees, as the crowd let out a roar. Silver Star had appeared in the stadium, his ninth mile almost completed.

When Morgan came into the stadium what seemed an eternity later the gap was only forty seconds. One mile to go.

"We'll never make it," groaned Flanagan. "Even Nurmi couldn't make forty seconds a mile on a horse!"

But Thurleigh went off hard into the final lap, gasping even in his first quarter-mile around the roaring stadium. As he left the stadium he looked up the hill at Silver Star. The horse appeared to have stopped. What had happened was that the bumpy track had loosened the nuts on the right wheel of the sulky and it would no longer rotate. Levy looked down the hill at the toiling Thurleigh and cursed. He jumped clumsily from the sulky and fumbled for the wrench in the repair bag on the back of the cart. Thurleigh plodded leadenly toward him, now only a hundred yards away and slowly gaining. Levy was still struggling with the wheel nut

as the Englishman staggered past. By the time Levy had tightened
the wheel nut Thurleigh was over one hundred and fifty yards
in front, with just over half a mile to go.

Ahead for the first time, with no clear idea of why Levy had
stopped, Peter Thurleigh was in agony. Somehow he managed
to maintain his running form, consciously keeping head and
shoulders still, but his breath came in deep, rasping gulps. He
wobbled down the hill to the stadium through a tunnel of noise,
his mind just sufficiently alert to prompt him to watch for rocks.
At the bottom of the hill, with almost a lap of the trotting track
to go, he again ventured a look above him. Silver Star was at the
crest of the hill, and gaining. Levy had brought back his fading
stallion to something approaching its trotting rhythm, although
the horse was now down to a sluggish twelve miles an hour. Levy
in turn could see Thurleigh staggering down the rocky path ahead,
but knew that he could not risk a foul or chance damaging a wheel
by forcing Silver Star down the hill after him. No, he would have
to pick Thurleigh up on the final circuit, on the track—where
Silver Star would be back in his element.

As he entered the stadium Thurleigh had three-quarters of a
lap to cover, counterclockwise, to reach the finish. His legs had
gone, his breathing was broken, and he knew that Silver Star was
closing in fast. He had completed a hundred yards on the soft
surface of the track when he heard the shouts and cheers behind
him. Silver Star had entered the stadium. On the smooth surface
of the track the horse's hooves thudded once more in perfect
balance. Thurleigh again looked back: Levy and Silver Star were
gaining fast.

Two hundred yards to go. For one final time Thurleigh dug
deep inside himself and launched his stricken body into a grotesque
parody of a sprint. Knees bowed and wilting, arms thrashing, he
entered the home stretch. The air was now poison to him, but
he was far beyond pain. He charged up the track, oblivious of
the hooves behind him. The tape seemed to be receding, but still
he kept running, his legs bowing on each stride.

He hit the finishing tape with his teeth, cutting his lips, and
fell full length on the ground, the dry dirt spuming in front of
him, Silver Star only a yard behind. He lay on the track, on his
face, spitting blood and grit, until Doc pulled him to his feet,
limp, like a rag doll.

"Congratulations, Peter," he said. "I reckon you've paid your dues."

All in all, the city of St. Louis was well pleased with Leonard H. Levy. He had provided the citizenry with right royal entertainments: two circuses, and two man-versus-horse races about which St. Louis men would spin yarns for many a year. Levy had lost $120,000 in bets, it was true, but every man in St. Louis knew that he had cleared $200,000 from spectator fees, concessions and the sale of programs. He might have lost the races, but he stood high in the respect of the citizens of St. Louis: first, because of the entertainment he had provided; second, because he had proved himself a real smart fellow.

The clink of champagne glasses therefore sounded throughout "Hambletonian," Levy's sumptuous house on King's Highway, the Nob Hill of St. Louis, as Levy entertained the Trans-Americans and over two hundred other guests. Hugh, Peter and Morgan, Dixie and Kate, splashed at each other in Levy's kidney-shaped swimming pool, while the gentlemen of the press refilled their glasses and swapped "exclusive" interviews.

Levy looked on indulgently from the side of the pool, the sweat from his day's driving still trickling down his face.

"Jesus," he said. "Your boys sure did put up a show out there at Coolidge Stadium today."

"They assuredly did, sir," said Colonel Carlsen, at Levy's right hand together with a beaming Flanagan. "I sincerely hope that you gentlemen feel that the proceedings were carried off with fairness and lack of prejudice?"

"Let me fill your glass, sir," said Levy. "Indeed, Colonel, I do. Although I feel that if I had not sustained a mechanical breakdown I might well have won." He paused for a moment, then looked up at Flanagan inquiringly.

"Tell me one thing," said Levy, "and I promise that it will go no farther. How in God's name did you win the sprint? I thought I had it all sewn up after the second race."

"Pigeons, cotton, and a little *savoir faire*," said Flanagan.

"Pigeons?" said Levy, gulping down his champagne.

Flanagan related Doc's story about the race between the grey-hound and the pigeon and how Dixie had held the handkerchief upon which Hugh McPhail had focused.

"And there's our pigeon," he said, as Dixie stood, trim and golden in her blue bathing suit, poised to dive into the pool.

"Some pigeon," said Levy.

"Some greyhound we had to run against," said Flanagan, raising his glass.

"And the cotton?"

Flanagan explained how Hugh had been told to shut out the noise of Silver Star's hooves.

"Hell," said Levy. "You boys had it all worked out. But you mentioned something about *savoir faire*."

Flanagan grinned.

"That, sir, may have been the difference between fifty thousand dollars and a kick in the ass. We figured that since a trotter's head moves from left to right, if we could get Silver Star's head held on the right that would lose you a yard at the start."

Levy laughed and kept on laughing until he started to cough.

"Did I say something funny?" said Flanagan.

"You surely did, sir," said Colonel Carlsen, smiling. "Silver Star is well known in the world of trotting as the only trotter who moves his head from right to left. Any advantage you gained was simply because the horse's mouth was held, not for any other reason. No, sir, you simply had the better man."

Hugh and the others at the pool looked up as they heard Levy's guffaws.

"For a loser, Levy's sure enjoying himself," said McPhail.

"Yes," said Doc, following his eyes. "I reckon all of this is worth about a hundred grand. Levy's no loser. Guys like him never are."

"Isn't there something wrong when we have people like we've seen on the road, people with nothing—" said Hugh.

"People like us," interrupted Kate.

"—and wealth like this?" ended Hugh.

"Nothing wrong with it, if you can get it," said Doc.

"That all depends how many faces you have to smash in on the way," said Morgan.

"Oh, I don't reckon that our Mr. Levy qualifies as a face-smasher," said Doc, slipping into the pool. He nodded across at Flanagan, Levy and Carlsen. "Looks like he's cooking up some deal over there with Flanagan. Wonder what it is this time . . ."

* * *

At that moment Levy was pointing a stubby finger at Flanagan. "I rate you, sir, as a sportsman of the first rank," he began.

"Wait for it," said Flanagan, winking at Colonel Carlsen. "The last time he said that back in Topeka I nearly lost my pants."

"Seriously, Mr. Flanagan—may I call you 'Charles'?" continued Levy. "Last night I received a call from a friend of mine in Bloomington, a General Aloysius Honeycombe."

"Honeycombe?" said Carlsen. "Never heard of him. In the army?"

"An honorary title, I believe, Colonel," said Levy. "He runs a traveling circus, and he'll be in Springfield, Illinois, in five days or so. When will your runners reach Springfield?"

Flanagan looked over at Willard. "Springfield?" he said.

"Down for May 14, boss," said Willard.

"Ideal," said Levy. "My friend, General Honeycombe, has a proposition for you. He's got a big circus and fairground just outside Springfield for a week. He'll offer you five hundred dollars a day for your circus, plus a slice of the profits."

"Keep talking," said Flanagan.

"What he really wants is some of your boys and Miss Sheridan to run a few exhibition handicap races," continued Levy. "You know, with some of the local boys. He'll give you five hundred for that as well."

"Done," said Flanagan.

"And Doc Cole," said Levy. "He must have Doc Cole."

"What for?"

"Not for running. But you know as well as I do that Doc's a national figure now—look over at the pool: all the matrons of St. Louis are after him. Well, my friend General Honeycombe wants Doc to put on a public appearance, giving some sort of lecture."

"How much?" said Flanagan.

"Five hundred dollars," said Levy.

"A thousand."

"Seven fifty."

"Done," said Flanagan.

Levy smiled. "The way I see it, no hard feelings on my part. We both came out well today. We can do the same up in Springfield." He paused. "One final matter," he said. "General Honeycombe would like one of your boys to take on a little fisticuffs."

"Boxing?" said Flanagan, frowning. "My boys are runners, not prizefighters."

"Well, the owner of the boxing booth at his carnival offers five hundred dollars if one of your boys can take his pug in four rounds."

"Impossible," said Flanagan, looking idly across the pool. "I told you, Mr. Levy, my boys are runners."

"Look, I owe Honeycombe some favors from way back," said Levy. "And after today, I can afford to be generous. How does five grand at five to one sound to you?"

"It would take us to Newark," said Flanagan quietly, still looking across the pool. "But I told you, Leonard, my boys aren't fighters, so how can I get some guy who's never boxed to go in against a trained fighter, and that after he's run over two thousand miles?"

"Eight to one," said Levy, pouting.

"I'm a fool to myself," said Flanagan, his gaze now fixing firmly on Morgan. "But you just make it ten to one and I think we might have ourselves another little deal."

Levy nodded. "Agreed," he said. "I'll be in Springfield at the end of the week to arrange the final details."

He turned to Colonel Carlsen. "Have you had any experience in boxing, Colonel?"

"Army light heavy champion 1907," said Carlsen, pushing back his shoulders.

"Then might I ask you to make the trip to Springfield to referee, to ensure that fair play is done? All expenses paid, of course."

"It will be an honor, sir," said Carlsen, before adding to Flanagan, "I'm afraid that you may have bitten off a little more than you can chew this time, sir."

"It certainly does appear that way, Colonel," said Flanagan, waving idly at Mike Morgan, who was at that moment being drowned by Kate.

Flanagan had never seen Morgan so mad.

"You're crazy," he said. "Either that or pig stupid." He shook his head and sat down on the downy couch in Flanagan's lush trailer. "First you set us up against a horse and damn near kill us. Now you want me to take on a professional fighter. What next? Pitch against Babe Ruth, tackle Red Grange? Why not? I've got just as good a chance."

"Have a beer, Mike," said Flanagan easily. "Look, you know the trouble I've had keeping this show on the road. It costs me over five grand a day just to stay alive. If you guys hadn't won today the Trans-America wouldn't even have got as far as Spring-field. And don't forget, if we don't make New York then we're all in the cellar."

As he filled Morgan's glass, Kate entered the trailer, concern on her face as she saw Morgan, head down, elbows on his knees.

"What's up? Just what have you asked him to do this time, Flanagan?" she asked suspiciously.

"Nothing much. Just another little deal I've set up," said the Irishman, pouring Kate out some orange juice. "Levy offered me ten to one on one of our boys taking on some stumblebum in a booth in Springfield. I've asked Mike here to deal with it."

"Fighting? Mike's no fighter," she said stoutly.

"He knows, honey," said Morgan quietly.

"I figured Mike for a fighter from the beginning," Flanagan explained. "I've seen hands like his before, and I've seen eyes like his too."

Morgan looked up. "So I fought in booths? I admit that. But Flanagan, last time I fought barefist I killed a guy. For all I know the cops are still looking for me."

"But not in Springfield," said Flanagan, his mind traveling back to his meeting with Bullard. "Look, I give you my solemn word, anything happens, then I put up ten grand for legal expenses. I'll get the very best—this time it'll really be Clarence Darrow. What do you say?"

Morgan looked at Kate.

"What sort of fighter is he going to be up against?" she asked.

Flanagan rubbed his chin. "No way of knowing. Some palooka. Who cares?"

"I do," said Morgan, standing up. "Flanagan, I know the booths—I've fought in them. There're two kinds of fighter there, the guys on the way up and the guys on the skids. The ones on the way up will take on a gorilla for a dime. They don't have much science, but they come out hitting like crazy. The ones on the skids *have* to take you if they're going to earn their oats. They know all the dirty tricks—the thumb in the eye, the dig in the kidneys, the knee in the groin. They sap you with wrestling, stand on your feet, elbow you until your ribs are raw. Then, when you're tiring, they straighten you up with a left and then right hook you into crazyland."

Flanagan had never heard Morgan speak at such length. He was taken aback. "Then it's impossible?"

"I'm not saying that. I'm saying that only one challenger in a hundred from the crowd ever lasts four rounds to pick up his ten bucks. As for *winning* against a booth fighter, I'd have to take in a machine gun."

He sat down and sipped his beer. "First question, who referees?"

"Colonel Carlsen, the man who umpired today. He was army light heavy champion."

"That's the first good news I've heard," said Morgan. He paused. "Second question. Where can I get some gloves and a sparring partner?"

Hugh felt as if he had been hit in the face with a club. Morgan circled around him, crouching, his left constantly breaking through Hugh's guard as if his arms were made of marshmallow. Hugh swung at Morgan with his right, hitting air, and received in return the full force of Morgan's left in the stomach. Gasping, he went down on one knee.

Dixie banged the tin drum that was serving as a gong and rushed to Hugh's side. He struggled to his feet and staggered to his stool, followed by Morgan.

"Had enough?" said Morgan, fingering the wound high on the scalp which he had sustained in the race.

Dixie answered for him. "Three rounds," she said. "That's enough."

Morgan ruffled Hugh's hair. "You did well," he said. "Landed some good ones. Hell, let's have a beer."

Hugh had been the only Trans-American willing to spar with Morgan, as the other runners saw it as a certain exit from the race. He had fought before, not with gloves but bare-fisted, during his time as a miner at Shotts. It had never been clear to him why the fights had begun, but once they had, they were fought with savagery and bitterness.

It was odd. The miners would always insist that a winner should "finish" his man. "He's entitled to the ground," they would say. He was glad that he had never met Morgan on such terms. Even three rounds with gloves with him had left his head ringing.

Saturday, May 9, 1931

St. Louis (1952 miles)

			Hrs.	Mins.	Secs.
1 =	H. McPhail	(Great Britain)	317	12	00
2 =	A. Capaldi	(USA)	317	25	00
3 =	J. Bouin	(France)	317	36	28
4 =	M. Morgan	(USA)	317	44	20
5 =	A. Cole	(USA)	317	56	10
6 =	P. Eskola	(Finland)	317	59	50
7 =	P. Thurleigh	(Great Britain)	318	08	10
8 =	R. Mullins	(Australia)	318	28	12
9 =	J. Martinez	(Mexico)	318	54	10
10 =	L. Son	(Japan)	319	10	47
11 =	P. Brix	(USA)	319	18	49
12 =	P. Komar	(Poland)	319	47	50
13 =	P. Dasriaux	(France)	319	49	10
14 =	J. Schmidt	(Poland)	320	06	21
15 =	P. Coghlan	(New Zealand)	320	08	27
16 =	P. O'Grady	(Ireland)	320	12	42
17 =	C. O'Connor	(Ireland)	321	01	08
18 =	P. Maffei	(Italy)	321	29	12
19 =	K. Lundberg	(Sweden)	322	01	12
20 =	R. Brady	(Ireland)	322	08	10

1st Lady: (392) K. Sheridan (USA)   390   24   06
Number of finishers: 1021
Average speed (leader): 9 mins. 45 secs. per mile

20

THE BIG FIGHT

General Honeycombe had been right, thought Flanagan, as he stood surveying the crowds milling around him on Coogan's Flats, just outside Springfield, Illinois. Hugh, Dixie and Kate stood at his side.

The appearance of the Trans-Americans at Honeycombe's fair had probably doubled the attendance. Flanagan wrinkled his nose and frowned. He should have held out for more back in St. Louis, he knew that now. But it was too late for tears; in less than an hour Morgan would face Professor Anderson's fighter and Flanagan again felt that sick, empty feeling that he had experienced back in St. Louis when Thurleigh had staggered off after Silver Star on the final lap.

He nodded to Hugh. "See you at the booth in half an hour. Don't forget you're acting as second for Mike. We got a lot riding on this."

Flanagan left them to wend his way through the crowds toward the booth.

Kate Sheridan nibbled at her cotton candy, her left arm loosely around Dixie's shoulder. That morning a crowd of over ten thousand people had watched a program of handicap footraces and novelty events featuring the Trans-Americans and local athletes and civic dignitaries. Kate herself had run a six-minute mile, beating a burly local sheriff to the post on the rough track improvised in the field beside the fairground.

Now the thousands attracted by the appearance of the Trans-Americans had transferred their attentions to the fair, and over in a grassy natural bowl outside the main fairground area, picnicking families were already beginning to assemble to hear Doc Cole's Chickamauga spiel later in the evening.

Hundreds of sun-blackened Trans-Americans, easily identifiable in their running shirts and shorts, threaded their way through the vast crowds, signing autographs for eager children as they walked. Others held court to clusters of ethnic groups, French, German, Finnish and Chinese, gesticulating and jabbering in their native tongues. Yet others delivered impromptu talks from the stages of shows as varied as *Ching the Elastic Man* and the *Octopus People of the China Sea*.

Turning, Dixie saw Carl Liebnitz approaching them, accompanied by Pollard, and smiled her recognition. Liebnitz could respond only with a half-smile. His day's intake of root beer, ice cream and popcorn, three rides on the roller coaster and two on the Krazy Train, had been sufficient to convince him that the days, if not the desires, of his youth were over.

"You reckon Doc Falconer's got some seltzer stowed away somewhere?" he asked.

Dixie pointed behind her to the Trans-America trailer a hundred yards away.

"The Doc's back there," she said. "I'm sure he'll have some handy, Mr. Liebnitz."

The journalist touched his hat and gave a weak grin before making his way toward the trailer.

"Looks like Mr. Liebnitz isn't too well," she observed.

"No," said Pollard, interrupting his demolition of a giant raspberry ice-cream cone. He removed from his head a paper hat which bore the request "Hold me, honey" and used it to fan his face. "I reckon Carl's finding that a sixty-year-old stomach won't quite take the sort of garbage he's been pouring into it today."

"I hope he'll manage to make the fight," said Dixie anxiously.

Pollard nodded and bit into the wafer of his cone.

"I hope so too," he said. "Me, I wouldn't miss it for anything."

Hugh was standing a few yards off, still absorbed in the tumult of the fair. He had never seen anything like it. He had experienced the fairgrounds which followed the Scottish Highland Games, but those were tame compared with this vast, blaring whirl. The fat woman of Katmandu; Dr. Faustus; the Syrian fire eater; the two-headed pig; Martha, the world's hairiest lady; Faido, the India Rubber Man: all were on show in a noisy, vulgar, dazzling display Dominating the carnival, at its center, was the boxing booth, a massive, grease-cloth frontage featuring grotesque colored paintings of gloved men embroiled in ludicrous battle. In front of the booth was a railed wooden balcony and there the barker, a stout little man in blue blazer, white flannels and sailing cap, was exhorting his audience to bring forth their champions.

"Four rounds!" he cried into an ancient-looking microphone. "Any man who stays on his feet for four rounds with *any* one of my boys"—he half turned to give the crowd a better view of the line of boxers standing impassively behind him—"will win himself ten dollars. And any man who wins, under *Queen*sberry Rules" —he stressed the word "Queen" as if it had royal connotations— "will take away the prize of one hundred—I repeat one hundred— silver dollars." The man, who proceeded to announce himself as Professor Anderson, held up a cloth purse, shook it, then poured out its contents onto the table beside him.

Anderson's boxers were a rugged bunch, all bearing the flat noses and cauliflower ears which were the marks of their trade. None of them looked fit, being puffy around the waist and short of hard muscle in the thighs. They were men who had long since seen their best days, men journeying toward a blurred and alcoholic middle age. However, though many of the reflexes of youth had gone, thousands of rounds of boxing lived behind those scarred eyebrows, and they were more than a match for the eager young farmhands whom they faced daily.

There was never any lack of takers, for these were hard times. The crowd, already cheering its heroes, had poured all day into the ramshackle tented booth. It was essential that each audience be given its money's worth, and Professor Anderson's men always provided the local boys with a few moments of glory. Occasionally the novices were allowed to make solid contact with the pugs' bodies, although usually only around the arms and chest. These contacts were greeted by Professor Anderson with "My, you good people have a veritable champion here, another Jack Dempsey!" or some other such phrase. It was generally enough.

In the first two rounds the "contenders" were permitted to exhaust themselves, to the baying of the crowd, as the pugs swayed away easily from their wild swings, occasionally answering with an eye-watering poke to the nose. But what the crowd had really come to see was big men being hurt, men who were the terror of Main Street being humiliated by experienced fighters. They came for that moment when a local big-boy would be hit solidly for the first time in his life, to see the look in his eyes when he realized that this time it was he who would be on the end of a beating.

And by the third round all was ready. First some hard thumps to the waist to lower the novice's guard: most men had never felt blows of such force, and they usually dropped their arms to protect their stomachs. This was immediately followed by a stiff, hard left to the chin to measure them, and finally by a clubbing right cross. Many men went down after the first punch; few survived the second. Some less fortunate souls, senses scrambled, blood pouring from mouth and nose, staggered about like stricken bulls, still encouraged by their supporters to hit back. One more clout and it was all over, and a bucket of cold water was sloshed over the now horizontal "Dempsey" of the town, while Anderson asked the crowd for a "big hand for such a worthy challenger," and passed on to the next.

Morgan had seen it all before, and was quietly taking it all in when he was joined by Hugh and Flanagan at the back of the crowd outside the booth. Morgan saw no one in the group of boxers on the platform whom he could not handle, for all of them looked about the same weight as himself. His main worry was about his legs; and deep inside he knew that he was ring-rusty. It had nothing to do with fitness; everything to do with timing, reflexes, sheer aggression. Anderson's men were daily putting leather to opponents, but whatever abilities Morgan had once possessed were furred over by months of distance running. He was going to have to rediscover his skills before he could use them, and by that time it might be too late.

Four rounds would be an eternity with a skillful pug wrestling, elbowing and kneeing, or grinding a bony head into his eyes.

No, it was always a hard time in that small square ring for those who did not daily live and breathe in it, no matter what one's strength and fitness. Occasionally a strong and nimble lad might last four rounds, but Morgan had never seen a challenger come out the victor.

As for his fight, Flanagan had put in a side bet of five thousand dollars at three to one with Levy that Morgan could stay on his feet for four rounds, so Anderson would also be in on another slice of the action if his man could put the Trans-American out early. And there was bound to be more money on the line when he put up his challenge.

At a nudge from Hugh, Morgan put up his hand. "A challenger!" shouted the Professor, and all heads turned toward Morgan. "Come right up, young fella!" Morgan and Hugh made their way through the crowd, up the steps onto the stage. There Anderson shook Morgan's hand before turning him toward the crowd.

"Your name, sir?" he asked, still holding his microphone to his mouth. Morgan duly answered.

"Mike Morgan!" bellowed Anderson. "*The* Mike Morgan of the Trans-America footrace?"

Morgan nodded, as the crowd responded with applause and shouts.

"Well, lad*ies* and gentle*men*," stressed Anderson. "This is one challenger who should stay the course."

He raised his hands above his head. "This, ladies and gentlemen, is indeed an honor. So let's hear it for Mike Morgan, a worthy challenger indeed." He started to applaud, both hands still above his head, and was immediately joined by the crowd now pressing hard against the flimsy wooden stage of the booth.

Morgan knew that Anderson was already sizing him up. The Professor had gripped Morgan's left arm to pull him up onto the stage, and now he tapped him jovially in the stomach to check his abdominal tone. The barker then nodded to one of his assistants, a nod which meant only one thing. They were going to put a heavier man against him, someone to whom Morgan would have to surrender at least twenty pounds. It was not going to be easy.

On cue, Professor Anderson picked out a sweaty Leonard Levy in the front row of the packed crowd. Levy's right arm was raised.

"Yes, sir," shouted Anderson. "What can I do for you?"

Levy pushed his way up onto the wooden steps leading to the stage and whispered into the Professor's ear. Anderson returned to the microphone, raising both hands for silence. "Ladies and gentlemen," he shouted. "We have a further, special challenge!"

He again raised his hands for silence and beckoned Levy, dressed in a white lightweight suit and Panama hat, to the microphone.

"Ladies and gentlemen. May I proudly introduce to you one of the truly great sportsmen of our time, the creator of last week's great race in St. Louis, Mr. Leonard H. Levy."

There was sustained applause, for Levy's St. Louis promotion had made him a considerable figure. Levy pulled the microphone to him and spoke in an unsteady voice.

"Most of you know," he said, "that Mr. Flanagan has already made a small side bet on the result of this match." He paused. "I wish to offer yet another challenge to Mr. Flanagan. I offer him an additional wager of five thousand dollars at the generous odds of six to one that his champion cannot beat one of Professor Anderson's picked men over four rounds. That, ladies and gentlemen, is my challenge."

There was applause, followed by whoops and cheers from the packed crowd in front of the booth.

Anderson swooped down on the microphone, and said, "Would Mr. Flanagan care to step up onto the stage?"

Flanagan, already prepared at the steps leading up to the stage, walked confidently up onto the platform and lowered his head to the microphone.

"I reckon everybody here knows me."

The crowd shouted their agreement.

"So I reckon everybody here knows that above all things I am a sportsman?"

The crowd again voiced their agreement.

"So what do you think, my friends? Should I take on Mr. Levy?" He turned to put his right hand on Levy's shoulder. "Yet again?"

There was no doubting what the crowd thought and they voiced it.

Flanagan smiled his cracked, toothy smile.

"Okay, okay," he said. "You good people have made up my mind for me."

He fished into his inside pocket, pulled out a wad of bills and peeled off a thick stack. He held it up to the crowd.

"Five grand more in the pot," he said, "says Mike Morgan, the Iron Man, can beat any man the Professor here puts up."

Levy responded by withdrawing an even thicker wad of dollars, and the men, with Professor Anderson standing between them, solemnly shook hands, Anderson placing both hands on top of theirs.

"The booth fight of the century," he bellowed into the microphone. "Mike Morgan, versus . . ." he paused for a moment. "Ladies and gentlemen, I think we'll keep you in suspense as to his opponent. Simply let me say that it will be the best man my booth can offer. So roll up, one and all, for the booth fight of the century."

There was almost a riot as crowds surged toward the narrow entrance to the booth on the right of the stage. Anderson's fighters had to be summoned to control them, eventually forming them into a noisy, jostling line which stretched for over a hundred yards. Flanagan followed Morgan and Hugh in, while Levy and Anderson stood in conference on the platform.

"We're gonna have to beat them back with clubs," enthused Anderson. "I reckon I can pack in more than five hundred—six hundred, say, if they stand on each other's feet."

"Great," said Levy. "But what about your man? Have you got him set up right?"

"No problem," said Anderson. "My best, a real pro. Anyhow, he'll spot Morgan more than twenty-five pounds. No way some goddam runner can beat a pro. But I gotta give the paying customer a show, Mr. Levy. So he's got to hold this Morgan guy up for a coupla rounds, make him look good. Then it's lights out in the third. That all right by you?"

Levy nodded. "Just make sure that he puts him out clean. I don't want any points decision."

"No," said Anderson. "Not with your fancy Colonel Carlsen as referee. I just saw him a few minutes ago. Looks as if he's come straight from West Point. There'll be no points decision. I just told my boy he'll be canned if he doesn't take Morgan in three."

Morgan and Hugh had meanwhile entered the silent, empty booth, leaving Anderson and the pressing crowds outside. Anderson, knowing of Morgan's challenge, had gutted the stage of its normal benches to increase its audience capacity, leaving only a rectangle of faded red-velvet chairs around the ring for local dignitaries. Morgan pulled himself up on the slack, greasy ropes which encircled the ring. He walked slowly into the center and looked around him, absorbing every detail.

The stale and bitter smell of sweat and sawdust was unchanged from his days of boxing in Kansas—the same sagging ropes, the same dirty, uneven canvas floor, the same low worn stools, the almost tangible atmosphere of human sweat mixed with the sweetness of wet grass and the sour smell of liniment.

He looked down at his gloves—brown, lumpy and patched—and picked them up as Anderson entered the booth with Colonel Carlsen. Anderson's eyes narrowed when he saw that Morgan had already started to tape his hands.

"You fought before?" he asked, climbing up into the ring.

"A little," said Morgan, putting his left hand into his glove and thudding it hard against the palm of his right.

Alan Carlsen was the next to push his way under the ring-ropes. He took the right glove from Morgan and shook his head. "Disgraceful," he said. "They might as well fight with bare fists. No bout will take place under my jurisdiction using these."

"This ain't no Golden Gloves tournament, Colonel," said Anderson testily.

"Perhaps not," answered Carlsen. "But these gloves are in an appalling condition. So change them, man, change them."

Anderson scowled, too surprised to say anything further, and after a moment's hesitation strode off toward the front of the booth.

Carlsen watched him go, then walked around the ring, checking the ropes. He frowned. After the formality of St. Louis this was not really what he had expected. Perhaps he should have stopped back at Coolidge Stadium, while he was still ahead. The gloves he could change, but there was little he could do about the slack ropes, the dirty, patched, uneven ring or the low beams.

A few moments later Anderson returned, levering his way through the crowds now pouring into the booth, up the narrow gangway leading to the ring. He pushed two pairs of gloves at Carlsen through the ropes. "Do these meet your honor's requirements?" he growled.

Carlsen put his fist into each glove, punched into the palm of his hand, and checked them thoroughly. "They'll do," he said, handing a pair to Morgan. "Only one more thing: timekeeping." He pointed to a neutral corner where a beefy, flat-nosed man in a polo-necked sweater was standing. "Sergeant O'Brien. He'll keep time."

Anderson scowled again. Timekeeping had always been flexible in his booth: long rounds to sap novices, short counts when they hit the canvas.

"If you insist, Colonel."

"I most certainly do," said Carlsen, pulling on the ropes. "And try to get something done about these."

Morgan sat quietly on his stool, gloves dangling between his legs, and looked around the ring. Undersize as usual, to give novices nowhere to hide. That suited him: he had not come to run. He looked above him. Low wooden beams, about six and a half feet up from the ring. Most novices would tend to duck under the beams, misjudging their height, and in that moment of doubt a left hook would put them away. He stood up and walked slowly around the ring, testing it for soft spots, areas where he would be liable to lose balance. Booth boxers knew such spongy areas by heart and would be ready for those moments in which balance was lost and a single punch could put their opponent down.

As usual even the stool was low, to make it uncomfortable, difficult to rest on between rounds. Anderson was indeed a sportsman of Olympic caliber.

But to Morgan it was like coming home. In 1930 he had spent three months in a booth, chinning bumpkins around Kansas and Nebraska in a certain Colonel Marshall's Academy of Boxing. There he had been schooled by Packy Paterson, an aging middleweight who had once hovered on the fringe of championship honors. Old Packy had taught him every trick of the booth boxer's trade—how to pull men into punches, to sap them by elbowing and wrestling, to dig to the kidneys, to thumb the eye. Packy's specialty was a long, looping, around-the-corner left to the head, followed by a short left hook to the chin. Both these punches were, admittedly, often amplified by the introduction of a lump of plaster of Paris inside his left glove, but the recipient was by that time past caring, the audience equally unconcerned.

The tent was now bulging, with more desperate, noisy spectators pressing in from the ticket booth at the entrance, causing those at the front to press forward, protesting, over the fragile rectangle of VIP seats with which Anderson had framed the ring. Air-conditioning was not yet one of Professor Anderson's amenities and the tent was like a sauna. Levy, sitting beside Flanagan in the VIP area, dripped sweat onto his immaculate suit, so that it stuck uncomfortably to his skin. He loosened his silk tie and undid his top shirt button.

"Looks like the Professor's got himself a full house," he said, looking to each side. "Nothing like good clean sport to bring people out." He held back a smile. His bet with Flanagan had nothing to do with money. Leonard H. Levy did not like to be outsmarted, and Flanagan was not going to make his way on to New York with Levy's scalp under his belt. He looked up at the ring. Anderson, who by some sleight of hand had changed into evening dress, had a megaphone to his lips. The din of the crowd diminished.

"It is my pleasure, ladies and gentlemen, to announce tonight's special challenge bout," he boomed. "In the corner to my right, the challenger, the Iron Man of the Trans-America, Mike Morgan, now placing fourth in the race and coming up fast. Entering the ring now, the undisputed champion of the booths of Illinois . . ." Behind him, a hunched, shadowy figure in a hooded dressing gown pushed his way through the crowd.

Flanagan groaned inwardly as Anderson's man ducked under the ropes to mixed cheers and boos. Kate, standing directly under Morgan's corner, looked across at Flanagan anxiously. The man was a burly 180 pounds, a classic booth boxer. Flanagan summoned a weak smile and made an even weaker fist. "Easy," he mouthed silently to Kate. "A piece of cake."

It was like the old days, only Doc had never before faced an audience of such size. A crowd of four thousand stood around him, only the first few rows clear in the pool of light from the stage, while in the background whirled and blared General Honeycombe's carnival. For Doc Cole was now a celebrity, and even if he had said nothing or simply run about on the spot his audience would probably have considered they had got their money's worth.

Doc stood at the microphone, a tiny sun-bronzed figure in the bright lights of the stage, standing in front of a wooden table on which rested a turtle shell and a row of colored glass bottles purchased that morning from the local drug store. At the side of the table stood a human skeleton, borrowed from the proprietor of the fair's "Haunted House." There was a roar of welcome and thunderous applause and the front rows of the audience pressed in on him.

He held up his hands for silence. "Ladies and gentlemen," he said. "I don't come to you tonight as Doc Cole, Trans-American. No, I come to you as the bearer of great and important news. Great news that will transform the life of every man, woman and child in this audience." Doc's voice had dropped an octave, for he was now Doc Cole, huckster extraordinary. It was also slower, as he gave weight to each key word and syllable.

"Let me first tell you a story, a tale from China. During the reign of the Whang Po dynasty the nation's birth rate suddenly dropped like a stone. Rich and poor alike were affected; there was no escape for anyone.

"The emperor offered ten million yen—that's one hundred thousand silver dollars in our money—for a remedy to restore normal vitality to China's population. But all efforts met with failure—until a scientist named He Tuck Chaw made a remarkable discovery."

Doc moved across the stage and picked up the turtle shell from the table, holding it in front of him with both hands.

"He Tuck Chaw," he said, "was exploring a volcanic area in Southern Mongolia when he noticed untold numbers of small, turtlelike animals. At first glance they seemed identical in appearance. Occasionally, however, he found one with beautiful golden stripes. One day it occurred to him: why was it that there were so few turtles with golden stripes? Why?"

Doc paused, put down the turtle shell, unbuttoned the middle button of his 1908 Olympic blazer, and held up seven fingers to the audience.

"He Tuck Chaw studied seven thousand—I repeat, *seven thousand* of these striped turtles. And do you know what they were? Do you have any conception?"

He did not wait for an answer.

"They were all, each and every one of them, males. Male turtles."

He paused again. "But the really important thing was that the ratio of male to female of this type of turtle was one male to twelve hundred females."

Doc paused a third time to allow the ratio to sink in.

"He Tuck Chaw was now certain that he was on the brink of a major discovery. And was not the fate of all China in the balance?

He must determine the source of this incredible vitality possessed by these pitiably few, but undoubtedly potent, male turtles."

He lifted a glass of water to his lips and sipped slowly. The audience was hushed.

"And what did he find, gentlemen? More to the point, what did he find, *ladies*?"

Doc lowered the glass to the table, raised a finger and wagged it at his audience.

"I'll tell you what he found, my good sirs and ladies," he said. "He found that, in contrast with the female, the male turtle possessed a small pouch at the base of its brain. This was known as the 'Quali Quah' pouch."

He held a small leather pouch over his head.

"The Quali Quah pouch," he repeated. "So He Tuck Chaw worked swiftly. He removed the pouches of hundreds of males, dried them and reduced them to powder, then rushed off back to the emperor's court. The emperor, desperate at the fall in population, told He Tuck Chaw that he should be immediately given several patients upon whom to experiment."

Doc put down his glass.

"Do you know, my friends, what sorry, hopeless victims of impotence the emperor presented to He Tuck Chaw? Each man had reached at least seventy years of age. One, the emperor's own cousin, had passed four score and nine. Just think of it! Some of them were too weak to stand, let alone perform their manly functions. These, then, were the poor wretches brought forth to test the goodness of Quali Quah . . ."

His audience roared with laughter.

Doc paused again, wagging his finger, maintaining his composure. "It was no laughing matter, I assure you, when He Tuck Chaw looked upon these—these virtual eunuchs—and contemplated his own fate were he to fail in his task. He knew that the emperor, tired of the charlatans of the past, had set him the supreme test."

He lowered his voice to a whisper and pulled the microphone to him.

"Gentlemen, in the space of four hours those feeble examples of manhood were flexing muscles unused for decades, and were crying aloud 'Pong Wook Ee!' which, as many of you know, is the Chinese equivalent of 'Eureka.'

"Delicacy does not permit me to reveal what happened next. Suffice to say that in a mere nine months the efficacy of Quali Quah was proved beyond all doubt. And what is the population of China now, ladies and gentlemen? I'll tell you. Six hundred million—a quarter of the population of this planet!

"Now, gentlemen, there is a sufficient quantity of Quali Quah in the Chickamauga remedy to restore you to the identical condition of virility that has made China a marvel, as well as a problem, to the modern world."

Doc picked up a bottle of Chickamauga.

"And gentlemen, I am not going to *sell* you bottles of Chickamauga tonight. No sir, I am going to *give them away*. Every one of you who buys my autographed photograph at one dollar gets a *five*-dollar bottle of Chickamauga free. Just think of that!"

There was a roar of applause. Times had changed, and few in the audience had much belief in the "virilizing" qualities of Quali Quah. But who cared? Doc was a voice from a lamp-lit, cozy past, when men believed in such nostrums as Vital Sparks, Perry Davis's painkiller or Dr. Perkins's Metallic Tractors. To them Doc Cole was John Philip Sousa, Jim Thorpe and Teddy Roosevelt rolled into one; within an hour he was out of Chickamauga and was selling the photographs alone at a dollar apiece.

Morgan sat on his stool and looked across the ring. Of course, it was old Packy. A year had put a little more fat around his waist, his pectorals were beginning to sag, but he had still the broad, muscle-slabbed back and shoulders of an old pro. Morgan had not fought Packy since that first time in 1930 when the veteran had danced with him for a couple of rounds before dispatching him in the third, but he knew that the older man must still have a good few shots in his locker.

Packy's immediate reaction was one of surprise, then one of pleasure. Wiping the smile from his face, he walked menacingly to the center of the ring where he was joined by Morgan.

"Great to see yuh again, Morgan," he said, assuming a scowl. His voice dropped. "I got problems," he whispered. "Anderson's cutting down on men. If I don't take you, I get canned. So lie down, for Christ's sake, in the third."

Morgan went back to his corner. The picture was clear. Packy was on his last chance. Another defeat and the old man was finished.

Below the ring, seated uncomfortably on one of the lumpy, faded velvet chairs Flanagan puffed uneasily on his cigar as he swopped pleasantries with the Mayor of Springfield and other local dignitaries, and fobbed off side bets from bettors behind him. From the shouts of the crowd Morgan seemed to have a lot of local support, news of his performance in the Trans-America having preceded him, and the audience also contained a fair number of Trans-Americans. Flanagan sucked hard on his Havana as he looked up again at Packy Paterson, then shivered. On the tightrope again. He forced a confident smile as Liebnitz passed by with Pollard, and made his way to a seat on Flanagan's left. The senior journalist, looking white-faced, was shaking his head gloomily.

Carlsen had meanwhile brought the two boxers together in the center of the ring, and stood between them, his hands on their shoulders.

"Gentlemen," he said. "I want this to be a clean fight. Break when I say break, and keep those punches above the waist. And remember, I am the sole arbiter within this ring. The very best of luck to both of you."

Packy stepped back, giving Morgan a knowing look. Morgan did not respond.

Sergeant O'Brien clanged the bell for the first round.

Packy came shuffling out, and the two men immediately clinched, with Packy pinning Morgan's arms to his body.

"Make it look good, Morgan boy," he whispered, cuffing him with a soft left as Carlsen pulled them apart.

Morgan circled Packy, poking out tentative lefts to find his distance: this was no bare-fist fight in which one clubbing blow would finish things. Morgan kept circling, trying to focus his thoughts. Packy's long, looping left came over and took him on the outside of his right cheek, and the runner cursed himself for his slowness. Packy followed in with his short left hook, but there was no power in it. Colonel Carlsen's pre-fight inspection had also made sure that there was no plaster of Paris either.

Packy then put in several showy rat-a-tat hooks to the body, but still there was no strength in the punches. "Let's show 'em some class, Morgan," he puffed, grinning as they clinched, the sweat already streaming down his hairy chest. Morgan responded with some light, fast blows to Packy's head, followed by hooks with both hands to the stomach, but he too made sure there was no steam in them. The two men gave the crowd some flashy toe-to-toe punching as the bell clanged for the end of the first round, but it was all show.

Morgan sat back on his stool. "What do you think?" asked Hugh anxiously, flapping a towel to cool his man, while Morgan rinsed his mouth. "You don't look too happy."

"I know him," said Morgan. He spat into the water bucket. "It's Packy Paterson. I've fought him before. He won't go down easy." He was not even sure whether that was what he wanted. Packy had been like a brother to him. The old man was finished if Morgan put him away. And yet . . .

His mind was at war with itself. Part of him searched desperately back into the past, trying to recall the mass of routines and combination punches which Packy had used, and the counters which the veteran had taught him. He knew that only the muscular memory of those days with Packy would save him, for he had taken every punch in the old man's armory at some time or other. But he was tired by thousands of miles of running, and already taking punches that a year ago would have glided harmlessly past. It was fortunate for him that Packy had waltzed the first round; had he taken it seriously Morgan would undoubtedly have been forced to take a count.

He thought of the hundreds of punches he had thudded into Packy's face and body, in those days when the old man had helped him survive. There had been no profit in it for Packy. Indeed, young men like Morgan were rivals, the natural successors of Paterson and the other ring-scarred veterans. It was impossible to tell a man, let alone a woman, of the comradeship that could develop between men who spent at least an hour every day knocking hell out of each other. But comradeship it was, and the cold certainty with which Mike Morgan normally approached combat melted away in that short minute on his stool, unheeding of Hugh's anxious advice at his side.

The bell clanged for the second round and Packy came out fast. Obviously, he was not going to wait until the fourth: someone must have told him to put Morgan down. Jab, jab went his left hand into Morgan's face, without reply. Jab, jab again, puffing Morgan's right eye. Morgan circled, making the older man move. Again Packy's left hand went out, this time followed by a right cross over the top of Morgan's left, splitting his lip on the right. The crowd roared: they had come to see blood, and here it was.

Morgan counter-jabbed, jolting Packy's head back like a whip.

He noticed the pained surprise in the veteran's eyes. Packy pulled him into a clinch in the neutral corner.

"Take the fall, for Chrissake," said Packy. "Don't wanna cut you up."

Carlsen parted them and Morgan moved away. He was still confused. All his reflexes told him to fight, but there was no way in which he could put Packy Paterson down.

The decision was made for him. Packy's sucker left came over the top. Morgan could see it coming from a long way back, as if in a nightmare, but could do nothing about it. It was inevitably followed in by the short, sharp left jab, straight to Morgan's chin. The runner went down like a stone, the blur of the booth lights blinding him as he fell. He landed flat on his back, his head striking the floor with a dull thud. He was dimly aware of Carlsen counting above him, and dragged himself up on to his elbows, only to fall over once more. One—two—three—four—five—six—seven—eight . . .

On the count of nine Sergeant O'Brien clanged the bell and Hugh rushed into the ring, put his arms under Morgan's armpits and dragged him back to his corner. In the front row of the audience Flanagan had his face in his hands, while beside him Dixie was comforting Kate Sheridan.

Morgan hung limply on his stool, his back resting on the corner support, arms dangling at his sides, eyes half closed. Hugh sponged his face with lukewarm water and Morgan's eyes opened. He shook his head, water and sweat spraying over them both. Hugh looked desperately down at Flanagan, who still sat head down, immersed in his own worries.

"Here, give him this."

It was Doc, from beneath the ring. He thrust a small bottle of smelling salts into Hugh's hand.

"Get them under his nose, and quick."

Hugh unscrewed the container, put his left arm around Morgan's shoulders and thrust the salts under the boxer's nose.

Morgan coughed as the acrid smell of the salts reached his nostrils. Hugh slapped his face lightly.

"You with me, Mike?"

Morgan nodded.

"Then listen. Just stay out of trouble for the next three minutes, till your head clears. Use the ring. Make him move."

Morgan pushed away the smelling salts, shook his head and

brushed the tears and sweat from his eyes. His head still spun. It was strange: breathing, legs, body were still in good condition, yet here he was, fighting to secure that level of concentration that would enable him to stay on his feet for another round. He felt his head slowly clear. It had been a good punch, but it had not been of knockout caliber. Perhaps Packy needed the plaster of Paris to put people away for good nowadays.

Colonel Carlsen walked over to him.

"You sure you're able to continue?" he asked.

"Try to stop me," growled Morgan, pushing his gloves together and baring his teeth. He looked across at Packy, who was swilling out his mouth, listening to the snarled advice of Professor Anderson, on his left. This was no time for aggression. He must do as Hugh had advised: stay out of trouble until he could clear his head completely and get back into his punching rhythm.

The humid atmosphere in the tent was now intense, with the Trans-Americans on their feet chanting out their man's name, but Morgan was no longer aware of it. His aim throughout the next minute had, simply, to be to survive, to stay on his feet. The bell rang. He circled, making Packy move to him. But he could not stay out of the way of Packy's sharp prodding left, which was rapidly closing his right eye. Hugh's words clung in his mind. *"Use the ring, make him move."* Somehow Morgan was able to keep on the balls of his feet, circling and swaying to the rhythm of past reflexes. Each time the old man missed, Morgan heard the sharp explosion of breath, the increased heaviness of his breathing. Packy was tiring. Throughout the whole round Morgan hardly threw a punch, circling and dancing, bobbing and weaving as his senses returned and some of the old rhythms and reflexes came back to him, though only in flurries. Packy plodded dourly after him, occasionally catching Morgan but never with a solid, punishing punch. The veteran was puffing hard as O'Brien signaled the end of the third round, to the boos of the local crowd.

"Get that man to fight, Colonel," hissed Anderson. "This ain't no dancing school."

"I'll thank you to keep your comments to yourself, Professor," spat Carlsen in reply.

Morgan meanwhile was back on the low stool, the sweat streaming down his lean body. He was back in the fight. Packy would have to put him away in the fourth to save Anderson his hundred dollars, plus whatever Levy had offered him. The old man would have to come to him. So this was the time to go for the big hit. If Packy did succeed in putting him out, what did it mean? For Packy, another couple of stumblebum years in the booth and a glassy senility in some asylum. And Flanagan now had over forty grand riding on the fight—the future of the Trans-America, not to mention all the bets the Trans-Americans had taken.

"Morgan!" He looked down to his right, below the ring. It was Flanagan.

"The belly," said Flanagan, putting together a fantasy combination of lefts and rights into the smoky air in front of him. "Go for the body and the head will die." He put another combination together and replaced his cigar on the left side of his mouth. "You can bank on it."

He made a fist to Morgan with his right hand and moved back to his seat.

Morgan turned to look at Hugh above him. "He's right," said Hugh. "Go for his gut."

Morgan spat his rinse water into the bucket, replaced his mouthpiece with a grimace and pressed his gloves together. He looked across at Packy. It was so obvious that he should have seen it himself. There were fear and uncertainty in the older man's eyes as Professor Anderson spat advice at him from beneath the ropes. Time was running out for him. He would have to put Morgan away.

With the sound of the final bell Packy came out crouching, balanced, and immediately took the initiative. The veteran led with a straight left which snapped Morgan's head back, then ducked to hook him with a right to the stomach, below the belt. Morgan gasped and went down on his left knee, his right glove on the canvas. The old man still packed a wallop: his hardest punch so far. And no longer legal. He looked above him at Packy's pouting, hairy belly. *"Go for the body and the head will die."*

He got up at the count of seven. Carlsen cleaned his gloves, held him by both cheeks, looked closely into his eyes, then released him. Left, left into Packy's face, forcing him into a corner. Then Morgan ducked and drilled six short jabs deep into Packy's stomach, feeling the old man gasp as he dug them home and the spray of sweat as Packy pulled him into a clinch.

Carlsen pushed them apart and Morgan again went in low, boring short lefts and rights deep into Packy's stomach. He heard the "oof" of Packy's breath as his punches sank home. He felt the veteran's legs go soft, and for a moment he considered holding him up.

But no. He again hit Packy with a left jab to the diaphragm. As the old man's right hand dropped, Morgan threw a left to the point of Packy's chin. From the moment the punch was thrown he knew that it was the final blow of the fight. Packy went down flat on his back. All the bellowing of Professor Anderson and his fighters could not bring him to his feet.

The Trans-Americans rose as one man, throwing hats, newspapers, jackets in the air. Flanagan had done it again. In the red-velvet seat beside Flanagan, Leonard H. Levy smiled limply and stood to shake his rival's hand. Flanagan ignored him, instead making a flurry of left and right jabs to an imaginary belly, as he continued to look up at the crowded ring.

"I told you, Morgan!" he shouted. "I told you."

Half an hour later, Mike Morgan stood alongside Kate Sheridan, Hugh McPhail and Dixie Williams in the darkness outside the deserted booth, and watched as the lights on the booth front went out one by one.

Morgan put both hands on Kate's shoulders and looked her squarely in the eye.

"There's something I've got to do," he said quietly. "Wait for me here." He nodded to the others then walked to the left of the booth and on to the cluster of trailers behind it. Some of Anderson's fighters were sitting at a wooden table outside the ring of trailers, drinking and playing cards.

Morgan strode over to the cardplayers; they continued their game, not once looking up.

"I'm looking for Packy Paterson," he said squarely. "He around?"

An unshaven, flat-nosed man took a cigarette from his mouth and dropped it to the grass, trampling it in with his feet. He jerked a thumb over his left shoulder.

"In there," he said. "What's left of him."

With a brief word of thanks Morgan made his way in the direction suggested, toward a small trailer painted in dull blue and gold. He could hear Anderson's voice even as he mounted the trailer's steps; the word "finished" was repeated several times. He could guess only too well what form the conversation was taking. He knocked on the door, to be greeted a moment later by a flushed Professor Anderson.

"S'pose you're here to see your old buddy?" said Anderson tersely.

Morgan nodded and walked past Anderson into the disheveled quarters beyond. At the end of the narrow trailer, on the edge of a bunk, sat Packy Paterson. His head was between his knees, his hands laced together on the back of his neck. Like the cardplayers, he did not look up either.

"How you feeling, champ?" asked Morgan, looking behind him to Anderson, who made a contemptuous thumbs-down sign as he left the trailer.

Paterson raised his head and attempted a smile, the sweat still streaming down his face.

"Great—a hundred per cent," he said bitterly. He pointed toward the door. "Looks as though I'm gonna have to find me a new boss, though."

"That'll be no problem," said Morgan. "I've got one already lined up."

He moved to Packy and pulled him to his feet.

"Got one? Who d'you mean?" The fighter's voice was cautious, and slightly bewildered.

"Me, that's who," said Morgan firmly. He grabbed Packy by his shoulders and looked him in the eyes. "Pack your things," he said. "You're with the Trans-America—as from now."

"Doing what?" asked Packy, still bemused, yet reaching up into the cupboard above him for his clothes.

"Taking care of me," answered Morgan. "Making sure I reach New York."

21

SHOWDOWN WITH TOFFLER

"Say those figures again."

Flanagan leaned back in his rocking chair and closed his eyes.

Willard sat down and took a crumpled sheaf of papers from the trailer desk. He looked at them gloomily, shaking his head.

"It's scrambled eggs, boss. Now I know what those Wall Street big shots felt like back in the crash of twenty-nine."

He glanced once more at the clip of papers, shrugged, then dropped them onto the desk.

"I got bills here for over a hundred grand, another hundred grand in the pipeline. Jesus, we got a lawyer's bill today for thirty G's and we haven't even seen court yet."

There was a knock at the trailer door.

"Come in," shouted Flanagan, scowling.

It was Levy, but no longer the smiling, confident Levy of St. Louis or Springfield

"Hope I'm not troubling you, gentlemen?"

"Never any trouble to pick up forty grand," said Flanagan, uncorking a bottle of whiskey with his teeth. "Drink?"

"You got your own stuff here?" Levy mopped his brow and sat down.

"Ice?" continued Flanagan unabashed.

Levy nodded, then took a bundle of bills from his pocket.

"Here you are," he said. "No one can say that Leonard H. Levy is a welsher."

He sipped his drink slowly, then leaned back in his seat.

"I don't know how you do it. They haven't stopped talking back in St. Louis about your runners and Silver Star. But I thought I had you cold with Anderson's pug."

"It's the Trans-America," said Flanagan. "Somewhere in the race we got poets, fighters, lords. You name it, we've got it."

"Looks like it," said Levy. "Anyway I have a message for you. It's from a Mr. Martin P. Toffler. You may know him. A personal friend of mine. He ran for Congress a few years back. I did some campaigning for him."

The smile left Flanagan's face. "I know him," he said, sharply.

"He'd like to meet you, urgently, tomorrow at seven-thirty P.M." He fished a card out of his pocket. "At this address."

Flanagan took the card, looked at it and passed it over his shoulder to Willard. His eyes returned to Levy's.

"Tell him I'll be there," he said. "Seven-thirty P.M. on the button."

May 18, 1931. The Columbia Hotel, Peoria, Illinois.

Toffler looked at his watch. He had seen it all before, with his old college friend, Commissioner K. M. Landis, in the Black Sox scandal of 1920. It had been a nine-game World Series between the Sox and the underdogs, the Cincinnati Reds.

In the first game Eddie Cicotte, the starting pitcher for the Black Sox, gave up five runs in four innings and the Reds won 9–1. The second game had been close until Lefty Williams walked three Cincinnati batters, then allowed a three-run triple by a powder-puff hitter, Larry Kopf.

The third game had gone to the Sox, but the fourth went to the Reds, when Cicotte again chipped in with a couple of errors. At 3–1 against, the players in on the fix decided to make it look good, for the next two games went to the Sox. But the roof fell in during the next game, when the Reds scored four times in the first inning and went on to win the World Series 5–3.

Eventually, early in September 1920, stories started leaking out that the previous year's series had been thrown and Toffler had been close to it from the beginning. Three Black Sox players, Jackson, Cicotte and Williams, signed confessions admitting their part in the scheme, but before they could be brought to trial there was a sudden turnover in the Illinois state's attorney's office and all the confessions mysteriously disappeared. When the case entered the courts the players repudiated their statements and the case was dropped.

That the players had been acquitted mattered little to K. M. Landis. He banned them all from major league parks, and even went as far as ensuring that they could not play even in the minor leagues.

Toffler sniffed, pulled back his cuff, and looked at his watch. It was 7:30. The Black Sox, Battling Siki, Ty Cobb, Jim Thorpe, Charles Flanagan, it was all the same. They all reeked of corruption, the fast buck.

He looked up to see Flanagan, lean and tanned, standing in front of him, dressed in an immaculate pin-striped gray double-breasted suit. Toffler forced a smile. "Mr. Flanagan?"

The Irishman nodded.

Toffler extended a limp hand. "Perhaps we should go over to the bar?"

Flanagan led the way and they perched themselves on two narrow stools.

After they had ordered and received their drinks Toffler began, stiffly. "Your men have come a long way, Mr. Flanagan."

Flanagan's teeth parted in a grimace as the whiskey hit the back of his throat.

"Farther than we ever expected," he replied. "Two thousand two hundred and ten miles, to be exact. Just over eight hundred to go."

Toffler smiled.

"Just so," he said. He laid down his glass.

"Mr. Flanagan, you must forgive me my frankness. Would it be fair to say that you devised the Trans-America for personal—"

"Profit?" asked Flanagan. "Say it, Mr. Toffler. It's not a dirty word, not in my vocabulary."

"I was going to say 'gain,' " said Toffler.

"Same thing," said Flanagan. "The answer's yes, that was my aim."

"Would it be impolite of me to ask you how much you expected to clear on the Trans-America?"

"It would be impolite," said Flanagan. "But I'll tell you. Close to one hundred and fifty grand."

Toffler nodded.

"What would be your response if I asked you if you would like to receive that sum from me tonight to stop the Trans-America now? Stop it dead?"

"I'd say that you must have some pretty good reason for doing such a thing."

Toffler's soft lips pouted affably.

"Mr. Flanagan, it cannot possibly have escaped your notice that next year the United States will host the tenth Olympic Games."

"No," said Flanagan, nodding to the barman to set up two more drinks. "It has not escaped my notice."

"Then you must realize," continued Toffler, "that, as matters stand, the Trans-America represents a considerable embarrassment to the American Olympic Committee—indeed, to the whole American Olympic Movement."

"You mean to Mr. Brundage, Aloysius P. Leonard, and the officers of the AAU?"

"Among others," said Toffler. "But please let me continue. A group of public-spirited businessmen have put together a fund to . . . to meet your expenses if the Trans-America is wound up."

"It'll take more than one hundred and fifty G's," said Flanagan. "You must know that we've come up against a lot of unexpected problems—damaged equipment, towns failing to pay up, legal bills. All told, I think my ball-park figure is a quarter of a million."

Toffler picked up his glass and seemed to be studying its contents intensely. He looked up.

"I think we can meet that figure," he said, quietly.

"Let me get this clear," said Flanagan, pointing a finger at Toffler. "You're willing to put up a quarter of a million bucks just to stop the Trans-America?"

"Exactly," said Toffler.

"Then that means you think you're beaten," said Flanagan.

Toffler flushed and put down his glass. "Just what exactly do you mean?" he asked, his voice rising.

Flanagan's voice was hard and even.

"Mr. Toffler, you know *exactly* what I mean. Since the Mojave I haven't been running a flat race, I've been in some goddam crazy steeplechase, with no rules. Hell, for the past six weeks the Trans-America has been like some moving disaster area. Natural catastrophes we could take—rain in the Mojave, snow in the Rockies. If you and your Ivy League buddies had anything to do with that you must have been on a ouija board to the Almighty Himself. But the rest has been pure Tammany Hall, no holds barred."

Toffler's face twisted into a scowl.

"I can see that I must lay my cards on the table, Flanagan. Do you realize, do you have any conception of the noble history of the Olympic movement? Have you any understanding of the honor, the privilege which accrues to the United States in securing the Games for Los Angeles? And now, because of the interest which your tawdry circus has excited, some of the world's greatest athletes may be tempted to forsake their precious amateur status to join you."

Flanagan reached into his inside pocket, withdrew a Havana and bit into it. He placed the plug in the ashtray beside him, then struck a match on the sole of his shoe and lit his cigar, puffing slowly. He put the match in the ashtray, withdrew the cigar from his mouth and tapped imaginary ash from its tip.

"Mr. Toffler," he said slowly. "You surprise me, you really do. You see, I always thought that America was a free country. As things stand, being an amateur athlete isn't a matter of choice, because we don't have any pros. At present, there is no choice. But the Trans-America and next year's Trans-Europe will give some amateur athletes that choice for the first time. A real profession, a career."

"You intend to hold a Trans-*Europe* next year?" gasped Toffler.

"Preparations are now well in hand," replied Flanagan. "All the way from London to Moscow, the White City Stadium to Lenin Stadium."

Toffler gulped down his sherry.

"Perhaps you'd like to join me in something stronger, perhaps a whiskey, Mr. Toffler?" smiled Flanagan. "But first, let me take you back a few years, to 1913 to be exact, to poor ol' Jim Thorpe, losing his Olympic medals because he took twelve bucks a week playing bush-league baseball. Who headed the commission that canned him?"

"I did," said Toffler.

"You surely did. Twelve bucks a week to a guy who didn't know amateur status from a salami sandwich. That was real justice. But let me take you on a few years more to 1925, to a young promoter trying to fix some indoor meets with Abrahams, Paddock, Scholz at the Garden—all the Olympic boys. It was a nice deal, five grand to the AAU, five grand to the YMCA for a new gymnasium, a couple of grand to the promoter. But it was no deal. That young promoter's face didn't fit with Mr. Martin Toffler, so the YMCA missed out on its gymnasium. Now, who do you think the promoter was? I'll give you three guesses."

Toffler reddened. "There were good reasons," he began.

"I'm sure there were," said Flanagan. "There always were, where I was concerned. The promoter was me, but apparently I wasn't the right kind of person to be promoting AAU meets. All right to fix the track and rake the pits, but no way I could get to wear the white tuxedo."

"That's all in the past," said Toffler. "No point in raking it up now. So I admit the Committee may have erred back in twenty-five, but this is a fresh situation."

"First let's get one thing clear," said Flanagan. "Do you admit that you have been behind all the blocks that have been put on the Trans-America?"

"I . . . I admit that I may have spoken to a few people."

"Vegas? Topeka? Kansas City? Columbia? Poliakoff? You seem to know quite a few people, Mr. Toffler."

Toffler bared his teeth. "Flanagan, have you any idea of where your ragged regiment lies in the world of sport? I'll tell you. Level with Shipwreck Kelly pole-sitting on the roof of the Wild West bar in the Bronx. In the same world as marathon dancers hanging onto each other in the smoky filth of dime-a-dance halls, Jimmy Dooley keeping a bike going for five days. That's your little world."

"So now it's all out," said Flanagan, leaning back on his stool. "Look, Toffler, I don't have to justify the Trans-America to you. Or to anyone else for that matter. It justifies itself every day out there on the roads of America. Hell, I don't know any more than you what makes one sports performance a stunt, like pole-squatting or spitting for distance, and another one people admire and want to emulate, like baseball or marathon. Perhaps it's because people see in it qualities they admire—skill, endurance, intelligence, will. I don't know. What I *do* know is that the Trans-America stands right up there with the marathon, long-distance cycling and swimming. It isn't people like you or me who'll decide whether or not those guys out there are athletes or freaks. Mr. Joe Public will decide. And he's *already* made up his mind. He likes what he sees."

"So you're going on with this . . . circus?" said Toffler, his mouth set tight.

"Let me say something," said Flanagan. "Because I've always wanted to meet one of you guys head on, face to face. People like you don't love sport; you love the committees, the parties, meeting Baron de Coubertin, shaking the President's hand, being Mr. Big. You haven't done much in your life, but in the AAU you suddenly find you can tell some of the greatest muscle in the world where to go and what to do. You think you've got some sort of God-given right to run sport, some sort of monopoly. So if an upstart like me threatens to spoil the garden party, then the answer is to fix him or to buy him off. You don't live *in* sport, you live *on* it."

"Is that your final word?" asked Toffler.

"You can bet your last two hundred and fifty G's it is," said Flanagan, gulping down the last of his whiskey. He turned to the man who had been sitting with his back to them on the stool behind Toffler.

"And now, Mr. Toffler, there's someone I'd like you to meet."

"Meet someone?" queried Toffler, puzzled. "Who?"

The man spun on his stool to face Toffler.

"FBI Agent Ernest J. Bullard," said Flanagan. "I think that you two may have a lot to talk about."

Charles C. Flanagan was back in his rocking chair again, eyes half closed. It had been good to get it all off his chest, after so many years. It would, of course, change nothing, for nothing could change the cold hellos, the eyes staring past him, which he had for years endured anyway from Toffler and his kind.

One thing, however, was clear. Any future problems of the Trans-America would no longer emanate from Toffler and his AAU cronies. Ernest Bullard had made sure of that. Bullard had taken detailed notes of the Toffler-Flanagan Peoria conversation, and these were more than enough to put FBI agents on Toffler's trail, should the need ever arise.

For the moment Bullard had put Toffler on probation, and the gray, shaking Olympic official had mumbled his good-byes through dry lips. But there were other troubles enough. From the beginning, the financial basis of the Trans-America had been fragile, since no one knew how many men would survive the three thousand miles from Los Angeles to New York. They had guessed at three hundred men lasting into the last thousand miles, and now, in fact, carried over a thousand, each one costing nearly ten dollars a day to feed and house. The Trans-America had been a step in the dark in more ways than one, and they were learning on the hoof. Flanagan's only profit would be experience, the sort of experience that would be invaluable in the Trans-Europe.

The Trans-Europe! Flanagan had only tossed the idea at Toffler to test the man's reaction, for not a single preparation had been made and Flanagan had only the vaguest idea of the countries lying between London and Moscow. Still, the world of sport was watching the Trans-America. Pro track and field had to start somewhere, and this might well be the beginning. Why not? He could see it all, the World Professional Track and Field Association, with a network of Trans-Continental races, supported by a capillary structure of national races. They could run parallel to the Olympics, perhaps even join up with it at some future point when the Tofflers of the world realized that there was nothing morally wrong in accepting money for competing in track and field athletics. The WPTFA would be the governing body, maintaining a rigid moral code, higher even than the Olympic movement, since payments would be open and above board. And at its head would be Charles C. Flanagan, the father of pro track and field . . .

Or would they simply go the way of roller pole, battle ball, Bronx bull-fighting, ice baseball, basketball on roller skates, aerial golf, water baseball? The line between sports and freak sports was a thin one, and Toffler had probably not been too far out when he had tried to compare Flanagan's men with marathon dancers and pole-sitters. To qualify as sports there had to be something noble about it, something which struck a chord in every spectator— Red Grange crazy-legging it through the broken field, Babe Ruth making the clean, long bop into the bleachers, Charley Paddock leaping for the tape, Nurmi striding, ice-cold, through lap after lap . . .

It had grabbed him. His first and only aim in holding the Trans-

America had indeed been the quick buck, but over the miles his motives had changed. Now he wanted to see who would come out on top, whether it was to be gabby little Doc Cole, the phlegmatic Morgan or the tough, vulnerable Scot, McPhail. Would it be Lord Thurleigh, the Finn, Eskola, or the rapidly closing pack of All-Americans led by Capaldi? And then there was the Australian, Mullins, the Japanese, Son, and the Frenchmen, Dasriaux and Bouin . . . Tonight, in Peoria, he could have stepped out clear, if not clean, with two hundred and fifty thousand bucks; but it had never entered his head.

For a brief moment it was as if the years had rolled back. Then Doc looked at Lily more closely. True, the structure of the strong, high-cheek-boned face was still there, the bright, even teeth, but Lily Carson's blue eyes were tired now, her face puffy, her makeup garish and contrived.

Doc smiled and kissed her right cheek

"How long has it been?" he asked.

"Ten years, come Thanksgiving Day," said Lily, sitting down in the candlelit bar of the Columbia Hotel, Peoria.

"You're looking great," lied Doc.

Lily smiled weakly, lit a cigarette, and nodded at the white-coated waiter hovering above them.

"Still drinking orange juice?" she asked.

Doc nodded.

"Two orange juices, one special, one straight." Lily pulled heavily on her cigarette. "I suppose you're still doing those crazy exercises too. What did you call 'em—sandwich exercises?"

"Sandow," he corrected her. "The Sandow Program." He smiled. "Every morning, without fail."

She shook her head. "Things don't change much, do they? Here you are, fifty-four years of age, still running, still doing kid's exercises. Where has it all got you?"

Doc puckered his lips. "It's got me this far, eight hundred miles short of New York. I'm placing second."

"And is this it, the Big One you always used to talk about?"

Doc nodded, as he accepted his orange juice.

"Yep. This is the one I was looking for all those years back."

"The Big One. The great race in the sky. You must have gypsy blood in you, Alex. You sure waited long enough, giving up just about everything that made life worth living, waiting around for it. D'you know, I used to lie waiting with the hots for you in hotel rooms from Austin, Texas, to Davenport, Iowa, while you were out on the roads running your heart out?"

Doc smiled and shook his head.

"And when you got back, your heart beating fit to bust, you would shower and lie down beside me and go to sleep, goddam you. Sometimes I could have killed you."

Doc shook his head once more and put his hand across the table to cover hers. "We got together a few times, didn't we?"

Lily smiled. "When it did happen it was good. But, after all, I was with the fittest man in the world. A little more quantity wouldn't have gone amiss."

Doc sipped his orange juice.

"Well, it's all panning out now, the golden pot at the end of the rainbow, in New York."

Lily looked at him across the table.

"Was it all worth it—really?"

"How do you mean?"

"Well," she said, her hands cupping her glass. "When you were competing as a pro, against Longboat and all those other crazy marathon runners, there was some reason for running. You won a few, you lost a few, but it all had some purpose. But when it all dried up, before the war, you still kept running. I never could understand why."

Doc bit his lip. "I don't know if I can explain it to you, honey. When the pro circuit died, in 1913, I couldn't get back as an amateur—the AAU wouldn't let me. Hell, I thought, I'm just beginning to get a grip on this long-distance running, so why stop now? So I decided to compete against myself. By 1924 I had cracked most world records from ten miles upward to marathon."

"But you were the only one who knew?"

Doc grinned and nodded.

"I reckoned that I was the only one who needed to know, though I seem to remember that I wrote you a few times."

Lily smiled wryly. "They sure meant one helluva lot to me, those clockings of yours." She looked down into her drink, then up at Doc. "You know why I left you?"

Doc shook his head.

"It was the running. Sure, at the time I said that I wanted to settle down, get off the medicine-show circuit. But I could have taken that, as long as I was with you. No, it was the running. That was where you lived—in your running—the only place you were really alive. Not with me."

Lily sighed and pushed back a wisp of graying blond hair. She looked across at him.

"What did you find there, Alex, out on the roads? You used to talk about how you could 'see inside yourself' when you ran— hell, I can't remember the half of it. But what else did you find there? Not me. Not any woman."

Doc shrugged. "You're right, though I didn't understand it at the time. What I found inside me was that one talent I had, the ability to run long distances, the capacity to push my body to its limits. It's like a drug, the stretching of your body out to the unknown. And once you get hooked it's difficult to come off it. As long as I was improving it was great. Then, when I got older, I had to con myself by running over odd distances—do you know I hold the world record for nine and a quarter miles? Then, just when it was all beginning to go sour and I was starting to have doubts, up came Flanagan and the Trans-America."

"And that made it all worthwhile?"

"Just about. It seemed to be what I had been preparing for, only without knowing it."

"The Big One?"

"Yes. And it hasn't been lonely, as I had expected. It's been like a sort of Swiss Family Robinson, trekking across the country. We've got a little team, a couple of Englishmen, a Mexican, and a guy called Morgan. I think you'd like them."

Lily fingered her glass.

"You want to know what happened to me?"

Doc nodded.

"Like you, I was waiting for the Big One, the knock on the door that was going to change it all. I met my Big One in Chicago in 1922."

She looked down at her empty glass.

"His name was Al Capone."

She paused to allow her words to sink in.

"He seemed a nice little guy at first, quite a gentleman, like most Italians. We had ourselves some good times."

She finished her drink with a quick gulp.

"In 1925 he set me up in my own hairdressing shop. A couple of weeks later he set up a speakeasy and a gambling shop at the back. I thought, so what, I was doing what I wanted."

Lily nodded again at the waiter.

"In twenty-eight he threw me over. Since then my job has been to set him up with young broads. So you see I found my Big One, my Wizard with the miraculous hat."

Doc drew his lips together tightly and again put his hand on hers.

"So we're both still looking, after all these years?"

"Sure looks that way."

Doc looked Lily in the eyes.

"One thing about never having grown up properly, you've still got plenty of stretch left in you. By my age, lots of guys have been married three times and have one foot in the grave. Me, I'm young. Jesus, I've got the body of a twenty-year-old and a mind not much older. I've got eight hundred miles left to finish this race and win it. With the money, I can set us up in any sort of business you like."

Lily shook her head.

"It's too late. We've come too far."

"No," said Doc. "Not too far. Perhaps not far enough. Wait till after New York. Give it a chance."

"*If* you make New York," she said suddenly.

"What do you mean?"

"I'm still close to Capone and his boys. The Trans-America's too big for them not to want a piece of it. A couple of his boys, Jake Guzik and Frank Nitti, have set up a syndicate. They've put a bundle on one of the local boys, Capaldi, winning the stage into Chicago."

"Capaldi could win it on his merits," said Doc. "He's coming on strong."

Lily grimaced. "Well, just make sure no one tries to head Capaldi into Chicago."

AMERICANA DATELINE MAY 22, 1931

Goose Lake Prairie, Illinois. C. C. Flanagan's Trans-Americans make the fifty-six-mile run into Chicago tomorrow. The race has now reached a remarkable pitch, with Doc Cole's group, which has led since Denver, being attacked from behind by the Williams' All-

Americans, led by the Chicago-born Italian, Capaldi, and by a four-man European team led by the Finn, Eskola. Other non-team runners Mullins, Son, and the Irish runner, Brady, are also starting to close in on the leaders.

The Mexican, Juan Martinez, who is now thirty-fourth and has been suffering from stomach trouble, looks likely to try to win this fifty-six-mile slog, as Chicago is the home of his brother, Emiliano. Chicago bookmakers are giving low odds of 2–1 against the Chicago-born Capaldi, who tells me that he wants to show well in front of newly appointed Mayor Cermak and his fellow citizens.

Also of interest to the sports-loving Chicago public will be the appearance of the now-famous Miss Kate Sheridan, whose last performance in Chicago was on the stage of the Roxy Theater, where she appeared in 1929 as a dancer. Miss Sheridan's legs, though now put to different tasks, are well worth the consideration of the Chicago public. Miss Sheridan still has nearly two hundred men between her and the $10,000 offered her by a national ladies' journal. All Chicago will be out to see if this splendid representative of the weaker sex can step still closer to that magic ten grand.

—CARL C. LIEBNITZ—

Saturday, May 23, 1931

Chicago (2246 miles)

			Hrs.	Mins.	Secs.
1 =	H. McPhail	(Great Britain)	368	43	06
2 =	A. Cole	(USA)	369	47	12
3 =	A. Capaldi	(USA)	370	02	14
4 =	M. Morgan	(USA)	370	21	24
5 =	P. Eskola	(Finland)	370	41	26
6 =	J. Bouin	(France)	370	59	42
7 =	R. Mullins	(Australia)	371	03	38
8 =	P. Brix	(USA)	371	21	36
9 =	P. Dasriaux	(France)	371	26	24
10 =	P. Thurleigh	(Great Britain)	371	41	07
11 =	L. Son	(Japan)	371	43	21
12 =	R. Brady	(Ireland)	371	45	01
13 =	P. Komar	(Poland)	371	48	07
14 =	K. Lundberg	(Sweden)	371	53	21
15 =	C. O'Connor	(Ireland)	372	03	28
16 =	P. Maffei	(Italy)	372	03	30
17 =	P. Flynn	(USA)	372	05	32
18 =	C. Charles	(Australia)	372	07	21
19 =	P. O'Grady	(Ireland)	372	12	28
20 =	P. Coghlan	(New Zealand)	372	14	30

1st Lady: (221) K. Sheridan (USA)   449   12   04
Number of finishers: 971
Average speed (leader): 9 mins. 51 secs. per mile

22

MEETING
MR. CAPONE

After Juan Martinez had won his village trial, and so the right to represent them in the Trans-America, it was decided that he would be sent to the mountains of the Sierra Tarahumare to train with a tribe of runners called the Tarahumares. He had taken almost a week to recover from the trial race, during which he had been daily massaged by the village's medicine man, Carlos. Meat was virtually unknown in Quanto, but an ancient goat was slaughtered to provide Juan with the necessary protein, and daily he had struggled to digest its tough, teaklike flesh, carefully watched by Carlos and his mother and father. Daily, he trotted five miles over dusty broken roads, and with each day he found that running was becoming a little easier. Perhaps, he thought, he might have a talent for this distance running; or perhaps it was only the goat meat.

In 1890 a Norwegian naturalist, Carl Lumholtz, had timed the Tarahumares running twenty-one miles in two hours while playing *rarahipa*, a ball-kicking game. His accounts were derided and forgotten. Much later, in 1926, the Mexican government had brought two Tarahumares to the high altitude of Mexico City for an exhibition run. The Indians had amazed sports writers by completing a sixty-five-mile course in nine hours thirty-seven minutes. A year later another Tarahumare had lopped over an hour from the record for the fifty-one mile distance between Kansas City and Austin, Kansas.

The Mexican government then asked a Tarahumares chief to send three of his runners to compete in a standard marathon. The chief responded by sending three women, one of whom finished in third place. The race organizers expressed surprise that the tribe's best runners had been women. The chief replied that a short race like twenty-six miles was ideal for women, and that was why he had sent them.

To the villagers of Quanto, Juan was an investment. If he came back successful from the Trans-America, then the subsistence economy of the village would be transformed. The villagers could lose little in this gamble; they had little to lose.

Juan had staggered home first of nineteen aspirants in the village trial, over a modest twenty-mile course around the village. Every salable item in Quanto had then been sold to get him to the Tarahumares for training, and to pay for his trip to Los Angeles. Even then there had not been enough, and there had been recourse to the local moneylender for a loan at heavy rates of interest. Letters of introduction had been sent ahead to Manuel, the leader of the Tarahumare tribe, and three weeks later Juan Martinez set off toward the Sierra Tarahumare.

Juan had taken the train, the Ferrocarril Chihuahua Al Pacifico, to Chihuahua, then traveled by mule to the home of the tribe to which he had been sent at the village of Chogita. Chogita lay in a long, narrow valley and consisted of an avenue of adobe huts, each about half a mile apart.

When he arrived groups of tribesmen, faces and legs daubed with white paint and wearing colored headbands or sombreros, were chanting and dancing outside a hut. Juan realized he had come in the middle of a religious holiday and so he squatted on the other side of the rough road munching his food until the Tarahumares had jogged down the valley to the next hut.

The Communidad, the town hall where all tribal matters were settled, was in the middle of the village, and it was there that Juan met Manuel. The wiry old man had been a great runner in his youth, and knew well why Martinez had come. He had come to Chogita to be absorbed into a running culture, and he was soon to gain his first direct experience of it, for the chief told him that a forty-mile race was to be held the next day. It was not a *rarahipa* or a *dowerami* (hoop race), but a simple footrace.

Juan had watched that night as the runners squatted in the flickering lights of their camp fires, oiling their legs with goat grease and massaging them with boiled juniper branches. This part of their preparation completed, they huddled around the fire, smoking, eating *tortillas* and drinking coffee.

The race was a nightmare: forty miles of running over rough stony country at high altitude, at a steady eight miles an hour. The Tarahumares, wearing thonged leather sandals, shuffled evenly over the dry, brown mountains with never a break in their rhythm. Martinez kept up with the leaders for the first ten miles, then gradually felt his breathing become more and more labored as he battled desperately in the thin air. Soon he was back among the youths and the old men, struggling to maintain even a modest six miles an hour. He finished last out of thirty runners, barely able to lift his feet from the ground as he staggered in the evening gloom toward the Communidad.

It took him three whole days to recuperate, lying on his back on a wool blanket on the dirt floor of the chief's hut, as Manuel and his guests sat above him on crude log stools around the primitive, wood-burning stove, drinking coffee and talking in the local dialect. In those three days of recovery he had eaten the last of the cheese and dried goat's meat which he had brought with him, but on the fourth day he began the spartan dietary regime of the Tarahumares. This consisted of corn, squash and beans, of which the corn, used for *tortillas*, ground into *pinole*, pulped for cornmeal mush or mashed into a thick gruel, was the most important element.

When he started to run again he did so with the women, slow, daily five- to ten-mile stints in the thin mountain air, covering forty miles in his first week. Then he followed the senior men on the forty-mile *rarahipa* runs in preparation for the competitions between Chogita and her neighboring villages. The *rarahipa* runners ran without shoes because this made the kicking of the ball easier, but Juan ran behind them in sandals. He was not allowed to take part in the intervillage competitions but was able to absorb every detail of the runners' preparations, down to the intricate personal tattooing of the legs, a ritual which each runner considered essential to success.

Within three months he was able to run over eighty miles a week, though he was never able to copy the low, clipped shuffle of the Tarahumares, his natural action being a prancing, high-stepping one. During this period his only confidante was Manuel, for whom Spanish was a second language. The hundreds of hours spent with the runners of the tribe contained only one language, the unspoken tongue of men linked by miles of running. The old man knew his purpose, though he could only have a dim idea of the great race in Los Angeles for which Martinez was preparing.

Then, after four months, he repeated his forty-mile race against the runners of the tribe. This time it was different. His body had now adapted, and he was able to stay with the Tarahumares all the way and use his greater basic speed to run away from them over the last three miles.

In the final two months he lifted his weekly mileage to one hundred and fifty miles and knew, at the end of this period, that he was now ready for the Trans-America. Manuel would accept no money for his stay at Chogita, only a wool blanket made by Martinez's mother. The whole village came out to see him go, running as always up the steep slopes to gather at the Communidad. The chief said little on his departure. "Distinguish yourself," he told him. "No man can ask more."

The fitness gained by Juan Martinez in the mountains served him well in the first blistering days of the Trans-America and he was able to pick up good money for early stage prizes, which he immediately sent back to a bank in Mexico City for onward transmission to his village. He was also able to handle the altitude of the Rockies because of his mountain experience. Slowly, however, the daily mileages across the Great Plains took their toll and like the other runners he began to experience pain, not only in the muscles but in the joints. Some days even his bones seemed to hurt, and Martinez wept dry tears across the dust roads of Kansas.

As with the Tarahumares the common experience of running daily drew him closer to runners of whose culture and background he knew nothing—men from Glasgow, from Pennsylvania, men like Doc who seemed to have no home. All possessed an inner assurance which at first frightened him, but gradually he was drawn into their company. It was strange. They were, after all, competitors. What bound them was the daily challenge of the miles and behind it all the test of traversing a continent by foot. His responsibility to finish in the prize money to rescue the economy of his village receded. Rather, he tried every day, as Manuel had said, to distinguish himself. He knew that if he could do that then there could be no dishonor, whatever the eventual outcome of the race.

He had felt himself become steadily weaker after St. Louis, particularly on the occasional hilly stretches. However, like McPhail and many others in the race, he had vowed that he would never walk. But this vow had often reduced him to a broken trot no faster than a walk, and more exhausting. Juan Martinez was now paying for years of malnutrition, and there was no way that by will alone he could overcome this handicap.

Doc and the others in the group could be of little help to him in his daily agonies, for they had to stay up with Capaldi, Mullins, Eskola and Dasriaux, all of whom were beginning to win stages and so creep up on aggregate time. By Wilmington, just over fifty miles from Chicago, Juan Martinez realized that his hopes of winning the Trans-America were dim; he was now in thirty-fourth place. He knew, as a member of Doc's group, that he would benefit equally from any shareout in New York, but that was not why he had come. He had come to make his mark, and that he had not yet done.

There was, however, still Chicago, the Windy City, to be approached in two separate stages, totaling fifty-six miles, with a stage prize for the final section of five hundred dollars. There his brother Emiliano, his wife and two children, lived and worked, and Martinez was determined to be first at the finish at Soldier Field stadium. His aim would be to save himself in the first stage, finishing back in the mid-fifties, and on the second stage to hang in with the leaders until the final mile and use his speed to leave them at that point.

Doc and his group knew that at least one man would be racing full speed on that second stage—Capaldi—who had been primed to win the section by a big-money syndicate in Chicago, led by Nitti and Guzik. Capaldi and the All-American team management knew nothing of the syndicate's connections with Capone's men. Indeed, they had laid two thousand dollars through the syndicate on Capaldi. There was nothing illegal or underhand in this. Every stage was up for grabs, and it was certain that money had also been laid on other runners for the final stage into Chicago, as it had been on other stages throughout the Trans-America.

Doc and Hugh spent most of the night preceding the Chicago stage arguing with Martinez, trying to impress upon him the ruthlessness of men such as Nitti and Guzik, but the little Mexican had been adamant. It was the first time they had ever seen him angry.

"You say I to run slow? You say I dishonor myself in front of my own brother?" He had looked unbelievingly at Doc, tears in his great brown eyes.

Try as he might, Doc could not explain to Juan the danger he might face if he beat Capaldi. "I get beat, too bad. But golly Jesus, I run all the way into Chicago. My brother, Emiliano, he loses a whole day's pay to see me!"

All they could hope for was that Martinez, now desperately weak, would not be able to hold the tough Italian-American into Chicago, and that the problem would resolve itself.

It was not for nothing that Chicago had been dubbed jocularly as "the armpit of the world." As early as the end of the Civil War it had established itself as the world's leading packer of meat, as Texas cattle drovers moved the herds through Jayhawkers, pestilence and Indians north to the Chicago stockyards. Then in 1870 the fertile mind of Joseph McCoy had conceived the idea of a railhead town where cattle ranchers could sell their herds at a point of intersection with the newly built Trans-Continental railway, choosing Abilene as his site. Though Abilene faded almost immediately to be overtaken by other western towns such as Ellsworth, and McCoy died in poverty, Chicago went from strength to strength, as a center for meat packing. The simple equation, established after the Civil War, that eighty cattle were required to meet the needs of one hundred people, made certain of that. It also made certain that Chicago stank of leather and excrement, and its winds made equally certain that the stink swept through the poorest areas of the city.

Like all the industrial cities of the north, Chicago had been devastated by the Depression, and its poorer sections had that quality of desolation which was indistinguishable from Glasgow,

Frankfurt or any of the other stricken cities of the Western world. In industrial wastelands, tin cans of soup and mulligan stew endlessly boiled beside packing-box homes, just as they had in the IWW workers' Camp Stand back in Nevada. Daily the soup kitchens fed endless lines of shuffling, unshaven men, and daily the same men wandered the windy, broken streets, seeking employment.

In this desolation Chicago was matched by most of the industrial cities of the north, but there was another aspect in which it was a clear leader, and that was the extent of its gangsterdom and civic corruption. One of the first results of Prohibition had been a massive increase in the consumption of alcohol. A second and more serious consequence had been the emergence of the bootlegger and the gangster, and the centralizing of power in a small number of these men. One such was Al "Scarface" Capone who, shielded for years by corrupt policemen, judges and politicians, had by the late 1920s come to dominate the town.

In 1930 local businessman Frank Knox, alarmed at the increasing power of Capone and his mobsters, had raised a fund of seventy-five thousand dollars and had formed a committee, "The Secret Six," to challenge Capone's authority. More important, Knox led a delegation to Washington to seek federal help in securing Capone's downfall. The appointment, by a 191,000 majority, of Mayor Cermak to supplant "Big Bill" Thompson further weakened Capone's position. Cermak had, however, agreed to honor Thompson's commitment to Flanagan and his Trans-Americans. Indeed, he was glad to do so, for the arrival of Flanagan's Trans-Americans was a ray of sunshine after the bleak winter of 1931. Commentators predicted that the streets of Chicago would be thick with crowds to greet the runners and Soldier Field stadium was packed to capacity when the first competitors arrived at just after 6 P.M. that evening.

The first stage to Chicago was a deliberately easy one for Juan Martinez, who finally finished in fifty-fourth position, the stage being won by "Digger" Mullins, with Doc, McPhail and Dasriaux close behind, and Capaldi well placed in twelfth position. A temporary camp was set up in a rocky field by the roadside, just north of Plainfield, and the runners given three hours' rest before the final twenty-seven-mile stage into Chicago.

Martinez felt tired even before Willard Clay fired the gun that sent nine hundred and seventy-one runners on their way toward Soldier Field stadium at 3 P.M. that afternoon in bright spring sunshine. For the first fifteen miles, covered in two hours and fifteen minutes, Martinez stayed in the center of the leading pack of twenty-odd runners, noting that Capaldi was always among the leaders.

Even in the first half of the stage Martinez ached from ankle to hip, his legs feeling leaden and sore, his high, prancing action pruned to a low clipped movement. But he gained heart as runner after runner dropped away, leaving at twenty miles a knot of six runners—himself, Capaldi, Mullins, Dasriaux, Bouin and Eskola. They moved through the industrial suburbs of Chicago, the murky, gray Illinois and Michigan canal on their right. Ahead of them, the Maxwell House Coffee Pot blared the inevitable "Whiffenpoof Song" while Flanagan or Willard Clay informed the growing crowds of the race positions from the Trans-America bus. Behind the runners, ignoring the police, cars threw up clouds of dust and heavy carbon monoxide fumes. The leaders gradually moved into the final three miles toward Lake Michigan, near whose shores Soldier Field stood.

With two miles to go, Capaldi and Martinez had shrugged off their four companions, who now ran in Indian file, forty yards or more apart, behind the two leaders.

Capaldi seemed tireless. He was a stocky, crablike runner, his swarthy legs beating a constant rhythm on the soft surface of the road. For once the wind of Chicago was a relief, and fortunately it was behind them.

Juan glued his eyes to Capaldi's sweating back, a technique Doc had taught him back in Nebraska. He dreaded the moment when he might no longer be able to preserve that visual thread that bound the American to him, like some spider clinging to its web.

As a small boy he had experienced the extraction of a tooth, without painkiller, at a free dental clinic. He had never forgotten the blinding sharpness of that moment; it was as if some insistent drummer were pounding on a drum called Pain, gaining strength with each strike. Thus it was now, and Juan ran locked in agony.

The stadium at last came into view, at the end of the long avenue, and together they ran oblivious to the crowds pushing against the chain of beefy policemen posted there to restrain them from spilling out onto the roadway. No contrast could have been

greater: the hairy, squat Italian-American and the wraithlike Mexican; Capaldi expelling his breath in deep grunts and Martinez
an octave higher in what was almost a sigh. Capaldi's eyes were
set under bushy, black eyebrows and his thin moustache dripped
sweat onto lips flecked with foam. In contrast, Martinez's eyes
stood out in his head as if he were straining to catch sight of a
stadium miles in the distance.

Only half a mile to go. Then suddenly, like a ship slipped off
its moorings, Juan Martinez was free. Capaldi was spent, and
although Martinez did not dare look back he could sense that the
American had broken and had dropped to a trot. The knowledge
gave him added strength and unconsciously he increased his leg
speed, leaving Capaldi even further adrift. The following cars and
motorcycles cruising slowly on his right honked in response to
his efforts, and he continued to pile on the pace, his breath issuing
from him in small rhythmic screams. But Juan Martinez, running
in a closed world of accepted pain, could not hear them. Nor
could he hear his brother's shout from the crowd on his left as
he came within two hundred yards of Soldier Field, with Capaldi
grunting over a hundred yards behind.

On his right, a black Ford limousine which had tracked him for
over three miles drew slowly in line with the little Mexican. The
driver's window descended revealing the swarthy unshaven face
of Frank Nitti, a spent cigar was thrown out, to land just in front
of the unheeding Martinez. Then, abruptly, the car swung in hard
to the left, its rear fender hitting Martinez with a sickening thud
on the right thigh. Somewhere in the crowd a woman screamed—
the last sound which Juan Martinez heard as he fell helplessly to
the pavement, his head landing with an audible crack on its hard
surface. As crowds burst through the police cordon to surround
the stricken Mexican, the limousine reversed, turned and accelerated
back the way it had come.

A few seconds behind, Capaldi, only dimly aware of what had
occurred, chugged past into Soldier Field entrance. Five minutes
elapsed before Doc and his following group heard the blare of
sirens as they approached the scene and knew from voices in the
crowd only that Martinez had somehow fallen.

Ten minutes later Doc, Mullins, Morgan and McPhail ran four
laps around the packed stadium to the roar of fifty thousand
excited Chicagoans, as Capaldi, standing on a podium, wreathed

in flowers and wearing a crown of laurel leaves, waved to the crowd. As Doc approached the finish line in third position, followed some fifty yards behind by Mullins and Morgan, with McPhail fading a hundred yards behind them, he caught sight of Flanagan. The Irishman sat on a bench on the home stretch, behind the podium, dressed in his immaculate Tom Mix costume and surrounded by flouncing majorettes. His elbows were on his knees, his face cupped deep in his hands.

It was common gossip in Washington that every week President Hoover would hold a "medicine balls" cabinet, an exercise session with the leading members of his government. Each time, as the session began, President Hoover would say, "Gentlemen, have you got that fellow Capone yet?" Fifteen minutes later, facing the red, perspiring members of his cabinet, he would stop. "Remember," he would say, "I want that man in jail."

It was easier said than done, but Treasury Agent Pat O'Rourke was sent to work on the weakest aspect of Capone's kingdom—his tax affairs. The first to be caught was the gangster's brother, Ralph "Bottles" Capone, whose only previous indictment had been for scaring a horse. "Bottles" got three years in the state penitentiary and a ten-thousand-dollar fine.

Capone himself was to take longer. However, by the time the Trans-America hit Chicago, on May 23, plans for his downfall were well in hand, and his indictment less than a month away.

Doc Cole and Ernest Bullard approached Flanagan's darkened trailer and knocked uncertainly on the door. It was a few moments before a light came on and Flanagan released the door lock. The two visitors blinked in the bright light as Flanagan took a large white handkerchief from his pocket and loudly blew his nose. They could see that he was red-eyed, though he turned quickly from them to pick up an almost empty whiskey bottle.

"Drink?" he asked gruffly.

They both shook their heads and sat down slowly.

"Hope you don't mind if I do," he said, pouring out the last of the bottle into a large glass before dropping it into the wastebasket beside his desk. He sat down on his rocking chair, then sniffed again.

"I've got one helluva cold," he explained. "One helluva cold."

He sat back, fingering his glass. "And it's been one godawful day," he added grumpily.

"Yes," said Doc. "It's sure been that."

Bullard spoke first. "The press boys have come up with some money for Martinez's next of kin. It isn't much—eight hundred and forty-seven dollars." He placed a crumpled brown envelope on the desk.

Flanagan summoned a smile. "Thanks. I'll see that they get it." He sat back in his chair. "Poor little guy. All this way, to be taken out by those animals."

"We think we know who did it," said Doc.

"Who?" asked Flanagan, sitting up.

"Two of Capone's boys," answered Doc. "Names of Nitti and Guzik. They had a couple of thousand dollars on Capaldi, at good odds, and Martinez got in their way. That's my guess."

Flanagan shook his head. "Two thousand lousy bucks. I would have given them the money." He paused. "Do you think Capone had anything to do with it?"

"Most unlikely," answered Bullard. "He's up to his neck in his own problems at the moment. In fact, Martinez's death is probably an embarrassment to him. No, I've talked to some of the betting fraternity; Guzik and Nitti were just doing a little work on their own behalf."

"So what do we do about it?" asked Flanagan. "Keep on the move to New York and just forget it ever happened?"

"I know it sounds callous," said Doc. "But we won't do Juan any good by folding up now. Even from a practical point of view, if my group ends up in the money Martinez's relatives will still get their cut, just as if he were alive. If we stop now, his family and his village both lose out."

Flanagan picked up his glass, saw that it was empty, and placed it back on the desk at his side. For a moment he rocked back and forth in his chair, head down, without speaking. Then he looked up at both men.

"It's just that I feel so . . . so goddam useless. After all, it was me who brought Martinez all the way from Mexico. And tomorrow we bury him in some unknown grave. So help me, I've got to do something or I'll burst."

"Cole's right," said Bullard firmly. "We know how you feel, Flanagan, but it would serve no real purpose to fold up now."

"Okay," said Flanagan thoughtfully. "So we go on to New York. But what do we do about the bastards who killed him?"

"Now that's where I come in," said Doc. "You see, I have this lady friend . . ."

At 11 A.M. on the morning of May 24, 1931, nine hundred and seventy-one Trans-Americans, the entire body of Flanagan's staff and the majority of the attendant press corps stood at Juan Martinez's grave in the light drizzle of Chicago's Oak Park Cemetery. To many of the Trans-Americans the scene was unreal. For two months the little Mexican had skipped across the dirt roads of America, through the Mojave, over the Rockies, across the flat, dry plains of Kansas, seemingly indestructible. To many there it seemed inconceivable that he would not be with them again at the starting line at three o'clock that afternoon.

Flanagan, head bowed, black armbands on his light summer suit, sprinkled moist earth into the grave, to be followed by Doc, Hugh and a score of other runners who had known the little Mexican well. Soon the gravediggers were at their task, scooping soil onto the brown casket below.

Flanagan looked up and turned to Morgan at his side. He glanced at his wristwatch.

"Five minutes past eleven," he said. "About four hours to go." He beckoned to Doc to join him. "But first," he said, his voice hardening, "we have a little business with a certain Mr. Capone."

Al "Scarface" Capone had always claimed that he received his scar as a machine-gunner in World War I. The true story was less to his credit: he had got himself cut during a brawl over a whore at a Brooklyn dance hall.

The Martinez affair had indeed come at a bad time for him, for the taxmen were closing in. It was ironic: ten years of bootleg booze, torturings and killings without a single conviction, and now he was about to be tied up by a load of pen-pushing tax inspectors.

Capone himself was a bundle of contradictions. He was an excellent man-manager, but like many men who come up the hard way he possessed a narrow view of money. Even a few years back, in 1924, when the tax inspectors had first zeroed in on him, he could have easily bought his way out legitimately for a relatively small sum. The dollars had poured in faster than he could count them and were stashed away in safety deposit boxes all over Illinois; but in his view what was his was his, and the opportunity to go legitimate had passed, never to return. Now O'Rourke had penetrated his organization, and Capone knew he was only weeks away from an indictment.

And those knuckleheads Nitti and Guzik! The Trans-America's arrival in Chicago was big news, and two minor hit men had managed to put the spotlight on the Capone organization, all for a few thousand bucks.

Capone sat back in his black leather chair in his suite in "Camp Capone," the Lexington Hotel, and prodded at his front teeth with a soft, medicated toothpick. He picked up the morning newspaper, which headlined Martinez's death, scanned it, then wearily replaced it on the desk in front of him. It was essential that he lower the temperature on the Trans-America tragedy. He had bigger fish to fry.

So the feds called him a bootlegger. Okay, so it was bootleg when it was on the trucks, but when your host at the country club offered it to you on a silver platter—hell, that was called hospitality. What had he done? He had supplied a legitimate demand. He called it business. They said he had violated the Prohibition laws. But who hadn't?

His reverie was broken by a knock at the door. Capone pressed the buzzer on his right.

Frank Nitti entered the room. He was wearing an expensive black pin-striped double-breasted suit which sat uneasily upon his squat muscular frame. Nitti was known within Capone's circle as "the enforcer." A ruthless killer, he had been employed as muscle for the Capone organization for the last two and a half years, following an undistinguished career as a prizefighter and speakeasy bouncer.

"Flanagan to see you, boss," he said apprehensively, his eyes on the thickly carpeted floor.

Capone beckoned in the Irish entrepreneur, who was followed by Mike Morgan, dressed in blue denims, a turtle-necked jersey and black leather jacket. They sat down in front of Capone's massive teak desk. For a moment even Flanagan was quiet, in awe of the most dangerous man in the United States; in contrast, Morgan showed no signs of concern.

Capone broke the silence first. "So what can I do for you, gentlemen?"

"You know what happened yesterday," said Flanagan. "It's all in the newspapers in front of you. One of my runners, Juan Martinez, was killed." The words poured quickly from him, uttered without any of his normal confidence.

"I'd heard. I've been following your boys since way back in Los Angeles," said Capone softly. "Real sorry to hear it. A bad business."

"We know who did it," Morgan interjected. "It was two of your boys—Nitti and Guzik."

Capone smiled, withdrew a cigar from his desk and beckoned Nitti to light it.

"You're a brave man to come here and say that, Mr.—?"

"Morgan."

"Mr. Morgan. Or a foolish one. I suppose you have proof?"

"You know we don't," said Flanagan, gripping the arms of his chair.

"So what exactly do you want me to do?"

The Irishman's voice grew stronger. "First, we want ten grand sent to Martinez's next of kin. We want it in cash, and we want it right now."

Capone puckered his plump cheeks and whistled.

"Ten G's. For something I didn't do, and you can't even prove. You got plenty of gall, Mr. Flanagan, I'll give you that."

Flanagan opened his briefcase and withdrew a crumpled piece of paper from it. He pushed it across the desk to Capone.

"Perhaps this might help you change your mind."

Capone picked up the paper and looked at it for a moment.

"How did you get hold of this?"

"That's none of your business," said Flanagan. "We've got plenty more, and it all goes straight to the Treasury in Washington unless you follow our terms."

"Your terms?" Capone's lips twisted in a scowl. "Flanagan, I just say the word and you guys end up in a marble ghetto."

"No," said Flanagan. "Any harm comes to us and two files of these documents are on their way to Secretary of the Treasury Mellon. When they do you'll be traveling down a corridor thirty years long."

Capone took the cigar from his mouth and threw it into the

wastepaper basket. He placed both of his soft, plump hands on the table in front of him and leaned forward.

"What guarantee do you give me that if I do what you want you still won't hand these papers to the Treasury?"

"You have my word," said Flanagan, simply.

"Your word? The word of some jumped-up Mick, with a load of clapped-out runners? What the hell do you think I am?"

"Well, that's all you've got," said Flanagan, reddening. "Take it or leave it."

Capone sat back in his chair and looked Flanagan squarely in the eye. Then he slowly opened the drawer of his desk and drew out ten crisp bundles of notes, counted them, and threw them across the table.

"There," he said. "Happy?"

"That's better," said Flanagan. "But we haven't quite finished yet."

"Well," said Capone, "what else do you want?"

"Just twenty minutes of your time."

Capone's face showed his perplexity.

"Our Mr. Morgan here wants ten minutes' time with each of your colleagues Nitti and Guzik," said Flanagan. "No guns, no knives; just fists."

Capone's plump face broke into a smile as he looked at Morgan, sitting impassively on Flanagan's left, then at Nitti, smiling behind him at the door.

He pressed a buzzer on the desk on his right and spoke into a speaker.

"Get Guzik in here." Turning back to Flanagan, he added, "I think your Mr. Morgan here may have taken on a little more than he can handle."

"We'll just have to see about that," answered Flanagan, gathering up the money into his attaché case and locking it firmly. He looked at his watch. "Let's say two o'clock, Mr. Capone, at Soldier Field, where we finished yesterday. And just you, Nitti and Guzik. No one else."

"You got my word," Capone said. "There'll be no one else. No need for it." His plump face creased into a smile.

Two hours later Capone's black Ford cruised into Soldier Field, driving through its black wrought-iron gates beyond the parking lot and on into the entrance to the track, located at the beginning of the home stretch. All around workmen were dismantling Trans-America banners or removing bottles and trash from the empty stands. The bare flagpoles stood gaunt in the cloudy afternoon sky, their ropes flapping sharply in the wind. Above them, white gulls wheeled and screamed, occasionally swooping to pick up a morsel of food left by spectators. The stadium was dead; all that had made it so alive the day before had gone.

Except the Trans-Americans. Like guards, they ringed the stadium perimeter, armed with baseball bats and fence posts. Capone's eyes narrowed as he noted their presence. The Ford stopped at the entrance to the track. Standing there, awaiting them, were Flanagan, Morgan, Packy Paterson and Lily.

Capone saw Lily Carson and his soft lips tightened.

There were no introductions or small talk. Flanagan simply beckoned Capone and his men to a side door leading to the area under the main stand. He knocked twice on the door, which was unbolted from the inside by a thin, grizzled old groundskeeper. He tipped his cap to Flanagan and looked at Capone.

"You got some business here?"

Flanagan answered for him. "Yes," he said. "Mr. Capone has some business here."

The Irishman ushered Capone, Nitti and Guzik into a gloomy corridor. Morgan and Paterson followed. Then he beckoned the old man to bolt the door and led the group along the stone-floored corridor, their feet echoing as they followed its curved path beneath the main stand. Finally, after walking some fifty yards, Flanagan stopped outside a door on the left and knocked twice. It was opened immediately, by Capaldi. The bronzed Italian-American gulped as he recognized the gangster.

"They didn't ought to have done it, Mr. Capone," he said, moving past him apprehensively. Capone did not answer, but together with his men entered the room, followed this time only by Morgan and Flanagan. Paterson and Capaldi remained guard outside.

In the center of the room stood a massive, sunken, tiled bath. Flanagan pointed to it then beckoned toward Jake Guzik. "Bath time," he said.

Guzik looked at Capone, who nodded. The hoodlum swallowed, loosened his tie, took off his gray jacket and placed it on a hook, then slowly released his cuff links and rolled up the sleeves of his blue silk shirt. Morgan's face was impassive. He took from his pocket a pair of black leather gloves and pulled them on. Then he pointed to the bath.

"In there," he said.

Guzik walked slowly down the steps onto the white-tiled surface of the bath, followed by Morgan.

"Let's leave them to it," said Flanagan to Capone and Nitti, ushering them from the room and closing the door behind him.

The five men stood uneasily in the silent, gloomy corridor outside the locker room. Flanagan was the first to break the silence, taking from an inside pocket two thick Havanas and offering one to Capone. As Capone took the cigar and Flanagan struck a match on the sole of his left shoe, there was a dull grunt from within the locker room: it sounded like Morgan. Capone smiled and bent to light his cigar. Packy Paterson glanced uneasily at Flanagan, who stood expressionless.

Then they heard a voice. It was Jake Guzik, screaming. The next clear sound was the scratching of fingernails on the inside of the door, followed by a body scraping down its side. There was a momentary whimper. Finally, silence.

The door opened and Morgan appeared, a trickle of blood seeping from his left nostril. He withdrew a handkerchief from the pocket of his denims and dabbed his nose.

"Looks like Mr. Guzik didn't want the full ten minutes," he said, pulling open the door to reveal Guzik face down on the locker-room floor, blood spilling from his nose and mouth.

"Didn't seem to like the bath too much either," said Flanagan.

Frank Nitti walked over to his fallen comrade and pulled him around onto his back. Guzik's face was a bloody mush. Nitti looked up desperately at his employer, then at Morgan.

"How'd he do this?" he said, turning to look around the room. "He got a club stashed somewhere?"

He continued to peer helplessly around the empty locker room, then finally his eyes went back to Capone. The older man was still sucking slowly on his cigar. As if making some inner decision, Capone suddenly tapped the ash of his cigar onto Guzik's shirt.

"It's your problem, Frank," he said. "You're a grown man. You got to take your licks."

Morgan looked at Frank Nitti and pulled on the top of his right glove as Flanagan pulled the door shut.

"Your turn," he said, as the door closed behind them.

When the Trans-Americans left Chicago, along with them went Lily Carson, while the documents she had supplied on Capone's finances were sent on to a safety deposit box in the Trans-America bank. In fact, for all the gangster's worries, the documents were superfluous; Treasury officials already had more than enough evidence to convict him. On June 5, 1931, he was indicted for tax evasion and on October 20 he was fined fifty thousand dollars with thirty thousand dollars in costs, and sent to prison for eleven years.

23

END OF THE ROAD

Kate Sheridan had read somewhere that the deepest love was unspoken. If that were so, she sometimes thought wryly, then she was having one hell of a love affair with Mike Morgan. Seven hours a day plodding two hundred places behind him on dirt roads, followed by a couple of hours each evening over a cup of coffee. And yet Kate felt both contented and secure as she stood beside Morgan in the cool of evening at the Maxwell House Coffee Pot on the road outside Florence, Ohio. They were both wearing gray sophomore sweatsuits, the gifts of Bloomington College.

"Twenty-one," she said, breaking the silence and putting down her cup.

"Twenty-one what?"

"Twenty-one more men to pass before New York."

"Don't think about it," said Morgan. "Just do your piece each day." He drained his cup and turned to the counter to have it refilled. "That's all I do—live a day at a time."

"You're beginning to sound like Doc," said Kate, smiling.

"Perhaps," said Morgan thoughtfully. "I'll admit, I've learned a lot from that old coot."

He picked up his fresh cup of coffee and looked out beyond the Trans-Americans standing in groups by the trailer. Below, in a field just off the road, the lights of the camp flickered. Then he saw Ernest Bullard approach them, determinedly making his way through the crowds of athletes.

Bullard nodded over Morgan's shoulder to the waitress at the hatch and smiled uneasily.

"I've got a confession to make," he said, turning to face his companions. A moment later he took his coffee from the hatch, paused, sipped it slowly, and sighed. "It's amazing," he went on. "All this way to find the best cup of coffee in the United States."

He looked directly at both of them.

"I won't flimflam you any longer," he said, taking out his Bureau card from his inside pocket, and opening it.

"FBI." He looked at Morgan. "I suppose you know why I'm here?"

Morgan nodded.

"Know what?" demanded Kate sharply, flushing.

Bullard gestured for his cup to be refilled. "I don't know what I would have done without this coffee," he said. He sipped his recharged cup and turned to face them.

"I know about Morgan," he said. Morgan made to speak, but Bullard silenced him, putting his finger to his lips.

"Have another cup of coffee," he said, smiling as he pushed their cups toward the colored waitress at the hatch of the Coffee Pot. "And don't start blaming Flanagan, either of you. I knew before that fight at Springfield. Just after St. Louis my people sent me this . . ." He fumbled in his inside pocket and withdrew from it a faded press clipping. He handed it to Morgan. "Some young free-lance photographer back in Pennsylvania got this picture of you in a warehouse way back in 1929."

"So what are you going to do?" asked Morgan sullenly, ignoring his coffee.

"For the immediate present, nothing," said Bullard. "You see, I've been keeping close tabs on you. I watched you handle yourself in St. Louis, in Springfield and then in Chicago. Back there in the booth you knew you were exposing yourself as a handy man with your mitts. It was the same in Chicago with Capone." He put down his cup and tipped back his hat. "But you never held back. You never hid. Most men—most guilty men—would have steered well clear on both occasions."

Bullard loosened his tie.

"No, as I said, I like your style. I've watched you both since Vegas. It's been an education." He replaced his empty cup on the hatch and shook his head as the waitress offered him yet another refill. Bullard sighed.

"One thing we're taught at the Bureau is never to let our feelings influence our decisions. Sort of like a doctor—you know what I mean? You start doing that in my line of work and you're on your way to getting killed." He smiled. "So I've got a job to do. And that places me in what you might call a predicament. If I go strictly by the book I should pull you in now."

Kate darted a fearful glance at Morgan, who remained impassive, waiting to hear what Bullard still had to say.

"But all the law isn't in the book. So let me put it to you straight. Do you give me your word that you won't abscond before New York?"

Morgan looked across at Kate, who nodded.

"You got it," they said simultaneously.

Bullard put out his hand to Morgan. "Fine. That way you'll pick up enough folding money to hire yourself some fancy lawyer to keep you out of a striped shirt. Leastways, that's how I hope it'll work out. For both of you."

"So what happens in New York?" asked Kate.

"The moment your man crosses that finishing line, he's mine," replied Bullard.

"And what happens if the Trans-America doesn't make New York?" asked Morgan.

Bullard looked him straight in the eye.

"Then neither do you," he said evenly.

It had been clear to Charles Flanagan, even before Springfield, that he would not be able to bring a thousand runners into New York, as he had hoped, for even the athletes who had survived the Mojave, the Rockies and the Great Plains were only mortal. Illness, injury and sheer fatigue had trimmed the Trans-America down to close to nine hundred runners even before Chicago.

By Maumee, Ohio, the Japanese runner, Son, in eleventh position, had succumbed to a throat infection and withdrawn, and soon after Elyria, the Italian Maffei, who had been closing in on the leaders, had to give in to crippling leg cramps. But the main volume of withdrawals were much farther down the field, in the area of certain failure, where seven hours a day at five miles an hour on hot roads was more difficult to bear.

At the top the position changed almost daily. Since St. Louis, Doc had steadily eroded McPhail's lead, but Capaldi always finished well up on each stage, and was within striking distance, in third position, by Chicago. Behind Capaldi, only an hour framed Morgan, Eskola, Bouin and Digger Mullins. Thurleigh, who had taken some days to recover from his St. Louis race against Silver Star, gained strength after Chicago, and now held tenth place, but was daily gaining on the leaders and edging toward the sixth position required by his London wager.

As the race had gained in popularity, so sponsors offered increasing numbers of stage prizes. These awards were often secured by runners who had no hope of winning the race but who were willing to exhaust themselves on a single stage in order to win a few hundred dollars, a car or a suite of furniture. No matter; as far as Flanagan was concerned these new names and faces added spice and variety to the Trans-America. And with Toffler at last off his back his troubles were melting away. The towns ahead looked likely to meet their obligations, and although the debts were still piling up there would be a modest profit once the race reached New York.

The Trans-America now moved directly east, toward Cleveland and Flanagan's final press conference.

Charles Flanagan looked down at the massed reporters in the audience in the Grand Metropolitan Hotel, Cleveland. Things had gone well. He had just learned that Fred Astaire had launched a dance in honor of Kate Sheridan called the "Sheridan Shuffle," while Irving Berlin had composed a ditty called the "Trans-American Rag." Neither work would make its way into the pantheon of American show business, but it was all good copy nevertheless. He checked his wristwatch: the first half hour of questions had presented no problems.

The race itself was now only four hundred miles from its conclusion, and should be gravy all the way. Already the request for places on the VIP platform at Madison Square Garden had exceeded the platform's capacity.

Flanagan had decided, on balance, against the races between midget jockeys on Shetland ponies. Better to finish with dignity.

After all, as he reminded himself, the Trans-America wasn't marathon dancing or pole-squatting. And anyway, the race was boiling up to one hell of a finish.

Carl Liebnitz raised his arm and, catching Flanagan's eye, got to his feet.

"Some of my colleagues of the press corps have been wondering about Madame La Zonga and Fritz the talking mule," he said, keeping his voice deadpan. "We don't seem to have seen them since Springfield?"

"I'm glad you asked that question, Carl," said Flanagan. "Back in Springfield, General Honeycombe made me an offer for the circus. I talked it over with Madame La Zonga—"

"And Fritz?" said Liebnitz.

"And Fritz, and the rest of the staff," grinned Flanagan. "And they agreed to go with the General. Last thing I heard they were doing great business in Scranton, Pennsylvania."

The exchange went down well. Flanagan peered down into the audience, scanning it for further questions. As he did so, at the back of the conference room a buttoned bellboy in a pillbox hat entered with an envelope, and after whispering with some of the journalists in the back row, made his way to Carl Liebnitz, tapped him on the shoulder and handed him a white envelope. Liebnitz looked up, ripped it open, scanned its contents, and stood up frowning.

"Sorry, Flanagan," he said. "I'm afraid it's bad news." He paused and took off his glasses. "I have a telegram here which states that the Trans-America Bank has today closed its doors to its depositors. In short, the bank has gone broke."

There was an immediate uproar and journalists scrambled over each other to get to their telephones, leaving Carl Liebnitz standing at the back of the room, the telegram hanging limply from his fingers.

Flanagan slumped back in his chair, face flushed, a lump in his throat.

"Conference over," he said gruffly, banging his hammer on the desk.

The next morning nine hundred and sixty-one Trans-Americans, Flanagan's road gang and the catering staff silently faced Flanagan in the same conference room at the Grand Metropolitan Hotel.

Flanagan stood up, forced a thin smile, and drew his fingers through his graying hair.

"I guess you've all heard the bad news by now. Carl Liebnitz got the first telegram, but I have since had the position confirmed by Leonard Evans, the vice president of the Trans-America Bank. The long and short of it is that, at twelve A.M. yesterday the Trans-America Bank closed its doors for good and is now in the hands of the receivers. I have at this moment no idea why the bank has gone broke—banks are going to the wall every day—but that isn't our immediate concern. What it means to us, to you, is that your three-hundred-and-fifty-thousand-dollar prize money isn't there anymore. There's nothing in the pot."

The sun-blackened Texan Kane stood up. "Just what options have we got? What's our financial position?"

"I'll level with you," said Flanagan. "I might have seventy thousand dollars in the pot after all the salaries and bills are paid. We have nine days to New York, the cost of that is forty thousand dollars, maybe thirty thousand if I cut it fine. That could leave thirty to forty thousand dollars for prize money."

"But surely," said Doc, interrupting, "those are your profits?"

"*Were* my profits," replied Flanagan gloomily. "No, boys, it all goes into the pot. If I come out of this without ending up in the Tombs then I reckon I'm ahead."

There was spontaneous applause from the Trans-Americans. Then Eskola got to his feet. "We could end here; split up the seventy thousand dollars now."

"Impossible." It was Doc again, moving to the dais on which Flanagan and his staff were seated. He faced the Trans-Americans. "Back in Hays, Kansas, Flanagan and my group laid out over seven grand at long odds on our making it all the way to New York. Flanagan chipped in about the same. That was for the cooks. Those guys went out on a limb for us back there in Kansas when we were in trouble. We've got to stand by them now."

Eskola put up his hands in a placatory gesture as Doc sat down. "My apologies, Doc. I was not thinking clearly."

"What if Mr. Flanagan went ahead to look for a new sponsor, while we keep racing?" It was the Frenchman, Bouin.

Flanagan shook his head. "Time," he said. "There's no way I can see me picking up that sort of money in a week."

Willard had meanwhile entered the room, and now placed a

sheaf of telegrams on the table, at the same time whispering in his employer's ear.

Flanagan smiled. "Looks like some good news for a change." He picked up a telegram. "From the IWW union boys back in Vegas. They're sending us five hundred clams." He picked up another. "Doug Fairbanks is sending a grand, and here's a wire from Levy in St. Louis—a grand." He picked up the sheaf of telegrams.

"What's the total we've got here?"

Willard scribbled on a pad in front of him and grinned.

"Twelve grand, I reckon. We even got a grand from those Scotsmen back in McPhee. Who says the Scots are tight?"

"Great," said Flanagan. "But still a long way from what we need."

Doc stood up again.

"Look, Flanagan, every man here is committed to finishing this race. Hell, we didn't come all this way just to end up in Cleveland. That much is certain. All you have to do is to feed and house us till we hit New York. If it comes to the worst we'll run for nothing."

There was a rumble of agreement.

"Wait a minute," said Flanagan, hands on his forehead. "See how this strikes you. Say we keep forty grand out of the total, just to get us to New York. That leaves us with around forty grand, with maybe more to come . . ." Flanagan closed his eyes.

"I'm getting it," he shouted. "It's coming through." At his side, Willard put his fingers to his lips, and the Trans-Americans became silent, as if attending a seance.

Flanagan's eyes opened, and he clenched both fists, knuckles down on the desk in front of him. "So we keep our forty grand safe, so we can get to New York, come what may. What's left is either prize money or . . ."

"Or what?" said Doc.

Flanagan smiled.

"Gambling money. We take a chance, like we did in McPhee, in St. Louis, in Springfield . . ."

"Like we been doing since Los Angeles," came a voice from the floor.

Flanagan nodded.

"Like we've been doing all the goddam way." He paused. "I know for certain there are some fancy hustlers here in Cleveland."

"Hustlers?" shouted Bouin.

"Gamblers. Poker. Dice," explained Flanagan. "So let's say I take the forty grand and put it in the pot . . ."

"You want to play cards with our money?" said Eskola. "*Cards*?"

"It's a chance," said Flanagan. "One that might be worth taking."

McGregor, the head cook, stood up.

"I know it's none of my business, but I saw Mr. Flanagan pick up seven G's in Las Vegas, on a five-hundred-dollar stake. He's good. He's a humdinger."

There was a flurry of discussion in some half-dozen different languages. Willard banged the gavel. "Order, gentlemen!" he shouted.

Doc stood at the base of the dais. "I'm in second place, and all of my group is in the first dozen, so I reckon I've got as much of a stake as anybody if all of us end up in the cellar. Forty thousand dollars split between the top runners—that's chicken feed compared to what we ran for at the start. Let's look at this carefully. First, we put the forty grand on ice. That can't be touched, and that means we get to New York. Then we allow Flanagan to play with the rest of the money. Hell, it's been a gamble from the beginning. Flanagan gambled on getting us to L.A., we all gambled when we came here, we've gambled one way or the other every single day since. Well, here's just one more gamble—the final one."

There was no need to put it to a vote. That night Flanagan made his way to the Biltmore Hotel with forty-two thousand five hundred dollars burning a hole in his pocket.

He entered the elevator and pressed the button for the basement. A few seconds later he stood before a heavy steel door marked "boiler room." He knocked and a hatch opened, revealing a pair of black bushy eyebrows and a bulbous nose.

"I'm Flanagan."

The eyes looked at him unblinkingly.

"This is a private game," said the nose eventually. Flanagan reached into his pocket and withdrew a thin wad of hundred-dollar bills. "How much to make it less private?"

The eyes looked down at the clip of bills which Flanagan was holding.

"What you got there," came the reply.

The next moment the door opened, and Flanagan entered.

9 A.M., June 3, the Grand Metropolitan Hotel, Cleveland, Ohio. Flanagan entered the conference room with a smile on his face and stepped onto the platform to face his Trans-Americans. He was impeccably dressed in a black-vested pin-striped suit and black patent-leather shoes. Before him stood the Trans-Americans and his staff and a sprinkling of reporters, including Liebnitz, who had got wind of what was in the air. This time there was no need for Flanagan to call for silence. The room was still.

"One hundred and fifty grand in the pot—all our stake," said Flanagan, his hands on the table in front of him. "Five card stud. Just me and Easy Eddy Arnold left in. A good player, but I'd played him in Vegas. A bluffer."

The silence was almost palpable.

"Easy Eddy has to fill in a run in diamonds." Flanagan drew in a deep breath. "I have a full house—aces and kings."

Capaldi was the first to speak.

"For God's sake tell us, Flanagan. Did the man fill in his run?"

"Yes," said Flanagan, dropping his head into his hands.

Willard Clay looked around him and shook his head. He sat at a table in the gloom of Gargan's speakeasy, Cleveland, along with Doc and his group and surrounded by other Trans-Americans. If he had visited any one of the ten speakeasies within walking distance of Gargan's he would have witnessed the same scene: men who had not let alcohol pass their lips since Los Angeles now in various stages of inebriation.

"I sure hope these guys can take it," he said, looking around him as he drained his glass. " 'Cause we hit the road again, eight A.M. tomorrow, rain, hail or snow, money or no money."

"They can handle it," replied Doc. "We can all handle it." Around the table sat his team—Thurleigh, McPhail and Morgan— along with Packy Paterson, Stevie, Kate, Dixie and Lily.

"Where's Flanagan?" Morgan asked.

"Haven't seen hide nor hair of him since morning," said Willard. "He took off right after he spoke to you guys. Just got into a taxi and vanished."

"He shouldn't take it too bad," said Doc. "Nothing he could have done. In his place I'd've done the same. A full house of aces and kings against someone trying to fill in a straight? He can't be blamed. Anyhow, he's kept this whole damn shebang on the road since Los Angeles. None of the boys blames Flanagan."

"So what are you going to do?" said Willard.

"Keep running," replied Doc. "That's what we came here to do." The others nodded agreement.

"Have you any idea of the number of people who have stopped us in the street today, telling us to keep going?" asked Doc.

"That's right," said Hugh. "People I don't even know. One pushed twenty dollars into my hand."

"One old guy stopped me in the street, gave me his running shoes. Said he had run a marathon back in 1912. That must have been about your time, Doc," said Morgan, smiling.

"Amazing how many marathon runners we seem to meet," continued Hugh. "Never heard of most of them. Jesus, it must be the American Dream to run a marathon. No, there's no doubt the man in the street wants us to keep going. For one thing, he wants to know who's the best man—"

"Or woman," interposed Kate. "A crowd of ladies from the Daughters of the American Revolution turned up at the hotel today, after we'd finished our meeting, and offered me food and accommodations all the way to New York." She turned to face Willard. "How much have you got left in the kitty?"

"Four thousand, three hundred and twenty-eight bucks in stage prizes, bets, et cetera. At least a grand of that will go back to Juan Martinez's folks. The rest of it we split up among ourselves, in New York."

"If I manage to make the first two hundred places into New York—and the *Woman's Home Journal* stay with their offer—then put that in the kitty, too. I reckon you guys have kept me in the frame since back before Vegas," said Kate.

Doc raised his glass, smiling sentimentally. "Here's to you, Kate. You're a lady. Where do you stand now?"

"Two hundred and twenty-first," interjected Willard. "Twenty-one runners to beat. You dropped a few places."

"But the big question is how many runners will stay in."

"We still have stage prizes left, don't we?" asked Dixie.

"Yes," said Willard. "About four thousand dollars' worth. That might keep a fair number in, especially those in the front group."

"Then the *Journal* will probably stay with me," said Kate.

"Whatever happens, we should all come up smelling like roses," said Doc. "How many of us haven't had offers of work or endorsements for products?"

"I've been asked to lecture at colleges and women's clubs all over the country," said Kate. "*Me*? I never gave a lecture in my life."

"You'll have no problem," said Doc. "You've been giving press conferences since Morgan bopped you way back in the Mojave. You've learned to stand on your feet. We all have. Of course it's a shame that we're not going to be able to finish off in real style, with the pot of gold at the end of the rainbow, but if it hadn't been for the Trans-America I'd still be serving milkshakes at five bucks a week." He squeezed Lily. "I reckon we've all come out of this in good shape. I certainly know *I* have."

He raised his glass.

"So, ladies and gentlemen, let me give you a toast. To Charles C. Flanagan, wherever he is."

For "Packy" Paterson the Trans-America had proved to be a new lease on life. He had not fully understood the implications of Morgan's offer to join the race back in Springfield but he had immediately accepted: to become, in effect, the "manager" of Doc's group, dealing with mail, laundry, massages and any details which might detract from the runners' concentration on their daily fifty-mile stints. In return, he was given an equal share of any winnings which Doc's group might accrue by New York.

Packy soon teamed up with Hugh McPhail's friend Stevie and, free of the physical demands of boxing, the veteran boxer soon learned the delights of the Scottish "half and half," which had felled Flanagan back at the McPhee Highland Games. Their friendship was perhaps not surprising. They had both lived through hard times in bleak places, the Scot in the depths of a Glasgow tenement, the American in New York's Hell's Kitchen. Together they made a formidably effective management team, the hulking boxer and the quick-witted, bandy-legged little Scot.

For Stevie, the rural sections of the United States, the vast wheat plains of Kansas and Nebraska, had been a revelation; but the industrial north was simply Depression Glasgow all over again. True, the faces were Polish, German and Negro, but they bore the same hopeless expressions that had haunted the "broo park." He could not escape from them—gaunt unshaven faces in the rear of excited crowds lining the streets as the Trans-Americans plodded through town after town toward New York.

His journalistic work with McLeod of the *Glasgow Citizen* was far from onerous; just to winnow out the human stories of the Trans-America in order to give color and depth to McLeod's formal reports. By Springfield Stevie was offering his pieces to McLeod with confidence and by Elyria he was submitting whole reports to the *Citizen* under the journalist's by-line. Like Hugh McPhail, he knew that there was no going back. You returned only to soil that would allow you to grow, and he owed no loyalty to Glasgow. True, times were hard in America too, but here there was room to breathe; and if he could not survive in America, he reasoned, he had no right to survive at all.

The immediate concern of the Scot and the American was, however, the location of Charles C. Flanagan, about whom nothing had been heard since Cleveland. Willard Clay, absorbed with the problem of setting the Trans-America on its way again, had asked Carl Liebnitz and the unlikely pair to find Flanagan.

Flanagan was not found, however, until three days after Cleveland, on the morning of June 6, when he was discovered face down, clad only in trousers and a woman's dressing gown, in a hotel bedroom in Akron, Ohio. Alongside him in the double bed were a trumpet and two German Shepherd dogs.

"Wake up, you dumb Mick," shouted Carl Liebnitz, pulling him onto his back. Packy Paterson slowly poured a pitcher of cold water over the recumbent figure, while the third member of the rescue party, Stevie McFarlane, pulled back the curtains.

Flanagan hardly twitched as the icy water splashed over his face.

"Aces on kings," he mumbled. "Aces on kings."

Liebnitz looked helplessly at his two fellow searchers.

Stevie took the initiative. "Just you go get some hot black coffee, Packy, lots of it, and plenty of ice."

Packy stumbled off downstairs, to return a few minutes later with a steaming jug of coffee and a box of ice cubes.

"You want I should give him the coffee now?" asked Packy, standing menacingly over Flanagan.

"Not yet," said Stevie. "Put the coffee and ice down there." He pointed to the bedside table. "And get those blasted dogs out of here."

Packy led the growling German Shepherds from the room.

Liebnitz sat down on the side of the bed and took off his jacket and tie.

"God, it stinks in here," he said. "Open that window, for God's sake, somebody." He bent close to Flanagan and grimaced.

"Give me the ice," said Stevie. "And bear with me a wee moment. I've never tried this before, but I've heard it works a treat. It's called the 'collision of opposites' method. When I say 'now,' I want you to pour the coffee down his trap. You got it?"

Packy nodded while Liebnitz propped the limp figure up against the headboard of the bed.

Stevie gingerly unbuttoned Flanagan's trousers and pulled out the elastic of his underpants. Flanagan's eyes did not even flicker. Then Stevie picked up a handful of ice cubes and rammed them down into Flanagan's groin.

"Now!" he shouted.

Packy pulled open Flanagan's lower lip like a drawer and poured down the hot coffee.

The effect was immediate. Flanagan sat bolt upright, his eyes staring, spraying coffee over them all.

"Mother of God!" He leaped to his feet, jumped off the bed and ran around the room, spraying out ice cubes as he ran.

Liebnitz smiled at Stevie.

"Looks as if your collision theory works," he said. "At that speed Flanagan could have beaten Silver Star on his own. I think we can all have coffee now. But this time without the ice."

Half an hour later a gray, shaven, sober Charles C. Flanagan sat in Jake's Diner, Akron, on a stool alongside Liebnitz, Stevie and Paterson.

"It was one of the boys from Morgan's old union who found you and got back to us," said Liebnitz. "He said you were doing some sort of Rudy Vallee impersonation in the speakeasy last night. That didn't go down too badly, but when you said Caruso couldn't hold a candle to Count John McCormack you got into a fight with some Italians and the barman threw you all out."

"That was the last I can remember," said Flanagan, rubbing his jaw. "Still, I think I dished out a few punches."

"Took a few too, by the looks of you," said Packy.

Flanagan gulped down his coffee and shook his head. "Why didn't you just let me be?" he said. "I've had it. I'll pick up the race outside New York."

"The race?" said Liebnitz. "The race is no problem. The boys are still pounding out the miles like there was still three hundred and fifty grand at the end of the road, and your man Willard is Mr. Efficiency as usual. It's all going like clockwork."

"Then what are you doing here?" asked Flanagan.

"Because I've got you an offer," said Liebnitz. "So just prick up your Irish ears."

Flanagan nodded blearily as a waitress served him his tenth cup of coffee.

"Transcontinental Airlines' new boss is one Clarence C. Ross. He only took over a couple of weeks ago. After Cleveland, I wired him about the Trans-America, to see if he could rustle up some loot from some of his New York banker buddies. He refused point-blank."

"And you three came all this way to tell me that?" muttered Flanagan morosely.

"Let me finish," said Liebnitz. "As I said, he refused point-blank. No, he said, I won't go to my banking associates, not on any account. I'll put the money up *myself*. Transcontinental will sponsor the race."

"God almighty!"

Flanagan sat up and coughed, again spraying coffee over Packy and Stevie.

"But on one condition," said Liebnitz, taking out his handkerchief to dab his spattered jacket.

"I thought there'd be a catch."

"No, listen, it's not all that bad. You see, Clarence Ross is marathon mad; has been ever since the 1908 Olympics. He even tried running in one himself at Boston but ended up with *rigor mortis* at twenty miles. He thinks marathon runners are the greatest thing since the vertical man."

Flanagan grimaced. "So what does he want us to do? Roller-skate into New York?"

"No. He wants us to put up the three hundred and fifty grand for a standard marathon into New York, the full classic twenty-six miles three hundred and eighty-five yards. So the slate's wiped clean for the past three-thousand-odd miles. All the money goes on the marathon alone."

They could almost hear Flanagan's mind clicking into place.

"Why not?" he asked, smiling. "Why not? The way things are no one gets nothing. Sure, the guys in the lead coming into New

York have got a beef after running three thousand miles, but it's either that or nothing. We've got to go along with it."

Flanagan looked around at Packy and Stevie. He shook his head.

"Well," he said. "It's sure not working out the way I planned back in L.A."

"Has anything?" growled Liebnitz.

Flanagan grinned.

"Not much."

Edgar J. Hoover's flat, square face crinkled into a smile. "Finley, that son of a bitch Flanagan has done it again." He laid down his newspaper. "There he was, dead on his feet in Cleveland, his bank gone bust, all his prize money gone. Then he lost all the rest of his money in a card game. What a son of a bitch!"

Finley allowed himself a smile. "Bullard reported that he vanished into the boondocks on a three-day binge. Took them a coon's age to wake him up once they'd found him."

Hoover laughed. "Then he digs up three hundred and fifty G's from this marathon nut, Ross of Transcontinental, and presto! he's back on his feet again."

"With a bound he was free," offered Finley.

"Come again?" said Hoover.

"Nothing, Director," said Finley, taking his glasses off his nose and polishing them.

Hoover sat back in his chair and closed his eyes.

"Finley, it is my belief that the Trans-America is about as political as Mom's apple pie." He opened his eyes and leaned forward on his desk. "Does that coincide with your views?"

"Precisely, Director."

"Then call Agent Bullard. Tell him I want to see him. And also tell him right now that if he values his job to get me on that VIP platform when Flanagan's boys hit New York, and to arrange all necessary hotel accommodations. I want to be in on this at the finish."

The cable Peter Thurleigh sent to his London club was addressed to Lord Farne and the others with whom he had made his wager all those long months ago on his reaching the top six in the Trans-America. It read: "Trans-America race discontinued through lack of funds. Now only final marathon. Does wager stand? Suggest all money on marathon. Thurleigh."

He now had in his blazer pocket a crumpled reply from London, received only a day after his own had been sent. It read, "Wager now on marathon. Still top six. Run for your life."

It was with some pride that on June 17, 1931, Charles Ross sat in the Roosevelt Room in the newly built Empire State Building, alongside an immaculate Charles C. Flanagan and his retinue, facing the world's press.

Flanagan stood up to the whirring of cameras and explosion of flash bulbs.

"Let me first say," he said, "that it is with great gratitude that we have received the sponsorship of Transcontinental Airlines and its distinguished owner, Clarence C. Ross."

"Wouldn't 'relief' be a better word, Flanagan?" quipped a voice.

"Yes," said Flanagan, smiling. "But don't quote me on that."

Bill Campbell of the *Glasgow Herald* had risen to his feet and stood patiently until the laughter had subsided.

"I'd like to ask Mr. Ross a question, Mr. Flanagan," he said finally, in his rich Scots burr. "Many of my readers at home, observing that a Scot, Hugh McPhail, had a two-minute lead in the Trans-America before the final marathon stage was placed on the present 'winner take all' basis, will ask if the present competition is entirely fair to him."

Flanagan flashed an uneasy sideways glance at Ross, who was growling under his breath. "Perhaps," said Flanagan, "that question should be addressed directly to Hugh McPhail himself."

Hugh stood up.

"No," he said, "I don't feel badly about it. I came out here to cross America by foot, and it looks as if I've just about done that. Even to have led a group of runners of this class all that way is an honor as far as I'm concerned. Mr. Ross has put up money that otherwise wouldn't have been there, so I'm content to fight it out over the marathon on Saturday."

"I think that answers your question, Bill," said Flanagan.

"I'd like to ask why we're finishing the race in Central Park instead of Madison Square Garden or the Polo Grounds," said Liebnitz.

Charles Ross stood up. At forty-five he still had the lean, hard build of a long-distance athlete.

"May I answer that question, Mr. Flanagan?" he said. Flanagan nodded and Ross continued. "It was my treat to the citizens of New York. I felt that everyone should see these great athletes who have trekked all the way across the roads of America. I consulted first with Mayor Jimmy Walker, and we were in full agreement. This way, I reckon, well over three million citizens will view the final miles of the race; the greatest crowd for a marathon in the history of track and field."

There was scattered applause as Ross sat down.

Pollard of the *St. Louis Star* stood up.

"Flanagan, do you see any possibility of Kohlemainen's Olympic best of two hours, thirty-two minutes, thirty-five seconds being broken in the race?"

Flanagan stood, shaking his head. "How many miles did Kohlemainen run in 1920 before that record? My boys have covered more than three thousand miles. They won't be looking for any Olympic records on Saturday. Anyhow, no athlete ever does. Athletics is about beating other men, and with three hundred and fifty thousand dollars in the pot this is the richest race of all time. So if I were you I wouldn't wear out your pencils talking about records."

"Kevin Maguire, *Irish Times*. What celebrities are you expecting to be at the finish, Flanagan?"

Flanagan rose and picked up a sheet of paper. "You boys will get the full official list after this meeting, though we're still getting calls from all over the States. We have Governor Roosevelt, J. Edgar Hoover—who has, throughout, shown a personal interest in the race—Walter Reuther, Miss Tallulah Bankhead and Miss Helen Hayes. Douglas Fairbanks is flying in from Los Angeles, accompanied by Miss Mary Pickford, and the British, French and Finnish ambassadors are going to be in attendance." He lifted a telegram from the table. "And I've just received a telegram from the famous evangelist, Miss Alice Craig McAllister, to say that she'll be at the finish. Gentlemen, all the world's going to be in Central Park three days from now."

Albert Kowalski of the *Philadelphia Globe* rose to his feet.

"Lord Thurleigh, with about one hundred miles to go, when it became known that the race money was going to be decided by a marathon you were just half an hour and two places short of the sixth position required by your wager. Do you think that you could have picked up those vital—and might I say lucrative—thirty minutes?"

Peter Thurleigh rose, smiling. "Yes, it was possible. All I had to do was to pick up fifteen minutes on two consecutive days over one hundred miles. My wager has been changed, and now relates to Saturday's marathon." He smiled. "So, gentlemen, when that gun goes off on Saturday I'll be running for the money like everyone else in the race."

"Charles Rae, *Washington Post*. Flanagan, three hundred and fifty thousand dollars is one heck of a pot, right in the middle of the hardest times the United States has ever faced. Have you any means of ensuring that no cheating takes place? I mean, like drugs?"

"Could I answer that one, Flanagan?" It was Doc Cole, who stood up in the audience, his face serious.

"I know that journalists are by nature a pretty cynical bunch," he said. "But I'd like to say this. I would trust every man in this race with my last buck. For the last three months we haven't just run together and raced together—we've *lived* together. Tell me, who wants to lie to his buddies and lie to himself for the rest of his life? Say there was something a guy could take—and I wouldn't know what that could be—that would help him win this final marathon. What would he feel like, living with that lie, wondering whether or not he could have won on his own merits? No, I don't think the question will arise, gentlemen."

There was an awkward silence, but Rae stayed on his feet.

"I'm sorry to pursue this point," he said, looking down to scribble on a pad in his left hand, "but it is common knowledge that many of the Trans-America competitors have formed themselves into teams and will split any winnings they have picked up during the race. Now, I'm not suggesting that there is anything corrupt in this. Far from it. What I *am* asking is whether or not such agreements might result in teams shepherding their favored runners or individuals sacrificing themselves for the sake of another team member. This would surely diminish the Trans-America marathon as a race."

"A very good question," said Flanagan. "I have yesterday asked all Trans-Americans to nullify any financial team agreements which they may have made, or at least those relating to the final marathon stage on Saturday. Any sign of runners using destructive team tactics will result in immediate disqualification."

"That answers my question," said Rae, resuming his seat to murmurs of approval.

Albert Kowalski rose to take his place. "A question for Miss Sheridan, please. I believe that, by virtue of being in one hundred and ninety-eighth position at the end of the penultimate stage, she has now been offered the ten thousand dollars originally set by the *Woman's Home Journal*. Since she has not completed the full distance, does she intend to accept the prize?"

Kate Sheridan stood up, eyes flashing. "No, I don't. I was offered the prize for finishing within the first two hundred positions over the whole distance across America. It's my intention only to pick up the prize if I finish in the top two hundred in the marathon."

There was immediate applause.

"That's the spirit of the Trans-America," shouted Flanagan, as the applause subsided.

Carl Liebnitz got to his feet, looked around him at his colleagues, and addressed himself directly to Flanagan.

"Flanagan, it seems to me that this may be the last time we're all going to be together in one room: athletes, journalists, you, your staff. And when that last man comes in on Saturday it'll be sort of like a family breaking up. It certainly will be for me, anyway."

He took off his glasses, rubbed his thin, hawklike nose, and looked around him at his silent colleagues.

"I'm not a sentimental man, Flanagan. As you know, journalism isn't a sentimental profession. But we've come a long way together, all of us, across some of the toughest country God ever made. I'd like to say on behalf of all my colleagues that it was worth it, every long mile of it. We're glad you made it."

The press corps rose as one man, applauding and, for the first and only time, a blush suffused Charles Flanagan's lean face. He nodded sheepishly, shuffled with his papers and made his way from the dais as the press broke up.

As Morgan was leaving the conference room he was stopped from behind by a tap on the elbow. It was Ernest Bullard, his face grim.

"Just got a cable from my boss," he said. "They want me to close the case and hightail it back to headquarters after the race."

"And what about me?" asked Morgan.

"How do you mean?"

"The Bronx Bomber?"

"The Bronx Bomber?" laughed Bullard. "What the hell would a prizefighter be doing in a footrace?"

"You mean—?"

"I mean you're still in trouble," said Bullard. "If you don't run your heart out, all the way into Central Park." He jammed his hat onto his head. "And forget about the Bronx Bomber. I never even met him."

AMERICANA DATELINE FRIDAY JUNE 19, 1931

Had the Greeks failed to whip the Persians at Marathon in 490 B.C. then it is unlikely that three million New Yorkers would tomorrow be watching the richest footrace in history. Similarly, had, in 1908, an Italian waiter called Dorando Pietri been a good judge of pace and finished the London Olympic marathon without the assistance of officials, then the distance to be run tomorrow would not be the exact twenty-six miles three hundred and eighty-five yards that Charles Flanagan's Trans-Americans will attempt to cover.

However, the Greeks did defeat the Persians, setting Pheidippides on his epic run to Athens; and Dorando Pietri was no judge of pace, and as a direct result Clarence C. Ross of Transcontinental Airlines has put up over a quarter of a million dollars on tomorrow's footrace from Denville, New Jersey, to Central Park, New York.

Everyone and his uncle is now on the Trans-America bandwagon, and many a Hollywood agent is in trouble for failing to secure his client a place on the VIP platform in Central Park, but it was not always thus. There were many doubting Thomases, not least your correspondent, when Charles C. Flanagan first set his tattered crew on their way east from the Coliseum Stadium, Los Angeles, way back in March. That day many competitors failed to survive the first stage, indeed some did not get much farther than the Coliseum parking lot, and my perhaps oversensitive nostrils began to sense something rotten in the state of California.

Those of my readers who have shown sufficient endurance to stay with me since those early days will know that I was an early convert to the Trans-America, as were the American people. Floods, riots, defaulting towns, snowstorms—nothing has stopped the onward rush of Flanagan's men across the United States. When, one day, the full story of the Trans-America is written, it will read like something between Homer's *Odyssey* and *Huckleberry Finn*.

One of my first reservations about the Trans-America was that it was obscene that in the middle of the worst Depression in our history men should be footracing for such massive prizes. I humbly admit my error. The athlete represents man at the edge of his limits in an area which few men glimpse, let alone inhabit. We identify with the athlete because we feel this, sense that he is one of the privileged few who can go close to reaching his potential, while most of us spend our lives unaware that such a potential even exists.

Some idea of the nature of Flanagan's Trans-America may be given when I reveal that every one of his runners insisted on completing the whole distance to Denville, New Jersey, in order that they could claim to have run all the way from Los Angeles to New York. These men had come to run across the United States, and they would be satisfied with nothing less.

So, tomorrow, even when you are looking at some veteran chugging along in seven hundredth position with no hope of ending up in the money, remember that *he* is the privileged one. For he is one of a select band of men who have made their way on foot across America. He is a Trans-American. And that is in itself an accolade.

—CARL C. LIEBNITZ—

Tuesday, June 16, 1931

Denville, New Jersey (3120 miles)

			Hrs.	Mins.	Secs.
1 =	H. McPhail	(Great Britain)	520	01	02
2 =	A. Cole	(USA)	520	03	06
3 =	A. Capaldi	(USA)	521	45	28
4 =	P. Eskola	(Finland)	521	50	27
5 =	M. Morgan	(USA)	521	52	05
6 =	R. Mullins	(Australia)	521	58	01
7 =	J. Bouin	(France)	522	14	07
8 =	P. Brix	(USA)	522	28	21
9 =	P. Thurleigh	(Great Britain)	522	29	18
10 =	P. Dasriaux	(France)	522	38	40
11 =	A. O'Rourke	(Ireland)	522	39	27
12 =	R. Brady	(Ireland)	522	42	18
13 =	P. Komar	(Poland)	522	51	21
14 =	C. O'Connor	(Ireland)	522	58	07
15 =	K. Lundberg	(Sweden)	522	59	01
16 =	P. Flynn	(USA)	523	07	18
17 =	P. Coghlan	(New Zealand)	523	18	20
18 =	J. Schmidt	(Poland)	523	20	24
19 =	C. Charles	(Australia)	523	27	05
20 =	D. Quomawahu	(USA)	523	40	06

1st Lady: (198) K. Sheridan (USA) 624 01 09
Number of finishers: 862
Average speed (leader): 6 mins. per mile

24

MARATHON

Clarence Ross had not been alone in being affected by the London marathon of 1908, for the race had touched the hearts of the world. The marathon event was not, however, one of great athletic antiquity. The first Olympic marathon, in Athens in 1896, had been the creation of the Frenchman, Michel Bréal, inspired by the feat of one Pheidippides who in 490 B.C. ran to Athens from the Plains of Marathon with news of the victorious battle with the Persians.

That first Olympic marathon of twenty-four and three-quarter miles in Athens in 1896 had been run by twenty-five athletes, mostly Greeks, most of whom had never competed beyond a mile. Some failed to survive the dust and heat and withdrew early in the race while others fell prey to the hospitality of villages they encountered on the route. Just beyond the village of Karvate, with only a quarter of the race to go, the French fifteen-hundred-meter runner Lermusiaux was brought to a halt with crippling cramps, and was passed by an Australian, Flack. Behind Flack plodded a Greek shepherd, Spyros Louis, who had doggedly threaded his way through a fading field.

Back on the marble stands of the Averoff stadium the crowd of sixty thousand was ignorant of the progress of the race until the thirty-seventh kilometer when a Greek cavalryman riding a white charger galloped into the stadium to announce that Louis was in the lead. Then, a few minutes later, the distant boom of cannons marked the arrival of the first runner at the outskirts of Athens.

Sixty thousand pairs of eyes strained to identify the leader as he entered the stadium. It was number seventeen—Louis! Pandemonium broke out, and men and women wept openly as the little shepherd trotted wearily toward the finish, dwarfed by the lanky Prince George of Greece, who had leaped from the royal box to run with Louis over part of the last lap.

It was only some years after the Paris Olympics marathon of 1900 that the runners realized that they had even competed in an Olympics; nothing on the medals they received gave any such indication. However, the Frenchman, Michel Théato, had chugged through the cobbled streets of Paris to win an undistinguished race.

The 1904 St. Louis race turned out to be a mixture of drama and farce. The Cuban, Felix Carjaval, who had trotted across America after losing his stake money in a shipboard card game, turned up at the start dressed in boots, jacket and trousers. Only a pair of scissors wielded by some Irish-American throwers brought Carjaval's apparel close to the athletic. The Cuban trotted off into the steamy heat and the carbon-monoxide fumes toward the St. Louis World's Fair, the site of the 1904 Olympics, to finish fourth.

The American, Fred Lorz, had been forced to stop running at ten miles because of cramps. He took a lift in a passing truck, and nine miles later, when the truck broke down, he jumped out, trotted into the stadium and was assumed by the crowd to be the winner. The American did nothing to disillusion the spectators and even paused to have his photograph taken with the President's daughter, Alice Roosevelt. Ten minutes later, Hicks, the real leader, trudged into the arena and, when race marshals later reported back, all hell was let loose on the wretched Lorz.

But it was the next Olympic marathon, in 1908, that captured the imagination of the world. Up till then the marathon had been run over varying distances from twenty-four to twenty-six miles. In 1908, the distance was set at exactly twenty-six miles three hundred and eighty-five yards—from Windsor Castle to the newly built White City Stadium, Shepherd's Bush, London. Legend has it that the three hundred and eighty-five yards was added so that the finish could be opposite the royal box. More likely, the extra yardage was simply the distance from the entry to the stadium around the track to the finish.

By this time, most Olympic nations held formal trials for their marathon entrants, and 1908 was the first Olympics in which athletes were entered as national teams. Thus the runners who faced the starter on the road beside the royal lawn at Windsor were worlds away from the untrained optimists of the 1896 Games or the rabble of St. Louis. Dorando Pietri (Italy) had already run the equivalent of two hours forty minutes, the Indian Tewanima (USA) was renowned over shorter distances and his countryman, John Hayes, was an outstanding endurance athlete. Tom Longboat (Canada), whom the Americans unsuccessfully claimed to be a professional, was a brilliant distance runner and the Englishmen Price and Lord, products of the renowned English cross-country system, were hard and durable.

At the unsuitable time of 2:30 P.M. on a sweltering July day, fifty-six runners set off toward London. Price and Lord led an overfast opening ten miles, ahead of Hefferon (South Africa) and Dorando. Then Hefferon took the lead and by fifteen miles he had set up a three-hundred-yard lead over Lord and Dorando. By twenty miles, Hefferon had increased his lead over Dorando to over half a mile. Dorando had by now detached himself from Lord, who was himself under pressure from the American Hayes. However, Dorando started to gobble up the yards between himself and Hefferon, and just before they reached twenty-five miles he passed the South African and began the final run in toward Shepherd's Bush.

Unfortunately, the blistering heat and his effort to catch Hefferon had drained Dorando, and though he entered White City first, he faced the crowd at the entrance to the stadium rubber-legged, and groggy with fatigue. He turned in the wrong direction and collapsed onto the track. There were sympathetic shouts for officials to pick him up and set Dorando in the right direction. The officials, bewildered, duly lifted the little Italian to his feet and pointed him toward the back stretch. Four times more he dropped to the cinders, and each time he was lifted to his feet. He was finally half carried across the finish line.

The next man to enter the stadium was the American John

Hayes, who had throughout run a solid, well-paced race. American team leaders immediately submitted a protest on behalf of Hayes, which was just as soon sustained. Dorando was taken to the hospital, where he lay for days in a dangerous condition. However, the Italian's efforts were not completely in vain, as he was later, at the prompting of Sir Arthur Conan Doyle, presented with a cup by Queen Alexandra in recognition of his courage.

The Dorando marathon triggered off a professional marathon craze which was to suck Doc Cole and some of the world's best long-distance runners into a whirl of marathon races held over the years immediately preceding World War I. Alas, with no central international governing body, the marathon boom faded just before the time of the Great War, leaving great runners like Cole, Longboat and Shrubb stranded in a sporting limbo.

The future of marathon running lay in the rapidly developing amateur movement. But Clarence Ross, fired by the 1908 Games and by his own unsuccessful attempt in the 1909 Boston marathon, had little time for amateurs. Regularly, in his nationwide chain of country newspapers, he had denounced the follies of the AAU and the American Olympic Committee, to the bewilderment of farmers and housewives from Maine to Oregon, for whom these organizations had as much significance as Glasgow Rangers Football Club. Thus, when Carl Liebnitz had informed him that the Trans-America was up for grabs Ross needed little time to consider the position. His only proviso had been that sponsorship would only be for the magic twenty-six miles three hundred and eighty-five yards into Central Park and not for the full Trans-America distance. Ross wanted only one title, "Mr. Marathon"; Flanagan and his Trans-Americans were happy enough to give him that.

8 P.M. Friday, June 19, 1931. Alexander "Doc" Cole sat on the edge of his bed in the Cranston Hotel, Denville, New Jersey, sand-papering his feet. Like many of the others he had forsaken the camp, for this final marathon stage required isolation, special preparation.

He looked across at his bedside table, stacked high with bundles of letters tied with string: his Trans-America mail had just caught up with him. Eighty-three offers of marriage, many of them from ladies old enough to be his mother or young enough to be his daughter, some suggesting activities which would have been far beyond his capacity even in his youth. Fifty-one offers of employment, ranging from radio announcer through salesman to college track and field coach. Whatever happened, he would never again want for work.

All day long he had been besieged by journalists. Naturally they wanted a prediction. Was he afraid of McPhail? Morgan? Perhaps Eskola or Bouin? Cole was afraid of none of them. He knew that in the end all sport was a contest against yourself. If you beat yourself you could walk away tall, no matter where you finished.

And yet behind this philosophy, which he knew to be sound and true, Doc knew that above all he wanted to prove that he was indeed one of the greats, fit to be mentioned in the same breath as Nurmi and Kohlemainen. Like most men, his ego required not only the present but the future to be marked by his acts. As he gently rubbed his feet he could already see himself in Central Park, feel himself break the tape, hear his own interviews with press, film and radio. It would be the Big Hello, the payoff for all the years of running on forgotten roads.

He thought of the race ahead, a whole life to be compressed into just over two and a half hours. And yet it was no different from the races of his youth except that the ratios had changed. Then, ten hours' training for each one of competition had always been his guideline, and it had been a demanding one. His years in the wilderness had simply changed the mathematics, and now it had to be about a hundred to one, perhaps a thousand. It didn't bear thinking about.

Doc knew that he had run as many miles as any man in the race, and yet behind his thoughts lay that nagging doubt that plagues every athlete, whatever his abilities. He looked down at his legs. All the running, all the exercise, had not prevented that dry, crêpelike quality of the skin, that hint of a bubbly blue varicose vein on his right calf which he had for years tried to ignore.

He knew that there was only one strategy, to run evenly, aiming at just over six minutes a mile, peeling competitors off as he ran; for marathons offered no possibility for showy tactical bursts. And yet, no matter how evenly you ran, no matter what your experience, there was always the wall to be breached at twenty miles. At that point, his medical friends had told him, blood sugar started to run out and the body had to resort to other mechanisms. No matter how many marathons you had run, no matter how strong you were feeling, the wall was always there, waiting for you.

The wall. He felt a bitter taste in his mouth, a hollowness in the pit of his stomach. Doc finished off his feet, put the sandpaper on the small table beside his bed and lay back on the pillow for a moment, staring at the ceiling. Sometimes, he thought, ignorance was your best friend. Most of the men he would run with tomorrow knew nothing of the wall, and that ignorance might be their strength.

He looked down at his wristwatch: only 8:35 P.M. The nights before a race were always slow. He sat up and began to work again on his feet.

His concentration was broken by a knock at the door. Doc continued to sandpaper his feet without looking up.

"Come in," he shouted.

Morgan and McPhail entered and closed the door behind them. They stood sheepishly at the entrance.

"What the hell is this?" said Doc, beckoning them in. "A staring competition? Sit down, both of you."

They sat down on the edge of Doc's bed as he continued to rub away with the sandpaper.

"You guys worked on your feet yet?" he asked, still without looking up.

Neither man answered.

"C'mon," said Doc. "What's the matter with you two? The cat got your tongues?"

"We'd like to thank you," blurted out Hugh.

"Thank me? For what?" He fished out a bottle of olive oil from his bag on the floor. "We had ourselves a deal to share, to run as a team. Ross put the kibosh on that yesterday, and I can't say I blame him. He's putting up the dough, and for that sort of money he's entitled to his race into Central Park."

He poured some oil onto his left palm, rubbed both hands together and, lifting his left foot across his right knee, started to massage it.

"It was more than just a deal," said Morgan. "You know that."

"Banana oil!" grinned Doc, lifting his right foot across his left knee and starting a similar massage. "We all had ourselves a good time. We picked up a few bucks. We'll come out well, whatever happens. Me, I'm going to enjoy it. Hell, it's taken me thirty years to become an overnight success."

"So no hard feelings?" said Hugh.

"Hard feelings? No time for them. I got me a race on tomorrow. So have you. And there's going to be some fancy running. Don't forget this time we're up against real marathon specialists. Eskola, Bouin, Mullins, Dasriaux—they all ran at the Olympics in twenty-eight, and all inside two hours forty."

He stopped massaging his foot and looked up at them.

"Just what's got into you guys? Have you forgotten everything I taught you? You are pros. *Pros.* Tomorrow it's devil take the hindmost, dog eat dog. So if either of you aren't after my balls—and each other's—all the way into Central Park, then I'll be ashamed of you!"

Hugh looked across at Morgan.

"It's just we didn't want you to think we didn't owe you," said Morgan.

"Okay, so you owe me," said Doc. "Now stop owing me and get the hell out of here and work on your feet."

10 P.M. *Friday, June 19, 1931.* Hugh McPhail lay on his bed, face down in his pillow. He had left Morgan at the door of the bedroom which he and Kate Sheridan shared. Hugh could not understand Kate and Morgan being together the night before the marathon. It was contrary to all the tenets of the preparation, by which Scottish athletes had for over a century conditioned themselves for match races. Still, he thought, Morgan probably knew his own business best.

He had not seen Dixie since midday. All of his trainers in Scotland had been strict, indeed puritanical, about women before big races. They were always on about "vital bodily fluids" and such things. Even Stevie, now with Packy in a Denville speakeasy, had spoken at length in the same vein. So Hugh had left Dixie to her duties at the camp and had returned to his hotel for a massage and an early night. They would have plenty of time together after the race, win or lose.

For Stevie, roped in to administer the massage, it was like the old days back at the mine.

"Of course you like Doc," he had hissed. "I do. We all do. But tomorrow afternoon it's eyeballs out. He's quite right. No prisoners taken."

"You've been seeing too many Hollywood pictures," drawled Hugh sleepily.

"Think so? Then don't forget there's one hundred and fifty thousand dollars for the first runner past the post. Man, you could *buy* the Broo Park with that sort of money."

But Hugh did not need Stevie to excite him or harden his will. He could no more dull his competitive desires than he could change the color of his eyes. If Doc was the better man, then so be it. But Hugh had learned a lot in the three months of the Trans-America, much of it from Cole himself, and tomorrow he was going to put it to good use. If anyone else was going to get first to Central Park, he was going to have to do some hard running.

10:30 P.M. Friday, June 19, 1931. Mike Morgan and Kate Sheridan lay naked, parallel to each other on single beds, each covered by a cool white sheet. Above them a fan whirred, stirring the heavy air. They lay still, like statues, the sweat beading on their sun-blackened arms and faces. They had not touched each other since the press conference.

"I feel sick," she said.

"Me too," replied Morgan. "So does every guy back in camp. You're running for ten grand tomorrow. Me, I'm running for a hundred and fifty. We all feel sick. Me, I'd be worried if I didn't."

Kate closed her eyes.

"You know Clare Marsh, the reporter from the *Woman's Home Journal*? She's going to keep me posted every five miles on my position."

"You got a lot of men to beat," observed Morgan.

"Over eight hundred," said Kate.

"One thing," said Morgan.

"Yes?"

"Back in the Mojave, when I bopped you. I'm sorry."

Kate smiled. "You've taken a helluva long time to tell me."

"And another thing."

"Yes?"

"Tomorrow, when it's all over—you fancy being a mother to a boy of two?"

"That a proposal?"

"It's as close to one as I'm ever going to get," said Morgan, turning onto his face.

Kate Sheridan smiled and closed her eyes.

"Reckon I do," she said.

2:15 P.M. Saturday, June 20, 1931. It was a massive white clock face, close to eight feet in diameter, its hands already set at the starting time of 2:30 P.M. Willard Clay had arranged that it be mounted on the back of a Trans-America truck and for it to start the moment that the crack of Will Rogers' Winchester set them on their way. Thus all the leading runners could obtain an accurate account of their speed by checking the clock and relating it to the markers which Flanagan had arranged at one-mile intervals all the way into New York.

Ross had built temporary bleachers at the side of the fields on the road east of Denville, accommodating over two thousand spectators on each side of the road from the start to a hundred yards up the course. On the soft tar surface of the road itself eight hundred and twenty-one men and one woman now trotted, pranced, stretched and fidgeted in the humid afternoon atmosphere. To the sweating, excited spectators the Trans-Americans seemed almost like the inhabitants of some other world. Lean, sinewy, sunburned, their shirts and shorts cut as close as modesty would permit, the runners appeared to live in a private world of their own. Some wore sun hats or caps, most wore wrist and head sweatbands, all bore cloth numbers pinned on their upper bodies, back and front.

Flanagan, again dressed in his favorite Tom Mix outfit, his spurs jingling, strolled among the runners, addressing each one by his first name, shaking a hand here, patting a shoulder there. His Trans-America family was on the road again, for the last time. The red-bearded McGregor and his catering staff, their normal duties over, sat at trestle tables at the side of the road, where they were to act as race stewards. Tomorrow, in New York, they would collect their bets.

Another group was the many journalists, who mingled with the runners to secure last-minute stories, taking photographs of likely winners or of national or regional groups, anything that would fill the early evening editions. The leading runners flitted from one interview to the next, dutifully answering the same questions, while Kate Sheridan was followed everywhere by a swarm of journalists, radio interviewers and clicking cameramen.

2:20 P.M. Saturday, June 20, 1931. The competitors were already beginning to gather in rows of fifteen, across the soft macadam road, with the leading Trans-Americans taking up the front rows. Willard Clay and other members of Flanagan's staff passed between the rows, making their final checks.

About a hundred yards ahead, standing under the "start" banner, the Maxwell House Coffee Pot, the time truck, the Trans-America van, the press buses and a dozen support trucks stood ready. Above them, like wheeling birds, circled newsplanes and a massive silver-gray Tiffany's airship in which the elite of Manhattan would dine from silver plate while they peered through binoculars at the runners toiling below.

Carl Liebnitz, perspiring on the bleachers in the crowd above the start, looked down on the throng of runners and sensed the change in atmosphere. Since Los Angeles, he felt, the Trans-America had been more like a tapestry unfolding than a race, and only in the battles for stage prizes had the racing element occasionally asserted itself. True, he had sensed the subtle daily struggles between Doc, Eskola, Morgan, Bouin, McPhail and the others, but there had been none of the quality of a real fight-to-the-finish race in these daily encounters.

Today was different. This was a marathon, the classic footrace for the greatest prize in the history of the sport. In observing each man and in allowing himself to absorb into his pores the ambience of these prerace moments, Carl Liebnitz experienced that same quiver of expectation that a competitive race triggers even in those who know nothing about sport.

The swarthy Frenchman, Bouin, prowled through the waiting competitors like a hungry cat. Eskola, the lean, blond Finn, pranced on the spot or endlessly doubled over to touch his toes. Capaldi nervously blinked and drew his hands through his black, crinkly hair. A few yards behind the starting line, in the front line of runners, Morgan stared down the long straight road to New York as if he could already see the finish line. Beside him, Peter Thurleigh, clad in his ragged and faded blue-fringed Oxford shirt and shorts, gnawed his knuckles or swung his arms in wide circles to loosen his shoulders. A few feet away, Hugh McPhail yawned the nervous yawn of the frightened athlete, while at his side Doc Cole was for once silent, lifting one knee after the other in front of him and hugging it to his chest, eyes closed. Twenty-five rows behind him, Kate Sheridan nervously pushed back for the twentieth time an imaginary strand of hair from her tanned face.

Every man in the race went through his personal, private prerace ritual, each, whatever his abilities, nursing the hope that this just might be that magic moment when he would run beyond himself. For most of the runners that was all they could hope for, for the prize money only went down to fiftieth place.

Liebnitz found Maurice Falconer standing beside him, mopping his brow with a handkerchief. The journalist looked around him and up at the cloudy sky. "What do you think of the weather, then, Maurice?" he asked.

Falconer scowled and shook his head. "At least eighty-five degrees down there on the road and over seventy per cent humidity—the worst we've had since Los Angeles."

Liebnitz scribbled on his pad. "So how much body-weight will the boys down there lose by Central Park?"

Falconer wrinkled his nose, causing drops of sweat to drop onto his white summer suit.

"Up to ten per cent. Anything from six to fourteen pounds. Though some of those boys have lost so much weight since Los Angeles they're going to have to get an overdraft."

Liebnitz smiled. "How many feeding stations?"

"Ten. I've made up a concoction of my own for the runners, a special saline drink which should help keep up body fluids and cut down on leg cramps."

Liebnitz looked at the map pinned to a clipboard in his left hand and traced the course with his finger.

"Looks pretty straight to me, for once. No deviations for Flanagan's 'appropriations' or Highland Games this time?"

Falconer smiled and shook his head.

"Not this time, Carl."

Liebnitz continued to scrutinize the map. "Down Pallington Boulevard, then Little Falls, Clifton through West Paterson—I had an aunt who lived there once—Teterboro, Lodi, then Ridgefield Park and across the Hackensack River."

He adjusted his glasses.

"Here's where it'll get tough—at Fort Lee," he continued. "Then the Hudson and the George Washington Bridge, and into New York proper. Down Lenox Avenue and into Central Park. And that's when it ends, for all of us."

He looked up from the map and pointed into the mass of runners at Kate Sheridan.

"And what about her? Do you think she can make it into the top two hundred?"

Falconer unfastened the top button of his shirt and loosened his tie.

"A couple of months ago I'd have laid long odds against it," he said. "But this Trans-America race, it's been an education for me. If you want my professional opinion, I'd put Miss Sheridan's chances at a good deal less than even. Carl, don't forget there's over eight hundred men down there. That's a lot of heart, of pride, on the line today."

Liebnitz nodded and pointed again, this time at Willard Clay.

"Looks as if they're all set to get started," he said, beginning to move off. "See you later in the bus."

Willard was nodding at Flanagan, who in turn now beckoned with his right hand to Will Rogers standing at the microphone on a podium directly in line with the start. Rogers was the ideal man for this final stage. Acknowledged as the All-American of wit, Rogers' homely, country-boy face was known and loved in every home in the land. Rogers had great respect for athletes, being himself one of America's greatest exponents of the lasso. He cleared his throat and began.

"Ladies and gentlemen, I don't reckon that there can be a single man, woman and child here who hasn't followed Mr. Flanagan's Trans-Americans since they first left Los Angeles, way back on March 21. They've been on show in Main Street, America for the past three months, and those of you who hadn't seen them in person till today have most certainly done so on the silver screen.

"So here we are, on the final stage because of the generosity of possibly the world's greatest follower of the marathon race, Mr. Clarence Ross of Transcontinental Airlines. I only saw a marathon once myself, back in Boston in 1924. I always remember watching the runners at the finish. You know how tired them runners always are, hobbling in, crawling about on hands and knees. Well, there was these two prim ol' Boston ladies sitting next to me at the finish. One says to the other, 'What a lovely race.' 'Yes,' says the other, 'I'm really looking forward to the finals.' "

The laughter came both from athletes and spectators, momentarily relaxing the tension.

"Well," said Rogers, raising his Winchester with his right arm. "I won't hold you folks up with my jawing much longer. The best of luck to each and every one of you."

There was silence as Rogers increased his pressure on the trigger, the athletes on the road frozen as if in a tableau.

"Get on your marks . . ."

The engines of the trucks started up.

"Get set . . ."

The trucks slowly started to move off up the soft hot road.

Crack! The gun fired, and like a greyhound released from a trap the Trans-Americans surged along the road to New York to the roars of the crowd, the explosion of cameras and the din of low-flying airplanes zooming in to secure closer shots of the start. They were on their way, for the last time.

From the beginning it was fast. By three miles the race had divided into three leading groups. In the lead were Eskola, Bouin, Dasriaux, Capaldi, Mullins and Komar, and a dozen other hopefuls who had never previously featured in the top twenty at any time in the Trans-America. A hundred yards or so behind them came the second group, consisting of Brady, Lundberg, Brix, Quomawahu and eight others. A hundred and fifty yards back ran Doc, Thurleigh, McPhail and Morgan, together with the Australian Charles, a little Irishman, Magill, and an American, Flynn. Three miles was run in a swift sixteen minutes twenty-one seconds, and Eskola's group ran past the first feeding station without stopping.

Doc eased off, drank a cardboard container of fluid on the run, then picked up a second from another table, again drinking it on the run and pouring the dregs over his head. "Drink," he said, almost to himself. "Keep drinking."

All along Pallington Boulevard crowds stood three or four deep, shouting and applauding, many of them in overalls and dungarees, all work having stopped along the route. Restraining them, beefy, grinning New Jersey cops, relieved to be coping with something other than strikers or rioting mobs, nodded and shouted encouragement as the runners streamed past.

Six miles in thirty-three minutes and nine seconds, and still Eskola's group held the lead, though six of the optimists who had been sucked into the fast early pace were now plodding dourly, broken and sweat-sodden, two hundred yards behind Doc's group and sinking steadily down the field. Behind them ran Brady's pack, now reduced to six runners. Doc's group remained unchanged, covering the first six miles almost three-quarters of a minute behind Eskola . . .

Another drama was being played over a mile behind the leaders. There Kate Sheridan fought her own war of attrition with the stream of runners stretching away from her into the distance.

As she passed down the crowd-lined avenue the cheers and shouting always took on a shriller note. Women and girls who had never in their lives run a mile screamed, whooped and applauded as Kate went past, their screams rising in pitch each time she overtook yet another male competitor. The "Lone Lady," as the press corps had dubbed her, had started cautiously, as Doc had advised her; perhaps too cautiously. By six miles, run in just over forty-five minutes, she was in three hundred and ninth position, her body already drenched in sweat . . .

. . . At the front, Eskola's pace was still remorseless; through Little Falls, down into Clifton, he continued to pump out mile after mile in just over five and a half minutes. By nine miles, achieved in fifty minutes fifty seconds, his group had been pared down to Bouin, Dasriaux, Capaldi, Mullins and Komar, with of the "unknowns" only the lean, turbaned Indian, Singh, hanging on. Those who had peeled off, their rhythm broken, now languished far down the field.

In the second group, a hundred and fifty yards behind, the little Indian Quomawahu was beginning to crumble, his feet now flapping on the soft tar road. But Brady, Lundberg and Brix stayed firm, having shrugged off the other earlier members of their pack.

Two hundred yards behind them it was now only Doc, Thurleigh, Morgan and McPhail, Charles and Magill, running in two lines through the cheering crowds. Behind them the field was strung out for well over two miles, back into the outskirts of West Paterson.

In the leading press bus Carl Liebnitz stood on the top deck with Bullard, Packy Paterson and Stevie McFarlane, scanning the race through binoculars. "Look," he said, handing the binoculars to Bullard. "Eskola's still piling it on. If he keeps this up what time will he run?"

"Close to two and a half hours," said Bullard, peering through the glasses. "Hey!" he said, handing them on to Stevie. "Doc's taking water again. That's more time lost."

Stevie took the glasses and scowled. "No, time drinking isn't time lost. Not on a day like this." He wiped the sweat from his brow and surveyed it on the back of his hand. "Have a look at this," he said. "Just think what it must be like for those lads down there. Like a bloody Turkish bath."

Liebnitz nodded and scribbled on the pad on his lap. "You may be right," he said, looking at the race clock. "Twelve miles in one hour nine minutes exactly for Eskola and company. Doc and his pack must be close to two minutes down and we're nearly halfway. I hope the old pro hasn't misjudged it."

"I asked him last night if he had ever dreamed about this race," said Bullard. "Know what he said? He said he'd run it so often in his dreams he'd have to get the sheets resoled!"

Stevie grinned. "He's a great old guy. A pity it'll have to be a Scot who'll beat him."

"Or perhaps an American, a Finn or a Frenchman," said Liebnitz, continuing to peer through his binoculars, but the drone of the newsplanes above drowned his answer.

"Two hundred and fifty-first!" screamed a remarkably unladylike Clare Marsh at Kate Sheridan as she loped past at fifteen miles on Sylvan Avenue on the outskirts of Teterboro. "Fifty-one to go!" she added, skipping to make herself visible over the heads of the crowds. Kate nodded weakly and took her drink and sponge as she went from the trestle table at the feeding station, squeezing the tepid contents of the sponge down the back of her neck. By drinking on the run, she passed three runners who had taken their drinks standing at the station. She was finding it hard, for, at just inside eight-minute miles, this was the fastest pace at which she had ever run. There was no breathlessness yet; just pain and heaviness all over, bringing her farther and farther down onto her heels . . .

. . . At the front, fifteen miles through Lodi in one hour and twenty-eight minutes. This time Bouin, Dasriaux and Mullins picked up drinks at the tables on the run, as did Eskola, Capaldi and Komar. Behind them Brady's pack were wilting and were over two hundred yards behind, Singh and Quomawahu having been dropped at fourteen miles. All of Brady's pack stopped at the refreshment table, their bodies spurting sweat. A mile farther on, at sixteen miles, they were passed by Doc's group, and Brady's pack began to disintegrate.

In the lead, Eskola's group pressed on through Ridgefield Park and across the Hackensack River and past the eighteen-mile marker. Below, on the black, oily water, tugs and barges whistled as the runners crossed, unheeding, behind Flanagan's trucks and buses. At the bridge, the Pole Komar suddenly dropped to a trot, clasping his right calf. The wall had claimed its first victim.

Behind, Doc and the others had burned off Magill and Charles, who labored in a limbo a hundred yards ahead of Brady's broken group, and it was now the old firm of Doc, McPhail, Thurleigh and Morgan, running in line together, their brown bodies streaming sweat. As they crossed the Hackensack River they knew from shouts from the crowd that they were pulling in Eskola's pack and were less than two minutes behind the Finn. For the first time in the whole Trans-America Doc had said nothing to the others, but the four men ran as if driven by a single will—on, down, looping northeast through Fort Lee, toward the Hudson and the George Washington Bridge . . .

. . . Kate Sheridan saw the figures "220" on a large white card above the crowd at the bridge across the Hackensack as Clare Marsh, holding the card aloft, shrieked above the noise of the milling mob. The sweat poured over Kate's eyebrows, sending the bitter mascara down her bronzed cheeks and into her mouth. She cursed, regretting her vanity in using eye makeup for the first time since the Mojave. All elasticity had gone from her legs, but the men in front of her seemed to be fading even faster. "Got you, you bastard," she growled under her breath each time she passed one . . .

In the press bus the journalists clustered at the end of the top deck. "Doc's getting to them," growled Liebnitz, standing as he looked at Doc's group through his binoculars. "He's pulling Eskola in on a long rope."

Ernest Bullard put a hand on Liebnitz's shoulder as he peered through his own binoculars at the race leaders.

"You're right," he said. "But I never thought I'd see you this deep in a footrace."

Liebnitz turned to face him. "This isn't a race, Ernest. It's a goddam battle. That Finn's thrown down the gauntlet and Doc and the boys have picked it up." He returned to his binoculars and thumped the seat in front of him with his right fist.

"C'mon, Doc," he said. "I've got five bucks right on your nose."

The bus bumped and lurched as it crossed a railroad track, causing Liebnitz to be thrown back onto his seat. Behind the bus, Eskola and his group passed across the rails and the gates clanged shut behind them. Over a quarter of a mile back, but catching Eskola with every stride, Doc and his pack were not immediately aware of what had happened. Then, two hundred yards from the crossing, as the clang of the approaching train was heard, Doc realized what had occurred. When they reached the five-foot-high wooden barrier the train to New York stood hissing and steaming on the other side, barring their way onward.

For a moment the four men, Cole, McPhail, Morgan and Thurleigh, stood irresolute. Then Doc started to climb up the white wooden gates, looking down over his left shoulder.

"Come on," he growled. "Over."

The others followed him, gasping as they scrambled untidily over onto the road beyond. Doc then turned right, followed by the others, up the soft cinders by the side of the line toward the engine, about a hundred yards back down the track. On reaching the front of the train Doc glanced at the engineer in his cabin above and winked. He looked up the line going in the other direction, and followed by the others crossed the rails and ran to his left toward the gates on the other side of the track. By the time the train began to ease out of the station they were already on their way. The pursuit was on.

With just over six miles to go they were just over three minutes down . . .

. . . Three miles back Kate Sheridan was fighting her own final lonely battle. With each mile she felt she had reached the limit of the pain which she could tolerate; then, that limit accepted, somehow a new limit was reached, broached and again accepted. Since the eighteenth mile she had been counting grimly; five more to go and she had made it. Five men to pass in eight miles . . .

The moment had come, the moment for which he had waited all his life, and Doc Cole sensed it. With six miles to go, he would have to go after Eskola and his group now or it would be too late. He was at the wall, on the razor's edge between success and failure. If he held back now, Eskola might be able to hang in to win. If he went off too fast, then he might blow up before the finish. It was a gamble, but one which he would have to take. Ahead he could hear the applause and the whistles of the boats on the Hudson signal the arrival of Eskola's pack at the George Washington Bridge only half a mile ahead. He started to accelerate, feeling his leg cadence increase as his will expressed itself in movement.

The others sensed what had happened, sensed the decision that Doc was making for them. As the pace lifted they stayed locked together and pressed in on the George Washington Bridge. Across the Hudson they thudded, oblivious of the crowds behind and ahead, the tugs whistling below, their eyes fixed on Eskola's group, whom they could see making their lonely way toward Lenox Avenue.

For a moment, Doc feared he was making no impression. Then he began to hear Capaldi's grunts as he dropped back, and with five miles to go, just before the right turn down Lenox Avenue into Manhattan, they passed the swarthy American, leaving him to struggle on in their wake. At the front Eskola, Bouin, Dasriaux and Mullins had broken and were running in single file, about two hundred yards ahead.

The leaders were running in a tunnel of sound through the deep canyons of Manhattan, blind to the crowds massed thick on either sidewalk. Above them confetti and tickertape drifted down from offices, occasionally resting on their necks and shoulders.

Eskola still ran fluidly, eyes glazed and fixed. But he was slowing, and at the final feeding station, at twenty-three miles, he again ignored the refreshment and kept on running, his stride growing increasingly choppy and labored. Behind him Doc's group had picked up Bouin, Dasriaux and Mullins and were making ground steadily. The Finn's speed and his failure to take sufficient fluid were taking their toll: slowly he was grinding to a halt.

Eskola gave no sign of acknowledging their presence, but hung on, drawing on the rhythm of Doc and his group for strength. He locked in on Morgan's left shoulder, on the outside of the group. But Doc continued to press, and suddenly Eskola grunted and dropped back. The Finn's stride dropped to a forlorn, pecking action. He was beaten.

With two miles to go, at Lenox and 125th, Doc made his final decision. He would leave them . . .

. . . Six miles behind, Kate could see the turbaned Indian Singh, an early leader, now down to a hobbling walk-trot. It took her only another fifty yards to pull him in and pass him. He gave a toothy, broken grin as she passed and raised his right hand in acknowledgment.

She was beginning to feel her breathing weaken, the air coming through lungs that seemed hedged with thorns. Kate ran against the rhythm of this pain, fixing her eyes on the sweat-stained shirt of the next runner, an Austrian, whom she slowly passed, hearing his grunt as she did so.

The next three ran together, the tall Texan, Kane, and two tiny Japanese, running in their now familiar split-toed shoes, a hundred-odd yards ahead. For a mile she did not seem to be gaining ground at all, could see no change in the space which separated her from them. Then she began to hear Kane's monotonous, high-pitched wheeze, and suddenly the distance between them seemed to shrink. With five miles to go, as she crossed the George Washington Bridge, she drew level, then squeezed past. Kane put his hand to his forehead in salute, and brushed the sweat from his eyebrows. Kate nodded, feeling herself for the first time on that day grow stronger as she ran on. Ahead, at the end of the bridge, a prim, angular woman stood holding aloft a large piece of cardboard. It was a jubilant Clare Marsh.

The board read "200."

Kate felt her leg cadence increase as she passed it, smiling. In the next mile, she passed three more men in the storm of confetti and tickertape that was now Lenox Avenue. She had made it . . .

. . Each man felt it, felt his body protest as Doc placed new demands on bodies already screaming at their maximum. But they held firm, stayed glued to Doc's sweat-drenched shirt as he pushed ahead of them to go into a five-yard lead. Hugh felt as if he was being torn apart, his breath roaring through his lungs as he fixed his eyes on Doc's back, picking up each infinitesimal flicker of muscle on its sweating surface. To his right Thurleigh and Morgan ran in step, Morgan low and flat-footed, Thurleigh's legs bowed and buckling, his mouth flecked with foam.

Doc could feel their eyes boring into him, feel the thread which bound them—for that was what he had always told them to do. But Doc was deeply imbedded in this final moment, while the others were simply struggling to become part of it. So he kept pressing, feeling his strength and their weakness as he piled on yard after yard down the length of Lenox Avenue, toward Central Park.

The three runners continued to focus their gaze on his back, desperately hanging on. But Doc was getting away, gradually slipping from them. With just over a mile to go, and the entrance to Central Park in view, Doc knew that he had the race in his pocket. His lead had stretched to over a hundred yards. It had not been hard, despite the excessive heat. Like all things done well, it had come almost easily; the race had only released what had been lying dormant in him for twenty years.

He accelerated again, through the park gates and along to the left toward the finishing tape at the Obelisk, now just over half a mile away. He took a last look at the clock as the timing truck and the press buses peeled off to get into position at the finish. Just over two hours thirty-six minutes: faster than he had expected.

Then he heard the crowds in the park.

"Doc! Doc Cole!" they roared, and as he passed through the park gates a beefy cop patted his shoulder.

Doc cruised easily through the park, passing the Lasker Pool Rink on his left, then curving down the left hand loop to Fort Fish, waving to acknowledge the crowd as he ran. Two hundred yards behind McPhail, Morgan and Thurleigh ran in line, still locked together.

He strode strongly down the cool, tree-lined shadows of East Drive past delirious crowds straining behind police cordons. All the years, all the miles, and now the big payoff, the place in the history books. He had done it.

He had shown them who he was. Yet as he ran Doc felt a moment's uncertainty. Hell, he knew who he was, had known for the past thirty-odd years. He had no need to prove it, to these people or to anyone else. Finally, in the Trans-America, he had got to the center of himself, beyond the fairground huckstering, beyond even the lost records on forgotten roads . . .

As he ran along the left side of the Reservoir he could see the brown-painted Obelisk on his right, three hundred yards away, and the massive wooden VIP platform which straddled East Drive just beyond the finish and which was crowded with celebrities straining to catch a glimpse of the first Trans-American. He looked over his right shoulder. Two hundred yards behind him, hugging the side of the Reservoir, McPhail, Morgan and Thurleigh ran as if held together by a magnet: only feet divided each one from the other.

Only just over a hundred yards to go. The noise engulfed him, the goodwill and affection drenching him as he glided in toward the finish. He heard Flanagan's voice on the microphone—"The leader is . . . Doc Cole, Doctor Alexander Cole!"

He was there, where he had for so long dreamed he would be. "Finish," said the banner above the tape. Suddenly he realized that he was weeping, indeed had been since he had entered the park. A hundred yards . . .

Doc glanced behind him. Two hundred yards away Hugh McPhail had at last broken clear and was wobbling toward the tape, eyes glazed, his head already jutting forward in a grotesque memory of a dip finish. Five yards behind him came Mike Morgan, legs bowed, arms thrashing desperately, while behind him Peter Thurleigh, foaming at the mouth, his thighs beginning to cramp, struggled to maintain a dignity quite beyond his powers.

Doc flowed in easily to the tape and the crowded mass of dignitaries seated beyond it. Without losing rhythm he looked behind him again, and in a glance absorbed the final battle between the following trio. The white finishing tape just over sixty yards ahead was at least six inches broad, stretching the whole breadth of the road, and about fifty yards beyond it was the VIP stand, on which the gathered luminaries were already on their feet, applauding, whooping and cheering.

With fifty yards to go Doc began to ease up—to the gasps of the crowds on each side of the park. Thirty yards from the tape he stopped completely, and the crowd suddenly became hushed. Doc slowly turned to face the oncoming runners, his palms uppermost. Hugh McPhail was the first to reach him, gasping as obediently he drew to a halt, to be followed by Morgan who, lungs heaving, draped his arms limply over Doc's shoulders. A moment later a sobbing Peter Thurleigh struggled toward them, eyebrows raised in surprise. He stopped, wiped the white foam from his lips and looked at Doc, his hands on Hugh's shoulders.

Doc looked ahead at the platform—to Flanagan, who had descended its steps to stand on the road, a few yards beyond the finish. He then linked hands with an uncomprehending McPhail and beckoned Morgan and Thurleigh to do the same. His and Flanagan's eyes met, as Doc raised Hugh McPhail's hands above his head. Morgan and Thurleigh, both still gasping, slowly raised their arms too, and the four men walked forward together in silence, across the finish line. It was impossible to separate them.

Doc was the first to reach the microphone, set up on the road below the VIP platform. For a moment he stood savoring his triumph, as the silence around them was broken by a babble of excited talk. Then he seized the mike in one hand, and smiled.

"We just got in," he said. "From L.A."

POSTSCRIPT

In September 1931 Kate Sheridan, newly arrived in Hollywood, appeared in the first of a series of supporting roles in *A Thousand and One Nights* with Douglas Fairbanks. Her husband, Michael Morgan, began that August a career as a stuntman for Universal and in the 1940s became one of Hollywood's most famous directors of stunt sequences.

In December 1931 Hugh McPhail and his wife, Dixie, went into business with Doc Cole, who had set up with his wife, Lily, the first of the now-famous Cole Health Spas.

Lord Peter Thurleigh, now again a rich man because of his winning wager, returned to England to fight a by-election, gaining a seat as Liberal MP for Epping. He lost his life on August 19, 1942, during the Allied raid on Dieppe, heading a battalion of the Coldstream Guards.

Charles C. Flanagan spent 1931 and 1932 managing a burlesque review called *Running Without a Stitch*, which toured successfully and was briefly filmed in a sequence in the *Gold Diggers of 1933*. The 1932 Trans-Europe Race did not take place; but Flanagan Foods received the catering contract for the 1932 Olympic Games, and in 1935 Charles C. Flanagan became a member of the American Olympic Committee, with Avery Brundage as chairman.

In 1960 Doc Cole was given a place in America's Track and Field Hall of Fame, and in 1961, at the age of eighty-four, ran the marathon from Denville to Central Park in four hours and eight minutes, a world record for his age group.

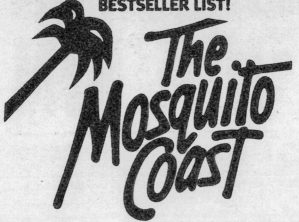

MURDER ON LOCATION

GEORGE KENNEDY

Internationally renowned actor George Kennedy
finds himself playing both star and sleuth
in his own novel when murder stalks the set
in Mexico for the filming of a
major motion picture.
Whether the motive is sabotage
or personal vendetta, nothing is certain
except that everyone's a suspect—
even stars Dean Martin, Glenn Ford,
Raquel Welch, Yul Brynner and
Genevieve Bujold.   83857-5/$2.95

